THE
WILD
ROSE

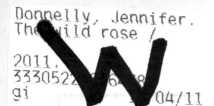

THE
WILD
ROSE

JENNIFER

DONNELLY

HY**P**E**R**I**O**N

NEW YORK

Library of Congress Cataloging-in-Publication Data

Donnelly, Jennifer.
The wild rose / Jennifer Donnelly. — 1st ed.
p. cm.
ISBN 978-1-4013-0104-0
1. World War, 1914–1918—England—Fiction.
2. Upper class families—England—Fiction.
3. Domestic fiction.   I. Title.
PS3604.O563W55 2011
813'.6—dc22
2011013278

Hyperion books are available for special promotions and premiums. For details
contact the HarperCollins Special Markets Department in the New York office
at 212-207-7528, fax 212-207-7222, or email spsales@harpercollins.com.

Design by Fritz Metsch

FIRST EDITION
10 9 8 7 6 5 4 3 2

THIS LABEL APPLIES TO TEXT STOCK

We try to produce the most beautiful books possible, and we are also extremely
concerned about the impact of our manufacturing process on the forests of the
world and the environment as a whole. Accordingly, we've made sure that all of
the paper we use has been certified as coming from forests that are managed, to
ensure the protection of the people and wildlife dependent upon them.

FOR
SIMON LIPSKAR
AND
MAJA NIKOLIC

It is not the mountain we conquer, but ourselves.

—SIR EDMUND HILLARY

THE
WILD
ROSE

PROLOGUE
August 1913—Tibet

DID ALL ENGLISH girls make love like a man? Or was it only this one?

Max von Brandt, a German mountaineer, wondered this as he stroked the hair out of the face of the young woman lying next to him in the dark. He'd been with many women. Soft, pliant women, who clung to him afterward, extorting promises and endearments. This woman wasn't soft, and neither was her lovemaking. It was hard and quick and without preliminaries. And when it was over, as it was now, she would turn away, curl into herself, and sleep.

"I don't suppose there is anything I can say. To make you stay with me," he said.

"No, Max, there isn't."

He lay on his back in the dark, listening as her breath slowed and deepened, as she drifted off to sleep. He couldn't sleep. He didn't want to. He wanted to make this night last. To remember it always. He wanted to remember the feel of her, the smell of her. The sound of the wind. The piercing cold.

He had told her he loved her. Weeks ago. And he'd meant it. For the first time in his life, he'd meant it. She'd laughed. And then, seeing that she'd hurt him, she'd kissed him and shaken her head no.

The night passed quickly. Before the sun rose, the woman did. As Max stared ahead of himself, into the darkness, she dressed, then quietly left their tent.

He never found her beside him when he woke. She always left the tent or cave or whatever shelter they'd found while it was still dark. He'd searched for her in the beginning, and always he'd found her perched somewhere high, somewhere solitary and still, her face lifted to the dawn sky and its fading stars.

"What are you looking for?" he would ask, following her gaze.

"Orion," she would answer.

In only a few hours, he would say good-bye to her. In the time he had left, he would think of their first days together, for it was those memories he would hold on to.

They'd met about four months ago. He'd been traveling in Asia for five months prior. A renowned Alpine climber, he'd decided he wanted to see the Himalayas. To see if it was possible to conquer Everest; to take the world's highest mountain for Germany, for the fatherland. The kaiser wanted conquests, and better to satisfy him with a beautiful mountain in Asia than a wretched war in Europe. He'd left Berlin for India, traveled north through that country, then quietly entered Nepal, a country closed to Westerners.

He'd made it all the way to Kathmandu before he was apprehended by Nepalese authorities and told to leave. He promised he would, but he needed help, he told them; a guide. He needed someone to take him through the high valleys of the Solu Khumbu and into Tibet over the Nangpa La pass. From there he wanted to trek east, exploring the northern base of Everest on his way to Lhasa, the City of God, where he hoped to ask permission of the Dalai Lama to climb. He had heard about a place called Rongbuk, and hoped he might find an approach there. He'd heard of one who might be able to help him—a woman, another Westerner. Did they know anything about her?

The authorities said that they did know her, though they had not seen her in several months. He gave them presents: rubies and sapphires he'd bought in Jaipur, pearls, a large emerald. In return, they gave him permission to wait for her. For a month.

Max had first heard of the woman when he'd arrived in Bombay. Western climbers he'd met there told him of her—an English girl who lived in the shadow of the Himalayas. She'd climbed Kilimanjaro—the Mawenzi peak—and had lost a leg on Kili in a horrible accident. She'd almost died there. Now, they said, she was photographing and mapping the Himalayas. She was trekking as high as she could, but the difficult climbs were beyond her. She lived among the mountain people now. She was strong like them, and had earned their respect and their liking. She did what almost no European could—moved over borders with goodwill, receiving hospitality from Nepalese and Tibetans alike.

But how to find her? Rumors abounded. She had been in China and India, but was in Tibet now, some said. No, Burma. No, Afghanistan. She was surveying for the British. Spying for the French. She'd died in an avalanche. She'd gone native. She'd taken a Nepalese husband. She traded horses. Yaks. Gold. He heard more talk as he made his way northeast across India. In Agra. Kanpur. And then, finally, he'd found her. In Kathmandu. Or at least he'd found a hut she used.

"She's in the mountains," a villager told him. "She'll come."

"When?"

"Soon. Soon."

Days passed. Then weeks. A month. The Nepalese were growing impatient. They wanted him gone. He asked the villagers again and again when she was coming, and always he was told soon. He thought it must be a ruse by the wily farmer with whom he was staying to get a few more coins out of him.

And then she'd arrived. He'd thought her a Nepalese at first. She was dressed in indigo trousers and a long sheepskin jacket. Her shrewd green eyes were large in her angular face. They assessed him from beneath the furry fringe of her cap. Turquoise beads hung from her neck and dangled from her ears. She wore her hair in a long braid ornamented with bits of silver and glass as the native women did. Her face was bronzed by the Himalayan sun. Her body was wiry and strong. She walked with a limp. He found out, later, that she wore a false leg made of yak bone, carved and hollowed for her by a villager.

"*Namaste,*" she'd said to him, bowing her head slightly, after the farmer had told her what he wanted.

Namaste. It was a Nepalese greeting. It meant: The light within me bows to the light within you.

He'd told her he wished to hire her to take him into Tibet. She told him she'd just returned from Shigatse and was tired. She would sleep first, then eat, and then they would discuss it.

The next day she prepared him a meal of rice and curried mutton, with strong black tea. He'd sat with her on the rug-covered floor of her hut and they'd talked, sharing a pipeful of opium. It killed the pain, she said. He'd thought then that she was referring to her damaged leg, but later he realized that the pain she spoke of went much deeper, and the opium she smoked did little to dull it. Sadness enfolded her like a long black cape.

He was astonished by the depth and breadth of her knowledge of the Himalayas. She had surveyed, mapped, and photographed more of the range than any Westerner had ever done. She kept herself by guiding and by publishing papers on the topography of the mountains for Britain's Royal Geographical Society. The RGS would soon publish a book of her Himalayan photographs, too. Max had seen some of them. They were astonishingly good. They captured the fierce magnificence of the mountains, their beauty and cold indifference, like no other images ever had. She never went to the RGS in person, for she would not leave her beloved mountains. Instead she sent her work to be presented there by Sir Clements Markham, the RGS's president.

Max had exclaimed over her photographs and the precision of her maps, amazed by both. She was younger than he—only twenty-nine—and yet she'd accomplished so much. She had shrugged his praise off, saying there was so much more to do, but she couldn't do it—couldn't get high enough to do it—because of her leg.

"But you've had to climb in order to do this much," he said.

"Not so high, really. And not on anything tricky. No ice fields. No cliffs or crevasses," she replied.

"But, it's all tricky," he said. "How do you climb at all? Without . . . without both legs, I mean."

"I climb with my heart," she replied. "Can you?"

When he had proved to her that he could do that, that he could climb with love and awe and respect for the mountains, she agreed to take him to Lhasa. They'd left Kathmandu with two yaks to carry a tent and supplies, and had trekked through mountain villages and valleys and passes that only she and a handful of sherpas knew. It was hard and exhausting and unspeakably beautiful. It was brutally cold, too. They slept close to each other in a tent, under skins for warmth. On the third night of the trek he told her he loved her. She laughed and he'd turned away, upset. He'd meant it, and his pride had been deeply wounded by her rejection.

"I'm sorry," she said, placing a hand on his back. "I'm sorry, I can't . . ."

He asked if there was someone else and she said yes, and then she took him in her arms. For comfort and warmth, for pleasure, but not for love. It was the first time in his life his heart had been broken.

They'd arrived three weeks ago at a bleak Tibetan village at the base of Everest—Rongbuk, where she lived. They waited there while the woman, who was known and well connected, used her influence to get him papers from Tibetan officials which would allow him to enter Lhasa. He stayed with her in her house—a small whitewashed stone structure, with a smaller building tacked on that she used to house her animals.

She'd taken photographs during those days. Once he'd seen her try to climb. She attempted an ice field when she thought he wasn't watching, with her camera strapped to her back. She was not bad even with only one leg. But then she suddenly stopped dead and did not move for a solid ten minutes. He saw her struggling with herself. "Damn you!" she suddenly screamed. "Damn you! Damn you!" until he feared she would start an avalanche. At whom was she yelling? he wondered. At the mountain? Herself? At someone else?

His papers had finally come through. The day after he received them, he and the woman left Rongbuk with a tent and five yaks. Yesterday, they'd reached the outskirts of Lhasa. It had been their last day together. Last night, their last night. In a few hours, he would begin the trek to the holy city alone. He planned to stay for some months, studying and photographing Lhasa and its inhabitants, while he tried to obtain an audience with the Dalai Lama. He knew his chances were slim. The Dalai Lama tolerated one Westerner—the woman. It was said that on occasion he would drink with her, sing Tibetan songs with her, and swap bawdy stories. She was not going into Lhasa this time, however. She wanted to get back to Rongbuk.

Max wondered now, as he rose in the cold gray dawn, if he would ever see her again. He quickly dressed, packed a few things into his rucksack, buttoned his jacket, and walked out of the tent. Four yaks, presents for the governor of Lhasa, were stamping and snorting, their breath white in the morning air, but the woman was nowhere to be seen.

He looked around and finally spotted her sitting on a large, jutting rock, silhouetted against the sky. She sat still and alone, one knee hugged to her chest, her face lifted to the fading stars. He would leave now. With morning breaking. With this image of her forever in his mind.

"*Namaste*, Willa Alden," he whispered, touching his steepled hands to his forehead. "*Namaste*."

PART ONE

MARCH
1914

LONDON

CHAPTER ONE

"AUNT EDDIE, STOP! You can't go in there!"

Seamus Finnegan, sprawled naked across his bed, opened one eye. He knew that voice. It belonged to Albie Alden, his best friend.

"For heaven's sake, why not?"

"Because he's asleep! You can't just barge in on a sleeping man. It's not decent!"

"Oh, bosh."

Seamie knew that voice, too. He sat up, grabbed the bedcovers, and pulled them up to his chin.

"Albie! Do something!" he yelled.

"I tried, old chap. You're on your own," Albie shouted back.

A second later, a small, stout woman dressed in a tweed suit threw open the door and greeted Seamie loudly. It was Edwina Hedley. She was Albie's aunt, but Seamie had known her since he was a boy and called her Aunt Eddie, too. She sat down on the bed, then immediately jumped up again when the bed squawked. A young woman, tousled and yawning, emerged from under the covers.

Eddie frowned. "My dear," she said to the girl, "I earnestly hope you have taken preventive measures. Otherwise, you'll find yourself with a baby on the way and the father en route to the North Pole."

"I thought it was the South Pole," the woman said sleepily.

"It was," Seamie replied.

"Has he told you about all the children?" Eddie asked the girl, lowering her voice conspiratorially.

Seamie started to protest. "Eddie, don't . . ."

"Children? What children?" the woman asked, her sleepy look gone now.

"You know he has four children, don't you? All illegitimate. He sends the mothers money—he's not a complete bounder—but he won't marry any of them. They're completely ruined, of course. London girls, all of them. Three left for the country. Couldn't show their faces anymore. The fourth went to America, the poor dear. Why do you think the whole thing with Lady Caroline Wainwright ended?"

The girl, a pretty brunette with a short bob, turned to Seamie. "Is this true?" she asked indignantly.

"Entirely," Eddie said, before Seamie could even open his mouth.

The girl wrapped the duvet around herself and got out of bed. She picked her clothes up off the floor and huffed out of the room, slamming the door on her way.

"*Four* children, Aunt Eddie?" Seamie said, after she'd gone. "Last time it was two."

"A gold digger through and through," Eddie sniffed. "I saved you just now, but I won't always be around at times like these, you know."

"What a pity," Seamie said.

Eddie leaned over and kissed his cheek. "It's good to see you."

"Likewise. How was Aleppo?"

"Absolutely splendid! Stayed in a palace. Dined with a pasha. Met the most extraordinary people. A Tom Lawrence among them. He traveled back to London with me. He's staying in the Belgravia place and—"

There was a loud, resounding boom as the house's heavy front door slammed shut.

Eddie smiled. "Well, that's the end of that one. Won't be seeing her again. What a tomcat you are."

"More of a stray dog, I'd say," Seamie said ruefully.

"I heard about Lady Caroline. It's all over London."

"So I gathered."

Seamie had come to Highgate, Eddie's beautiful Georgian brick house in Cambridge, to recuperate from a brief and heady love affair that had soured. Lady Caroline Wainwright was a privileged young woman—wealthy, beautiful, spoiled—and used to getting what she wanted. And what she wanted was him—for her husband. He'd told her it would never work. He wasn't good husband material. He was too independent. Too used to his own ways. He traveled too much. He told her any bloody thing he could think of—except the truth.

"There's someone else, isn't there?" Caroline had said tearfully. "Who is she? Tell me her name."

"There's no one else," he'd said. It was a lie, of course. There was someone else. Someone he'd loved long ago, and lost. Someone who'd ruined him, it seemed, for any other woman.

He'd finished with Caroline, and then he'd hightailed it to Cambridge to hide out with his friend. He had no home of his own to go to, and when he was in England, he tended to bounce between Highgate, his sister's house, and various hotels.

Albie Alden, a brilliant physicist, taught at King's College and lived in his aunt's house. He was constantly being offered positions by universities all over the world—Paris, Vienna, Berlin, New York— but he wanted to stay in Cambridge. Dull, sleepy Cambridge. God knew why. Seamie certainly didn't. He'd asked him many times, and Albie always said he liked it best here. It was peaceful and quiet—at least when Eddie was away—and he needed that for his work. And Eddie, who was rarely home, needed someone to look after things. The arrangement suited them both.

"What happened?" Eddie asked Seamie now. "Lady Caroline break your heart? Didn't want to marry you?"

"No, she *did* want to marry me. That's the problem."

"Mmm. Well, what do you expect? It's what happens when you're a dashing and handsome hero. Women want to get their claws into you."

"Turn around, will you? So I can get dressed," Seamie said.

Eddie did so, and Seamie got out of bed and grabbed his clothing off the floor. He was tall, strong, and beautifully made. Muscles flexed and rippled under his skin as he pulled his pants on, then shrugged into his shirt. His hair, cut short on the sides, long and wavy on the top, was a dark auburn with copper glints. His face was weathered by the sun and the sea. His eyes were a frank and startling blue.

At thirty-one years of age, he was one of the world's most renowned polar explorers. He'd attempted the South Pole with Ernest Shackleton when he was still a teenager. Two years ago, he'd returned from the first successful expedition to the South Pole, led by the Norwegian Roald Amundsen. In demand all over the world, he'd embarked on a lecture tour shortly after returning from Antarctica and had traveled nonstop for nearly two years. He'd come back to London a month ago and already he felt it, and everyone in it, to be dull and gray. He felt restless and confined, and couldn't wait to be gone again on some new adventure.

"How long have you been in town? How are you liking it? Are you going to stay for a bit this time?" Eddie asked him.

Seamie laughed. Eddie always talked this way—asking a question, and before you could answer it, asking ten more.

"I'm not sure," he said, combing his hair in the mirror above the bureau. "I may be off again soon."

"Another lecture tour?"

"No. An expedition."

"Really? How exciting! Where to?"

"Back to Antarctica. Shackleton's trying to get something together. He's quite serious. He announced it in the *Times* last year, and he's already drawn up some very detailed timetables. All he has to do now is scare up some funds."

"What about all the war talk? Doesn't that worry him?" Eddie asked. "People talked about nothing else on board the ship. In Aleppo, too."

"It doesn't worry him a bit," Seamie replied. "He doesn't give much credence to it. Says it'll all blow over, and wants to sail by summer's end, if not earlier."

Eddie gave him a long look. "Aren't you getting a bit old for the lad's life? Shouldn't you settle down? Find a good woman?"

"How? You chase them all away!" Seamie said teasingly. He sat down on the bed again to put his socks on.

Eddie flapped a hand at him. "Come downstairs when you've finished dressing. I'll make us all some breakfast. Eggs with harissa sauce. I bought pots of the stuff back with me. Wait till you taste it. Simply marvelous! I'll tell you and Albie and his boffin friends about all my adventures. And then we'll go to London."

"To London? When? Right after breakfast?"

"Well, perhaps not right after," Eddie conceded. "Maybe in a day or two. I've got the most fascinating man staying in my town house whom I want you to meet. Mr. Thomas Lawrence. I was telling you about him just a moment ago, before your paramour nearly slammed my door off its hinges. I met him in Aleppo. He's an explorer, too. And an archaeologist. He's traveled all around the desert, knows all the most powerful poohbahs, and speaks flawless Arabic." Eddie suddenly stopped speaking and lowered her voice. "Some people say he's a *spy*." Eddie said this last word in a whisper, then resumed her normal, booming tone. "Whatever he is, he's thoroughly amazing."

Eddie's words were punctuated by a sudden clap of thunder, followed by the pattering of rain against the mullioned windows, one of which had a cracked pane.

"Water's coming in," she said. "I must call the glazier." She sat watching the rain for another minute. "I never thought I'd miss the English weather," she added, smiling wistfully. "But that was before I'd seen the Arabian desert. It's good to be back. I do love my creaky old house. And creaky old Cambridge." Her smile faded. "Though I do wish the circumstances of my return were different."

"He'll be all right, Eddie," Seamie said.

Eddie sighed heavily. "I hope so," she said. "But I know my sister. She wouldn't have asked me to come home if she wasn't terribly worried."

Seamie knew that Mrs. Alden, Albie's mother and Eddie's sister, had wired Eddie at Aleppo, asking her to return to England. Admiral Alden, her husband, had taken ill with some sort of stomach complaint. His doctors had not yet figured out what was wrong with him, but whatever it was, it was bad enough to keep him in bed and on pain medication.

"He's made of tough stuff," Seamie said. "All the Aldens are."

Eddie nodded and tried to smile. "You're right, of course. And anyway, that's about enough moping for one morning. There's breakfast to attend to and then I must call the glazier. And the gardener. And the chimney man, too. Albie's done nothing in my absence. The house is dusty. My mail is up to the rafters. And there's not one clean plate in the entire kitchen. Why doesn't he get that girl from the village up here to do some cleaning?"

"He says she disturbs him."

Eddie snorted. "I really don't see how she could. He never comes out of his study. He was in it when I left two months ago. And he's in it now, working harder than ever, even though he's supposed to be on sabbatical. He's got two more boffins in there with him. I just met them. Dilly Knox, one's called. And Oliver Strachey. They've got blackboards and charts and books strewn all over. What on earth can they be doing in there? What can possibly be so fascinating?"

"Their work?"

"Hardly. It's all just numbers and formulas," Eddie said dismissively. "That boy needs a wife. Even more than you do, I daresay. He's far too odd and absentminded to continue without one. Why is it that you have more women after you than you can possibly cope with and poor Albie hasn't any? Can't you push some of your admirers in his direction? He needs a good woman. And children. Oh, I would so love to hear the happy noise of little ones in my home again. How wonderful those years were when Albie and Willa were little and my sister would bring them here and they'd swim in the pond and swing from that old tree—that one right there," Eddie said, pointing at the huge oak outside the bedroom window. "Willa would climb so high. My sister would plead with her to come down, but she wouldn't. She'd only climb higher and—"

Eddie suddenly stopped talking. She turned and looked at Seamie.

"Oh, crumbs. I shouldn't have spoken of her. Do forgive me."

"It's all right, Eddie," Seamie said.

"No, it isn't. I . . . I don't suppose you've had a letter from her recently, have you? Her own mother hasn't. Not for the last three months anyway. And she's been writing to Willa twice a week. Trying to get word to her about her father. Well, I suppose getting letters to and from Tibet is a rather tricky business."

"I suppose it is. And no, I haven't heard from her," Seamie said. "But I never have. Not since she left Africa. I only know as much as you do. That she nearly died in Nairobi. That she traveled through the Far East afterward. And that she's in the Himalayas now, looking for a way to finish the job."

Eddie winced at that. "You're still pining for her, aren't you?" she said. "That's why you go through women like water. One after another. Because you're looking for someone who can take Willa's place. But you never find her."

And I never will, Seamie said to himself. He had lost Willa, the love of his life, eight years ago, and though he'd tried, he'd never found a woman to come close to her. No other woman had Willa's lust for life, for adventure. No other woman possessed her bravery or her passionate, daring soul.

"It's all my fault," Seamie said now. "She wouldn't be there, a million miles away from her family, her home, if it hadn't been for me. If I'd handled things properly on Kilimanjaro, she'd be here."

He would never forget what had happened in Africa. They'd been climbing Kilimanjaro, he and Willa, hoping to set a record by being the first to climb the Mawenzi peak. Altitude sickness had plagued them both, but it had hit Willa especially hard. He'd wanted her to go down, but she'd refused. So they went up instead, summitting much later than they should have. There on Mawenzi, he'd told her something he'd felt for years, but had kept to himself—that he loved her. "I love you, too," she said. "Always have. Since forever." He still heard those words. Every day of his life. They echoed in his head and in his heart.

The sun was high by the time they'd begun their descent, too high, and its rays were strong. An ice-bound boulder, loosened by the sun's heat, came crashing down on them as they were heading down a couloir. It hit Willa and she fell. Seamie would never forget the sound of her screams, or the twisting blur of her body as it flew past him.

When he finally got to her, he saw that her right leg was broken. Jagged bone stuck through her skin. He went down the mountain to their base camp to get help from their Masai guides, only to find they'd been murdered by hostile tribesmen. He'd had to carry her off the mountain, and through jungle and plains, alone. After days of walking, he'd found the train tracks that run between Mombasa and Nairobi. After flagging down a train, he managed to get Willa to a doctor in Nairobi, but by the time they got there, the wound had turned gangrenous. There was no choice, the doctor had said; it would have to be amputated. Willa begged and pleaded with him not to let the man cut her leg off. She knew she'd never climb without it. But Seamie hadn't listened to her pleas. He'd let the doctor amputate to save her life, and she'd never forgiven him for it. As soon as she was able, she left the hospital. And him.

I wake up every morning in despair and go to sleep the same way, she'd written in the note she left for him. *I don't know what to do. Where to go. How to live. I don't know how to make it through the next ten minutes, never mind the rest of my life. There are no more hills for me to climb, no more mountains, no more dreams. It would have been better to have died on Kilimanjaro than to live like this.*

Eddie reached for his hand and squeezed it. "Stop blaming yourself, Seamie, it's not your fault," she said resolutely. "You did everything a human being could have done on that mountain. And when you got her to Nairobi, you did the only thing you could do. The right thing. Imagine had you not done it. Imagine standing in my sister's drawing room and telling her that you did nothing at all, that you let her child die. I understand, Seamie. We all do."

Seamie smiled sadly. "That's the hard thing of it, though, Eddie," he said. "Everyone understands. Everyone but Willa."

CHAPTER TWO

"PARDON ME, MR. Bristow," Gertrude Mellors said, poking her head around the door to her boss's office, "but Mr. Churchill's on the telephone, the *Times* wants a comment from you on the trade secretary's report on child labor in East London, and Mr. Asquith's requested that you join him for supper at the Reform Club this evening. Eight o'clock sharp."

Joe Bristow, member of Parliament for Hackney, stopped writing. "Tell Winston if he wants more boats, he can pay for them himself. The people of East London need sewers and drains, not dreadnoughts," he said. "Tell the *Times* that London's children must spend their days in schools, not sweatshops, and that it's Parliament's moral duty to act upon the report swiftly and decisively. And tell the prime minister to order me the guinea hen. Thanks, Trudy luv."

He turned back to the elderly man seated on the other side of his desk. Nothing, not newspapers, not party business, not the prime minister himself, was more important to him than his constituents. The men and women of East London were the reason he'd become a Labor MP back in 1900, and they were the reason why, fourteen years later, he remained one.

"I'm sorry, Harry. Where were we?" he said.

"The water pump," Harry Coyne, resident of number 31 Lauriston Street, Hackney, said. "As I was saying, about a month ago the water started tasting funny. And now everyone on the street's ill. Lad I talked to works down the tannery says they're dumping barrels of lye on the ground behind the building at night. Says the foreman don't want to pay to have the waste carted away. Water lines run under that building and I think the waste from the tannery's getting into them. Has to be. There's no other explanation."

"Have you told the health inspector?"

"Three times. He don't do nothing. That's why I came to you. Only one who ever gets anything done is you, Mr. Bristow."

"I have to have names, Harry," he said. "Of the tannery. The man in charge. The lad who works there. Anyone who's been ill. Will they speak to me?"

"I can't answer for the tannery man, but the rest will," Harry said. "Here, give us that pen." As Harry wrote down names and addresses, Joe poured two cups of tea, pushed one over to Harry, and downed the other. He'd been seeing constituents since eight o'clock that morning, with no break for lunch, and it was now half past four.

"Here you are," Harry said, handing the list to Joe.

"Thank you," Joe said, pouring more tea. "I'll start knocking on doors tomorrow. I'll pay a personal visit to the health inspector. We'll get this solved, Harry, I promise you. We'll—" Before he could finish his sentence, the door to his office was wrenched open. "Yes, Trudy. What, Trudy?" he said.

But it wasn't Trudy. It was a young woman. She was tall, raven-haired, blue-eyed—a beauty. She wore a smartly tailored charcoal gray coat and matching hat, and carried a reporter's notebook and fountain pen in her gloved hands.

"Dad! Mum's been arrested again!" she said breathlessly.

"Bloody hell. *Again?*" Joe said.

"Katie Bristow, I've told you a hundred times to knock first!" Trudy scolded, hot on her heels.

"Sorry, Miss Mellors," Katie said to Trudy. Then she turned back to her father. "Dad, you've got to come. Mum was at a suffrage march this morning. It was supposed to be peaceful, but it turned into a donnybrook, and the police came, and she was arrested and charged, and now she's in jail!"

Joe sighed. "Trudy, call the carriage, will you? Mr. Coyne, this is my daughter, Katharine. Katie, this is Mr. Coyne, one of my constituents," he said.

"Very pleased to meet you, sir," Kate said, extending a hand to Mr. Coyne. To her father she said, "Dad, come on! We've got to go!"

Harry Coyne stood. He put his hat on and said, "You go on, lad. I'll see meself out."

"I'll be on Lauriston Street tomorrow, Harry," Joe said, then he turned to his daughter. "What happened, Katie? How do you know she's in jail?" he asked her.

"Mum sent a messenger to the house. Oh, and Dad? How much money have you got on you? Because Mum says you need to post bail for her and Auntie Maud before they can be released, but you can do it at the jail, because they were taken straight there, not to the courts, and crikey but I'm parched! Are you going to finish that?"

Joe handed her his teacup. "Did you come all the way over here alone?" he asked sternly.

"No, I have Uncle Seamie with me and Mr. Foster, too."

"Uncle Seamie? What's he doing here?"

"He's staying with us again. Just for a bit while he's in London. Didn't Mum tell you?" Katie said, between gulps of tea.

"No," Joe said, leaning forward in his wheelchair and peering out of his office. Amid five or six of his constituents sat Mr. Foster, his butler, upright, knees together, hands folded on top of his walking stick. Upon seeing Joe looking at him, he removed his hat and said, "Good afternoon, sir."

Joe leaned farther and saw his usually brisk, no-nonsense secretary fluttering madly around someone. She was blushing and twisting her necklace and giggling like a schoolgirl. The someone was his brother-in-law. Seamie looked up, smiled, and gave him a wave.

"I wish Mum had let me go to the march. I wanted to. Would have, too, but she said I had to stay put in school," Katie said.

"Too right," Joe said. "This is the third school we've put you in this year. If you get thrown out of this one, it won't be so easy to find another that will take you."

"Come *on,* Dad!" Katie said impatiently, ignoring his warning.

"Where were they taken?" he asked.

"Holloway," Katie said. "Mum wrote in her note that over a

hundred women were arrested. It's so unfair! Mum and Dr. Hatcher and Dr. Rosen—they're all so accomplished and smart. Smarter than a lot of men. Why won't Mr. Asquith listen to them? Why won't he give them the vote?"

"He feels it won't go over well with the Liberal Party's voters, all of whom are men, and most of whom are not yet ready to acknowledge that women are every bit as smart, if not smarter, than they are," Joe said.

"No, I don't think so. That's not it."

Joe raised an eyebrow. "It isn't?"

"No. I think Mr. Asquith knows that if women get the vote, they'll use it to throw him out on his bum."

Joe burst into laughter. Katie scowled at him. "It's not funny, Dad. It's true," she said.

"It is indeed. Stuff those folders in my briefcase and bring it along, will you?"

Joe watched her as she put her pad and pen down and then collected his things, and as he did, his heart filled with love. He and Fiona had six children now: Katie, fifteen; Charlie, thirteen; Peter, eleven; Rose, six; and the four-year-old twins, Patrick and Michael. Looking at Katie now, so tall and grown-up, so beautiful, he remembered the day she was put into his arms, the day he became a father. From the moment he held her, and looked into her eyes, he was a changed man. He'd held that tiny girl in his arms that moment; he would hold her in his heart forever.

Joe loved all his children fiercely, and delighted in their differences, their passions, their opinions and abilities, but Katie, his first-born, was more truly his child than any of the others. In looks, she was a younger version of her mother. She had Fiona's Irish loveliness, her slender build and her grace, but Katie had got her driving passion—politics—from him. She was determined to go up to Oxford, read history, and then go into politics. She'd declared that once women were fully enfranchised, she would run for office on the Labour ticket and become the country's first female member of Parliament, and already her ambitions had gotten her into hot water.

Six months ago, she'd been asked to leave the Kensington School for Young Ladies after she'd single-handedly got the school's cleaners and groundsmen into a labor union. He and Fiona had found her a place at another school—Briarton—and then, three months ago, she was asked to leave that school, too. That time, it was three unexplained absences from her afternoon French and deportment classes that had gotten her into trouble. After the third infraction, the headmistress—Miss Amanda Franklin—had called Katie into her office. There, she asked Katie why she had missed her classes and what could possibly be more important than French and deportment.

For a reply, Katie had proudly handed her a single sheet newspaper, printed front and back. On the front, at the top, were the words *Battle Cry,* in twenty-two-point type. Followed by KATHARINE BRISTOW, EDITOR-IN-CHIEF, in eighteen-point.

"I should have told you about it, Miss Franklin. I would have, but I wanted to wait until it was finished, you see," she said proudly. "And here it is, hot off the presses."

"And what exactly is it, may I ask?" Miss Franklin had asked, raising an eyebrow.

"My very own newspaper, ma'am," Katie replied. "I just started it. I used my allowance money to get the first edition printed. But money from advertisements will help with the next one. I intend for it to be a voice for working men and women, to chronicle their struggle for fair working conditions, higher wages, and a stronger voice in government."

Katie's newspaper featured a story about the prime minister's refusal to meet with a delegation of suffragists, another about the appalling work conditions at a Milford jam factory, and a third about the enormous turnout for a Labour rally held in Limehouse.

"Who wrote these stories?" Miss Franklin asked, her hand going to the brooch at her neck, her voice rising slightly.

"I did, ma'am," Katie said brightly.

"You spoke with factory workers, Miss Bristow? And with radicals? You sat in upon debates in the Commons?" Miss Franklin said. "By yourself?"

"Oh, no. I had our butler with me—Mr. Foster. He always goes with me. Do you see those there?" Katie asked, pointing at advertisements for men's athletic supporters and bath salts for women's troubles. "I got those by myself, too. Had to knock on quite a few doors on the Whitechapel High Street to do it. Would you like to buy a copy, Miss Franklin?" Katie asked her eagerly. "It's only three pence. Or four shillings for a year's subscription. Which saves you one shilling and two pence over the newsstand price. I've already sold eleven subscriptions to my fellow students."

Miss Franklin, whose students included many privileged and sheltered daughters of the aristocracy—girls who had no idea that men had bits that needed supporting, or that women had troubles only bath salts could solve—went as white as a sheet.

She declined Katie's offer, and promptly wrote to her parents to inquire if their daughter's extracurricular activities might be more fully fostered at another school.

Joe supposed he should have been stern with Katie after she was sent down for a second time—Fiona certainly was—but he hadn't been able to. He was too proud of her. He didn't know many fifteen-year-old girls who could organize a labor force—a small one granted, but still—or publish their very own newspapers. He'd found her a new school, one that offered no deportment lessons and that prided itself on its progressive teaching methods. One that didn't mind if she missed French to attend Prime Minister's Questions—as long as she made up her homework and did well on her tests.

"Here you are, Dad. All packed," Katie said now, handing Joe his briefcase. Joe put it on his lap and wheeled himself out from behind his desk. Katie picked up her pad and pen and followed him.

Joe had been paralyzed by a villain's bullet fourteen years ago and had lost the use of his legs. An East End man by the name of Frank Betts, hoping to discredit Fiona's brother Sid—then a villain himself—had dressed like Sid, appeared in Joe's office, and shot him twice. One of the bullets lodged in Joe's spine. He'd only barely survived and spent several weeks in a coma. When he finally came to, his doctors gave him no hope of a normal, productive life. They said he would be bedridden, an invalid. They said he might well lose both his legs, but Joe had defied them. Six months after the shooting, he was healthy and strong. He'd had to give up the Tower Hamlets seat he'd won just before he'd been shot, but in the meantime, the MP for Hackney had died and a by-election had been called. Joe went out campaigning again, this time in a wheelchair. He won the seat for Labour handily and had held it ever since.

Joe rolled himself into his waiting room now and explained to his constituents what had happened to his wife. He apologized and asked them to please come back first thing in the morning. All agreed to his request, except a group of church ladies outraged over the posters they'd found plastered all over Hackney advertising a racy new musical revue—*Princess Zema and the Nubians of the Nile*.

"Lass has got about as much clothing on her as she had the day she was born!" one indignant lady—a Mrs. Hughes—said.

"I have to cover me grandkiddies' eyes when they walk down the very street we live on!" another—Mrs. Archer—exclaimed. "We've got the kaiser making ructions, and Mrs. Pankhurst and her lot throwing bricks through windows. Our young girls are smoking and driving, and to top it all off, we've now got naked Egyptians in Hackney! I ask you, Mr. Bristow, what's the world coming to?"

"I don't know, Mrs. Archer, but I give you my word that I will personally see to it that the posters are removed by the end of the week," Joe said.

After he'd mollified the women, and they'd left his office, Joe, together with Katie, Seamie, and Mr. Foster, took the elevator to the street, where Joe's driver and carriage were stationed. Another carriage, the one Katie and her escorts had traveled in, waited behind his.

"Thanks for coming to get me, luv," he said to Katie, squeezing her hand. "I'll see you at home."

"But I'm not going home. I'm going with you," Katie said.

"Katie, Holloway is a prison. It's not a Labour rally, or a jam factory. It's a terrible place and it's not fit for a fifteen-year-old girl,"

Joe said firmly. "Go with your uncle and Mr. Foster. Your mother and I will be home shortly."

"Come on, Kate the Great," Seamie said.

"No! I won't go home! You're treating me like a child, Dad!" Katie said hotly. "The suffrage movement is something that will affect me. It's politics. And women's rights. It's history in the making. And you're putting me on the sidelines! I want to write about the march and the arrests and Holloway itself for my paper and you're going to make me miss the whole thing!"

Joe was about to order Katie home when Mr. Foster cleared his throat. "Sir, if I may make an observation," he began.

"As if I could stop you, Mr. Foster," Joe said.

"Miss Katharine does present a most persuasive argument—a skill, I might add, which will serve her well in Parliament one day. What a remarkable boon for the country's first female MP to be able to say she was on the front lines of the fight for women's suffrage."

"You've got *him* in your pocket, too, haven't you?" Joe said to his daughter.

Katie said nothing. She just looked at her father hopefully.

"Come on, then," Joe said. She clapped her hands and kissed him.

"We'll see if you're so happy once you're inside Holloway," he said. "Don't say I didn't warn you."

"Can you use a hand, Joe?" Seamie asked. "I'm feeling a bit useless here."

"I could," Joe said. "And an extra bit of dosh, too. Since it seems I'm expected to liberate half the prison. Have you got any?"

Seamie checked his wallet, said that he did, and handed Joe twenty pounds. Joe asked Mr. Foster to take the second carriage home.

"I will, sir," Mr. Foster replied. "And I shall have the maid ready a pot of tea."

"Good man," Joe said.

He, Seamie, and Katie got into his carriage, a vehicle custom made to accommodate his chair. The driver carefully urged his pair of bay horses into traffic, then headed west, toward the prison. In only a few minutes they were at London Fields, the park where the suffrage march was to have terminated. The three passengers had been talking during the ride, but they all fell silent as the carriage rolled past the green.

"Blimey," Joe said, looking out one of the windows.

Wherever they looked, they saw devastation. The windows of a local pub and several houses were broken. Costers' carts were upended. Apples, oranges, potatoes, and cabbages had rolled everywhere. Banners, torn and tattered, hung limply from lampposts. Trampled placards littered the ground. Residents, costermongers, and the publican were trying their best to restore order to the square, sweeping up glass and debris.

"Dad, I'm worried about Mum," Katie said quietly.

"Me, too," Joe said.

"What happened here?" Seamie asked

Joe could hear a note of alarm in his voice. "I'm not sure," he replied, "but I don't think it was good."

As the carriage rolled out of the square, Joe saw the publican throw a bucket of water over the cobbles in front of his pub. He was washing something red off them.

"Was that—" Seamie started to say.

"Aye," Joe said curtly, cutting him off. He didn't want his daughter to hear the word, but it was too late.

"Blood," she said.

"Blood?" Seamie said, shocked. "Whose blood?"

"The marchers'," Joe said quietly.

"Wait a minute . . . you're telling me that women—*women*—are being beaten up on the streets of London? For marching? For asking for the vote?" Seamie shook his head in disbelief, then said, "When did this start happening?"

"You've been off tramping across icebergs for quite a few years, mate," Joe said wryly. "And then off on your lecture tours, too. If you'd stayed in London, you'd know that no one's *asking* for much of anything anymore. The have-nots—whether they're the poor of

Whitechapel, or national labor unions, or the country's suffragists—
are all demanding reform now. Things have changed in dear old England."

"I'll say they have. What happened to the peaceful marches?"

Joe smiled mirthlessly. "They're a thing of the past. The struggle
for suffrage has turned violent," he said. "We've now two factions
pushing for the vote. There's the National Union of Women's Suffrage Societies—led by Millicent Fawcett, with Fiona a member—
which wants to work constitutionally to achieve its aims. And then
there's the Women's Social and Political Union, let by Emmeline
Pankhurst, which has become fed up with Asquith's foot-dragging
and has turned militant. Christobel, Emmeline's daughter, is a firebrand. She's chained herself to gates. Thrown bricks through windows. Heckled the PM in public. Set things on fire. The Pankhursts'
activities get a lot of press coverage. Unfortunately, they also get
the Pankhursts—and anyone who happens to be near them—
arrested."

Joe glanced at Katie as he spoke, and saw that she'd gone pale.
"It's not too late, luv. I can still get you home," he told her. "I'll have
the driver take us there first, then Uncle Seamie and I can continue
on to Holloway."

"I'm not afraid, Dad. And I'm not going home," Katie said quietly. "This is my battle, too. Who's Mum doing this for? You? Charlie? Peter? No. For me. For me and Rose, that's who. The least I can
do is go with you to fetch her. And write about what I see for my
paper."

Joe nodded. Brave girl. Just like your mother, he thought. Bravery was good and bravery was noble, but bravery couldn't protect
one from horses and batons. He was anxious about his wife, worried
she might've been hurt.

"I guess that old dear was right," Seamie said.

"What old dear?" Joe asked.

"The one in your office. The one complaining about the musical
revue. She asked you, 'What's the world coming to?' I thought she

was just a cranky old bat, going on about naked Egyptians, but now I'm wondering if maybe she had a point. England, London . . . they're not the same places that I left back in 1912. I sound like an old dear myself, but stone me, Joe—roughing up women? What *is* the world coming to?"

Joe looked at his brother-in-law, whose expression was still one of astonishment. He thought of his wife and her friends in some dank holding cell in Holloway. He thought of the strikes and labor marches that were nearly a daily occurrence in London now. He thought of the latest volley of threats from Germany, and of Winston Churchill's telephone call, which had almost certainly been about garnering support for the financing of more British battleships.

And he found that he had no answer.

CHAPTER THREE

SEAMIE FINNEGAN THOUGHT he knew about prisons. He'd been in one for a few days once, years ago in Nairobi. His brother Sid had been incarcerated there for a crime he had not committed. Seamie and Maggie Carr, a coffee plantation owner and Sid's boss, had contrived to break him out, which had involved Seamie and Sid trading places. It hadn't been a difficult thing to do. There had only been one guard on duty and the building itself was, as Mrs. Carr had put it, "a two-bit ramshackle chicken coop of a jail."

Now, however, as he gazed at the building looming in front of him, Seamie realized he knew nothing about prisons, for Holloway was like nothing he'd ever seen.

It looked like a dark medieval fortress, one with a keep, an iron

gate, and crenellated turrets. A pair of gryphons flanked the entrance—
an arched passage wide enough to permit carriages—and through it
he could see the cell blocks—long, rectangular structures with row
upon row of small, high windows.

He felt suffocated just looking at it. His explorer's soul craved
the vast, open places of the world—the snowy expanses of Antarctica and the soaring peaks of Kilimanjaro. To him, the mere
thought of being confined behind Holloway's ugly stone walls was
crushing.

"Uncle Seamie, this way. Come on," Katie said, tugging on his hand.

Joe had already rolled through the passage in his wheelchair and
was halfway across the lawn and heading toward an inner building
marked RECEIVING. Seamie and Katie quickly caught up with him.

The scene inside the receiving area was chaos. As Joe counted out
Fiona's and her friend Maud Selwyn Jones's bail money to a uniformed
man seated behind a desk, and Katie interviewed a woman holding a
bloodstained handkerchief to her head, other women—many wearing
torn and bloodied clothing, some with cuts and bruises—angrily de-
nounced the wardresses and the warden. Family members and friends
who'd come to collect them pleaded with them, trying to convince
them to leave, but they would not.

"Where's Mrs. Fawcett?" one of them shouted. "We won't leave
until you release her!"

"Where are Mrs. Bristow and Dr. Hatcher?" another yelled.
"What are you doing with them? Let them go!"

The chant was taken up. Scores of voices rang out as one. "Let
them go! Let them go! Let them go!"

The noise was immense. Over it, a wardress yelled that they must
all leave, right now, but she was soon shouted down. Seamie saw an
older man in a black suit and white collar going from guard to guard,
a worried expression on his face.

Joe saw him, too. He called to him. "Reverend Wilcott? Is that
you?"

The man turned around. He wore spectacles, was clean-shaven, and looked to be in his fifties. His hair was graying, his expression kindly and befuddled.

He squinted at them, lifted his glasses, and said, "Ah! Mr. Bristow. Well met in Islington, eh?"

"Hardly, Reverend. Jennie's been arrested, too, then?"

"Indeed she has. I've come to collect her, but she doesn't appear to be here. I'm most concerned. The warden has released many of the women to family members, but not Jennie. I've no idea why. I spotted Mr. von Brandt a moment ago, looking for Harriet. Ah! Here he is now."

A tall, well-dressed man with silvery blond hair joined them. Introductions were made and Seamie learned that Max von Brandt—German and from Berlin originally, but currently living in London—was Dr. Harriet Hatcher's cousin and had been sent by Harriet's anxious mother to fetch her.

"Have you found her?" Joe asked him.

"No, but I did see the warden briefly, and he told me that Harriet and several other officers from the National Union of Women's Suffrage Societies are being held elsewhere in the prison."

"Why?" Joe asked.

"He said it was for their own safety. He told me that he'd had to separate officers of Mrs. Fawcett's group from those of Mrs. Pankhurst's. There were some harsh words between them, apparently, and he feared further hostilities would take place. He said they would be released shortly, but that was an hour ago and there's still no sign of them."

Joe, frustrated, wheeled himself over to a harried wardress to try to find out more. Max went with him. Katie continued to interview marchers and scribble notes. Seamie and the Reverend Wilcott attempted to make polite conversation. The reverend knew Seamie's name and asked about his adventures in Antarctica. Seamie learned that the reverend headed a parish in Wapping and that his daughter Jennie, who lived in the rectory with him, ran a school for poor children in the church.

"It's also a de facto soup kitchen," the Reverend Wilcott explained. "As Jennie always says, 'Children who are hungry cannot learn, and children who cannot learn will always be hungry.'"

As Reverend Wilcott was talking, a gate at the far end of the receiving room was opened and a group of dazed and weary-looking women walked through it. Seamie recognized his sister immediately, but his relief at seeing her soon turned to dismay. Fiona's face was bruised. There was a cut on her forehead and blood in her hair. Her jacket was torn.

As the women entered the receiving area, a cheer went up from their fellow marchers—those who had been released but had refused to leave. There were hugs and tears and promises to march again. Joe and Katie hurried to collect Fiona. Seamie followed them. Women's voices swirled around him as he made his way across the room. Seamie didn't know most of the women, but he recognized a few of them.

"God, but I need a cigarette," one woman said loudly. Seamie knew her. She was Fiona's friend Harriet Hatcher. "A cigarette and a tall glass of gin," she said. "Max, is that you? Thank God! Give us a fag, will you?"

"Hatch, is that a cigarette? Have you got an extra?" Seamie knew that voice, too. It belonged to Maud Selwyn Jones, the sister of India Selwyn Jones, who was married to his and Fiona's brother Sid.

"You all right, Fee?" Seamie asked his sister when he finally got to her. Joe and Katie were already on either side of her, fussing over her.

"Seamie? What are you doing here?" Fiona asked.

"I was at home when your message arrived. I accompanied Katie."

"Sorry, luv," Fiona said.

"No, don't apologize. I'm glad I came. I had no idea, Fiona. None. I . . . well, I'm so glad you're all right."

He was upset to see the marks of violence on her. Fiona had raised him. They'd lost both parents when she was seventeen and he was four, and she'd been both sister and mother to him. She was one of the most loving, loyal, unselfish human beings he had ever known, and to think that someone had hurt her . . . well, he only wished he had that someone here now, right in front of him.

"What happened?" Joe asked her.

"Emmeline and Christabel happened," Fiona said wryly. "Our group was marching peacefully. There were crowds there, and police constables, but very little heckling or baiting. Then the Pankhursts showed up. Christabel spat at a constable. Then she lobbed a rock through a pub window. Things went downhill from there. There was a great deal of shouting. Fights broke out. The publican's wife was furious. She walloped Christabel, and went after other marchers, too. The police started making arrests. Those of us who had been marching peacefully resisted and, as you can see, paid for it quite dearly."

"The warden told us you were being held downstairs for your safety," Joe said. "That there was scuffling between the two factions here at the prison."

Fiona laughed wearily. "Is that what he told you?"

"It's not true, Mum?" Katie asked.

"No, luv, it's not. The warden held us downstairs, but not for our safety. There was no scuffling between us. The warden wanted to scare us, and he did. But he didn't scare us off. He'll never succeed in doing that."

"What do you mean, scare you off?" Seamie asked.

"He put us all in a cell next to one in which a woman, another suffragist on a hunger strike, was being force-fed. He did it on purpose. So we would hear it. It was terrible. We had to listen to the poor thing scream and struggle, and then she was violently sick. So they did the whole thing over again. And again. Until she kept the food down. They made sure we saw her, too. Afterward. They marched her right by our cell when it was over. She could hardly walk. Her face was bloodied. . . ."

Fiona paused, overcome by emotion. When she could finally speak again, she said, "We were all quite undone, sickened ourselves, and cowed, every one of us. Except Jennie Wilcott. She was the only one amongst us with any presence of mind. She was magnificent. As the woman was marched by us, Jennie started to sing. She sang 'Abide with Me,' and the woman heard her. Her head was hanging down, but when Jennie sang, she looked up. And then she smiled. Through the blood and the tears, she smiled. And then we all started singing. I think the whole prison must have heard us and taken heart. And it was all because of Jennie."

"Fiona, what exactly is force—" Seamie had started to ask, when a young woman suddenly stumbled and bumped into him. She was small and blond, about twenty-five or so, he guessed, and she had the ugliest black eye he'd ever seen.

"Pardon me! I'm ever so sorry," she said, embarrassed. "It's this eye. I can't see terribly well with only one." She was holding tightly to the Reverend Wilcott's arm.

"There's no need to apologize," Seamie said. "None at all."

"Mr. Finnegan, this is my daughter Jennie Wilcott," the Reverend said. "Jennie, this is Seamus Finnegan, Fiona's brother and a very famous explorer. He found the South Pole."

"Very pleased to meet you, Miss Wilcott," Seamie said.

"Likewise, Mr. Finnegan. How on earth did you get from the South Pole to Holloway? Some great misfortune must have befallen you."

Before Seamie could answer her, Katie tugged on his arm. "Uncle Seamie, we're leaving now. Are you coming?"

Seamie said he was, then turned back to the Wilcotts. "Please, take my arm, too, Miss Wilcott. It'll be easier for you with someone on either side of you. I know it will. I went snowblind once. On my first trip to Antarctica. Had to be led around like a lamb."

Jennie took Seamie's arm. Together, Seamie and the Reverend Wilcott walked her out of the receiving area, toward the long, gloomy passageway that led from the prison to the street.

"Fiona's just been telling us about your ordeal," Seamie said as they walked. "You must be the same Jennie who sang 'Abide with Me'?"

"Did you now, Jennie?" the Reverend Wilcott said. "You told me about the force-feeding but you didn't tell me that. I'm glad you sang that one. It's a lovely old hymn. It must have given that poor woman a great deal of comfort."

"My motivation had more to do with defiance than comfort, I'm afraid, Dad," Jennie said. "I sang to that woman, yes. But also to her tormentors. I wanted them to know that no matter what they do to us, they will not break us."

"What is force-feeding?" Seamie asked. "And why were the wardresses force-feeding a prisoner?"

"Do you not read the London papers, Mr. Finnegan?" Jennie asked. There was an edge to her voice.

"Indeed I do, Miss Wilcott," Seamie replied. "But they are hard to come by in New York, Boston, or Chicago. To say nothing of the South Pole. I only returned to London a month ago."

"Forgive me, Mr. Finnegan. For the second time. It has been a very trying day," Jennie said.

"Once again, there is nothing to forgive, Miss Wilcott," Seamie said. He turned toward her as he spoke. Her eye was horribly swollen. He knew it had to be very painful.

"It was a fellow suffragist the wardresses were force-feeding," Jennie said slowly. "One who'd been arrested for damaging Mr. Asquith's carriage. She's been in prison for a month now and is in the process of starving herself."

"But why would she do that?"

"To protest her imprisonment. And to call attention to the cause of women's suffrage. A young woman starving herself to death in prison makes for a good news story and elicits a great deal of sympathy from the public—which makes Mr. Asquith and his government very unhappy."

"But surely you can't force a person to eat if she doesn't wish to."

Jennie, who'd been looking straight ahead as she walked, turned her head, appraising him with her good eye. "Actually, you can. It's a very dreadful procedure, Mr. Finnegan. Are you sure you wish to know about it?"

Seamie bristled at her question, and at her appraisal of him. Did she think he couldn't handle it? He'd handled Africa. And Antarctica.

He'd handled scurvy, snowblindness, and frostbite. He could certainly handle this conversation. "Yes, Miss Wilcott, I am sure," he said.

"A female prisoner on hunger strike is subdued," Jennie began. "She is wrapped in a sheet to prevent her from flailing and kicking. Of course she does not wish to cooperate with the wardresses, or the prison doctor, and so clamps her mouth shut. Sometimes, a metal gag is inserted between her lips to force her mouth open and she is fed that way. At other times, a length of rubber tubing is forced into her nose and down her gullet. Needless to say, that is very painful. The doctor pours nourishment through the tube—usually milk mixed with powdered oats. If the woman is calm enough, she can breathe during the procedure. If she is not . . . well, if she is not, then there are difficulties. When the allotted amount of milk has been fed, the tube is removed and the woman is released. If she vomits it up, the doctor begins again."

Seamie's stomach turned. "You were right, Miss Wilcott," he said, "it *is* a dreadful thing." He caught her glance and held it. She knew a great deal about the procedure. He shuddered as he guessed the reason why. "It's been done to you, hasn't it?" he asked. As soon as the words were out of his mouth, he regretted them. It was not the sort of thing one asked a woman one had only just met.

"Yes, it has. Twice," Jennie said, unflinchingly. Her frankness surprised him.

"Perhaps we should find a pleasanter subject to talk about with Mr. Finnegan, my dear," the Reverend Wilcott said gently. "Look! Here we are. Out of the lion's den and into the light. Just like Daniel."

Seamie looked ahead of himself. They'd come to the end of the long stone passageway and were now outside of the prison. He saw that his family had preceded him to the street. Darkness was coming down and the streetlamps were glowing.

Fiona was sitting on a bench, her eyes closed. Katie sat next to her scribbling in her notepad. Joe, Seamie guessed, had gone off in search of the carriage. The street had been filled with carriages when they'd arrived, and his driver had not been able to park in front of the prison. Harriet Hatcher, standing next to the bench, had found a fresh cigarette. Max and Maud were with her. Maud was laughing throatily over something Max had just said.

"I must find a hackney cab. Mr. Finnegan, would you be so good as to stay with Jennie while I do?" the Reverend Wilcott asked.

Seamie said that he would. "Let's get you to a bench, Miss Wilcott," he said.

They passed under a streetlight on their way, and Seamie, glancing once again at Jennie's face, let out a low whistle. He examined the puffed and blackened flesh in the lamplight and winced.

"Is it very bad?" Jennie asked.

"It is. It's awful."

"Why, thank you," Jennie said, laughing. "Thank you very much! Ever hear of something called tact?"

Seamie laughed, too. He had seen something else when he'd looked at her just now—that she was very pretty, even with a black eye. A few seconds of awkward silence followed, and Seamie found he didn't want their conversation to end. He quickly thought of something to say to make sure it didn't.

"Your father mentioned that he heads a church in the East End."

"Yes, that's right. In Wapping. St. Nicholas's. Are you familiar with the saint?"

"No," Seamie said, suddenly worried that she would give him some dull, proselytizing description of the saint and all his miraculous doings, and then admonish him to start attending church on Sundays, but again she surprised him.

"He's the patron saint of sailors, thieves, and prostitutes," she said. "Which means he's perfect for us, really, since we have plenty of all three in Wapping. You should see the High Street on a Saturday night."

Seamie laughed again. "Have you been in Wapping a long time?" he asked her.

"We've been there for twenty-five years now. Well, my father has," Jennie said. "Dad took over a poorly attended church and made it vital again. My mother opened a school for neighborhood children about twenty years ago. I took it over six years ago. One hundred percent of our children stay until they're fourteen. And twenty percent of our graduates go on to a vocational school," Jennie said. "Of course, we don't do it alone," she continued. "That the school is still open is due mostly to the generosity of your sister and brother-in-law, Mr. Finnegan. It is their school as much as mine. In fact, they just gave us money for ten more desks and a blackboard."

Seamie found that he was very interested in the work she was doing. He wanted to ask her more about it, but they'd reached the bench. Fiona and Katie moved over to make room for Jennie. Harriet, Max, and Maud, having finished their cigarettes, walked over to join them.

"Were you just talking about your school, Jennie?" Fiona asked, opening her weary eyes.

"I was," Jennie replied. "In fact, I was just telling your brother about yours and Joe's contributions."

Fiona smiling tiredly, pointed at a poster stuck to the side of an idling omnibus. "I was just thinking about the school myself. I see that one of your former students, little Josie Meadows, has done quite well for herself," she said. " 'Princess Zema, Ancient Egypt's Most Mysterious Enigma.' Mysterious *and* an enigma. Top that if you can!"

Jennie, looking at the poster now, too, sighed. "I suppose she has. If you call dancing around half-naked and carrying on with villains doing well."

"Villains?" Fiona echoed.

"Half-naked?" Seamie said.

"Princess Zema?" Harriet said. "Why do I know that name?"

"Because it's on every billboard, every telephone pole, and every bus in London," Jennie said, shaking her head. "Josie Meadows, a girl I used to teach, is the lead."

"In *Princess Zema*," Fiona said. "Eighty exotic dancers, twenty peacocks, two panthers, and a python bring to life the story of an

Egyptian princess, stolen from her palace bed on the eve of her wedding, sold into slavery by a false, fierce, and felonious pharaoh."

"Sounds fantastically fabulous," Max joked.

"My goodness, Fiona, how do you know all that? You haven't seen it, have you?" Jennie said.

Fiona shook her head. "Charlie, my eldest boy, had the poster. God knows where he got it. I took it away from him. It's rather risqué, as you can see."

"Josie was actually more than just a student of mine," Jennie explained to Seamie and the others. "She was like a sister to me. I'd taught her since she was ten years old. She's nineteen now. She desperately wanted to be on stage. And now she is. As an exotic dancer. She does a number with veils, I'm told, that leaves very little to the imagination."

"What's this about villains?" Fiona asked.

"Rumor has it that Billy Madden's taken a fancy to her," Jennie said quietly.

"Billy Madden," Fiona said grimly. "My god, what a foolish girl. She doesn't know what she's gotten herself into."

She traded glances with Seamie. They both knew who Billy Madden was—the most powerful crime lord in all of London. Sid, their brother, and once the boss of the entire East End crime world, had told them Madden was one of the most brutal, vicious men he'd ever known.

"Oh, I think she does know," Jennie said sadly. "I saw her the other day. Diamonds on her fingers and bruises on her face."

"Yegads, how ghastly," Maud said. "As if today wasn't depressing enough already. Let's change the subject. Or better yet, let's have another smoke. Harriet, darling, care to join me? Max?"

"I guess I had better, Miss Selwyn Jones," Max said. "Since I'm the one with the cigarettes."

As Maud, Max, and Harriet headed to the curb so as not to blow smoke all over the others, Fiona turned back to Jennie. "Never mind Josie and her villains. Tell Seamie about one of our successes," she said. "Tell him about Gladys."

But before Jennie could tell him, Joe arrived with his carriage. Fiona and Katie said their good-byes and offered to take Maud with them and drop her at her home. Maud thanked them, but said she would go to the Hatchers' house with Harriet and Max. Seamie said he would wait with Miss Wilcott until her father returned, and then get his own cab to Fiona and Joe's house.

"I'd love to hear about the other girl," he said to Jennie, when they'd left. He was glad the others had gone—glad for the chance to talk with her alone.

"The other girl?" Jennie repeated.

"The success story. You were starting to tell me about her when Joe came with the carriage."

Jennie smiled. "Yes, I was. Gladys Bigelow *is* a success story," she said. "Truly. She was a student at our school. A very bright girl. Came from a dreadful situation—a drunken, violent father, who's since died, and a very poorly mum. She was destined for some dreadful job in a factory, but instead she's working for Sir George Burgess, second in command under Mr. Churchill at the Admiralty."

Seamie watched Jennie's expression change as she talked about her former student. Her face became radiant.

"She attended our little school, then went on to secretarial studies. I'd originally asked Fiona and Joe if they might have a place for her. They didn't at the time, but Joe knew Sir George was looking for a capable girl and he gave him Gladys's name. And Sir George hired her."

"That's a wonderful story, Miss Wilcott," a voice said from behind them. It was Max von Brandt. Seamie hadn't been aware that Max was listening. He hadn't even known Max was there. He'd thought he was still out by the curb, smoking.

"Yes, it is, Mr. von Brandt," Jennie said, turning toward Max. "That job has changed her life. Gladys was a bit shy. A bit withdrawn, you see. All she had in her life was her sick mother and her Thursday-night knitting group. And now, because of her studies, she also has a job she loves. At the Admiralty, no less! She has purpose and independence, and they mean the world to her. Why, she's even become a suffragist. She attends the evening meetings. Isn't it amazing? These are the things an education can do."

"Jennie! Over here, my dear!"

It was the Reverend Wilcott. He'd finally found a cab.

"Take my arm," Seamie said. "I'll walk you to the street." Jennie did so. She said good-bye to Max, waved at Maud and Harriet, then Seamie led her toward the cab.

"I wonder, Mr. Finnegan . . . I wonder if I might ask you to come and speak to the children. At the school," she said as they walked. "Perhaps next week? You're a very dashing figure, you know. You've achieved so much, done so many amazing things. I know they would be so excited to see you. And so grateful. And so would I."

Seamie had speaking engagements planned for the week, and a meeting with Sir Clements Markham at the Royal Geographical Society. Markham had rung him up at Fiona's house and told him he wanted to speak with him about a position at the RGS. In addition, Seamie had long-standing plans with his friend George Mallory to go on a pub crawl. They were all reasons for saying no—but they weren't the main reason. The main reason he wanted to say no to Jennie Wilcott was that he was afraid to say yes. He was afraid to see her again. She stirred something in him. Admiration, he quickly told himself. But it was deeper than that, and he knew it and it scared him. The other women he'd been with over the last few years . . . they'd stirred something in him, too—his lust. This was a different feeling. Jennie Wilcott, in just the few moments he'd known her, had touched his heart. No woman had touched that part of him for a very long time.

Don't do it, he told himself. You've just finished with Caroline. The last thing you need right now is some new entanglement. "I'm not sure I can, Miss Wilcott. I'll have to look at my schedule," he said to Jennie.

"I understand, Mr. Finnegan," she said, trying to hide her disappointment. "You must be incredibly busy." She tried for a smile, but winced instead. "Oh! Ouch!" she exclaimed. "This eye's so big and fat, it hurts to even smile now."

"That shiner's getting worse, I'm afraid," Seamie said. And then without thinking, he gently touched the bruised skin around her eye. "It's going to swell a bit more and then, in a day or so, it'll start to go down, though the bruising will last a bit longer, I'm afraid."

"I take it you've had a few black eyes yourself," Jennie said.

"One or two," he admitted. "Good night, Miss Wilcott," he said, handing her into the carriage,

"Good night, Mr. Finnegan," Jennie said. She sat down, then leaned toward the door before he could close it. "You will try to visit our school, won't you? You'll think about it at least?"

Seamie looked at her, at her poor eye, nearly swollen shut now, at her blouse stained with blood. He thought of what she had endured in her fight to obtain the vote—beatings, imprisonment, force-feeding. He remembered how only days ago, at Cambridge, he'd felt that London, and everyone in it, was dull and gray, and wondered now if he'd been mistaken.

"Yes, Miss Wilcott," he finally said. "I will."

CHAPTER FOUR

WILLA ALDEN STOPPED her heavily laden yak. For several long minutes she did nothing but stare at the sight before her. She'd seen it too many times to count. She'd looked at it through a camera lens, a telescope, a theodilite, and a sextant. She'd photographed it, sketched it, mapped it, measured it. And still, it took her breath away.

"Oh, you beauty," she whispered. "You cold, impossible beauty."

Rising before her, all peaks, ridges, and sheer cliff faces, was Everest. A white plume swirled around the summit. Willa knew it was high winds blowing the snow around, but she liked instead to think it was the mountain spirit dancing around her high, remote home. *Chomolungma* the Tibetans called Everest—Goddess Mother of Mountains. '

From where she stood, a few miles south of Rongbuk village, on the Rongbuk Glacier, Willa could see the mountain's north face rising. Time after time, her head told her there was no way up that bloody mountain, and time after time, as she looked at the north face, all forbidding rock and snow, her heart wouldn't listen. What about that ridge? Or that spur? it said to her. And that cliff . . . it looks like a tough nut from here, but maybe if a very experienced climber were to tackle it, in good weather, a very gifted climber, one equipped with an oxygen tank . . . what then?

There was no way up Everest, no way at all, without oxygen— of this she was certain. She had suffered badly from altitude sickness climbing Kilimanjaro's Mawenzi peak, and that was only about seventeen thousand feet. What would happen to a human being at twenty-nine thousand feet?

Willa knew the first symptoms of altitude sickness—the ceaseless nausea and vomiting; the swelling of the face, hands, and feet; and the crucifying difficulty of pulling air in and out of your lungs. She had suffered all of them. And as one climbed higher, the symptoms became more serious. Altitude sickness often attacked the lungs. A dry, hacking cough would set in, and then fever—both of which signaled fluid in the lungs. A climber might then find himself coughing up bright red froth. If the height didn't get the lungs, it often got the brain. A nagging headache became a crashing one. Confusion followed, and then blurred vision. The climber started losing control over his hands and feet. If he didn't get down, and fast, paralysis and coma were next. Then death.

"Why?" people asked her, unable to understand that which made alpinists risk everything to achieve a summit.

If only I could show them this sight, this magnificent Everest soaring into the blue sky. Untouched, pristine, wild, and fearsome, she thought. If only I could show them that, they'd never ask why again.

And soon she would. Soon her pictures of the Himalayas would be published. She had almost all the shots she needed. Soon the world would see for itself what mere words could never adequately describe.

"Come on, old stick," she said to her yak.

She pulled her fur cap down tightly around her ears and clapped her mittened hands together. A small, thin grimace stiffened her features as she and her animal started walking again. Her leg was playing up. Just a bit. But a bit often turned into something more, and she had no time for it today. She wanted to be well upon the Rongbuk Glacier and have her camp set up by early afternoon. She had a great deal of work to do.

During the time she'd been in the Far East, she'd sent the Royal Geographical Society photographs—shots of India, of her temples and cities and villages. Of her mighty rivers, arid plains, her lush hills and valleys. She'd sent pictures of China and its Great Wall. Of Marco Polo's Silk Road and Genghis Khan's Mongolia. Sir Clements Markham had shown her pictures at the RGS. He'd turned them into books—books that had made her a bit of money.

Two years ago, she'd written Markham with a new proposal—a book of photographs on the Himalayas. Of Annapurna. The Nilgiris. And Everest.

A few months later, she'd received his one-line reply—*Himalayas. Yes. How soon?*—and ever since, she'd been working nonstop, pushing herself mercilessly in the pursuit of the perfect shot—a shot that would be stunning and beautiful, so good it would make people gasp, or quiet them into a reverent awe. She now had more than two hundred images for her Himalayas book—of the mountains in all their moods, the villages that surrounded them, the people who lived at their feet.

And the route. She had that.

She had pictures of what might be a way up Everest.

And they would make her famous. Cement her reputation as an Alpine explorer. They would sell a great deal of books and make her money, which was something she desperately needed now. Her aunt

Eddie had given her five thousand pounds when she was younger, but she'd already spent a good deal of it. On a passage to Africa. And then one to India. On her travels throughout the Far East. On bribes to officials to let her cross borders. On food and tea and shelter. On cameras and film, darkroom equipment, tents and cots, and the animals needed to carry it all.

The route, the path, the way, she thought now, squinting up at the mountain as she trekked along. Markham wanted it. The Germans wanted it. The Italians and the French and the Americans, too. Alpinists were a competitive lot; being first was all that mattered to them. And being first up the highest mountain in the world—well, there was no prize greater than that. Willa knew that well enough. She'd been first once. First up the Kilimanjaro's Mawenzi peak. It had cost her her leg and nearly her life. It had cost her her heart.

"Hup, hup!" she said to her yak, urging him up the snowy shoulders of the glacier.

They walked on, over the white vastness, for an hour, then two, until Willa had what she wanted—an unobstructed view of the north col. She stopped then, hammered an iron stake into the snow, and tied the yak. Slowly, methodically, she unloaded her animal and set up camp.

It took her an hour to unpack her gear, pitch her tent, and build a fire pit. She always traveled and worked alone. She preferred it that way, but even if she hadn't, there was no other choice. There were not many women who wished to live as she did, in a cold, foreign, and forbidding environment. Without any domestic comforts. Without a husband or children. Without any guarantee of safety or protection.

And as for men . . . Willa would have gladly signed on to any number of expeditions sponsored by the RGS, but they would not have her. Their expeditions were conceived and executed by men, and it was still unthinkable for a woman to be included in an exploratory party to the North Pole or the South Pole, or down the Nile, or up Everest, because she would have to trek, climb, eat, and sleep with men. And that was unacceptable. Not to herself or the men she might be climbing with, but to British society, and it was British society that was footing the bill. They were the ones contributing monies to the RGS, and they were the ones financing its expeditions.

When Willa finished setting up camp, she loaded her rifle and placed it on the ground beside her cot. The rifle was protection against wolves; the kind that went around on four legs and the kind that went around on two. When she was satisfied that everything was in its proper place, she fed her yak and then fixed herself a small meal of hot tea and sampa—a mixture of barley flour, sugar, and a pungent butter made from yak's milk. She deliberately ate little to keep herself thin. The thinner her body, the less likely she was to suffer her menses—an encumbrance at the best of times, and even more so when one was a world away from flush toilets and running water.

When she'd finished her meal, she decided to do a bit of trekking. It was late afternoon, she still had two, maybe three hours of light. She stood up to wash her dishes, and gave a small gasp. The yak bone prosthetic was lighter and more comfortable than the wooden one she'd had made in Bombay, when she'd first arrived in India, but after a long day's trekking, it still hurt her. The pain was growing stronger now. She knew what was coming and she dreaded it. People talked of the feeling of a phantom limb, of the odd, unsettling sensation that the lost arm or leg was still there—people who hadn't lost a limb, that was. Those who had knew of something different. They knew of the dull, hard aches that often turned into an unbearable agony. They knew of the lost days, the restless nights.

How many times had she screamed herself awake? How many nights had she torn her sheets to bits, wept and shrieked and banged her head against the wall, nearly blind from pain? Too many to count. Dr. Ribiero, the man who'd amputated her leg, had given her morphine in the days following her surgery. She'd left Nairobi on crutches only a few days after her amputation, with a few bottles of the drug, and had traveled east. And there, after her morphine supply had run out, she'd discovered opium. She'd bought it in the markets of Morocco and Marrakech, from farmers in Afghanistan, and from peddlers in India, Nepal, and Tibet. It dulled the pain in her leg, and it dulled a pain that was even sharper—the one in her heart.

She took some now. She reached into her coat pocket, for she always kept it close, drew out a small hardened chunk of brown paste, cut a piece off, and proceeded to smoke it in a pipe. Within minutes, the drug had beaten back the pain and she could walk again. She quickly cleaned her dishes, checked that her yak was tied securely, then set off.

Untethered and alone, trekking across the pristine snows of the glacier, she felt as wild and free as a falcon circling, a winter fox loping across the snow, a wolf howling at the moon. As she approached the lower foothills of Everest, the trek became a climb, but still she went on over an ice field, across some jagged moraine. The terrain became more challenging, and her artificial leg more of a hindrance, but she could not stop. Everest, soaring high above the glacier, was glorious. It pulled at her, cast its spell upon her, and she was powerless to resist it.

The low foothill became a proper slope, and still she pressed on, heedless and unaware, seduced by the mountain, refusing to remember that she could no longer climb. She used her good leg to push herself up the slope, and she used her bad one, too—jamming the carved, unfeeling toes into cracks and crevices, using the foot to pivot and the leg to hold her weight. She used her strong, sinewy arms to pull herself up to a hold, and her powerful hands to keep her there.

Up she went, higher and higher, intoxicated by the cold whiteness, the sound of her own breath, the incredible feeling of ascending. Of gaining the slope. She was climbing, well and fast, and then it happened. She lost a handhold and slipped. Down she hurtled, screaming, as the fall jammed the edge of her false leg into her flesh. Ten feet. Twenty. Thirty. At forty, she managed to arrest the fall, clawing at the side of the slope. She ripped off two nails doing so, but she'd only feel those later.

She clung there, shaking and sobbing, her face pressed into the snow. The pain of her injuries was terrible, but it wasn't that pain that was making her cry. It was the terrifying memories of Mawenzi. This fall had woken them up and they rushed at her now, paralyzing her. They were so intense, so harrowing, that she could not move an inch, she could only clutch at the slope, eyes closed, sick with fear.

She remembered the fall and the impact. She remembered Seamie getting her down off the mountain and then pulling her shattered leg straight. She remembered him carrying her for miles and miles. And the pain—she remembered the red, ragged, unspeakable pain.

She'd been out of her mind from it—and from fever—by the time Seamie got her to Nairobi. The doctor there had taken one look at her and decided to amputate immediately. She'd begged him not to, begged Seamie not to let him. But the doctor had taken her leg anyway, right below the knee.

Seamie had told her she would've died if he hadn't allowed the operation. What he hadn't understood is that she *had* died, at least a part of her had. She would never climb high again. She couldn't. Her artificial leg didn't allow the flexibility, the stability, and the fluid physical finesse that were required to undertake challenging ascents. In some ways, what had happened to her was worse than death, for all that was left to her now was working to ensure that others would one day climb the highest mountain in the world. It was a leftover life. A second best. She hated it, but it was all she had.

She had hated Seamie, too. Almost as much as she loved him. She'd cursed him, and her useless leg. She'd blamed him, too. Because it was easier that way—having somebody to blame for what had happened to her, someone other than herself.

She remembered leaving Nairobi, and taking a boat from Mombasa. Her wound was still seeping blood; she could barely hobble on her new crutches, but she was so wild with grief and anger, so overwhelmed by the conflicting emotions she felt for Seamie, that she'd wanted to put as much distance between herself and him as possible. She'd managed to get herself all the way to Goa, where she'd taken a small house on the coast. She'd stayed there for half a year, waiting for her leg to heal properly and mourning her lost life. When she'd gotten her strength back, she traveled to Bombay, where she'd found a doctor who could fit her with an artificial leg. She allowed herself a month in that city to learn how to walk properly on the new leg, and then, loaded with cameras, a few pieces of clothing, a chunk of her aunt's money, and little else, she left Bombay. She could never climb again, but she could still explore, and she was determined to do so. She left the civilized world, hoping to leave her heartbreak behind as well, but it followed her. Wherever she went, whatever she saw, or heard, or felt—it was Seamie she ached to share it with—whether it was the breathtaking vastness of the Gobi desert, the sound of a hundred camel bells announcing the arrival of a merchant's caravan, or the sun rising over the Potala Palace in Lhasa. She had tried to run away from him and had failed, for he was in her head and in her heart, always.

There had been times—so many of them when, longing for him, she would impulsively decide to return to London. And to him. If he would have her. As she began to pack, she would imagine seeing him again, talking to him, holding him in her arms—but then just as quickly, she would stop packing and tell herself that she was a fool because surely Seamie wouldn't even wish to see her, much less talk to her or take her in his arms. She had left him eight years ago. She'd run away. Blamed him. Broken his heart. What man could forgive those things?

A strong wind blew down upon Willa now, making her shiver, whirling away her memories of Mawenzi and of all she had lost there. She stopped trembling, stopped crying, and got herself down the last thirty feet of the climb.

Dusk was falling by the time she made it back to the glacier. She didn't have her gun with her, but she wasn't afraid. Camp was not far. She knew she would make it there before the light faded entirely. She was limping. Her leg was bleeding; she could feel it. Her hands, too. Opium would dull the pain of those wounds, and the wound to her heart as well.

Willa walked slowly across the snow, the sun setting behind her— a small, broken figure, lost in the shadows of the soaring, ageless mountain, and in the shadows of her own broken dreams.

CHAPTER FIVE

SEAMIE HAD BEEN a guest in Edwina Hedley's London house on many occasions. He should have been familiar with it, but every time he set foot in it, it looked completely different. Eddie was forever traveling and forever bringing home plunder from her adventures with which to redecorate it.

There might be a new bronze Buddha in the dining room. Or a stone carving of Kali. Or a Thai demon, a dragon from Peking, a beaded fertility goddess from the Sudan. There might be Indian silks draping the windows, or Afghan suzanis, or fringed shawls from Spain. Once when he'd visited, a massive Russian icon was hanging from the foyer's ceiling. Right now, a huge, ornate mosaic fountain was burbling in the middle of its floor.

"It looks like Ali Baba's cave," he said, turning around in circles.

"It looks like a bloody souk," Albie muttered. "How can anyone move with all this rubbish strewn about?"

"Good evening, my dears!" a voice boomed from the drawing room.

A few seconds later, Eddie was kissing them hello. She wore a flowing turquoise silk tunic over a long, beaded skirt, and heavy necklaces of amber and lapis. Her thick gray hair was piled high on her head, held in place by two silver combs. Bracelets of silver studded with onyx jangled on her wrists.

"I like the new decor, Eddie," Seamie said. "That fountain's a smasher."

"Oh, that's nothing!" Eddie replied. "Most of what I bought is still on a boat in the middle of the Mediterranean. I can't wait until it arrives. I bought an entire Bedouin tent! I shall have it installed in the backyard. And furnish it with rugs, skins, and pillows. And we shall have the most wonderful garden parties in it. I shall have to find some belly dancers, however, for the proper effect."

"Might take some doing here in Belgravia," Seamie said.

Albie handed her a box. "From Mum," he said.

Eddie peered inside. "An almond sponge! What a darling! She knows it's my favorite. But she shouldn't have taken the time to make it for me. Not with all that's going on. How is your father, dear?"

"About the same, Aunt Eddie. No change, I'm afraid," Albie said. Then he quickly changed the subject.

The admiral was not well, not at all. Seamie and Albie had visited him that afternoon. He was gaunt and gray-faced and barely had the energy to sit up in bed. Seamie knew that his old friend didn't like talking about his father's illness; he knew that it worried him terribly.

The admiral's illness had changed Albie. In fact, Seamie barely recognized his friend these days. Albie's entire personality had changed. He'd always been the befuddled academic—even when he was ten years old. He'd always been bookish and distracted, dreaming of formulas and theories. But he was more than distracted now. He was tense. He was haggard-looking and short-tempered. And how could he not be? Seamie wondered. He never stopped working. Seamie thought the constant work was likely Albie's way of coping with his fears for his father's health, but he wished he wouldn't push himself so hard. Albie spent almost all of his time poring over documents with Strachey and Knox and other Cambridge lads. They were already at work when Seamie rose in the morning, and were still at it when he went to bed at night. Seamie didn't know exactly what they were all doing—dreaming up more incomprehensible equations, he imagined—but whatever it was, it was damaging Albie. He barely ate or slept. Seamie had had to drag him out of his office and practically push him onto the train to London today. He was certain that if Albie kept up this punishing pace, he would soon find his own health broken.

"Come in, my dears! Come in and meet my other guest," Eddie said now, taking Seamie's arm and Albie's hand and leading them into her drawing room. Seamie saw that she'd gotten rid of her furniture and replaced it with low, painted wooden beds, each topped with bright silk cushions. The place looked like an opium den.

"Tom, this is my nephew Albie Alden, and his friend Seamus Finnegan, the dashing Antarctic explorer," Eddie said, as a young man, holding a glass of champagne, stood up to greet them. "Albie and Seamie, may I present Tom Lawrence. He's an explorer, too, but he prefers the warmer climes. He's just returned from the deserts of Arabia. We met onboard a steamer out of Cairo. Spent some lovely days together."

Seamie and Albie shook hands with Tom, then Eddie handed them glasses of champagne. Seamie guessed that Lawrence was in his mid-twenties. His skin was bronzed. His eyes were a light, Wedgwood blue; his hair was blond. He stood awkwardly in Eddie's overdone drawing room and looked so uncomfortable in his suit—as if he would like nothing better than to chuck it off, pull on some trousers and boots, and head back to the desert. Seamie liked him immediately.

"I believe we've met, Mr. Alden," Lawrence said. "I was visiting friends at Cambridge several years ago. The Stracheys. George Mallory. I met you and Miss Willa Alden, too. In the Pick. Do you remember?"

"Why, yes. Yes, I do," Albie said. "One of the Stephen girls was with you. Virginia."

"Yes, that's right," Lawrence said.

"I'm very pleased to see you again, Tom," Albie said. "I wouldn't have recognized you. The desert's turned you from a pasty English lad to a golden boy."

Lawrence laughed warmly. "You should have seen me a year ago," he said. "Not golden at all, but as red as a radish and peeling like an onion. How is Miss Alden? I've seen her photographs of India and China. They're quite remarkable. Superb, actually. Is she well?"

Albie shook his head. "I wish I could tell you. Unfortunately, I have no idea."

"I don't understand," Lawrence said, puzzled.

"She had an accident. About eight years ago. On Kilimanjaro. She was there with Mr. Finnegan," Eddie said, her eyes resting on Seamie as she spoke. "She took a fall and broke her leg. It had to be amputated. The fall broke her heart, too, I fear, for she never came back home. Took off to the East instead, the headstrong girl. To Tibet. Lives there with the yaks and the sheep and that bloody great mountain."

Seamie looked away. The conversation pained him.

Lawrence noticed. "I see. I fear I've treaded rather harshly on tender ground," he said. "Please forgive me."

Eddie flapped a hand at him. "Don't be silly. There's nothing to forgive. We've all moved past it. Well, most of us have."

Seamie looked out of a window. Most of the time he appreciated Eddie's honest nature, her candid words, but there were times he wished she could at least *try* to be subtle.

"Why is everyone still standing? Sit down," Eddie said. "Albie, you take those pillows . . . yes, those right there. Seamie, you sit here, next to Tom." Eddie's voice dropped to a whisper. "He's a spy, you know. I'm certain of it."

"What rubbish, Eddie," Lawrence said.

"What do you talk about with all those Arab sheiks, then, Tom? Camels? Pomegranates? I doubt it. You talk uprisings. Rebellion. Freedom from their Turkish masters."

"We talk about their lives, their ancestry, and their customs. I take photographs, Eddie. Of ruins and tombs and vases and pots. I make notes and sketches."

"You make maps and alliances, my dear," Eddie said knowingly.

"Yes. Well. Turkish delight, anyone?" Lawrence asked, passing a plate of sugared rosewater jellies.

"Tell me, Mr. Lawrence, how did you come to find yourself in Arabia?" Seamie asked diplomatically.

"Archaeology. I love digging up old things. Went to Syria while I was an undergraduate. Studied the crusaders' castles there and did my thesis on them. After I left university, I was offered work with

D. G. Hogarth, an archaeologist with the British Museum. I took it. Did quite a bit of digging in the ancient Hittite city of Carchemish. In fact, I think we dug up both banks of the Euphrates," Lawrence said happily.

"I don't know if I could take the desert," Seamie said. "All that heat and sand. I need snow and ice."

Lawrence laughed. "I understand your love of all things pristine and cold, Mr. Finnegan. I enjoy mountains, and Alpine scenery, but the desert, Mr. Finnegan . . . oh, the desert."

Lawrence stopped speaking for a few seconds and smiled help-lessly, and suddenly his was the face of a man in love.

"I wish you could see it," he said. "I wish you could hear the sound of the muezzins calling the faithful to prayer. And see the rays of the sun coming through the minarets. I wish you could taste the dates and the pomegranates, picked in a lush desert garden. And sit in a Bedouin tent at night listening to their stories. If you could meet the people—the imperious sheiks and sharifs. The veiled harem women. If you could meet Hussein, the sharif of Mecca, and his sons. If you could feel their hunger for independence, for freedom." He shook his head suddenly, as if embarrassed by the depth of his feeling. "If you could do these things, Mr. Finnegan, you would turn your back on Antarctica in a heartbeat."

"Oh, I don't know, Mr. Lawrence," Seamie said, baitingly. "I don't think your sand dunes can live up to my icebergs. To say nothing of my seals and penguins." His voice turned serious. He matched Lawrence's poetry with his own. "I wish you could see the sun ris-ing on the Weddell Sea, its rays striking the ice and exploding into a million shards of light. I wish you could hear the song the wind sings to you at night and the shrieking of the ice floes shifting and shattering on the restless seas. . . ."

Tom listened raptly as Seamie spoke. They were talking about such vastly different parts of the world, and yet their kinship was immediate, for each understood the passion in the other. They were explorers, and each felt the force that called one into the great unknown. They knew the pull that made one give up the comforts of hearth and home, the nearness of friends and family. It was no accident that they were both unmarried, Seamie and Lawrence. They belonged to their passion, their yearning to see, to discover, to know. They belonged to their quest, and to nothing else.

For a few seconds after he finished speaking, Seamie's heart clenched with sorrow. It was so good to sit with these people. So few understood what drove him, but they did. There was another who understood. But she wasn't here and he wished—with his heart and his soul and everything inside him—that she was.

"I'm going back as soon as I can," Lawrence said, breaking the silence, giving voice to the urge they were both feeling. To get out of this gray, smothering London and back into the wild, beckoning world. "I'm going back to Carchemish. I've been working under William Ramsey most recently, the renowned New Testament scholar. He's with the British Museum. I'm back here to give a report on our findings. It has to be done, of course, but as soon as I've finished, I'm heading back to the desert. There's so much more to do. And you, Mr. Finnegan? Have you any further adventures planned?"

"Yes," Seamie said. "And no. And . . . well, *possibly* I guess."

"That's a strange answer," Lawrence said.

Seamie admitted that it was. "Ernest Shackleton is getting up another expedition to Antarctica, and I'm very interested in going," he explained. "But I have a compelling reason to stay in London now, too."

"Really?" Eddie said, raising an eyebrow. "Who is she?"

Seamie ignored her. "Clements Markham offered me a position at the RGS. Just yesterday in fact. He wants me to help with the money-raising efforts for new expeditions. I'd have an office and a fancy brass plaque on the door and a salary, and he tells me I'd be a fool not to take it."

"He's right," Albie said. "You would be. You're getting too old for this *Boy's Own* adventure stuff."

"Why, thank you for pointing that out, Alb," Seamie said.

A melancholy quiet descended on both Seamie and Lawrence at those words. Perhaps he is thinking himself too old for further adventures, too, Seamie thought. Or perhaps, he—like me—travels the world because he's lost someone and hopes that if he goes far enough afield, if he's cold enough or hot enough, in deep enough danger, hungry enough or sick enough, he might just forget that person. He never does, of course, but he always keeps trying. The strange, sad mood persisted until Lawrence said, "And what do you do, Mr. Alden?"

"I'm a physicist," Albie said. "I teach at Cambridge."

"He writes the most horrible, inscrutable, incomprehensible equations you've ever seen," Eddie interjected. "On a blackboard in his office. All day long. He's supposed to be on sabbatical, taking it a bit easy. Instead, he's working all hours. It's absolutely inhuman."

"Aunt Eddie . . . ," Albie protested, smiling embarrassedly.

"It's true, Albie. You never rest. Never have a nice long lunch. Never go for a ramble. You're as washed-out-looking as a pair of old knickers. You need a holiday. I know you're the country's leading and most exalted boffin, Albie dear, but surely England can wait another month or two for whatever it is that you're working on?"

"No, Aunt Eddie, England can't," Albie said. He was still smiling, but there was suddenly an edge to his voice and a grim look in his eyes. Seamie stared at his old friend, startled. Albie never spoke in anything but polite and measured tones.

As quickly as it had come, though, the hard edge was gone, and Albie's voice was mild again. No one else seemed to have noticed the lapse and Seamie wondered if he'd only imagined it. Frowning slightly, he decided he would get Albie out of the house this week for a hike across the fens, no matter how much he protested.

Prodded by his aunt, Albie told them all a bit about his work, and about the current preoccupation of physics professors the world over: the rumor that Albert Einstein would soon publish a set of ten field equations that would support a new theory of general relativity. Albie was in the process of trying to explain geodesic equations when the butler appeared in the doorway and said, "Beg your pardon, ma'am, but dinner is served."

"Oh, thank God!" Eddie said. "My head is spinning!"

The party rose. Eddie led the way out of the drawing room and down the hallway to the dining room.

As they reached the dining room, Lawrence stopped suddenly and placed a hand on Seamie's arm. "Never mind Clements Markham," he said to him quietly and with feeling. "Come out and visit me, Mr. Finnegan. You're not too old for adventures; you can't be. Because if you are, then I am, too. And if I was, I shouldn't know what to do. I shouldn't know how to live, and, frankly, I wouldn't wish to. Do you understand that feeling?"

Seamie nodded. "I do, Mr. Lawrence. All too well."

"Then do come. Bake your cold bones in Arabia's desert heat for a while."

Eddie, who'd been standing inside the doorway to the dining room listening, said, "Tom's right, Seamie. Sod Markham and Shackleton, too. Go to the desert. Bake your bones in Arabia." She smiled, then added, "And thaw your heart while you're at it."

CHAPTER SIX

"FOURPENCE, MISTER. YOU won't regret it," the girl in the red shawl said, smiling seductively. Or trying to.

Max von Brandt, head down, shoulders hunched against the cold, shook his head.

"Two, then. I'm clean, I swear. Only been on the game a week." The false brazenness was gone. She sounded desperate now.

Max glanced at her face. She couldn't have been more than fourteen. A child. Thin and shivering. He pulled a sixpence from his pocket and tossed it to her. "Go home," he said.

The girl looked at the coin, then at him. "God bless you, mister. You're a good man, you are."

Max laughed. *Hardly,* he thought. He opened the door to the Barkentine, hoping the girl had not seen his face, or that she would not remember it if she had. The Barkentine, a den of thieves in Lime-house, on the north bank of the Thames, was the sort of place Max von Brandt occasionally had to visit but was careful never to be seen doing so.

He had done his best to blend in. He'd worn the rough clothes of a workingman, he hadn't shaved for three days, and he'd hidden his silvery blond hair under a flat cap, but it was harder to hide his height, his sun-bronzed skin, or the fact that his legs weren't bowed from rickets. These things came from good food and fresh air, and in the East End of London, there was precious little of either.

Once inside the pub, Max approached the bartender. "I need to see Billy Madden," he said to him.

"No one here by that name," the man said, not bothering to look up from the day's racing sheet.

Max looked around. He knew what Madden looked like; he had a picture. He knew what Madden was, too: a thief with a boatyard— which was exactly what he needed. He inspected the faces in the room. Many had scars. Some ignored him, others eyed him insolently. He saw a woman, young, blond, and pretty—despite the faded bruises on her face—sitting alone by a window. Finally, he spotted Madden at the back, playing a game of solitaire, and walked up to his table.

"Mr. Madden, I'd like to speak with you," he said.

Billy Madden looked up. He wore a bright scarf knotted around his neck and a gold hoop in one ear. A scar puckered his brow. His mouth was filled with decaying teeth. He was a large man, physically imposing, but most unsettling were his eyes. They were preda-tor's eyes—dark, soulless, and keen.

"Who the fuck are you?" Madden growled, his free hand going to a large flick knife on top of the table.

Max knew he would have to tread carefully. He'd been warned that Madden was violent and unstable. He wished he didn't have to deal with him, but he had no choice. The boys from Cambridge were hot on the scent. He had to find some new way of evading them, and fast, or everything would be ruined.

"My name is Peter Stiles. I'm a businessman. I would like to make a deal with you," he said, in a perfect London accent.

"You're a dead man, is what you are," Madden said. "You've a lot of bloody cheek. Maybe I'll cut some off. Throw it in the river. Throw you in after it. What's to stop me, eh?"

"A good deal of money," Max said. "I need your help, Mr. Madden. I'm prepared to pay you well for it. If you kill me, we can't do business."

Madden sat back in his chair. He gave a curt nod. He kicked a chair out from under the table. Max sat down.

"I've heard you've a boatyard," Max said. "I need a boat. A motorized one."

"For what?" Madden asked.

"To take a man from London to the North Sea. To certain coordinates there. Every fortnight. I also need a man who can pilot that boat. A man who is well known to the river authorities, who has been seen coming and going on the Thames for years, and whose movements will raise no eyebrows."

"Why do you need all this?"

"I have something that needs passing into other hands."

"Swag?" Madden asked.

"I would prefer not to say," Max said.

"If I'm risking my boat, and my man, I've a right to know," Billy said.

"Jewels, Mr. Madden. Valuable ones. I need to get them out of England, to the continent," Max said. He took his money clip out of his pocket, peeled off five twenty-pound notes from it, and laid them on the table. He rested his hand on top of them. "I'm prepared to make generous terms with you," he said.

Madden's small eyes lit up. He reached for the money, but Max did not release it.

"I'm paying you for your boat, your man, and your silence. Are we clear on this? If one word of this gets out, our deal is off."

"I hardly go looking for publicity in my line of work. Your secret's safe with me," Madden said.

Max nodded. He pushed the money over to him. "This is a down payment only. My man will bring more each time. His name is Hutchins. He will be on the dock behind the Barkentine two weeks from tonight. At midnight. Have your man meet him here."

Max stood up. He tipped his cap to Madden, then left. Madden was a grim and horrible man, and Limehouse a grim and horrible place. He was glad to be leaving both, but the meeting had been productive. Very productive.

He had something to pass into other hands, yes—but it wasn't jewelry. And he needed a chain to do it. A strong, unbreakable one stretching between London and Berlin.

And tonight, the first link had been forged.

CHAPTER SEVEN

"VOTES FOR WOMEN NO?" Seamie said, reading aloud the words on a huge banner stretched across his sister's dining room table. "That's not going to help your case, Fee," he added, as he kissed her cheek.

Fiona laughed. She had a needle in her hand and was bent over the banner, stitching. "I still have to add the W," she said. "Get yourself some breakfast, Seamie, luv."

"I think I will, thank you," Seamie said, sitting down at the table. A maid was clearing dirty plates, smeared with egg and jam, where the younger children had been sitting. They'd just gotten up from the table and had run past Seamie in the hallway. Only Katie and Joe remained at the table.

"Good morning all," Seamie said, but he got no response. Katie, her eggs untouched, her tea going cold, was shifting photographs around on a mocked-up layout of the *Battle Cry*. Joe, sitting at the head of the table, was writing furiously. The morning's newspapers lay open on the table near him. Crumpled sheets of paper littered the floor all around him.

"Pass us those kippers, Joe, will you?" Seamie said, as he put his napkin in his lap. "Joe? Oi! *Joe!*"

Joe looked up, blinking. "Sorry, lad," he said. "What is it?"

"Can I have the kippers?" Seamie said. Joe passed them over. "What are you doing?" Seamie asked him.

"Working on the speech I'm due to deliver in the Commons asking Parliament for more money for schools."

"Will you get it?" Seamie asked, spearing a fish from the platter Joe had handed him.

"It's doubtful," Katie said, before Joe could reply and without looking up from her newspaper. "Mr. Churchill's speaking, too. Right after Dad. He wants more boats and he has a good deal of support for them from both benches. Germany's saber rattling has many in England eager to build up our military. Calls are being made for monies to fund a new fleet of dreadnoughts and Dad thinks they'll be heeded—based on precedent. Five years ago, Lloyd George tried to cut naval spending—back when he was chancellor of the exchequer—and was roundly defeated."

Seamie shook his head, laughing. "Is that so, Kitkat?" he said, calling Katie by a nickname he'd given her—one that he knew she hated. "Don't you ever talk about anything other than politics?

You're fifteen years old, and a girl, for goodness' sake. Don't you ever talk about dances or dresses or boys?"

Katie looked up at him, narrowing her eyes. Seamie laughed. He liked to spar with her.

"You really oughtn't to tease her," Fiona said, still stitching. "She gives as good as she gets. You know that."

"Come on, Kitkat," Seamie said, not heeding his sister's warning. "I'll buy you a new dress. From Harrods. A frilly pink one with bows on it. And a hat to match. We'll go today."

"Yes, let's," Katie said, smiling like a shark. "And while we're there, let's buy a suit, too. For you, Uncle Seamie. A gray worsted cut nice and tight with miles of buttons. We'll get a tie, too. To keep your shirt collar nice and tight around your throat. Just like a noose. Today a desk job at the RGS, tomorrow a nice little wife who'll darn your socks for you, and next week a semidetached in Croydon." She sat back in her chair, crossed her arms over her chest, and started humming Chopin's Funeral March.

"Tomboy," Seamie said, bested and genuinely annoyed by it.

"Pencil pusher," Katie retorted.

"Hoyden."

"Office boy."

"I haven't even taken the job yet!" Seamie said defensively.

"Oi, you two!" Joe said. "That's enough."

Seamie, still glowering—for Katie had touched a nerve—speared himself a broiled tomato from a platter.

"I warned you," Fiona said to him.

"Can you take me to the *Clarion*'s printing presses tomorrow afternoon, Uncle Seamie? Please? I need to get the next edition of the *Battle Cry* printed and Mum and Dad are busy and they won't let me go alone," Katie said.

"I don't see why I should," Seamie said, huffily.

Katie smiled again. It was a real smile this time, broad and engaging. "Because you're my uncle and you love me to bits," she said.

"*Did*," Seamie said. "I did love you to bits."

Katie's face fell.

"Oh, I'm just joking. Of course I'll take you," Seamie quickly said. He couldn't stand to see her sad, even if she was just putting it on.

"Thank you, Uncle Seamie!" Katie said. "I was just joking, too. You'd never take that job, I know you wouldn't. And you'd never move to Croydon, either."

Katie went back to her paper. Joe continued to write, Fiona to stitch. The younger children's voices carried to Seamie from another part of the house—they were shrieking and laughing and undoubtedly having fun.

Seamie stopped piling food on his plate and looked at them—Fiona, Joe, and Katie. He was happy, being here with his sister and her family, but it struck him now that it was her family, not his. As much as they loved him, and as much as he loved them, he was an uncle—not a father, not a husband. And he had never felt that distinction as keenly as he did right now. He had no idea why. Perhaps it was Katie teasing him about having a little wife who would darn his socks. She was right, of course—he wouldn't take the RGS job, much less move to Croydon—but as he looked at his sister and her family—together around the table, busy and contented, always happy to spend time in one another's company—he wished, just for a moment, that he had someone in his life who could make him *want* to move to Croydon. An image of Jennie Wilcott popped into his head, but he quickly pushed it out again. Connecting her to this odd, uncharacteristic longing for domestic bliss was madness; he barely knew her.

"Give us a paper, will you?" he suddenly said to Joe, wanting to dispel his strange mood.

Joe handed him one. Seamie spread it out next to his plate, picked up his fork, and glanced at the headline. KAISER'S DREADNOUGHT LAUNCHED, it read. And below it, CHILL WIND BLOWS ACROSS BELGIUM AND FRANCE.

Neither the ominous headline nor the story that followed it did anything to dampen Seamie's appetite. He was starving. He added broiled mushrooms, bacon, poached eggs, and buttered toast to the herring and tomato already on his plate, then poured himself a cup of tea. It was an Assam, bright, brick red, and strong enough to bring the dead back to life. He needed that. George Mallory was in town. They'd gone out on a pub crawl last night and he hadn't gotten home until three A.M.

It was nine o'clock now on a clear and crisp March Saturday. Seamie was spending a long weekend with Joe and Fiona at their Greenwich estate. Easter was only a month away, and Fiona had come out especially to check on the progress the painters were making. She had invited fifty people for Easter dinner and wanted several rooms freshened up before the holiday.

"The post, madam," Foster said now, placing a silver tray piled high with letters on the table.

"Thank you, Mr. Foster," Fiona said, not bothering to look up from her work.

"I believe that a missive from California is included among the invitations and tradesmen's bills, madam. I believe the cancellation reads Point Reyes Station."

"Point Reyes? How wonderful!" Fiona said. She put her needle down, dove into the mail, and fished out a large, stiff envelope.

"How are the painters faring, Mr. Foster?" Joe asked.

"Quite well, sir. They've finished in the drawing room and have moved on to the foyer."

"Oh, Joe! Seamie! Look!" Fiona said with emotion. "India's sent us a beautiful likeness of herself, Sid, and the children. How lovely they are!"

Seamie snorted. "Our brother? Lovely?" he said.

"Well, his children are," Fiona said, laughing. "Just look at Charlotte. What a beauty. And the baby. And Wish, who looks just like his father." She paused for a few seconds, then softly said, "And ours."

Seamie tried to read his sister's expression as her eyes traveled over the images in the photograph. He saw love in it, and happiness, and loss.

He knew she still grieved for their parents. Their father, Paddy, had been killed back in 1888 at the docks where he worked. His death had looked like an accident, but it had been the work of his employer, William Burton. Paddy, a union organizer, had been trying to get his fellow dockers at Burton Tea to join the dockworkers union. Burton, together with an East London thug named Bowler Sheehan, had arranged the so-called accident to put an end to Paddy's unionizing. And Kate, their mother, had been murdered the same year by a madman known as Jack the Ripper.

Their baby sister, ill and weak, had died shortly thereafter. And then they'd lost their brother Charlie. He hadn't died. He'd been driven mad by the sight of his mother dying in the street by their house. He'd run away, and then killed another lad in self-defense. Too afraid to return to his family, he'd taken the dead boy's name— Sid Malone   and descended into a life of crime.

Years later, Fiona had met up with him again. They had a falling out, and Sid disappeared back into the dark streets of East London. Heartbroken over what he'd become, Fiona made the decision never to tell Seamie what had really happened to the brother he'd loved.

He had found out anyway, though—years later, in the most horrible way. Joe, the newly elected MP for Whitechapel, had sought out Sid, to warn him to stay on the straight and narrow or there would be consequences. Joe hadn't been able to see Sid, but he'd seen his henchman—Frankie Betts. They got into a terrible fight, and Frankie, worried that Sid would desert him and the other hard men who worked for him, had shot Joe and blamed the shooting on Sid— hoping to make it impossible for him to return to the straight world.

Sid, on the run and wounded by a detective's bullet, had come to Fiona's house late one night to tell her that he hadn't shot her Joe. She'd taken him in and hidden him until it was safe for him to get out of London. He'd gotten himself hired on the first ship he could find, a cargo ship bound for Africa. He'd left everything behind: his life, his family, and the woman he loved—a young, aristocratic doctor named India Selwyn Jones. He'd left her because he believed she'd abandoned him to marry a man of her class—a corrupt and heartless politician named Freddie Lytton. India only married Freddie, however, because she believed Sid was dead, and because she was carrying Sid's child and wanted a father, if only on paper, for that child.

Sid and India met again in Africa. Sid was living there under an assumed last name—Baxter—and Freddie, a rising star in the Colonial Office, had been sent there on government business. When he realized that Sid was still alive, he had him arrested and thrown in jail, in hopes of having him hanged. And then Freddie had nearly killed both India and the child—a girl named Charlotte—by abandoning them in the African bush. He'd been killed himself, however, by hyenas as he was on his way back to the bungalow where they'd all been staying. With Seamie's help—for he had been in Africa himself at the time, at Kilimanjaro—Sid escaped from jail, barely in time to save India and Charlotte. He brought them to safety, and then, still fearing arrest, he rode off, leaving them with only a note telling them to meet him in America, in California, where India owned land. They would begin again there. He promised them that. At Point Reyes on the coast, where he and India had once dreamed of going, where the sea met the sky.

"I wouldn't believe it if I wasn't seeing it," Seamie said now, as Fiona handed him the photograph. He looked at the faces of the beaming children, the beautiful woman, and the man, tanned and smiling. "Our brother—married, happy, and raising cows."

"Steers," Joe said.

"Cow, steers . . . does it matter? I couldn't be more surprised if he was raising daffodils," Seamie said.

"He's so fortunate," Fiona said. "To have survived that journey, all those miles across Africa, and then the passage to New York, and the trek to the west."

Seamie nodded. He remembered waiting desperately for news of his brother. They had all waited, and worried, and suffered, for the better part of a year, until finally they'd had a letter from India in Point Reyes telling them that Sid had come home to her and Charlotte, and that he was all right. Or would be, in time.

He had journeyed west across the entire continent of Africa with a horse and little else—including little money. He'd had his gun with him and so was able to hunt his food. His horse grazed. And water was free wherever he could find it. Halfway across, he'd come down with malaria. Tribesmen found him and doctored him. He pulled through, and when he got his strength back—about a month later—he continued on to Port Gentil. There, he sold his horse and worked the docks until he'd saved up enough money for a passage to New York. He worked the docks again when he arrived in the States, this time in Brooklyn, until he'd earned enough money for train fare to San Francisco.

He almost made it, too, but he was coshed and robbed in Denver one night as he made his way to a cheap hotel where he'd planned to spend the night before catching a train west the next morning. He'd had to hunt for work again and found it in a slaughter yard. He worked there for two months, and nearly had his fare earned, when he was injured. A steer got loose, trampled him, and broke his leg. A man in the tenement where he lived—an orderly at a pauper's hospital—set his leg to save him the doctor's fee, which was why he walked with a cane. He'd gotten five dollars out of the yard's foreman. That, together with the money he'd saved, got him to San Francisco, and then up the coast. He'd arrived at Point Reyes with forty-six cents in his pocket.

Seamie had asked him once, in a letter, if he'd ever had a moment where he wondered if he should be making the journey. He hadn't spoken to India since he deposited her, half-delirious, back at the bungalow in Kenya, where she had been staying. What the hell would he have done if she hadn't been there?

Sid wrote back that the thought had never crossed his mind. Of course she'd be there. And he'd have made a hundred such journeys, if that's what it took to get to her and Charlotte.

"I know some people might think I'm mad," he wrote. "But I'm not, I'm lucky. So bloody lucky."

Seamie had smiled at that and folded the letter away. Sid had married India only days after he arrived. They'd had another child, a boy, in 1908. They named him Aloysius—Wish for short—for India's cousin. And then baby Elizabeth had arrived four months ago. She was named for Elizabeth Garrett Anderson and Elizabeth Blackwell, two of the first women doctors. They were happy, Sid and India. Seamie hadn't been to visit them yet, but Fiona and Joe and their children had. Fiona said that their house was filled with light and love and laughter, and that one could see and smell and hear the ocean from every room.

Seamie thought now that both his sister and his brother had had lives that seemed as if they'd come from a fairy story, complete with happy endings. He thought it must be nice to have those things. Not everyone got to have them. He hadn't. His happy ending had run away from him, all the way to the other side of the world.

"Oh, Joe, we must go to California again next year. I miss them all so much," Fiona said, still gazing longingly at the photograph. "The baby's already four months old, and we've never even seen her. Well, Maud's going at the end of the summer. That's something."

Maud Selwyn Jones was India's sister and now Seamie's, Fiona's, and Joe's sister-in-law. She was also Fiona's good friend. The two women had worked together for years on women's suffrage, and a close bond had developed between them. A widow and enormously wealthy, Maud scandalized British society by doing exactly what she pleased, when she pleased—whether it involved traveling to unsuitable places, indulging in unsuitable substances, or dallying with unsuitable men.

"I'm going to give Maud a trunk filled with presents for the children to take with her. She said she'd be happy to do it. I saw her the other day, you know. We talked about the trip, and how much she was looking forward to seeing her nieces and nephew. She joked that she's finally become the thing she most feared—an old spinster aunt." Fiona laughed. "Hardly! She's still very beautiful. She must've been something else when she was younger. Well, weren't we all?"

Seamie looked at Joe. He looked mortified. Seamie knew Joe and Maud had been lovers once, many years ago, before Fiona and Joe were married.

"Oh, sorry, luv!" Fiona said sheepishly, noticing Joe's expression. "Forgot about all that. I suppose I should be jealous, shouldn't I? I would be, Joe, but the problem is, good women friends are so hard to find." She reached over and patted his hand. "Almost as hard to find as good husbands. And anyway, Maud's not after you anymore. I think she's quite taken with Harriet's cousin, that handsome Max von Brandt. She told me he's too young for her, but then again, Jennie Churchill married a man twenty years her junior, didn't she? It's the fashion now, and why not? Men have been doing it for ages. I saw Lady Nevill in the park the other day. She's in her eighties now and as wicked as ever. She was walking amongst a whole gaggle of children. I asked her what she was doing there, and she said, 'Well, if you want to know, my dear, I am searching in the perambulators for *my* next husband!' "

Joe rolled his eyes. Seamie laughed. He poured himself a second cup of tea, downed it, finished the last of his kipper, then said, "Well, I'm off, Fee. I've a busy morning. I'm going to visit Admiral Alden again."

"How is he?" Fiona asked.

"Worsening, I'm afraid," Seamie said.

"I'm so sorry to hear it. We'll go to visit him soon. In the meantime, please give him and Mrs. Alden our best."

"I will, Fee. And after I've seen him, there's a lunch at the Royal Geographical Society. Shackleton's going to be there."

"Oh, no," Fiona said, frowning. "Not again! We just got you back."

"Very possibly," Seamie said, grinning. "Rumor has it his latest expedition's actually coming together. Don't wait for me for tea. I'll be back late."

Fiona was looking at him thoughtfully as he spoke. He knew his sister well enough to be worried when she did that.

"Seamie, luv . . ."

"Yes, Fiona?"

"Since you're going into the city anyway, would you do me a favor?"

"Uh-oh."

"What? Why uh-oh? All I wanted you to do was to drop off a check at the Wilcotts'. Joe and I are making a donation to Jennie's school."

Katie looked up, giggling. "Croydon, here I come!" she said.

Seamie ignored his niece. He gave his sister a long look. "Ever heard of a post office, Fee?"

"In fact, yes. I have. I thought you taking it would be safer, that's all."

"Fine. I'll take it. All I have to do is slide it through the Reverend Wilcott's mail slot, right?"

"Well, it *would* be nice if you could give it to the Wilcotts in person. It's for a rather large amount, you know. I wouldn't want it to go missing."

Joe, still working on his speech, snorted. "You're about as subtle as a freight train, lass," he said.

"What?" Fiona said, feigning innocence. "You don't . . . you *can't* think I'm matchmaking?"

"Yes, I can," Seamie and Joe said together.

Fiona made a face at them. "All right, then," she admitted. "I am. So what? Jennie Wilcott's a lovely young woman. Any man in his right mind would be madly interested in her."

"Stop, Fiona," Seamie said. "Just stop."

"I'm only concerned about you, you know. Concerned about your happiness."

"I'm perfectly happy," Seamie said. "Deliriously happy."

"How could you be? With no home of your own? With no wife and family? I don't worry about Sid anymore—"

"Lucky sod," Seamie said under his breath.

"—but I do worry about you. I wish you had what he had. You can't spend your best years alone at the South Pole with only icebergs and penguins for company, you know. What kind of life is that?"

Seamie sighed.

"I just want you to be happy, Seamie. Truly happy, I mean. As happy as Sid and India are. As happy as Joe and I are. I just want—"

Fiona's words were cut off by the sound of a loud and terrible crash. It was followed by shouting, swearing, barking, and crying.

"Bloody hell," Joe said.

Two seconds later, the dogs, Tetley and Typhoo, came tearing into the dining room, yipping and covered in paint. Six-year-old Rose, eleven-year-old Peter, and the twins, Patrick and Michael, who were four, followed, clutching on to their thirteen-year-old brother, Charlie. All five were also covered in paint. The three painters came next, covered in paint, followed, most alarmingly, by Mr. Foster, also covered in paint.

Rose stamped her foot and sobbed that it was all Peter's fault and he'd ruined her favorite dress. Peter blamed Charlie. Charlie just blinked through the blobs of white paint dripping off his head onto his clothing. Patrick and Michael, howling, blamed no one. They just sought comfort—in their father's lap. Joe tried to fight them off, but in no time at all he, too, was covered in paint. The dogs trotted about, tracking paint everywhere. Then one of them shook himself, spraying paint all over Fiona. The head painter swore he wouldn't come back, not ever.

Seamie shook his head in disbelief. He had sailed to Antarctica, often on rough seas, in a small ship with men and dogs and livestock, but that had been a peaceful stroll through the park compared to the noise and commotion he was witnessing now. He poured himself another cup of tea, drank it, then said, "You lot can keep Croydon. I'll take the South Pole any day of the week!"

CHAPTER EIGHT

THE LONDON OMNIBUS turned onto Wapping's High Street. It bumped and banged over the rutted cobblestones, belched and sputtered as it picked up speed, then careened dangerously around the bends and turns of the narrow and winding dockside thoroughfare.

Seamie, sitting on the bus's open top deck, lifted his face to the sky. It was a fair day, but the locals wouldn't have known it. The sun didn't shine on the streets of Wapping; the warehouses, dark and looming, blocked it out. A stiff breeze carried the smell of the Thames on it, muddy and low, with a tang of salt.

An image suddenly shimmered across Seamie's mind, a quick, fleeting picture of a handsome man with black hair and blue eyes. They were sitting together on a flight of stone steps at the river's edge. He was small, only a tiny boy, and the man had his arm around him. The man's voice was low and beautiful and full of the music of his native Ireland. He was telling him the names of all the ships in the river and what they were carrying and where they were from.

And then the picture faded. As it always did. Seamie tried to call it back, but he couldn't. He wished he remembered more about the man, his father. He was only four when his father died and his memories of him were few, but he knew he'd been happy then, sitting by the river. He knew even then, at the age of four, that he loved ships and the water, but not nearly as much as he loved his father.

The bus slowed, coughed, and came to a stop at the Prospect of Whitby, an old riverside public house. Seamie hopped off. Fiona had told him that the Reverend Wilcott's church was on Watts Street, just north of the pub. He planned to say a quick hello to the Wilcotts, drop off the check, and be on his way.

He'd just come from visiting the Aldens and would have to go all the way back west again to get to the dinner at the Royal Geographical Society. He was running late, too, for he'd stayed at the Aldens' house longer than he'd planned.

Seamie was no doctor, but he didn't need to be to see that the admiral's condition was worsening. His face was waxen and he was in a great deal of pain. He'd been happy to see Seamie and eager to hear about Ernest Shackleton's plans for another trip to Antarctica, but he'd needed morphine twice in the scant hour that Seamie had been with him.

"It's cancer of the stomach," Mrs. Alden had said tearfully, as he'd sat with her in the drawing room afterward. "We've known it for a while, but we haven't talked about it much. I suppose we should have. But we're not terribly good at talking about such things, Albie and I. Dogs and the weather, those are our preferred topics."

"Does Willa know?" he asked.

Mrs. Alden shook her head. "If she does, she's given us no word. I've written her. Albie has, too. Several times. But I've received nothing from her. Nothing at all."

"She'll come," Seamie said. "I know she will."

He'd promised Mrs. Alden to call again soon, given her Fiona's and Joe's regards, and then left for Wapping. It was too much for him, seeing the admiral suffering so, and seeing all the photographs of Willa in Mrs. Alden's drawing room.

He tried to shake the sadness off now, as the church of St. Nicholas came into sight. It was old and unlovely, as was most everything in Wapping. Seamie first tried the door to the rectory—a sooty stone building built cheek-by-jowl to the church, but it was locked. He then tried the church door. It was open. He went inside, hoping he might find the Reverend Wilcott in there, tidying the altar or some such thing. Instead, he found Jennie Wilcott and two dozen children.

They weren't in the classroom he passed, but were all seated— some on chairs, some on tea chests—around a small black stove in the sacristy, reading words chalked on a portable blackboard. Jennie looked up at the sound of his footsteps, startled. He was startled, too—startled to see how pretty she was. She looked so different from the last time he'd seen her. Her eye was no longer swollen; the bruising around it had faded some. Her blond hair was neatly combed and pinned up in a twist. Her clothes, a white cotton blouse and blue twill skirt, were clean and pressed and showed off her lovely curves and tiny waist.

She's more than pretty, he thought. She's beautiful.

"Hello, again, Miss Wilcott," he said. "I'm Seamus Finnegan. Fiona Bristow's brother. We met a few weeks ago. At the . . . um . . . well, at the prison."

Jennie Wilcott's face lit up. "Yes, of course! What a pleasure it is to see you again, Mr. Finnegan!" she said.

"Cor, miss, was you sent down *again*?" a little boy asked.

"It's '*Were* you sent down again?,' Dennis. And yes, I was."

"You're in the clink more than me dad, miss!" a girl said.

"Do you think so? I'd say it's pretty close. Luckily, I had Mr. Finnegan to help get me out last time. Boys and girls, do you know who Mr. Finnegan is?"

"No, miss," twenty-four voices said in unison.

"Then I shall tell you. He is one of our country's heroes—a real, live explorer!"

There were cries of "Get out of it, miss!" and "Blimey!" and "Pull the other one, it's got bells on."

"Yes, he is. He went with Mr. Amundsen to the South Pole in Antarctica, and he's here now to tell you all about it. He promised me that he would come and here he is!"

Jennie's voice was excited. Her eyes, as she looked at the children seated all around her, shone.

Seamie had quite forgotten about the promise he'd made. "Actually, Miss Wilcott, I came to give you this," he said, pulling an envelope from his breast pocket. "It's from Fiona and Joe. It's a donation."

"Oh. Oh, I see," Jennie said, disappointment in her voice. "Forgive me, Mr. Finnegan, I thought . . ."

Twenty-four little faces, upturned and eager, suddenly fell.

"Is he not going to talk to us, miss?" one boy asked.

"Miss, won't he stay?"

"Won't he tell us about Ann Tartika?"

"Now, children. Mr. Finnegan is very busy and—" Jennie began to say.

"Of course I'll stay," Seamie said hastily, finding that he couldn't bear the disappointment in the children's faces. Or Jennie Wilcott's.

He hastily stuffed the envelope back into his pocket, then sat down among the children. One boy stood to give him his seat, which was close to the stove, but Seamie told him to sit down again. The child was poorly dressed for a March day.

Seamie began by telling them about his first expedition. He'd gone to the Royal Geographical Society one night to hear Ernest Shackleton speak about his upcoming trip to Antarctica, and his quest to find the South Pole. He'd been so impressed with Shackleton, and so determined to be a part of his expedition, that he'd followed the man home and stood outside his house for thirty-three hours, never moving, never so much as flinching, not when night fell, not when it poured rain, until Shackleton invited him in. He'd impressed the explorer with his enthusiasm and his steadfastness, and Shackleton had taken him on.

The children's eyes grew wide as Seamie told them what it had been like to set off for the South Pole at the age of seventeen. He told them of the endless seas, the vast night skies, the lashing storms. He told them of life on board the *Discovery*—Shackleton's vessel—and of the hard work, the discipline, and the tedium of being cooped up for months in such a small space with so many men. He told them about his more recent journey to the pole with Amundsen. He told them what it was like to finally feel the air turn frigid and see ice in the water. To be watched by seals and penguins and whales. To work at twenty below zero, to set up camp, run dog sleds, take measurements and readings, to trek over treacherous pack ice, to force the body to perform miracles of physical endurance when it hurt just to breathe.

And he told them that it was worth it. The long voyage, the

loneliness, the bad food, the agony of cold—it was worth every second of pain and doubt, just to stand where no one had ever stood
before, in a pristine wilderness of snow and ice. To be the first.

He talked to the children for nearly two hours. He didn't notice
the time passing. He never did when he talked about Antarctica.
He forgot time, and he forgot himself. He was aware of only one
thing—his desire to make his audience feel the passion he felt for
Antarctica and to see—if only in their imaginations—the beauty
he'd seen there.

When he finished, the children applauded loudly. Seamie smiled at
their enthusiasm, at the curiosity and excitement in their faces. They
had a million questions for him, and he did his best to answer them.
But suddenly it was four o'clock and time for them to go home. They
thanked him and begged him to come back, and he said he would.
They readied themselves to leave, and as they did, Jennie said, "There's
one more thing, children. One thing Mr. Finnegan forgot to tell you.
Do any of you know where Mr. Finnegan was born?"

They all shook their heads.

"Who can guess?"

"Buckingham Palace!"

"Blackpool!"

"Harrods!"

"He was born in East London," Jennie finally said. "Just like you.
He lived with his sister and brother in Whitechapel."

There were expressions of disbelief, then searching glances and
shy smiles—all evidence of some small, secret hope held in each heart.

"I'm so sorry, Mr. Finnegan," Jennie said, when the children
were gone. "I didn't mean to put you on show. I didn't know you'd
come to bring a donation. I thought you'd come to speak with the
children."

"Please don't apologize. I enjoyed it. Really."

"Then thank you. It was very kind of you."

"It was nothing, Miss Wilcott. I hope I gave them a bit of entertainment."

"You gave them more than entertainment," Jennie said, with a sudden intensity. "You gave them hope. Their lives are very hard, Mr. Finnegan. Very hard. Everything and everyone conspires against them. Every voice they hear—a weary mother's, a drunken father's, a grasping employer's—tells them that the bright and shining things of this world are for others, not for them. Today, you silenced those voices. If only for a few hours."

Jennie turned away then, as if embarrassed by her emotion, and busied herself with banking the coals in the stove. "I don't know why I bother," she said. "It's a useless stove. It heats nothing. But at least it's a stove. We don't have any heat at all in our actual classroom."

"It's Saturday, Miss Wilcott."

"Yes, it is," she said, raking the embers into a pile with a poker.

"You hold school on Saturdays?"

"Yes, of course. It's a day when I can actually persuade the children's parents to send them to me. Most of the factories and warehouses close at half day on Saturdays, you see. There's no work to be had in the afternoons, so they can come here."

"Don't they go to regular schools?"

"In theory, yes," Jennie said, closing the stove's door.

"In theory?"

"Families must eat, Mr. Finnegan. They must pay their rent. Pay for coal. Children can do piecework at factories. They can stuff tickings with straw. They can scrub floors." She gave him a wry smile. "When you weigh a pound of sausages bought with a child's wages against maths equations or writing out Tennyson, the sausages always win."

Seamie laughed. Jennie took her coat off a hook, shrugged into it, and put her hat on. She pulled a pair of leather gloves from her coat pocket, and as she did, Seamie saw that a long, faded scar ran across the back of one hand. He wondered what had caused it, but thought it rude to ask.

"I'm off to the market," she said, picking up a willow basket off the floor. "There's one on Cable Street on Saturday evenings."

Seamie said he was going that way, too. Which he wasn't, of course. Until now. They left the church, leaving the doors unlocked.

"Aren't you worried about robberies?" he asked.

"I am. But my father's more worried about people's souls. So we leave the doors open," she said.

They set off north.

"Your life sounds so exciting, Mr. Finnegan," Jennie said, as they walked together.

"It's Seamie. Please."

"All right, then. And you must call me Jennie. As I was saying, your life sounds amazing. What incredible adventures you've had."

"Do you think so? You should go exploring," Seamie said.

"Oh, no. Not me. I can't bear the cold. I wouldn't last two seconds at the South Pole."

"What about India then? Or Africa? The dark continent," Seamie said, echoing an expression used by mapmakers about Africa, because so much of it was unknown and hence left dark on the maps.

Jennie laughed. "*England* is the dark continent. Take a walk in Whitechapel, down Flower and Dean Street, or Hanbury, or Brick Lane, if you need convincing. I've always felt that British politicians and missionaries should make certain their own house is in order before marching off to set the Africans to rights." She paused, then looked up at him from under her hat brim. "I sound terribly righteous, don't I?"

"Not at all."

"Liar."

It was Seamie's turn to laugh.

"It's just that I feel there are such important discoveries to be made right here, Mr. Finnegan."

"Seamie."

"Seamie. One doesn't have to travel far. Watching the children who come to my school learn their letters and numbers, watching them read pages of Kipling or Dickens and thrilling at the worlds and the people those books contain, watching their small faces light up as they make their own discoveries . . . well, I know it's not mountains or rivers, but there's nothing more exciting. To me, at least."

Seamie noticed the way Jennie's own face lit up as she talked about the children. The sparkle in her eyes, the flush on her cheeks, made her look even prettier.

They arrived at Cable Street, where the bustling and noisy Saturday market was in full swing. Costers of all stripes sang their wares. A greengrocer juggled last autumn's apples. Butchers hefted chops for their customers' appreciation. Fishmongers cleaved the heads off salmon, plaice, and haddock. At a clothes stall, women tussled over secondhand shoes for their children.

"That's an awful lot of potatoes for two people," Seamie said, as Jennie bought five pounds from a greengrocer.

"Oh, it's not just for my father and me, it's for the children, too."

Seamie felt puzzled. "The children?" he said, trying to keep the surprise from his voice.

"Oh, yes. I cook for them. Cornish pasties usually. They're very partial to them."

"I didn't know you had children," Seamie said.

"I don't," Jennie said. "I meant for the schoolchildren. They're always hungry. There are times when the pasties are all they get to eat in a day."

"Oh, right. Of course," Seamie said. He'd felt an unwelcome twinge of jealousy at the thought of her with children—and a husband.

Jennie finished loading the potatoes into her basket, paid the coster, then struggled to lift the basket.

"Please, Miss Wil—Jennie. May I carry that for you?"

"You don't mind? It would be a great help."

"Not at all," he said, taking the basket. He also took a loaf of bread from a baker, two pounds of lamb from a butcher, and nutmeg from a spice seller, and put them all in her basket. He noticed how expertly she negotiated with the costers, shaving pennies off prices at every stall. He wondered what sort of salary a minister made. It couldn't be much. And he was willing to bet a good deal of it went on food and books for the children and coal for the church stove.

"I believe I'm finally finished," Jennie said, after tucking a half pound of butter into the basket. She looked at her watch. "My goodness,

I'd better be getting back. The reverend will be home shortly and expecting his tea. He'll be tired, my dad. Today's his day to visit the sick of his parish. There was a rumor of a cholera outbreak on Kennet Street. I hope it's only a rumor."

"*Cholera?*" Seamie said. "That must be very dangerous work."

Jennie smiled sadly. "Very. It's how my mother died. She caught typhoid on one of her visits to a parish family. That was ten years ago."

"I'm sorry," Seamie said.

"Thank you. You would think it might've stopped my father, wouldn't you? Losing his wife and all. But it didn't. He believes God is watching over him." She shook her head. "His faith is so strong. So absolute. I wish I had it, but I don't. I'm afraid I spend more time arguing with God than I do praising Him."

Jennie took a deep breath, then blew it back out again. She looked as if she was trying to gather her composure. Seamie wondered what it was like to tend mortally ill people. To visit slum houses that most doctors were afraid to set foot in. To lose one's mother to typhoid. To brave ignorance and poverty every day of one's life. Looking at Jennie, Seamie realized that courage took many forms.

"I'm sure I've taken enough of your time," she said. "Thank you again for talking to the children and for carrying my marketing. You've gone above and beyond the call of duty today."

She reached for her basket, but Seamie didn't give it to her. "Don't be silly. It's far too heavy," he said. "I'll carry it for you."

"No, really. I couldn't ask you to."

"You didn't," Seamie said. "I offered."

Twenty minutes later, they arrived at the rectory. The Reverend Wilcott was already home. "Come in! Come in!" he said, opening the door for them. "Why, Mr. Finnegan, is that you?"

"I'm afraid so, Reverend," Seamie said, taking the man's out-stretched hand.

"It's wonderful to see you again, my boy! Have you come to join us for tea?"

"No, sir, I haven't. I was just helping Jen—Miss Wilcott with her marketing," Seamie said, suddenly formal again in front of the reverend.

"Nonsense! Stay and have a bite of something with us. There's plenty. Jennie's had a hotpot simmering on the stove all day."

"Won't you stay?" Jennie said. "It's the least I could do after all you've done for me today."

Seamie knew he was supposed to be at the RGS. At a talk. And a dinner. And the interminable drinks session that was bound to follow. "All right, then. Yes. I'd love to," he said.

Jennie led the way through a short, narrow hallway, into a brightly lit kitchen. The reverend took a seat by the hearth. Seamie put the heavy basket on a bench under a window, then stood around feeling foolish. He looked out of a window and saw a small yard.

"Our garden," Jennie said, smiling. "Such as it is. It looks much nicer in summer." She took his jacket and told him to sit down next to her father. The next thing he knew, she was handing him a cup of tea, hot and reviving.

He looked around the little kitchen as he sipped his tea. It was tidy and warm. White lace curtains hung in the window. Bright rag rugs dotted the floor. A little earthen pot, filled with purple crocuses, sat atop the table. The fire gave off a delicious heat, and whatever Jennie had in the oven gave off a delicious smell.

"Did you put the parsley in, Dad?" Jennie asked her father, laying a gentle hand on his shoulder.

"Hmm? What was that?" the Reverend said, taking her hand in his.

"Did you put any parsley into the hotpot? You were supposed to. To finish it off."

"I'm sorry, my dear. I quite forgot."

"Oh, you." She scolded him fondly.

He patted her hand, bade her sit down beside him. "It will be a wonderful dish, parsley or no." To Seamie he said, "Jennie is a marvelous cook."

"I look forward to it," Seamie said. "My bachelor existence doesn't allow me home-cooked meals very often."

"How were the children today?" the reverend asked Jennie.

"Just wonderful!" she said. "Mr. Finnegan came to talk to them. He told them all about his expeditions. Oh, you should have seen their faces, Dad. They were so excited!"

"Did you now, lad? That was very good of you," the reverend said.

"How were your visits? Is it as bad as you feared?" Jennie asked.

The Reverend Wilcott shook his head. "Thankfully, the cholera scare was only that—a scare—and I pray to God it stays that way. Cholera moves like lightning through the slums, Mr. Finnegan. It's the closeness that does it, of course. Too many people jammed into too little space. Sharing rooms and beds and privies. Water lines running close to the sewers. Bad air. All it takes is one person, and before you know it, the entire street's down. But for today at least, we are spared."

Jennie squeezed his hand, then went back to her stove.

"Can I help you with anything?" Seamie asked.

"No, thank you. I can manage," Jennie said.

"I'm quite handy. I cooked onboard the *Discovery,* you know," Seamie said.

"Did you?"

"Yes. For the sled dogs."

Jennie narrowed her eyes. "Are you making comparisons, Mr. Finnegan?" she asked.

"What? No. No! Oh, blast. I just meant that I know my way around a kitchen. It was one of the most important jobs on the entire expedition. If the dogs hadn't been well fed and healthy when we made land, we would have gone nowhere."

"Well, *I* won't be needing your help, but perhaps you can go with my father on his visits. You could feel his parishioners' noses. See if they're cold and wet," Jennie said.

The reverend laughed out loud. "Did you say you're a bachelor, lad? Can't imagine why!"

"At least let me set the table," Seamie said sheepishly, trying to make good.

"That would be helpful. The feed bowls are above the sink," Jennie said.

She teased Seamie a bit more, then served the dinner—a Lancashire hotpot—a casserole of lamb chops, potatoes, and onions—with hunks of crusty brown bread and fresh, sweet butter. They all sat down, and the reverend gave the blessing. Seamie bowed his head. He knew he should close his eyes, but he didn't. Instead he looked at Jennie. Her color was high from the heat of the stove. The light from the lamps picked out the threads of pure gold in her hair. When the blessing ended, she opened her eyes and saw him looking at her, and she did not look away.

"This is delicious," he said as he tucked into his meal. "Truly."

Jennie thanked him and didn't make any more dog jokes, and Seamie realized as he ate that he was hungry—for something other than food. He was hungry for the warmth and ease he felt here, in Jennie Wilcott's tiny kitchen.

There was something about her—something lovely and comfortable. He felt contented in her presence. Peaceful. Not stirred up. Not wild. Not angry and sad and desperate, the way he felt every time he thought of Willa Alden.

He liked the home she had made for herself and her father. He liked the ticking of the mantel clock, the smell of furniture polish and the freshly washed tablecloth. He found himself wishing, to his great surprise, that he had such a thing himself—a home, a real home.

After Seamie and the Wilcotts had finished their meal, and topped it off with a dish of apple crumble doused with cream, the reverend declared he would pour everyone a sherry, but Seamie said he was not to do it until he—Seamie—had done the washing up. He made Jennie take a seat by the fire, then he rolled up his sleeves and got busy. He didn't sit down again until every plate, glass, and piece of cutlery was clean and dry.

He stayed with the Wilcotts, sipping his sherry, until the clock struck eight, and then he said he must be going. He knew tomorrow was Sunday and that both the reverend and Jennie would have an early start in the morning. He didn't want to leave, though. He didn't want to go out in the cold, dark night alone, always alone, and make his way across the river, to his sister's house, to the empty room, and the empty bed, that awaited him there.

"Thank you," he said to the Wilcotts as he took his leave. "For the supper and for your company. I enjoyed both immensely."

Jennie and the reverend both walked him to the door. He had just put his hat on, and was buttoning his jacket, when something crinkled in his front pocket.

"Oh, the check!" he said, laughing. It was the only reason he'd come here, and he'd forgotten it completely. He gave it to Jennie and told her it was for her school. She thanked him and said she would thank Fiona in person.

"You'll come back and see us again soon, won't you, my boy?" the reverend said, seeing him to the steps.

And Seamie, who, earlier in the day, had found himself so annoyed that Fiona had asked him to come here at all, said, "Yes, Reverend Wilcott. I will. Very soon."

CHAPTER NINE

MAX VON BRANDT checked his watch: 8:05 P.M. The bus he was waiting for would be here any minute now. He'd been standing under the awning of a tobacco shop on the Whitechapel Road for the last fifteen minutes to make certain he didn't miss it.

A chill crept up his spine. He hunched his shoulders against the cold, damp night. He hated the filthy English weather, but he was glad it was raining. It served his purpose.

A few feet away from him, a hissing gas lamp cast its weak glow over the slick black cobbles, the dreary shop fronts, the sooty brick buildings. Nowhere was there a pot of flowers, a green park, a cheerful coffee shop. If ever he had a mind to commit suicide, he thought, he would do it here in Whitechapel. It was made for it.

Max was not wearing his usual uniform tonight—a beautifully tailored suit, crisp white shirt, and silk tie. Instead, he wore a navy sailor's jacket, a cap, canvas trousers, heavy boots, and wire-rimmed spectacles with fake glass inserts.

Another minute passed. Two. And then he heard it, the sputter and pop of an omnibus engine. The sound grew louder as the bus rounded a bend. The engine grumbled as the driver stopped at a bus shelter across the street and waited for a handful of passengers to step off. Max watched them as they did, inspecting their faces.

There she is, he thought, watching as the last passenger—a young woman—stepped into the street. She had a plain, round face, framed by dark, wavy hair. Her eyes were small behind her glasses, her teeth large and rabbity. Looking at her, he knew his plan would succeed. In fact, it would be easy. The knowledge made him feel a deep and dreadful regret. He quickly quashed the feeling, though, for he could not afford to indulge it. There was work to be done, another link to be forged.

He waited. Until she was on the pavement, struggling with her umbrella. Until the conductor had rung his bell. Until the bus had pulled away from the curb, spewing black exhaust. And then he crossed the street and started walking toward her, hands in his pockets, head down against the rain.

He knew she would walk toward him. From a window high above the street he'd watched her take the exact same path for four nights in a row. He heard her steps coming closer and closer, his head still down. He waited until he could feel her. Smell her. Not yet, he told himself, not yet . . . hold on . . . *now.*

With a quick, fluid motion, he clipped her hard with his shoulder, knocking her satchel out of her arms and her glasses off her face.

"By gum, I'm sorry!" he exclaimed, in a flawless Yorkshire accent, quickly bending to pick up her things. "I didn't see you. Are you all right?"

"I . . . I think so," she said, squinting at him from under her umbrella. "Do you see my glasses anywhere?"

"Right here," he said, giving them to her.

She put them on with shaking hands, then took her satchel back from him.

"I'm very sorry. What an oaf I am. I feel terrible about this," he said.

"It's all right, really," the woman said.

"I'm afraid I'm a bit lost. I'm coming from Wapping. My ship just docked an hour ago. I'm looking for a lodging house by the name of Duffin's."

"Oh, I know Duffin's," the woman said. "It's just that way," she pointed east, "two streets down. On the left. But Duffin's is dear, you know. You might've been better off finding a lodging house closer to the river. Wapping's full of them."

Max shook his head. "I can't imagine you've ever stopped in one, miss. They're terrible, no better than a doss-house. I have a few days until my ship sails again, and I want to be in a decent place. One near a church."

He noticed the girl's eyes widen a bit at that.

"I'd actually been looking up at the street signs. Just before I smacked into you. I still feel terrible about it. Could I make it up to you? Buy you a cup of tea in a nice tea shop? Is there one around here?"

"No, everything's closed now," the girl said. She bit her lip.

It started raining harder. Perfect, Max thought. He pulled his collar up around his neck and shivered visibly.

"Here . . . ," she said, holding her umbrella so that it covered them both.

Max made a show of looking around. "There's a pub," he said. "The Blind Beggar. Would you accompany me there?"

The girl shook her head. "I don't frequent pubs," she said.

"There might be a ladies' area in that one," Max said hopefully.

The girl still hesitated, but her eyes looked hungry and sad. She was lonely, as he'd known she would be from the way Jennie Wilcott had described her when they'd all been waiting for cabs and carriages outside Holloway: a single woman with a poorly mother, a knitting group, suffrage work. She was desperate for a man's company. He could see that. Anyone could.

"Right. Well, I won't keep you," he said, tugging on the brim of his cap. "Good night, miss."

"Maybe just one drink," she suddenly said. "A lemonade or some such. My mother waits up for me. But I don't think she'll miss me. Not just yet. I sometimes get home a bit late from my knitting circle."

Max smiled. "That's wonderful. I'm glad you changed your mind. Just one drink, then. It's the least I could do after nearly knocking you down. I'm Peter, by the way. Peter Stiles," Max said, offering her his arm.

The woman's glasses had slid down her nose. She pushed them back up and gave him a shy smile.

"I didn't get *your* name," he said.

"Oh! Right. Silly me," she said, with a nervous laugh. "It's Gladys. Gladys Bigelow. Very pleased to meet you."

CHAPTER TEN

"THE STOVE GOES where, guv? *There?* Are you quite certain? It's a church," Robbie Barlow, the deliveryman, said.

"It's a very cold church," Seamie said.

"Is the door open? This thing's bloody heavy, you know. Once we get it off the cart, we'll want to get it straight inside."

Seamie nodded. "It's always open. The reverend keeps it that way." He jumped off the cart, trotted up the church steps, opened the door, and called out, "Hello? Anyone here? Reverend Wilcott? Jennie?"

There was no answer, so he went inside and tried again.

"Hello? Is there anyone here?"

He heard footsteps, and then a young woman, a very pretty young woman in an ivory blouse and beige skirt, came out of a room off the church's vestibule.

"Seamie Finnegan? Is that you?" she said.

"Jennie! You're here!"

"Yes, of course. I finished with the children a few minutes ago. I was just tidying up."

"I was hoping you'd be here."

Hope had nothing to do with it. It was a Saturday, the day Jennie taught school. He knew she would be here.

Just then the church door opened again. "Pardon me, missus, but where's the stove going?" Robbie said. He and another man had just carried it inside and were straining under its weight.

"What stove?" Jennie asked.

"I've brought you a new stove," Seamie said. "To replace the old one. You said it didn't work. And the children looked so cold the other day."

"I can't believe you did this," Jennie said.

"It's nothing. Really," Seamie said. "I just wanted to help."

It was true. Mostly. What he'd really wanted was to see her again. Very much. He hadn't stopped thinking about her since he'd said good-bye to her a week ago. He hadn't wanted to think about her. Hadn't wanted to remember the color of her eyes, the curve of her waist, or the sound of her laughter, but he couldn't help it. It was a bit crazy—coming here like this with a delivery wagon and a stove—he knew it was, but he didn't care. It gave him a reason to see her again.

"I don't know what to say. Thank you. Thank you so much," Jennie said now, visibly moved by his gift.

"Oi, missus!" Robbie wheezed. "Save the thank-yous for later. Where the devil do you want this thing?"

"I'm so sorry!" Jennie said. "This way, please."

She turned and led the men into the small sacristy that served as her classroom. They put the stove down with a bang, then stood bent over, hands on knees, chests heaving.

"Is the old stove hot?" Robbie asked when he'd caught his breath.

"No, it isn't. We couldn't use it today. I couldn't get it to work. I think the flue's finally broken."

"Do you want it removed?"

Seamie said they did. The two men detached it from its vent pipe and took it to their cart.

"I . . . I don't know what to say," Jennie said after they'd left. "It's far too kind of you."

Seamie waved her thanks away, took off his jacket, and rolled up his sleeves. He opened the bag of tools he'd brought with him from Joe's house and got busy installing the new stove. He'd tinkered with Primus stoves and the stove on board the *Discovery* so often that hooking up this one was no great challenge. Half an hour after he started, he was finished.

"There!" he said, crawling out from behind the stove. "You'll all be warm as toast in here now."

Jennie looked at him and burst into laughter.

"What?" he asked, looking back at her.

"You're black as a chimney sweep! You should see your face. You look like you fell down a coal hatch. Wait there. I'll get a basin and some water."

She was back in a few minutes with water, soap, and a flannel. She bade him sit down, then scrubbed at the soot on his cheeks and neck. He closed his eyes as she washed him. Her hands were soft and gentle and he liked the feeling of them. So much so that he let his feelings get the better of him. He'd planned to be very proper, very formal. He'd planned to go to her house and speak with her father first. Instead, he reached up, caught her hand in his, and said, "Jennie, come walking with me."

"Yes. All right. I'd like a walk. I've got to go to the market, and—"

"No. I mean tomorrow. After services. In Hyde Park."

"Oh," she said softly. "That sort of a walk." She looked down at their hands and did not pull hers away.

"I'd call for you in a carriage. All proper."

She looked up at him then and smiled. "Yes, all right, then. That would be lovely."

"Good."

"Yes. Good."

"I'll . . . um . . . I'll walk you home."

"My home is right next door, Seamie."

"I know that. I'd like a word with your father."

"About the stove?"

"No."

"You don't have to. He doesn't expect it. I'm twenty-five, you know. All grown up."

"I know. I still want to talk to him, though."

She laughed. "All right, then. If you insist."

The Reverend Wilcott was seated at the kitchen table with a pot of tea, working on his sermon. He looked up when Jennie and Seamie came in.

"Seamus! Good to see you again, my boy! Will you have a cup of tea?"

"No, Reverend. No, thank you."

"What brings you our way?"

And Seamie, who'd braved uncharted seas, howling gales, and subzero temperatures, suddenly found that his nerve had deserted him. He felt like a six-year-old lad in short pants asking for tuppence to spend at the fair. He'd never asked permission to take a woman walking. The women he'd been with in the last few years—well, walking wasn't in it—and he found now that he didn't know how.

"I . . . uh . . . well, sir I . . . I want . . . I mean I'd *like* to ask your permission to take Jennie walking tomorrow."

The Reverend Wilcott blinked at him, but didn't say a word.

"Unless that would be a problem, Reverend," Seamie said nervously.

"No, no! It's not that at all," the reverend said, laughing. "It's just that I'm not used to being consulted, that's all. My Jennie does what she likes. She always has. She's a very independent girl. But if it makes you happy, then yes, you have my permission to take her walking tomorrow."

"Thank you, sir," he said. "I'll call at two, shall I?"

"Call whenever you like," the reverend said.

"Two would be lovely," Jennie said.

Seamie bid the reverend good day, and Jennie walked him to the door.

"You didn't need to do that," she said, before she opened it.

"Yes, I did."

"Next you'll be insisting on a chaperone."

He hadn't thought of that. "It would be all right. If you want one, I mean," he quickly said.

"No, I don't," she said. And then she went up on her tiptoes and kissed him.

Before he even had time to respond, she'd opened the door. "Until tomorrow," she said.

"Right. Yes. Until tomorrow," he said.

She closed the door then and he knew he should go. But he didn't. Not right away. For a few seconds, he just stood there, touching the place she'd kissed, touching his fingers to his cheek, wonderingly.

CHAPTER ELEVEN

"DARLING, HAVE YOU seen my new German?"

"No, Elinor, I haven't. Have you misplaced him?" Maud Selwyn Jones asked.

"Cheeky girl," Elinor Glyn said. "Do come. He's playing piano across the hall and making all the ladies swoon. You'll adore him. He's positively glorious. His name is Max von Brandt. He came with his cousin, Harriet Hatcher. The lady doctor. Do you know her?"

"I do. And him, too."

"Wonderful! The Hatchers were great friends with the Curzons, of course. Mrs. Hatcher and Mary Curzon were like sisters, I'm told."

A servant walked by carrying a tray of crystal goblets filled with champagne. "Here," Elinor said, plucking one. "You look parched."

"I am. Thank you," Maud said.

"Drink up. We've plenty. I found twelve cases in George's cellar this afternoon," Elinor said, winking. And then she was off, trailing silks and perfume. "We're just across the way, darling!" she trilled over her shoulder.

Maud smiled. Across the way was no short distance at Kedleston Hall, the sprawling ancestral home of George Nathaniel Curzon, First Marquess Curzon of Kedleston, and a widower. She had come up for a weekend party at Elinor's urging, and though she'd been at Kedleston several times, she never failed to marvel at the size and beauty of the Adam-designed house. It was very old and very beautiful and quite excessive, and she loved it.

Elinor adored it, too, Maud knew, and would love nothing more than to become its mistress. She was already Curzon's mistress, and made no secret of her desire to become his wife as well. But there were impediments. Her reputation, for one. She was a scandalous lady novelist whose books included *It, Three Weeks,* and *Beyond the Rocks*— racy stories no respectable woman would be caught dead reading. And then there was her husband—Sir Richard. Once wealthy, he had become a spendthrift and a debtor. Elinor had started writing back in 1900 and churned out a book a year now to pay the bills. They sold by the lorry load.

Maud didn't particularly feel like music tonight. She was bored by George and the other politicians who were visiting Kedleston for the weekend. Even her good friend Asquith, the prime minister, bored her tonight. She'd been feeling awfully restless, actually, and had been thinking about taking a stroll through Kedleston's gardens, or simply going to bed with a book. But now Max von Brandt was here and that changed things. She remembered him. Very well. A woman never forgot a man with a face like his. In fact, she'd thought about him ever since she'd met him that day at Holloway.

She placed her empty champagne glass on a table, took a cigarette from her purse, and lit it. It was a special cigarette, one with a touch of opium mixed into the tobacco—courtesy of a Limehouse drug lord named Teddy Ko. She'd visited him a few days ago for a fresh supply. She'd improved over the years. She didn't frequent the East London opium dens anymore, and she didn't even smoke as many of these things as she used to, but she still allowed herself the odd one. Every now and again.

She inhaled deeply, blew out a plume of smoke, then walked to the music room. It was enormous, of course, like every other room at Kedleston, and filled with a thousand distracting things—paintings, porcelain, furniture, and people—but even so, she spotted Max immediately.

He was seated at the piano playing "In the Shadows." His silver-blond hair was brushed back from his forehead. He was beautifully dressed in a black tuxedo and every bit as impossibly handsome as she'd remembered.

He looked up suddenly and smiled at her, and she felt herself go weak in the knees. Like some silly sixteen-year-old girl. It had been a long time since a man had had that effect on her.

He sang the next few songs to her, all songs she loved—"Destiny," "*Mon Coeur S'ouvre a la Voix*," "*Songe d'Automne*"—never taking his eyes off her, and to her dismay, she found herself looking away and, worse yet, blushing.

As the last notes of "*Salut d'Amour*" rose and faded, he declared himself exhausted and in need of a drink and abruptly left the room. There was applause and shouts of "Bravo!" but Maud felt as if the whole world had suddenly gone dark.

"Do get hold of yourself," she whispered.

She walked out of the music room and down the hall to the ball-room. It was empty, but a pair of French doors was open, and she quickly walked through them, badly in need of some air. Kedleston's marble terrace was bathed in moonlight. No one else was outside.

"Thank God," she sighed.

The quiet and the coolness of the night calmed her, but her hands still trembled slightly as she fished another cigarette from her purse.

"I wonder at you. I really do," she told herself. She was too old for this sort of schoolgirl behavior. At least, she thought she was.

"Ah. There you are," a voice said from behind her. A warm, rich voice, colored by a German accent. Maud slowly turned. Max was standing a few feet away. He held a bottle of champagne in one hand. "I thought you'd left. I thought all I'd find was your glass slipper," he said.

"I . . . I went outside. To take the air," she said.

Max smiled. "Yes, I see that. May I?" he asked, reaching for her cigarette.

"What? This? No, you don't want this," Maud said, hiding the cigarette behind her back.

"Yes, I do," Max replied. He leaned close, so that his face was only inches from her own. She could smell him—champagne and sandalwood and leather. He reached behind her and pulled the cigarette from her fingers. He took a deep drag and blew the smoke out slowly. His brown eyes widened. "You must tell me the name of your tobacconist," he said, coughing.

"Give that back," she said.

"Oh, no. Not yet," he said. He took another drag, smiling at her. "It's so nice to see you again. I didn't expect to."

"Nor I you," Maud said. "I enjoyed your playing. It was beautiful."

"I enjoyed you. Your dress is beautiful."

She didn't reply. He was playing with her. Teasing her. Mocking her. He must be.

"Fortuny, no?" he said.

"Very good," she replied. "Most men wouldn't know Fortuny from a tuba."

"Amethyst is your color. You should only ever wear amethyst.

I'll buy you a dozen amethyst dresses. A rare jewel should only have the very best setting."

Maud burst into laughter. She couldn't help it. "Oh, Max. How absolutely full of shit you are!"

Max laughed, too. "Yes, I am, and it's a relief to hear you say so." He took a slug from the champagne bottle. "So you're a woman who likes to hear the truth, eh?" He handed her the bottle, motioned for her to take a drink. "Here it is then: I want to make love to you. I have since I laid eyes on you. I won't be happy until I do."

Maud nearly choked on the champagne. She wasn't shocked by much, but she was shocked by that.

"Cheeky sod," she said, wiping bubbly off her chin. She handed him the bottle, then turned to go back inside.

"I see," Max called after her. "Like most women, you only thought you wanted the truth. Should I have lied to you? Sent you roses? Chocolates? Spouted poetry?"

She stopped.

"You *are* poetry, Maud."

Slowly, she turned around again. And then she walked back to him, took his face in her hands, and kissed him. Hard. Hungrily. She felt his hands on her waist, her back. He pulled her close and she felt the heat inside him, and inside herself, and suddenly she wanted him as she had never wanted a man. Wildly. Desperately.

"Where?" she whispered.

"My room," he said. "In half an hour."

He pressed a key into her hand. It had a number on it. All the bedrooms in Kedleston were numbered. She kissed him again, biting his lip, and then she quickly left him, her heels clicking against the marble tiles as she walked across the terrace, her heart pounding in her chest.

She didn't look back. Not once. So she did not see the smile that played upon Max von Brandt's lips. A smile tinged with sorrow. A smile that did not touch his eyes.

CHAPTER TWELVE

"ORDER! ORDER!" THE speaker of the house boomed, pounding his gavel. "Order, please!"

No one listened. On both sides of the aisle, MPs cheered and jeered.

"You've done it again, Joe," Lewis Mead, a Labour MP for Blackheath, whispered to him. "Can't you ever take the easy road? Suggest something uncontentious for a change? New flower boxes at Hackney Downs? More benches at London Fields?"

Joe laughed. He leaned back in his wheelchair, knowing it would take several minutes for the speaker to restore the peace. He looked around the room as he waited, taking in its soaring ceiling, its graceful Gothic windows and paneled galleries. These, plus the room's high, leaded windows and long, raked benches, always made him feel he was in a cathedral. It was an association that pleased him, for there was no place in all of Britain as sacred to him as this one, the House of Commons' chamber, and no calling as holy to him as that of member of Parliament.

Politics was Joe's religion, and this chamber his pulpit, and only moments ago, he had been speaking with all the zeal and eloquence of a fiery evangelist preacher. He wished now that he had some brimstone to hurl as well, for he saw he would need it.

"This is my last warning!" the speaker bellowed. "I ask the honorable gentlemen to sit down immediately! Or I shall have them removed!"

One by one those who had been standing sat—Conservatives, Liberals, and Labourites. Joe saw that Churchill was glowering. Henderson and MacDonald were beaming. Asquith was rubbing his brow.

Joe had opened today's session by introducing his new education bill with its demands upon the state to enlarge existing schools, build seventy new ones, raise the leaving age, and inaugurate education programs in ten of His Majesty's prisons. It had been given quite a reception.

"This is preposterous!" Sir Charles Mozier, owner of five clothing factories, had sputtered, as soon as Joe had finished speaking. "Government cannot afford this bill. It will bankrupt the state."

"Government *can* afford it. The question is—can capital?" Joe shot back. "Educated children become smart children and smart children ask questions. We can't have our seamstresses suddenly asking, 'Why am I paid seven pence to make a blouse Sir Charles sells for two quid?' They might take it in their heads to strike. And then it will be you, Sir Charles, not the state, who is bankrupt."

That had gotten half the room bellowing. What came next finished the job.

"Perhaps we can mandate tea and crumpets in the prisons, too," shouted John Arthur, whose Welsh mines had lucrative contracts to supply coal to prisons and Borstals. "We can have china teapots brought to the convicts on silver trays! Tell me, sir, have you any idea what such a program would cost?"

"Nothing," Joe replied.

"I beg your pardon?"

"I said, 'Nothing.' In fact, it'll save the state money. Educate every man in Wandsworth, every woman in Holloway. Give them the opportunities education brings, help them lift themselves out of poverty, and you can close those hellholes forever," Joe had said.

He waited now, until every man had sat down, until it was quiet once more. He looked at the faces he knew so well, faces of friends and adversaries. He looked up at the Strangers' Gallery, where his mother, Rose, his wife, Fiona, and his daughter Katie sat. Looking at them, he thought how easily they could not be sitting there. How easily he and his family could be shivering in some dank room in East London, with little to eat, not enough coal for a warm fire, or enough money to pay their rent. They had escaped that life, he and

Fiona. But so many hadn't. He thought about all the ones who were still there, still working for pennies an hour, still hungry, still cold. And then he started speaking again.

"Prime Minister, Mr. Speaker, honorable colleagues, it is time. Time to educate every child in Britain to the fullest of his or her potential. Time to bring every girl and every boy in Whitechapel, in the Gorbals, in the Liverpool courts, out of destitution and hopelessness. Only education can accomplish this. Only education can empty the workhouses and prisons, the slums and rookeries.

"Our government is, at last, beginning to recognize the dire plight of working people. It is beginning to work on behalf of the many, not the few. Look how far we have come in the last decade alone. Look at our accomplishments: better protection for children against abuse and exploitation, pensions for the aged, and national unemployment insurance—to name but a few.

"The naysayers said these things could never be. They called those who proposed the Children's Act and the National Insurance Act dreamers. As some of you—the kinder ones among you—have called me. If it is the dreamers who keep six-year-olds out of mills, if it is the dreamers who strive to end illiteracy and ignorance—then I am proud to be called a dreamer."

Joe paused for a few seconds, then delivered the closing lines of his speech.

"We now come to a crossroads in Britain's history," he said. "Do we proceed down the new and shining path, and in so doing, secure the future for *all* of Britain's children? Or do we turn back? Back to business as usual. Back to failure. Back to deprivation and despair. I cannot tell you how to vote. I can only tell you this: It is time to set aside self-interest, it is time to set aside politics, and it is time to consider the very ones who put you in the seats you now occupy. Look to your constituents, gentlemen, and to your consciences."

It was quiet when Joe finished speaking, so quiet that he could hear the chamber clock ticking. And then the applause began. And the cheering. Labour MPs to a man stood and clapped. Many of their Liberal colleagues joined them. Only the Tory benches were quiet.

The applause lasted for two minutes straight, and then the speaker once again called for order.

When the vote was called, enough ayes were counted to get Joe's bill to a second reading. The ayes were not unanimous, not by a long shot. The bill still had a long way to go before it became a law, but at least it had passed its first reading; it had not been killed. It was as much as Joe could have hoped for today.

As he wheeled himself back to his customary place near the front benches, he glanced up at the gallery. Fiona and Rose were smiling triumphantly. Katie, notepad in hand, gave him a quick wave.

There was a brief break, and then the speaker called upon the Honorable Winston Churchill, first lord of the admiralty and head of Britain's navy.

"What's Winston after now?" a man seated behind Joe whispered.

"More bloody boats," Lewis Mead replied.

As Churchill began to speak, it became clear that it was not mere boats he was after, but dreadnoughts.

Britain's first dreadnought had been launched in 1906. An entirely new breed of battleship—one armed with enormous guns and driven by steam turbines—the fearsome dreadnought had sparked an arms race with Germany.

After the kaiser had built two similar such ships, Parliament—in 1909—voted to fund the construction of four more dreadnoughts, with provisions for another four to follow in 1910.

Authorizing the battleships had pitted the Liberals against the Conservatives in an epic battle. The Liberals, hoping to reduce military spending, had wanted to fund only four ships. The Tories would have none of it. Joe well remembered the scene in the Commons when the number had been debated, with the Tories yelling, "We want eight and we won't wait!" until they'd defeated the Liberal chancellor, David Lloyd George, and won their boats. And now Winston wanted even more.

Churchill spoke at length now, with great command of figures and facts, and in his usual impatient tone, about Germany's increasingly aggressive stance toward France and Belgium. He raised the

possibility of a coming conflict and the possibility of Turkey align-
ing itself with Germany should that conflict actually occur.

"What would such an alliance mean for our ally Russia?" he
asked the chamber. "For the Balkan states? And most importantly,
what would it mean for Britain's continued access to her Persian oil
supplies and her Indian colonies?"

He paced the chamber for a moment, letting those dark scenarios
hang in the mind of every man in the room, and then he quietly said,
"The country with the superior naval fleet is the country that will
control the Dardanelles, gentlemen. And the country that controls
the Dardanelles controls passage to the Middle East, to Russia, and
to the Orient. I ask you today to authorize a new dreadnought to
make absolutely certain that that country is Britain, not Germany."

The Conservative benches were not quiet at the end of Churchill's
speech, as they had been at the end of Joe's. Instead, they positively
erupted. Tory MPs whistled, cheered, shouted, and applauded. Joe
expected them to burst into the chorus of "Rule Britannia" any second. The speaker nearly splintered his hammer trying to quiet them.

"Hmm . . . slum rats or ships? Which will it be?" Lewis Mead
said to Joe. "I know which one my money's on."

"Mine, too," Joe said. "When it comes to a second reading, Winston's bill will pass and mine will be killed. Winston's got everyone
convinced that the Germans are two seconds away from marching
on Buckingham Palace. My schools won't stand a chance, Lewis. Not
against his ships."

A vote was taken, and Churchill's bill, too, passed its first reading. The speaker then called a recess for lunch and the members
stood up to leave.

Joe, of course, could not stand, but as he wheeled himself out of
the chamber, he could see. Quite clearly. He could see the writing on
the wall. He could hear the conversations of the men around him. The
chill wind he had read of in the papers only days ago was strengthening. A storm was gathering, blowing west from Germany across Europe and the Channel, all the way to London.

Several MPs came up to congratulate him on his speech. Among them was the former Tory prime minister A. J. Balfour.

"Fancy a spot of lunch, old boy?" he asked Joe. "Yes? Excellent! Brilliant speech you gave, I must say. Not that any of them gives a toss. They've all got a raging case of war fever. Time to give the kaiser a black eye and all that. Next thing you know, Winston will have them all marching up and down Trafalgar Square with saucepans on their heads."

Joe nodded solemnly. Balfour might joke, but they both knew he was right.

"Now, now, old boy. Don't look so glum," Balfour said. "It's all saber-rattling, really. We'll stay well out of it, mark my words. You know as well as I do that a strong military is the best way to avoid a war."

"Not this time, Arthur," Joe said, with a bitter laugh. "Not with that madman in Berlin," he said. "In fact, I'm quite certain it's the best way to start one."

CHAPTER THIRTEEN

"MUM'S BEEN ASKING me about you, Peter. 'What's he like, Gladys?' and 'What does he do, Gladys?' and 'Why don't you bring him home, all proper like, Gladys?' and I thought . . . well, hoped really . . . that maybe you could come for tea next Sunday."

Max von Brandt looked down at his hands, then back up at the dowdy young woman sitting across from him. He hesitated for a few seconds—just long enough to terrify her—then said, "I'd like that, Gladys. Very much."

"You would?" she whispered, her voice incredulous. "I mean, you would! How wonderful! Mum'll be ever so pleased." She looked at him shyly, her brown eyes blinking behind her thick glasses, then added, "I know I am."

Max smiled at her. "How about another shandy?" he said. "To celebrate."

"I shouldn't. I've had two already," Gladys said, biting her lip.

"No, you're absolutely right, pet, you shouldn't," Max said. "A moment like this deserves something better—champagne."

"Oh, Peter! Champagne!" Gladys said. "I love champagne, me. But we shouldn't, really. It's awfully dear."

"Nonsense. Nothing's too good for my girl," Max said, patting her hand.

He stood, walked to the bar, and ordered a bottle of plonk and two glasses. As he waited for the publican to bring it, he watched Gladys in the mirror above the bar. She was fussing with her hair. Her cheeks were flushed. She was smiling. This was almost too easy.

Tonight was the fifth time he had taken her out. They'd gone for drinks twice. A stroll in Greenwich once. To the music hall another time. And now they were here again, back to the pub where he'd taken her the night he'd staged their first encounter.

He'd been a perfect gentleman on each outing. Solicitous, polite, happy to pay for everything. He'd taken her hand to help her on or off the omnibus, asked about her mother, talked of his work and his church and his parents up north in Bradford. He'd made sure to disappear now and again for several days at a time, as a seaman on a run north to Hull or south to Brighton would be expected to.

"Here we are!" he said, bringing the champagne back to their table.

He poured two glasses, then made a toast.

As he leaned toward Gladys, her eyes flickered to his neck.

"My goodness! What happened to you?" she asked.

"It's nothing," Max said.

Gladys hooked a finger in his collar, pulled it open. "It looks terrible," she said.

Max knew it did. It was a deep scratch, and livid.

"I was carrying a trunk for the captain," he said. "It had a rough edge. Caught me in the neck."

"Poor thing. Let me make it better," Gladys said coyly.

She kissed her the tip of her finger, touched it to his neck, then giggled behind her hand. She always held her hand over her mouth; she was embarrassed by her large, crooked teeth.

He caught her other hand in his and kissed it. "That's much better. Thank you, darling Glad," he said.

Gladys blushed a deep, unbecoming shade of red. "Naughty boy," she said, giggling again. "Don't be going and getting any ideas, now."

Max felt leaden inside. It was awful to watch this sad, plain dumpling of a woman, with her thick stockings and her sensible shoes, trying to be flirtatious and gay. It was cruel what he was doing, and he suddenly wanted to stop this charade, to apologize to her, bundle her into a hackney, and send her home. But he did not. There were times he hated what he did—times when he hated himself for doing it—but he would no more run from his duties than his father would have in 1870 on the battlefield at Metz. Duty had always come first, for every generation of von Brandts, and it did now for Max.

He closed his collar, wincing as the cloth rubbed against the wound, and feigned interest in Gladys's chatter. He had lied to her about the wound, as he had lied to her about everything else. It was no trunk that had caused that scratch, or the ones on his back. It was his lover who had done it, Maud Selwyn Jones.

As Gladys burbled on about the dinner she would cook for him on Sunday, Max remembered making love to Maud.

The first time, in his room at Kedleston, they'd knocked over a table and broken a vase.

The second time, at Wickersham Hall, her Cotswold estate, he'd had her in the woods. Or maybe it had been the other way around. He'd simply leaned over to kiss her as they stopped to rest the horses, and the next thing he knew, they were tumbling onto the ground. She'd somehow kept her riding hat on the whole time, and her silk stockings. Her teasing smile, just visible under the hat's black net veil, had driven him mad with desire. They'd certainly frightened the horses.

The third time, they'd been on their way to his flat after the opera. Just as the hackney driver had pulled away from the curb and into the dark London night, she'd kicked off her shoes, then lifted the hem of her dress, slowly, teasingly, an inch at a time, until it was quite apparent that she was wearing nothing under her gown. That time, they'd frightened the driver.

And then there was last night. At her flat. She'd had what seemed like a hundred candles burning in her bedroom when he arrived. Champagne in a silver cooler. Oysters on ice. She'd trailed a chunk of that ice down his body when they started, and had held another chunk to the scratches on his skin when they finished. The memory alone made him hard as stone now. She was everything he craved in a woman—exciting, exhausting, beautiful, and wild. She gave him what he wanted most—a few hours in which he could forget what he was, and the things he did.

". . . or a Victoria sponge? Which one do you think, Peter? Peter?"

Gott verdammt noch mal. He'd been miles away.

"Yes, Gladys?" he said, quickly putting Maud out of his mind. Thoughts of her made it impossible to concentrate on Gladys, and that would not do. He had things to accomplish this evening.

"I asked you which pudding you'd like," she said anxiously. "For tea on Sunday. Weren't you listening?"

"No, not entirely."

"Oh," she said, looking upset. "I'm sorry. I must be boring you, talking of puddings. How stupid of me. I don't know why I rabbit on so, I just—"

He took her hand in his. "If you must know, Gladys, I was thinking about how much I want to kiss you. It's something I think about a lot. Much more than I think about puddings."

Gladys blushed again, visibly flustered. "Oh, Peter, I . . . I don't know what to say."

"Say you'll give me a kiss, Glad. Just one."

Gladys looked around nervously, then gave him a quick peck on the check. He caught the scent of her as she did—wet wool, talcum powder, and camphor.

"That's much nicer than Victoria sponge," he said. "Now, let me give you one."

He leaned forward and kissed her mouth, lingering slightly. She could barely look at him afterward. He looked at her though, and saw that her chest was heaving and her hands were trembling. Good. He poured her more champagne. Several times. And half an hour later, Gladys Bigelow was drunk.

"Oh, Peter, this champagne is delicious!" she said. "Let's have some more."

"I think you've had plenty, pet. It's time we got you home."

Gladys pouted. "Don't want to go home."

"Yes, you do. Come on now, upsy-daisy, there's a good girl. . . ."

Max got her up on her feet, into her coat, and out of the pub. She swayed a bit on the sidewalk. He had to take her arm as they walked toward the bus stop. Before they'd gone five steps, she tripped, and he only just managed to stop her falling flat on her face.

Things were going perfectly.

"Gladys, dear," he said. "I think you've had a bit too much. You can't go home like this. We've got to get some coffee into you first. Only there's no place around here for tea or coffee, is there?" he said, pretending to look up and down the street.

"Kiss me, Peter," Gladys said. Only it came out sounding like *Kish me.*

He sighed deeply. "I'd love to," he said. "Only what sort of cad would I be, then? Kissing a girl who's had too much champagne?"

"Oh, Peter, you're not a cad," Gladys said, with feeling. "You're the most wonderful, wonderful, *wonderful* man I've ever met."

Max smiled. "Now I know you're drunk, Gladys. Listen, this is what we're going to do. I'm going to take you back to my room."

"I . . . I don't think that's a good idea," Gladys said, worriedly.

"Just for a bit. Just until you sober up a little. I can make you a pot of coffee there."

"No, I'm all right. I can get home. Really."

Max shook his head. "I can't let you go on a bus all by yourself in this state, Gladys. And I can't take you home to your mother like this, either. What on earth will she think of me? She'll never let me come to tea on Sunday. Never."

At these words, Gladys's eyes grew wide. "All right then," she said anxiously. "I'll go with you. But just long enough to drink some coffee. I've got to get home right after."

"Of course," Max said. "Just for a few minutes. Then I'll walk you to the bus."

Max put an arm around Gladys and led her down the dark cobbled streets to Duffin's, his lodging house. He helped her up the stoop, then unlocked the front door and poked his head inside to make sure no one was hanging about in the hallways. As he'd expected, no one was, for Mrs. Mary Margaret Duffin did not tolerate smoking, swearing, spitting, or loitering. He hurried Gladys inside, locked the door, then held a finger to his lips. She nodded, giggled, tried to kiss him again, then allowed herself to be helped up the stairs.

"Oh, Peter, my head's spinning," she said, when they were inside his room. "I don't feel very well."

"Lie down for a minute," he said, leading her to his bed.

"I shouldn't. I should go," she protested.

"Gladys, it's all right," he said easing her down onto the mattress. "Just lie back and close your eyes. The spinning will stop soon, I promise."

Gladys did as she was told. She sank back against his pillow, moaning slightly. Max lifted her legs onto the mattress, unlaced her boots, and took them off. He wasn't surprised that she felt awful. After all, he'd made sure that she drank most of the bottle.

He talked to her soothingly, telling her that the coffee would be ready in a minute. And it would be. He needed it to be there when she woke up. Later, he would tell her she'd drunk some and then fallen asleep. After a few minutes had elapsed, he called her name and got a mumbled response. He waited a bit, then called her again. Nothing. She was out.

Moving quickly, Max went to the one closet in the room, opened the door, and took out a tripod and camera. He had it set up in seconds. There was no need to pull the blind down; he'd done that earlier. He took the shade off the gas lamp on the wall, then lit two kerosene lamps, positioning them close to the bed. When he was satisfied with the light, he moved the camera close to the bed, then turned his attention to Gladys.

He sat her up and started to undress her. It was heavy going. She had layers of clothing on. Her thick wool jacket had to be unbuttoned and pulled from under her. There was also a suit jacket and skirt. A high-necked blouse. And a corset. He had just got it unlaced and was pulling it off her when her eyes suddenly opened and she sleepily protested. For a few seconds, he was worried that she was coming round, but then her eyelids fluttered and she was out again.

Max was relieved. He didn't want to have to use chloral hydrate on her. It kept people under for hours, and he didn't have hours. If he didn't get her back to her mother by ten at the latest, the old woman might worry and ask a neighbor to fetch the police.

He threw her corset on the floor, then quickly unbuttoned her camisole and bloomers and pulled them off. She stirred again, murmuring slightly, but did not waken. By the time he got her stockings off, he was sweating, but he didn't pause to catch his breath. Instead, he arranged her hands behind her head, tucked a fake flower behind her ear and turned her face toward the camera. He stood back to take in his handiwork, hesitating for a few seconds, then brusquely pushed her legs apart. It wasn't a pretty picture, but then again, it wasn't meant to be.

Max dropped a dry plate into the camera. He glanced at the naked woman on his bed one more time, focused his lens, and started to shoot.

CHAPTER FOURTEEN

"BLOODY HELL, BUT she's beautiful," Seamie said.

He stood on the dock, head back, eyes wide and full of wonder as he took in every proud and graceful inch of the ship in front of him. She was a three-hundred-and-fifty-ton barkentine, with her forward mast square-rigged and the other two masts rigged for fore and aft sails, like a schooner's. The subtle curves of her hull, the thrust of her prow, the soaring height of her mainmast—they all took his breath away.

"She's more than beautiful, lad," said the man standing next to him. "She's the strongest wooden ship ever built."

Seamie raised a skeptical eyebrow.

"The *Fram* comes close, I'll give you that, but this one's stronger."

Seamie knew the *Fram*, every inch of her. He'd sailed in her, with Roald Amundsen, to the South Pole. That ship had been specially designed to cope with pack ice. Built stouter, its hull more rounded, it rose up on top of the ice when the ice closed in, almost floating on it, instead of being crushed by it. It was an ingenious design and an effective one, but not beautiful. Compared to the ship in front of him, the *Fram* looked like a washtub.

"She won't do as well in the ice," Seamie said.

"She won't need to. She's to be used for loose pack only."

"Is that so? What do you call her?"

"Her name's *Polaris*, but I'm thinking of calling her *Endurance*. After my family motto: *Fortitudine vincimus*—'By endurance we conquer.'"

"*Endurance*," Seamie said. "It's a perfect name. Perfect for anyone, or anything, connected with you, sir."

Ernest Shackleton laughed loudly, his shrewd eyes sparkling. "Come aboard her, lad," he said. "Let's see what you think. Still have your sea legs?" Before he'd even finished speaking, Shackleton was halfway up the rope ladder dangling down the ship's side.

Seamie shook his head, smiling. He could see where this was leading. Shackleton hadn't said too much over the telephone. He hadn't needed to.

"How are you, Seamus, lad?" he'd bellowed. Seamie had recognized the voice on the other end of the line immediately. He'd heard it daily for more than two years in the Antarctic, when he made his first polar expedition aboard another of Shackleton's vessels, the *Discovery*.

Before he'd even give Seamie time to answer his question, Shackleton had launched into the reason for his call. "I need your help," he said. "There's this ship I'm thinking about. Norwegian built, but currently in dock at Portsmouth. Could you come out and take a look? I'd love to know what you make of her." He'd paused for a breath then, and Seamie could hear the teasing note in his voice as he added, "If you aren't too busy sipping tea and nibbling biscuits with Clements Markham at the RGS, that is."

"You heard about the job offer?" Seamie said.

"I did. And I assume you turned him down."

"Not yet."

"Why not?"

"It's a good job, doing good work on behalf of the RGS, a place that means a great deal to me and to us all," Seamie said. "I may take it. Why not? I haven't had any better offers," he added pointedly.

After they'd sounded each other out a bit more, Seamie had agreed to meet his old captain in Portsmouth and give him his frank opinion of the boat, quite certain that Shackleton would ask him to sign on.

But would he agree to go? A few weeks ago, he would have had no hesitation, but that was before he'd met Jennie. Before he'd started courting her. Before he'd taken her hand as they walked, talking about her life and his. Before he'd held her close and kissed her lips and felt her heart beating against his own. Before he'd started to think—for the first time in his life—that there might be another woman for him besides Willa Alden.

Seamie looked at the ship again now. He climbed up the rope ladder and stood next to Shackleton on the deck.

"Her keel's seven feet thick. Sides are anywhere from one-and-a-half-feet to two-and-a-half-feet thick. She's got twice the number of frames any other ship her size has. Bow's over four feet thick where it meets the ice," Shackleton said, answering Seamie's questions before he could even ask them.

Seamie nodded, impressed—even though he didn't want to be. He almost wished there was something wrong with the ship. He wished it had some terrible flaw in its design or construction—something that would give him a reason not to go. To stay in London and take the job at the RGS. To stay with Jennie.

"And her engine?" he asked.

"Coal-fired steam. She'll do just over ten knots," Shackleton said.

He talked on, telling Seamie about the ship's many qualities and how it was purposely built to handle polar conditions. He went on about the oak, Norwegian fir, and greenheart wood that was used in her construction. He talked for over an hour, leading Seamie up and down her deck, then below it to the crew's and captain's quarters, the engine room, the kitchen, and the hold. When he'd finished the tour, he brought Seamie abovedecks again.

He lit a cigarette, offered it to Seamie, then lit another for himself. He took a deep drag, blew the smoke out, then said, "Well, lad, I might as well tell you, I didn't bring you to the seaside for a box of taffy."

"No, I don't expect you did, sir."

"I'm getting up another expedition."

"I'd heard as much."

"You lot found the South Pole, but that doesn't mark the end of exploration in the Antarctic. I want to do another journey—a transcontinental trek. Two parties. Two ships. The *Endurance* will sail to the Weddell Sea and put a party ashore at Vahsel Bay, where they will begin a trek to the Ross Sea, via the pole."

"What about supplies?" Seamie cut in, remembering how crucial the proper planning of food, drink, shelter, and warmth was to Amundsen's success in obtaining the pole. "The Weddell Sea party won't be able to carry enough to get them all the way across."

Shackleton smiled. "That's where the second party comes in. As the first party heads to the Weddell Sea, a second ship will take a second party to McMurdo Sound in the Ross Sea, where they'll establish a base camp. From that camp, they'll trek toward the Ross Sea, laying down caches of food and fuel across the Ross Ice Shelf to the Beardmore Glacier, supplies that will sustain the first party as they complete the crossing. The Weddell Sea group eventually joins the Ross Sea group, and there you have it—the first land crossing of Antarctica."

Seamie mulled Shackleton's plan. "It could work," he said at length.

"*Could?* There's no could about it. It *will* work!" Shackleton bellowed.

Seamie heard the excitement in the man's voice. He'd heard that same excitement the first time he'd met him—at a lecture at the Royal Geographical Society, right before he'd talked Shackleton into taking him along on his *Discovery* expedition.

He smiled now. "You're never happier than when you have a quest, sir," he said.

"The quest is all, lad," Shackleton said. "You know it as well as I do. So what's it going to be? I'd love to have you with me. Are you in? Or are you going to let Clements make a file clerk out of you?"

Seamie laughed, but then found, to his consternation, that he had no answer.

Am I in? he wondered.

He remembered the *Discovery* expedition and the South Pole trek. He remembered the stark, aching beauty of Antarctica—the steel gray seas, the ice-blasted landscape, and the vastness of the night sky. It was nothing like London's sky, or New York's, where man-made light and smog obscured the stars. It was so clear there, so unspeakably still, that he'd felt as if he was seeing the heavens for the very first time. On so many of those nights, he'd felt as if he could reach up and touch the stars, as if he could gather them in his hands like diamonds.

Most of all, he remembered the life-threatening push to the pole. The first time, with Shackleton, they'd had to turn back only a hundred miles away from it. If they hadn't, they would have died. The second time, with Amundsen, they'd made it. He remembered how much each of the expeditions had taken out of him. He remembered the hunger, cold, and exhaustion. Two years had elapsed since the South Pole expedition, and he was only just now getting back to any sort of a real life, and the expedition Shackleton had outlined for him would take two more. Maybe even three. He'd be that much older when he returned. And what about Jennie? Would she wait for him? Was he sure he wanted her to?

"Well, lad?" Shackleton pressed.

Seamie shrugged helplessly. "Can I think about it, sir? I'm afraid I just don't know."

"You don't know?" Shackleton said, disbelief in his voice. "How can you not know? For God's sake, where's your heart, lad?"

Good question, Seamie thought. Where, indeed? Had he left it at Kilimanjaro? Was it lost somewhere out in the icy oceans of the Antarctic? Was it in London with Jennie Wilcott?

As he looked out over the harbor, past Shackleton, past all the ships moored nearby, he realized, with an aching sadness, that he knew the answer. He didn't want to admit it, because it was so painful to always long for something you would never have, but he knew it nonetheless. His heart was where it had always been—in the keeping of a wild and fearless girl, a girl he'd never see again. How he wished it wasn't.

Shackleton sighed. "It's a woman, isn't it?"

Seamie nodded. "Yes, it is."

"Wed her, bed her, then come sailing with me."

Seamie laughed. "I wish it was that simple, sir."

Shackleton softened. "Look, lad, it's only March. I won't be sailing until August, at the earliest. Take your time. Think it over. I want you with me. You know that. But you must do the thing that's right for you."

"I know that, sir. Thank you. I will," he said to Shackleton.

And to himself, he added, "If I only knew what the right thing was."

CHAPTER FIFTEEN

MAX VON BRANDT took a deep drag on his cigarette, then exhaled slowly. He was glad of the plume of smoke that hung about him. It helped mask the stench.

Max was sitting on the one and only chair in his room at Duffin's. Across from him, on the bed, sat Gladys Bigelow. She was sobbing and shaking. She'd already vomited twice, all over his bed, and she looked as if she would soon be sick again. He'd gathered up the quilt, the sheets and the pillows, and had taken them downstairs to the rubbish bin, but the smell still lingered.

Spread out on a table in the center of the room was the cause of Gladys's tears—a set of photographs, ugly and obscene. They showed a woman lying in a bed, naked, her legs splayed. The woman's face was clearly visible. Max knew the photos well. He had taken them himself, only a few days ago.

"Please," Gladys sobbed. "I can't. I can't do it. Please."

Max took another drag on his cigarette, then said, "You have no choice. If you refuse, I'll send the pictures to George Burgess. You'll lose your position immediately and the resulting disgrace will ensure you don't find another. That job is your life, Gladys. You told me so yourself. On several occasions. What else do you have? A family? A husband? No. And you're not likely to. Not if I make these photographs public."

"I'll kill myself," Gladys said in a choked voice. "I'll walk to Tower Bridge and jump off."

"Who would look after your ailing mother if you did?" Max asked. "Who would pay her doctor's bills? Buy her food? Pay her rent? Who would take her to the park on Sunday in her wheelchair? You know how much it means to her. She looks forward to it all week. Do you think the orderlies in the institution where she'll end up will do it? She'll be lucky if they remember to feed her."

Gladys covered her face with her hands. A low, animal moan of anguish escaped her. She retched again, but there was nothing left inside her.

Max rested his cigarette on the edge of an ashtray and crossed his arms over his chest. He wished he was not here in this filthy place, breathing in the smell of vomit and despair. He closed his eyes briefly, summoning an image in his mind of the place he did want to be—a place that was wild and free and untouched by men.

It was white and pure and cold this place, it was Everest, the rooftop of the world, and the hope that he would go back there one day when all of this was over, and that he might find her—Willa Alden—still living there, as wild and beautiful as the mountain itself, sustained him.

Thinking of that place, and that woman, made him want to stand up and leave. Leave the wretched room he was sitting in. And the wretched woman nearby. And wretched, ugly Whitechapel. He'd put his life in danger every time he came here. He knew he had. He'd heard that the Cambridge lads were on to him, that it was only a matter of time. Well, that was as it must be, and to leave before the job was done was to put other people's lives in danger. Millions of them. And so he stayed.

He waited a few more minutes, giving Gladys a little more time to recover, then he said, "Will you do it? Or do I send the pictures?"

"I'll do it," she replied, in a hollow voice.

"I knew you'd see reason," Max said. He stubbed his cigarette out, then leaned forward in his chair. "I want copies of every letter that leaves George Burgess's office."

"How? How am I to do that?" she said. "He's in and out of my office. So are other people."

"Carbons. You make a copy of every letter for his files, don't you?"

Gladys nodded.

"Use a second carbon. One for each letter. The carbons are all placed in a special basket, dumped into an incinerator at the end of the day, are they not? It's a tremendous waste and expense, but necessary for security. At least, that's what you told me."

"Yes."

"Make sure the second carbon does not go into the basket."

"*How?*" Gladys asked. "I told you that people—"

"I would suggest you fold each one twice and tuck it into the top of your stockings. Wait until you are alone. Or pretend to reach under your desk for a dropped pencil. Use your good mind, Gladys. Your bag is searched every night, but you are not because Burgess trusts you completely. That's another thing you told me. I also want notes on the documents you can't copy. Incoming correspondence, for example. Blueprints. Maps. Tell me what they are and what they contain. Leave nothing out, I warn you. If I hear about naval plans or acquisitions from other sources, the pictures go in the mail. Do you understand?"

"Yes."

"Every Wednesday, my agent will meet you on the bus you take home from work. He'll board at Tower Hill and sit next to you. You will be sitting on the top deck. He'll be wearing a suit and carrying a doctor's bag. He'll also be holding a copy of that day's *Times*. So will you. Inside your paper will be the carbons you've obtained for me. You will put your paper on the seat between you. The man will exchange yours for his. Afterward, you'll get off the bus at your usual stop. That's all you have to do. Do anything else, Gladys, anything at all, and you know what will happen."

Gladys nodded. Her face was gray. Her eyes were dull and expressionless. She looked dead inside.

"May I go now?" she asked.

"Yes," Max said. "This is the last you will see of me unless you give me some reason to doubt you."

He stood then and pulled an envelope from his pocket.

"This is from the kaiser," he said. "To show his appreciation for your efforts. It contains one hundred pounds. To help with your mother's medical bills."

Gladys took the envelope from him and tore it to bits, letting the pieces flutter to the floor. When she was finished, she staggered out of the room, slamming the door behind her. Max listened as the sound of her shoes on the stairs faded, then disappeared, and as he did, an expression of almost unbearable pain crossed his face. He knelt down, picked the pieces up off the floor, and fed them into the fire.

CHAPTER SIXTEEN

"ARE YOU COLD?" Seamie asked Jennie, as he pushed the punt they were in up the River Cam.

"Not at all. It's so warm today, it feels more like June than April. It's glorious, isn't it? After that dreary, endless winter," she said, smiling at him from under the brim of her straw hat.

She was wearing a dress of robin's egg blue faille. A sash of ivory silk set off her tiny waist. Her color was high and her eyes were sparkling. Fetching, he thought, as he looked at her. That's the perfect word. That's exactly what she is.

They'd come up to Cambridge together on a train last night, along with Albie Alden and Aunt Eddie, and were spending a long weekend at Eddie's house. Eddie had taken to Jennie immediately and, in typical Eddie fashion, had made all sorts of inappropriate comments during the train ride, such as "You'd be stark raving mad to let this one go, old chap." And "Best get a ring on her finger, before she finds out what you're really like." And Seamie couldn't forget this one—delivered sotto voce, or Eddie's best attempt at sotto voce, which meant only half the train heard it: "If you take my advice, you won't trifle with this girl. She's not a gin-swilling, gold-digging hussy like all the rest of them."

By the time the train had pulled into the Cambridge station, Seamie had been utterly mortified, but he also knew deep down that Eddie was right. He'd been seeing Jennie for nearly two months now. They'd done something together every weekend—whether it was walking in Hyde Park, or seeing a show, eating fish and chips at Blackheath, or taking tea at the Coburg Hotel. Jennie was undoubtedly wondering what his intentions were. Her father, too. He would gladly tell them, if only he knew.

"I'm a bit worried about the clouds over there," he said now, pointing ahead of them. "It was a bit of a mad idea, this. People don't usually go punting until high summer."

"Mad ideas are often the best ones," Jennie said. "I love being here, Seamie. Truly. I love being on a river. My father used to take us punting on the Cherwell all the time when I was a girl. My mother's father left her a cottage at Binsey. We would holiday there, and often go into Oxford and rent a punt at the Cherwell Boathouse. It's mine now, the cottage. My mother left it to me. Though I don't go there nearly enough."

"You'll have to show it to me someday," Seamie said, expertly guiding the boat around a downed tree limb.

"I don't know if you'd like it. It's very small. Lots of antimacassars and teacups and pictures of the royal family."

Seamie laughed.

"How did it go with Sir Clements?" Jennie asked him. "You never told me."

Seamie had met with Clements Markham at the RGS yesterday

morning to talk further about the position Markham was offering him.

"Well, there's an office," he said flatly.

"What's wrong?" Jennie said. "Is it not a nice one?"

"It's very nice, actually. Grand. Spacious. With a desk in it. And a chair. And filing cabinets and rugs. And views of the park from the window. And a secretary sitting outside waiting who'll bring me tea and biscuits anytime I like."

"It sounds rather splendid."

"It is rather splendid. That's the whole problem."

"No icebergs or penguins," Jennie said.

"No," he said ruefully. "No icebergs or penguins."

No sunrises that stop you dead with their unspeakable beauty, either, he thought. No whales breaching only yards from the ship, showering your awestruck self with a cold ocean rain. No songs and whiskey belowdecks at night while the wind plucks at the ship's rigging and the ice beats against her hull.

He thought these things but didn't say them, because he thought they might be hurtful to Jennie and he did not wish to distress her. She wanted him to stay here, to take the job at the RGS. He knew she did. She had never said so, had never once pressured him, but he'd felt it in her touch. In the kisses she gave him. He'd heard it in her words—how she would talk about wanting to visit Brighton with him over the summer, or the Lake District, or some such thing, then suddenly stop herself, realizing he would not be here over the summer if he signed on for Shackleton's expedition.

She turned away from him now, feigning interest in a pair of ducks, but the unspoken words lay heavily between them. He had a choice to make: take the position Markham had offered him and stay here in London, or go on another Antarctic expedition with Shackleton, one that would take him away for years. Much depended on that choice and they both knew it.

"What do you think about that barn over there for our picnic?" Seamie said, nodding at a small tumbledown stone building at the edge of a field. "It's looks a bit ramshackle, but I bet it's dry inside. Drier than the bare ground, at least."

"It looks perfect," Jennie said.

Seamie poled the boat over to the bank, jumped out, and pulled it ashore. He helped Jennie out and then reached for their picnic basket and the tarpaulin.

They'd planned to go into town for Sunday lunch at a pub, but as they walked across the Silver Street bridge, Seamie had glimpsed Scudamore's, which hired out punts—narrow, flat-bottomed boats that were not rowed, but rather pushed along the river by long, thin poles. Workmen had taken a few out to repair them, and Seamie, never able to resist the intoxicating combination of boats and water, asked Jennie if she'd like to go punting. She'd agreed immediately but the Scud's proprietor had been a bit hesitant. The boats weren't officially out yet, he said, and the Cam was high just now from all the spring rain. But then he'd recognized Seamie and said he reckoned if a man could get himself to the South Pole and back, he could get himself up the Cam.

Seamie had ducked into the nearby Anchor pub and arranged a picnic lunch. He'd placed the basket in the boat and asked the Scud's proprietor for a tarp to put on what would surely be sodden ground. Then he handed Jennie into the punt, and they were off, poling through the ancient village, past the colleges, and into the countryside.

Jennie led the way now, up the riverbank toward the field. Seamie trailed behind her with their lunch. He nearly crashed into her when she stopped suddenly.

"Oh, Seamie! Snowbells!" she exclaimed. "Look at them all!"

His eyes followed where she was pointing. To the right of them, on the crest of the bank, were clumps of small white flowers, their tiny blooms dangling above slender green stalks.

"Oh, what a lovely sight," Jennie said. She went closer to the flowers, taking great care not to step on any, and bent down to touch one of the blooms. "It's been such a dreadful winter," she went on, all in a rush. "So cold and long. And I've been so worried about so many things. About my father doing too much. About some of the children—a little boy in particular whose own father is far too handy with his belt. About a friend of mine, a lovely girl caught up with the wrong people." She turned to him and he saw a shimmer of tears in her eyes. "I'm sorry. It's daft, I know, but snowbells always make me cry. They're so tiny and fragile, yet they push themselves through the cold, hard soil. They're so brave. They give me hope."

Seamie looked at her, at her beautiful face turned up to his, at the tears in her eyes, at the smile on her lips despite them. She was so good, this woman. So gentle and kind. She worried about others always, never herself. His heart clenched inside him, full of emotion. It wasn't what he'd felt before—the blind, tearing, wild yearning he'd felt for Willa—but it must be love all the same, he thought. It must be.

Overcome by his feelings, he put the picnic things down, knelt beside her, and kissed her. Her lips were sweet and yielding and he would have kept on kissing them, but it started to rain. He looked up, saw that the dark clouds he'd spotted earlier were now directly over them, and knew there would soon be a downpour.

"Come on," he said, picking up the basket and tarp. "We'll have to make a run for it."

They dashed across the field—Jennie pressing her hat to her head— and made it inside the barn just as the skies opened. The barn wasn't much—only three of its walls were standing—but it still had most of its roof and would do to keep the rain off them.

"It must've been abandoned some time ago," Jennie said, spreading the tarp over the earthen floor. "Seamie, would you hand me the basket? I'll set the luncheon out and . . . Oh!"

Seamie didn't give a toss about the lunch or the basket or any of it. He had taken Jennie into his arms and was kissing her again. He wanted to feel what he'd felt only moments ago. He wanted to savor that feeling and know it for love. He wanted that so much.

Jennie kissed him back. Shyly at first, then more passionately. And then she sank down onto the tarp, pulling him with her. "Make love to me, Seamie," she whispered.

He had not expected that. "Jennie, I . . . ," he started to say.

"Shh," she whispered, taking off her jacket. "I want you to." She unbuttoned her blouse and shrugged out of it. Seamie could see the shape of her breasts through her camisole, full and round, and before he knew what he was doing, he was unbuttoning it, and then fumbling with her skirts. She was beautiful and he wanted her. Very badly.

He put his jacket on the tarp and laid her down. He began to kiss her, his lips traveling over her neck, her breasts, down to her belly, and then he saw it—a long, jagged scar running from the bottom of her rib cage, across her belly to her opposite hip.

"My God, Jennie . . . what happened?"

He heard her take a deep breath, then let it out again. "An accident. When I was a child. I was hit by a carriage."

"Were you in hospital?" he asked.

"For six months," she said. "I don't remember the accident. I was nine. I remember the recovery, though."

"My poor girl," he said, tracing the long jagged line with his fingers.

"Don't look at it. Please," Jennie said, stopping his hand. "It's so ugly."

He took her hand in his and kissed it. "Nothing about you is ugly, Jennie Wilcott. You're beautiful. In every way. God, but you're beautiful." He lost himself then, in the sweet softness of her body. In the depth of her lovely eyes. In the taste and smell of her. In the sound of her voice, whispering his name.

It was over too fast. He hadn't meant it to be, but he couldn't help himself. "I'm sorry," he said smiling sheepishly. "Couldn't help myself. I'll make it up to you. I swear," he said, nibbling on her earlobe and making her giggle. "It'll be wonderful. Simply fantastic. So good, you won't be able to stand it. You'll be begging me for mercy." She was laughing now. He loved the sound of her laughter. Loved knowing that he was making her happy. He bit her shoulder gently, making her laugh even more, then kissed her throat, the place between her breasts, her hip. He put his hand between her legs, wanting to kiss her there, too, until he looked down and saw the blood on her thighs.

Oh, hell. Bugger. Damn it all, he thought.

"Jennie . . . are you . . . You're not . . . ," he started to say.

"A virgin?" She laughed. "Not anymore."

A wave of remorse washed over him. He had wanted her so much, he hadn't stopped to consider whether she might or might not have had a lover before him. He shouldn't have done it. Not with her. He'd only ever bedded experienced women. He was a blackguard. A cad. An utter bounder. She was a reverend's daughter, for God's sake. Upright and upstanding, and all those sorts of things. Of course she was a virgin. How could he have been so thoughtless and stupid?

"I'm sorry, Jennie. I didn't know or I wouldn't have done it. Truly," he said, expecting tears and remonstrance.

But Jennie surprised him. Just as she'd done that day at Holloway.

"Sorry? Why? I'm not," she said, laughing. "I've wanted you since the day I first saw you, Seamus Finnegan." And then she kissed his mouth and pressed her body against his, making him want her, too. Again.

He went slowly the second time, holding himself back until he heard her breath hitch, felt her twine her legs around his and shudder against him, and then he came again, hard and fast and calling her name. He was in thrall to her beauty. To her sweet face. To her body—so full and lush and achingly lovely. She looked like something the old masters had carved, a flawless Galatea come to life. The curve of her breast, so softly heavy in his hand now. Her tapered waist. The generous flare of her hips. The unspeakable softness of her thighs, and what lay between them.

Willa had not looked like this. She had not felt like this. She was muscular and thin, not lush. They had never made love, he and

Willa, but he had held her close and kissed her. Right before her accident. He'd felt the bones of her hips pressed against him. The strong, thumping beat of her fearless heart. And after the accident, he'd set her hopelessly broken leg. Carried her injured body for miles, through African jungle and veldt, feeling her fever-racked cheek against his. He'd made her eat and drink. Held her when she vomited. Cleaned the blood and pus from her wounds. He knew her body. Better than he knew Jennie's. He knew her soul. Her spirit. Her heart.

Willa. Again, he thought, his heart suddenly heavy. Always Willa. Even now as he lay naked next to Jennie. Would he never be free of her? Of the memories? The longing? The torment? He wished he could rip her out of his head. And his heart.

By God, he would rip her out of himself. He'd do it. He'd rid himself of her. Break her hold over him. End the misery he felt whenever he thought of her. Here. Now. Forever.

He propped himself up on one elbow. "I love you, Jennie," he said.

Jennie, who'd been drowsing, opened her eyes. "What?" she whispered.

"I love you," he said, hoping she couldn't hear the desperation in his voice. "I do."

I do love her, he told himself. I do. Because she's beautiful and wonderful and I'd be completely mad not to.

Jennie blinked at him. She looked as if she wanted to say something but couldn't get the words out. Seamie's heart sank. He'd said too much. Or maybe he hadn't said enough. Yes, that was the most likely thing. He should've followed up his mad declaration with a proposal. He'd just made love to her, taken her virginity. He should be on bended knee now, asking her to marry him. But he couldn't do it. Because it wasn't her lovely hazel eyes he saw when he imagined asking that question, it was Willa's green ones. Still. Always.

"I'm a fool, Jennie," he quickly said. "You don't have to answer. I understand," he said. "I probably shouldn't have said anything. I—"

"You're not a fool, Seamie," she said. "Not at all. I . . . I . . ." She took a deep breath, then said, "I love you, too. Madly." A tear rolled down her cheek, and then another.

Seamie brushed her tears away. "Don't cry. Please don't cry. I don't know what I'm doing, Jennie. I don't know if I'm going to be on a ship bound for Antarctica in a few months, or behind a desk at the RGS. I don't know if . . ."

He wanted to be honest with her. He wanted to tell her that he wished he knew what to do. Whether to go or to stay. He wanted to tell her that he loved her, he did, as best he could. He wanted to ask her, to beg her, to somehow make him love her more. Enough to make him forget Willa Alden forever. But he didn't know how to say those things, not without hurting her. He tried. He stuttered and stammered, until she finally stopped him.

"Shh," she said, touching her finger to his lips. "It's all right, Seamie."

"Please don't be sad," he said. "I can't bear to see you sad."

She shook her head and kissed him. "I'm not sad. Not at all. I'm happy. Very, very happy. I have your love. It's all that I want and more than I ever thought I'd have."

He wondered at her words. How could a woman as beautiful and good and smart as Jennie have thought for a second that a man's love was more than she'd ever have? Jennie Wilcott could have a thousand men, and every last one of them would have counted himself beyond lucky to have won her. Why on earth didn't he love her as much as he loved Willa? Why couldn't he ever get over Willa—the woman who'd smashed his heart and left him to pick up the pieces? What was wrong with him?

These questions hounded Seamie now; they tortured him. He wanted to get up, to get dressed, and go walking in the rain-soaked fields. He wanted to walk until the anger was out of him. Until the despair was gone. Until he had his answers.

But Jennie didn't let him. She kissed him softly and pulled him down to her.

"It's all right," she said again.

And in her arms, for a few sweet hours, it was.

CHAPTER SEVENTEEN

"AH! THERE SHE is! My green-eyed heretic!"

Willa Alden smiled. She stood up and bowed to the man who'd just walked into Rongbuk's one and only public house—a corner of an enterprising villager's yak barn.

"*Namaste, Rinpoche,*" she said warmly, greeting him—an elder and a lama—first, as tradition demanded. She addressed him not by his name but by the honorific *Rinpoche*—"precious one."

"*Namaste,* Willa Alden," the lama replied. "I should've known to look for you in Jingpa's. Have I not often told you that alcohol obscures the path to enlightenment?" His words were chiding, but his eyes were kind.

Willa lifted the bamboo cup she was holding. It was filled with chang, an ale-like drink made from barley. "Ah, *Rinpoche,* I am in error!" she said. "I thought Jingpa's chang *was* the path to enlightenment."

The lama laughed. He pulled up a low wooden stool and sat down at Willa's table—a plank stretched across two tea chests, placed close to the fire. He pulled off his sheepskin hat and mittens and unbuttoned his coat. The night was brutally cold, and the wind was howling outside, but inside Jingpa's stone barn it was warm, for his fire and his animals gave off a great deal of heat.

"Will you have a sip of something hot, *Rinpoche?*" Willa asked. "The night is cold and the body desires warmth."

"My body desires little, Willa Alden. I have mastered my desires, for desire is the enemy of enlightenment."

Willa suppressed a smile. It was a game they played, she and this wily old man. He was the village's spiritual leader, head of the

Rongbuk Buddhist monastery, and must not be seen to be enjoying himself in a public house. Tomorrow Jingpa, a gossip, would talk to the entire village of the lama's visit. If he stayed to drink with her, he must be seen to be doing it for her sake only.

"Ah, *Rinpoche*, have pity on me. I am not as fortunate as you. Enlightenment eludes me. My desires control me. Even now, for I greatly desire the pleasure of your esteemed company. Will you deny a poor heretic the comfort of your light and knowledge?"

The lama sniffed. "Since you ask it, I will take a small cup of tea," he said.

"Jingpa! Po cha, please," Willa called out.

Jingpa nodded. He began whisking together the ingredients for the restorative drink—hot black tea, salt, yak milk, and butter. When he was finished, he poured the steaming mixture into a bamboo cup and brought it over. The lama held the hot cup in his hands, warming them, then took a sip and smiled. Jingpa bowed.

"What brings you here, *Rinpoche*?" Willa asked.

"A group of men, traders from Nepal, has just come through the pass on their way to Lhasa. They are staying overnight in the village. There is one among them—a Westerner—who is asking for you," the lama said.

Willa felt her heart leap at his words. For a wild, hopeful second, she allowed herself to believe that it was him—Seamie Finnegan— here somehow and wanting to see her. Then she silently scolded herself for her foolishness. Seamie wanted nothing to do with her. Why would he? She had left him, told him to live his life without her.

"His name is Villiers. He is a Frenchman, I believe," the lama continued. "A heretic like yourself. Determined to climb that which cannot be climbed, our holy mountain mother. He wishes to hire you as a guide. Shall I tell him where to find you? And endanger your soul? Or shall I say that there is no such person in Rongbuk and, by doing so, bring you closer to the Buddha?"

"I thank you for your concern, *Rinpoche*, and though my soul longs for transcendence, my body longs for sampa, po cha, and a warm fire at night. I must have the money I earn from guiding to buy these things, and so I will meet your Frenchman now, and the Buddha not quite yet, but soon."

"Soon. Always soon. Never now," the lama sighed. "As you wish, Willa Alden."

The lama finished his drink quickly and readied himself to return to the monastery.

"Will you please tell the man to meet me at my hut, *Rinpoche?*" Willa asked him as he pulled his mittens on.

The lama said he would. Willa thanked him, then asked Jingpa to fill an earthen bowl with hot chang and cover it with a plate. She knew the Frenchman would need it after trekking over the pass. She put her outer things on, paid Jingpa, and took the pot from him. She walked home through the village holding the pot close to her body, warming it as it warmed her.

As she passed by the monastery, she could smell the incense, smoky and thick, wafting from under the door and through cracks in the shutters. Under the wind's banshee howl, she could hear the monks chanting, their strong voices carrying through the monastery's walls. She loved the deep-voiced chants and was greatly moved by them. They sounded older than time, like the mountain itself speaking.

Willa stopped for a minute to listen. She had been inside the temple often and knew the saffron-robed monks would be seated to either side of their Buddha, eyes closed, palms turned up. She knew the Buddha would be gazing down on them, his face radiant with kindness, acceptance, and serenity.

She remembered the lama's words now and how he had wished to bring her closer to the Buddha. He wanted her to accept the Buddhist way. To detach herself from desire, to transcend it.

Willa knew the lama meant well for her, but what he was asking . . . well, it was like asking her to transcend the need to breathe. She simply could not do it. Her desire, her drive, they were what kept her going. They got her up and out in the morning when it was twenty below. They kept her working, photographing, trying to find a route up the mountain, even though she was hobbled by the loss of her leg. They kept her here year after year, though she was lonely and often longed for her family. She *was* her desire. To not want Everest, to not want to explore as much as she could of this magnificent mountain, was inconceivable to her. To stop desiring, to stop questing, was to die.

The lama called her, and all those who came to Rongbuk wishing to climb Everest, heretics. The mountain was holy, he said, and must be left undefiled by man. Yet he was kind, and though he tried his best to convert Willa and the other Westerners who made their way to Rongbuk, he also allowed them to stay in the village. He made sure they were provided for and prayed for their acceptance of the Buddha.

Willa walked on, certain the lama had worn out many beads praying for her, and certain he would wear out many more. She continued toward her home, more than a bit reluctant to meet the stranger who waited for her there. She needed his money—for food and drink and supplies, as she'd told the lama, and also for opium. Her leg was playing up something fierce. Her supply had dwindled and she would need to buy a fresh stock of the drug from the trading party that had stopped in Rongbuk, if they had any.

Willa always needed money, but solitude was what she wanted now, not visitors and their money, for she was finishing up her photographs and maps of her proposed route up Everest, and she needed to keep that route a secret. She didn't want anyone—and certainly not this man Villiers—to go back to Europe and claim her findings as his own.

Hopefully he wouldn't be too much trouble. He'd likely been trekking for weeks, and would need a few days to rest and recover from his exertions. That would give her the time she needed to do the climbing she wanted to do, finish taking notes, and write up her findings. Then she'd have to post them to Clements Markham at the RGS, which meant surrendering them to the first trading party heading to India and the British post office at Darjeeling.

As Willa neared her small, one-roomed hut at the eastern edge of the village, she spotted him, standing by her door, stamping his feet and clapping his hands to keep warm. As she got closer to him, she saw that he was gaunt and trembling. His lips were puffy and blue. There were white patches on his nose and chin.

"Miss Alden?" he called out.

"Mr. Villiers, I presume," she replied.

"Yes. M-M-Maurice Villiers. From France. I'm . . . I'm an alpin- ist, Miss Alden, and h-h-have heard of your f-f-familiarity with the north face of Everest. I w-w-wish to retain a guide and was w-w- wondering if you would consent—"

Willa laughed. The man was shivering so hard he could barely speak. "Stop talking and come inside," she said. "Before you drop dead."

She pushed her door open, then pushed him in, shaking her head as she did. She had begun to see Europeans as the Tibetans did. This man would insist on formalities and politenesses and the proper form of address even as he was freezing to death.

"Sit down. There," she said, pointing to a chair by the hearth. He did as he was told, putting his pack down first, while Willa immedi- ately set about warming the room. She built up the fire she'd banked earlier, then lit a lamp. Then she pulled off her guest's hat, inspect- ing his ears, cheeks, and chin. Next she took off his mittens and turned his blue, swollen hands over in her own.

"They look worse than they are. You won't lose any fingers," she said. She poured a cup of Jinpa's chang, still steaming, from the earthen bowl and handed it to him. He took it gratefully, drank it quickly, and asked for more.

"In a minute," Willa said. "First let's see about your toes."

The fire had thawed his frozen laces. She untied them, opened his boots, and took them off. He made no protest. Not when his boots came off. And not when his socks wouldn't—because they were fro- zen to his swollen, blackened toes. She waited until the socks had thawed, too, then carefully peeled them off.

"How bad is it?" he asked her, not looking.

"I don't know. We'll have to wait and see."

"Am I going to lose my toes?"

"One or two."

He swore and raged. Willa waited for him to stop, then gave him a bowl of sampa. He was still shivering convulsively even after he'd finished eating, which worried her greatly. She quickly took his coat off and then his clothing. His underwear was sodden. She took a pair of scissors and cut the legs of it so that she could ease it over his damaged feet. He didn't want to take it off, but she made him.

"It's wet," she said. "You can't get in my bed in wet underwear. Here, put these on. I won't look," she added, giving him a tunic and a pair of wide-leg trousers. She turned away. When he'd dressed himself, she wrapped him in a wool robe and helped him hobble to her bed. The bed was piled high with sheepskins and furs.

"Get in and turn on your side," she said. He did. She got in next to him, pressed her body to his, and wrapped her arms around him.

He turned suddenly and kissed her violently, then grabbed her breast.

She slapped his hand away. "Do that again," she said, "and I shall beat you with the poker."

"But . . . but you touched me . . . you held me . . . ," Maurice said, through his blue lips.

"You're hypothermic, you bloody fool," Willa said. "I'm trying to save your life. Turn around now. Unless you want to be buried in Rongbuk."

Maurice Villiers did as he was told, and Willa put her arms back around him, holding him tightly, giving him her warmth. The heavy pelts held the heat around them. After an hour or so, his shivering stopped. A little while later, he fell asleep. When Willa heard his breathing deepen and even out, and felt his chest rising and falling steadily, she got out of bed and stoked the fire. She hoped he would sleep until morning. He needed it. She knew that eventually the pain in his thawing feet would wake him, and when that happened, she would give him some of her opium.

Willa was tired herself. She quickly tidied up the room—hanging up her visitor's wet things and opening up his boots so that they would dry properly. She was just about to douse the lamp and go to bed herself when Maurice Villiers rolled over in bed.

"The letters," he said groggily. "I forgot them. . . ."

"Go to sleep, Mr. Villiers," Willa said, not bothering to look at him, certain he was talking in his sleep.

". . . letters . . . in my pack."

Willa turned to look at him. "What letters?"

"For you. In my pack," he said, blinking at her. "Postman in Darjeeling gave them to me. I told him I was coming here." Then he rolled over again and went back to sleep.

Willa crossed the room, unbuckled his pack, and rooted through it. At the very bottom, bundled together with twine, was a thick stack of letters. The top one had a British stamp. She pulled the bundle out and flipped through the envelopes. Most were addressed in her mother's hand. Some were in her brother's. There were so many of them—too many of them. The post was dependent on traders and travelers coming and going, and was often delayed on its way north from Darjeeling, but even allowing for that, there were still too many letters here. Looking at them all, she was suddenly gripped by fear. Something was wrong, she knew it. Whatever news these letters contained, it was not good.

Willa pulled the top letter out of the stack. With trembling hands, she opened it and started to read.

CHAPTER EIGHTEEN

"MAUD?" THE PRIME minister said.

"Hmm?"

"It's your turn."

"My turn for what, darling?"

"Your turn to play! Ye gads, woman, where are you?" Asquith said petulantly.

"Here, Henry. Right here." She quickly looked at her cards, couldn't make heads or tails of them, and said, "No bid."

The turn passed to Margot, Asquith's wife, who made a whacking great bid, then Max.

Asquith oughtn't to have asked me "Where are you?" Maud thought. But rather "Where were you?" Because in her head, she was back in the Coburg, in Max's room. She was in Max's bed, naked. He'd tied a silk cravat around her eyes, tied her wrists to the headboard.

"We'll miss the train," she'd said.

"I don't care," he'd said.

"Max, he's the prime minister."

"So what?"

He'd kissed her mouth, then proceeded to nibble his way down her body, slowly and gently, biting her earlobe, her neck, her breast, her hip. He pushed her legs apart and kissed the place between them.

"Now, Max," she'd whispered throatily. "Now."

"No," he'd said, kissing her knee, biting her calf. "Not now."

She'd moaned and twined against him, wishing she could get her hands free and pull him to her, pull him inside of her. "Bastard," she'd hissed. But he'd only laughed and nibbled her toes. Her belly. Her shoulder.

THE WILD ROSE   131

He went on like that, teasing her with his lips and his tongue, until she was nearly mad with her need of him. And then suddenly he was inside of her, and her release, when it finally came, was so strong, so hot and violent, that it frightened her. She'd cried out, she remembered that. Actually, she'd screamed. It was amazing the manager hadn't come knocking on the door. Or the police. Never had a man made her feel so good. She was addicted to Max von Brandt. Her body craved him like a drug. He was all she could think about.

They'd drunk champagne afterward, made love again, and missed the damned train. They had to take Max's motorcar to Sutton Courtenay in Oxfordshire, where the Asquiths had their country home, and where the PM had invited them both for the weekend. Max had driven like a demon and they'd only been half an hour late.

Maud knew Asquith well. She was friends with his wife Margot and with his grown daughter, Violet. Violet's mother had died when she and her brothers were young, and Asquith had later married Margot, one of the beautiful and vivacious Tennant sisters.

Maud and Max had had a spot of tea with Margot and Violet, and the Asquiths' other weekend guests, when they arrived, then they'd bathed and changed for dinner. After they'd dined, Asquith suggested bridge. Maud and Max had been paired with the prime minister and his wife. The other guests played against one another at tables nearby. Maud was a good, competitive player and usually enjoyed the game, but memories of the afternoon's activities had her so hot and bothered tonight, that she could barely keep her cards straight.

"It's your turn *again*, Maud," Asquith said, a note of irritation in his voice. "What's distracting you? You usually go for your opponent's throat at the bridge table."

"Millicent Fawcett," Maud said abruptly.

Millicent and the suffragists were actually the farthest thing from her mind, but she was the best Maud could come up with. She could hardly tell the PM what she'd really been thinking about.

"She's making noises about going over to Labour. Doing her all to support and campaign for their candidates. She feels the Labour Party will be more sympathetic to the cause of women's suffrage," Maud said. "You'd best not ignore her, Henry. She may not have got us the vote—*yet*—but she does have clout, you know."

"Are you trying to rattle me, old girl? If so, it's very unsporting of you and it won't work."

"All's fair in bridge and war," Maud said. "Seriously though, you would be well advised not to underestimate Millicent. She is not altogether what she seems. She is polite and reserved, but she is also resolute, tough, and relentless."

Asquith raised his eyes from his cards. "I would say that no one, and nothing, is as it seems," he said, and Maud noticed it was not herself he was looking at as he spoke these words, but her partner, and that his expression had become most somber. "Wouldn't you agree, Mr. von Brandt?" he added.

"I would, yes," Max said, meeting Asquith's steely gaze unwaveringly.

For the briefest second, Maud had the inexplicably unsettling feeling that the two men were not still talking about bridge, but about something else completely. Then Margot started chattily asking questions, and as quickly as it had come, the strange feeling was gone.

"Maud tells me you've been to Everest, Mr. von Brandt," Margot said.

"I have, yes. I spent most of last year in Nepal and Tibet," Max replied.

Margot was about to say more, when the door to the drawing room opened.

"Excuse me, sir. . . ." It was Asquith's secretary.

"Mmm? What is it, man?"

"A telephone call, sir. From Cambridge."

Asquith was silent for a few seconds, then he turned in his chair. "Cambridge, you say?"

"Yes, sir."

The prime minister nodded. He turned back to the table and looked at Max, and Maud noticed, again, that the look in his eyes had become a hard one.

"I believe it's your turn now, Mr. von Brandt. I wonder . . . how will you play your hand this time? A bold move, perhaps?"

Max shook his head and smiled tightly. "With so many seasoned players about me, I must be cautious," he said. "I think I will play it safe for the present."

Asquith nodded. He rose from his chair.

"Will you take the call in your study, sir?" his secretary asked.

"I suppose I shall have to, to spare everyone my wittering," Asquith said, placing his cards facedown on the table. "Wish the blasted study wasn't so far away, but I shan't be a moment." He stood up, wagging a finger at Maud as he did. "No peeking, old girl. Margot, see that she doesn't."

It felt to Maud as if Asquith had suddenly remembered he had guests and must be genial toward them. She found the man's mood odd and hard to follow, but she chalked it up to the pressures of his office and the bother of having to take what were very likely difficult phone calls at all hours.

"Is the study so far?" Max asked.

"No, it's upstairs. Right above us. Henry's just being cross," Margot said.

Max nodded, then stood. "Would anyone like a top-up?" he asked.

"I would, darling," Maud said. "Claret, please."

Max took her glass. He smiled at her seductively, and Maud found herself wondering what sort of excuse she could come up with to get herself out of this beastly card game. She didn't want to be sitting here in the drawing room, concentrating on suits and trumps and tricks. She wanted to be lying in bed, reveling in Max's glorious body.

Margot had seen Max's smile, too. As he crossed the room to a cabinet containing decanters of spirits and wines, she gave Maud a mischievous look. "Is it just me? Or is it warm in here?" she whispered, fanning herself with her cards. Maud swatted her.

As they whispered and laughed together, neither woman saw Max glance up at the ceiling, his smile gone, a grim, determined look in his eyes.

CHAPTER NINETEEN

"YOU WANT TO break it off. That's it, isn't it?" Seamie said quietly, a stricken expression on his face. "That's why you wrote me." He was sitting on a blue silk settee in the Wilcotts' parlor.

Jennie, who'd been pacing back and forth, stopped and turned to him. "No!" she quickly said. "That's not it at all, Seamie. Would you let me finish, please?"

"Well, what is it, then? Something must be wrong. I can't imagine you asked me to come here in such a big fat hurry for a cup of tea."

"No, I didn't," Jennie said. She opened the parlor door, glanced down the hallway to make sure her father was nowhere near, then shut it again. Seamie was right—there was something wrong. She'd written to him last night, at his sister's Mayfair address, asking him to come this morning because she had something she needed to tell him, something urgent. It had been worrying at her for days. Ever since she'd been to see Harriet Hatcher. He was here now, and she had to tell him. She couldn't keep it to herself any longer.

"Seamie," she said quietly, "I'm pregnant."

Seamie's eyebrows shot up. "Pregnant? You mean you're going to have a baby?"

"Yes. That's what pregnant means—that one is going to have a baby."

Seamie, ashen-faced, slowly stood up.

Jennie looked down at her clasped hands. "I know it's a shock," she said. "And I know you have many plans, some of which do not include me. I've looked into homes for unwed mothers. Places where I could go to have the baby. Places that would find a good home for the child—"

"Never," Seamie said swiftly and harshly, cutting her words off. "Don't speak of it, Jennie. Don't even think of it." He crossed the room to where she stood, took her hand in his, and went down on one knee. "Marry me, Jennie," he said.

Jennie stopped speaking. She looked down at him, her eyes wide and searching.

"Marry me," he said again. "I want a life with you. A home. I want this child, and many more children. Lots of them. Three or four. Six. Ten. I want you to be my wife."

"But, Seamie," she said softly, "what about Ernest Shackleton and the expedition?"

"Shackleton will just have to trek off across Antarctica without me. My place is here now. With you and with our child. Marry me, Jennie. Say yes."

Jennie shook her head. In a small, anguished voice she said, "Seamie, I . . . I need to tell you . . ."

"What? Need to tell me what? Do you not want me? Is there someone else?" he asked, a mixture of hurt and surprise in his voice.

She raised her head. "*Someone else?*" she said, wounded. "No, there isn't. How could you say such a thing? There's only you, Seamie. And yes . . . yes, I *do* want you. So very much. That's what I wanted to tell you. Only that." She took a deep breath, then said, "Yes, Seamie. I *will* marry you. Yes. Oh, yes." And then she burst into tears.

Seamie brought her over to the settee, pulled her onto his lap, and kissed her. "I'm so happy about this, Jennie. Really. This is what I want—you, me, our children. I love you, Jennie. I do. I told you that in Cambridge and nothing's changed. I love you as much this very second as I did then."

Jennie let out a long, deep breath that it felt like she'd been holding for days. "You're not upset, then?" she said.

"Upset? I'm delighted! Why? Are you?"

"Well, no, not exactly. But, well, you see . . . I'm only a few weeks along. That's what Harriet—Dr. Hatcher—says. So for now, everything's well and good. But in a few months it won't be."

Seamie grinned at her mischievously. "You're worried about

waddling down the aisle with a big fat belly and everyone in the church knowing we had it off long before our wedding night?"

"Yes," Jennie said, coloring. "I am."

"It's nothing to worry about," Seamie said.

"It isn't?"

"No. If anyone says anything, I'll just tell them that we *did* have it off . . ."

"Seamie!"

". . . in an old cow barn by the Cam." He kissed her mouth. "I'll tell them how you lured me inside in a rainstorm and took advantage of me," he said, undoing the top buttons of her blouse. "I'll tell them I was completely helpless and . . . ," he hooked a finger in her camisole and peeked down it, ". . . and good God, woman, if they could see these, they'd believe me, too."

"For goodness' sake!" Jennie said, pulling her camisole closed.

"They get bigger, don't they? When you're pregnant, I mean. That's what I've heard. I hope so. I love too much of a good thing."

"Seamie, don't joke!"

"Why not?" he said, looking up at her. "What's the matter?"

"What's the matter? Have you not been listening to me? I can't walk down the aisle of a church with a huge belly!"

"I have been listening. I've heard every word. Let's get married tomorrow."

"*Tomorrow?*"

"Yes, tomorrow. We can take a train to Scotland. To Gretna Green. Spend the night there. Get married in the morning."

Jennie knew she should feel relieved. Even grateful to him for suggesting such a quick solution. Instead she began to cry again.

"Jennie . . . darling, what's wrong now?"

"I can't go to Gretna Green, Seamie. I can't get married without my father there."

"No worries, then. We'll have our wedding here. We'll post the bans this Sunday, all right? How long do we have to post them before we can have the actual ceremony?"

"For three weeks."

"Then we'll have our wedding three weeks from this coming Sunday. Your father can do the honors and I'm sure my sister will want to do something, too—a breakfast, a luncheon, something." Seamie was excited. He was speaking quickly. "I'm going to go to an estate agent's as soon as I leave here. I'll find us a nice flat. Near Hyde Park. And then I'm going to a furniture shop and find a bed. With a big cushy mattress. So I can throw you in it and make love to you again the very second we're married," he said.

He undid more buttons on her blouse as he spoke, then pulled open her camisole and cupped her breasts. He kissed them, and then her throat, her mouth, and the soft hollow beneath her ear. Jennie surrendered to his hands and his lips. She wanted him, too. So much. She couldn't wait until they were married and in a home of their own, in a bed of their own. She wanted to feel him reach for her in the darkness, to hear him whispering her name, and know he was hers, truly hers.

Seamie suddenly broke the kiss. "Oh, no," he said. "Oh, bloody hell."

"What is it?" Jennie asked him, pulling the sides of her camisole together.

"It's just dawned on me that I'm going to have to go and tell your father that you're pregnant. After I promised him I'd take good care of you in Cambridge."

"Don't worry . . . ," Jennie started to say, buttoning her blouse.

"Don't worry? I *am* worried. I'm flipping terrified!" he said. "Icebergs, leopard seals, blizzards—none of those things ever scared me. Telling the Reverend Wilcott that I've put his daughter up the spout—now, that scares me."

"Let's not tell him. Not right away," Jennie said, biting her lip.

"No, we have to. *I* have to. It's the right thing to do." He stood up, and Jennie did, too, smoothing her skirts and her hair. "No, you stay here," he told her. "This is a conversation between your father and me. I'll be back. Sit down."

Jennie smiled at him as he left the room, but as soon as the door closed behind him, her face crumpled. She put her head in her hands.

She was happy, she was, but she was also sick with worry. This pregnancy—it was more than she could have hoped for. It was nothing short of a miracle, actually, and Seamie had no idea. Because she hadn't told him the truth. Not about the scar running down the right side of her body. And not about the accident that caused it.

They'd been playing, she and her friends. Their ball had gone into the street and she'd run after it. She never saw the carriage, and thankfully, she didn't remember it striking her, didn't remember her body going under the front wheel. It had nearly crushed her. After a long, risky surgery, the doctor—Dr. Addison—told her parents that the carriage had broken five of her ribs, ruptured her spleen, collapsed a lung, destroyed an ovary, and punctured her uterus. He also told them that he had done his very best for her, but that they must prepare themselves for the likelihood of losing her. If the trauma her body had suffered did not kill her, infection probably would.

"We put stock in his opinion, of course," her mother had told her, months after she'd recovered, "but we put our faith in God."

Jennie was in the hospital for six long months, and though she didn't remember the accident, she remembered the recovery. It was an agony to her—the pain of the injuries, the infections and raging fevers, the bedsores and boredom, and the endless process of healing.

When she finally left the hospital, she was weak, pale, and horribly gaunt, but she was alive. It took another six months for her to put on a few pounds, and even longer for her to regain her strength, but with her parents' help she did it. The doctor came to visit her several times over the course of her convalescence. The last time he saw her, he brought her a beautiful china baby doll. A consolation prize, she'd thought as she grew older, for the real baby she would never have. The doctor had said good-bye to her in the parlor, then he'd taken her mother out in the hallway to speak privately. Jennie wasn't supposed to hear what he said, but she listened at the door.

"Her uterus is still inside her, Mrs. Wilcott, but it was badly damaged. She may have her menses, but she will never carry a child. I'm sorry. It's a blow to you now, and it will be a cross for Jennie later, but not all women need husbands to be happy. Jennie is a very bright girl. She would do well to enter the teaching profession or indeed my own. There is always a need for good nurses."

She'd hadn't understood his words then, for she was nine years old and innocent and could not imagine ever needing a husband for anything, never mind happiness. But when she was thirteen, and her menses started, and her mother sat her down and explained the facts of life and how they no longer applied to her, she then understood what Dr. Addison had been trying to say: that no man would ever want her, for she would not be able to bear children.

As she grew older, she told herself it did not matter. If she could not marry, she would find satisfaction in her work. If she could not have children of her own, she would love the little ones she taught at her school. Once, a young man, a deacon in her father's church, wanted to court her. He was fair and slender and kind. She did not love him, but she could have liked him well. Because she did not love him, she was honest with him, and when he learned that she could not give him a family, he thanked her for her frankness and promptly transferred his affections to a cloth merchant's daughter.

There had been two others—a teacher like herself and a young minister. She had been honest with them, too, and had lost them both. It had hurt a little, but not too terribly much, for she had not been in love with them, either.

And then she'd met Seamie Finnegan and had fallen in love, deeply and passionately.

That afternoon, in the cow barn on the River Cam, she had asked him to make love to her and she had not been worried about any re-percussions, for she knew there could be none. She knew, too, that once she told him the truth about her scar, he would leave her, just as the others had, for she was damaged and could not give him what a normal woman could. And so she had not told him the truth.

I'll tell him afterward, she'd silently promised God before she gave herself to Seamie, but let me have him first. Let me have love, just this once, she'd prayed, and I'll never ask for anything more.

And when it was over, and she was lying there, happy and sated, loving the smell of him on her skin, the taste of him on her lips, she had remembered her promise and begun to frame the words, to think of the right thing to say, when out of the blue, he'd told her that he loved her. And she found she could not say the words she knew she ought to. Because she could not bear to lose him. The others, yes— but not him.

So she'd said nothing.

Not during their trip on the River Cam. And not moments ago, when he'd proposed to her. She'd tried. Very hard. She'd almost got the words out, but she'd failed.

"I want a life with you. A home. Children. Lots of them. Three or four. Six. Ten. I want you to be my wife," he'd told her. At those words, her resolve had deserted her and she'd said yes. She'd let him believe she could give him the sons and daughters he wanted. She'd lied to him. Not by what she'd said, but by what she hadn't.

She'd told herself she would tell him the truth about herself. Over and over again. Weeks ago, on their way back to Cambridge. Then at Aunt Eddie's house. On the train back to London. But she hadn't. Every morning after their trip, when she first woke up, she told herself that today was the day she would tell Seamie the truth, no matter what it cost her. And every day he made it harder and harder for her to say anything.

And then, she realized her monthlies had not come. She'd thought little of it at first. They'd always been a little off—early one month, late the next. But then she'd started to hope. Could it be? What if Dr. Addison had been wrong? What if she *could* carry a child?

Hoping against hope, she'd gone to see Harriet Hatcher. Harriet had examined her and then said the words Jennie Wilcott never thought she would hear: "You're pregnant." Of course Harriet, who was Jennie's doctor and knew of her injuries, warned her not to get her hopes up. "You've conceived, yes," she said, "and that's wonderful, but it doesn't change the damage that was done to your reproductive organs. We don't know if your womb can carry a child to term."

Seamie had not hesitated to do the right thing when she told him she was pregnant. Though he'd been torn during the last few weeks, he now wanted to settle down. He wanted children. Many children. He'd said so. Why would he marry a woman who couldn't give them to him? No man would. Least of all a man like him—a man who was young and handsome and famous. A man who could have any woman. Who'd had many women, including the dazzling Willa Alden.

Jennie knew who Willa was. The magazines sometimes published photographs she'd taken in the East. They always mentioned how she and Seamie had set a record together, years ago on Kilimanjaro. They said how a terrible accident on the mountain had taken her leg and that she hadn't returned to England, but had gone instead to Nepal and Tibet.

Jennie had asked Seamie about her once. She asked if he still had feelings for Willa. He'd assured her that he did not, and that what he and Willa had had was firmly in the past. But his face had changed as he spoke about her, and the look in his eyes had not been one of indifference. He wasn't over Willa. He loved her still. Of that Jennie was certain.

Willa was like him, and she, Jennie, was not. And she wondered now, as she had so many times in the past few weeks, exactly what Seamie was doing with her. She who was not daring and bold and had not even explored west London, never mind the South Pole. She couldn't offer him what Willa could—the shared passion for discovery, for taking risks and setting records. What she could offer was the domestic pleasures—a comfortable home life, a family. And if she couldn't even give him these things, what then?

"I love you, Jennie. I do," he'd said to her when he'd proposed. It had almost sounded desperate to her. As if he very much wanted to love her and was trying to convince himself that he *did* love her. Her, not Willa. If she lost the child she was carrying, if he ever found out the truth about her, he *would* leave her. She was certain of it.

Tears threatened to overwhelm her again. Instinctively, her hands went to her belly. "Can you hear me?" she whispered. "Stay with me, little one. Please, please stay."

Footsteps came toward the parlor. Jennie quickly brushed her tears away. The door opened and her father stepped inside. He gave her a stormy look at first, then he crossed the room, took her by her shoulders, and quietly said, "I wish this had happened after the wedding, I must say, but I'm happy it's happened at all. I'm glad for you, Jennie. Truly. There is no greater joy than a child. I know this, for I know what joy you've given me."

"Thank you, Dad," she said, her voice breaking.

"Yes. Well. Come in, lad!" the Reverend Wilcott bellowed. The door opened and Seamie walked into the parlor. "I've some sherry in the kitchen," the Reverend said. "I'll fetch it and some glasses, too. I think we could use a nip."

As soon as he was gone, Seamie gathered Jennie into his arms. "He didn't kill me!" he whispered to her. "He'll post the bans this Sunday and marry us in three weeks."

"Oh, Seamie! That's wonderful!" Jennie said.

"It is. I'm so relieved. He was much better about it than I would have thought. Much better than I would have been in the circumstances." He put his hand on Jennie's belly. "If this baby is a girl, I'll make sure to protect her from the likes of me." He laughed, then said, "I can't wait to become your husband. And our child's father. It's everything I want, Jennie. Truly."

Jennie smiled weakly. A feeling of dread gripped her as she looked at him. She tried to shake it off. Tried to tell herself to stop being silly and to be grateful instead for the tiny life growing inside her. For the miracle she'd been given.

Nine months, she thought. That's all I need. Nine months from now, he'll be holding our child and he'll be happy. Happy with the baby. Happy with his life. Happy with me.

CHAPTER TWENTY

"THREE MILLION POUNDS. For boats," Joe Bristow said. He was sitting behind his desk in the study of his Mayfair home. "How many do we get for that? Two? Three?"

"Eight. And they're ships not boats," said the man sitting across from him. "The finest warships ever built." He drained the glass of whiskey he was holding, stood up, and walked to the window.

George Burgess never sat still for long, Joe thought as he watched him. Pale and freckled, his reddish-blond hair already receding, Burgess, at the tender age of twenty-nine, was a war hero, an acclaimed author, and had already held the offices of MP and secretary of state for the colonies. It was in his current role as second lord of the Admiralty that he'd paid a visit to Joe this evening, to harangue him into supporting Churchill's call for more dreadnoughts.

Joe was supposed to be downstairs at a family dinner. It was a lovely April evening, and Fiona had invited Joe's parents; his brothers and their families; her brother Seamie, and his fiancée, Jennie Wilcott; and a dozen close friends to dine with them. Jennie and Seamie were to be married in two weeks' time, and a great deal of planning was taking place tonight. Just as Joe had sat down, Burgess had arrived, saying he had urgent state business to discuss with him, and adding that another man from the Admiralty would be joining them shortly. Joe had excused himself and taken George upstairs in the elevator to his study, where the two men had engaged in a tense and heated discussion, for over an hour now, with George adamant on the need for Britain to acquire not one new dreadnought, as Churchill had originally asked of Parliament, but a whole new fleet of dreadnoughts, and

Joe intransigent on the idea of government releasing three million pounds with which to do the acquiring.

"I don't care how fine they are, George," he said now. "My constituents don't need warships. They don't want them. They want schools, hospitals, and parks. And jobs. Jobs would be very nice."

"Oh, they'll get them," Burgess retorted. "In the kaiser's munition factories. He plans to build several on the Thames docks as soon as he invades England."

"This is war-mongering, pure and simple," Joe said hotly. "You say you want to head off military aggression by making a show of strength, yet you take every opportunity to stir up feeling for the very war you wish to avoid!"

"I do not need to stir up feeling. It is already there. Furthermore—"

Burgess's words were cut off by a knock at Joe's door. "Come in!" Joe barked.

The door opened, and then Albie Alden, Seamie's friend from Cambridge, was suddenly standing in the room.

"Hello, Albie lad," Joe said. "The dinner's downstairs. Seamie and Jennie—"

Burgess cut him off. "He's here to see us," he said.

"Hold on," Joe said. "Albie's your man from the Admiralty? Albie Alden?"

"Finally, the other shoe drops," Burgess replied. He motioned impatiently at Albie. "Do come in, old boy," he said. "And lock the door, will you?"

Albie did as he was asked, then crossed the room, opened his briefcase, and handed Burgess a thick dossier. Burgess opened it, paged through its contents, snorting and nodding and sometimes swearing, then slapped it down on Joe's desk.

"Read that," he said. "Read it, *then* tell me we can't have our ships."

Joe looked at Burgess, then at Albie, wondering what could possibly be in the dossier. He opened it. The documents it contained were all stamped with the seal of the Secret Service Bureau, a department within the Admiralty whose presence was known to very few.

By the second or third page, Joe realized what he was reading: reports on various men and women, German nationals all, whom the SSB suspected of spying. One name in particular caught Joe's eyes—Max von Brandt. Joe knew the man; he'd met him a few weeks ago, after a suffragists' march at Holloway prison. He'd seen him several times since in the company of Maud Selwyn Jones.

Joe was greatly relieved to read that while von Brandt's name had been put forward as a possible spy, the author of the report had concluded that it was unlikely he was one. He had an independent income, family in England, and no ties to the German military other than carrying out his compulsory service.

Furthermore, Max had had a public falling-out with his industrialist uncle—his father's older brother—over the kaiser's aggressiveness. The argument had occurred in a Berlin restaurant. Both men ended up shouting at each other. Max's uncle had thrown a plate at him. The event was reported by three different, reliable eyewitnesses, and Max had left Germany for England a week later. Reportedly, his uncle was pleased about Max's departure. He openly accused him of being an embarrassment to the family and of costing him, the uncle, business. Max von Brandt, the report concluded, was an accomplished alpinist, a playboy, and a philanderer, but he was not a spy. Others were, though. Dozens of them. Joe flipped past page after page of names and grainy gray photographs. When he'd gone through them all, he looked up.

"How did you find all of these people?" he asked Albie.

Burgess answered. "Albie here, together with Alfred Ewing, Dilly Knox, Oliver Strachey, and various other Cambridge geniuses, has been very busy cracking codes over the last year. They've confirmed the existence of a widespread and effective German espionage ring in the UK, and as you can see, they've identified many of its foot soldiers."

"Then why haven't you arrested them?" Joe asked, alarmed.

"Because we are hoping the foot soldiers will lead us to the spymaster himself," Burgess said. "He's the one we dearly want to catch. Our own agents in Germany tell us that he's very effective.

Frighteningly so. He's already gathered and conveyed a great deal of very valuable information to Berlin. Our agents also tell us that Germany will invade France at the first possible opportunity and that they will do it via Belgium."

"It's nonsense, George," Joe said. "It can't be true. Even if the Germans wanted to invade France, they can't do it by going through Belgium. It's a treaty violation. Belgium's a neutral country."

"Why don't you ring up the kaiser and tell him so?" Burgess said. "Others—plenty of them—have already tried. To no avail."

He crossed the room now and sat down across from Joe. He poured himself another scotch, sat back in his chair, and said, "I am worried about Germany, Joe. Extremely so. I am also worried about the Middle East. About Germany's growing friendship with Turkey and about England's Persian oil fields and our ability to defend them should war be declared. We've got spies there, too. Some rather unlikely ones— a Mr. Thomas Lawrence among them. They've been mapping the whole bloody desert, forging bonds with many Arab leaders. Lawrence was debriefed only a fortnight ago."

"Lawrence? The young man who just gave a presentation at the RGS?"

"The very same. It was an important presentation, that one. Not so much for the ruins and rocks and bits of pottery he was nattering on about, but to keep the impression going that he's simply an impassioned archaeologist and nothing more."

Joe closed the dossier and pushed it across his desk. "Why are you doing all this?" he asked him. "Why all the cloak-and-dagger? Bringing Albie here? Showing me the dossier? Telling me about German spies in London and British spies in the desert?"

Burgess put his glass down. He leaned forward. When he spoke, his voice was low and urgent. "In the desperate hope that by doing so, I can underscore for you the dire seriousness of the German military threat and the very pressing need for Britain to counteract it. Now."

Joe went silent. He knew George wanted an answer from him, but he could not give it. He knew George wanted his support in his bid to build up Britain's military defenses. All efforts, all funds,

George felt, should go to strengthening the navy, the army, and the nascent air force. He wanted Joe to stop fighting him, to stop calling for funds for social reform programs.

As if reading his mind, Burgess spoke. "We in government must present a united front to the voters," he said. "I, and many others in the Liberal Party, are very aware of your influence with the workingman, and frankly, we wish to harness it to our cause. We need the weight of public opinion with us, not against us. Help me in this, Joe, and I will help you. I will back your calls for social reform, and for funding for your schools and hospitals."

Joe raised an eyebrow. "When?" he asked.

"After the war is over and won," Burgess said.

Joe knew what this request meant—that the things that mattered so dearly to him, and to his constituents, would be swept away in a mad burst of war fever. The suffrage question would be pushed aside. Monies for his projects—for the soup kitchens, the libraries, the orphanages—would dry up. And who would suffer when they did? Who would go hungry and cold? Not the children of the rich. Not the Asquiths and the Cecils and the Churchills, no. It would be the children of East London. As always. Men would go to war and would not come home. Women would lose their husbands, children their fathers.

After some time, Joe finally spoke. "I do not want this war, George, and you must promise me that you will do everything in your power to keep us from it. Everything. Use our diplomats. Use trade sanctions. Embargoes. Buy your boats. Buy ten of them. Twenty. If having more of them makes the kaiser draw back, then it will have been worth the cost. It's better to lose money than human lives."

Burgess nodded, then he said, "And if, even then, even after we have made every effort, war still cannot be avoided . . . then what is your choice?"

"Then there is no choice, George," Joe said. "And there never was."

CHAPTER TWENTY-ONE

JENNIE WILCOTT WAS helping her father get ready for his weekly parish visits. "Do you have your scarf, Dad?" she asked him.

"I don't need it, my dear. It's a sunny day."

"And a blustery one. You do need it. Here, put it on. And wear your other coat. It's warmer."

The Reverend Wilcott smiled. He took her face in his hands. "Ah, my darling Jennie. You take such good care of your old father. What will I do when you go?"

"Don't, Dad. You'll start me crying again," she said.

He kissed her cheek. "Only tears of joy, I hope. You'll make such a beautiful bride. I only hope I can get through the ceremony without crying myself. And speaking of the ceremony, did my best suit come back from the tailor's? I'm worried they won't get it back to me in time."

"It's in your wardrobe, Dad. A man from the shop brought it yesterday."

"Good. Well, I'm off then." He stopped in the doorway and turned around. "You're not to do too much today. You must rest yourself. Promise me you will."

"I promise," Jennie said, smiling.

As soon as she closed the door behind him, she went to the parlor, where she'd begun to make a list of all the errands she needed to run and notes she needed to write and gifts she needed to buy before Sunday.

"Why is it that lists only get longer, never shorter?" she wondered aloud. The wedding, which would be held at Seamie's sister's home in Greenwich, was only five days away and there was still so much to do. After the reception, they would leave for Cornwall for a honeymoon—a short one only, as Seamie was due to begin at the RGS the following Monday. When they returned from Cornwall, they would take up residence in a lovely, spacious flat in Belsize Park. Seamie had found it for them, just as he'd said he would, but they had very little furniture in it and no carpets or curtains whatsoever.

Jennie had been to see a seamstress about the curtains, and had even selected fabric, but it would be weeks before they were finished. Whenever she fretted about all that they still needed, Seamie would kiss her and shush her and tell her not to worry herself or the baby. He had means and would provide whatever they needed.

And he did. All she had to do was mention something, and he was off to the shops and back a few hours later with cutlery, towels, a mop bucket—whatever she wanted. He didn't mind doing these things one bit, he would tell her. He'd never gone shopping before—not for lamps and antimacassars, at least—and he found it all very interesting. He was always so good to her. So cheerful and willing. Excited about their wedding. He was always so happy. Too happy.

She thought now, as she looked out her parlor window, that he reminded her at times of the drunks who came to her father—men and women broken by alcohol. They'd lost everything—jobs, homes, their families. They shook and wept and promised to do anything, even swear off the demon drink forever, if only he would help them. He always did. He got them cleaned up, let them sleep on a cot in the sacristy, and tried to find them work. He prayed with them and made them take the pledge. And his efforts always succeeded—for a little while. They tried hard, all of them. They were eager, bright-eyed, and willing, full of good intentions. Happy to tell anyone and everyone that their drinking days were behind them. But deep inside, they struggled. They thought about drink constantly. Dreamed about it. Craved it. And many, unable to resist the ever-present temptation, went back to it.

Seamie was the same way. He wanted so much to embrace his new life. He talked excitedly about his new position at the RGS. He'd leased a flat, bought a bed, a set of sheets, cutlery, and a box of crockery. But

Jennie knew that underneath the bluff good cheer, under all the pro-
testations of happiness, he still dreamed about his old life.

She had seen him unpack a box of his belongings in their new flat
one evening when he wasn't aware she was watching him. He'd
taken photographs out of the box. Field glasses, book, maps, an old,
battered compass. He'd held the compass in his palm, then closed his
fingers around it. And then he'd gone to the window and stood
there, just stood there, gazing up at the night sky.

He was thinking about past adventures, Jennie was sure of it.
And about Willa Alden. Looking at him, she had been convinced
that if, at that very moment, the compass in his hands could have
shown him the way back to Willa, he would have followed it.

Jennie's hands went to her belly, as they did all the time now when
she was nervous or worried. As always, she prayed for the tiny life
inside to stay with her. A fortnight had passed since she'd told Seamie
she was pregnant. She was two weeks closer to being the mother of
his child. The love of a wife, of a child, these were good things, too,
Jennie told herself, the very best things. And in time, as Seamie got
older, as they had more children, he would grow to want them—and
her—more than he wanted other things and other people.

A knock on the door startled her out of her thoughts.

"Dad? Is that you? What've you forgotten now?" Jennie shouted,
trotting out of the parlor and down the hallway. "It's your specs,
isn't it?" she said as she opened the door. "How many times . . ."

Her words died away. It wasn't her father who was standing on
the stoop. It was Josie Meadows, a young woman whom she used to
teach. Josie had no coat on. The front of her dress was bloodied and
torn. More blood dripped onto it from a cut on her cheek. Her eyes
were bruised and swollen.

"Hello, duck," Josie said.

"Josie?" Jennie whispered. "My God, is that you?"

"Aye. I'm afraid so. Can I come in?"

"Of course!" Jennie said, ushering her inside and closing the door.
"I'm sorry, I . . . I just . . . Josie, what on earth happened to you?"

"Billy Madden happened to me," the girl said, walking past Jennie, down the hallway to the kitchen. She went to the sink, stoppered it, and turned on the taps. "Can I clean myself up?" she asked. "Borrow a dress? I've got to get out of here before he twigs where I've gone. Bastard's threatened to kill me."

Jennie saw that Josie was shaking. The cut on her cheek was still dripping blood. Her nose had started to bleed, too. Most women in Josie's shape would have been weeping. Not Josie. Josie Meadows was a Wapping girl, and Wapping girls did not cry. They were hard, loud, and tough as nails. Jennie had taught many of them and knew that the lives they led—the lives they endured—made them so. Josie would shake. She would drink, smoke, shout, and swear, but she would never, ever cry.

"Sit down," Jennie said, turning the taps off.

"Can't, luv. Haven't the time."

"Josie Meadows, you sit down. Right now."

Josie smiled, though it made her wince. "Yes, miss," she said. "You always get your way when you use your teacher voice, don't you?"

"Let me help you, Josie. We'll get everything sorted. Only sit down, please, before you fall down."

Josie took a seat at the kitchen table and Jennie put the kettle on. Then she got a bowl of hot water, some clean rags, and a bottle of rubbing alcohol and set about cleaning Josie's face. She tried not to let her emotions show on her own face—the shock she felt, the anger that a man could hurt a woman as badly as Billy Madden had hurt Josie. The kettle sang just as she was finishing up. She made the tea, then got two cups and saucers off a shelf and put them on the table. As she set a pitcher of milk and a sugar bowl down, she asked Josie what had happened.

"He put me up the spout, didn't he?" Josie said bitterly. "Man's bloody insatiable. Always got his cock out. Fucks me nine ways to Sunday—in bed, in the bath, up against the wall . . . Oh, sorry, luv! Forgot where I was. Well, anyway, he does me right and proper two, three, four times a day, and then he has the nerve to get angry at me—me!—when I tell him there's a little Billy Junior on the way." She reached into her dress pocket, pulled out a cigarette and a box of matches, and lit up. She took a drag, let out a long plume of smoke, then said, "Tells me I'm to get rid of it. Doesn't want his wife to find out, you see. He's scared to death of her. Doesn't want his three sons to know, either. Thinks the world of them three. I tell him I'm not getting rid of it. Been down that road a few times already. First time, I had no money, so the doctor who did it took his payment in kind, if you know what I mean. Last time, I had a woman. She was old. Her hands shook. She cut me up so, I almost bled to death. I'm finished with those butchers. I'm having this baby, Jennie. I swear to God I am. I'll give him up to a good home when he comes, but I'm damn well having him. I can't go through that again." She paused to take another drag, then continued. "So when I tell Billy all this, what does he do, the gobshite? He hits me. Hard. In the stomach. I bend over, like this," she curled up, arms crossed over her stomach, "so he can't get at my belly again, and I catch it in the face. He's yelling at me. Hitting me. Trying to kick me. Telling me he'll get rid of it himself. Well, I managed to get away from him. I had a few quid in my pocket and I ran out of the Bark, found a hackney, and paid the driver to bring me here. And here I am. I'm sorry to drag you into it. I didn't know where else to go. If I can just borrow a dress, any old thing, I'll be on me way."

Jennie, too upset to speak, said nothing. Instead she poured the tea. Josie picked up a spoon and tried to shovel some sugar into her cup, but her hands were still shaking so badly, she got more on the table than she did in her tea.

Jennie looked at those small hands, at the pretty rings on them, and the bitten nails, and her heart ached. Josie was only nineteen. She was bright. She was lively and funny and pretty. She could have done so many things with her life, but instead of studying to be a nurse, or taking a secretarial course, she'd taken to the stage and fallen in with a fast lot—chorus girls on the make, prostitutes, wide boys, married men, and finally, Billy Madden. Billy had set her up with her own flat and carriage, with diamonds and clothing, but as Josie soon learned, Madden did no favors. People paid for what they got from him. One way or the other.

"Where are you going to go?" Jennie finally asked her.

"Paris. To the Moulin Rouge. I'll get work there. I can sing and dance with the best of them."

"Now you can, but what about when you're seven months along?"

"Hadn't thought of that."

"And what about money?"

"I've got some squirreled away in a bank. My wages from the halls. Billy don't know about it."

"Is it enough to get you to Paris? To keep yourself until you find work?"

"I don't know," Josie said. "Probably not. I've got jewels. Plenty of them. But I can't get them. They're in my flat and Billy'll have his lads watching it. I don't know what I'm going to do, but I'll figure something."

"Stay here, Josie."

"It's good of you to offer, and I thank you for it," Josie said, "but I can't. I couldn't go outside, you see. Wouldn't dare risk being seen. So I'd have to stay inside. For months. I'd go mad."

Jennie went quiet again. She racked her brains trying to think up the best way to help Josie. She had to help her. She could not let the girl go out on her own. From her description of the beating Madden had given her, Jennie was quite sure he'd finish the job if he found her. She thought of friends she had in the south, near Bristol. And others in Leeds and Liverpool. They would help her if she asked them to, but what if she ended up endangering them, too? She needed a hotel, a house, a cottage . . . someplace private and quiet, but neither Josie nor she had the money required to rent a house or cottage. And then, suddenly, she had the answer. "Binsey!" she said, quite loudly.

"What's that?" Josie asked.

"You can go to Binsey."

"Where the flippin' hell is Binsey?"

"In Oxfordshire. Not too far, but far enough. I have a cottage there, Josie. It was my mother's. I barely ever go there anymore. You can stay there as long as you need to. It's not far from the village. You can buy everything you need. You can have the baby; then, when you're recovered and strong again, you can go to Paris. I could help you with the boat fare."

"Could you really? I'll pay you back. Every bleedin' penny. I swear I will."

"I know you will, Josie. I'm not worried about that. What I'm worried about is getting you there. Quickly. Let me think for a minute." She looked at the clock on the wall. "It's still early. Not even ten." She bit her lip. "We could do it, I think. In fact, I'm sure we could."

"Do what?"

"Make it to Binsey."

"Today?"

"Yes, today. We'd have to get you changed. And pack a few things for you. But if we could get to Paddington by eleven, and then get a train out by noon, we could be at the cottage by two at the latest. It's only a short walk from the station. I could settle you there, then come right back." She went quiet, then started thinking out loud again, almost unaware that she was talking. "My father will be home before I get home, and he'll wonder where I've gone. I'll have to leave a note. Say I went out to do some errands for the wedding. I'll pick up some cards on my way back. Nip into the florist's. So it's not entirely a lie."

"What wedding? Who's getting married?"

"Oh . . . um . . . I am," Jennie said.

"That's wonderful news! When is it?"

"This Sunday," Jennie said, hoping that the conversation would end. But it didn't.

"This Sunday," Josie echoed. Then she smiled cheekily. "That's awfully sudden, isn't it? I didn't even know you were engaged."

Jennie colored. "Yes, well, it is, but . . ." She stammered, at a loss for a convincing lie.

Josie gave her a close look, then said, "Oh, Jennie, you didn't! Not you!"

"Well . . . um . . . yes. I'm rather afraid I did," Jennie said.

Josie screeched laughter. "You little hussy," she said. "Sitting here like butter wouldn't melt in your mouth, and all the time you've a bun in the oven yourself. Same as me."

"Josie, we really have to get going if we're to make the train."

But Josie paid her no attention. "Is he nice?" she asked.

"Very nice."

"Handsome? Strong?"

"Yes, both of those."

"Is he a good kisser?"

"Josie Meadows," Jennie scolded. Then she laughed. "Yes. Yes, he is."

"Good," Josie said. "I'm glad he's nice. You deserve a nice one, miss. It's nice when they're nice, isn't it? In bed, I mean. When they've washed and shaved and they've brought you flowers and champagne. When they say sweet things and take their time. Cor, I do like the feel of a man in my bed. Makes me half-mad sometimes, the wanting of them." She dropped her voice to a whisper. "Does it make you feel that way, too?"

Jennie was about to tell her no, to tell her to hurry and change for they had a train to catch. But then she thought of that afternoon on the River Cam. And how it had felt to lie in Seamie's arms. She thought of how much she loved him, and how that love had made her do things she never thought she would, and hope for things she never should have.

And so she didn't tell Josie no. Instead she smiled and, with a rueful note in her voice, said, "Yes, Josie. It does."

CHAPTER TWENTY-TWO

"THERE'S NOT ENOUGH champagne. We'll run out. I just know it. I should've ordered more," Fiona whispered tersely.

"Are you mad, lass?" Joe whispered back. "There's enough champagne in the house to drown all of London."

"And the ice creams, Joe. I should've ordered four flavors. Not three. Four. How could I have been so daft?"

Joe took her hand in his. "Stop now. There's more than enough of everything. The luncheon will be beautiful. The house is beautiful. The day is beautiful." He smiled and kissed her cheek. "Most of all, you're beautiful."

Fiona smiled and kissed him back. Then she frowned again. "You do think he'll show up?" she said. "He won't do a runner or some such thing?"

Joe laughed. "I've just seen him. He's right inside the conservatory looking as happy as a sand boy."

Fiona sighed with relief. "Good. Maybe this will all go off without a hitch after all."

"Of course it will," Joe said. "Stop worrying and enjoy the day."

Fiona nodded. She turned her head and, smiling at this one and waving at that one, she looked at the people seated behind her in neat rows of white rattan chairs. The chairs had been divided into two groups and arranged with a little aisle between them. In ten minutes or so, at precisely one o'clock, her brother Seamus would walk down that aisle, to the bower the florists had made, turn around, and wait for his bride. It almost felt unreal to her. She couldn't quite believe that this day had come, that wild and reckless Seamie had given up roaming, found himself a job in London and a wife, and was ready to settle down. For so long he had mourned the loss of Willa Alden. No woman had ever been able to replace her.

And then he'd met Jennie Wilcott, who was as different from Willa as chalk was from cheese. Perhaps that was what had been needed all along to break Willa's spell. Jennie was blond and pink-cheeked, soft and feminine. She had a marvelous womanly figure and a quiet but determined way about her. Yet for all her sweetness and light, Jennie had tamed Seamie somehow. God knew how. Well, actually, they all did, Fiona thought, smiling—and the evidence would arrive in about eight months' time. She didn't think that Seamie was marrying Jennie because he had to, though. He wanted to marry her. So much. He'd told her so. Over and over again.

So many times that it unsettled her, if the truth were known. It made her uneasy, this sudden change on Seamie's part. Had Seamie really changed? Was he really over Willa?

Fiona had confided her doubts to Joe just a few days ago. He'd thrown up his hands in frustration and said, "For years, all I've heard from you is how much you want Seamie to meet a good woman and settle down. Now he has. He's met a very good woman. And you're still worrying. There's no pleasing you, Fiona!"

Maybe Joe was right. Maybe there was no pleasing her. And yet she could not quell the niggling little voice, deep down inside, the one that was always right, the one that was saying now that it had all happened so fast.

She looked at her watch—only ten more minutes to go—then felt an arm twine around her shoulders and lips upon her cheek. She looked up. It was Maud. Max von Brandt, tall, charming, and stylishly dressed, was with her. Fiona kissed Maud back, greeted Max, and then Maud and Max went to find chairs.

Fiona noticed that a few more late arrivals had seated themselves— the Shackletons, George Mallory and his fiancée, Ruth Turner, Mrs. Alden. She looked again at all the faces of her family and friends— Joe's parents, Peter and Rose; his brothers and sisters; all their children. Her own beautiful children. The Rosens, the Moskowitzes, Harriet Hatcher and her parents, Mr. Foster, friends of Seamie's—men whom he'd sailed with—and friends of Jennie's, so fetching in their spring dresses and hats.

A soft breeze caressed Fiona's cheek. She looked up, hoping it was not a harbinger of rain—it was May, but still early in the month, and the English weather could be so changeable—but no, the sun was still shining. The sky was blue. And all around them, buds were bursting into life. She was suddenly overcome by the beauty of it all and found herself wishing that she could stop time, that she could keep this perfect spring day forever. She saw suddenly, with a piercing clarity, that instead of worrying so much, instead of always looking for problems, she should feel deeply blessed, and deeply grateful, to be surrounded by so many dear people on such a joyous day. For joyous days were not always so plentiful.

She had lost loved ones years ago. Once, she had nearly lost Joe. Those losses, the terrible grief they had caused her, had made her ever fearful of losing another person she loved. It made her think dark thoughts too often, made her dwell on the bad—real and imagined—and blinded her to the good.

And today was good. Seamie had found someone wonderful. And if he was a little overexcited about marrying her, well, he had every right to be. She was the sort of woman any man would be excited to marry. Fiona told herself that she was being silly for worrying, and she resolved, once and for all, to stop it.

A few minutes later, the string quartet that she'd hired began to play the wedding processional. Everyone stood. Albie Alden, Seamie's best man, came striding down the aisle, smiling. He was followed by Seamie, looking so handsome in a gray morning suit. Next came the ring bearer and the flower girl—Joe's sister Ellen's two youngest—a maid of honor, and then the bride herself, lovely and radiant on her father's arm.

A moment in time, Fiona thought again, as she watched the Reverend Wilcott kiss his daughter and place her hand in Seamie's.

"Let it last forever," she murmured. "Please let it last."

CHAPTER TWENTY-THREE

"I ALWAYS WONDER how the sun can shine on days like today," Seamie said sadly.

"I wondered the same thing the day my mother died," Jennie said, slipping her hand into his. "My father says it's to remind us that brightness follows darkness, and that happiness will one day follow our grief."

They were in the Aldens' parlor, standing by a coffin. Admiral Alden had lost his battle with cancer two days ago, and Seamie was paying his last respects before the admiral's body was taken to Westminster Abbey for a funeral service, and then to the cemetery for a small, private burial.

"He was one of the old breed," Seamie said. "Duty and service above all. He was one of the finest men I have ever known." He paused to master his emotion, then said, "I used to sail with him and his family. As a lad. He gave me my first lessons in navigation. He saw how much I loved the sea and loved to explore, and he encouraged that. He was like a father to me."

Jennie leaned her head against his arm. "Would you like a few minutes alone with him?" she asked.

Seamie nodded, unable to speak.

"Take all the time you need," she said, kissing his cheek. "I'll be with Fiona and Joe."

Seamie took a handkerchief from his pocket. He wiped his eyes with it and blew his nose. He knew he should join the others, but he couldn't. Not yet. His feelings were still too close to the surface. So he walked around the parlor instead, looking at the books on the shelves, at paintings and family mementoes.

Seamie remembered this house so well. He remembered sliding down its banister, chasing Albie through its halls, drinking hot chocolate and eating biscuits in its warm and cozy kitchen. But he remembered this parlor best of all. He and Albie had built teepees here out of Mrs. Alden's sheets and blankets too many times to count. They'd sat by the fire at night as the admiral told them of his adventures on the high seas. Played draughts on the rug. Sung along to songs Mrs. Alden played on the piano.

He touched an ivory key now, listening as the sound it made faded. He looked at the photographs standing on top of the piano. Photos of ships the admiral had commanded, of boats he'd sailed and raced. There were family pictures, many taken on the water. Pictures of the Aldens, and Seamie with them, on the admiral's yacht *Tradewind*. One from July of '91, another from August of '92, a third from June of '93—all the endless summers of his youth.

There were pictures of Albie as a boy and as a young man. There was one of him receiving his doctoral degree at Cambridge. And there were pictures of Willa. As a toddler in braids and a pinafore. As a girl in trousers, standing on top of a boulder, or at *Tradewind*'s wheel. As a fetching young woman in an ivory dress and stockings.

Seamie picked that photo up and gazed at it. He remembered that dress, remembered that night. They'd been teenagers then. He'd been seventeen years old. The Aldens had had a party, that was why Willa was dressed up. They were in the backyard, the three of them, lying on a blanket and gazing up at the sky. He'd been about to leave, in just a few days, on his first expedition. It would be years before he saw his two friends again. Albie had gone inside to get them something to eat, and then Willa had kissed him, and told him to meet her one day again, under Orion.

He remembered how they'd met again. Years later in the Pickerel, a Cambridge pub. She'd challenged him to a climb—up the side of St. Botolph's Church—and bet him he couldn't beat her. If he won, she was to buy him a new pair of hiking boots. If she won, he was to accompany her to Africa, to Kilimanjaro. She'd won. She'd won the bet, the wager, the summit, and his heart.

And then he remembered coming home from Africa without her. He remembered standing here, in this very room, and telling her parents what had happened. He thought they would blame him for it—he blamed himself—but they didn't. Instead, they'd guessed his feelings for their daughter and said they were sorry that things had ended up as they had. Both the admiral and Mrs. Alden had taken Willa's decision to travel east instead of coming home very hard.

"How could you do it?" he asked the girl in the photograph now. "How could you not come home? Not once in all this time?"

The admiral had loved his daughter and she had loved him. She'd looked up to him and sought his respect and admiration in everything she did. How on earth could she have ignored her mother's and brother's many letters of the past few weeks begging her to return to London and see her father before it was too late? How could she be so cruel? She had certainly been cruel to him, true—but he was only her brokenhearted lover; Admiral Alden was her father.

Seamie put the photograph back, knowing he would never have an answer to that question. Willa should've come. She should've said good-bye to her father. She should've been here to help her mother mourn the loss of the man she'd been married to for more than forty years. She should've been here for Albie, her brother, who had struggled manfully to comfort his devastated mother, organize the wake and funeral service, the burial and the mourners' luncheon, all while trying to cope with his own grief. Willa should've been here, but she was not.

Seamie walked back to the coffin. He reached into his pocket, pulled out a pebble, and placed it under the admiral's folded hands. It was one of a handful he'd brought back from the icy shores of the Weddell Sea—a place he would never have got to if it hadn't been for this man. He swallowed hard, snapped the admiral a smart salute, then left the parlor for the drawing room.

There, he found Jennie again, sitting on a settee. She was talking with Mrs. Alden, who was seated in the chair across from her. Seamie took the empty spot next to her on the settee. As he sat down, Jennie wordlessly reached for his hand, and her gentle touch made his grief a bit easier to bear. He thought, as he had so many times over the last few weeks, how very good to him she was and how glad he was that he had married her.

He smiled to himself now, though, as he recalled that he'd been something other than glad when she'd told him she was pregnant. He'd been shocked, actually. In fact, he'd seen his life flash before his eyes, as men sometimes said they did when they thought they were going to die. But he'd also immediately seen what he must do. Jennie was pregnant and he had made her so; he could not possibly take off to the Antarctic and leave her in London, alone and unmarried, to bear their child. Only an utter blackguard could have done that. And so he had done the right thing, the honorable thing, the only thing—he had proposed to her.

He'd felt afraid as he spoke the words to her, and painfully torn. By asking her to marry him, he knew he was finally saying goodbye to Willa, once and for all. But to his great surprise, Jennie's acceptance had made him happy. The fear had left him as soon as she said yes, and in the days that followed, he'd felt only contentment and relief.

The thing was done, his decision made. In fact, all his decisions were made. He would stay in London. He would take the RGS job and leave exploring to other men—men who were younger, or crazier. Men who had nothing but themselves to lose. He'd been mistaken, he told himself, in his belief that Willa Alden was the only woman he could ever love, and he resolved to let go of the sad, destructive love he felt for her and to embrace the love Jennie offered. He took his memories of Willa—the sound of her laughter, the way she looked when she climbed, the taste of her lips—and locked them in a strongbox in the deepest recesses of his memory—a box that was never to be opened again.

For the first time in many years, he felt at peace with himself—calm, contented, light and easy. Not restless, not churned up. Not feeling as if he was always bleeding inside from a wound that never healed.

Yes, he told himself now, as he squeezed Jennie's hand, I was mistaken all those years ago. He'd found love, at last, he knew he had. And happiness, too. With the woman sitting next to him. Willa Alden belonged to the past. And the past was where she would stay. His future was with Jennie Wilcott.

Mrs. Alden excused herself and rose to greet some distant cousins who'd just arrived, and Jennie asked Seamie if he'd like another cup of tea.

"No, thank you, my darling," he said. "I've had three already and I'm bursting. I'm going to head to the loo. I'll be right back."

On his way there, he passed the parlor, where Admiral Alden lay, and as he did, he heard voices coming from it—a man's and a woman's. They sounded strained. They rose, then quickly fell again. He hurried past, thinking that whatever was being discussed, it was none of his business, and that whoever was doing the discussing would soon finish and leave.

But he was wrong. As he passed the parlor again on his way back from the loo, he discovered that the voices had only grown louder. Well, one of them had—the man's. To his surprise, he realized he knew that voice—it belonged to Albie.

Worried for his friend, Seamie stuck his head in the doorway. He saw Albie pacing back and forth. There was another man with him—an odd-looking chap who was tall and thin and dressed in loose trousers and a red cotton jacket and had a scarf wound round his head. Seamie could only see the man's back, but he looked dusty and rumpled, as if he'd traveled a long way. Seamie wondered where the woman was. He could've sworn that he'd heard a woman's voice, too.

The discussion continued, only it sounded more like an argument now, and Albie was doing all the talking. Seamie could see that he was angry but trying to contain himself.

Why was this person bothering him? Now? In a time of such distress? Seamie stepped inside the room, very concerned now. As he did, the strange man took a few faltering steps toward the coffin and Seamie saw that he walked with a slight limp.

With a sharp, gut-wrenching suddenness, Seamie realized who the man was. He tried to back up quickly, to get out of the room before he was seen, but in his haste he backed into a pedestal with a heavy Chinese vase on it. The vase teetered and, before he could catch it, fell. It hit the floor and shattered. The man turned around. Her huge green eyes, swollen with tears, widened in recognition, and pain.

"Hello, Seamie," Willa Alden said.

CHAPTER TWENTY-FOUR

SEAMIE STOOD STOCK still, emotions ripping through him like a howling arctic wind. He felt sorrow and anger for what she'd done to him, to them. Pity and guilt for what had happened to her. And love. Most of all, he felt love.

He loved her. Still. As much as he did when he'd first told her so, on top of Kilimanjaro. As much as he did when she'd told him good-bye.

"Hello, Willa," he said quietly, unable to take his eyes off her.

Willa's face worked as she looked at him; tears slipped down her cheeks. She took a few hesitant steps toward him, then stopped.

"The prodigal has returned," Albie said acidly, breaking the silence.

Willa winced at that, stung. Albie looked like he didn't care that he'd hurt her. Instead of embracing the sister he hadn't seen for years, he stood apart from her.

Seamie remembered that last time they were all together, in the Pick. It felt like a lifetime ago. Seamie and Albie had been drinking there. Willa and George had come in unexpectedly. She'd been dressed in men's clothes—tweed trousers and a bulky sweater. Her wavy brown hair had been cut short, setting off her long fawn's neck and high cheekbones. Her eyes had been merry and challenging and full of life.

The Willa standing before him now looked very different from the girl in his memory. This Willa looked gaunt. Haunted. Her face was tanned and weathered. Her hair, under her cap, was no longer short but gathered into a long, thick braid. She was still beautiful, though. Her eyes had lost none of their challenging intensity. Looking into them now, Seamie saw what he had always seen inside them— the same restless, questing soul that lived inside him.

He opened his mouth, wanting to tell her what he was feeling, wanting to say something that would make things right, that would bridge the gulf between them, all three of them, but all that would come out was "Well, then. Shall we have a cup of tea?"

"No, we shall not," Albie said, giving him a filthy look. "This isn't bloody Epsom and I don't want a bloody cup of tea on the bloody lawn!" And then he stormed out, slamming the door behind him, leaving Seamie and Willa alone.

Willa wiped the tears from her cheeks with her sleeve. "He's so angry with me. He called me cruel," she said in a choked voice. "I never meant to come so late. I didn't even know my father was ill. The letters were delayed—the ones from Albie and my mother. I set out the day they arrived—six weeks ago—and got here as quickly as I could." She shook her head. "It doesn't matter to Albie, though. My mother's already forgiven me, but he won't." She smiled sadly. "Well, at least I made the funeral," she added. "It's still a good-bye of sorts, isn't it? Not the one I'd have wanted, but the one I've got, it seems." She went silent for a long moment, gazing at the coffin, then said, "I never thought he'd die. Not him. He was so strong. So full of life." And then she broke down, covering her face with her hands.

Seamie went to her, wanting to comfort her. The man in the coffin was her beloved father, this house was her home. And yet she seemed so utterly out of place here, so totally alone. He put a tentative hand on her back. "I'm sorry, Willa," he said. "I'm so sorry."

She turned to him, helpless and heartbroken. "Oh, Seamie, I wish I could have said a real good-bye," she said, sobbing piteously.

"I wish I could have told him what he meant to me and how much I loved him. If only I'd got here sooner!"

Her grief was so deep, so harrowing, that tears came to Seamie's eyes for her. He forgot himself entirely, folded her into his arms, and held her close. Her sorrow came out of her in great, wrenching torrents. He could feel her chest heaving, her hands clutching bunches of his shirt. He held her as she wept agonizing tears, until she was spent and limp in his arms. And then he kept holding her, overwhelmed by their shared grief, overwhelmed by her nearness. Willa—whom he thought he'd never see again, whom he'd loved and sometimes hated.

"I miss him, Seamie. I miss him so much," she whispered, when she could speak again.

"I know. I miss him, too."

They both heard the door open at the same time, heard the voice, a woman's, say "Seamie? Are you in here . . . Oh! Pardon me, I . . . Seamie?"

It was Jennie.

Bloody hell, Seamie thought. He released Willa immediately.

"Miss Alden?" Jennie said, uncertainly, looking first at him, then at Willa.

Seamie was mortified. He felt terrible. Jennie would be hurt when she found out that the woman he'd been holding was indeed Willa Alden. She'd be furious. He only hoped that she would not make a scene. Not here. He hoped that whatever she had to say to him could wait until they were in their carriage.

He cleared his throat, expecting the worst. "Jennie, this is Albie's sister and my old friend, Willa Alden," he said. "Willa, may I introduce Jennie Finnegan, my wife."

He waited then, watching Jennie's face, expecting fireworks and tears. But Jennie indulged in neither. Instead, she walked up to Willa, took her hand, and said, "My condolences, Miss Alden. My husband has told me something of the admiral, enough for me to know that he was a wonderful man. I cannot imagine your pain and am so very sorry for your loss."

Willa nodded, unable to speak, and wiped her face on her sleeve again. Jennie opened her purse, took out a lace-edged handkerchief, and handed it to her.

"Thank you, Mrs. Finnegan," Willa said. "Forgive me, please. I wish we were meeting under better circumstances."

"I wish it, too," Jennie said, "and there is nothing to forgive." She looked at Seamie. "The hearse has arrived. We are expected to leave for the abbey in ten minutes' time."

"I'll get our coats," Seamie said.

Jennie shook her head. "Perhaps you should stay with Miss Alden for a few more minutes." She turned to Willa. "Pardon me, Miss Alden, but you do not look to be in a fit state to travel. May I bring you a cup of tea? And perhaps a damp facecloth?"

Willa nodded gratefully. Jennie bustled out of the room, and Seamie watched her go, marveling at her goodness and compassion. Another woman might've shouted and carried on. Not Jennie. She saw the best in people always. The most noble explanation for what she'd just seen was that her husband was simply comforting a grieving friend, and that was the only explanation she could accept. Seamie was touched, and not for the first time, at her faith in him, and in most everyone else. And he resolved, then and there, to always be deserving of that faith. To never hurt the good woman he had married. Whatever he had felt moments ago belonged to the past, and that was where it would stay.

"She is very kind and very beautiful. You are lucky," Willa said, sitting down tiredly on an overstuffed chair.

"Yes, I am," Seamie replied.

Willa looked at her hands. "I'm happy for you. Happy you found such a wonderful person," she said quietly.

"Are you?" he said. The words came out bitingly harsh. He hadn't meant them to.

Willa looked up at him, a stricken expression on her face, and the promise Seamie had made to himself, only seconds ago, was lost in a rush of emotion. "Why?" he said. "Why did you—"

But then the undertaker's men were suddenly in the parlor,

excusing themselves and closing the coffin, and Jennie was right behind them.

"Here you are, Miss Alden," she said, handing Willa a facecloth and putting a cup of tea down on the table beside her.

Seamie turned away from Willa and Jennie and feigned interest in an old sailing trophy. What am I doing? he wondered. I'm letting my feelings get the better of me. Stop it, he told himself. Now. It's utter madness.

"Thank you," he heard Willa say to Jennie. "I probably need more than a cat lick with a facecloth, though. I should change my clothes before we leave for the abbey. I've been in them for weeks."

"Was the journey very arduous?" Jennie asked.

"Yes, and very long," Willa said.

"Will you be going right back or staying in London for a while?" Jennie asked lightly.

Seamie closed his eyes, willing her to say she was going back east tomorrow. For his sake. For all of their sakes.

"I don't know. I actually hadn't thought about it," Willa said, and Seamie could hear the weariness in her voice. "I left in such a hurry, you see. I'll be here for a few weeks I should think. Perhaps a month or two. I shall have to do something to earn my fare back. I spent almost all I have getting here."

"Perhaps we can help you," Jennie said. "With the fare, I mean. Seamie, darling, could we?"

The realization of exactly what was occurring here hit him like a bolt of lightning. Oh, Jennie, he thought, you might be kind and good, but you're no fool, are you? He'd thought that she saw only the best in everyone, and that's why she behaved so generously to a rival. Well, he was wrong. She'd seen exactly what was going on between him and Willa, but had behaved generously anyway. He thought then that she was the most admirable human being he'd ever met, and told himself once more that he must never do anything that would hurt her.

"Of course, Jennie," he said. He'd gladly pay Willa's entire fare back. First class all the way if she liked. Anything. As long as she would go and leave him in peace and let him forget the feeling of her in his arms, the smell of her, the sound of her voice. As long as she'd leave him to the life he now had—a life with Jennie and their child.

"Thank you—you are both very kind—but that won't be necessary," Willa said. "I'm due to publish a book of photographs with the RGS. On Everest. I brought all the photos with me. I'm handing the materials all in a bit sooner than expected, and I'm hoping Sir Clements will pay up a bit earlier. I shall also speak at the RGS about Everest." She smiled tiredly, then added, "For a fee, of course. I brought my maps with me. Couldn't risk leaving them in Rongbuk. They might not be there when I returned."

Albie stuck his head in the door. "The hearse is leaving," he said. "Mother wants you to ride with us, Willa." And then he was gone again.

"So much for changing my clothes," Willa sighed. She stood up and looked from Seamie to Jennie. An uncomfortable silence descended, and Seamie found himself wishing to be at the abbey, where they would not have to talk. Where Willa would sit with her mother and brother, and he would sit with Jennie, far away from her.

"Well, thank you again, both of you, for your kindnesses to me," Willa said awkwardly. "And you'll come, won't you? If I speak at the RGS? Please say you will."

Jennie, smiling brightly, said they would make every effort to be there. Then she excused herself to fetch their things.

Willa started walking toward the door, and Seamie followed her. Before she reached it, she stopped, turned, and put a hand on his arm. "Seamie, wait. About before . . . I . . . I'm sorry. I never meant—" she began to say.

He smiled politely, the master of his emotions again. "Don't, Willa. There's no need to speak of it. Once again, my condolences. I'm so sorry for your loss."

He paused slightly, then ruefully added, "And for mine."

CHAPTER TWENTY-FIVE

IT WAS CLOSE to midnight. Joe Bristow had been working at his office in the House of Commons since three o'clock that afternoon. He was tired and wanted to go home, to his wife, to his bed. But he could not. Because George Burgess was sitting across from him, drinking his whiskey and talking about airplanes.

Most of London was asleep, but not Sir George. He'd been working late, too, going over facts and figures for a speech he was to deliver at the Commons tomorrow, on the need for the Royal Naval Air Service to be brought under the wing of the Admiralty as part of the Royal Navy's military branch.

First Churchill and his boats, Joe thought. Now Sir George and his planes. Every day there was some new call for increased military spending, usually fueled by the latest petulant remark, naval acquisition, or military parade put on by the kaiser.

"You simply cannot imagine it, old man," Burgess said. "The speed and maneuverability are unparalleled. And to be up in the clouds, safely able to see the exact position of an enemy encampment, the number of troops and cannon, well, the implications for reconnaissance are nothing less than staggering, to say nothing of the potential for the deployment of aerial munitions. I'll take you up myself, Joe. I can witter on about it all day, but you must see a war plane's capabilities for yourself."

"I'm going to hold you to it, George," Joe said. "We can fly right over Hackney. I'll show you where I plan to build a new school."

"I shall put it in my calendar," Burgess said, ignoring the arch note in Joe's tone. "We'll go to Eastchurch during the August recess, to the navy's flying school there. I'll take you up in a Sopwith and you'll be convinced. The Service is only in its infancy now," he added, "and it must grow up quickly. It has only forty airplanes, fifty seaplanes, and a hundred or so pilots, and it must be enlarged. We're being left behind. The Italians, the Greeks and Bulgarians, even the Americans are miles ahead of us with the development of combat planes, and—"

Burgess's words were interrupted by a battering on Joe's door.

"Does no one in this city sleep anymore?" Joe said. "Come in!" he bellowed.

"Sir George? Thank goodness I've found you. Hello, Mr. Bristow." It was Albie Alden, breathless and disheveled. He'd clearly been running.

"What is it, man?" Burgess asked.

Albie struggled to catch his breath. "We've had a bit of bother at the SSB," he said, glancing at Joe uncertainly.

"Speak plainly," Burgess said impatiently. "This man's as loyal to his country as the king."

"Two German spies were nearly apprehended tonight."

"Nearly? What do you mean by nearly?"

"Sit down, Albie," Joe said, pouring another glass of whiskey and pushing it across his desk.

Albie took the empty chair next to Burgess. He knocked the drink back in one gulp, wiped his mouth with the back of his hand, then continued speaking.

"Four days ago, our code work, plus intelligence from a paid informant, revealed that a man named Bauer—Johann Bauer—has been working at Fairfields."

Burgess, who'd been shaking his head as Albie spoke, suddenly swore. Joe knew why. Fairfields was a shipyard in Scotland. On the River Clyde. They built ships for the Royal Navy.

"Johann Bauer?" Burgess thundered. "That name's as German as sauerkraut! How the hell did a man with a name like Johann Bauer get work on the Clyde?"

"By changing it to John Bowman," Albie said. "He had all the documents. A forged birth certificate from an Edinburgh hospital. School leaving papers. A reference from an iron monger's. Nobody suspected a thing."

"But his voice," Burgess said. "His voice would have given him away."

Albie shook his head. "His accent's impeccable. *Was* impeccable."

"What happened?" Joe asked, pouring Albie another drink.

"As I said, we were on to Bauer, but we didn't move right away. We wanted to watch him for a few days first, to see if he might lead us to anyone else. I think he figured out we were on to him, though, because he suddenly left Govan last night and took a train to London. He was followed, of course. By one of our men from the SSB. When he got off the train, he traveled to East London, to a pub called the Blind Beggar."

"I know that pub. It's in Whitechapel," Joe said.

Albie nodded. "Bauer met another man there, Ernst Hoffman— he goes by the name of Sam Hutchins. They ate supper together, then left the pub and walked to Duffin's, a boardinghouse. Our man slipped in after them and watched them go upstairs to one of the rooms—a room we later found out had been let to a man called Peter Stiles. That's when our man—Hammond's his name—decided he had to act. He went to the police to get help, then he and five constables moved in. Hammond banged on the door to the room where Bauer and Hoffman were. A man answered. He yelled 'Who's there?' and when Hammond said it was the police, he said he'd be right there, he just had to put his trousers on."

Albie took a swallow of his drink, then continued. "Immediately after that, two gunshots were heard. The constables broke the door down, but it was too late. When they got inside the room, they found Bauer and Hoffman dead on the floor and the dormer window wide open. The third man—Stiles—apparently shot both of them in the head, then climbed out of the window to the roof and escaped. Hammond immediately went to the fireplace. Papers were burning in it. Stiles must've been worried that he might be caught and didn't want to be caught with the papers on him. Hammond managed to pull a few of them out before they were completely burned."

"What were they?" Burgess asked, his voice somber.

"Blueprints."

"Not the *Valiant*," Burgess said.

"I'm afraid so," Albie said.

Burgess picked up his own whiskey glass. For a few seconds, Joe thought he would fling it across the room, but he restrained himself.

"What's the *Valiant*?" Joe asked.

"Our best hope," Burgess replied. "A new and very advanced class of warship."

"One of the dreadnoughts?" Joe asked.

"A super-dreadnought. Only four are being made, and they're supposed to outdo anything the Germans have come up with."

"We must look on the positive side," Albie said.

"I didn't realize there was one," Burgess shot back.

"Two enemy spies are dead. Their plans to pass the blueprints to Berlin have failed."

"We were lucky this time, damned lucky," Burgess said. "The next time we might not be." He stood up and started pacing the room. "We have to find the other man—Stiles. He's the spymaster. I know it. I feel it in my bones."

"We are working on it, sir. We've gone through the contents of the room, and we're questioning the Duffin's landlady, and each one of her tenants, trying to get descriptions of Stiles—his habits, his movements, everything we possibly can."

"Good man," Burgess said.

"Can you get him?" Joe asked, alarmed at the thought of this vicious man at large in East London.

Burgess didn't reply at first. Big Ben's chimes, loud and somber, were sounding the hour—midnight.

When the last echoing tone finally faded away, he spoke. "Oh, we'll get him, the wily bird," he said, his voice hard. "We shall stalk him, carefully and patiently. We shall flush him out, and when he tries to fly back to Berlin . . . *bang!* We shall send a bullet straight through his black and treacherous heart."

CHAPTER TWENTY-SIX

SEAMIE FINNEGAN, STANDING wide-eyed in the foyer of 18 Bedford Square, a tall Georgian town house, turned to his friend, Albie.

"Does one *have* to be exotic and stylish to be here?" he asked him, watching a young man with kohl-rimmed eyes swan by, all perfume and silk scarves.

"No, or we wouldn't be here," Albie said. "You just have to know the hostess, Lady Lucinda Allington."

"And how, exactly, does a nearsighted swot like yourself know such people?" Seamie asked, smiling awkwardly as a girl with short hair, rouged lips, and a cigarette in a holder blew smoke rings at him and giggled.

"I was at Cambridge with Lulu's brother Charles. He died some years ago now, poor bastard. Typhoid. It was a terrible blow to the family. I've remained friends with his sister. Come on, let's see if we can find her."

Seamie and Albie hung their coats and set off in search of their hostess. They wound their way through the high-ceilinged rooms of the house, each painted a shockingly bold hue—peacock blue, crimson, chartreuse—past all sorts of equally colorful people talking, drinking, or dancing to the songs played on a gramophone. Albie pointed out various painters, musicians, and actors, telling Seamie that if he didn't know who they were, he should. They found their hostess—Lulu—in the dining room, having her palm read by a stunning Russian ballet dancer named Nijinksy. He was wearing a silk turban, a fur-trimmed jacket, and red silk trousers tucked inside brown suede boots.

Lulu was slender, with a swan's neck, red hair, and hazel eyes. Her voice was deep and dramatic, her face intelligent and lively.

"Albie Alden," she said, taking Albie's hand with her free one. "Why on earth are you here?"

"Lovely to see you, too, Lu," Albie said, bending to kiss her cheek.

"Why aren't you at your sister's lecture?" she asked. "Everyone I know is there. Virginia and Leonard, Lytton, Carrington . . ."

"Everyone?" Albie asked. "What are all of these people doing here, then?"

Lulu looked around the room. "Oh, these," she said. "They're not people. They're actors, most of them. Or dancers. They've all just come off one stage or another and are looking to cadge as much free champagne as they possibly can. But you . . . why aren't you at the RGS?"

"Have I introduced my friend, Seamus Finnegan?" Albie said.

"Finnegan? The explorer? I'm quite honored to meet you," Lulu said to Seamie. "Though I would have thought that you would be at the RGS, too. Aren't you interested in Everest? Having been to the South Pole, I should think that—"

Albie took Lulu's hand from the palm-reading dancer. "I say, old boy, what have you got there? Ah! Her tact line. Damned short, isn't it?"

Lulu looked from Albie to Seamie. "Oh, dear. Am I being tedious? Is Willa not a good topic?"

Albie smiled ruefully. "Most people would have figured out by my reticence on the subject and by my Herculean efforts to change it that no, she is not."

"I'm sorry. I had no idea. I'll make it up to you by telling you where I've stashed the champagne." She lowered her voice. "It's in the oven."

Albie thanked her and started to move off. "I'll want to know why!" she called after them. "You'll have to tell me everything." Then she turned back to the handsome dancer. "Now, Vaslav," she said. "Tell me if I've got a chance with that delicious Tom Lawrence."

Seamie followed Albie into the kitchen. A beautiful and bored woman was sitting on the kitchen table, smoking, as a man spouted poetry to her. Across the room, a wiry young man was balancing a plate on top of a wooden spoon, the end of which was positioned on his chin, while he stood on one leg. A group was egging him on in Russian.

Seamie was glad they'd got away from Lulu and her talk of Willa. He had resolved to put Willa out of his mind the day of her father's funeral, and he was doing his best to stick to that resolution. He thought now, as Albie opened the oven door, took out a bottle of Bolly, and poured two glasses, that maybe he shouldn't have come to this party at all. Maybe he should have just stayed home. It had been a last-minute decision. Albie had dropped by to visit with the Finnegans at their new flat. He said he'd been going mad cooped up at his mother's house.

"Where's Jennie?" he'd asked, after Seamie ushered him into the living room and started to open a bottle of wine.

"She's gone to the country. To her cottage in the Cotswolds," Seamie said. "Felt in need of a bit of quiet."

"The baby tiring her?" Albie asked.

"Yes," Seamie said.

"Why didn't you go with her?"

"She wanted to go for the week."

"So?"

"So I've work. At the RGS."

"Oh, yes. Forgot about that. You've become an upstanding and respectable member of society, haven't you?"

Snorting, Seamie chucked the wine cork at him. Work *had* kept him from going to Binsey, but the truth was, there was another reason he hadn't gone, one that he did not share with Albie: He'd sensed that Jennie had not wanted him to.

"Seamie, darling," she'd said to him two days ago, "I hope you don't mind, but I won't be able to attend Miss Alden's presentation at the RGS with you. I'm feeling a bit weary, and I thought I might go to Binsey for a few days. To my mother's cottage. For a bit of a rest."

"Are you not well?" Seamie had asked her, immediately worried.

"I'm fine. Just tired. It's completely normal. Harriet says so."

"I'll come with you," he said. "We'll go at the weekend. I've never seen the cottage and I'd like to. Besides, you shouldn't make the trip alone."

"You are so sweet to me," she said, smiling, but her voice had a slight edge of something in it—anxiousness? nervousness? He wasn't quite sure. "I think that's a lovely idea, of course I do, but I don't want to drag you all the way there just so you can watch me nap. It's a beautiful place, but it is rather dull. I don't plan on doing much while I'm there. Just a bit of reading, I should think. I'll also catch up on some correspondence, and perhaps I'll arrange for a man to come and look at the roof. The last time I went, I noticed some shingles were missing."

Seamie didn't know much about pregnant women, but he knew they could be moody and odd, prone to frets and tears. Maybe Jennie needed a break from noisy London, he thought, from all the demands of her life: checking in on her father, supervising the new teacher she'd hired to take over her duties at the school, attending suffrage meetings. Maybe she needed a break from him but did not know how to tell him—a break from running their home and cooking his meals and attending an endless number of RGS dinners.

"Of course," he'd said, not wanting to press her any further. "You must do what you think best, but you must write to me. Every day. So that I know you're safe and well."

She kissed him and said of course she'd write and that she would miss him terribly. He'd put her on the train just this morning at Paddington Station and promised to pick her up again next Saturday evening.

"Well, since you're a bachelor again, let's go live it up," Albie had said later. "We can head to a pub—there must be something decent

around here—and then a party. Some friends of mine who live on
Bedford Square are having a do."

"Live it up, Alb? Since when do *you* live it up?" Seamie asked
him.

"Every single day of my life," Albie said, looking at him over the
top of his glasses.

Seamie laughed. "Really? And since when do you like parties?"

"I love parties. Quantum physics is one big endless party," Albie
said.

They'd finished their drinks, gone to a pub for a few more, then
made their way to Bedford Square. Seamie noticed that no matter
how much he might be joking, or talking about parties, Albie looked
weary, yet again. Seamie had told him so and asked him if there was
anything wrong.

"The funeral . . . work . . . it's all got to me," Albie replied. "I
shall take a holiday at Easter. Go to Bath or some such place and restore myself, but for now, I must rely on Theakston's Bitter, and old
friends, to do the job."

Seamie had nodded, but had been unconvinced. He knew that the
death of a parent, combined with a heavy workload, would be enough
to exhaust anyone, but deep down, he still felt there was more to Albie's ever-present air of nervous strain than his old friend was letting
on. Perhaps it's Willa, he thought, and Albie—considerate fellow
that he is—isn't mentioning her out of tact. He knew that Willa and
Albie were both staying at their mother's house. Perhaps they still
weren't getting on. Seamie thought about pressing Albie on it, but
he didn't wish to speak of Willa either, so he decided against it.

"Shall we mingle?" Albie asked him now, glancing about the room.

"After you," Seamie said, sweeping his hand before him, still
wondering at his friend's newfound sociability.

As they moved through the various rooms of the house, Seamie
met a writer named Virginia Stephen, her sister Vanessa Bell, who
was a painter, and Vanessa's husband Clive, a critic. He met the poet
Rupert Brooke, bumped into Tom Lawrence, who'd come from the

RGS, and whom he was glad to see again, then chatted with an econo-mist named John Maynard Keynes.

Albie had explained to him, on the way over, that Lulu was at the center of a colorful coterie of artists and intellectuals called the Bloomsbury Group. "It's a very forward-thinking bunch," Albie had said. "Not terribly mindful of proprieties, morals, or much of any-thing else, as far as I can see."

Seamie enjoyed meeting these people, enjoyed their dramatic clothes and gestures, but for some reason, when they found out who he was and what he'd done, the talk always turned to Willa and the RGS lecture. Time and time again, he'd found himself explaining that no, he had not gone to hear it, but he was certain it must've been fascinating.

An hour had passed this way when Seamie decided he could take no more. He decided to find Albie—who'd earlier said he was going to make the acquaintance of two painters he'd heard about, young Germans visiting from Munich—and let him know he was leaving. The only problem was, he couldn't find him anywhere. It was getting on; the party had become loud and crowded. More people were ar-riving by the minute, making it difficult to move through the rooms.

A woman wearing a long silk kimono and ropes of pearls around her neck made her way over to him, cornering him by the dining room mantel. "You're Seamus Finnegan, aren't you?" she said. "I recognize you from your pictures. Were you at the Royal Geographical Society tonight? I've just come from there. Saw that smashing girl, Willa Alden. The one who's mapping Everest. She gave a marvelous presentation. Completely spellbinding."

"Good God," Seamie muttered. Desperate to get away from the chatterbox, he excused himself. The only place in the whole house where people were not congregating was on the staircase, which was across from the foyer. He made his way to it, getting jostled as he did, and nearly knocking over a marble bust of Shakespeare with green laurels on his head. When he got to the stairs, he climbed half-way up them and sat down. This was a good vantage point. And a quiet one. He would wait for Albie to walk by, tell him good-bye, then make his way home.

As he waited, finishing off the champagne still in his glass, the front door banged open yet again. A new, and noisy, group had just come in—two men and a handful of women. The men, in suits and overcoats, were tipsy. The women, in long, slim-cut silk dresses with ropes of glass beads around their necks, were laughing at something. One of them, Seamie noticed, was not wearing a dress. She was wearing trousers and a long silk coat.

He couldn't quite see her face. Her head was down because she was unbuttoning her coat. But his heart started to hammer nonetheless.

"No," he said to himself. "It's not her. It just looks like her, but it's not. It's just a coincidence. A bloody great coincidence. Everyone here dresses strangely."

"All hail our conquering hero!" one of the men suddenly shouted, grabbing the laurel wreath off Shakespeare's head and placing it on the woman's.

"Oh, do stop, Lytton," the woman said, looking up and laughing. "You're embarrassing me."

"Fucking hell," Seamie said.

It was Willa.

CHAPTER TWENTY-SEVEN

A VOLLEY OF cheers rang out. Applause echoed in the foyer. Willa Alden looked around herself shyly, mortified by the attention. She gave a quick bow and tried to back out of the foyer into the dining room, but a drunken man swooped down on her, lifted her up, and deposited her on the table in the center of the hallway, banging her false leg against the table as he did. She clamped down on a groan of pain as she struggled to find her balance. The leg was throbbing. If she didn't get some laudanum down her throat quickly, she was going to be in trouble.

She tried to get down, but some silly woman was throwing roses she'd swiped from a vase. Guests in the other rooms craned their necks to see what was happening, or ran into the foyer to join in the applause.

"I give you the mountain goddess Cholmolungha!" Lytton Strachey shouted, bowing and salaaming. Willa had known Lytton, a brilliant, acerbic writer, before she'd left London, known he could be a bit dramatic. His antics had amused her in the past, but now she very much wished he would stop.

"Thank you," Willa said awkwardly, to the people who were clapping for her. "Thank you so much." Then she turned to Lytton and hissed, "Get me down!"

Lytton did as she asked, taking her hand as she jumped off the table. The leg sometimes made such jumps tricky. The last thing she wanted to do was to knock the damn thing off in front of so many people. That would be quite the party piece.

"Willa Alden," Lulu said, striding into the foyer and enfolding her in an embrace. "Leonard Woolf just came to fetch me. He saw you at the RGS. He said you'd just arrived, and here you are! I thought so often that I'd never see you again." Lulu released her. "Oh, just look at you. You're positively swashbuckling."

"It's so good to see you, Lu," Willa said, forcing herself to smile and be charming. "It's been ever so long. You are impossibly ethereal and more beautiful than ever. You look as if you exist on air alone."

"Air and champagne," Leonard Woolf said. He was Virginia Stephen's fiancé and a literary critic. He was clever and bookish, like the Stephen girls and all their friends. He'd come to the RGS with Lytton tonight. Willa had met him after her lecture.

A man, tanned and blond and handsome, came up to them. "Lulu, I just wanted to say thank you and good night," he said.

Thank God, Willa thought. While Lulu was talking to him, she could slip off and take her pills. But no such luck.

"Tom, you're not leaving, are you?" Lulu cried. "You can't! Not until you've met Miss Alden. She's another adventurer, just like you."

Willa smiled at him. She was in such terrible pain. She'd just given an hour-long presentation, then fielded questions for another hour and a half. She had thought this was going to be a small gathering of friends, where she might be able to quickly take some medicine, get a bite to eat, and then collapse in a soft chair. She had not expected this—a large and noisy party. There would be so many people to meet. So many hands to shake. So much chattering.

"It's an honor, Miss Alden," Lawrence said. "I was at the RGS tonight. Your lecture was wonderful. There is much I would still like to know, but I will not keep you. I'm sure you're quite spent. I've given one or two talks at the RGS myself and I know how draining they can be."

"On what topic, Mr. Lawrence?" Willa asked, struggling not to show her pain, to be interested and polite. She wanted no one to think about her leg or guess at her pain. She wanted no one's pity.

"Carchemish. The Hittites. That sort of thing," Lawrence replied. "I would just like to say that you must come to the desert. There's so much to be discovered there, and you won't have to suffer altitude sickness to do it."

"Oh, the desert won't do for our girl," Strachey said. "She prefers her quests to be impossible. She likes to chase that which she can never have. It's so hopelessly noble. So impossibly romantic."

"Are we still talking about a mountain, Lytton? Or your newest boyfriend?" Lulu asked archly.

They all laughed. Lulu invited Tom to lunch; Tom accepted and then invited Willa to supper. Lytton swanned off in pursuit of a drink. Leonard said that Willa must be famished, and then he and Virginia went off to the kitchen to make her up a plate, and Willa found herself suddenly alone in the midst of the huge roiling party.

Thank God, she thought. The pain was nearly blinding now. She reached into her jacket pocket and pulled the pill bottle out. She spotted a half-empty bottle of champagne on the floor by Shake-speare's pedestal and grabbed it to wash the pills down. She knew she should join the party and be a sociable guest, but she couldn't, not until she got the pain under control. She decided to sit down on Lulu's staircase. Just for a few minutes. Just long enough to swallow a few pills and rest her leg.

She walked over to the steps stiffly, trying not to limp, and saw that someone had beaten her to them. A man was sitting halfway up the stairs, looking at her. Her heart leapt as she recognized him—Seamie Finnegan, the man she'd once loved. And still did.

"Seamie?" she said softly.

He raised his glass to her. "Congratulations, Willa," he said. "I hear the lecture was quite a success."

"You didn't come," she said.

"No. I didn't."

"Why?"

"I was busy."

She flinched, feeling as if she'd been slapped, but quickly recovered. She wouldn't show him her hurt feelings. She had no right to. She was the one who'd left; she wasn't allowed to have hurt feelings.

"Yes," she said, trying to keep her voice steady and light. "I can see how busy you are. Well, the lecture was a success. I met some fascinating people, too. Quite a few of them, in fact. I see more people here in an hour than I do in a month in Rongbuk." She paused, then smiled and said, "If you'll excuse me, I must get by you. Have to freshen up a bit."

Seamie moved over on the step to let her pass.

"Lovely seeing you again," Willa said.

"Yes," he said tersely. "Lovely."

Willa, who'd been resting her weight on her good leg, took a step forward now onto her false one. As she did, a white-hot bolt of pain shot up into her hip. She cried out, stumbled, and fell. She hit the steps hard, losing her grip on the champagne bottle and her pills. Immediately, Seamie was at her side, lifting her back onto her feet.

"What's wrong?" he asked her, alarm in his voice.

"My leg," she gasped, nearly blinded by the pain. "Where the hell are my pills?" she said, desperately looking about herself. "Do you see them anywhere?"

"They're here. I've got them."

"I need them. Please," she said, her voice ragged with pain.

"Hold on, Willa. This is no good," Seamie said. "If your leg is that bad, you should be lying down, not standing on it."

She felt him pick her up and carry her upstairs. He knocked on a door, opened it, then carried her inside a room. It was someone's bedroom. He put her down on the bed and lit a lamp. He disappeared for a few agonizing seconds, then reappeared with a glass of water.

"Here," he said, handing her the glass, then opening the pill bottle. "How many?"

"Four," she said.

"That's a lot. Are you certain that—"

"Give me the bloody pills!" she shouted.

He did. She swallowed them down then fell back against the pillows, desperately hoping they would do their work quickly.

Seamie walked down to the foot of the bed and started unlacing her boots. She didn't want that. She didn't want anything from him; she remembered his cutting words to her on the stairs.

"Don't. I'm all right. Just go," she said fiercely.

"Shut up, Willa."

She felt his hands pulling her boots off, rolling up one of her trouser legs. Felt him undoing the buckles and straps of her fake leg. Then she heard him swear. She knew why. She knew what the flesh below her knee looked like when she overdid it.

"Look at you," he said. "Your leg's a mess. It's swollen and bleeding." He looked up at her. "This is what you've been wearing?" he said angrily, holding the leg up. "What is it? Animal bone? It's barbaric."

"Yes, well, there aren't many prosthetic factories at the base of Everest," she snapped.

"There are in London. You have to see a doctor and have something proper built for yourself. You're going to lose more of your leg if you don't. Your body can't take this kind of punishment. No one's can."

And then he was gone. Willa looked at the ceiling, teeth clenched, as she waited for her pills to kick in. They weren't as good as the thick brown opium paste that she smoked in the East, but she'd run out of that weeks ago, somewhere around Suez, and had to make do with what she could buy aboard the ship, and then laudanum pills from London chemists.

A few minutes later, Seamie returned carrying a basin of warm water, clean rags, carbolic, salve, and bandages.

"I'm sorry I shouted at you," she said, her voice more civil now, for the pain had backed off a little.

"It's all right," he said, placing the basin on the night table and sitting down next to her on the bed.

"No, it isn't. I . . . Ouch! Blimey! What are you doing?" Willa said, as Seamie dabbed at her leg.

"Cleaning up this mess."

"It hurts. Can't you just leave it alone?"

"No, I can't. You'll get an infection."

"I won't. I haven't in Rongbuk."

"Probably because it's so bloody cold there. Germs can't survive. This is London, remember? It's warmer. And dirtier. So . . . how have you been?"

"How have I been?" Willa asked incredulously.

"Since the funeral, I mean," Seamie said. "How's your mother? Your family?"

She saw what he was doing—making conversation to take her mind off the pain, but steering away from anything contentious, from anything smacking of the past.

"Mother and I get along as well as can be expected. Albie and I don't. He barely speaks to me."

"He'll get over it," Seamie said.

And what about you, Seamus Finnegan? she wondered, looking at him, at his handsome face. How have you been? But she did not ask him that question. She thought, again, that she had no right to.

Instead she talked about her father's funeral, and about all the people who'd come to the abbey to pay their respects.

"The burial was the hardest part," she said. "Going through the tall black gates of that cemetery, so gray and dreary. With the hearse all draped in black, and the horses with their ghastly black plumes. All I could think about as they carried my father's coffin to the grave site was the Tibetan sky burial ceremony, and how I wished he could have had one."

"What is it?" Seamie asked, ripping a length of gauze with his teeth and tying it around the dressing he'd made for her leg.

"When someone dies in Tibet, the family takes the body to their priests and the priests take it to a holy place. There, they cut the flesh into bits and crush the bones. Then they feed it all—flesh, bones, organs, everything—to the vultures. The birds take the bodily remains, and the soul, liberated from its earthly prison, goes free."

"It must be a hard thing to watch," Seamie said, rolling her trouser leg back down over her knee.

"It was at first, not anymore," Willa said. "Now I prefer it to our own burials. I hate to think of my father, who so loved the sea and the sky, buried in the cold, sodden ground." She stopped talking for a bit, as her emotions got the better of her; then she laughingly said, "Though I can't quite imagine how I'd convince my very proper mother to feed her husband to a pack of vultures."

Seamie laughed, too. "He was a good man, your father," he said. "Proud of you, I can tell you. Proud of your climbing. Of what you'd achieved on Kili. He was so distraught to hear of your accident, but even so, he was proud you'd summitted. I remember that, I remember—" He suddenly stopped talking, as if he'd forgotten himself and now regretted what he'd said.

Willa, anxious herself not to bring up what had happened on Kilimanjaro, quickly started talking, desperate to fill the awkward, painful silence.

"You must tell me about the South Pole," she said. "It must've been so wonderful, to be part of that expedition. I can't even imagine it. To do what you've done. See what you've seen. To have been the first party to ever reach the South Pole. How amazing. You've achieved so much, Seamie, really. You've got everything, haven't you? Everything you ever wanted."

Seamie looking at the roll of gauze he still held in his hand and didn't reply immediately. Then he said, "No, Willa. Not everything. I don't have you."

Willa, stricken by the sadness in his voice, could not speak.

"I promised myself not to see you again," he said. "Not to ever talk about this. But here you are. And I need to know. For eight long years, I've needed to know how you could do it, Willa. How you could tell me you love me, and then walk away from me."

Willa felt as if he'd seared her with his words. His pain—the pain in his voice and in his heart—hurt her more than her leg, more than the fall at Kili had. It hurt her more deeply than any pain she'd ever felt. "I was angry," she said quietly. "I blamed you for what had happened, for the loss of my leg. And I was jealous. You could still climb. I couldn't."

"Blamed me?" he said, his voice rising. "*Blamed* me?" He stood up, anger contorting his face. "What was I supposed to do?" he yelled at her. "What the hell was I supposed to do? Let you die?" Furious now, he threw the wad of gauze across the room, then smacked the basin off the night table, sending bloodied water everywhere.

"What was *I* supposed to do?" Willa yelled back. "Pretend everything was rosy? Return to England? Have a nice church wedding? Cook and sew and play housewife while you went off to the South Pole? I'd rather have died!"

"No," Seamie said brokenly. "You weren't supposed to do any of those things. But you could have talked to me. That's all. Just talked to me. Instead of leaving and ripping my heart out."

Willa balled her hands into fists. She pressed them against her eyes. The pain inside her had become an agony. She reached for her prosthesis and started to put it back on, desperate to get away from Seamie.

"Go, Willa. Run away again. That's what you do best," he said, watching her.

Willa turned to him, tears of anger and grief in her eyes. "I was wrong! All right?" she shouted. "I know that. I've known it for the past eight years. I knew I'd made a mistake the minute I set foot on the train out of Nairobi, but I couldn't turn around. It was too late. I was afraid—afraid you wouldn't have me back after what I'd done."

Seamie shook his head. "Oh, Willa," he said, his voice cracking. "I loved you, for God's sake. I still love you."

Willa began to cry. "I love you, too, Seamie," she said. "I never stopped loving you. I've missed you every day since I got on that train."

Seamie crossed the room, took her tearstained face in his hands, and kissed her. She pulled him down on the bed next to her. They sat there, facing each other. Willa started laughing. Then she cried again. Then she kissed him hard, twining her fingers in his hair. To have him in her arms again, to feel him so close to her, it was nothing short of joy. A joy she had not felt for eight long years—mad, intoxicating, and dangerous.

"I love you, Seamus Finnegan," she said. "I love you, I love you, I love you."

Seamie kissed her back hard, as she'd kissed him. He slid his hands under the tunic she was wearing, and the sweet shock of his touch made her gasp. He pulled the tunic off her, cupped her small breasts and kissed them. She fought with the buttons of his shirt, fumbling with them, until she got them undone, then she pulled him down to her, loving the feeling of his skin against hers, the warm, heavy weight of him on top of her.

She wanted this. Wanted him close to her. So much. She caught one of his hands in hers and kissed his palm. And as she did, she saw it—his wedding ring, gold and shining.

"Oh, God," she said in a choked voice. "Seamie, wait . . . stop. . . . I can't do this. We can't do this. It's not right. There's another person involved now, not just us. There's Jennie. Your wife. You can't betray her."

Seamie rolled onto his back. He stared into the gloom of the small, lamplit room, then said, "I already have. I betrayed her when

I first saw you again. In the parlor of your parents' house. And I'm going to keep on betraying her. Every day of my life. A hundred times a day. By wishing I was with you."

Willa rested her head against his shoulder. "What are we going to do?" she whispered.

"I don't know, Willa," he said. "I wish to God I did."

CHAPTER TWENTY-EIGHT

"YOU CAN'T GO back to London, Jennie. I won't let you. Who will I talk to? There's nothing here but squirrels and cows. I've only been here for three weeks and that was enough to drive me barmy. How am I going to manage for another seven months?" Josie Meadows wailed.

Jennie, sitting by the cozy fireplace of her Binsey cottage with a pile of knitting and a pot of tea, gave Josie a stern look. "Would you like to go back to London?" she asked her. "I hear Billy Madden's in quite a state over your departure."

Josie paled. She quickly shook her head no.

"I didn't think so," Jennie said. "You'll find things to occupy yourself. You can knit. I know you can. I taught you myself. Knit something for the baby. She'll need a few things. And you can read, too. Improve your mind. You can even study a bit of French for when you go to Paris. I'll find a lesson book and post it to you." Josie nodded miserably and Jennie softened toward her. "It's only a few months, you know, and then you'll have the baby, and I'll take her to an orphanage, and you'll be free to go to Paris and start a new life."

Jennie thought Josie might smile at her words—she'd tried to make them sound encouraging—but Josie did not.

"She'll go to an orphanage then, my baby?" she said quietly.

"Yes. Where else would she go?"

"I don't like orphanages. Me mum was in an orphanage. Back in Dublin. And cor, the stories she tells. They make your hair stand on end. I don't want that for her, Jennie. I don't. Can't we find her a family to go to? A good one, with a sweet mum and a kind dad? With people who will love her and care for her?"

Jennie put her knitting down and thought about this. "We could try," she said. "I'm not sure how to go about it, but I can ask some friends. Some doctor friends who care for expectant mothers. They might know how to make inquiries."

"Would you?" Josie asked. "She can't go to an orphanage, my baby. She just can't."

"I'll do it as soon as I get back. Don't fret about it, Josie. We'll figure something out. We've got time. The most important thing right now is that you're safe and well and far away from Billy Madden."

"You're right. Of course you are. Only, I still wish you weren't leaving tomorrow," Josie said, suddenly petulant again.

"I'll be back again in a fortnight. I promise," Jennie said.

"A fortnight?" Josie said. "I can't take another two weeks here all by myself. I just can't!" She started to cry.

"Now, Josie," Jennie said soothingly.

"'Now Josie' my arse!" Josie raged. "It's not you stuck here. I wish it was you instead of me. I wish I was you. You're so lucky. You can go back to London tomorrow. You're married to a good man and carrying a baby you both want. You've a wonderful, wonderful life and no worries at all!"

Jennie almost laughed out loud. No worries? She had nothing but worries. She worried Billy Madden would find out where Josie had gone. She worried Seamie would find out what she was really doing at Binsey. She worried he was going to find out the truth about her accident. She worried, with every twinge and ache and cramp, that she was going to lose the baby. And she worried that he was going to leave her for Willa Alden. She had seen his face when he was holding Willa. In the parlor at her father's funeral. She had seen that he loved her. Still. It was in his eyes, in the softness of his expression, in the tender way he'd rested his cheek against hers.

"We all have worries, Josie," she said now softly.

Josie cried even harder. "Oh, Jennie, I'm so sorry. What a selfish git I am. Of course you have worries. You're due the same time as me, and you've got to worry about me and my baby as well as your own. Can you forgive me?" She got up from her chair, knelt down, and put her head in Jennie's lap.

"Don't be silly. There's nothing to forgive," she said, stroking Josie's hair. "I know it's hard on you. I do. But you've only seven more months to go. It's not so long. You'll see."

Josie snuffled and nodded. And Jennie, still stroking her hair, raised her head and looked out of the sitting room window, at the evening's gathering gloom.

Only seven more months, for you, too, she said to herself. It's not so long. You'll see. Only seven more months.

CHAPTER TWENTY-NINE

"WELL, WELL, IF it ain't Mr. Stiles. Always a pleasure," Billy Madden said, looking up from his newspaper.

"I need to speak with you," Max said tersely. "Alone."

Billy gave a curt nod, and the three men sitting with him stood up and made their way to the bar. Max sat down with Billy.

"You see this?" Billy said, pointing to a story on the front page of his paper. "Two blokes in Whitechapel shot each other over a few quid a few nights ago. One of 'em was called Sam Hutchins. Wasn't he one of yours? The one who was taking your swag out to meet the boat in the North Sea?"

"Yes, he was," Max said tersely. "The other one worked for me, too. Apparently, they fought over payment for a job I had them do. It's buggered everything for me. That's why I'm here."

It was not a total lie. The papers hadn't printed the real story about the mess at Duffin's. Max knew the government would never have allowed it. They'd printed what they were told—that two friends had been drinking and started to argue violently over money. One man pulled a gun out and shot his rival. When he realized what he'd done, he shot himself.

There was no mention about the third man who'd been there. The man who'd realized they'd been followed, shot the others, then escaped through a window. No, nothing about him.

Max remembered the horrible scene. He remembered pulling the pistol out. The look of horror on Bauer's face. The stoic resignation on Hoffman's. It had been quick, at least. He was an excellent marksman and had hit them both squarely between the eyes. And then he'd run, managing to elude the police and the man from the SSB, but only barely.

Two agents gone. The chain to Berlin hopelessly broken. And all because that fool Bauer had panicked and come to London when he should have stayed in Govan, at the shipyard. It was unspeakably frustrating. The system Max had set up had worked like a perfectly calibrated piece of machinery—Gladys to Hoffman, Hoffman to the boatyard, and then a quick trip to the ship waiting in the North Sea. And now that machine was smashed. Berlin desperately wanted the information from the Admiralty in London, and from the shipyards on the Clyde, that Max had been supplying to them, and now he no longer had any way of doing so.

Max had received a message from Bauer two days before the shooting. In it, Bauer had said that they were on to him; he was certain of it. He'd said he had something for Berlin, something big, and he had to get it to London. Now. Max had sent word that he was to stay put and wait for a courier. But he hadn't. He'd got on a train and shown up on Hoffman's doorstep—Hoffman, of all people—Max's most valuable courier. Hoffman had got word to him, Max, that Bauer had arrived in London, and Max had told Hoffman to bring Bauer to Duffin's.

Bauer must've been followed the entire way to Duffin's, for the knock on the door and the constable telling them to open up had happened only moments after he and Hoffman arrived. Max had had only seconds in which to execute the two men, throw Bauer's documents into the fire, and flee. That he had not been caught was a miracle. They'd shot at him, and one bullet had come uncomfortably close. They would've killed him if they could have.

"The boat is off," Max said to Billy now. "That's what I came to tell you."

"For how long?"

"I don't know," Max said. "As long as it takes me to find a new courier."

"Why can't you get your swag to the boat yourself?" Billy asked. "Business as usual."

"It wouldn't be wise right now."

"The busies are making things a bit hot?"

"Yes," Max said. "They are."

That, too, was not completely a lie. It wasn't the London constabulary Max was worried about, though. It was the British SSB. Max was a German in London and, as such, was under suspicion. He knew that he'd been followed on more than one occasion. He also knew that he was in the clear, for among all the documents Gladys had brought to him were letters bound for his own dossier, all of which showed that the SSB did not consider him a threat.

He must remain above suspicion, though, and that meant making no unusual movements. It wouldn't look right for a West End playboy, one accustomed to staying at the Coburg and dining in London's most stylish clubs and homes, to suddenly be seen hanging around a ramshackle East End boatyard.

Billy, who'd been blowing smoke rings, now said, "Could you get yourself to Whitechapel? Or Wapping? At night?"

"Why?" Max asked. He'd gone to Whitechapel many times, but it would be risky now after what had happened. He couldn't afford to be seen and identified by Mrs. Duffin or any of her boarders.

"The tunnels, lad," Billy said, stubbing his cigarette out.

"What tunnels?" Max asked, his interest piqued.

"The ones that run under East London. From Whitechapel to Wapping to Limehouse and all the way under the river to Southwark."

Max sat forward in his chair. "I had no idea such tunnels existed," he said.

"They do. They're a right maze. Very dangerous if you don't know your way through them, but very handy if you do. For avoiding the busies and for moving swag."

"Where, exactly, are they, Billy?"

"All over. One even runs from the basement in a church—St. Nicholas's—right to my boatyard. If you could get yourself to the church and drop the goods there, I could send my man Harris through. He'd pick them up and get them to your man in the North Sea. Many's the time one of my lads has hidden something in St. Nick's and another's picked it up by coming through the tunnels. Couldn't be easier."

"Doesn't the Reverend Wilcott mind this?"

"Oh, you know him, do you? Nah, he's a daft old git. Leaves the doors open all day long just in case someone's soul needs saving. Easy as can be to nip down to the basement."

"But doesn't he see the things you put down there?"

"He doesn't have a clue about any of it. Doesn't even know there's a door down there, or where it leads. I don't think he ever goes down himself. There's no reason to. It's a right nasty place. Dark and damp. Only thing down there is rats. Some old, rotted church pews. And a broken statue of St. Nicholas. It fell and smashed several years ago, when some yobs dropped it as they were trying to steal it. It's all in pieces now. Good thing is, the head's hollow. Makes a great place to hide guns and jewels and other smalls. Or forget Wapping and go into the tunnels in Whitechapel. At the Blind Beggar. Then walk to the boatyard from there. It's a longer walk, but my men have done it loads of times. You want to give it a go?"

Max thought about what Billy had said. There was something in it. He liked the idea of moving the documents underground, away from prying eyes, but he couldn't quite figure out how to make it work. At least, not yet.

"It's a good idea. But I can't do the trip myself. I still need a new courier."

A man, thick-browed, bald, and built like a barrel, came over to Billy. Billy looked up at him. "Any word?"

"No, guv. There's no sign of her. Nothing whatsoever."

Billy slammed his fist on the table. "Fucking cunt!" he shouted. "I'm going to gut her when I find her!"

"Lady troubles?" Max asked.

"It's this tart I was shagging. Little actress from the halls. A blonde named Josie Meadows. You ever see her here?"

Max nodded. He recalled a young, blond woman with bruises on her face, sitting by a window. "Once, I think," he said.

"She disappeared on me."

"Actresses are thick on the ground in London. Can't you find another one?"

"This one took something with her that belongs to me," he said.

Max had the feeling there was more to the story than Billy was telling him, but he didn't push him for the details.

"You know, I'm thinking you might come across her," Billy said. "Might see her skulking around somewhere."

"It's possible," Max said, hesitantly.

"You don't have to get your hands dirty, if that's what you're worried about," Billy said. "All I'm asking is that you let me know if you see anything or hear anything. I'd be grateful."

Billy smiled his horrible, black smile. Looking at it, and at the cruel, soulless eyes above it, Max thought that this girl, this Josie Meadows, would do well to get out of London. Max had known men like Billy before, men who took pleasure in hurting and killing, and he knew that if Billy ever found this girl, she would sorely wish that he hadn't.

Well, that wasn't his worry. Reestablishing the links in the chain, that was his worry. That and staying alive. He took an envelope from his jacket and put it on the table.

"Keep the boat ready for me," he said.

Billy nodded. He picked the envelope up and tucked it inside his jacket.

"I'll be in touch again when I can," Max said, standing up to leave. He thought about Duffin's again, about his narrow escape, and the bullet whizzing past his cheek. "*If* I can," he added.

CHAPTER THIRTY

SEAMIE TOOK A swallow of the whiskey he'd poured for himself. It burned his throat. Made his eyes water. He took another.

Glass in hand, he walked to the window of his hotel room, at the Coburg, and looked out of it. Night had come down. The street lamps were all aglow. He gazed at the street below but did not see the person he was looking for. He turned from the window, caught sight of himself in a mirror, and quickly looked away.

"Leave," he said out loud. "Now. Get out of here before it's too late."

He could do it. He still had time. He *would* do it. He put his glass down and grabbed his jacket. He was across the room in a few quick strides, had his hand on the doorknob—and then he heard it: a knock at his door. He stood there, frozen. Ran a hand through his hair. The knock came again. He took a deep breath and opened the door.

"I didn't know if you'd really be here," Willa said.

"Neither did I," he replied.

"Can I come in?" she asked.

He laughed. "Yes, of course," he said. "Sorry."

He took her jacket and hat and placed them on a chair with his own jacket. She was wearing a cream silk blouse under it and a navy skirt. He commented on her outfit and she told him she hated it, but had worn it to blend in. She didn't want to be recognized here.

He offered her tea, but she wanted whiskey. He was so jittery, he sloshed some on her as he handed it to her.

"It's all right, Seamie," she said. "We can just talk, you know. Like adults. We can try to sort things out."

That's what they'd decided to do at Lulu's party. They hadn't made love. Instead, they decided they would meet in a private place, at a time when emotions were not running as high, and there they would put the old ghosts to rest. They would talk about Africa, and about what had happened there, and when they'd finished, they would go their separate ways. They would part friends—not enemies and not lovers, but friends.

Seamie laughed mirthlessly now. "I told myself that, too, Willa. On my way over. I told myself all we would do tonight was talk. But I knew if I came here, I'd do more than talk. And I think you knew that, too."

He had booked a suite—a room with settees and chairs and a desk—so that the large, inviting hotel bed would be firmly out of sight. He'd hoped that would help. It hadn't. He wanted her so badly right now, it was all he could do not to take her on the floor.

She nodded at his words, looking at him as she did. Her eyes were frank and unflinching. He could see the love in them, and the longing.

"One time, then, all right?" she said quietly. "Just this one time and never again."

As she spoke, she put her drink down and started undoing the buttons of her blouse. She shrugged it off and let it fall to the floor. She had nothing on underneath it. She undid her boots and stockings. Then unbuttoned the waistband of her skirt and let that fall, too.

She stood before him, unashamed of her nakedness, or of the scars on her body, and he moved toward her as if in a trance. He knew what he was doing was wrong, and he knew, too, that he would pay a heavy price for his sins. The memories of this night would torture him for the rest of his life.

But he would pay that price. He'd pay any price to be with her.

He didn't take her in his arms. He would, but not yet. He wanted to see her, to discover and know every inch of her. And so he went slowly, taking his time.

He kissed her gently on the lips. Then on her neck. He took her hand, held her arm out, and kissed his way from her shoulder to her palm, brushing his lips along her muscled upper arm, the hollow of her elbow, over the veins and sinews of her forearm, to her hand, scarred and strong.

He kissed her throat, the bronzed skin of her chest. His mouth moved to her breasts, and he felt her arch against him as he teased her small, hard nipples with his tongue and teeth.

He turned her around and kissed the nape of her neck, ran his hand over the graceful flare of her back. He traced the knotted pearls of her spine one by one, kissed the jutting bones of her hips. He knelt down then and turned her once more. Toward him.

He slid his hands to her bum and pulled her hard against him. He kissed the place between her legs, and touched her there. She was soft, so soft. And warm and wet. He felt her fingers dig into his shoulders, felt her shudder against him, heard her cry his name.

That sound, the sound of her crying his name, maddened him with desire. He wanted to have her, to possess her body and soul. He wanted to hear her call his name again. His name. He'd wanted it for so long.

He picked her up and carried her into the bedroom. He had his own clothes off in seconds. And then he was on top of her. She pulled his face down to hers and kissed him. Then she pushed him off of her.

"No," she said in a rough, husky voice, her green eyes glittering. "It's my turn."

She pushed him down on the bed, onto his back, then lay next to him on her side. He grabbed her hips, wanting only to be inside her again, but again she told him no. She took hold of his wrists and pinned them to the pillows. Then she kissed his mouth, biting his bottom lip. She kissed his forehead and his chin. Bit his shoulder. She kissed his chest, trailing her tongue down his torso. Bit his hip and made him shiver, as he'd done to her. She went lower, tormenting him with her mouth. "Jesus, woman," he groaned.

And then she was kissing his mouth again, taking him inside her, moving with him, her eyes closed. He cupped her face in one hand, touched his forehead to hers.

"Tell me, Willa," he said, his voice barely more than a gasp. "Tell me."

She opened her eyes and he saw that they were bright with tears. "I love you, Seamie," she said. "I love you so."

He came then. Wildly. Helplessly. Overwhelmed by lust and love and sorrow and pain. And she did, too. When it was over, he held her close. He kissed her, brushed a stray tendril of hair from her sweaty cheek.

There was a vase of roses on the bedside table, lush and bright, their perfume strong and enticing. They were no scentless, lifeless hothouse blooms. They'd been cut for their perfume and their color, cut from a hedgerow in the country where they'd grown wild and brought to London. They didn't belong here in this hotel room, in this gray city. Neither did Willa. Seamie took one out and tucked it behind her ear. "A wild rose for my wild rose," he whispered to her. He smoothed a piece of hair out of her face, then said, "Why did you come back into my life, Willa? You've ruined it. Ruined me. You're the best thing that ever happened to me, and the worst."

"I told myself it would only be once," she said. "I told you that, too. But it can't be, Seamie. I can't leave here tomorrow morning knowing I'll never have this again. Never be with you like this again.

What are we going to do?" she asked desolately. Just as she had at Lulu's party. "What on earth are we going to do?"

"Love each other," Seamie said.

"For how long?" she asked, her eyes searching his.

He took her in his arms and held her close. "For as long as we possibly can," he whispered. "As long as we can."

CHAPTER THIRTY-ONE

MAUD HURRIED ALONG the third-floor corridor of the Coburg, the key to Max's suite of rooms in her hand. She'd just bribed a bellboy handsomely to get it. In her other hand, she carried a small, beautifully made traveling case. It contained two tickets to Bombay, a compass, and a pair of field glasses. They would go in the autumn, after she returned from visiting India in Point Reyes. Bombay was only the first leg of the journey, of course. Once there, they'd have to make their way north to Darjeeling, then to Tibet. And Everest.

It was a birthday surprise for Max, one she'd been planning for ages. He would turn thirty-four tomorrow and she wanted him to find the gift when he came home today. He'd been away in Scotland for a few days. "Shooting with friends, darling," he'd said. "Men only, I'm afraid. I'll miss you horribly."

Maud smiled now, as she fit the key into the lock, imagining the look on his face when he opened the case. He adored Everest. He was forever talking about it, and always with such passion, such longing. In fact, if Everest had been a woman instead of a mountain, she would have been quite jealous. She opened the door and quickly went inside. The plush, luxurious rooms were dark and silent. She could hear the echo of her heels as she walked across the foyer's marbled floor.

Now . . . where should I leave the gift? she wondered. Here in the foyer? No, he might trip over it. On the sitting room table, perhaps. That wouldn't do either. He'd likely walk right by it.

She decided to leave it on his bed. He'd be sure to see it there. She walked into the bedroom and laid the case on his pillow. It looked a bit lonely there, so she decided to leave a note as well. She sat down at his desk, placed her large silk clutch purse down next to the blotter, and shrugged out of her fur coat. Then she pulled open one of the desk drawers and rooted about for a pen and a sheet of paper. She found the first, but not the second. She opened another drawer, and then another, but still no paper. Frustrated, she picked up the leather desk blotter, to see if there might be a few sheets under it, but there was nothing. She'd tilted it slightly as she'd lifted it, and when she went to put it back on the desk, she noticed that something had slid partially out of it—out of a thin slit, one that had been cut almost invisibly into the bottom edge of the blotter.

It looked like the corner of a photograph. She tugged it all of the way out and saw that it was a black-and-white photo of a naked woman. "Why, Max, you dirty little bugger," she said aloud. She had no idea he collected pornography.

She shook the blotter and the edges of more photographs slipped out. Five in all. A whole collection. Maud looked at them, expecting something seductive and erotic, but there was nothing alluring about these pictures. They were wretched. Disgusting. The girl in them looked drunk or drugged. Her legs were spread. Her hands were behind her head. And her face . . .

Her face. Maud gasped. She recognized it. She knew this woman. "My God," she said out loud. "It's Gladys. Gladys Bigelow."

She knew Gladys from suffrage meetings. She'd been one of Jennie Wilcott's students and was now Sir George Burgess's secretary. What was she doing in these horrible photographs?

Maud scrabbled in Max's drawers until she found a letter opener. She poked it into the blotter, widening the slit. There was something else inside, she could see it. She wedged her fingers in, expecting to pull out another awful photograph. Instead she pulled out a thin sheaf of folded carbon papers.

She held one up to the light. It took her a minute to read the backward type, but as soon as she did, she realized she was holding a letter from George Burgess to Winston Churchill regarding the acquisition of fifty Sopwith airplanes. Another, from Burgess to Asquith, requested further funds for something called Room 40.

The horrible pictures of Gladys, the carbons of sensitive letters written by her employer—Maud put the two together and realized that Gladys was being blackmailed by Max.

There were more letters from Burgess, but she didn't read them all. With her heart in her mouth, she reached into the blotter again, dreading what she would find.

She pulled out a folded blueprint of what seemed to be a submarine. All the words on it were written in German. She found more carbons, but these, too, were written in German. They were addressed to a man whose name she recognized—Bismarck.

The blood froze in her veins as she pulled out the last item inside the blotter—a white card, with printing on the front, measuring about five by seven inches. She recognized it—it was the invitation Max had received to the Asquiths' country home, the Wharf. She had received one just like it, and they'd gone there together about a fortnight ago.

She turned it over. There was handwriting on the back—Max's. The words were in German. Maud spoke and read some German, enough to understand what she was seeing: Asquith's name and the names of French, Belgian, Russian, and American diplomats, as well as place names, times, and dates.

With horror, she remembered their first evening at the Wharf. She remembered Asquith's secretary coming into the room and telling the prime minister that there was a telephone call for him. Asquith had decided to take the call in his study. He'd left them, and after he had, Max had asked where the study was.

It's upstairs. Right above us. Henry's just being cross. He doesn't like stairs, Margot had replied.

"He's a spy," Maud whispered now. "My God, he's a German spy. And he used me, and my friendship with Margot, to get to Asquith."

The names and dates—they were notations of meetings the prime minister had had with foreign diplomats, or was going to have, Maud thought. They were very likely secret meetings, or else why had Max bothered to note them down? If they weren't secret, they'd be reported on in the daily papers, where anyone could read about them. Max must've gone to Asquith's study later that night, riffled through his diary and his papers, and written the information down.

But why, if he was passing British information to the Germans, did he also have a blueprint of a German submarine and carbons of letters written to Bismarck?

Maud didn't have an answer for that, and she knew she had no time to find one. With shaking hands, she shuffled together the papers she'd pulled out of the blotter into a stack, folded them over, tucked the photos inside, and put the whole bundle into her purse. She had to get out of here. Now. She didn't know exactly when Max was returning to London. He could arrive at the Coburg at any minute. She decided to take the traveling case with her so he'd never know she'd been here. Once she was outside of the hotel, she'd flag down a hackney cab and tell the man to take her to Downing Street. To Number 10. There, she would tell Asquith where she'd just been and give him the papers. He would know what to do.

Maud positioned the blotter exactly as she'd found it, then made certain all the desk drawers were closed. She stood, pulled her coat on, and was about to grab the traveling case off the bed, when a sudden movement in the doorway startled her. She gasped out loud. It was Max.

"Max, darling, you gave me such a fright!" she said, pressing a hand to her chest.

Max smiled, but his eyes were cold. "What are you doing here, Maud?" he asked her.

Maud was terrified, but knew she mustn't show it. She must appear simply to be flustered, and to use that to her advantage. It was her only chance.

"Well, if you must know, I was trying my hardest to surprise you. For your birthday. I was just trying to write you a note, but I can't seem to find any bloody paper in your desk."

"You were trying to surprise me?"

"Yes. Seems I've failed miserably though. There it is," she said, pointing to his bed. "Go on, open it."

Max looked past her. He smiled again. It was a real smile this time, warm and engaging.

"I can't wait to see what it is," he said. "But let's make it a proper celebration. Hold on . . . stay right there. I'll bring some wine."

He disappeared into another room and Maud let out a ragged breath. A few seconds later, she heard him pull a cork. She'd fooled him, she was sure of it. Why wouldn't he believe her? The present was on his pillow. He'd open it in a few minutes, and thank her, and then she'd suggest they go out for dinner. As soon as she was downstairs, in the lobby, she'd say that she forgot something in his room and would he be a dear and run back up for it. When he did, she would make a dash for it.

"Here we are," he said, returning with two glasses of red wine. He handed her one. "A Pomerol. 1894. I had one just last night. It was wonderful."

She touched her glass to his and smiled. "Happy birthday, darling," she said, kissing him for good measure. She took a generous swallow for courage, then licked her lips and said, "You're right. This *is* wonderful."

"I'm glad you like it. Drink up. I've plenty more."

She took another sip, then said, "Go on, then. Open your present."

"All I really want is you," he said, sitting down on the bed.

"You already have me," she said, laughing and taking another large gulp of wine. She must steady her nerves. He mustn't see her hands shaking. "Open your present," she said again, sitting down next to him.

"All right, then, I will." He reached behind himself for the case.

As Maud watched him opening the locks, she began to feel dizzy.

She suddenly saw two cases on his lap. Then one again. A low buzzing started in her ears. She looked away from Max, at the floor, trying to clear her head. But it didn't work. The dizziness only got worse. Was she drunk? On half a glass of wine?

"Max, darling . . . I feel rather strange," she said, putting her wineglass down.

She looked at him. He wasn't holding the box anymore. He'd put it down. He was watching her.

She tried to get up, tried to stand, but her legs went out from under her and she hit the floor. She closed her eyes, tried to take a deep breath. When she opened them again, Max was standing over her.

"I'm so sorry, Maud," he said quietly.

"No, Max," she said, though it was difficult to speak. "It's my . . . it's my fault. Too much wine, I think. Can you . . . can you help me? I . . . I can't seem . . ."

"Don't fight it," he said. "It's easier if you just let go."

Let go? Let go of what? Hadn't she put the wineglass down already?

The wineglass. He'd put something in her drink.

She tried once more to get up, but her arms and legs seemed as if they were made of lead. The room was whirling. Her vision began to fade.

"Max, please . . . ," she said, reaching a hand out to him.

He looked at her, but did not move to help her. There was a strange expression on his face. Maud didn't recognize it at first, but then suddenly she did; it was grief.

"Let go," he whispered.

"Oh, God," she pleaded. "Somebody help me . . . somebody, please help me. . . ."

CHAPTER THIRTY-TWO

"BEG YOUR PARDON, ma'am," Mr. Foster said, stepping inside Fiona's study. "I'm terribly sorry to intrude. I did knock."

Fiona looked up from the plans she'd been studying—blueprints for a new tearoom to be built in Sydney. She'd been so deeply absorbed by them she hadn't heard him.

"What is it now, Mr. Foster?" she asked. "No, let me guess . . . Katie's led a march on the House of Commons, Rose has taken a necklace without asking and now she's in tears because she can't find it, and the twins have jumped off the roof."

"I wish it was so, madam. All except for the twins jumping off the roof, of course. But I fear it is something of a graver nature."

"What's happened?" Fiona said, instantly alarmed. "The children . . . are they—"

"The children are well, madam. It's Dr. Hatcher. She is most distressed. She's in the drawing room and would like to see you."

Fiona was out of her chair immediately. She hurried by Foster and ran down the stairs. Harriet Hatcher was never distressed. She was rarely so much as perturbed. Nothing fazed her—not the blood and gore she dealt with on a daily basis, not the constant threats hurled at her when she took part in suffrage marches, not even the harsh treatment she received when she was arrested. Whatever it was that had upset her, it had to be grave indeed.

"Harriet?" Fiona called out as she opened the door to the drawing room. "What's the matter? What's happened?"

Harriet was sitting on a settee, ashen and trembling. Her eyes were red from crying. Fiona quickly closed the door and sat down beside her. "What is it?" she said, taking her hand.

"Oh, Fiona. I have the most terrible news. Maud is dead and the police are saying it's a suicide."

Fiona shook her head, stunned. She thought that perhaps she had not heard her correctly. "You must be mistaken," she said. "Do you know what you're saying? You're saying that Maud . . . our Maud . . . that she—"

"Killed herself," Harriet said. "I know how it sounds, Fiona. I can't believe it myself, but it's true."

"How do you know this?" Fiona asked.

"A police constable. He came to my house a few hours ago. He told me that Maud was found dead in her bed this morning by Mrs. Rudge, her housekeeper. The police questioned Mrs. Rudge, then asked her for names and addresses of Maud's family and her friends. They're going to question everyone. I imagine they'll come here. They've already been to see Max. He's in an awful way."

"I can imagine he would be. The poor man," Fiona said woodenly, still in shock.

"He's beyond distraught. He blames himself completely."

"Blames himself? Why?" Fiona asked.

"They'd had some kind of row, apparently, he and Maud, and he'd broken it off with her."

"Oh, no."

"Oh, yes. And it gets worse. The police believe that he was the last person to see her alive. So not only has he been questioned by a constable, but a detective inspector is going to question him again. Later today."

"I still can't believe this. Not any of it. How could Maud take her own life?" Fiona said. "Harriet, how . . . how did she—"

"An overdose," Harriet said. "Morphine. She injected herself. The police found two bottles and a hypodermic on her night table. The coroner found marks on her arm."

"I had no idea she even knew how to do something like that," Fiona said. The shock of Harriet's news had receded a little, and Fiona felt as if she could think straight again. She was trying to reason now, to make sense of it all.

"It's not hard to use a hypodermic, Fiona. You don't have to be a doctor. Anyone can do it," Harriet said.

"But I thought it was all over with, her drug use," Fiona said. "I know that she used to visit opium dens. In Limehouse. Years ago. And she used to smoke opium-laced cigarettes. She had mostly stopped, though. She still had the odd cigarette, but the trips to Limehouse were a thing of the past. India saw to that. It made her furious that Maud went there, and . . . and—oh, Harriet!"

Fiona's voice cracked, she covered her face with her hands and started to weep. Now that her mind had cleared a bit, she'd realized that there was someone else who must be told. Someone else who would be devastated by Maud's death, even more so than she and Harriet were.

"What is it, Fiona?" Harriet asked, putting an arm around her.

"How am I going to tell her, Harriet? How?"

"Tell who?"

Fiona lowered her hands. "How am I going to tell India that her sister is dead?"

CHAPTER THIRTY-THREE

"DO YOU MIND if I smoke?" Max asked the man seated across from him.

"Not at all," the man, Detective Inspector Arnold Barrett, said. "Nice place," he added, looking around Max's spacious receiving room, at the luxurious furnishings, the silver tea tray on the table, the blazing logs in the fireplace.

"Yes, it's very comfortable," Max said, sitting back in his chair.

They were in Max's hotel suite. Barrett had arrived a few minutes before. Max had offered him tea, which he'd gratefully accepted, and then they'd sat down.

"Thank you for seeing me, Mr. von Brandt," Barrett said, taking out a notebook and fountain pen. "I know this has been a very difficult day for you and I won't take up any more of your time than I have to."

Max nodded.

"Now, then, according to P.C. Gallagher, the man who interviewed you this morning, you believe you were the last person to see Miss Selwyn Jones alive," Barrett said.

"Yes, I believe so," Max replied.

"I would like to go over the events leading up to Miss Selwyn Jones's death. To begin with, the doorman here at the hotel, one William Frazier, remembers seeing you helping Miss Selwyn Jones into a hackney cab. Mr. Frazier has said that Miss Selwyn Jones appeared to be inebriated."

"Yes, that's correct," Max said. "Maud was very drunk."

"Alfred Ludd, the cabdriver, has stated that he heard Miss Selwyn Jones crying at times during the cab ride to her flat, and saying, and I quote, 'Please, Max. Please don't do this.'"

"That is also correct."

Barrett gave Max a long look. "You're hardly helping yourself here, Mr. von Brandt."

"There is no help for me, Detective Inspector. As I told P.C. Gallagher, and will now tell you, it was all my fault."

Barrett paused, weighing Max's words, then he resumed his questioning. "According to Ludd, when he arrived at Miss Selwyn Jones's building, you paid him, then helped Miss Selwyn Jones out of the cab and into her house."

"Yes."

"You yourself told P.C. Gallagher that you then carried Miss Selwyn Jones to her bedroom and laid her down on her bed. You covered her, then left the premises via the front door, locking it behind you."

"Yes. Maud had given me a key. I gave it to P.C. Gallagher this morning."

"A note was found on the deceased's bedside table, in what appears to be her handwriting. In it, she wrote that she was distraught over her breakup with 'Max.' That would be you."

Max nodded and took a deep drag of his cigarette.

"The note was hard to read," Barrett said. "It was scrawled more than it was written, but then again, Miss Selwyn Jones, as everyone seems to agree, was drunk. However, we could make it out well enough. It went on to say that she was sorry for doing what she was about to do, but she couldn't live without you."

Max rubbed at his forehead with one hand. The other hand, still holding his cigarette, shook slightly.

"Miss Selwyn Jones was found facedown in her bed, a tourniquet around her arm. An empty syringe and two empty morphine bottles were found nearby her," Barrett said, watching Max closely.

"I'm to blame," Max said in a choked voice. "If it wasn't for me, she would still be alive."

"What exactly happened last evening, Mr. von Brandt?" Barrett asked, his keen eyes on Max. "Why did Miss Selwyn Jones leave here so drunk she could barely stand? Why did she kill herself?"

Max lowered his hand. He brushed at his eyes awkwardly. "We had a fight," he began. "She had come here to give me a birthday present. A trip to India. With her."

"A very nice gift," Barrett said.

"Yes, it was. It was a very lovely gesture. But it was too much."

"The gift was?"

"No, her expectations."

"I don't understand."

"The relationship we had . . . our romance, if you will . . . well, for me it was only ever intended to be a short-lived thing. A fling between two grown, unattached people. I thought Maud understood that, but she didn't. She wanted more from me and I couldn't give it to her."

"Why not?" Barrett asked.

"Because expectations have been placed upon me. Family obligations. Maud was older than I. She had been married before. . . ."

"Not the kind of girl to bring home to Mama," Barrett said.

"No, not at all the kind of girl. I'd recently had a falling out with my uncle, you see. He now runs the company my grandfather started. I came to London to cool off, but I know that eventually I will have to return home, take my place in the family business, and marry a suitable girl—a respectable girl from a good family who will give me many children. My mother has several candidates picked out for me," Max said, with a bitter smile. "Maud knew this. I never lied to her. I was honest from the beginning. She said it didn't matter to her, and for while, it did not seem to. We had a very good time together, but lately she'd become unreasonable."

"How so?" Barrett asked.

"She began to pressure me constantly. She wanted me to not return to Germany. To stay in London. She wanted to get married. She told me I didn't need to go back, to join the family firm. She said she had plenty of money, more than enough to keep us both in a very high style. The gift was the last straw."

"Why?"

"She suggested it could be our honeymoon trip. I refused to accept it. I told her it was over between us. She got very upset with me. She yelled and screamed and started drinking. Quite a lot, in fact."

"You're an odd duck, Mr. von Brandt. Some men would have had no hesitation in marrying a very wealthy woman. A woman whose company, and whose bed, they happened to like."

"You are quite right, Detective Inspector. Some men would have no hesitation. They are called gigolos," Max said coldly.

Barrett held up a hand. "Now, now, Mr. von Brandt," he said. "I didn't mean to offend you. Tell me what happened next."

"Maud became very drunk. I couldn't listen to her anymore and I thought the best thing would be to take her home. So I did. And the rest you know." Max paused for a few seconds, then he said, "She told me I'd be sorry. She was right. I am. Very sorry. I shouldn't have broken it off with her. I wouldn't have if I'd known how fragile she was."

"Do you have any idea where she got the morphine? It was a very strong concentration. Stronger than you can buy at a chemist's."

"No. I know she used the drug, somewhat frequently, but I don't know where she got it," he said. He hesitated, then said, "Detective Inspector Barrett?"

"Yes?"

"I do know that she sometimes smoked cigarettes with opium in them. She told me once that she got them in a place called Limehouse. Does that help you?"

Barrett laughed. "Mr. von Brandt, there are a hundred places in the place called Limehouse where Miss Selwyn Jones could've bought those cigarettes. And the morphine, too." He capped his pen and closed his notebook. "Thank you for your time, Mr. von Brandt. We won't be bothering you again."

Barrett stood up. Max stood, too. He walked Barrett to the door and opened it for him.

"Now, if you'd married Miss Selwyn Jones, and then she ended up dead, her being such a rich woman, then we'd have more questions," Barrett said, pausing in the doorway. "But as things are, you've got no motive. None whatsoever. Miss Selwyn Jones's death was suicide, plain and simple. The papers won't be happy. They always like a good story—some sort of nefarious motive, some mystery novel nonsense—but sometimes death is just what it looks like—sad and sorry. Nothing else. My condolences on your loss, Mr. von Brandt. Good day."

"Thank you, Detective Inspector," Max said. "Good day."

As he was about to close the door behind him, Barrett turned and said, "Mr. von Brandt?"

"Yes?"

"A piece of advice . . . if I may."

"Of course."

"Don't be so hard on yourself. If breaking hearts was a crime, every jail in London would be full."

Max smiled sadly. Detective Inspector Arnold tipped his hat and then he was gone. Max closed the door, poured himself a glass of wine, and sat down heavily. Dusk was starting to fall, but he did not turn on a light. He sat staring into the fireplace, and as he did, a tear rolled down his cheek, and then another.

This was no false emotion, put on for a police officer's benefit. His sorrow was real. He had felt something for Maud. He had enjoyed her company and her humor and her bed, and he missed her. She did not deserve what had happened to her. And he was full of remorse for it.

But he had had no choice. He'd known she was in his room the minute he opened the door. He'd smelled her perfume. He'd prayed then, that she had come to welcome him home, that she was merely waiting for him, naked in his bed. His heart had clenched in sadness and anger when, having quietly walked to the doorway of his bedroom, he saw the photographs and documents spread out over his desk. He watched as she put the papers into her purse, and he knew what she was going to do with them, knew she would go to the police, or to somebody she knew in the government. Joe Bristow, perhaps. Or Asquith himself. And in so doing, she would have brought his carefully constructed house of cards crashing down.

He'd known, too, what he would have to do, and he'd done it unflinchingly. Indeed, he kept a small supply of the necessary drugs on hand for such occasions. And yet it had hurt him terribly, far more than he'd thought it would, to drug her, bring her to her home, stick a needle repeatedly into the soft skin inside her elbow, and empty two bottles of morphine into her veins.

As he sat in his chair now, still staring into the fireplace, unmoving, he heard a small, soft, sliding noise. He raised his head and looked toward his door. An envelope had been pushed under it.

"Further orders," he said to himself, wondering if it would be written in German or in English. Regardless, the envelope would have no return address, no postmark. It never did.

For a few seconds, a violent anger possessed him. He stood up, shaking with rage, grabbed a vase from a table, and hurled it against a wall. It shattered explosively, raining glass everywhere.

Maud didn't matter to them. She was expendable. Bauer, Hoffman—they were expendable, too. He himself was expendable; he knew that. No one mattered to them.

"One life," they would say. "What is one life against millions?"

He had cared for this one life, though. He'd almost loved this one woman. But he realized now, as he mastered his emotion once more, that getting close to Maud, letting himself feel things for her, had been a stupid mistake—one he must be sure never to repeat. Had he not gotten so close to her, she might never have come to his room, and might never have found what she shouldn't have.

Max toed the larger shards of glass into a pile, then telephoned to the concierge to have a maid come clean the mess up. He crossed the room, picked up the envelope, and read the letter inside it. It was time to get to work again.

Maud was gone. His heart was heavy with grief for her. And he knew it didn't matter. No one's cover had been blown. That was what mattered. That was all that mattered.

Love is dangerous, he told himself now. Far too dangerous. You learned that lesson already, but you chose not to remember it.

Max walked over to the fireplace. As he fed the letter, and its envelope, into the flames, he made himself a promise never to forget again.

CHAPTER THIRTY-FOUR

SEAMIE STARED OUT of the hotel room's window. The sun was in the western sky. It was probably five o'clock already. He looked at the light coming in the window, slanting across the bed, across Willa's naked body as she lay next to him, dozing. He knew this light well now. It was the sad, gray light of unfaithfulness. Married people—

well, the happy ones, at least—did not know it. They made love in the darkness, or in the clear and hopeful light of morning.

He pulled Willa close now and kissed the top of her head. She mumbled sleepily.

"I've got to go soon, my love," he said.

Willa looked up at him. "Already?" she said.

He nodded. There was a dinner at the RGS tonight. For donors. He was expected to attend, and Jennie, too. He had told her he would be talking with possible donors all day long, and that he would meet her there, at the RGS. He wanted to get there before she did. He wanted to not give her any reason to suspect he was lying. He and Willa worried all the time that she would find out. Or that Albie would.

"Let me see your photos before I go," he said to Willa now.

"Oh, yes. The photos. Forgot about those," she said. "I forget everything when I'm with you."

He did, too. He forgot so many things he shouldn't have—that he was married, that his wife loved him, that she was carrying their child.

It can't last, this, he thought, as he watched Willa get up and shrug into her shirt. He knew it couldn't. They both did. But he couldn't bear to let it go. Not yet.

She rummaged in a large satchel she'd brought with her, then got back into bed, carrying a pile of black-and-white photographs. They were of Everest. He hadn't seen them because he hadn't gone to her lecture at the RGS. But he wanted to. Very much. He wanted to see her work, to see Everest and Rongbuk, where she lived. He'd asked her to bring them with her today.

"I'm going to use this lot in my book," she said, depositing the stack in his lap. "The text is finished. The RGS has put an editor onto the project. It should be ready to be printed in three months or so."

"That's wonderful, Willa. Congratulations," Seamie said. "I'm sure it'll be a smashing success. Let's have a look." He held up the first picture and immediately fell silent, stunned by the beauty and clarity of the photograph, by the unspeakable majesty of Everest.

"That's the north face," Willa explained. "Taken from on top of the glacier. I'd been camping there for two weeks. Trying to get a clear shot. But I couldn't. There were always clouds. On the last day, in the morning as I was making tea, the clouds suddenly broke. I knew it wouldn't last. Knew I had about thirty seconds. The camera was set up, thank God. I fumbled a plate into it, and just before the clouds closed again, I got the picture."

"It's incredible," Seamie said.

He looked at the next shot. And the next. Of the mountain and the glacier and the clouds and Rongbuk and its people. Of Lhasa. Of Everest's south face, shot from Nepal. He saw the streets of Kathmandu. Peddlers and priests. Traders coming over a treacherous pass. Imperious nobles in their tribal dress. Shy and bright-eyed children, peering out at the camera from tent doorways.

And all the while, Willa told him stories. Stories of how she got the shot. Or what the laughing priest in the photo was like. How beautiful the mayor's wife was. And what an absolute bugger the Zar Gama Pass was.

He asked about Everest, and she told him that she was convinced the south face—in Nepal—was the easier way up, but the Nepalese were not at all amenable to Westerners messing about on their mountain. The Tibetans were slightly more welcoming. Any serious European climber would have to come into Tibet from Darjeeling and attempt the north face, if a climber were to attempt the mountain at all.

"Can you imagine it?" Seamie said. "To be the first up that mountain? The first up Everest? Everyone at the RGS wants that mountain for England."

"England's going to have to move fast, then," Willa said. "Germany and France want Everest, too. Success is going to depend on preparation, not only on technical skill. Stamina, too. You've got to set up a good base camp, and then a string of camps after that. Half the party does the setting up and provisioning with the help of sherpas. Then they come down and rest, before the altitude kills them. Then the other half goes up—the best climbers. The best and the toughest. They have to get up incredibly fast, and get down just as fast. And the weather, the wind, and the temperature all have to be on their side."

She pointed out the places on the north face that she thought would be best for the camps. Seamie listened, nodded, asked her question after question. He felt excited as he had not since his expedition with Amundsen, carried away by the very idea of climbing the world's tallest mountain. For a few brief and happy moments, they were once again as they had been in Africa, when they'd traveled together, camped together, planned their assault on Kili together. They were one.

Seamie looked at her now, as she pointed out a dark spot below a col and said she couldn't work out if it was a shadow from a passing cloud or a crevasse, and his heart ached with love for her. He craved her body, thought about making love to her all the time, but he craved this—this union of their souls—even more.

He looked away, unable to bear the intensity of his longing for her, and picked up the first photograph again. "It's so beautiful," he said.

Willa shook her head. "It's beyond beautiful, Seamie. My pictures don't do it justice. They don't begin to capture the beauty of that mountain. Oh, if only you could see it. I wish I could show it to you. I wish I could see your face as you first glimpse it. I wish—"

She stopped talking suddenly.

"What? What's wrong?" he asked her.

"We never will, though, will we? See Everest together."

He looked away. The light from the window was fading. Evening was coming down. He would have to leave now. To go to the RGS, where he was expected. And then home, where he belonged.

As if sensing what he was feeling, what he was thinking, Willa leaned her head against his. "We have to stop this," she said softly.

He laughed sadly. "I would, Willa," he said. "If only I knew how."

CHAPTER THIRTY-FIVE

"THIS WILL PROVE to be the spark in the tinderbox," Churchill said hotly. "There can be no denying it."

A chorus of voices rose in enthusiastic support.

"And we can fan the spark or douse it," Joe said, just as vehemently. "This is the twentieth century, not the tenth. We must solve our disputes in staterooms, not on battlefields."

A volley of "Hear! Hear!"s went up in response.

Joe was sitting in a private room at the Reform Club, the political headquarters of the Liberal Party. He loved the venerable old building, with its marble and its mirrors, its palazzo-like gallery and impossible crystal roof, and he usually took time to admire it when he visited, lingering in its many rooms and corridors, gazing at portraits of past Whig leaders or perusing volumes in the vast library.

Tonight, however, he was in no mood to admire the architecture.

Only hours ago, Archduke Franz Ferdinand, heir to the Austro-Hungarian throne, had been assassinated, together with his wife, in Sarajevo. The royal couple's killer was a young Serbian nationalist by the name of Gavrilo Princip.

News of the archduke's death had sent shock waves of alarm through both the Commons and the Lords. The day had been dreadful, with the government publicly promising a calm and considered response to the calamitous event, and privately scrambling to head off an international disaster. Austria-Hungary had immediately demanded justice from Serbia, and Germany was raging, promising to rush to the defense of its wronged neighbor. Sir Edward Gray, Britain's secretary for foreign and commonwealth affairs, had been quickly dispatched on a diplomatic mission of the utmost delicacy.

And now, at eleven o'clock, the prime minister had adjourned to the Reform Club with members of his cabinet and a small group of key frontbenchers from all parties to discuss further response to Austria-Hungary, Serbia, and Germany.

"Sarajevo is exactly what Germany has been looking for," Churchill thundered, "and the kaiser will use it, by God. He'll use it to march right into France and trample Belgium on the way. We must inform Germany immediately and in no uncertain terms that their interference will not be tolerated in this affair."

"Can we not wait until they tell us they wish to interfere?" Joe asked, to jeers and laughter.

Winston waited until the noise died down, then he said, "The honorable member for Whitechapel is blind. He cannot see the consequences of hesitating."

"No, I cannot," Joe shot back. "I can, however, see the consequences of rushing. I can see the consequences of hotheaded, blundering responses when patience and forbearance are required. I can see the consequences of forcing Germany's hand. I can the see the bodies of hundreds of thousands of dead Englishmen."

"Can you? I cannot. I can only see the Hun defeated. Belgium spared. The women and children of France throwing flowers at our brave lads' feet."

Joe tried to respond, but his words were drowned out by cheers and calls for God to save the King. He gave up. He recognized war fever when he saw it. He turned to Asquith, who was seated at his right, and said, "Henry, you can see what's coming, can't you? You must do all that you can to hold out against the dogs of war."

Asquith shook his head slowly. "I can control my own dogs, Joe—even that hothead Winston. What I cannot control is the pack across the channel."

"You think it's unavoidable, then?"

"I do. We will go to war. All of Europe will," he said. "It's no longer a case of if, but of when."

"I don't believe that, Henry. I can't."

Asquith sighed deeply. "Believe what you like, Joe. But be glad your sons are too young to fight and pray that it all ends quickly."

CHAPTER THIRTY-SIX

MAX STEPPED OUTSIDE of the elevator into the Coburg's sumptuous lobby. He thanked the operator, smiled at a woman waiting to enter the elevator, and made his way to the front desk. His tanned, handsome face looked smooth and untroubled.

Only because he wanted it to.

Inside, he was jittery and rattled. His nerves were frayed. Everything was going badly. Bauer, Hoffman, Maud . . . and now this new catastrophe—Sarajevo.

He had just received orders from Berlin, brought to his room hidden in a stack of freshly laundered shirts by a hotel maid on the kaiser's payroll. They wanted as much information as he could possibly get them on British ships, planes, and cannon—and what could he get them? Not a bloody thing.

The chain was still broken, and until he could forge a link between Gladys Bigelow and John Harris—Billy Madden's man—he had no way of fixing it. What had that lunatic in Sarajevo been thinking? What had he and his fellow anarchists hoped to do? Set the world on fire? If that was the goal, they might well succeed.

Lost in his thoughts, Max did not the see the woman walking toward him, her head down, until it was too late. He collided with her, knocking her hat and her purse to the ground.

"My goodness," he said, horrified. "How incredibly clumsy of me. I'm so sorry. Please let me get your things." He bent down, picked up the hat and purse, and handed them to her. "Again, please accept my . . ." He stopped talking, stunned. He took a step back, recovered himself, and said, "Willa Alden? Is that you?"

Willa looked up at him. "Max? Max von Brandt?"

"Yes!" he said excitedly. "What a pleasure it is to see you." He embraced her, then released her and looked at her, shaking his head. "I hardly recognize you in your Western outfit," he said.

Willa laughed. "I hardly recognize myself. You're looking well, Max. What are you doing in London? The last time I saw you, you were headed to Lhasa."

"Yes, I was. I got there, too. And was granted an audience with the Dalai Lama, thanks to your influence," he said. He then explained the falling out he'd had with his uncle, and that he'd come to London to get away from his family for a bit. "You look well, too, Willa," he said, when he'd finished. "What are you doing here? I didn't think anything could tempt you away from your mountain."

Willa told him about her father.

"I'm so sorry," he said, taking her hand and squeezing it.

She squeezed back. "Thank you, Max. That's very kind of you," she said. "It's still so hard for me to accept that he's gone."

They talked more, and as Max looked into her large, expressive eyes and listened to her voice, so full of life, everything he'd felt for her in the Himalayas came flooding back. His heart was full of emotion. He wanted to take her in his arms, right here in the lobby, to hold her close and tell her what he felt.

Stop it. Now. Before it goes too far, a voice inside him said. It's too dangerous. You know that. This woman, these feelings . . . they'll be the end of you.

He ignored the voice. As Willa started to say good-bye, as she told him she must be going, he pressed her to stay.

"But you haven't even told me what you're doing here," he asked her. "What brings you to the Coburg?"

"I'm . . . um . . . I'm meeting an old friend," she said. "For lunch."

She was lying; he knew she was. She suddenly seemed agitated and nervous. Max was experienced in identifying the tells that betrayed liars—the too-quick laugh, the darting eyes, the rising voice—and Willa was exhibiting all of them.

"Join me for a drink first," Max said. "You must. I insist. And your friend, too. Where is she?"

"I . . . I'm afraid I can't. I'm meeting her in her room, you see, and I'm late as it is."

"I understand," he said. "But you must give me your address, and you must allow me to take you to supper while you're in London."

Willa looked at him, her green eyes frank and appraising. "I don't know if that's such a good idea, Max," she said.

Max held his hands up, stopping her protests. "It will just be two old trekking companions catching up, that's all. I promise you, I've no ulterior motives," he said, smiling warmly.

Willa smiled back. "All right, then," she said. "Supper it is. I look forward to it."

"Tomorrow?"

"I can't tomorrow, I'm afraid. I already have plans. I'm meeting Thomas Lawrence."

"Ah, yes. The archaeologist. I've heard of him. Sounds like a fascinating chap. How about next week, then?"

They set a date—Monday—and a place—Simpson's. Then he kissed her cheek and walked her to the elevator. The smell of her, the marble smoothness of her cheek thrilled him. How did she do this to him?

"Good-bye, Willa," he said, working to keep his voice even. "Until Monday."

"Until Monday," she said, and then the elevator doors closed.

He stood there, watching the hand on the floor indicator until it stopped on five. Another elevator had just stopped next to this one. The doors opened. The occupants stepped out and Max quickly stepped in.

"Hold the door!" a man bellowed from across the lobby.

"Ignore him," Max said, handing the operator a pound note. "Get me to five. Now."

The man did as he was told, whisking Max to the fifth floor in seconds. He stepped out quietly, in case she was nearby, and the elevator doors closed silently behind him. He looked left, then right, and spotted Willa walking down a long corridor. Her back was to him. He pressed himself against the elevator doors in case she turned around. But she did not. She stopped halfway down the corridor, turned to her right, and knocked twice on a door. The door opened and she stepped inside. As soon as Max heard it close and lock behind her, he made his way down the corridor.

She had come here to be with a man. Max felt it in his bones. Why else would she have acted the way she did—so odd and skittish? Jealousy seared him. He knew it was a childish and stupid emotion, and he tried to damp it down, but he could not. He wanted her for himself and hated to think of her in the arms of another man, but at the same time, he had to know who the other man was. He reached the door that she'd entered, glanced quickly at the number, and kept on walking. To the end of the corridor and the fire stairs.

When he was back downstairs in the lobby, he collared a bellhop, a lad he'd tipped generously on many occasions. "I need you to do me a favor," he said quietly.

"Anything, Mr. von Brandt."

"Find out the name of the man in room 524. I'll be over there." He pointed to a group of plush chairs.

The bellhop nodded. A few minutes later, he was standing by Max's chair, bending to his ear. "It's a Mr. O. Ryan, sir," he said. "But I think that's a false name."

"Is it?"

"Aye. Pete, my mate, gave the bloke his key. Said he knew him instantly and he wasn't no Mr. Ryan."

"Who is he, then?"

"He's that famous explorer. The one who went to the South Pole. Finnegan's his name. Seamus Finnegan."

CHAPTER THIRTY-SEVEN

"I COULD EAT every berry in Binsey, me," Josie said, plucking another strawberry from her basket and popping it into her mouth. "Blimey, but they're good."

"If you don't stop, we'll have nothing for our tea," Jennie said, laughing. "We haven't even got ourselves outside of the village yet. Wait until we get back to the cottage before you eat any more."

They had just come from the village square, where a market was held every Monday. They'd bought strawberries freshly picked that morning, a pint of clotted cream, rich and crumbly scones, a wedge of sharp cheddar, another of Caerphilly, a loaf of brown bread, some smoked trout, and a pound of pale yellow butter.

Jennie knew she would only pick at the feast, for her stomach was upset most of the time now. Josie, on the other hand, would devour it. She had not been troubled by nausea in the least and was hungry all the time.

Jennie looked at her as they walked along. Josie was the picture of health. Her cheeks were pink and her eyes were sparkling. Her belly had already begun to pop out. Jennie, whose due date was three weeks later than Josie's, had not begun to show. She couldn't wait until she did. It would make it more real. It would show her—and Seamie, too—that the baby was healthy and growing. She had just seen Harriet Hatcher last week and was due to see her again in a few days' time. Harriet said that she'd heard a heartbeat and that so far all seemed well, but she'd still reminded Jennie of the delicate nature of her pregnancy and cautioned her against too much hope.

"What shall we do today?" Josie asked, swinging her basket. "Pick flowers? Make jam? God knows we bought enough berries. I know! Let's go to the river and dip our toes in. It's already beastly hot and it's only nine o'clock."

"The river . . . that sounds like a wonderful idea," Jennie said. It *was* hot, far too hot for June. Jennie was perspiring heavily. Her cheeks were flushed. A wade in the river would be just the thing to cool them both off. "Let's just put the marketing away, and then we'll go."

Jennie had come up from London the day before. It was her third trip to Binsey in two months. She'd told Seamie, yet again, that she needed some quiet time—time to rest and relax. He had been agreeable to the trip and had not questioned her or protested.

But then again, why would he? Her absence meant he could spend more time with Willa Alden.

Jennie didn't know where he was seeing her, or when, because he was always home at night, but she knew in her heart that he was.

He was always preoccupied now. He spent more time in his study. And even when he was in the very same room with her, he was miles away. He was still kind to her, though—solicitous of her health, concerned about the baby, anxious that she was overtaxing herself. But he didn't kiss her much anymore. Not like he used to. And at night, in their bed, he would turn out the light, roll on his side, and go right to sleep. They hadn't made love in weeks. She had tried to interest him a few times, but he had said they shouldn't. He didn't want to do anything to hurt the baby.

She thought of them together sometimes, Seamie and Willa—she couldn't help it. In her mind's eye, she saw him in bed with her, saw him kissing her and caressing her, and the images made her feel sick. There were days when she was so distraught that she vowed she would confront him. She would ask him about Willa. Ask him if they'd been together, if he was still in love with her.

But what would she do if he said, *Yes, Jennie, I am?*

And so she pretended. She pretended to him that she didn't know. Pretended to herself that she didn't care. That it didn't matter. And she hoped and prayed that one day it wouldn't. That one day soon, Willa would leave London and go back to the East. And that

Seamie would come back to her, Jennie. To their home. Their life. Their bed.

"We could go fishing," Josie said suddenly, as they passed a small sporting goods shop. "I saw fishing rods in the coat closet."

Jennie laughed, grateful for Josie's companionship, for her cheerfulness, and for the distraction Josie provided from her own dark thoughts.

"Yes, we could," she said. "If either one of us knew the first thing about fishing."

"All we would need are some worms," Josie said. "And hooks. We could get the hooks here. Right inside this shop."

"And line. I think we need some sort of fishing line. I think we need . . ." Jennie gasped suddenly, as a pain—dark and horrible—gripped her deep inside.

"Jennie? What is it?" Josie asked.

"Nothing, I . . ." She stopped talking as another cramp, stronger than the one before, shuddered through her.

She took a few more steps, and then she felt something warm and wet between her legs. It was coming out of her, seeping into her underthings. She didn't have to see it to know what it was—blood.

"Oh, no," she said, in a small, scared voice. "Please, no."

"Jennie," Josie said, her eyes large and worried. "What's wrong?"

"I think it's the baby . . . I . . . I'm bleeding," Jennie said. She started to cry.

"Come on," Josie said, taking her arm. "There's a surgery at the edge of the village. It's not far. Dr. Cobb's the man's name. I saw the shingle once. When I first got here. I made a point to remember it. Just in case something happened and I needed someone. It's not far."

"No!" Jennie said, shaking Josie off. "I'm not going to any doctor."

"Are you mad? You need help. The baby needs help."

"I won't go," Jennie said. "He can't know. Nobody can know."

"Who can't know?" Josie asked. "The doctor?"

"Seamie. My husband. He can't know," Jennie said, her voice rising. She was becoming hysterical, she couldn't help it. "If the cramps don't stop, if I keep bleeding," she said wildly, "I'll lose the baby, and him, too."

Josie looked at her with pity and understanding. "That's how it is between you, eh?" she said softly.

"Yes, that's how it is," Jennie said miserably. She didn't want to be telling Josie these things, but she couldn't seem to stop herself. "He's got someone . . . another woman. And all I've got is this baby. It's the only thing keeping him with me. I'm sure of it."

Josie nodded. "All right, luv. Calm down. Nobody's losing anybody," she said. Her voice was soothing, but her eyes were hard and determined. "We won't tell Seamie about this, right? Because they'll be nothing to tell. But we are going to see Dr. Cobb now. If you want those cramps to stop, we've got to see him. We'll just nip in, you and I. He'll check you over and give you something, and half an hour from now, you'll be right as rain again. Here we go now, you and me . . . just a few more steps . . . come on now, duck."

Josie took her arm once more and Jennie started walking again, desperately hoping that her friend was right, that there was something Dr. Cobb could do to stop the bleeding and the pain, but then another cramp gripped her.

"Oh, God," she sobbed. "It's no use, Josie. I'm going to lose this baby."

"Now, you listen to me," Josie said fiercely. "I'll sort it for you, Jennie, don't you worry. I'll take care of you. I'll take care of everything."

"How, Josie?" Jennie sobbed. "How? You can't! No one can!"

"Oh, but I can. You'd have to be a right git to have spent as much time around villains as I have and not pick up a trick or two," she said.

"I . . . I don't understand," Jennie said.

"You don't have to. All you have to do is remember something when we get to Dr. Cobb's. Just one small thing. Can you do that for me, Jennie? Jennie, luv, can you do that?"

"Yes," Jennie said. "What is it?"

"That my name is Jennie Finnegan," Josie said. "And that yours is Josie. Josie Meadows."

CHAPTER THIRTY-EIGHT

"HARRIET, MY DEAR," Max said, as he entered her office.

"My, goodness, Max. Is it noon already?" Harriet Hatcher asked, looking up from a patient's file. She closed the file. Her expression was troubled. "Sit down, won't you? Just clear the things off that chair."

Max did so, shifting a copy of the *Battle Cry* and a VOTES FOR WOMEN banner from the chair to a credenza. "How goes the struggle?" he asked.

"Well, and not so well," Harriet said. "You heard about the by-election in Cumbria, I'm sure. Labour won a seat that had long been held by the Liberals. So there's another MP sympathetic to our cause, which is wonderful, of course. . . ."

"But . . ." Max prompted.

"There's always a but, isn't there?" Harriet said wryly. "In this case, the but is the sudden bout of war fever that's gripped government. We in the movement fear that the push for women's suffrage will take a backseat to military concerns."

"Even if it does," Max said, "you must keep fighting."

Harriet nodded, a determined smile on her face now. "Oh, we will. Millicent Fawcett is like a glacier—slow but implacable. There is no stopping her. She will not give up and neither will the rest of us."

"Then you must be well fortified for the fight," Max said. "Where shall we dine tonight? I was thinking of the Eastern."

"It's a bit far and I don't have long today. I've lots of appointments to get through this afternoon. What about something closer? There's a nice pub only a street away."

Max feigned interest in her suggestions, pretending he was game for anything, but really, the very last thing he wanted to be doing right now was swanning off to lunch.

A war of words was heating up between Austria-Hungary and Serbia. The kaiser had signaled his readiness to jump into the fray. Berlin was waiting on Max for crucial information, and yet he could get nothing to them, for he still could not come up with a way to get the documents from Gladys Bigelow to the North Sea.

He had risked one meeting with her, on her bus, to tell her to keep bringing carbons out of Burgess's office, but to hold them in her home for now, until she received further instructions. There were times when he'd felt so desperate, he'd nearly decided to put on his old disguise, the one he'd used to seduce Gladys, and get the papers from her himself. But he knew that would be foolish. He must not be seen in those clothes anywhere near Duffin's again.

Max knew he had to be patient, as hard as that was. He had always dined with Harriet on Thursdays, and so he must continue to dine with Harriet on Thursdays. He must appear to be as predictable as the English rain after the disaster with Bauer and Hoffman, and the one with Maud, in case he was now being watched.

"And there's always the Moskowitzes' cafe, of course," Harriet said. "What do you think of that? Max? Max?"

"I think it's a fine idea," he said quickly, hoping she hadn't noticed that he'd been miles away.

"Good," Harriet said. She closed the file she'd been reading and put it on top of a stack of folders on her desk. He glanced at the name on the file—Jennie Finnegan. "Suzanne!" she called out.

A few seconds later, Harriet's receptionist stuck her head in. Harriet handed her the stack of folders. "After you go to lunch, could you file these, please?" she asked. "But don't file the three on top— Mrs. Finnegan's, Mrs. Erikson's, and Mrs. O'Rourke's. Put those in my briefcase. They're all coming in for appointments tomorrow, and I want to study my notes at home tonight." Suzanne nodded, took the stack of folders, and returned to her office.

Max had seen the slight frown on Harriet's face as she'd read Jennie Finnegan's file. Her reaction piqued his interest, accustomed as he was to reading people's facial cues. Something in Jennie Finnegan's file was especially bothering her. He remembered seeing Willa at the Coburg—how could he forget?—and discovering that it was Seamus Finnegan—Jennie's husband—whom she'd gone there to see. He wondered what it was that was troubling Harriet about Jennie, and he wondered if it had any connection to what was going on at the Coburg. He decided to press Harriet, ever so subtly, to see if he could find out more. Other people's private matters often proved useful.

"Mrs. Finnegan . . . ," he said now. "Would that be the former Jennie Wilcott? I haven't seen her, or her husband, since their wedding. What a lovely bride she was. What a perfect day that was. Blue skies. Flowers. All of us together. Who would think that only weeks later . . ." He let his voice trail off, swallowed hard, then picked up a wooden rattle that was lying on Harriet's desk and fiddled with it.

Harriet reached across her desk and covered his hand with her own. "It's not your fault, Max. You know that. Everyone knows that."

He nodded, then said, "We should talk of happier things." He held up the rattle, shook it, and smiled. "Like babies. What could be happier than a baby? Jennie and her husband must be very excited to have a little one due soon. How is she? Is she well?"

"As far as I know, yes," Harriet said, a bit distractedly.

What an odd answer, Max thought, but he decided to push it no further. He knew Harriet was a stickler for doctor-patient confidentiality. He didn't want to make her uncomfortable. Or suspicious.

"Perhaps we should get going," he said. "Before Moskowitzes' gets crowded."

"Yes, I think we should. Let's have a glass of wine while we're there, Max, shall we? Let's forget about struggles and sadnesses for an hour. Excuse me for a moment. I'm just going to go freshen up," Harriet said, disappearing down the hall.

As soon as he heard the door to the loo open and close, Max rushed out of Harriet's office and into her receptionist's, hoping that the woman had already gone to lunch. Luckily, she had—and she'd left all the folders Harriet had given her on her desk. Jennie Finnegan's was on top. Max flipped it open and began to read its contents.

He learned that Jennie Wilcott Finnegan's due date was a bit less than eight months after her wedding. Eight, not the usual nine. Furthermore, he learned that she had been horribly injured in an accident as a child, an accident that had damaged several of her organs, including her uterus. There were diagrams of Jennie's scars, sketches of what looked to him like a misshapen womb. There was a note that Jennie was taking time to rest quietly at her cottage in Binsey, Oxfordshire.

And finally, Max learned that his cousin, Dr. Harriet Hatcher, did not expect Jennie's due date to be reached. She had written in her notes that she did not believe the pregnancy would advance to full-term and that she had counseled Jennie on this very concern, telling her that she should prepare herself for the very real possibility of a miscarriage.

As Max put the folder back exactly as he'd found it and hurried back into Harriet's office, he found himself feeling newly optimistic.

He'd learned so many valuable things in the past few days—and they all centered on Jennie Finnegan, the Reverend Wilcott's daughter. He'd learned that she was pregnant before she was married, that she would likely never have the child she was carrying, and that her husband was making secret trips to the Coburg, where he was meeting Willa Alden. It was true—people's private matters *did* prove useful.

"Are you ready?" Harriet asked, as she walked back into her office.

"I am," he said, rising from the chair.

He helped Harriet into her coat—a linen duster—and complimented her on her hat, a pretty straw affair trimmed with silk flowers. When they got outside, they discovered that it had started to drizzle. Max quickly put his umbrella up and took Harriet's arm.

"Of course," she sighed. "How perfect. Dreary skies to match our dreary moods. I think we should cheer up, Max. What do you say? I think we should endeavor to enjoy our afternoon despite the gray clouds."

"Ah, my dear, Harriet," Max said, smiling, "I'm enjoying it already."

CHAPTER THIRTY-NINE

JOSIE PUT ANOTHER shovelful of coal on the fire. The summer evening had turned cool. She stoked the flames until they were burning brightly, leaned the shovel against the wall, and turned to look at her friend.

Jennie was sitting in a nearby chair. Her eyes were open, but dull. Her face was gray. She had stopped weeping—that was something—but now she just sat lifelessly, staring into the fire, not speaking.

The little life inside her had died this morning. And it seemed to Josie as if Jennie had died along with it. She was wrung out. Empty. A shell. There was no spark left in her.

It hurt Josie terribly to see her this way. Jennie had been like a second mother to her. She'd made sure Josie had learned how to read and write. She'd coached her on how to speak properly. At least, she'd tried to. She'd encouraged her love of music and singing. When Josie's father drank his wages, leaving nothing for food, Jennie had fed her. When he came home from the pub and started hammering on Josie's mother, and Josie ran away because she could not bear it, Jennie had taken her in and let her sleep in her bed.

Jennie was the only reason Josie was on stage. She'd saved her, years ago, from a life of drudgery in the factories of Wapping or Whitechapel, and she'd saved her again, just a few weeks ago, when Madden had put her up the pole. There wasn't anything Josie wouldn't do for Jennie—if only Jennie would let her.

Josie took a deep breath now and pulled a wooden chair over to where Jennie was sitting. She sat down in it, so close to Jennie that their knees were touching, then she took Jennie's hands in hers and said, "We can do this. I know we can. The two of us together."

Jennie shook her head. "It'll never work," she said.

"Yes, it will. If we want it to. If *you* want it to."

Jennie said nothing, but her eyes flickered from the fire to Josie's face and back to the fire again. Josie took this as a hopeful sign.

She'd hatched a plan—a plan that was clever and perfect. She'd thought it up as she was rushing Jennie into Dr. Cobb's, and then she'd refined it that afternoon, after she'd got Jennie home from the doctor's and into bed. She'd made herself a pot of tea, sat down at the kitchen table, and thought the whole thing through once more, carefully and slowly, testing it for flaws, just as she'd seen Madden and his men do when they were planning some new piece of villainy.

Only this wasn't villainy. This plan wouldn't hurt anyone. It would only help.

Jennie, out of her mind with both grief and laudanum, had told Josie everything after they'd come home from Dr. Cobb's. She told her about the accident and how it meant she couldn't have children. She told her about meeting Seamus Finnegan and falling in love with him and marrying him without having told him the truth about herself. And she told her about Willa Alden.

Josie knew her plan would solve both Jennie's problems and her own, but she hadn't been able to convince Jennie of that. She'd tried to explain it to her earlier, but Jennie, distraught and inconsolable, refused to listen, telling her it was impossible. Josie decided now to try one more time.

"The hardest bit's already taken care of, the rest will be a doddle," she said. "Dr. Cobb thinks you're Josie Meadows and I'm Jennie

Finnegan. He's written it all down and has his notes all safely tucked away in a file."

Josie had done all the talking at Dr. Cobb's. She'd told him that her friend Mrs. Meadows was visiting her at her cottage for the week and had started experiencing terrible pains.

It hadn't taken Dr. Cobb long to confirm Jennie's greatest fear— that she was indeed miscarrying her baby. He did only a cursory exam, gave her laudanum, and told her to expect cramping and bleeding for the next few hours, as her uterus expelled its contents. He told her that this was an unfortunate occurrence, but not an uncommon one, and that she would surely conceive again within the year.

"All we have to do now is go on exactly as we have been," Josie said to her.

"How, Josie? I lost the baby. Even if I don't tell a soul, everyone will know. My belly won't be growing," Jennie said.

"Yes, it will. Because you'll stuff a pillow under your skirt."

Jennie shook her head. "Josie, it's impossible. It won't work," she said.

"No, listen to me! It *will* work. We do it all the time at the music hall. For a gag. A girl goes off stage left, hand in hand with some rake, then comes back stage right crying and carrying on with a big fat belly. You start with a small pillow and change it for bigger ones as the weeks go by. I'll show you how to do it. The only tricky part will be your husband. If he wants relations, I mean. You'll have to put him off. Say you're poorly and it's bad for the baby. Doctor's orders."

"That won't be a problem at all," Jennie said bitterly. "My husband doesn't want relations. Not with me, at least."

"All right, then. So that part won't be hard. You keep the act going for a few months, and you come here when you need to take a break from it. In a few months, my baby comes. Dr. Cobb delivers it and writes out a birth certificate for baby Finnegan. Just make sure to figure out a name well in advance, right? I'll get word to you when the baby arrives. You come to Binsey immediately. You don't write home for a day or two, then you ring your husband from the pub, tell him what's happened—that you stumbled and fell, and your pains came on, and the baby came a little earlier than expected. He'll probably throw a wobbly and say that he wants to come to Binsey straightaway to collect you, but you tell him that the baby came easily and that you feel fine, and that you've engaged a girl from the village to travel to London with you and help you with your bags."

"A girl from the village? What girl?" Jennie asked.

"Me, of course," Josie said. "I'll get some sort of frumpy farm girl outfit together, put on a bonnet, and ride to London with you. I've never met your husband, so he won't know who I really am. There's always a chance he saw the *Zema* posters, but I had a wig on in those and not much else. I'm sure he wouldn't recognize me. Before you ring off, you tell him what time the train's arriving at Paddington and ask him to collect you. He does. I say hello and good-bye, then pretend I'm getting on a return train to Binsey, get on a train to the coast instead, and then on the ferry to Calais."

Josie paused to let her words sink in, then she said, "When your husband sees his baby, the baby he wanted so much, he'll be happy, and maybe he'll remember his wedding vows. And then you've got your child and your husband. And I escape to Paris, far away from Billy Madden, knowing my child won't grow up in some horrible orphanage, that she will grow up with the best woman in the world for a mother."

"Do you really think it could work?" Jennie said, her voice a whisper.

"I do."

"What if the baby looks nothing like me? Or Seamie?"

"We're both blond, you and I," Josie said. "And we both have hazel eyes. So if the baby looks like me, she'll look like you, too."

"It's ever so risky. So much could go wrong," Jennie said.

"No, luv," Josie said. "So much could go right."

Jennie looked Josie in the eye then, and for the first time since they left the market, Josie saw a spark there—faint and struggling, but a spark nonetheless. "Well?" she said hopefully, squeezing her friend's hands.

Jennie nodded, and squeezed back.

CHAPTER FORTY

"GOOD NIGHT, MR. Bristow. Safe trip home," Sir David Erskine, sergeant at arms for the House of Commons, said to Joe.

"Good night to you as well, Sergeant," Joe said, as he wheeled himself down St. Stephen's Hall, out the door, and toward Cromwell Green.

Outside, the air was soft and warm and the sky twinkled with a million stars. It was a beautiful summer night—a night to make anyone feel glad to be alive. But Joe didn't even notice it. He'd just come from another late session in the Commons. Earlier that day, Austria-Hungary had declared war on Serbia. Fearing the worst—Germany's imminent involvement—a wary Britain was now in constant contact with France and Russia, its Triple Entente allies, trying to determine a plan of containment should the kaiser actually declare war. Fortunately, the *Entente* had been put in place long before Franz Ferdinand's assassination.

France, who'd suffered a bruising defeat in the Franco-Prussian War of 1870 and had seen her territories of Alsace-Lorraine annexed to Germany, had aligned with Russia at the end of the last century, both countries finding common ground in their shared mistrust of the kaiser. Russia was especially concerned about Germany's warm relationship with Turkey. The tsar feared that if Germany gained a foothold in Turkey, the kaiser would try to take control of the Dardanelles and Bosporus straits—waterways that connected the Mediterranean to the Black Sea and which were crucial to Russia's ability to trade with the rest of the world.

Britain—already aligned with France as the result of the Entente Cordiale, a treaty signed in 1904 after both countries had settled their skirmishes over colonial territories in Africa—saw an alliance with Russia as also advantageous, and so the Anglo-Russian Entente had been signed in 1907. Britain had pledged to come to the defense of both France and Russia should they be threatened by Germany, and they had pledged the same for her.

In addition to strategizing with his country's allies, the prime minister had also approached Britain's own Field Marshal Horatio Kitchener—a soldier and statesman who'd distinguished himself on several major battlefields—and asked him to become secretary of state for war.

Joe had spoken with Kitchener and had learned that, unlike many of Asquith's advisors, the field marshal did not expect a war with Germany to be quickly fought and won. On the contrary, he had made the dire and unpopular prediction that such a war would last at least three years and would result in enormous casualties—a prediction that gave Joe renewed energy with which to argue against the warmongers in the Commons.

But his arguments were all to no avail. Joe could see that. Everyone could. Kitchener himself had come up to Joe in the Commons dining room, after he had spent the day giving a speech in the House and listening to many more. "Save your breath, old chap," he'd counseled Joe. "It doesn't matter what I say. It wouldn't matter what God said, had He the patience to sit in the Commons and endure Churchill's endless harangues. They will have their war."

It would be soon, Kitchener felt. Perhaps as soon as the coming autumn.

Weary and dispirited now, Joe wheeled himself across Cromwell Green to the line of carriages waiting just past it on the street. He saw his carriage in the queue and knew that Tom, his driver, would be nearby—fetching water for the horses or talking to one of the other drivers. As Joe drew up to his carriage, he saw a flower girl walking up and down the queue, trying to sell bouquets of roses. She was having little luck.

Joe stopped to watch her. He watched as people walked by her, deaf to her entreaties, blind to the holes in her shoes and the hollows in her cheeks. And he felt as if his heart was breaking. For he knew that while this child—she couldn't have been more than ten years old—walked the dark streets of London, desperately trying to make a few bob, men who had been raised in great homes and palaces, who had all the privileges wealth and power conferred, swept their make-believe armies across maps of the world. While she shivered and pulled her threadbare shawl around her thin shoulders, they poured more port into their crystal glasses and lit cigars.

They thought of borders broken and territories taken, these men. They thought of victories won and of medals gleaming, but they did not think—not once—of the struggle this child endured, every day, to simply survive. And they did not think to wonder what would become of this child and of every child like her, poor children in every town and every village in Britain and Europe, if they lost their fathers to bullets, their houses to cannons, their fields and animals to the pillaging of foreign invaders.

It was this child I fought for, Joe said to himself. And it's this child I've failed.

He wanted to go to her now. He wanted to tell her that he'd tried. But she would think him mad if he did that. So instead he wheeled himself over to her and told her that he wanted to buy all her flowers, everything she had.

"What? All of them?" she asked, stunned.

"Yes," Joe said. He turned to Tom, who had joined him now. "Tom, could you put these in the carriage, please?"

"Right away, sir," Tom replied, picking up the child's heavy basket.

Joe gave the child more than the price of the flowers. "You keep the extra for yourself," he said.

"Thank you, sir! Oh, thank you!"

"You're welcome," Joe replied.

Tom gave the child her basket back, and Joe watched as she hurried off, her money still clutched in her hand.

"That was good of you, sir. To help that child," Tom said.

"I didn't help her, Tom," Joe said. "A year from now, she'll likely be worse off than she is. With her father at the front. Her brothers, too, if she has any. Men earn a lot more than women do. It'll be her and her mum and her sisters, all shifting for themselves on factory wages and what they can make selling flowers. Poor little thing should be in school, learning how to read and write. Not out on the streets at all hours."

"Can't fix the entire world, sir. Not even you. Not tonight, leastways," Tom said.

Joe watched the child as she turned the corner and disappeared into the night. "Ah, Tom," he said, shaking his head. "Why did I tell her 'You're welcome'? When I should've told her 'I'm sorry.'"

CHAPTER FORTY-ONE

MAX VON BRANDT loved churches.

Churches were quiet and peaceful. Sometimes they had magnificent works of art to look at or wonderful choirs to listen to. But what he loved best about churches was that they were full of good people and good people were so easily used.

He opened the door of St. Nicholas's, in Wapping, removed his hat, and went inside. He moved quietly through the foyer into the nave. The church was empty, except for one person—a young blond woman. Gladys Bigelow had told him the woman would be here, that she cleaned the altar and brought fresh flowers for it every Wednesday.

She wasn't cleaning now, though. She was kneeling in a church pew near a statue of the Virgin Mary, her blond head bent, praying. He could see her belly, looking rounder. How interesting. It had not looked that way last week, when he'd seen her hanging out the washing at the back of her cottage at Binsey.

Max had decided to take a look around the village after learning from notes Harriet had written in her file that Jennie was staying there. He'd had to stay out of sight for most of the time he was there—skulking in the woods behind the cottage during the day, listening at the window at night, cooling his heels in his room at the pub—but even so, it had been such a productive trip. He'd discovered so much.

As he stood patiently now, waiting for Jennie to finish her prayers, he heard a sob escape her. And then another. She was weeping. Max was certain he knew why. He was certain, too, that her tears—and the reason behind them—would make his present task easier.

My God, he thought watching her, what havoc love wreaks. What damage it does. And had done. To Gladys Bigelow. Maud. Jennie. To Seamie. And Willa. And to him.

Even he had not escaped love's destruction, try as he might. He'd had his dinner with Willa. She had been friendly and lovely, but that was all, for she was in love with another man. And he? He had sat next to her for two hours, tortured the whole time by his feelings for her—feelings he knew she did not return. Afterward, he had made a vow, again, never to be so dangerously moved by his emotions.

He walked up the aisle to where Jennie was seated. "Mrs. Finnegan?" he said, gently touching her arm.

Jennie quickly sat up and wiped her eyes. "Mr. von Brandt . . . this . . . this is very unexpected," she stammered.

"Forgive me, Mrs. Finnegan, I didn't mean to disturb you. I tried the rectory first, but no one was there," Max said. He paused, then hesitatingly continued, "It grieves me to see you so upset. If I may be so bold . . . what is troubling you? Tell me. Perhaps I can be of help."

"Nothing. Nothing at all, really," Jennie said, trying hard to smile.

"It's my condition, I'm afraid. It makes me rather prone to moods and tears."

Max looked down at his hat. He fingered its brim, then said, "I don't believe you, Mrs. Finnegan." He looked up again and said, "Is it Willa Alden?"

Jennie paled. She looked as if she wanted to be sick. "Willa?" she said, working to keep her voice even. "No. Of course not. Why do you ask?"

Max affected a flustered look. "No reason," he said. "I misspoke. Please forgive me."

But Jennie pressed him, as he'd known she would, until finally, with feigned reluctance, he said, "I thought you knew. I shouldn't have said anything. It's just that I was so certain that's why you were crying."

"Mr. von Brandt . . . please," Jennie said, her voice strained. She made room for him in the pew, and he sat down next to her. "What do you know about Willa Alden?"

"I know that Willa and your husband are having an affair," Max said. Jennie said nothing. It was very quiet inside the church. Max could hear horses clopping past the open window, hear their traces jingling and their driver shouting at someone to get out of his way. "I'm sorry," he said.

Jennie nodded. She sat back in the pew. Then she put her head in her hands and wept again. Max patted her hand. He waited until she composed herself, then he said, "I'm sure that I can help you."

"How?" Jennie asked miserably.

"I'm acquainted with Miss Alden. I may be able to prevail upon her to stop seeing your husband."

Jennie laughed unhappily. "But will my husband stop seeing her?" she said.

"I will convince her to leave London."

"She might not wish to."

"I think she will."

He knew she would. He'd met Willa's brother at Jennie and Seamie's wedding. Albie was still in London. Max would contrive to meet him, seemingly by chance, and make sure to mention that he'd bumped into both his sister and his good friend Seamus at the Coburg recently.

Jennie looked at Max with anguished eyes now. "If you could do that, Mr. von Brandt, if you could get Willa to leave London, I would be forever in your debt." She wiped her eyes again, and then, as if remembering herself, she said, "I'm certain you did not come here today with the intention of discussing my marital problems."

Max smiled. "No, I didn't actually. I came here to ask for your help."

Jennie looked surprised. "I cannot imagine how I could be of help to you, Mr. von Brandt."

"It's very simple," he said. "I need you to help me pass along some information. Some rather crucial information. If you decide to help me, every fortnight Gladys Bigelow will give you an envelope containing documents. She will do this at your women's suffrage meetings. You would bring them here to the church during your Wednesday visits. You would go into the church, just as you always do, then go down to the basement. There's a statue of St. Nicholas down there. It's broken. All you would have to do is put the envelope inside the statue's head."

Jennie's expression changed from one of surprise to one of anger. "Do you take me for a fool, Mr. von Brandt?" she said.

"I do not," Max said.

"I know where Gladys works," Jennie said. "And for whom she works. What will be in those envelopes? Secrets? Information for your government?"

Max had anticipated this question and was prepared for it.

"Forgeries will be in those envelopes, Mrs. Finnegan," he said earnestly. "Fake travel papers, fake histories. Fake work contracts. Fake lives. They are to be delivered to dissidents in Germany— high-ranking professors, scientists, and ministers—pacifists all. Men who have been vocal critics of Germany's militarization. We are trying to help them and their families get out. Now. Before it's too late. We've already lost some. A physicist, a professor at one of our universities, tried to leave the country two days ago. His papers were confiscated. No one has heard from him or seen him since. Two ministers were jailed last week for speaking out against war. We are doing our best to get to them quickly, but sometimes we are not quick enough."

"Who is 'we'?"

"Britain's Secret Service. I am a spy, Mrs. Finnegan. A double agent. The kaiser thinks I am working for Germany. I am not. I am working against her. Germany is trying to start a war. An unjust war. I am doing all I can to stop it."

Jennie looked as if she was wavering, just a little. "And Gladys . . . is she a willing participant in this?" she asked.

"She is," Max replied. "But you must never discuss it with her. You must simply accept the envelope she gives you, put it in your own bag, and then bring it to St. Nicholas's basement. Everyone is watched. Gladys, too."

"But why me?" Jennie asks. "Why couldn't you get someone else?"

"Because you had the misfortune to be perfectly placed."

"I don't understand."

"We needed a friend of Gladys Bigelow's, someone whom Gladys sees regularly and has for years. If Gladys suddenly changed her daily patterns—if she suddenly started meeting a new person and traveling to a new place to do so—it would raise suspicions."

"Whose suspicions?"

"My fellow spies. Both British and German. There are double-agents everywhere. There are British agents who are feeding secrets to Germany as we speak. For money. If they figure out what Gladys is doing, the people we're trying to help are lost."

"Surely Gladys has other friends besides me," Jennie says.

"Yes, of course, but none with ties to this church. There is a network of tunnels under Wapping, Mrs. Finnegan. And under St. Nicholas's. Our man will be using them to move the documents. So you see, you are the critical link. Of course you must say nothing of this to anyone. Not your husband. Your father. No one. The more people who know about this, the more dangerous it becomes for all involved."

"I cannot do it, Mr. von Brandt. I cannot keep secrets from my husband," Jennie said resolutely, shaking her head.

Max had thought that perhaps he had her, but no, he'd lost her. No matter, he would get her back. He'd hoped it wouldn't come to this, but it had.

"I understand your reservations, Mrs. Finnegan," he said. He was no longer feigning earnestness, concern, or anything else. His voice was quiet now and deadly serious. "Let us discuss it with your husband, then. Perhaps he would like to join us—all of us—you, myself, and Miss Meadows, in that lovely cottage of yours in Binsey. I took the train there last week. What a beautiful little village. I stayed at the King's Head."

Jennie's eyes widened. Her hand came up to her mouth. "No," she said. "Stop. Please, stop."

But Max didn't stop. "Of course, if we were to do that," he said, "we might have to explain more than my request, mightn't we? We might have to explain Miss Meadows's presence at your cottage. We might also have to explain the contents of your file—the one I read a few weeks ago in Harriet Hatcher's office while Harriet was in the loo. And we might have to explain what, exactly, you have up under your skirts. I don't think it's a baby, is it, Mrs. Finnegan? Not anymore. At least, that's what Mrs. Cobb, Dr. Cobb's wife, said to Mrs. Kerrigan, the publican's wife, as Mrs. Kerrigan was doing her washing last week. I'm sure they thought no one could hear them, but my window faced the yard. Of course, Mrs. Cobb thinks it was Josie Meadows who lost her baby. Which, I must say, was an exceedingly clever idea. Tell me, was it yours? Or Josie's?"

"My God," Jennie said, a look of horror on her face. "You are a monster. A *monster*."

"Your husband will be leaving the RGS in about a half hour's time, I believe. I shall ask you one more time, Mrs. Finnegan . . . will you help me? Or do I tell him what's been going on at Binsey?"

Jennie looked at the altar, at the statue of Christ on the crucifix. Then she looked at her hand, the one with her wedding ring on it.

"I will help you," she said. "And God help me."

"Thank you, Mrs. Finnegan. Regarding the other matter we discussed, I shall do all that I can. Immediately. Good day."

"Good day, Mr. von Brandt," Jennie said woodenly.

Max moved quickly once he was outside of the church. He headed west, toward the Katharine Docks, where he hoped to hire a hackney cab. He did not want to be seen and recognized in Wapping.

He thought of Sarajevo as he walked. Of the kaiser's determination to go to war. Of the armaments on both sides. War was coming, of this he was certain. He had seen war, and what it did, and he wanted a quick and decisive battle, with as few lives lost as possible.

He thought of all the young German men ready and willing to fight, and of all the young men in England and France and Russia and Austria ready to do the same. They had no idea what they were in for. Young men never did. They thought it was all a great adventure. Which made it that much easier for old men to send them to the slaughter.

By the time Max found a cab, he felt good—better than he'd felt in many weeks. He'd finally been able to reestablish the chain of communication to Berlin, and not before time. Berlin was getting restive. They were doubting him, and that was not good.

Thank God for good people, Max thought again, as he climbed into the cab and shut the door behind him. Good people were loving and kind and charitable. They had the best intentions. Like Jennie Finnegan. She only wanted to save her marriage, to give her husband a child so that he might love her. Max closed his eyes. He leaned back in his seat and sighed. How very odd, he thought, that it's always people's best intentions, not their worst, that bury them.

CHAPTER FORTY-TWO

"MADAM, I BELIEVE—"

Mr. Foster didn't get to finish his sentence. Fiona was already out of her chair, out of the drawing room, and racing down the hallway to the foyer of her home.

The front door was open. The driver and the under-butler were carrying bags. Miss Simon, the governess, was corralling the excited children. In the midst of it all stood a weary-looking blond woman holding a small boy by the hand and a baby in her arms. A willowy, beautiful girl, blond with huge gray eyes, stood next to her.

Wordlessly, Fiona ran to them. She threw one arm around the woman's neck, enfolding her and the baby. With her other arm, she gathered the girl and the little boy into her embrace. The blond woman hugged her back. Fiona could feel her tense, hitching breaths, and knew that she was trying hard not to cry. Tears ran down Fiona's own cheeks.

"Oh, India," she said, releasing her. "I'm so happy to see you. Thank God you and the children made it here safely."

India Baxter nodded. She tried to speak, but burst into tears. "I'm so sorry, Fiona. I promised myself I wouldn't cry about Maud anymore. Not in front of the children," she said.

India's small son looked at his mother, saw that she was crying, and promptly burst into tears, too. The baby, tired and flushed, followed suit.

"I'm sure he's wet," India said tiredly. "And hungry. I'll just go change him and then—"

"No, India, you must sit down. Miss Simon, where's Pillowy?" Fiona asked.

"Right here, ma'am!" a large voice boomed.

It was the children's nurse. Her real name was Mrs. Pillower, but when Katie was tiny, she had christened her Pillowy because she was large, soft, and comforting.

"I've just drawn baths—one for Miss Charlotte and another for Mrs. Baxter's wee ones," she said. "I'll get them washed and dressed in fresh clothes, and then we'll pop down to the kitchen for a nice meal."

"Come on, Charlotte," Katie said, taking her cousin's hand. The two girls were almost the same age. "You're sleeping in my room. I'll show you where it is, and then you can have your bath."

Charlotte followed her cousin, and Mrs. Pillower offered her hand to six-year-old Wish, but he shook his head.

"I don't want a bath and I'm not hungry," he said, hiding behind his mother's skirts.

Mrs. Pillower put her hands on her large hips and shook her head sadly. "You aren't? What a pity! Cook's just made the loveliest berry pudding and a big dish of whipped cream to go with it. I suppose I shall have to eat it all myself now."

"No, Pillowy! Don't!" Patrick, one of Fiona's twin boys, said. "We want some!"

"And I would love to let you have some, my ducks, but I can't, you see. I've got to get Master Aloysius here bathed, and I can't very well let you two loose in the kitchen on your own. Cook will have my head."

"Oh, come on, Wish!" Patrick said. "Just get your bath, will you? It'll only take a minute and then we can all have pudding!"

"Pudding! Pudding! We want pudding!" Michael, the other twin, started chanting.

"Pudding," Wish said solemnly, taking a tentative step out from behind his mother. "Pudding!" he said again, with more conviction.

"That's the spirit, old son," Mrs. Pillower said. "Now, tell me, do you like a little demerara sugar sprinkled on top of your cream? I do. Gives it a bit of crunch. Sometimes I like to put a few fresh raspberries on top, too."

"I like raspberries," Wish said shyly.

"Course you do! Who doesn't? Nutters, that's who." Mrs. Pillower paused and affected a worried look, as if she'd just thought of something disturbing. "You're not a nutter, are you?" she asked Wish.

The little boy giggled. He quickly shook his head no.

"Didn't think so," Mrs. Pillower said. "But it pays to ask. You can't be too careful these days." She gently took Elizabeth from India's arms, and when she started to fuss, Mrs. Pillower produced a rattle from her pocket, which made the baby smile again. "Oh, you're damp as a mop, you," Mrs. Pillower said. Then she turned to India and added, "I'll have them back in an hour, washed, fed, and good as new."

India smiled. "Thank you, Mrs. Pillower," she said. "I'm very grateful to you."

As Mrs. Pillower disappeared upstairs with Wish and Elizabeth, the twins and Charlotte following her, Fiona led India into the drawing room, where a pot of tea and a tray of scones, cakes, and biscuits had been thoughtfully set out.

"Mr. Foster, no doubt," India said when she saw it. "How is he?"

"Well," Fiona said. "Getting on a bit, as we all are. The under butler's doing more of the heavy work, but Mr. Foster is still captain of the ship. Thank God. It would be utter chaos without him."

The two women sat down on a settee. India rested her head against the back of it as Fiona poured the tea. She handed India a cup. "This will knit body and soul back together," she said. "Sarah, the maid, is unpacking your things. After you've rested a bit, I'll have her draw you a bath."

"Thank you," India said. "It's so good to finally be here, Fiona. There were days when I thought we'd never make it. Two weeks to get from California to New York," she said. "And then three more on the ship from New York to Southampton. I don't ever want to see a train, a boat, or a hackney cab again. At least not until the children are grown. I had no idea Wish would be seasick. Charlotte isn't. I think it's because she's constantly out with Sid on his boat."

"How is my brother?" Fiona asked.

India smiled. "Happy and well. Delivering a calf one minute, off to meet the fishing boats to collect our supper the next. I've never seen anyone take to a new life so quickly. It's as if he'd been born at Point Reyes. We all miss him, of course. It's been weeks and weeks since we've seen him, and it'll be months before we return home."

"I wish he could have come," Fiona said.

"He wishes it, too. We all do," India said. "But it's not safe for him in London, given his past."

Fiona nodded. Her brother had spent many years in London's underworld, as one of the East End's leading crime bosses. Many of the people he'd known were dead, but many were still alive—and possessed of long memories.

She looked at India, who was too thin and too pale, and had dark smudges under her eyes, and said, "And how are you?"

India shook her head. "I don't know, Fiona. I'm heartbroken, of course. But I think I'm mostly still in shock, really. Maud died nearly six weeks ago now, and yet I still cannot get her death through my head. It makes no sense to me. Suicide, of all things. That's something I'd never thought she'd do in a million years. Not Maud."

"But if she was addicted to morphine, perhaps she was not in her right mind," Fiona said.

"That makes no sense, either," India said. "She used to smoke opium, quite frequently, but she'd stopped. For the most part. I think she still indulged in the odd doctored-up cigarette, but that was all."

"Perhaps she'd started again," Fiona said gently. "Max von Brandt—the man she was seeing at the time of her death—seemed to think that she had."

"That must be it, then," India said. "She must've started taking drugs, and more heavily than she ever had before. There's no other way her death can be explained. I can't imagine Maud killing herself over anything, least of all a man, if she was in her right mind."

India drained her teacup. Fiona poured her more.

"She left everything to me," India said. "The London flat, the Oxford estate. I'll have to sell them both, and most of her things. And I can't bear to even think about it. The thought of going into her house, and her not being there, is too painful."

"No, don't think about it right now," Fiona said. "I've already engaged an estate lawyer to help you. You can meet him in a few days, after you've rested and recovered from your journey. I'll help you with Maud's belongings, too. I'll go with you, if you like, to sort through them."

"Would you?" India said. "I feel like it's too much to ask of you. I've already descended upon you with the children, when I should probably just have gone to Maud's house. You have enough on your plate without us moving in."

"Don't be silly, and don't you dare say another word about going to Maud's house. Joe and I want you here, and so do the children. They were wild with excitement when they heard you were coming."

India looked down at her teacup. "I think I'll go to her grave site first, before anything else," she said.

"I'll go with you. We'll take the train," Fiona said. Maud had been buried in Oxford. In a small churchyard on her estate.

India looked at her, her eyes suddenly fierce and full of tears. "And I'm going to the police, too," she said. "I'm going to look at the coroner's pictures. I want to see her for myself. See the needle marks on her arms. See the bruises. Maybe that will make it real for me. Maybe that will help me make some sense of it."

Fiona shuddered at the idea of India doing any such thing. How could cold, black-and-white photographs of Maud's lifeless body offer her any comfort? It was her grief speaking—mad and wild and searching for answers.

Fiona put an arm around her. "I know you are very upset, India, but are you certain you want to do that?" she asked her. "Wouldn't it be better to remember Maud the way she was—beautiful and funny and full of life?"

India leaned her head against Fiona and gave vent to her grief.

"Full of life," she sobbed. "That was my sister. My God, Fiona, what went wrong?"

CHAPTER FORTY-THREE

WILLA SAT AT a table for two at the Dorchester, fiddling with her napkin.

The tearoom, with its low tables and silver trays and overstuffed chintz chairs, had been Albie's idea. She would never have chosen to come here. But then again, the idea to have afternoon tea together, out of their mother's house, was his idea, too.

"Why, Albie? Why can't we talk in the parlor, for God's sake?" she'd asked him earlier this morning, after he'd proposed the idea.

"We need to talk, Willa, and it will be easier without Mother nearby," he'd said.

He was right about that. They were still not on the best of terms, and their frequent silences or brusque exchanges upset their mother.

Willa was relieved her brother finally wanted to talk, and she hoped he would say what he had to say, get it off his chest, and get over it. He was mad about their father's funeral—and her coming home so late—but there was nothing else she could have done. She had loved their father, too. She hadn't meant to be away from him when he was ill, and as soon as she'd found out about his condition, she'd tried to get home as quickly as possible. It wasn't her fault letters took as long as they did to reach her in Rongbuk. She hoped she could make Albie understand that.

Willa checked her watch again. Albie was late and she wished he'd get here. She planned to see Seamie after she'd finished with her brother, and she didn't want to miss even one minute of the precious little time she had to spend with him. She would see him tonight and then, a few days later . . . in Scotland. They'd made plans to go to Ben Nevis next week, she and Seamie, and she was counting the hours.

"I can get away, Willa. For a whole week," he'd told her a few nights ago, in bed at the Coburg. "Come to Scotland with me. To Ben Nevis. Let's try for a climb."

He told her that Jennie often went to a cottage she owned in Binsey to rest and relax and that she'd be going the following week. It was August now, and people were taking their holidays. He himself was entitled to a bit of time off from the RGS. He planned to say that he was going to Scotland on a climbing trip. It was nothing out of the ordinary; he often went hiking or climbing.

He would rent a cottage, a tiny place situated somewhere wild and remote. They would travel up separately, avoiding any risk of being seen together. They'd each buy some provisions and meet at the cottage. And then they would spend an entire week together. Seven glorious days. Of hiking and climbing. Of eating every meal together. Talking. Going to bed in the dark together. Waking up in the light.

"Please come, Willa. Say you will," he said.

She'd tried to say no. She'd tried to do the right thing, and once again she'd failed. She wanted to be with him, and more than anything, she wanted to climb with him again. And she would.

On Seamie's advice, Willa had spent a good deal of her time in London investigating artificial limbs. Her inquiries had finally led her to Marcel and Charles Desoutter, two brothers who'd recently invented something called the duralumin alloy leg—a prosthetic leg made from light metal. It was half the weight of a wooden leg and had a frictional knee control that would allow Willa to manage the speed and length of her stride. Best of all, it had a feature called a cushion-joint foot, which moved and flexed in the manner of a real human foot.

Willa had tried one and had been so excited by its possibilities that she'd had one made for herself immediately, using the advance she had from Clements Markham for her Everest book to pay for it.

The new leg was nothing like her old one. Its comfort and lightness left her less fatigued and bruised at the end of the day and its flexibility broadened her range of movement considerably. She was hopeful now that it might even allow her to attempt a climb. A real one. She couldn't wait to try it out on Ben Nevis.

Willa looked at her watch now. It was a quarter past four already. Maybe Albie had got caught up in work and wasn't coming. She would give him ten more minutes. In the meantime, she went back to fiddling with her napkin. She'd just made a rabbit's head out of it, when she heard a voice say, "Hello, Willa."

Willa looked up. "Albie?" she said, confused.

He looked flushed and a little disheveled. He looked like a man who'd been drinking, and he was, in fact, carrying two glasses of scotch. He put one down in front of her, then sat down across the table from her and knocked his back in one gulp.

"Albie, what are you doing?" she asked him.

"Drinking," he replied.

"Yes, I can see that. But why?"

"What do you intend to do, Willa?" he asked her.

Willa felt even more confused. "About what?" she said.

"Are you planning on returning to Everest?"

"I'm not sure. Not yet. Why—" she began.

"Because I think you should. Father's funeral is over. Mother is coping now. And I think you should go back. As soon as possible."

Willa was taken aback—by her brother's questions and his tone and the smell of scotch coming off him. Her confusion turned to anger.

"Albie, just what do you mean by coming in here and speaking to me so rudely? I've explained over and over why I couldn't get home before Father died and—"

"I know, Willa," he said, cutting her off.

"You know? Know what?" she asked.

"What the hell do you think? About Seamie."

Willa felt as if he'd struck her. "How do you know?" she asked in a small voice.

"I figured it out. After I found out you've been visiting the Co-burg. And Seamie, too."

"Who told you that?"

"I'm not going to tell you, so don't bother asking."

Willa continued to press him, but he would not reveal who'd told him. And then it hit her. How could she have been so stupid? "It was Max von Brandt, wasn't it?" she said, knowing that Max and Albie had met.

Albie didn't reply right away, but Willa could see from his ex-pression that she was right, and she said so.

"Yes. All right, then. It was him," Albie said. "He didn't do it on purpose, though. I bumped into him on the street. He told me that he'd seen you in the lobby of his hotel, and that you'd had dinner together and he'd had such a nice time. He said he'd seen Seamie at the Coburg once, too. Max might have thought it a coincidence, but I didn't. I waited in the lobby one afternoon. I saw Seamie come in, saw him take the elevator to the fifth floor. You were about ten min-utes behind him. You also went to the fifth floor."

Willa, stricken, said nothing.

"The next evening, I went to Seamie's flat, intending to have it out with him. He wasn't there. Jennie was, though. She was upset. She'd been crying. I sat down with her and we talked. She knows, too, Willa."

"But that's not possible. She couldn't know," Willa says. "We've been so careful."

"Not careful enough, apparently," Albie said. "Jennie's distraught. She isn't sleeping or eating properly, which is not good for her baby." He leaned forward in his chair, his eyes hard with anger. "Did you ever think about that, Willa? Either of you? Did you ever think about the damage it would do to other people? To Jennie? To me? To our mother, if she ever found out?"

"Stop it, Albie. Please."

"No, I won't stop. I can't imagine either of you did think about anyone else. You never do. You never have. You've always done just as you pleased. Doesn't matter who gets hurt, does it? Doesn't matter who worries, who suffers, who gets left behind. All that matters is the bloody quest. Being first. Getting to the top. Getting what you want. Or, in this case, whom you want. And icebergs and mountains, and people—yes, even people—are all just obstacles to be got round."

Willa's defenses crumbled. Albie was right. All along, she had been so wrong, so selfish. She'd wanted Seamie so badly, and so she'd taken him, with no thought for the woman he'd married, the woman who was going to have his child. Shame and remorse engulfed her now.

"I never meant to hurt her, Albie. Or you. I love him, that's all. I love him more than my own life and I wanted to be with him. Oh, God," she whispered, covering her face with her hands. "What have I done?"

Albie must've heard the sorrow in her voice, for he softened slightly. "You have to stop this, Willa. For Jennie's sake. And Scamie's. And their child's. And for your own sake, too. It's an impossible situation, can't you see that?"

Willa lowered her hands and nodded. Tears were running down her cheeks. She was frightened suddenly. She, who had climbed Kilimanjaro and nearly died, who'd journeyed to one of the most forbidding places on the planet and made it her own. She was terrified, because she knew now what the worst thing was that could ever happen to her—and it wasn't losing a leg, or not being able to climb. It was losing the one she loved most in this world. Again.

"What will I do?" she asked her brother, though she already knew the answer.

"You have to leave, Willa," he said. "You have to leave Seamie. You have to leave London. There's nothing else you can do."

CHAPTER FORTY-FOUR

SEAMIE POURED HIMSELF another glass of wine. His third. If he didn't stop, he'd be tipsy when Willa arrived.

He walked to the window and looked out over the rooftops of London. Where was she? She was supposed to have been here an hour ago. It was already six o'clock. They had so little time together, he didn't want to miss a second spent with her, never mind an entire hour.

He had a surprise for her—a key to their cottage near Ben Nevis. He'd finalized the arrangements just this afternoon and the agent had given it to him. They would leave for Scotland in a few days' time. Seven days they would have together. Seven days of walking and climbing. Of looking up at the stars at night and searching for Orion. Of sitting by the fire. Cooking breakfast together. Reading. Doing the washing up. Six nights of making love to her without watching the clock, of lying next to her in the dark and listening to her breathe.

Jennie had looked unhappy this morning when he'd told her of his plans to climb Ben Nevis. She'd looked as if she were about to protest, but then she'd forced a smile and wished him a wonderful trip. He'd wondered then, just for a moment, if she suspected. How could she? They'd always been so careful, he and Willa. They'd never taken chances.

He told himself he was being foolish, and yet something still nagged at him. Something in Jennie's eyes as he'd put her on the train to Oxford. Not suspicion exactly, no. It was more like sadness. It *would* have to stop one day. What he and Willa were doing. And likely the day would come soon. One day, yes, he thought. But not yet, he begged the fates. Please, not yet.

He heard a knock at the door. Finally, he thought. But when he opened it, a bellhop was standing there, not Willa.

"Letter for you, sir," the man said, handing Seamie an envelope. There was no name on it, just his room number.

"A letter? When did it arrive?" Seamie asked.

"Just a few minutes ago."

"Who brought it?"

"I didn't see, sir."

Seamie reached into his pocket, gave the man a tip, and closed the door. He opened the envelope and unfolded the sheet of paper inside. It was covered with Willa's handwriting.

My dearest Seamie,
I cannot do this anymore. It's not right and it never was. Jennie deserves better. Your child deserves better. I am sorry for leaving a note—again. But if I come upstairs right now, and say good-bye to you in person, I will do what is wrong, not what is right. I love you, Seamie. I always have and I always will. Wherever you go in this wide world, and whatever you do, never forget that.
                                                              Willa

"Well," he said aloud. "It looks like the day has come. Sooner rather than later."

He folded the note, put it back in its envelope, and tucked it in his jacket pocket, next to his heart. He was not angry. Not this time. He knew that Willa was right—that she'd somehow found the courage to do what he could not.

He knew, too, that he must try to forget her now. That he must go back to the woman he'd married and try his best to love her again. To be a proper husband to her and a good father to their child. She needed him. He had made her a promise, had taken a vow.

A long time ago, Willa had lost her leg, and she had learned to live without it. He had lost his heart. Twice now. He would have to learn to live without that. And without her—the woman who shared his soul.

He poured himself another glass of wine, emptying the bottle, and took his time in drinking it. He didn't have to be home at any particular hour tonight. Jennie was in the country. When he'd finished his drink, he collected his things and left a few coins on a table for the maid. He settled his bill downstairs and told the receptionist that he would not be needing the room again.

Dusk was coming down by the time he left the hotel. The doorman asked him if he required a hackney and he told him no. It was a mild night—warm and overcast. He would walk. He took off his jacket, slung it over his shoulder, and set off. He looked up at the sky once as he walked London's dark streets, but he could not see the stars.

CHAPTER FORTY-FIVE

"ALL THAT'S LEFT for tonight is the sleeper to Edinburgh . . . or the ferry train," the man in the ticket booth said.

"What time does that one leave?" Willa asked.

"Nine-twenty. Which one will it be, luv?"

"I . . . I don't know. How much is the Edinburgh fare? And the other one? The fare to Calais?"

The ticketing agent patiently explained the different prices, depending on whether she wanted a berth and, if so, whether she wanted it in first, second, or third class.

Willa was standing at a ticket window in Kings Cross Station, dazed and heartbroken, two large suitcases nearby. She had left the note for Seamie at the Coburg, then hailed a hackney cab back to her home, where she'd quickly packed her bags, said good-bye to her brother and tearful mother, and promised to write soon.

"But why are you leaving so suddenly, Willa?" her mother asked. "You only just got here."

"Now, Mother, that's not true. I've been here for quite a while," Willa said. "I've done my presentations. Finished the text for my book and turned it in. It's time I went back east. I've so much more to do. I've got to get back to my work."

"But we should have a going-away dinner. You can't just leave."

"I must, and anyway, I hate long good-byes. I'll write. I promise. And with any luck, the letters will go back and forth between us more speedily than they have been. Oh, please don't cry, Mum. You're making it even more difficult than it already is."

Albie had put a hand on their mother's shoulder. "We mustn't be selfish, Mother," he'd said. "We must think of Willa and let her get back to her mountain."

But Willa wasn't going back to her mountain. Not just yet. She couldn't bear to get there and look at yet something else she loved and could never have. She would go to Paris instead. Or Edinburgh. And knock around either place for a few days until she figured out what to do next. The important thing was that she put distance between herself and Seamie.

"Have you decided yet, miss?" the ticketing agent asked her. "Where will it be?"

She was just about to say Edinburgh, when she heard a voice calling her name. She turned around and saw Tom Lawrence hurrying toward her. He was wearing a linen suit and looked handsome and dashing.

"I say, Willa, I thought that was you!" he said cheerfully. "How are you? Where are you headed? I hope you're on my train—the ferry train to Calais. I'm going to visit Paris for a few days, then head to Italy."

"Whatever will you do there, Tom?"

"I'm taking a steamer across the Mediterranean to Turkey, then it's through the Straits to Cairo. I hope, at least. If the Germans haven't got hold of them by then. I've officially joined up, you see. I'm working under General Murray at the Bureau of Arab Affairs. I do hope you're on my train. I'd love to have a spot of tea with you en route. Hear more about Everest and Tibet."

"Miss? What train do you want?" the ticketing agent asked impatiently. "There are people behind you waiting."

Willa suddenly got an idea—a mad, impossible idea.

"Take me with you, Tom," she said.

Lawrence blinked at her. "I beg your pardon?"

"Take me to Cairo with you. I don't want to go back to Tibet. Not just yet, at least. I want to do something else. I can pay my way. I have enough money. And once I'm there, I'd be happy to work for the place you mentioned—the Bureau of Arab Affairs."

"Willa, you can't be serious. It's a bloody long way, you know. And I can't guarantee you any sort of employment once we arrive."

"Couldn't you find me something? I can survey. Make maps. Ride a camel. Type letters. Mop floors. Empty rubbish bins. Anything, Tom. Anything at all. Just please, please take me with you."

"You *are* a damned good surveyor," Lawrence said. "Good navigator, too. I'm sure Arab Affairs could find some way to make you useful." He frowned thoughtfully. "Well, General Murray will have my head, but what the devil." He turned to the ticketing agent and said, "Good evening, sir. We'll take two for Calais, please."

CHAPTER FORTY-SIX

MAX VON BRANDT sat in his hotel room, smoking.

He was attending a supper at the Asquiths' tonight. The PM would not be there, of course. He had things other than dinner parties to occupy him just now. But many others would be. Margot was a shimmering social butterfly, and her circle was not limited to politicians. There would be writers and artists, people who knew people. He was sure to learn things there. He always made it a point to learn things.

He would have to leave shortly, but not just yet. He would relax for a little while longer, savoring both his cigar and the moment.

The chain was whole. The information so critical to Berlin was moving along it smoothly once more. Just in the nick of time.

Gladys was handing copies of everything that went in and out of Burgess's office to Jennie. Jennie was hiding it all in the basement of her father's church. And a new man, one who'd come up to London from Brighton—Josef Fleischer, also known as Jack Flynn—was picking the material up every fortnight and taking it through the tunnels to Billy Madden's man, John Harris. Together Fleischer and Harris were sailing out of London with the documents twice monthly, on the fifteenth and the thirtieth, to meet the boat in the North Sea.

All the links were sound. John Harris would do what Billy Madden told him to. Gladys would do what he, Max, told her to, or some very unsavory pictures would be sent to her boss, and Jennie . . . Jennie would also continue to do as he wished, if she didn't want her husband to find out that his child, the one that Max guessed would happen to be born in Binsey, was really Billy Madden's bastard.

Of course, Jennie's continued tractability depended a great deal upon her husband. She wanted him. And he wanted Willa. If he had left Jennie for Willa, Jennie might well have given up her charade of a pregnancy and Max would have had no leverage over her. So he'd removed *that* particular impediment as well—by enlisting Albie Alden's help.

Willa Alden was gone. Nobody knew where, not even her brother, for Max had questioned him.

"Willa's left London," Albie had said to him, at a party they'd both attended, after Max had asked how she was.

"That was rather sudden, no?" he said. "I assume she's gone back east?"

"I suppose so," Albie had said. "To be truthful, though, I actually don't know where she's gone. We'll have a letter at some point. Or perhaps not. Willa follows her own rules."

"Indeed she does," Max said to himself now. He had no doubt that Willa would turn up again—in a place that was just like she was—beautiful, desolate, and wild.

For a moment, Max felt a heaviness in his heart, and he wished—desperately—that things had been different. He wished that he and Willa had been different people and that she could have been his. She was the only woman he'd ever truly loved, and he wished he could have spent his life with her in a place like Tibet—far away from Europe and its madmen.

He stubbed out his cigar and stood. He smoothed his lapels, tugged his cuffs straight, boxed his feelings away. It was eight o'clock, time to get going. Margot Asquith started her evenings punctually.

Max smiled grimly as he thought about Margot. They had formed a sudden and close bond, he and the prime minister's wife, having found themselves united in their sorrow over Maud's death.

Max had let her find him sitting alone in the drawing room at Maud's Oxford estate after the funeral, staring down at a ruby ring he was holding in his palm—a ring he'd found only moments before on the mantel.

"Max? Is that you? Whatever are you doing in here all alone?" Margot had asked him.

"She asked me to marry her once, Margot. Did you know that? She took this ring off her hand and put it on my little finger and said we were engaged." He had smiled sadly, then said, "She tried to say she was only joking and that she wanted it back, but I wouldn't give it to her. I'd . . . I'd hoped to find a way, you see . . ." His voice broke. He brushed at his eyes.

"Max, darling. Don't," Margot said, hurrying to his side.

"The thing that hurts me, the thing that is so hard to bear, is that no one knows the truth," he said.

"What is the truth? Tell me."

"The truth is that I cared for her a great deal. And if things had been different, if I hadn't had the family obligations that I do, I would never have broken it off. I would have married her."

Margot, greatly moved by this admission of love, had taken him to her heart then. She rang him up constantly, invited him to all her soirees and weekends, made sure he was not too much alone. He was spending every weekend, and many weeknights, in the homes of politicians, military men, cabinet ministers. Which made Berlin very happy.

A man's tears were a powerful enticement to a woman, he knew. Women could not resist them. Let a woman see you cry and she thought she owned you. But actually, you owned her—heart and soul.

Dusk was just beginning to fall as Max walked out of the Coburg's lobby. He waited patiently as one doorman hailed a cab for him, and watched with interest as two more took down the Union Jack that always flew above the hotel.

He wondered, as he watched them fold the flag with care and respect, if the Union Jack would always fly over the Coburg. And the Houses of Parliament. Buckingham Palace. He wondered if one day the kaiser's troops would march down Pall Mall. Germany's army and her navy were unsurpassed now in size and strength. The kaiser had put it about that he'd be in Paris in a week or two and in London shortly thereafter. Max was not quite so optimistic.

It would begin soon, though—in a mere matter of days, if his sources were to be trusted—a war that would span all of Europe, if not the entire globe. Sarajevo had merely been a convenient excuse. If it had not happened, the kaiser would have found another one.

Max's cab arrived. He climbed inside and gave the driver the Asquiths' address. Then he sat back in his seat and opened the window. He wanted to smell the air. It was a warm night, and beautiful in a fragile, fleeting way—as only English summer nights could be.

It was the first of August today. Already, Max thought. Summer would soon be over. For a very long time.

As the carriage skirted Hyde Park, so full of leafy trees and lush flowers and couples enjoying an evening stroll, Max's heart, hidden and unknowable, clenched. He was suddenly very glad that Willa had left London. He hoped she climbed to the top of Everest and stayed there, far away from what was about to come. He was glad, too, that he had nothing and no one now—no wife, no children—to love.

For the world was about to change. Suddenly, violently, and forever.

And love had no place in it.

CHAPTER FORTY-SEVEN

FIONA, BUSILY PUTTING the finishing touches on a birthday cake for Rose Bristow, her mother-in-law, glanced out of the dining room window of her and Joe's Greenwich estate and groaned.

"Katie, luv," she said, "can you get your brothers down out of the tree? And can you tell your little sister to get out of my dressing room? I know she's in there, spraying perfume all around. I can smell it. The whole house stinks. This cake is going to taste like Narcisse Noir."

Katie put an arm around her mother and kissed her cheek. "Calm down, Mum. Everything's fine. Nothing stinks and Gran's in no hurry for her cake. She's only just finished her supper and she's having a wonderful time. Auntie India gave her Elizabeth to hold and you know she's never happier than when she's got a baby on her lap."

"And your grandfather? He's all right?" Fiona asked fretfully.

"He's having a better time than anyone. Who do you think bet the twins they couldn't get up that tree?" Katie said, laughing. "Don't worry so much, Mum. Come outside and enjoy the party."

Fiona smiled. "All right, then. I will," she said. Then she walked through the dining room's huge French doors into a gloriously beautiful summer evening.

Her smile broadened and her blue eyes sparkled as she regarded the scene before her. A huge table had been set up on the lawn and decorated with a white lace cloth and masses of tea roses, all clipped from her gardens. Seated around it talking and laughing—or racing up and down the lawn, or hanging from trees, or playing croquet—was her large and boisterous family. Nearly every one of them.

Her children. Her brother Seamie and his wife, whose first child would soon arrive. Joe's sisters and brothers and their many children. Rose and Peter Bristow, Joe's parents. And Fiona's sister-in-law India and her three children. Fiona wished, with a deep pang of longing, that her brother Sid was here, too. But it could not be.

They were all here to celebrate Rose's birthday, and looking at them now, Fiona felt her heart swell with love and gratitude. And she, who had spent so much of her life arguing with God, sent Him a quick and heartfelt thank-you—thank you for these people, thank you for this incredible day, and thank you for not letting the twins fall out of the tree onto their heads.

She talked for a bit with Rose, who was completely taken with Elizabeth, allowed the twins to tie a serviette over her eyes for a game of blindman's buff, admired the latest edition of Katie's newspaper, which Katie had passed out to nearly everyone present, and then sat down to drink a glass of punch with India. As she did, Sarah, the maid, came up to Fiona and said, "Excuse me, ma'am, the supper dishes have all been cleared. Shall I bring the cake now?"

"Oh, my goodness. I'd quite forgotten about the cake. Yes, Sarah, do. No! Hold on a moment," she said, looking around. "Where's Mr. Bristow? He should be here."

Fiona realized she hadn't seen Joe for quite some time—at least an hour.

"Have you seen him, Ellen?" she asked his sister. But Ellen had not. No one had. Not since the party began.

"He must be in his study working, as always," Fiona said. "I'll drag him out. Wait on the cake, please, Sarah, until I return."

Fiona hurried into the house and up the stairs to Joe's study, but he was not there. She checked their bedroom, thinking perhaps he'd tired himself and gone to lie down for a few minutes, but he wasn't there, either.

As she was walking back downstairs, she happened to glance out the huge round window at the top of the second-floor landing and spotted him. He was in the orchards. Sitting in his wheelchair. Alone.

"What is he doing all the way down there?" she wondered aloud, a bit put out. It was just like her husband to go off and admire his fruit trees when his mother's cake was about to be served.

She hurried back down the stairs, over the east lawn, and down the gently sloping hill that led to the orchards. Joe had planted the trees long ago, years ago, before he and Fiona were married. Their limbs were dotted with ripening fruit. In another month or so, she and the children would be picking pippin apples and rosy Anjou pears.

Joe was sitting at the far end of the orchard, where the trees gave way to another hill and the River Thames beyond it. Fiona could just see him from where she stood. He was gazing out over the water, his face lifted to the flawless evening sky. It was nearly eight o'clock. The soft summer light had begun to wane. Dusk would come down soon and, with it, the night's first silvery stars. Fiona would have stopped and left Joe to his enjoyment, if she hadn't been so irritated with him.

"Joe!" she called loudly, waving at him. He must've heard her, but he didn't answer. He didn't even turn around.

Red-faced and flushed now, she hoisted up her skirts and started running, making her way between two rows of pear trees. When she was ten or so yards from him, she called to him again.

"Joseph Bristow! Have you not heard me calling you? Your mother's cake is about to be served, and—"

Joe turned to her now and her words fell away. His face was a picture of devastation. She saw that he held a piece of paper in his hand. It looked like a telegram.

"Joe, what is it? What's wrong?" she asked.

"It's all going to change soon, Fee. It's all going to end," he said softly.

"What will, luv? What's going to change?"

"This. Our lives. Others' lives. England. Europe. All of it. It's begun," he said. "Three days ago, Germany declared war on Russia and France."

"I know that," Fiona said. "The whole world knows it. It's been in all the papers. But England's not involved in it. We still have hope, Joe. The war is only on the continent. It's a European war and there's still a chance of containing it."

Joe shook his head. "The Germans invaded Belgium this morning," he said, "a neutral country. All our diplomatic efforts have failed." He held the paper he'd been holding out to her. "It's from Downing Street," he said. "A messenger brought it about an hour ago."

"Asquith needed to send a messenger? He couldn't have rung?" Fiona asked.

"No. Not for this."

Fiona took it from him.

Classified, the first line read.

3 August 1914, the second line read.

And then the third line, and Fiona knew that Joe was right, that their lives would never be the same.

At 1900 hours this evening, Great Britain declared war on Germany.

PART TWO

FEBRUARY
1918

HEJAZ, ARABIA

CHAPTER FORTY-EIGHT

WILLA ALDEN SPOKE loudly and heatedly to the man kneeling down by the railroad tie, pointing at him for emphasis with the slender red cylinder she was holding.

"You know what pictures like that could do for the cause, Tom," she said. "They'll bring interest, support, and money. You need all three. Especially now with the push to Damascus."

"I won't hear of it. It's far too dangerous. You're to stay behind the dunes with the rest of us."

"I can't get the shot from behind a bloody sand dune!"

"You also can't get shot behind a bloody sand dune," Lawrence said matter-of-factly. "Stop waving that dynamite around, please, and hand it to me."

Willa did so, sighing. "I suppose you'll want the charges next?" she said.

"Rather difficult to blow up a train without them," Lawrence replied, carefully placing the dynamite next to several other sticks in the hollow he'd dug underneath the tie.

Willa crouched down by a wooden box, carefully lifted out two gelatin charges, and handed them to him. One slip and they'd both be blown sky high. She should've been frightened by the thought, but she'd long ago learned that only those with something to lose were afraid of dying.

Lawrence connected the charges to a pair of wires stretching away from the tracks, across the sands, and over the nearest dune, then carefully positioned them. Willa helped him as he worked, handing him wire strippers, screwdrivers, whatever he asked for. Sweat, caused by the brutal Arabian sun, poured down his deeply tanned face. His blue eyes, made even bluer by the white head scarf he wore, were focused on his task.

They were on a raid, Lawrence and his men. They were rigging explosives just north of Al-'Ula, under the tracks of the Hejaz Railway, a line that ran from Damascus to Medina and had been built by the Turks to strengthen their hold over their Arab domains. Lawrence's mission was to blow up a train known to be carrying Turkish soldiers, guns, and gold, for a strike against Turkey was a strike against Germany and Austria-Hungary, Turkey's Central Powers allies. It was also a strike for Arabia's independence from its Turkish masters.

Willa was there to document the raid, as she had many times before. Her images, and the copy she wrote to accompany them, were couriered to Cairo, where Lawrence's commanding officer—General Allenby—reviewed them, then released them to Downing Street, who, in turn, released them to the press.

This time, however, Willa didn't want to stay behind the dunes during the action, photographing only the befores and afters. She'd got her hands on a Bell & Howell, a small motion picture camera—she'd been hounding Allenby for it for more than a year—and she wanted to shoot live footage as the raid was happening.

She wanted to capture the victories, as she'd told Lawrence, because victories would rally support, but there was another, equally urgent reason why Willa wanted to film the raid—she desperately wanted to show the West the brutal, beautiful place that was Arabia, and to document its people's fierce struggle for autonomy.

Large swaths of Arabia had been—and still were—under the control of the Ottoman Empire, but Britain wanted to change that, for the British had seen an advantage in helping the native tribes rise up and throw off the Turks. If Turkish troops were engaged fending off guerrilla fighters in Arabia, they could not attack the Suez Canal and attempt to take it from the British, as they had already tried to do. Furthermore, with the Turks gone from Arabia, and the Arabs their allies, the British would have new access to, and greater influence in, the Middle East.

To achieve this aim, the British had cultivated ties with Hussein, sharif of Mecca, and his son, Faisal. Faisal, it was determined, would lead the revolt against the Turks, and Britain would help fund it. Lawrence, who had spent his postgraduate years traveling in Arabia, digging among its ruins and studying the people, their customs, and their language, was made advisor to Faisal. With Lawrence's help, and the use of guerrilla tactics, the desert fighters—known as the Arab irregulars—had already taken a number of garrison towns. They were also able to tie up Turkish troops by blowing up sections of the Hejaz Railway—preferably when a Turkish train was passing over them—thereby forcing the Turks to defend it constantly.

Willa had been in the desert for three years now, and she had come to love this wild, impossible place, and its wild, impossible people. She loved the proud and fierce Bedouin men, the tribal women with their blue robes, their veils and jewels, their language and songs. She loved the shy, darting children. And she loved Tom Lawrence.

She didn't love him as she loved Seamus Finnegan. Seamie had her heart and her soul, and he always would. She loved him, still, even though she knew she could never again have him. The pain of that knowledge tortured her every day, as did the pain of her remorse for loving a man who belonged to someone else. There had been times, during the long passage to Cairo, that she'd sat alone in her cabin, pills in one hand, a glass of water in the other, ready to take her own life. She hadn't been able to do it, though. Suicide was the cowardly way out. She deserved her pain, deserved to suffer for what she'd done.

Lawrence she loved as friend and brother, for he was both those things to her. Back in 1914, when she'd left Seamie and was leaving London, brokenhearted, guilt-ridden, and despairing, Lawrence had brought her to Cairo, to the Intelligence Department's Arab Bureau, and had found her work in the Maps Department. It was her job to alter and expand the map of the Arabian Peninsula as information on the Turks' movements and encampments, and those of the various desert tribes, became known.

The position Tom Lawrence had secured for her was an important one, one that kept her so inundated with work during the day that she had no time to think of anything else. No time to remember and grieve. He'd helped her forget, if only for a few hours a day, that she had lost Seamie Finnegan forever. The opium she bought in the back streets of Cairo helped her forget at night. And that was the only thing she wanted now—a way to forget. A way to forget Seamie and what they'd had. A way to forget she'd ever loved him, for their love was not a good thing, it was dangerous and destructive. To them and everyone around them.

When Lawrence had left Cairo to go into the desert and fight with Arab troops under the command of Emir Faisal, Willa had followed him. She had resigned her position, cut her hair off, donned britches and a head scarf, packed her cameras, and set out into the desert on a camel. Everyone at the Arab Bureau said Tom was going to get himself killed out there. Maybe he could get her killed, too. Dying in service of one's country was an honorable death, she thought, a far better death than suicide.

Lawrence was furious with her when she caught up with him, at a rough campsite near Medina. General Allenby was furious with her, too. He sent word from Cairo telling her that she couldn't be at a campsite with men. She couldn't be a lone woman in the desert. She couldn't stay. She would have to return to Cairo. Both Lawrence and Allenby badgered her and would not stop.

Until they saw her pictures.

Pictures of the blond, blue-eyed Lawrence, striking in white Arab robes, a golden dagger at his waist, and of the dark-haired, handsome Faisal, with his shrewd and piercing eyes. Pictures of Auda Abu Tayi, a fierce Bedouin, a Howeitat chief who fought with Lawrence, and of the defiant desert fighters—the Arab irregulars. Pictures of the Bedouin encampments. The red cliffs of Wadi Rum, the Valley of the Moon. The endless dunes. The shimmering waters of the Red Sea.

"So?" she'd said to Allenby as she slapped a stack of them down on his desk back in Cairo. She'd returned with him under the pretense of cooperating with his demands, but really she'd only gone back to develop her film.

The general had picked the photographs up, one after the other, and though he'd tried his best to hide it, Willa saw that he was impressed. And that he saw the possibilities the images presented.

"Mmm. Yes. Quite nice," he said.

"They're better than nice, sir, and you know it. They'll capture people's imaginations. Their sympathies. Their hearts. Everyone in the world will be rooting for Lawrence and for Arabia. He'll become a hero. I'll write dispatches to go with them. Reports from the desert front."

Allenby looked out of his window, brow furrowed, saying nothing.

"Can I go back?" Willa asked him.

"For now," he replied.

That was in 1915. Willa had ridden with Lawrence and his men ever since. She'd photographed them and written about them, and her reports had been published in every major newspaper in the world. Because Allenby was worried about the public's reaction to a woman riding with soldiers, Willa filed her reports under a pseudonym: Alden Williams. Because of her, Tom Lawrence was now Lawrence of Arabia. Every man who read about him admired him. Every woman fell in love with him. Every schoolboy wanted to be him.

Against all odds, Lawrence and his desert fighters had pulled off some stunning victories against the much stronger Turkish Army, but the final routing of the Turks hinged on the Arabs' ability to push northward and capture Aqaba, and then the biggest prize: Damascus. Willa had followed Lawrence this far, and she would follow him farther yet, until they won the fight and gained independence for Arabia, or died in the attempt.

As she watched him now, finishing with the charges, her hands unconsciously went to her camera, and before she knew what she was doing, she was shooting him again.

"Trying to get footage of me blowing myself up?" he asked her.

"Let me do it, Tom. Let me shoot the whole thing," she said, "the train coming, the explosion, the heat of the battle, and the victory.

What amazing footage that would be. Cairo will send it to London and London will give it to Pathé and it will be on every newsreel in the world and Allenby will get more funds."

"You'll spook them, Willa," Lawrence said. "If the Turks see you, they'll know something's up. They'll stop the train, search for our device, and disable it. Then they'll search for us."

"I won't spook them. I'll wait until the countdown and run out on three. Three seconds are all I need. I know it. I've timed myself. Out on three and not before. No one can stop a locomotive in three seconds. You know that."

"He is right, *Sidi*," a voice behind her said, using a very respectful term of address. "You should let him do this thing. If anyone can do it, he can. He is the bravest man I know."

It was Auda abu Tayi. Auda called Willa "him" because he refused to believe she was a woman. Even now after years together in the desert. No woman could handle camels as she did, or shoot a rifle. No woman could navigate as well.

"It's *Sidi* now, is it, Auda?" Lawrence said. "That makes a change. Usually you roar at me like I was your camel boy."

"You must let him do this. His pictures bring money from Cairo. We need money for the push to Damascus. My men must eat."

"Victories are important, Tom," Willa said quietly.

"Yes, Willa, they certainly are," Lawrence said.

"I meant to the people back home. It keeps up their morale. Gives them hope. Lets them know that their sons and brothers and fathers have not died in vain."

Lawrence turned his blue eyes, troubled and searching now, upon her. "What happened to you?" he asked her. "What are you trying to forget? Or whom?"

Willa looked away. "I don't know what you mean," she said.

"Something must've happened. Something terrible. Why else do you insist on taking such chances? None of us is mad enough to go over the dune before the charge goes off. None but you."

"He is a warrior, *Sidi*. He is brave," Auda said.

Lawrence shook his head. "No, Auda. Bravery is feeling fear but doing the thing anyway. Willa Alden feels no fear."

"Let me do it, Tom," Willa said stubbornly.

Lawrence looked away from her, down the track, deliberating. "Out on three," he finally said. "Not one tenth of one second before."

Willa nodded. She was excited. She'd never filmed a full attack, start to finish. "How much longer have we got?" she asked.

"By the best of my calculations, a half hour," he replied. "How are the men coming with the wires?"

"They are almost done," Auda said.

"Good," Lawrence said. "All we've got to do now is connect the wires to the plunger box. Then wait."

Willa looked at the tall sand dune. Close to the top of it, men were scooping out a shallow trench in the sand with their hands. More were laying wires in it, then smoothing the sand back over them. They stayed close together as they worked, so as not to make footprints all over the dune.

Lawrence was still speaking, asking Auda if the men behind the dune, about a hundred in all, were ready, when he abruptly stopped speaking and placed his hand on the iron rail. He was perfectly still, listening, it seemed, with his entire being.

Willa looked down the track. She could see nothing, only the two iron rails stretching away into the desert.

"They're coming," Lawrence said crisply. "Auda, get the men in position. Willa, brush our tracks away. I'll take care of the wires. Go!"

As Lawrence and Auda picked up the boxes of dynamite and charges and hurried over the dune with them, Willa stuffed her camera into the carrying case dangling from her neck and grabbed the broom lying on the tracks. Moving quickly, she swept sand over the hole Lawrence had dug for the dynamite, then began working her way backward up the dune, brushing away all evidence of their presence, taking care not to disturb the wires lying only inches under the sand. She was panting by the time she finished. Sand, with its constant shifting, was hard on her artificial leg and took more effort to maneuver in.

As soon as she got over the top of the dune, she threw the broom down, crouched low, and pulled her camera from its case. She tossed the case aside and started shooting. She panned over the men crouched only a few feet below her, rifles ready, then focused in on Lawrence, who was feverishly attaching the wires to the plunger box. She could see the tension in his face. They could hear the train now. It was traveling fast.

There was no guarantee any of this would work and they all knew it. The connection might be bad. The charges, or dynamite, might be faulty. Their work, the deadly risks they were taking, might all be for nothing.

Lawrence finished with the wires. He readied his own rifle, slung it over his back, then bent his head, listening. They could chance no lookout at the top of the dune. The Turks were wary. They'd have their own lookout, and very likely a sharpshooter, in the front of the train. Lawrence would start his countdown when he heard the engine pass them by. By the time he got to one, the middle of the train would be over the dynamite. That's when he'd press the plunger. There would be a tremendous explosion. Train cars would be blown apart. Those that remained would likely tumble off the tracks. Then Lawrence, Auda, and the men would rush down the dune, rifles raised, to complete the attack.

They waited silently now, nerves taut, as the train drew closer. Lawrence with one hand on the box, the other on the plunger.

"Ten, nine, eight, seven . . . ," he began.

The men closed their eyes, took deep breaths, and prayed.

Willa inched closer to the top of the dune, her camera ready. Please let this work, she said silently. Please. For Lawrence. For Arabia. For the whole wretched war-torn world.

". . . six, five, four, three . . ."

Like a racehorse out of its gate, Willa shot over the top of the

dune. She knelt in the sand, trained her camera on the section of track
where the dynamite lay buried, and started her film rolling. For what
seemed like an eternity, there was nothing, just the train . . . wary
faces in its windows . . . a mouth opening in surprise . . . a rifle barrel pointed at her . . . and then it came—the explosion.

There was a blinding light and then a sound like the end of the
world, as the force of the explosion tore two cars apart and sent three
more tumbling down the embankment. Willa felt herself pushed violently back into the dune. She felt sand, sharp as needles, driven
into her hands and face. Felt shrapnel raining down around her. A
piece of charred wood hit her arm, tearing her shirt and ripping
her skin. She barely felt it; she was only relieved it hadn't hit her
camera.

And then there was smoke, thick and black, and the shouts and
screams of the injured. A battle cry went up behind her, a lone voice.
It was joined by others, and then the men were streaming down the
dune past her, already firing on the train.

Willa raced down with them, stumbling in the shifting sand,
nearly falling, righting herself, all the while keeping her film rolling.

She heard the sound of bullets flying past her—felt the impact of
one lodging itself in the sand only inches from her left foot. A man
next to her fell, his head blown off. She felt his blood, warm and wet,
on her cheek. And still she ran on, panning over the train, focusing
in on the skirmishing, capturing the expression of a tribesman as he
thanked Allah that his bullet had found its mark.

The battle raged for nearly an hour. And then it was over. The
Turkish commander surrendered. Prisoners were taken. Loot plun-
dered. The remaining train cars were set on fire. Auda had lost eight
men. The Turks, many more. And Willa had got it all on film, stopping only once, when the shooting was over, to load a new roll.

Lawrence would later say that it had been a close battle, that the
Turks had nearly won it. They all knew what that meant. If they'd
lost, they'd be dead now. The Turks might've taken Lawrence prisoner, but they'd likely have shot everyone else.

Willa didn't care. She'd never felt fear, not for a second. She'd felt only a mad determination to film Lawrence and his men at battle. And a wild and raw hope that for a few moments there would be no pain, no sorrow, no guilt, just the sweet nothingness of forgetting.

CHAPTER FORTY-NINE

CAPTAIN SEAMUS FINNEGAN, standing on the bridge of his destroyer, *Hawk,* looked out over the sparkling waters of the southeast Mediterranean with a pair of binoculars. The expression on his deeply tanned face was troubled.

They were out there. Under the calm blue waters, German U-boats were gliding, as dark and silent as sharks. He could feel them, and he would find them.

As he lowered his binoculars, his lieutenant, David Walker, appeared by his side. "They want to draw us out. Away from the coast," he said.

"I am aware of that, Mr. Walker," Seamie said. "They cannot hit us unless they do. Nor, however, can we hit them."

"Our orders, sir, are clearly stated. They say we are to patrol the coastline for German vessels."

"Our orders, Mr. Walker, are to win this war," Seamie said curtly. "And I, and this crew, of which you are a part, will do our utmost to carry them out. Is that clear?"

"Eminently. Sir," Walker said tightly.

Seamie raised his binoculars again, ending the conversation. David Walker was a coward, and Seamie could not abide cowards. Walker constantly tried to couch fear for his own personal safety in a feigned concern for protocol. Seamie had been trying to have him transferred off the *Hawk* for the last four months. He made a mental note now to redouble his efforts.

Unlike Walker, Seamie, a heavily decorated naval captain, had been personally responsible for sinking three German warships and had been a member of various crews on dreadnoughts and destroyers that had together sunk another eight. It was an impressive record, and one that had not been achieved by fretting over his own safety.

He had joined the Royal Navy a day after Britain declared war on Germany. Because of his extensive seafaring experience and knowledge, and the courage he'd demonstrated on two Antarctic expeditions, he was made an officer—a sublieutenant—directly upon enlisting. His courageous conduct during the hellish Battle of Gallipoli in 1915, when the Allies tried and failed to force their way through the Dardanelles to Istanbul, had gained him the rank of full lieutenant, and his bravery during the Battle of Jutland, off the coast of Denmark in the North Sea, in which his ship had sunk two German battle cruisers, had made him a captain.

Many called him brave; some, like Walker, called him reckless— behind his back, of course. But Seamie knew that he wasn't reckless. He took risks, yes, but that was what one did in a war, and the risks he took were very carefully calculated. He knew his crew and what they could do, and he knew his ship—every nut and bolt of her. The *Hawk* was no great tub of a battleship, a sitting duck for U-boats. Lighter and faster than the dreadnoughts, she was made for patrolling, for raiding enemy harbors, harrying minelayers, and ferreting out U-boats. The *Hawk*'s bow had been specially fortified for ramming surfacing submarines. Her shallow draft made it difficult for their torpedoes to hit her. She'd been equipped with hydrophones for detecting submerged U-boats and depth charges for destroying them.

Seamie lowered his glasses again, mulling the question. They were only half a mile out from Haifa, a port town in western Arabia. They could play it safe and travel north or south along the coastline, searching for suspicious-looking vessels, or they could make for the open water—a more dangerous proposition.

The Germans had an effective intelligence-gathering force, for too often they knew the exact positions of British ships in the Mediterranean. It was as if they had some shadowy phantom of a chess master, constantly moving his pieces closer and closer to the *Hawk* and her sister ships. Seamie often wondered where this master was. In Berlin? London? Arabia? He thought it most likely that the man, whoever he was, was here. He had to be. Seamie and the other ships' captains rarely relayed messages on their ships' whereabouts by radio, fearing they would be intercepted. For someone to know so much about their movements, that someone—or his sources—had to be nearby. Watching the ships. Overhearing talk in the port towns, the bazaars, the officers' messes.

Thanks to Britain's own highly effective Secret Service Bureau, Seamie and the Allied captains often knew where Germany's ships were, too, but not her U-boats. The U-boats were a different thing completely, much harder to track—even with the advantage of intercepted German messages.

Seamie well understood the consequences of failing to find a U-boat before it found them. He had seen the devastation a submarine's torpedoes could wreak. He'd seen the explosions and the fires, heard the screams of dying men, had helped recover the broken and charred bodies. He had read, as had the entire world, of the sinking of the *Lusitania*, and the deaths of nearly twelve hundred of its passengers, civilians all—an act so reviled, it had pulled the United States, a country reluctant to sacrifice its sons on foreign battlefields, into the war.

But he did not allow himself to think about those consequences. He did not think about the possibility of his death, or his men's. He did not think about the wives and children his crew had left back in England. He did not think of his own child, James, the young son whom he loved so dearly, or his wife, Jennie, whom he did not. He did not think of the woman he did love, Willa Alden. All he thought of was the necessity of sending enemy sailors to their graves before they sent him, and his crew, to theirs.

"Mr. Ellis," he said now to his quartermaster, "set a course bearing three hundred degrees north."

"Aye, aye, sir," Ellis said.

"Open waters, sir?" Walker asked.

"Yes, Mr. Walker. Open waters."

"But sir, the report from SSB said——" Walker began.

Seamie knew what report Walker meant. The SSB had received intelligence that Germany had increased the number of U-boats in the southeastern Mediterranean, with an eye toward wiping out the Allied naval presence there and, by so doing, weakening Britain's grip on the important strongholds of Port Said, Cairo, Jaffa, and Haifa.

"The reports are only that—reports," he said now. "They may have been planted by the Germans to keep us close to shore. They may be entirely false."

"And they may be entirely real," Walker said.

Seamie gave the man an icy, dismissive glance. "Cold feet, Mr. Walker? Perhaps we should stay right here and knit. We'll knit you some socks to warm them," he said.

Walker flushed red. "No, sir. Of course not. I just——"

But Seamie had already turned his back on the man.

"Full speed ahead," he said.

CHAPTER FIFTY

FIONA, DRESSED IN a handsome cream silk suit and standing in an ornate and cavernous room in Buckingham Palace, held her breath as Britain's sovereign, King George V, raised his pen.

For a few seconds, a strong, dizzying feeling of unreality gripped her. For a few seconds, she simply could not believe that this was happening, that she was here, with Joe and Katie, with the prime minister, with Millicent Fawcett and Sylvia Pankhurst and other suffragist leaders, watching the king giving his royal assent to the Representation of the People Act of 1918, the Fourth Reform Act.

Joe, at her side in his wheelchair, took her hand. Katie, on her other side, whispered, "Are you all right, Mum?"

She nodded, tears glistening in her eyes. She had worked for this, fought for this, spent time in Holloway prison for this, and now here she was, watching the king signing an act of Parliament that would grant voting rights to a large segment of British women.

Fiona had read the bill many times. She practically knew it word for word. It decreed that women over the age of thirty, who were married, or who were single but met certain basic property requirements, could vote in Parliamentary elections. A separate act had additionally decreed that women over the age of twenty-one could stand for Parliament.

Fiona knew that the act had come about because Millicent Fawcett and her group—to which Fiona belonged—had quietly, but forcefully, continued to nonviolently petition government for the vote all during the war, at the same time that the Pankhursts and the WSPU had stopped their violent protests and supported the war effort. In addition, the young women of Britain had made a splendid example of themselves as they took up the jobs British men left when they enlisted, especially jobs in the munitions factories.

Fiona knew that the women of Britain had earned this day, and yet she could still barely comprehend it. It was a proud day, a historic day, and as the king bent over the document, she was filled with emotion that the dream had become reality, that she, at the age of forty-seven, finally had the vote, and that her daughters would have it, too. It was not enough, she knew that—the voting age for women must be lowered—but it was a start, and a very sweet victory after such a long and bitter struggle.

As she watched the king scribble his signature across the document, a million memories raced through her mind. For a moment, she was not a wife and mother, not a successful tea merchant; she was a seventeen-year-old girl, a poor tea-packer in Whitechapel, struggling to make ends meet. Then, after her father's and mother's murders, she was a young woman on the run, struggling to survive.

She remembered her early battles—to get herself and Seamie out of London, to get to America and start a business there. She remembered how she'd fought to make her first shop—a shop she shared with her uncle Michael, her father's brother—a success. She remembered fighting for her first husband's—Nicholas Soames's—health, and his life. For justice against William Burton, her father's killer.

She'd fought for her own life after William Burton had threatened to kill her and had tried to make good on that threat. She'd fought for her brother Sid's life after he'd been wrongly accused of murdering Gemma Dean, an East London actress. She'd fought for Joe's life after he'd nearly been murdered himself at the hands of the villain Frankie Betts.

And she continued to fight now, she and Joe both. Together they'd set up two hospitals—one in France and one in Oxfordshire, at Wickersham Hall, Maud's old and sprawling estate, which now belonged to India—for wounded British veterans, and they fought constantly for funding.

Katie, now nineteen, fought, too. She was reading history at Magdalene College and hoped to graduate with a first this coming spring, when she would promptly leave the dreaming spires of Oxford for the teeming streets of Whitechapel. There she planned to set up a proper office and print shop for the Labour newspaper she'd started four years ago, the *Battle Cry*. Her circulation was two thousand strong now and growing. Though still only an undergraduate, she routinely got interviews from leading political figures, keen to put their policies and arguments across to the young readership the *Battle Cry* served. She'd been arrested several times at suffragette marches, had had her eye blackened, and had even had the windows of her room at the college put out by thugs working for an Oxfordshire factory owner whose abusive practices she'd publicized. Not easily intimidated, Katie shrugged these damages off, considering them mere bumps and bruises from the rough-and-tumble of politics and journalism.

And then there was Charlie, Fiona's eldest boy. He fought every day of his life now—on the front lines in France. He'd enlisted two years ago at the age of fifteen. He'd told his parents he was going on a camping trip with some mates, but he'd gone to see a recruiting sergeant instead. He'd lied about his age, joined the army, and three days later, he was shipped off to the Somme. Fiona and Joe found out from a postcard he sent them from Dover. And by then it was too late; he was gone. Fiona had wanted him found and brought back, but Joe said it was pointless—even if they managed to bring him home, he'd just slip off again the first chance he got. She worried about him constantly now and dreaded every unexpected knock on the door, every telegram, every official-looking envelope that arrived in the post.

Three and a half horrible years had passed since August of 1914. The jaunty, boisterous mood that had greeted the declaration of war had quickly changed with the first reports of heavy fighting in Belgium and then that brave country's defeat. The ones who had said there would be a few quick, decisive battles and then the Germans would limp back home defeated had been dead wrong. The Germans had pressed on through Belgium into France, and the resulting carnage had been unspeakable. Millions had been killed, soldiers and civilians. Lives, towns, entire countries had been ripped apart. Every day, Fiona hoped to hear that it was ending, hoped to hear of some decisive victory that would tip the scales in the Allies' favor. And every day passed without one.

It seemed to her sometimes as if the struggles never ended. She had come so far in her life, she and Joe both, and she'd tried to bring others with her—through her charitable endeavors, through the East End schools she and Joe funded, and through her fight for women's suffrage. And today, for one brief, shining moment, it seemed as if she'd finally won a battle—she and the other women who'd fought so hard for the right to vote. For once, they'd won. The knowledge of the victory they'd achieved at home gave her hope that victory could be achieved abroad as well. America was now involved in the fighting. With her men, money, and might added to the Allies' side, the war would end soon. It had to. Before there were no men left to fight it.

The king finished signing. He raised his pen. There was applause—some polite, some, like Fiona's, a bit more boisterous—and then there were photographs and tea and cakes and champagne.

Joe was buttonholed by another MP. Katie hurried off to try to get a quick interview with the new prime minister, Mr. Lloyd George. Millicent and Sylvia were busily giving interviews, and Fiona, overwhelmed by her emotion, slipped away for a few minutes, to a corner of the huge state room, to collect herself.

She pulled a handkerchief from her purse, dabbed at her eyes, discreetly blew her nose, then stood by a window, staring out at the wintery February day until she felt she could converse once more without bursting into tears. She was just about to turn around and join the rest of the king's audience when she felt a soft cheek pressed against her own and an arm around her shoulders. It was Katie.

"Mum, are you really all right?" she asked.

"I'm fine, luv."

"Then why aren't you with everyone else? You should be clinking champagne glasses with the king and Mr. Lloyd George, instead of moping in a corner."

Fiona smiled. "You're absolutely right. And I will. I was just feeling a little tired, that's all. As you do at the end of big things," she said.

Kate took hold of Fiona by both shoulders now. Her excitement was palpable. "But, Mum," she said, "it's not the end of anything. Not at all."

"It isn't?" Fiona said, looking at her daughter's bright, beautiful face, looking into her fierce, intelligent blue eyes.

"No. I've decided that I'm going to stand for Parliament on the Labour ticket. I can't wait until I'm thirty to participate in my own government. I just can't. Mr. Lloyd George might've placed a high age bar on voting—he couldn't have us women wielding too much influence in government, now, could he? But he set a lower one on standing for Parliament. I can't vote for eleven more years, but I can run as soon as I turn twenty-one—which is less than two years away. And I will. As soon as I'm out of university, I'm going to start planning my campaign."

"Oh, Katie," Fiona said, her eyes shining. "That's the most wonderful news. I'm so excited. And so proud."

"Thank you, Mum. I hoped you would be. Oh, look! The king's free. Be right back!"

"The king? Katie, you're not going to . . ." Her voice trailed off. It was too late. Katie was making her way over to the monarch.

Fiona felt someone take her hand and squeeze it. It was Joe. "Looks like she's gone off to buttonhole old King George," he said.

"You don't think she's going to give him a copy of this week's *Battle Cry*, do you?" Fiona said. "She's got articles by Ben Tillet, Ella Rosen, Annie Besant, and Millicent Fawcett in there. Every firebrand in London. She'll give him heart palpitations."

"She's already giving him heart palpitations," Joe said, "and it's not because of her newspaper."

Fiona laughed. The king was looking at Katie, motioning for her to come forward. He was smiling at her. Of course he was, Fiona thought. Katie had that effect on men. With her black hair, blue eyes, and slender figure, she was a beauty.

"Have you heard her news, then?" Joe asked.

"I have," Fiona said. "You wouldn't have had anything to do with it, would you now?" she added, raising an eyebrow.

Joe shook his head. "Katie makes her own decisions. She's her own girl, you know that."

"I certainly do."

Joe smiled roguishly. "I *will* say I'm pleased she's going into the family business, though," he said.

"Politics, the family business," Fiona said wonderingly. "It used to be barrows and the docks. Who'd have thought it, Joe? Back when we were our children's ages, I mean. Who'd ever have believed it?"

Katie dropped a curtsy to the king, then stood up straight, squared her shoulders, and started talking. Joe and Fiona couldn't hear what she was saying, but they both watched as the king, nodding his head, leaned in closer to listen.

"Poor sod," Joe said. "He has no idea what he's in for."

Fiona shook her head, then she said, "You know, luv, earlier tonight, I thought it was ended. I thought the struggle—at least one of them—was over. I thought . . ."

Joe was about to answer, but his words died away also, as he and Fiona, both incredulous, watched their daughter pull a folded copy of the *Battle Cry* from her purse and hand it to the king.

"Yes, Fee? What were you saying?" Joe said, when he could find his voice again.

"Forget what I was saying," Fiona said, laughing. "Nothing's over. Nothing's ended. With our Katie in the fray, it's only just beginning."

"Joe! There you are!" a familiar voice said. Fiona turned. David Lloyd George was at Joe's side. "Greetings, Mrs. Bristow. How are you today? Well, I trust. I must tell you both, that daughter of yours is a firecracker of a girl. Just had the most fascinating conversation with her. All about her newspaper. She gave me a copy and made me promise to subscribe. She's an excellent saleswoman, and as smart as a whip!"

"Takes after her mum, she does," Joe said proudly.

"She also told me that she planned to run for Parliament just as soon as she turned twenty-one," Lloyd George said. He smiled at Joe and added, "I think you'd better watch out for your job, old boy."

Joe smiled back and said, "Actually, Prime Minister, I think you'd better watch out for *yours*!"

CHAPTER FIFTY-ONE

"THEY SAY NOW that the Yanks are in, it'll be over soon," Allie Beech said.

"I heard it might be as soon as this year," Lizzie Caldwell said.

"Wouldn't that be wonderful? Having them all home again?" Jennie Finnegan said.

"I remember when my Ronnie enlisted. It was all a big lark, wasn't it? The boys were going off to give old Gerry a big black eye. They'd be home in two months, three at the most. It would all be over before we knew it," Peg McDonnell said.

"And here we are, March of 1918, going on four years," Nancy Barrett said.

"And millions dead. And so many others badly injured and in hospital," Peg said.

"Peg, dear, pass me the teapot, won't you? I'm parched," Jennie said, wanting to stop any talk about dead and injured men before it got started.

Jennie was sitting in the kitchen of her father's house, the rectory house of St. Nicholas's parish. She'd moved back here to be with her father after Seamie had enlisted. He'd wanted that. He hadn't wanted her to be alone in their flat with a new baby. He'd felt it would be good for all of them—herself, the reverend, and little James—to be together during this long, hard, horrible war.

She put her knitting needles in her lap now, poured herself another cup of tea, then set the pot on the table. She and half a dozen women from the parish were knitting socks for British soldiers. They met here every Wednesday evening at seven o'clock.

It had been Jennie's idea to start this knitting circle. She knew the women of her father's parish and knew that many of them were suffering greatly. They were lonely for their men and worried they'd never see them again. They were raising their children alone, without enough money, and—thanks to the German U-boats that prevented supply ships from getting to Britain—without enough food, either. Rationing had made them all thin. Jennie scrimped on her own rations to provide a pot of tea and a few thin biscuits for these evenings. But she did it gladly, for their lives—and hers—were difficult and uncertain and it bolstered all their spirits to spend an evening sitting together and talking, to make socks and send them off and feel that they were contributing, if only in a small way, to the comfort and well-being of the men on the front lines.

"Gladys, can I pour you more tea?" Jennie asked the woman sitting on her right.

"No, thank you," Gladys Bigelow said, never taking her eyes off her knitting.

Jennie set the pot down on the low tea table in front of her, frowning with concern. Gladys no longer lived in the parish, but Jennie had asked her to join them anyway. She was worried about her. As the years of the war had dragged on, she'd watched Gladys turn into a shadow. Once plump and bubbly, she'd become thin, pale, and withdrawn. Jennie had asked her several times what was troubling her, but Gladys would only smile wanly and say that her work was demanding.

"Sir George is always the first to hear what ship was torpedoed and how many were lost," she'd explained. "It takes a toll on him. Takes a toll on us all, doesn't it? But I mustn't complain. So many have it so much worse."

Jennie had taken her hand then and had quietly said to her, "At least we have the comfort of knowing that we're doing our part, along with Mr. von Brandt, to help save innocent lives. And perhaps even hasten the end of this dreadful war."

Perhaps she'd only imagined it, but it had seemed to her then that Gladys, already pale, had gone even whiter at the mention of Max's name.

"Yes, Jennie," she'd said, pulling her hand away. "We always have that."

Jennie had not mentioned Max again, but she had continued to take the envelope Gladys gave her, after every Tuesday night suffrage meeting, just as Max von Brandt had asked her to do three and a half years ago.

This very evening, before the women had arrived, while her father was busy giving James his bath, Jennie had quietly slipped down to the church's basement to tuck this week's envelope inside the broken statue of St. Nicholas.

She had often wondered if the man who took the envelope was nearby when she placed it under the statue. Was he in the tunnel, waiting for her to leave? Was he in the basement itself, watching her? The thought made her shiver. She was quick about her work, never tarrying, and felt glad only when she'd climbed back up the steps and closed the basement door behind her.

Jennie had never opened the envelopes, not once, though she had been tempted. Sometimes, on a long, sleepless night, she would lie quietly in her bed and wonder if Max von Brandt had told her the truth, if he was really on the side of peace. She would remember how he'd mentioned Binsey to her, and the cottage there, and how her heart had stuttered inside her at his ugly threat. And then she would resolve to open the very next envelope Gladys gave her, to find out the truth once and for all.

But then the night would give way to day, and her resolve would give way with it, and she would tell herself she must not open it. Max von Brandt had told her not to and he'd likely had a reason. Perhaps to do so might somehow breach security. Perhaps the envelope might not be accepted if it was opened. Perhaps she might even endanger an innocent person's life with her foolish curiosity.

Jennie told herself these things, because to believe otherwise—to believe that Max was not what he said he was, that he was using her to aid Germany and harm Britain—was simply unthinkable. And so she refused to do so. She had become very practiced, over the last few years, at not thinking about difficult things.

"I hear that a lot of soldiers are coming down with the influenza," Lizzie said now, diverting Jennie's thoughts from Max and Gladys. "The new one . . . the Spanish flu. Supposed to be worse than any other kind. I've heard it can kill you in a day."

"As if there wasn't enough to worry about," Allie sighed. "Now that."

"Allie, how's your Sarah doing at the secretarial school?" Jennie asked, trying, yet again, to steer the conversation away from worrisome topics.

"Oh, she's getting on like a house on fire!" Allie said, brightening. "Her teacher says she's top of the class and that she's going to put her name in for a position at Thompson's—it's a boot factory in Hackney—in the Accounts Department."

"Oh, I'm so pleased!" Jennie said. She'd taught Sarah at her school.

"She always was a bright one, your Sarah," Lizzie said approvingly.

As the talk drifted to other children and their doings, Jennie finished the sock she was working on. She had cast it off her needles and was just starting the second of the pair, when she heard the sound of small feet in the hallway and a little voice calling, "Mummy! Mummy!"

She looked up and saw a blond, hazel-eyed, pink-cheeked boy run into the kitchen—her son, James. Her face broke into a radiant smile. She felt her heart swell with love, as it always did at the sight of him. He stopped a few feet past the doorway and said, "May I please have a biscuit, Mummy? Grandpa says I might have milk and a biscuit if I ask nicely."

Jennie never got the chance to answer him. The others beat her to it.

"Of course you may, my duck!" Peg said.

"Come here and sit with your auntie Liz, you little dumpling!" Lizzie said.

"Wait your turn, you lot. I'm closest and I get him first," Nancy said.

James, giggling, allowed himself to be squeezed and kissed, passed around and cuddled and fed too many biscuits. He'd single-handedly managed to do what Jennie could not—take the women's minds off the war and their absent men and their worries.

"Look at the color of his hair. And those eyes!" Nancy exclaimed. "Why, he's the spitting image of his mother."

Jennie forced a smile. "Yes, he is," she said aloud, silently adding, His real mother—Josie Meadows.

Anyone glancing at her and then at three-year-old James would think them mother and child. They both had blond hair, hazel eyes, and porcelain skin. But if that same person were to look closer, he would notice differences.

Jennie looked at James now, as the women around her continued to fuss and chatter, and she saw Josie in the shape of the eyes, the tilt of his nose, and the curve of his smile. She remembered, with a sudden, startling clarity, the day the letter had arrived from Binsey—the letter from Josie telling her that she'd had the baby, that Dr. Cobb from the village had delivered him, and that he'd written Jennie Finnegan's name on the child's birth certificate, for that was what Josie had told the doctor her name was. When Dr. Cobb had asked Josie who the father was, she'd smiled and said, "My husband, of course. Seamus Finnegan."

Jennie, still faking her own nonexistent pregnancy, had left for Binsey that very same day. She'd met Josie at the cottage that evening, and then she'd met her son—James.

Josie was holding him and cooing to him, but as soon as she saw Jennie, she put the baby in her arms. Then she put her jacket on.

"You're not leaving, are you?" Jennie said, surprised. "I only just got here. You have to stay. At least for a day or two. And you said you'd travel to London with me. That we'd say you were a girl from the village."

Josie, her eyes bright with tears, had shaken her head no. "I'm sorry, Jennie. I can't," she said. "It gets harder every second I'm with him. If I don't go now, I never will."

Jennie looked into her friend's eyes, and in them she saw what it cost to surrender a child. "I can't do it," she said. "I can't take him from you. He's your baby."

"You have to take him. I can't stay here. You know that," Josie said. "Billy Madden doesn't forget and he doesn't forgive. He'll beat me within an inch of my life and put the baby into an orphanage—and that's if he's in a good mood. This is the best thing, Jennie. The only thing." She'd buttoned her jacket, put on her hat, and picked up her suitcase. "I'll write. Under a different name. Once I have a flat and get myself settled," she said. "Write me back and tell me about him. Send a picture now and again, if you can."

"I will. I promise. He'll be loved, Josie. Loved and cared for. Always. I promise you that."

"I know he will," Josie said. She kissed baby James and then Jennie, and then she left, suitcase in hand, never once looking back.

Jennie had spent a strange and terrifying and wonderful week alone with her new son, and then she'd got on a train back to London. She told her father and her friends and Seamie's family that the baby had come a bit early. There was some surprise, and she'd had to endure a bit of scolding for going off to the country on her own so close to her due date, but mostly there was joy and delight in the tiny new life in their midst. No one suspected her of passing off another woman's child as her own—why would they? Only her father and Harriet knew the exact nature of the injuries her accident had caused. Her father, being a man of faith, simply accepted James's birth as yet another of God's miracles. Harriet Hatcher, being a woman of science, had posed a bigger problem, but Jennie had got round it by telling Harriet that as she was spending so much time in Binsey, she had decided to see the doctor there, Dr. Cobb, for her check-ups. Harriet said she understood and told Jennie to come back to her after the baby was born, but Jennie never did. And never would.

It would have been a far trickier thing to pull off had Seamie been in London. He would have seen that her body had not changed during her pregnancy, and that her breasts were not full of milk, and would likely have wanted to know why. She told any woman friend who asked if she was nursing James that her milk was scanty and so she'd decided to bottle-feed him instead. Seamie might also have wanted to go to Binsey, to see Dr. Cobb and thank him for delivering his son, but Seamie had been hundreds of miles away on a British warship when James arrived, so that had not happened.

Jennie'd had a photograph taken of the baby, which she'd enclosed in a letter to Seamie, informing him he was now the father of a strapping son. She'd written that she hoped he didn't mind, but she'd named the boy James, after him. When he'd come home on furlough, nearly a year later, he'd fallen in love with the child at first sight and made Jennie promise to send him photos of James every month.

And so, amazingly, Josie's mad plan had worked—perfectly. Josie herself was safely away from London, working as a chorus girl in Paris under a stage name. Her child was safely in Jennie Finnegan's care. And no one was the wiser.

Jennie should have been happy. She had the child she'd desperately wanted. James was hers. He was her pride and her joy, her beautiful, golden boy. And she loved him fiercely. She had her handsome, war-hero husband. She had the love of family and friends.

But she was not happy. She was tortured and miserable, for her happiness had all been built upon lies. She had lied to Seamie about her ability to have children. She hadn't told him about her miscarriage. And she'd lied again by telling him James was their son. And though she'd got away with those lies, she knew that God was nonetheless punishing her for them, because Seamie, her beloved husband, no longer loved her.

He had never said as much. He was good to her. Concerned about her. He signed all his letters to her with love. He tried his best to love her, but he did not. There was no fire in his touch anymore. His eyes, when he looked at her, were kind, but distant. There was a sadness and a heaviness to him always, as if the fire that had burned so brightly inside of him, the fire that had carried him to places like Kilimanjaro and the South Pole, that had made him brave and daring, that had kept him always on a quest, had gone out forever.

She had found the letter Willa had written to him, the one in which she told him good-bye. It was crumpled in the pocket of one of his jackets. And she'd found one he started to write to her after she left—torn into pieces at the bottom of the rubbish bin in his study. In it, he'd told her that she'd done the right thing by leaving, that she'd been stronger than he had. He told her that he was sorry for being unfaithful to his wife and that he was going to spend the rest of his life being a good husband to her and a good father to their child, but that he wanted her, Willa, to know that no matter what happened, no matter how many years passed, even if he never laid eyes on her again, he loved her and he always would. She was his heart and his soul.

Jennie had cried when she'd read those words. For her sorrow and for his. Knowing that he was sorry for what he'd done, that he wanted to try to be a good husband even at the expense of his own happiness, didn't make anything better. It just made it sadder and harder. Willa Alden—not she, Jennie—was Seamie Finnegan's heart and his soul, and Willa had left him. And the loss of her, for the second time in his life, had gutted him. Emptied him. Turned him into a shell.

"Come on, you little monkey," her father said to James now. "We have to leave these ladies to their work. Our boys can't march without nice warm socks."

James finished the biscuit he was holding and kissed Jennie good night. She pressed him close and held him tightly, inhaling his little boy smell. He was all she had to love now, the best and brightest thing in her life.

"Ow, Mummy! You're squooooshing me!" he squeaked.

The women all laughed. Jennie kissed his cheek one more time, then released him. She watched him take his grandfather's hand as they walked out of the kitchen, and for a few seconds, the depth of her feeling for him completely overcame her. She desperately hoped he would never find out what she'd done. She imagined him doing so, when he was older, and hating her for it. The thought alone caused her a deep and terrible anguish. She closed her eyes and put a hand to her temple.

Lizzie noticed immediately. "Are you all right, Jennie?" she asked her.

Jennie opened her eyes again. She nodded and smiled. "I'm fine, thank you. Just a bit tired, that's all."

Peg grinned wickedly. "Maybe you're expecting again," she said.

"Peg McDonnell! What a terrible thing to say. Her husband's away!" Lizzie scolded her.

"Oh, keep your knickers on, will you? I was only joking," Peg said.

Jennie smiled, pretending she thought the women's ribbing was all good fun. Deep down, though, she knew it wouldn't have mattered if Seamie had never left, for she'd never be expecting his child. Never. Even if he still wanted to make love to her, which he did not, she couldn't have given him a child.

"At least Jennie's husband writes to her. I haven't heard from Ronnie for over a week now," Peg said, and her voice, usually loud and boisterous, had gone quiet. Now that James was gone, Peg's mind had returned to its anxious thoughts.

Looking at her, Jennie thought she saw a shimmer of tears in her eyes. Allie must've seen them, too, because she suddenly said, "He hasn't written because he's thrown you over and taken up with a French girl. Her name's Fifi LaBelle."

The women all screeched laughter. Peg wiped her eyes and scowled. Allie winked at her, then elbowed her in the ribs, jollying her out of her tears. Allie knew, as they all did, that Peg wasn't worried about her Ronnie taking up with a French girl. She was worried he'd been shot and was lying dead on the cold, hard ground somewhere far away.

"Fifi LaBelle has bubs as big as melons and feathers in her hair and she wears pink silk knickers with diamonds on them," Allie added.

"Fine by me," Peg sniffed. "Fifi's welcome to him. Randier than a goat, that man. Never gives me a minute's peace." She sighed deeply, then added, "Oh, how I miss him."

There was more laughter at that, followed by more bawdy chatter. Jennie watched them as they talked, and listened to them, and envied them. She knew that French girls were not her problem. Her husband was not in love with a French girl. He was in love with an English girl and he always would be.

CHAPTER FIFTY-TWO

WILLA SAT, HER bare feet tucked discreetly beneath her, on a soft, woven rug in a *bayt char*, or house of hair—a black Bedouin tent woven of goat's hair. The tent was enormous and richly decorated with exquisite rugs and hangings—all signs of its owner's wealth and power—but Willa barely noticed. Her attention was focused on the glass of hot tea in her hands, flavored with mint and sweetened with sugar. She, Lawrence, and Auda had been riding across the desert for five days, with nothing to sustain them but water, dates, and dried goat's meat. The tea tasted so good to her, and was so restoring, she had to remind herself to sip it politely, not gulp it like a glutton, for she knew well that the Bedouin placed a high value on mannerly conduct and would not treat with those they deemed boorish and rude.

Lawrence had been searching for the Beni Sakhr, the sons of the rock, a Bedouin tribe, and their sheik, Khalaf al Mor. Earlier today, they had found his encampment. Khalaf had sent an emissary to meet them and inquire after their purpose.

"*Salaam aleikum,*" Lawrence said to the man, bowing slightly, his hand upon his heart. "Peace be upon you."

"*Wa aleikum salaam,*" the man replied. "Peace be upon you, too." He told them his name was Fahed.

"I come with greetings from Faisal ibn Hussein," Lawrence said in Arabic. "I wish to speak with your sheik. To ask him for his counsel and his aid in our war against the Turks. I am Lawrence, from England. This is Auda abu Tayi, a Howeitat chief. This is Willa Alden, my secretary."

Fahed's eyes widened. He looked Willa up and down, frowning. Willa had never so much as typed a letter for Lawrence, but in Bedouin culture, where women were kept apart from the public life of men, it was the most easily accepted explanation for her presence at Lawrence's side, and the one most likely to gain her admittance to the sheik's tent, instead of banishment to his wives' quarters. Willa didn't give a damn what the sheik thought of her, or of any other woman; all she cared about was getting photographs of these remarkable people, their homes, their lands, their animals, their way of life.

Fahed frowned a bit more, then he said, "I will bring this news to the sheik," giving them no promises and no commitments. He showed them where to water and rest their camels, and had water brought to them as well, and then beetled off to the largest tent in the encampment.

Half an hour later, he returned. "Sheik Khalaf al Mor instructs me to tell you that you may attend him in his tent this evening."

Lawrence bowed. "Please tell the sheik he does us a great honor."

Fahed then took Lawrence and Auda to one tent to wash themselves, and Willa to another. Clean robes were unpacked from their satchels. It would not do to appear before a sheik in dusty ones. Willa was grateful for the bath. It was only April, but already the days were warm, and she was sweaty and dirty after her long ride through the desert. While they waited for evening and the sheik's summons, Lawrence and Auda talked of strategy and how best to win Khalaf al Mor to their cause, while Willa took photographs of the Beni Sakhr women and children. The women were shy, but the children were as curious about her as she was about them. They pulled up her sleeves to see her skin, pulled off her head scarf to touch her hair. They felt her artificial leg, then demanded to see how it attached to her body. They clasped her face between their hands so that they could look more closely at her green eyes. As they touched and inspected her, Willa laughed, marveling at how these desert children were so different from English children, and yet—with their shy giggles, their curiosity, their mischievous smiles—they were so very much the same.

Willa asked them in their language if any of them belonged to Khalaf al Mor. They went silent then and looked at one another. She asked what was wrong, if she had given offense. And then one, a boy of ten or so, Ali, told her in a hushed voice that the sheik's children, and their mothers, were all in his first wife's tent. Her eldest child—the sheik's firstborn son—was very ill and not expected to live. The sheik's entire family was praying for him, beseeching Allah to spare his life.

Willa was gravely concerned when she heard this—for the child first and foremost, and for Lawrence's petition. How could Khalaf al Mor even listen to them, much less favor them with counsel and men, when his child was dying?

As the sun was beginning to set, Fahed came for them. Willa had told Lawrence and Auda of Ali's news. It had made them both solemn. They went along nonetheless, all three of them, carrying gifts—pearl-handled revolvers, daggers in intricately worked sheaths, compasses in brass cases, plus beautifully worked dog collars and jesses with golden bells for hunting birds—for Khalaf was known to keep salukis and hawks.

Greetings and bows were made, gifts were presented and warmly accepted. The guests were welcomed by Khalaf. He was charming and gracious, and betrayed no sign that anything was troubling him, but Willa could see the worry deep within his eyes. She knew, too, that his Bedouin pride would not allow him to share his private grief with strangers.

Instead, he expressed a jovial curiosity at her presence. "Is your sheik Lawrence so poor he cannot afford a proper secretary?" he asked her jestingly. "And must make do with a woman?"

"Ah, *Sidi*! My sheik is so clever that for me he pays half what he would pay a man, yet gets twice the work . . . and ten times the brains!" she replied.

Khalaf laughed uproariously at that, his worries forgotten for a moment, and beckoned Willa to sit beside him. Lawrence was invited to sit at his right, and Auda was seated next to Lawrence. *Day'f Al-lah*, Khalaf called them—"guests of God." Finger bowls were brought, then a delicious minted tea, which Willa was now sipping. She knew that a lavish dinner would be laid on as well. The Bedouin code of hospitality demanded it. To offer guests anything less than a feast would have been unthinkable.

There was talk of superficial things to begin with—weather and camels, mainly—for to launch directly into the purpose of their visit would have been seen as awkward and unsubtle. After an hour or so, the meal was brought.

It was mansaf, a Bedouin dish of stewed lamb in yogurt sauce, spiced with baharat—a mixture of black pepper, allspice, cinnamon, and nutmeg—cooked over an open fire, sprinkled with pine nuts and almonds, and served on a bed of rice on a large, communal platter. It was one of Willa's favorites.

Well versed now in Bedouin etiquette, Willa washed her hands in the nearest finger bowl, then rolled up her right sleeve. Only the right hand was used for eating, never the left, for the left was the hand one wiped one's backside with.

Everyone knew why they were here, but as the desert saying advised, "It is good to know the truth, but it is better to speak of palm trees."

"*Al-hamdu illah*," Khalaf said—"Thanks be to God"—and the dining began. Willa moistened a portion of the mansaf with jamid, the yogurt sauce, then used her right hand to delicately fashion it into a small ball. She lifted the ball to her mouth and popped it in, careful not to touch her lips, or to drop any of the rice or meat from her hand or her mouth. She was careful, too, to keep her feet well tucked away beneath her robe, for showing the sole of your foot to an Arab was the very height of rudeness.

After the meal, sweets were served, and Khalaf had his prize salukis and his favorite hawk brought out to be admired. Auda, a Bedouin, too, was much moved by the beauty of the hawk and pronounced it an exceptional bird. Lawrence inquired after the dogs' bloodlines. And then they got down to the reason for their visit.

"Faisal ibn Hussein has asked us to convey his respectful greetings, and to petition you and your men to join with him in the battle for Arabia's independence," Lawrence said. "We have four thousand men ready and willing to march north upon the Turks in Aqaba, and then Damascus. I need more. I need the men of the Beni Sakhr."

Khalaf made no reply. Instead he gave Auda a long, assessing look. "And my Howeitat brothers?" he asked him. "Have they joined with Faisal?"

"We have," Auda said.

Willa held her breath, waiting for Khalaf's reaction. Auda's reply might have brought favor, or it might not have. The Bedouin could be extremely distrustful of one another. Allegiances between tribes often went back for generations, but so did rivalries and feuds.

Khalaf opened his mouth to speak, but before he could, a long and piercing wail ripped through the walls of the tent—a woman's cry of grief. All heard it, but none remarked it. Khalaf al Mor's stony look forbade it.

The cry shook Willa terribly. She was certain it had come from the sheik's wife, the mother of his very ill son. She longed to go to the woman, to help her care for her dying child. She had Western medicines with her—quinine, aconite, and morphine. She always carried them. People who trekked across glaciers at the foot of Everest, who rode for days in the desert, she had learned, had to be their own doctors. If the first two medicines did no good, the third would at least ease the child's suffering. She could not go, however—not without the sheik's permission. If she asked him for it, he might grant it— or he might be gravely insulted. He might take her request as her suggesting that his own efforts to care for his child were inadequate. If that happened, if she offended Khalaf, here in his own tent, among his own men, he would never agree to join with Lawrence and Faisal.

"The Turks are very powerful," Khalaf said now, still evasive. "Faisal may win a few battles, but they will win the war."

"That is true, *Sidi* . . . unless you were to help us," Lawrence said.

"Why should the Bedouin fight for Hussein? For the English?

The Bedouin do not belong to Hussein, or to the English, or to the Turks. We belong to no man. We belong only to the desert."

"Then you must fight for that desert. You must expel the Turks."

"What will Faisal give?"

"Gold."

"And the English?"

"More gold."

"Why?"

"Because we have interests in Arabia," Lawrence said. "We have our Persian oil fields to defend, and access to our colonies in India to protect. We wish also to tie up the armies of the Turks and the Germans, to draw their resources away from the western front."

"What guarantees have I that once our Turkish masters are ousted, the English will not try to replace them?"

"You have my guarantee. And that of Mr. Lloyd George, England's great sheik. England wishes to have only influence in the region, not control."

Khalaf nodded. "And what of—" he started to say, but his words were cut off by yet another wail. He rose quickly, crossed the floor of his tent, and feigned interest in his hawk, perched in a large cage behind him, in order to hide his face and the despair etched upon it.

Damn these men and their wars, Willa thought angrily. She could sit still no longer. She rose and approached Khalaf.

"*Sidi,*" she began. "I have medicines with me—strong, good medicines. Allow me please to go to your son."

Khalaf looked at her. The pain in his eyes was searing. He shook his head no. "It is Allah's will," he said quietly.

Willa had expected this response. It was the only one he knew how to give. She understood the hardship of his life, of all the Bedouins' lives. Death stalked them always. They died of disease, of battle wounds, or in childbirth. How many times had she seen a Bedouin man walk into the desert with the shrouded body of a wife or child in his arms? She had expected the response, yes, but she could not accept it.

"Great sheik," she said, humbly bowing her head before him, "is it not also Allah's will that I am here this night? He, who with infinite care painted every speckle on every feather of this magnificent hawk? He, who sees the sparrow fall. Does He not also know that I am here with you now? Did He not will that, too?"

It was dead quiet inside the tent. Willa, a woman, had just countered the decree of a sheik. She had been heard to do it by every man there. She might well have just ruined any chance Lawrence had to secure Khalaf al Mor's support. She raised her head slowly and looked at Khalaf. She did not see a great sheik before her then, but a heartbroken father.

He nodded. "*Inshallah*," he said softly. "If Allah wills it."

Fahed was sitting nearby. She hurried to him. "Please," she said, "take me to the child."

Willa gasped as she saw the boy. He was so dehydrated, he looked like an old man. He was burning with fever, delirious, and in a great deal of pain from the violent spasms that gripped his gut. She laid a gentle hand on his chest. His small heart was racing. It was cholera. She was sure of it. She'd seen enough cases of it in India and Tibet to recognize its symptoms.

"You will help him, please. Please. Allah in his goodness has sent you here to help him, I know He has. Please help my child," the boy's mother said. Her name was Fatima. She was weeping so hard now that Willa could barely understand her.

"I'll do my best," Willa said. "I need tea. Mint tea. Cooled. Can you get me some right away?"

She knew that the child needed liquids inside him, immediately. His mother had been giving him water, but Willa didn't want to give him any more. Cholera was a waterborne disease. He might have got it from a tainted well here. Or he might have got it at the last encampment. There was no way to tell. The Bedouin traveled frequently, staying in no one place longer than a fortnight. The tea would be safe, though, for it had been boiled. She would give him some with sugar in it and a few drops of the aconite tincture she always carried with her. She'd learned about aconite in the East. It was used there against cholera. It helped to diminish a fever and slow a too-rapid heartbeat.

The tea was brought, dosed, and administered. The boy fought against it, splashing it everywhere, but Willa thought she'd managed to get at least half a pint down him. A few minutes later, however, it all came gushing out of him. Willa asked for more tea and gave him a few more ounces. Again, spasms racked his small body, and again the life-giving liquid came out of him.

Willa changed tactics. She used what tea she had left to bathe him. The liquid evaporating from his skin, and the cooling properties of mint, helped to take some heat from him, but he was still delirious, still moaning with pain. When she was finished washing him, she asked for more tea to be brought and gave him, yet again, a few ounces of it. She waited. Two minutes. Four. Ten. There were no spasms. No diarrhea. Had some of the aconite she'd put in the first cup of tea been absorbed by his body? Willa desperately hoped so. Stopping his body from trying to expel every drop of liquid she tried to put in it was his only chance. His bones poked through his skin. His breathing was labored. She touched her fingers to his neck, underneath his ear. His pulse fluttered. He was truly on death's doorstep. They would have to fight, very hard, to pull him back.

"Might I have a pot of coffee?" she suddenly asked Fatima.

Fatima's eyes widened. "Coffee? But it's so strong. Will it help him?"

"No, it will help me," she said. "It's going to be a long night."

Hours passed, then the night, and then the following day. Willa refused to sleep. Over and over again, she raised the boy's head, held the glass of tea to his lips, and coaxed him to drink. Over and over again, she bathed his thin body. And somehow the child, Daoud was his name, hung on. He did not open his eyes. His fever did not break. But his diarrhea stopped, and somehow, he held on. Willa gave him another dose of aconite. And then one of quinine. She drank more coffee, ate flatbread and roasted goat, and waited.

They talked, she and Fatima, while they kept vigil. About the sheik. About the desert. About camels and goats. About Lawrence. About Willa's accident. About Fatima's wedding day. About their lives.

"There is a sadness in you," Fatima said, as the first night gave way to day. "I see it in your eyes."

"I'm not sad, I'm tired," Willa said.

"Why have you no husband? No child of your own?"

Willa didn't answer, so Fatima pressed.

"There was someone once. A man. I loved him very much. I still do. But he's with another," Willa finally said.

Fatima shook her head. "But why can he not marry you both? This other woman and you. He would have to give his first wife more jewels, of course. And a better tent. That is her due. But you would be his second wife and that is not so bad."

Willa smiled wearily. "I'm afraid it doesn't work that way where I'm from," she said. "They don't let men have more than one wife in London, and there's no place to pitch a tent."

"I do not understand these English."

"Neither do I," Willa said.

"Fatima," she said later, as the day lengthened into night again and still Daoud would not open his eyes. "Do you and the other women of the Beni Sahkr ever mind your lot in life? Do you ever long for something different?"

"No," Fatima said slowly, as if she'd only just now—for the first time—even considered having a different life. "Why would I? This is the life Allah ordained for me. This is my fate. Do you mind your life?"

"No, but that's the whole point, isn't it? I've nothing to mind. I have my freedom."

Fatima laughed out loud. "Is that what you think?"

"Yes, that's what I think. What on earth is so funny?" Willa asked.

"You are. You might have your freedom, Willa Alden, but you are not free," Fatima said. "You are a driven creature. Possessed by something. What, I do not know. But whatever it is, it haunts you. It takes you from your home, causes you to chase phantoms in the desert with madmen like Auda abu Tayi and the sheik Lawrence."

"It's called a war, Fatima. I'm fighting for my country. It will be different when it's over. I'll go home then. I'll buy myself a nice little house in the country and be peaceable and contented and sew by the fire."

"No, I do not think so," Fatima said.

"But I thought you *did* think so!" Willa chided her. "I thought I was supposed to find a husband and have children. Isn't that what you told me last night? Isn't that what you want me to do?"

"Yes, but what I want is of no consequence. It is Allah's will that matters, and He has much work for you yet, and it does not involve sewing."

Willa was just about to tell Fatima that she was an impossible woman, when they both heard a small, raspy voice say, "Mama?"

It was Daoud. His eyes were open and clear. He was gazing at his mother. Fatima, who'd been pouring tea into a glass, dropped both the pot and the glass and flew to him, praising Allah as she embraced him.

"I'm thirsty, Mama," he said, still weak and confused.

Willa got the child more tea, and then she ran to find his father. They hurried back to Fatima's tent together, and then Willa left the family to themselves. For some reason, the sight of the fierce Bedouin sheik sitting on his child's bed and kissing his small hands made her cry.

"He's out of the woods," she told Lawrence. Then she staggered back to the Khalaf's sixth wife's tent—where she'd gone to wash when she first arrived at the encampment—sank down on some cushions, and slept for fifteen hours straight.

When she awoke, Fatima was sitting across from her, smiling. "He is doing well," she said.

Willa smiled back. She sat up. "I'm so happy, Fatima," she said.

"Khalaf wishes to see you once you have eaten. But I wanted to see you first," she said. She stood up, crossed the small room, and knelt down by Willa. She drew a necklace from the folds of her robe, and before Willa could protest, she fastened it around her neck.

"Khalaf gave it to me when Daoud was born. A present for the woman who gave life to his first son. You gave my child life again, Willa Alden. Now you are his mother, too."

Willa, speechless, looked down at the necklace lying against her chest. It was made of gold medallions set with turquoise and strung together with red amber and agates. Fatima picked the necklace up off Willa's chest and shook it. The medallions made a soft jingle.

"Do you hear that? It is to ward off evil spirits."

The necklace was very valuable. Willa wanted to give it back, she wanted to tell Fatima that it was too great a gift. But she could not. To refuse a gift gave great offense to the Bedouin.

She embraced Fatima. "Thank you," she said, her voice husky with emotion. "I will wear it always, and think of the one who gave it to me."

Willa washed, dressed herself in clean clothes, and went to Khalaf al Mor's tent. The sheik smiled when he saw her. His smile broadened when he saw the gift his wife had given her. He bowed to her, then thanked her for the life of his son.

Two days later, with promises of five hundred men and two hundred camels from Khalaf for the march on Damascus, she, Lawrence, and Auda said their good-byes. They had a long ride ahead of them back to Lawrence's own camp.

"I wish you would stay with us, Willa Alden," Khalaf said as he stood outside his tent, watching them mount their camels and bidding them farewell. "I must tell you, I tried to buy you from Lawrence, but he will not part with you. Not even for twenty thousand dinars. I do not blame him."

"Twenty thousand dinars?" Auda thundered. "*I* blame him! Twenty thousand dinars would buy us all the guns we need!" He stuck his chin out at Willa. "I would have parted with you for five," he said. Then he snapped his crop against his camel's haunch and rode off.

Laughing, Willa and Lawrence said a final good-bye to Khalaf, then set off after Auda.

"Twenty thousand dinars," Willa said, as they rode out of the Beni Sakhr encampment. "My word, but that's an awful lot of money. And you didn't take it. I think you like me, Tom. I really do."

"No, that's not it all," Lawrence said, looking at her, mischief sparkling in his eyes.

"It isn't? Then why didn't you sell me to Khalaf?"

"Because I'm holding out for thirty."

CHAPTER FIFTY-THREE

BEN COTTON, TWENTY-ONE years old, from the city of Leeds, and a patient at Wickersham Hall, a hospital for injured veterans, sat on the edge of his bed, hands clasped, head down. A new artificial leg, complete with flexible knee joint, lay on the floor next to him where he'd thrown it only moments before.

Sid Baxter, standing in the doorway to Ben's room, his cane in one hand, a pile of clothing in the other, looked at the fake leg and then at Ben. Tough nut, this one, he thought. Ever since he'd arrived, the lad had barely eaten, barely spoken, and had refused to wear his new leg. Dr. Barnes, the head psychiatrist, had given up. He couldn't do a thing with him, he said, so he'd asked Sid to have a go.

"Ben Cotton, is it?" Sid said now.

"Aye," Ben said, not raising his head.

"I brought some clothes for you. A pair of trousers. Shirt and tie. A jumper," Sid said. He got no response.

"I thought you might need them," he continued. "There's a girl down in the visitors' room who wants to see you. Says she came all the way from Leeds. Says she's staying in a little inn in the village but she can't stay much longer. It's costing her quite a bit, you see. She's been coming here every day for a week, hoping to see you. I figure you haven't gone down yet, because all you've got to wear is that silly bloody nightshirt."

"I told Dr. Barnes to tell her to go home," Ben said.

"Who is she?"

"My fiancée."

"A bit rude of you to stay in your room when she's come all this way to see you, wouldn't you say so, lad? It's a beautiful June evening. Sun's still out. Birds are singing. Why don't you go down and sit out in the garden?"

Ben picked his head up and looked at him then, and Sid saw that his eyes were filled with anger.

"Just waltz downstairs on my one good leg and say hello, will I? Maybe have a nice stroll round the grounds and a spot of tea while I'm at it?"

Sid shrugged. "Why not?"

"Why not? *Why not?* How can I go down to her? How can I let her see me?" he said bitterly, gesturing at his missing leg. "I'm not even a man anymore."

"You're not?" Sid said. "Why's that? Did Gerry blow your nuts off, too?"

Ben blinked. His mouth dropped open.

"I guess he must've. It's the only thing that might explain why you're sitting up here on your bed whinging and moaning and feeling sorry for yourself instead of going to see that pretty little lass of yours."

Ben scowled; he started to tell Sid off, but then burst into laughter instead. The laughter grew until it became hysterical, and then it turned into great, wrenching sobs. Sid had seen it before. The doctors here were a fine and educated lot, but they didn't speak to the men as bluntly as he did. And sometimes bluntness was exactly what was needed to draw them out.

Sid sat down on the bed, patted Ben's back, and waited patiently for his emotion to subside. "You finished?" he said when the lad had gone quiet.

Ben nodded. He wiped his eyes on his sleeve.

"I know your story," Sid said. "I read your records. You signed up right away. Fought for your country. You spent over three years on the front in France, earning yourself some nice commendations for bravery while you were at it, until one of Gerry's bombs took your leg. You almost bled to death in the mud. Then an infection almost took you. The field doctor who fixed you up wrote that it was a miracle you didn't die. 'One of the toughest, bravest lads I've ever seen,' he wrote. You're a man all right, Ben Cotton. You're more of a man on one leg than most are on two."

Ben said nothing, but Sid could see his jaw working. He reached down, picked the artificial leg up off the floor, and handed it to Ben, hoping he'd take it. Ben did. He started to buckle it on.

"I can't walk on it properly," he said. "I hobble around on it like an old man."

"You can't walk on it properly *yet*," Sid said. "It takes a bit of practice. Give it some time."

"What happened to your leg?" Ben asked. "I've seen you around here. You walk with a limp. Was it the war?"

"No, it was a steer. And a bad doctor. Years ago. In Denver. I broke it in a slaughterhouse. Steer rushed at me and knocked me down. Doctor set it badly. It didn't heal right. Mostly I can manage. Sometimes, if it's paining me, I need a cane."

"You're married, aren't you?" Ben asked. "To the lady doctor?"

Sid could hear the worry in his voice. "I am," he replied. "She liked me before my leg was broken. And she liked me after, too."

Ben nodded.

"Here's the clothing I brought," Sid said. "The docs have you lot running around in these bloody nightshirts all the time, I don't understand it. No wonder you don't feel like a man. You've got no trousers on."

Ben thanked him. He reached for the clothes, pulled them on, then stood up. He took a few clumsy steps, then turned around in the doorway, fists clenched, and looked back at Sid. "I'm afraid," he said.

"I don't blame you, lad. Women are scarier than anything in Gerry's whole bloody arsenal."

Ben smiled bravely. Then he squared his shoulders, turned around again, and started walking.

Sid waited for a few minutes, then he followed him downstairs, casting a quick, casual glance into the visitors' room. The girl, Amanda was her name, was crying, but she was laughing, too, and Sid could see that her tears were tears of joy.

As Sid ducked out of the doorway, Dr. Barnes walked by, wearing his overcoat and hat, and carrying his briefcase. He, too, peered into the visitors' room, then ducked out again, smiling.

"Well done, Mr. Baxter! Bravo!" he said quietly.

Sid smiled. "I expect we'll see Ben eating and talking a bit more. Maybe even trying a bit harder with the new leg. Amazing, isn't it, how women make us want to buck ourselves up?"

Dr. Barnes laughed. "What's amazing is your effect on the hard cases," he said.

"I suppose it takes one to know one," Sid said.

Dr. Barnes told Sid he was leaving for the night and asked if he was heading home, too.

"Soon," Sid replied. "But I thought I might visit Stephen first. If you've no objection."

"Of course not," Dr. Barnes said. He frowned, then added, "Any signs of life there?"

"Maybe," Sid said cautiously.

"Really?" Dr. Barnes said eagerly.

"Don't get excited, mate. I said *maybe,* didn't I? I really don't know. I thought I saw something. Yesterday, when I took him into the stables. I found out his people are farmers, you see. . . ."

"How did you find that out? Stephen doesn't speak."

"I wrote his da. Asked him to tell me as much as he could about Stephen's life. Before the war, I mean."

Dr. Barnes nodded, impressed.

"Anyway," Sid continued, "I got the idea to take him into the stables and walk with him past the horses and the cows, and I thought—like I said, maybe I only imagined it—but I thought I felt the trembling subside a little, and I saw his eyes go to Hannibal, the big plow horse. Just for a second. I thought I'd take him again this evening. When they've all come inside from the fields and the cows are being milked."

"You've a most unorthodox method, but please, by all means, keep it up. Good night, Sid."

"Ta-ra, Doc."

Sid made his way down a long hallway to a set of rooms at the back of the hospital, rooms that had padded walls and no beds, only mattresses—rooms for men suffering from the horrors of shell shock. Many of them had no physical signs of injury, and yet Sid knew that of all the patients at Wickersham Hall, these men were the most damaged, and the hardest to reach.

He remembered now how he and India had barely any idea of what shell shock was when they'd opened the hospital. They'd been prepared for amputees, for men who'd been badly burned, even brain-damaged by bullets or shrapnel to the skull, but they'd been woefully unprepared for the wretches who came to them shaking and trembling, or sitting in wheelchairs, impossibly still. Some came with their eyes screwed shut, others with eyes downcast and blank, or impossibly wide open, as if still staring at the carnage that had driven them mad.

Dr. Barnes had wanted them to talk about their experiences on the battlefield, to share what had happened to them and not keep it inside. Sometimes the talking cure worked, sometimes it didn't. Sid observed the doctor's method, and knew that his intentions were the best, but privately he wondered how reliving the hell that these men had suffered through was supposed to help them.

"Who'd want to talk about it over and over again?" he'd asked India. "Wouldn't a geezer just want to forget it all? To look at a tree or pat a dog and forget he'd ever set foot in a trench? At least until he regained a bit of strength and could cope with the memories?"

"Sounds like you have an idea," India said.

"Maybe I do," Sid replied. "Maybe I do."

The next day, he'd gone to see Dr. Barnes and asked if he might take some of the men outside, for a stroll around the grounds. He said he thought the fresh air might do them good. Dr. Barnes, overwhelmed as he was by the needs of his patients and desperate for any helpful measures, quickly agreed to Sid's request.

Sid had started with a nineteen-year-old boy named Willie McVeigh. Willie's entire unit had been slaughtered on the Somme. Willie himself had been shot in the side and had lain on the battlefield, next to his dead and dying comrades, for two days before a field doctor had found him. When he'd arrived at Wickersham Hall, his body was rigid and his eyes were as wide, and as wild, as a frightened horse's.

Sid had taken Willie by the arm that April morning, and they'd set off around Wickersham Hall's grounds—all three hundred acres of them. As they walked—slowly, for Sid had a cane and Willie's gait was stiff—Sid had pointed out the daffodils and tulips poking through the ground. He'd showed Willie the new green willow leaves and the lilac buds about to burst open. He'd sat him down in the freshly tilled kitchen garden and put his clenched hands into the rich, wet dirt.

He did these things for five weeks straight, with no discernible effect whatsoever. And still he persisted, until, after two months of strolls and hikes and nature walks, Willie suddenly bent down in the garden, picked a strawberry from one of the plants growing there, ate it, and asked if he might have another.

Sid gave Willie another strawberry. He gave him a whole basketful. He'd have picked every strawberry in the garden if the lad had asked him to. He stood there watching Willie eat them, wanting to whoop and twirl and click his heels together.

The next day, he asked Henry the gardener if Willie might help hoe weeds between the plants.

"What if he throws a wobbly? Hacks me plants to bits?" Henry asked unhappily.

"He won't, Henry. I know he won't," Sid said.

He knew no such thing. In fact, he half expected Willie to try to hack *him* to bits, but Willie didn't. Sid sat in a chair at the edge of the garden, watching Willie as anxiously as a new mother watches her darling infant take its first steps. And Willie did marvelously. He hoed the weeds, carefully hilled the soil around the base of the plants, and then helped Henry harvest the berries.

When, at the end of the day, Henry complimented him, Willie simply said, "Me dad had an allotment. I used to help him with it." It was the most he had said since he'd arrived.

They'd had setbacks, of course. A thunderstorm had sent Willie diving under a bench, and it had taken Sid and Henry two hours to coax him out again. A backfiring motorcycle sent him running inside, howling in fear, and he'd refused to go out again for three whole days. But there was more progress now than there were setbacks. With Willie and with others, too. With Stanley, who, Sid had discovered, liked to knead bread, for the repetitive motion calmed him. He now helped Mrs. Culver, the hospital's cook, with her baking. And Miles, who refused to stop playing an imaginary piano until Sid bought him a real one, and who now played Brahms, Chopin, and Schubert for the other patients.

But not with Stephen. Poor, mad Stephen, who'd arrived at the hospital six months ago with red, raw marks around his neck from trying to hang himself.

Stephen was Sid's greatest challenge. Sid had worked with him day in and day out, trying everything he could think of. When nothing had had any effect, he'd hit upon the idea of writing to Stephen's father, to ask about his life at home. His father had written back, telling him all about their farm and their fields and livestock, and Bella, their huge workhorse, an ornery creature that had only ever been tractable for Stephen.

Immediately Sid had thought of Hannibal—Wickersham Hall's own plow horse, a very large and very cross animal, whom only Henry could handle, and even Henry had trouble with him. Sid had asked Henry if he could leave Hannibal in the pasture a little longer tonight, instead of putting him in his stall, for Hannibal was better behaved outside and Sid needed him in an amenable mood. He planned to coax Hannibal to the fence with some carrots, then to place Stephen's hand on the horse's withers.

As he reached Stephen's room, he paused and took a deep breath—to calm himself. He was excited, but he didn't want to betray his excitement to Stephen or Hannibal, in case he spooked either of them. He thought his plan might actually work, that Hannibal might offer a way to break through to Stephen. Then again, Hannibal, the little bleeder, might just kick them both straight into the next county.

Sid hurried across the meadow that separated the hospital from the house where he was now living—the Brambles, the caretaker's cottage on Wickersham Hall's grounds.

It was dark. India would certainly scold him for missing his tea—again. He hadn't meant to be so late, but he'd had a breakthrough with Stephen and he'd lost track of the time. He was so excited, so happy about it, that he couldn't wait to tell India. She was concerned about Stephen. She asked for him, or visited him herself, nearly every day.

Sid saw her now, his wife, as he drew closer to the cottage, through the mullioned windows of the kitchen. She was sitting at the table, reading. He stopped for a moment and stood still in the darkness, watching her. Just as he had once, long ago, outside her flat in Bloomsbury. Before she was his wife. Before their children were born. Before he'd ever imagined that he could know the kind of happiness she'd given him.

She was leaning her head on one hand, turning the pages of whatever she was reading with the other—the *Lancet,* no doubt. She was a new doctor when he'd first met her, a woman dedicated and driven to improve the health of her patients, and she hadn't changed. She'd only grown more dedicated as the years passed.

Wickersham Hall had been her idea. When the first injured men started coming home, she'd volunteered to care for them at Barts Hospital, in London. She'd soon seen that a busy city hospital could not address the long-term needs of wounded veterans, and that something more was needed. She'd written him.

> *My darling Sid,*
> *I've had the most marvelous idea today. I don't want to sell Wick-*
> *ersham Hall anymore. I want to make it into a hospital—a hospi-*
> *tal for those wounded in the war. A place where they can receive the*
> *very best of care, and stay, in comfort, for as long as is needed to*
> *make them whole again. It is a way to turn a sad, unhappy place*
> *into something useful and hopeful. I can't think of a better way to*
> *honor the memory of my sister, and I know in my heart that this is*
> *what Maud would want. . . .*

That had been back in January of 1915. They'd been apart for months. After she'd received news of Maud's death, India and the children had gone to London, so she could try to find out why her sister had taken her own life and also settle her affairs. Maud had left everything to India, and India, who had no use for Maud's Oxford estate and couldn't even bear to be in her London house, had decided to sell them. She thought she'd stay for two months, three at the most, then return to their home in Point Reyes, California.

But things hadn't quite worked out as they'd planned. War broke out. India had managed to sell Maud's London town house, but it was more difficult to sell Wickersham Hall. People were anxious and un-certain and not eager to spend on large estates.

With European navies engaged in battles and blockades, ocean travel became perilous. Sid cabled India shortly after Britain de-clared war on Germany and told her that under no circumstances were she and the children to travel back to the United States—not until the war was over. At that point, Sid, like most of the rest of the world, thought it would take a few months, possibly a year, for the fighting to end, but it had not. The Germans had taken Belgium, then France, and it looked as if Italy and Russia would fall, too. For a few months, the kaiser looked to be unstoppable. Sid realized that he might well invade England, and that his wife and children were in London, without him to protect them. He left his ranch in the hands of his capable foreman and began the long journey to Southampton. He didn't tell India he was coming, for he knew she would worry. He simply showed up one day—having crossed America by train and the Atlantic Ocean by steamer—on Joe and Fiona's doorstep.

India was furious at him for coming. "Haven't you heard that German U-boats are targeting civilian ships?" she angrily asked him, but she kissed him and hugged him and told him how very glad she was that he was there.

By the time he arrived, she'd already made Maud's estate into a hospital. She'd staffed it and supplied it herself. She already had a great deal of her own money, and Maud had left her another very large fortune. Joe and Fiona also contributed to the hospital's upkeep. When India suggested that they leave London for the hospital, because she wanted to work there, Sid quickly agreed. London was not a good place for him. He had long ago been cleared of any wrongdoing regarding Gemma Dean's death, a former girlfriend for whose murder he'd once been blamed, but that was not his only worry—there were those in the London underworld who undoubtedly remembered him—and not with great fondness. The sooner he left the city, the better.

As they journeyed to Oxford on the train, he wondered how he would occupy himself while India was busy doctoring all day long. He had thought of enlisting when he arrived in England, but he knew he'd never be accepted—not with his dodgy leg and not with the scars on his back, the ones the screws had put there with a cat-o'-nine-tails when, as a young man, he'd done hard time. Those scars said *prison* loud and clear, and the recruiting sergeants were not terribly fond of ex-convicts.

Sid hadn't had to wonder how to make himself useful for long, however. Every spare pair of hands was needed at the hospital. He helped dig the hospital's kitchen garden—an absolute necessity in a time of rationing. He helped drive ice, crates of eggs, sacks of flour, and sides of meat from markets and shops and farms into the kitchen.

He helped feed, wash, and dress the damaged bodies of soldiers and sailors and airmen, and as he did, he talked with them, to calm them and reassure them and try to lift their spirits, as well.

Young, working-class lads—boys who were uncomfortable talking to educated medical men with their clipped accents and soft hands— heard Sid's voice, still full of East London even after so many years away from it. They saw his rough worker's hands, and they recognized him as one of their own. They trusted him, felt comfortable with him, and they talked to him. They told him about their lives, about their injuries, about their fears—things they would not tell their doctors.

And Sid, to his great surprise, discovered that he liked the talking and the listening and that he was very good at it. His life, the part of it he'd spent in England, had been all about taking—taking money, and jewels, and many other things that hadn't belonged to him. Now he was giving, and he found it the most rewarding thing he'd ever done.

"Ever think of medical school, Mr. Baxter?" India had asked him one day, as she watched him work his magic on yet another broken body, broken mind.

"Nah, I hear it's a doddle. Got better things to do, me," he said, teasing her. "I'm getting a football team together. The lads are all mad for it. I figure it'll get them all out and running around. Excuse me, luv, will you?" And then, a clipboard in hand, he'd tried to hurry off to the gymnasium, which had been set up in one of the stables, but before he could, India grabbed his sleeve, pulled him close, and whispered, "You're a good man, Sid, and I love you."

He loved her, too. More than his life. And he thought now, as he looked at her, silhouetted in the warm light of the kitchen, that his heart would surely burst, it was so full of emotion.

He went into the house, took off his jacket and boots and left them in the mudroom, then made his way into the kitchen.

She looked up at him, smiling, happy to see him. "There's rabbit stew on the stove. Mrs. Culver made it. She made biscuits, too."

"Ta, luv. Where are the children?"

"In bed, you daft man. It's after nine."

"Is it? I'd no idea." Sid shoveled some of the stew onto a plate. As he did, he told her all about Stephen.

He'd taken the lad to the pasture to see Hannibal, the workhorse. Hannibal, true to his ornery nature, had flattened his ears and stamped ominously the very second Sid had approached him, but before he could start snorting or kicking or any other horsely nonsense, he'd spotted Stephen. His eyes had widened and his ears had gone up. Sid didn't know if horses were capable of curiosity, but at that moment, that's how Hannibal had looked—curious.

Stephen wouldn't raise his eyes, he wouldn't make direct contact with Hannibal, and yet he saw him. Sid knew he did; he could feel it. Stephen saw the horse with something inside of him—his heart, his soul maybe—Sid didn't know. What he did know was that for the first time in six months, Stephen's trembling had stopped.

Hannibal trotted over to the fence, ignoring Sid, looking only at Stephen. For a few seconds, Sid's heart was in his throat, so certain was he that Hannibal was going to open that huge mouth of his and take a chunk out of the lad; but he didn't. He sniffed Stephen. He whickered and blew. Then he pushed his great velvety nose against Stephen's cheek. Once, twice, three times. Until slowly, miraculously, Stephen raised his hand and placed it on Hannibal's neck.

The look on that lad's face at that moment . . . well, it was something Sid would never forget as long as he lived. He'd seen that look before, on the faces of men coming home on furlough and embracing the wives and children, the ones they hadn't seen for years and had often thought they'd never see again.

Stephen was too young to have a wife or a child, but he'd had a horse once. Long ago. In another, better, lifetime.

They stood that way, the boy and the horse, silent and still, for five, and then ten minutes, and then Stephen said, "He should be in his stall now. It's damp out tonight."

"Right. Yes. He will be, Stephen. Straightaway. Henry's coming for him," Sid said, trying to keep his voice even.

"Henry led Hannibal to the stables," he said to India now, "and I took Stephen back to his room. I told him we'd go see the horse again tomorrow night. He didn't say anything to that, but I saw that his trembling hadn't come back."

"Sid, that's wonderful news!" she exclaimed. "Oh, I'm so pleased to hear it!"

"We've still a long, long way to go," he said. "But it's a start." He grabbed a biscuit and sat down at the table across from her. As he did he saw that her eyes were red. "Can't you put that away now?" he asked her. "Give medicine a rest for the night?"

"It's nothing," India said. "Just a bit of eyestrain."

Sid glanced at the journal lying open in front of her. "The *Lancet*, is it?"

"Yes," she said. "There's a very disturbing report in it, about the new strain of influenza—the Spanish flu. It says that it's killing thousands in America and has started moving into Europe. Soldiers on all the European fronts are being hit heavily, and now it's supposedly started cropping up in Scotland and in some of the northern English cities."

"It's bad?" Sid said, between bites of stew.

"Very," India replied. "It starts out as a typical flu. The patient becomes very ill, seems to rally, but then grows worse. Bleeding from the nose and eyes may occur, followed by a virulent pneumonia. It's the pneumonia that's actually killing people. And oddly enough it's not the usual victims who are succumbing to it—babies and the elderly. It's carrying off young, healthy men and women. The United States already has quarantines in place. I just pray it doesn't hit the hospital. The men here have been through so much already."

She closed the journal then, and Sid saw that there was something underneath it. He recognized it. It was a photo album that had belonged to Maud. It contained pictures of Maud and India when they were children.

"It's not the *Lancet* that's made your eyes red, it is, luv?" he said quietly.

India looked down at the photo album. She shook her head. "No, it isn't," she said. "I shouldn't have got it out, but I couldn't help it. It's her birthday today. Or rather, it would have been."

Sid reached across the table for her hand and squeezed it. "I'm sorry," he said. She nodded and squeezed back.

He remembered how shattered India had been when the letter arrived from Fiona telling them that Maud was dead. She'd cried in his arms, sobbing "Why, Sid? Why?" over and over again.

She hadn't accepted the coroner's verdict on Maud's death. She simply could not believe that her sister would take her own life. Other people, yes; Maud, never. When she'd arrived in London, she immediately went to see the officer who'd investigated Maud's death. She asked the man—Arnold Barrett—for the mortuary photographs. He tried hard to talk her out of looking at them, but she would not be swayed. She steeled herself, made herself view them as a doctor, not a sister.

Holding a magnifying glass over the photos, India had examined the puncture wounds inside Maud's elbow. They had definitely been made by a hypodermic needle, but they were all fresh-looking wounds, not old.

"Yes, of course they are," Barrett said. "A hypodermic only holds so much and she'd injected herself several times, to make sure the dosage she received was lethal."

"But her lover, von Brandt . . . you told me that he said she was using morphine regularly. Someone who was an addict, who was getting and using morphine regularly, would have had old bruises where she'd injected the drug on previous occasions—not just fresh needle marks. There are no faded bruises anywhere on her. No old, scabbed punctures. And furthermore, Detective Inspector, my sister hated needles. She hated blood. She nearly fainted at my medical school graduation because she thought there were cadavers on the premises. How could she, of all people, have injected herself repeatedly?"

"Drug addiction forces its victims to do things neither they nor anyone else ever thought them capable of," Barrett said. "And hadn't

Miss Selwyn Jones had a past history of visiting Limehouse opium dens?"

"At one point in her life, yes," India said. "But my sister was not an addict. Not at the time of her death. She doesn't look overly thin in these pictures, as addicts do. No one who'd seen her or been with her in the last few weeks of her life—except for von Brandt—ever described anything that matched the behavior of a drug addict." India had paused for a few seconds, and then she'd said, "I want you to reopen the case, Detective Inspector. My sister did not kill herself. I am certain of that. Which means someone else did kill her."

Barrett had leaned forward in his chair and in a kindly voice told her that he could not possibly do what she was asking.

"I'm afraid there simply isn't enough to warrant a reopening of the case," he told her. "I know that she was your sister, and that this is terribly hard for you to accept, but if you go home now and think it over, I believe you will see, as I do, that your suspicions sound, well . . . a little bit mad."

India had bristled at that.

"Hear me out . . . listen to me . . . think carefully about what I'm about to ask you: Who on earth would have wanted to kill your sister?"

"What about the man she was seeing . . . Max von Brandt?" India asked.

Barrett had shaken his head. "If anything, I believe Miss Selwyn Jones might have wanted to kill him," he said. "I interviewed von Brandt. The very next day. I've been at this for thirty years, and I can tell you that he was genuinely and deeply upset. Furthermore, he had corroboration for all of his movements leading up to her death. He was seen with Miss Selwyn Jones leaving his hotel. The cabdriver who took them to your sister's home backed up von Brandt's story one hundred percent. At no time did Mr. von Brandt attempt to conceal his movements. Are these the actions of a criminal trying to cover his tracks, Doctor?"

India had found she could not answer him.

He had given her a kind smile and said, "It's a very bitter thing, suicide. The ones left behind always look for another explanation. But I am convinced that Miss Selwyn Jones's death was just that—a suicide."

"I miss her, Sid," India said now, in a small, choked voice. "I miss her so much."

Sid stood up and pulled India up out of her seat. He put his arms around her and held her close and let her cry. Her cousin Aloysius had been killed several years ago and now her sister was gone. They were the only members of her family she had been close to. If only he could do something for her. She was not getting over Maud's death. She was still sad, still grieving.

"I wish I could just believe what Barrett told me," she said now, wiping her eyes. "If I could believe it, I could let it go. Let her go. But I can't."

Sid wished she could let it go, too. He wished *he* could, but like India, he couldn't quite believe Maud had killed herself, either. And yet perhaps Barrett was right. Perhaps she'd become an addict, and the morphine, combined with the loss of her lover, had caused her to behave irrationally.

If Maud was an addict, though, someone had to have supplied her with the drugs, Sid thought. He wondered, for the briefest of seconds, if it could possibly have been his old colleague, the East End drug lord Teddy Ko. It was Ko's establishment that Maud used to frequent. It was at Ko's that Sid had first met India, as she was trying to convince Maud—and every other poor sod in the place—to leave it.

As he thought about those sad, smoke-filled rooms, Sid knew what he had to do; he knew how he could help his wife. He would go to see Teddy Ko and ask him if he'd sold drugs to Maud, or if anyone he knew had. He and Teddy went back a long way. If Teddy knew something, he might tell him. Then again, he might not. Either way, though, Sid had to try. He wanted to get answers for India, to give her some peace over her sister's death.

He would go back. Not right away; Stephen and the other lads needed him too much right now, but before the summer was out. He'd been steering clear of London, and India knew it, so he would have to cook up a story about why he was suddenly going—maybe he'd say that he was after supplies for the hospital—so that she wouldn't worry about him. It was the last place he wanted to go, but he would do it for her.

Back to the East End. Back to the past. Back to the scene of so many crimes.

CHAPTER FIFTY-FOUR

"MAKE IT QUICK, Wills, or Johnny Turkey'll blow us both to hell!" Dan Harper shouted over the noise of his biplane's propeller.

Willa gave him a thumbs-up to signal that she'd heard him. He gave her one back, then the biplane banked sharply right. Willa unfastened her safety belt, raised her camera, leaned as far out of her seat as she dared, and started to film.

Bedouin raiders had told Lawrence about the Turkish Army encampment in a valley to the west of the Jabal ad Duruz hills. Lawrence had no idea if they were telling the truth or if they'd been paid by the Turks to spread false information. He immediately sent a messenger to Amman, where the British had troops garrisoned and two biplanes, and asked the commander to undertake aerial reconnaissance for him. Willa had gone with the messenger. She'd never filmed from the air and thought this would be the perfect opportunity to start. For once, Lawrence had taken little convincing. The Bedouins' reports troubled him, and he knew she would bring back good pictures. The rumored encampment was close to Damascus. Had the Turks got wind of Lawrence's plan to march on the city? Were they building up troops to defend it? It was early August now, and Lawrence and his troops had taken Aqaba last month without too much difficulty, but Damascus, which was well defended, and which Lawrence wanted in British hands before autumn, would be a much harder nut to crack.

Willa saw now that the Bedouins had got the camp's position right—it lay roughly a hundred and fifty miles southeast of Damascus, in a shallow valley, but they'd vastly underestimated its size. Canvas tents covered at least fifty acres of ground. Soldiers were drilling—at least a thousand of them. There was a huge livestock pen full of the goats and sheep needed to feed the men. Another pen held camels—which would undoubtedly be used by the Turks for reconnaissance missions of their own.

Luckily there were no airplanes on the ground. The Germans had far fewer aircraft in the desert than the British did. Consequently, their air reconnaissance wasn't as good as Britain's, and their air attacks were less frequent. There were guns on the ground though: two large antiaircraft guns. She and Dan had seen them immediately, and both had known that they had only minutes to get the film they needed and get gone. The Turks obviously did not want their position discovered, or if it was, they wanted to make sure the discoverers did not live to make their findings public.

As Willa looked through her viewfinder, she saw soldiers running out to man those guns. Only seconds later, the barrels had been aimed—at them.

"Go, Dan!" she shouted, still filming. "Get us out of here!"

Dan was way ahead of her. The plane, a Sopwith Strutter, was quick and maneuverable, and he now put it through its paces, swooping down suddenly, then banking left, climbing again, flying fast and erratically in a bid to evade the guns.

Willa heard them blasting and hoped—because she still had not put her camera down—that she'd caught it all on film.

Only a minute or so later, though it felt much longer, the plane shot over the first of the Jabal ad Duruz hills, out of range of the guns.

Dan whooped loudly, raising his thumb again, and Willa leaned back in her seat, eyes closed, relief flooding through her. They'd done it. She'd got her film, Dan had got them out alive, and Lawrence would get the recon information he so desperately needed.

Willa wondered, as Dan passed over the hills completely, what the Turkish troops were doing. If they were meant to defend Damascus, why weren't they garrisoned there? She felt the plane bank sharply left and knew they were heading south now, to Lawrence's camp. Dan would drop her there then continue back to Amman. She had just started to breathe a little easier, when—about seventy miles south of the hills—she heard Dan suddenly swear, panic in his voice.

"What is it?" she shouted.

"Sandstorm!" he shouted back. "Out of bloody nowhere! I'm going to try to set us down!"

Two minutes later, the storm hit them, buffeting the plane badly, driving sharp, stinging grains of sand everywhere. Willa felt them against her face. Her goggles protected her eyes from being scratched, but they afforded her no vision. The winds were so wild, and the sand was whirling so thickly, she could barely see a foot in front of her.

She felt the plane descending, felt it bucking and jumping as it did. She heard Dan swear again and again as he struggled to control it, and then she heard nothing—nothing but the fierce screaming of the wind—for the propeller had stopped.

"It's jammed!" Dan shouted. "Sand's got inside it. Hang on!"

"How high are we?" Willa shouted, refastening her safety belt. If they'd got down low enough, they might have a chance.

But Dan didn't answer her. He couldn't. He was struggling to keep the plane level, so he could bring it down like a glider. Willa felt the plane lurch and then dive, level itself, and then dive again.

The film, she thought. The camera. No matter what happened to her, the film had to survive. She put the camera on her lap, then curled her torso over it, head down, hoping to cushion it from the impact of the landing—or the crash—with her body.

She heard screaming—she didn't know if it was coming from

her, Dan, or the wind. And then there was a roaring noise as the plane went down. It hit the ground hard, knocking the landing gear off. It skidded along at speed, hit a large rock, and flipped over, tearing its wings and propeller off, tearing its pilot apart.

Willa felt the plane roll over and over. She felt sand and rock pelt against her, felt the plane's body crush in against her. The belt that held her in her seat felt as if it would cut her in two. The plane rolled over a few more times, then stopped and toppled onto its left side.

Willa spat sand from her mouth. "Dan!" she cried out hoarsely, but she got no answer.

Dazed and shaking, hardly daring to believe she was alive, Willa raised her head. There was no more wind, no more driving sand. The storm had stopped. There was sand in her eyes, though. Blood, too. Her goggles had been ripped off. She lowered her head again, horribly dizzy, and felt for her camera, but it was gone. She was taking a few deep breaths, trying to clear her head, to make the spinning stop, when she smelled something, something acrid—smoke. The plane was on fire.

"Dan . . . Dan, are you there?" she called again, more weakly. And again there was no answer. He must've been knocked out, she thought.

She sat up all the way, gasping from a horrible pain in her side, and tried to pull herself out but could not. She remembered her restraints and unbuckled them, then crawled out of her seat. It was difficult. The harness on her artificial leg had been damaged in the crash and the leg was hard to control. When she was finally out of the plane, she turned around—ready to pull Dan out—and screamed.

Dan Harper had been decapitated by the impact.

She didn't have long to mourn him, for smoke from the burning engine, thick and choking, enveloped her. She stood up, panting with pain, and staggered away from the plane.

It was then that she saw them—four Bedouin men, their faces wrapped protectively against the storm. They were about ten yards away. Staring at her. They must have seen the plane go down, she thought.

They spoke among themselves in a dialect she couldn't understand. Then they shouted at her. In Turkish.

Oh, God, she thought. Oh, no. They were in the employ of the
Turks. No matter what, they must not get her camera, for they would
take it to their masters, and the Turks would see what was on it and
know that the English had seen the Jabal ad Duruz camp. But where
was it? She looked around frantically, then spotted it on the ground,
about halfway between herself and the Bedouins.

Willa knew she only had seconds. She started hobbling toward
the camera, as fast as she could go, but one of the men, seeing her
intent, got to it first. The others started moving toward her.

Willa was trapped. She knew she must not let them take her, for
they would bring her to their masters, along with the camera, and she
well knew what the Turks were capable of. They had captured Lawrence once, when he was spying in Amman. They had thrown him in
prison, beaten him, and raped him.

She pulled up her right trouser leg. She was reaching for the knife
she always wore strapped to her calf when the first man got to her. He
backhanded her hard and sent her reeling. She hit the ground; the
knife went flying from her hand. She tried to get up, to go after it, but
the man who'd hit her grabbed the back of her shirt and flipped her
over. She felt his rough hands on her, tearing her shirt open. Felt him
rip Fatima's necklace from her.

Again she lunged for the knife, but a second man kicked it away.
Two other men grabbed her arms and hoisted her to her feet. She
struggled and fought ferociously, hoping to make them angry enough
to kill her. She screamed insults at them, shouted curses at them.
Begged for death.

Until a fist, aimed to the side of her head, finally silenced her.

CHAPTER FIFTY-FIVE

"FUCKING HELL! IT *is* you!" Teddy Ko bellowed.

Teddy was standing in the doorway of his Limehouse office, wearing a gold ring, diamond cuff links, and a striped flannel suit—one that all but shouted *wide boy*.

"Couldn't believe me ears when Mai here said Sid Malone wants to see me. Fucking Sid Malone! I thought you was dead, Sid. Last I heard, you was floating facedown in the Thames."

Sid forced a smile. "Can't believe everything you hear, Teddy."

"Come in! Come in!" Teddy said, waving Sid into his office. "Mai!" he shouted at his secretary. "Bring us some whiskey. Cigars, too. Hurry up!"

That's our Teddy, Sid thought. Always a charmer.

Teddy sat down at a huge desk, fashioned from ebony and embellished with paintings of dragons, and motioned for Sid to take one of the chairs across from him.

As he did, Sid looked around the large and opulently appointed room. On the walls hung richly embroidered ceremonial robes from China, crossed swords with jeweled hilts, and hand-colored photographs of Peking. Tall blue and white urns stood in the corners of the room. Thick rugs with more dragons on them covered the floor.

Sid remembered when Teddy worked out of a room in one of his laundries. Back when he paid Sid protection money. Back when Sid was the governor—the biggest, most feared crime lord in all of London.

"You've come up in the world, Teddy," he said.

Teddy chuckled, pleased by the compliment. "Got fifty-eight

laundries now, me. All over London. A big importing business, too—porcelain, furniture, artworks, silk, parasols, you name it—direct from Shanghai to London." His voice dropped. "That's the legit side. I'm still going gangbusters with the drugs. Branched off into prostitution, too. Got whorehouses in the East End and the West. Twenty-three and counting."

"That's wonderful, Teddy," Sid said. He couldn't quite muster a warm *Congratulations*.

"What about you? Where have you been? What have you been doing with yourself all these years?"

"It's a long story," Sid said. "I've been out of the country."

Teddy nodded knowingly. "Busies made it too hot for you here, did they?" he said. "Had to go farther afield? Well, I imagine the villainy's just as good in Dublin or Glasgow or wherever it is you are now."

Sid smiled. It was fine with him if Teddy thought he was up to no good elsewhere. He was not about to tell Teddy Ko, or anyone else from his old life, about his new life or his new last name. His wife, his children, America—it was all off-limits.

Teddy's secretary entered his office. She placed a silver tray on the table. On it was a bottle of scotch, a bucket of ice, two crystal glasses, and a small wooden humidor. She poured the men their whiskey, trimmed and lit their cigars, then quietly disappeared again. Sid didn't want either the drink or the smoke, but he felt it would be rude to refuse them.

"So, Sid," Teddy said, glancing at his watch, "what can I do for you? What brings you here? Business or pleasure?"

"Neither," Sid said. "I'm here as a favor to a friend."

Teddy, puffing away on his cigar, raised an eyebrow. "Go on," he said.

"A few years ago, right before the war started, a former customer of yours, Maud Selwyn Jones, overdosed on morphine."

"I remember. It was a shame, that."

"Did she get it from you?"

Teddy leaned forward in his chair. His smile was gone. "Maybe she did, maybe she didn't. Either way, why the fuck would I tell you?" he said. "You've been gone a long time, Sid. Things have changed. You're not the guv anymore. You want something from me now, you can pay for it. Just like everyone else."

Sid had anticipated this. He reached inside his jacket. He pulled out an envelope and pushed it across the desk to Teddy.

Teddy opened the envelope, counted its contents—which came to a hundred pounds—then said, "I didn't sell the morphine to Maud. I barely sold her anything anymore. She'd quit coming to the dens years ago. After that bloody doctor, her sister or whatever the hell she was, tried to drag her out. Meddling bitch, she was. Bent on wrecking my business."

Sid's jaw tightened at that, but he said nothing. A bust-up with Teddy wouldn't serve his purposes. "Did she look like an addict to you?" he asked. "The last time you saw her?"

Teddy shook his head. "No, she didn't. She was thin, but she was always thin. She didn't have the hop-fiend look. You know, all pale skin and dark circles under the eyes and desperate. I know a lot of addicts. Maud didn't look like one."

"Did you hear anything about it at the time? From anyone else in the business? Did anyone else you know sell Maud any morphine?" he asked.

Teddy shook his head. "Not that I know of. But I hardly went round asking, did I?"

"Can you ask now?"

Teddy shrugged. "For a hundred quid I can do a lot of things," he said. "But it was over four years ago, wasn't it? I'm not sure how much I can find out. Why is it so important to you?"

"I'd appreciate anything you can do, Teddy," Sid said, stubbing out the rest of his cigar.

"Where can I get hold of you? If I find out anything?" Teddy asked.

"I'll get hold of you."

"When? I'm a busy man."

"How about we meet right here again? In a month's time. Same day. In September."

"I'll try me best," Teddy said.

Sid rose to take his leave.

"You're not leaving already, are you?" Teddy said. "You only just got here. Let me show you round the place."

Sid noted that Teddy looked at his watch again as he spoke. He'd said he was a busy man. Undoubtedly he had places to go and things to do, but oddly, it seemed to Sid that Teddy wanted to keep talking, to hold him here. Sid didn't want to stay. He couldn't wait to get out of the East End, to get away from all the memories and all the ghosts.

Teddy wouldn't hear of his leaving, though. He had to at least see the warehouse first. Sid agreed, reluctantly. He wanted Teddy to do him a favor, and if admiring the warehouse was what it took to get Teddy's goodwill, he would do it.

They walked out of Teddy's two-story office building, to the four-story warehouse that abutted it. As he stepped inside, Sid felt as if he'd stepped into a giant, sprawling Chinese bazaar. There were huge brightly painted beds. Tables inlaid with mother-of-pearl, ebony, and ivory. Giant blue-glazed statues of lions and dogs. Urns large enough to plant trees in. There were vases and teapots and gongs. Rolled up rugs were propped against the walls. Bolts of silks and satins were stacked on shelves. There were open crates containing beaded necklaces, bracelets carved of cinnabar, and tiny jade figurines. Teddy reached into one crate, pulled out a small carved Buddha, no taller than two inches, and gave it to Sid.

"For good luck," he said, winking.

"Thank you, Teddy," Sid said, putting the figurine in his jacket pocket.

"Here, this'll interest you. Come take a look," Teddy said.

He led Sid upstairs to the second floor. It was filled with tea chests. Teddy pried the lid off one, dug deep down into the rich black tea that filled it, and pulled up a large, dark brown lump, roughly the shape and size of a cannonball.

"Chinese opium. The purest. The very best. It comes in buried in tea chests. Stuffed inside statues. Teapots. Furniture. And it goes out through my laundries, cut up and wrapped in brown paper like a bundle of napkins or shirts. And Old Bill's none the wiser."

"You were always a clever one, Teddy. Always going places," Sid said. "I've got to hand it to you."

Teddy didn't give a damn about the people the drug enslaved. He didn't care whether they could afford it or not. Whether they went without shoes, or clothes, or food to fund their habit. Or whether their children did. He'd made himself a bundle in the opium trade, stood to make a lot more, and that's all that counted. Sid knew this, for he'd been the same as Teddy once, done the same things. A long time ago. In another life. Before he'd met India.

Teddy held the fat brown lump out to Sid now. "You want a taste? I'll have Mai fix us a pipe. Get us a couple of girls, too. Just like old times."

"Thanks, Teddy, but I have to be off."

Out on the sidewalk, Sid said his good-byes. Teddy shook his hand, glancing up the street as he did, and said, "I'll start asking around on the other thing. Hopefully I'll get something for you. Same day next month, right?"

"Right-o," Sid said. He hunched his shoulders against a sudden August rain shower and started walking west. He passed by several small, dreary shops, a rope-maker's, and two dingy pubs. On the corner, three little girls, not one of whom was dressed for the weather, were jumping rope and singing a morbid rhyme.

There was a little bird, her name was Enza.
I opened the window and in flew Enza.

The Spanish flu had already cropped up in Scotland, India had said. Sid shuddered to think what would happen if it hit the East End. The area, with its notorious overcrowding and poor sanitation, would provide an ideal breeding ground for the disease. It would move through the slums like wildfire.

Five minutes later, he found a hackney cab, climbed inside, and told the driver to take him to Paddington Station. He was well on his way out of Limehouse by the time a carriage, sleek and black, pulled up in front of Teddy's offices, so he did not see the two men step out of it—one wearing the rough clothes of a riverman, the other in a flash suit, tugging on a gold earring and smiling with a mouthful of black, rotted teeth.

CHAPTER FIFTY-SIX

"HELLO, MAI, DARLING," Billy Madden said. "Where's that boss of yours?"

"He's in his office, Mr. Madden," Mai said. "He's expecting you. What may I get for you? Tea? Whiskey?"

Billy put his hands on Mai's desk. He leaned in close to her and smiled horribly. "How about yourself, you lovely little lotus flower? Buck naked on a bed in the back? I've always wanted to see what's under those pretty silk dresses of yours."

The man with Billy looked away, clearly uncomfortable. Mai colored, but her polite smile didn't falter. "If you would like, Mr. Madden, I can arrange a girl for you when your are finished with Mr. Ko," she said.

Billy's smile faded. His eyes turned hard. "I told you what I would like. You. On your back. Now get up and get your knickers off, you useless . . ."

Teddy, hearing Billy's voice, stepped out of his office and saw what was going on.

"Oh, for fuck's sake, Billy, you don't want her," he said, trying to defuse the situation. "She's got smaller tits than you do. Why do you think she's here doing my typing instead of working in one of my whorehouses?"

"Is that so?" Billy said.

He walked around Mai's desk, behind Mai herself. Then he reached around her and cupped her small breasts, weighing them in his hands. Mai stiffened. She swallowed hard, stared straight ahead, and did not make a sound.

Anger rose in Teddy. He liked Mai. She was a nice girl, not a tart. She was good at her job. She didn't deserve this. But Billy was the guv'nor. He took what he wanted. If he wanted Mai, he'd have her, and there wasn't a damn thing Teddy or anyone else could do about it.

"You're right, Teddy," Billy finally said. "Not enough here to keep me happy. Back to your typing, darlin'."

Mai picked up a pencil. Teddy saw that her hands were shaking. He swore under his breath. Scenes like this were becoming more frequent. Billy Madden was a bastard and always had been, but he was getting worse. Bothering women. Losing his temper. Starting fights for no good reason. He'd bashed a lad's skull in a month ago at the Bark because he thought he was laughing at him. He'd got this mad, wild look in his eyes, then did for the poor sod.

"Come have a glass of whiskey with me, Billy," Teddy said now. "You and John, both. Afterward, I'll fix you up with a girl who's worth your while. Two girls, if you like. From Shanghai. They'll have you begging for mercy. Come on, come inside now, I've got things I need to discuss with you."

"And I've got things to discuss with you, Edward," Billy said, sitting down behind Teddy's desk. "You were short. Two weeks in a row." Billy's man, John, stood behind him.

"I wasn't short. That was twenty-five percent. Same as always. Your cut was less because I sold less. My supplies were low. Got another shipment in at Millwall as we speak. Soon as I get it, and get selling it—"

Billy cut him off. "John here is going with you to unload your tea from the *Ning Hai* tonight. Him and three more of my men."

"Tonight? Why tonight? It's supposed to be unloaded tomorrow afternoon," Teddy asked.

"Because the next high tide's at two A.M.," John Harris said.

"And because I don't want you offloading any of the cargo before tomorrow," Billy said, picking his nails with Teddy's letter opener. "John and the others are going to get it, bring it here to the warehouse, open it, and see just how much hop you're bringing in. So I can figure out myself what you should be paying me."

"You think I'm cheating you out of your cut," Teddy said.

The anger Billy had kindled in Teddy flamed into a hot fury. Billy was the guv'nor, yes, but even so, he was taking a few too many liberties. Accusing him, Teddy, of cheating him out of money, the cheek of it. Teddy *was* cheating him, of course, but still—he shouldn't just come in here, rough up his help, and make Teddy look small on his own turf.

"I'm just keeping my eye on things, that's all," Billy said.

"Is that so? Well, you know what, Billy? You might want to start keeping both eyes on things," Teddy said hotly

Billy leaned forward. "Oh, aye? And just what do you mean by that?"

"Sid Malone's back in town."

Billy stopped picking his nails. He looked up at Teddy, and Teddy saw, to his satisfaction, that Billy had paled. Teddy knew that there was only one thing Billy hated more than another villain cheating him out of money, and that was another villain making a play for his manor—a manor they both knew used to belong to Sid.

"What did you say?"

"I said Sid Malone's back in town."

"Now I know where all your hop's gone, Teddy. You've been smoking it yourself."

"He was here. Right in this office. Not ten minutes ago."

"Sid Malone was fished out of the Thames years ago. He's dead."

"Not anymore he isn't."

"Are you sure, Teddy?"

"I'm sure. I know him. I used to work for him. Remember? It was Sid Malone in my office, sure as I'm standing here."

Billy glowered at him. Then he slammed his fists on the desk and stood up. "Why didn't you tell me that?" he shouted.

"I wanted to!" Teddy shouted back. "But you were too busy interfering with my girl, and with my business! I even tried to keep him here until you came. Tried to stall. But he said he had to be off."

"What the fuck was he doing here?" he said. "What did he want?"

"He wanted information on that woman's death—Selwyn Jones. The rich one. The one who topped herself a few years back. He wanted to know if I'd sold her the drugs."

"What? Why the hell would he want to know that?"

"I asked him. He didn't tell me."

"You tell him about Stiles?"

Teddy shook his head.

A man named Peter Stiles had bought quite a bit of morphine from Teddy only days before Maud Selwyn Jones died. Billy knew about it; he was the one who'd sent Stiles to Teddy. Both Billy and Teddy had wondered at the time if there was any connection between Stiles and the Selwyn Jones woman's death.

"Why is he nosing into this?" Billy asked. "What's this Jones woman's suicide to him?"

"I have no idea," Teddy said. "It makes no sense."

Billy made no response at first, then, at length, he said, "Yes, it does. Sid Malone's back and he wants his old manor back. He has to get me out of the way first, though, and he's looking to see if there's any way he can land me in the shit with Old Bill. He's trying to do it through you. Wants to have me sent down for the Selwyn Jones woman. Do it all nice and clean-like. No violence. No blood. At least not to begin with, that is."

Billy lit up a cigarette as he spoke, and started pacing the room. Teddy wasn't quite sure that Billy had it right. Sid Malone certainly hadn't acted like a man planning to launch a big turf war. But Teddy also knew that once Billy Madden got an idea into his head, there was no getting it out.

"Did you tell him anything at all?"

"I said I'd dig around, see what I could come up with. We're supposed to meet again next month. Right here."

"Good. Well done, Teddy lad."

"What do you want me to do when he comes back? Give him something? Give him nothing?"

"Just keep him here, Teddy. Keep him talking."

"You're going to do for him," Teddy said.

Billy Madden shook his head. His eyes had that mad look in them. The one Teddy knew all too well, and wished he didn't.

"No," Billy said, "I'm going to beat him bloody first. Make him tell me what he's got on me. Who he's working with. And then I'm going to do for him."

CHAPTER FIFTY-SEVEN

WILLA OPENED HER eyes.

The world, bright and sand-colored, spun sickeningly beneath her. She tried to move, but pain, breathtaking and horrible, shot through her side. She tried to right herself, tried to sit up, but she could not make her arms and legs work.

She wondered, for a few seconds, if she was dead.

She managed to pick her head up, but was seized by a dizziness so strong that she was sick. Her stomach heaved again and again, but nothing came up. She lowered her head. Her cheek pressed into something thick and soft. It seemed to be moving. She seemed to be moving.

"Water," she moaned, closing her eyes. Her throat was parched. It felt like it was on fire. Her lips were cracked. "Water, please . . . ."

A voice was yelling. A man's voice. The words sounded like Bedouin, but she couldn't understand them.

She opened her eyes again, and this time they focused. She saw rocks and sand going by. She saw a camel's leg. And her own hands, tied at the wrists by a length of rope, hanging down in front of her.

She realized she was lying across the back of a camel, bound fast against the back of the rider's saddle. How long had she been like this? Hours? Days?

She struggled, trying again to right herself, to sit up. The rider must have felt her movements, or heard them, for he turned around to shout at her. He was telling her to stop, to lie still, but she did not understand him, and would not have heeded him if she had. Frenzied by pain and fear, she kept struggling, kept pleading for water.

The camel driver was angered by this, for her movements were spooking his animal. He shouted once more for her to be still, then he struck her where he could easily reach her—on her side. Willa screamed with pain as her damaged ribs received his blows.

Pain filled her senses. She could see nothing, hear nothing, feel nothing but it's awful suffocating blackness. She cried out once more, and then she was still.

CHAPTER FIFTY-EIGHT

"COME ON, ALBIE. What's the news? Did Lawrence take Damascus yet? Are Gerry and Johnny Turkey chasing him all around the sand dunes?" Seamie Finnegan said. He was sitting in a chair in Albie's office in the building that housed the Bureau of Arab Affairs in Haifa.

"I could tell you," Albie Alden said, not looking up from the document he was reading—a telegram, taken from a stack that his secretary had just delivered. "But then I'd have to kill you."

Seamie shook his head. "I still can't believe it: Albie Alden, spy catcher. The Secret Service Bureau. Room 40. And you cool as a cucumber the whole time. Never said a word."

Albie looked at Seamie over the top of his spectacles. "Stop pestering me and let me get these telegrams read. Or else I'll have the guards come and escort you back to hospital. Where you should be. In your bed. Recovering."

"Bugger that. I can't stand it anymore. I'm going mad in hospital. I shouldn't be there at all. I'm fit enough to take command of another vessel right now, but the bloody doctors won't let me. I'm getting a new ship, the *Exeter*, but not for another five weeks."

"Fit? Didn't you just take a two-inch chunk of shrapnel to the torso? Lift up your shirt. No, go on. Lift it up. . . ." Albie stared at Seamie's torso, shaking his head. "Your dressings haven't even come off yet," he said. "They're covering your entire right side. What happened anyway? You still haven't told me the whole story."

"My ship, *Hawk*—she was a destroyer—tangled with a German gunboat about twenty miles west of here. We took a hit to the hull, just above the waterline. And then another to the foredeck. I caught a piece of it."

"Bloody hell," Albie said.

"Yes, it was," Seamie said, with a sardonic smile. "The shrapnel missed my ribs and my vitals, but it took a chunk of flesh out of my side. Luckily, we'd sited the gunboat and were able to radio one of our own boats about fifteen minutes before we were hit. They got there too late to stop the attack, but in time to rescue us." His smile faded. "Well, most of us. I lost five men."

"I'm sorry," Albie said.

Seamie nodded. "I am, too. The gunboat got us back to Haifa and the hospital here, but I swear, if I'd known they were going to keep hold of me for so long, I'd have stayed in the water. I'm going off my nut with boredom. I was so happy when I heard you'd arrived in Haifa. I still can't believe it."

"How *did* you hear about it? I'm supposed to be keeping a low profile here."

"Completely by chance. I overheard one of the nurses talking to her friend about you. Seems you were in for some sort of stomach trouble."

Albie made a face. "Yes. Dysentery. Picked it up in Cairo. Bloody awful thing."

"Anyway, I guess she gave you some medicine and fell in love at the same time. God knows why. The heat must be affecting her head. When I heard your name, I asked her to describe you. When she had, I knew it was you. Couldn't possibly be two gangly, four-eyed boffins in the world with the name of Albie Alden."

Albie laughed. "Can you keep quiet for two more minutes so I can finish reading these telegrams?"

"I'll do my best," Seamie said, picking up a folder and fanning himself with it, for the August heat was brutal.

He had knocked on Albie's door about half an hour ago. His old friend had been so surprised to see him. He'd invited him in and had him sit down, and Seamie had learned that Albie had arrived in Haifa two days ago. After Albie had sworn him to secrecy, he'd also learned that Albie had been posted from London, where he'd been working since 1914 for Room 40, a group of code breakers under the aegis of the Royal Navy, to head intelligence and espionage in western Arabia.

Seamie was astonished to learn that his shy, quiet friend was part of Room 40. He remembered Albie back in 1914, remembered how weary and tense he'd been. He'd thought it had all been caused by his father's illness and by overwork. Now he knew that Albie and a team of brilliant Cambridge academics had been working feverishly, before the war had even begun, to intercept and unravel German intelligence communications. He had always admired Albie greatly; he admired him even more now, knowing how relentlessly he had worked—literally night and day—even when he had lost his beloved father.

Albie, finished with the stack of telegrams now, rose and called for his secretary. He asked her to file them all before she left, then he picked up his briefcase.

"Sorry to be so distracted. It's been a bit hectic. I just have to gather some things for an early meeting tomorrow and then we can go," he said. He stopped shuffling papers for a few seconds, looked at Seamie, and earnestly said, "It's ever so good to see you here. Truly."

"It's good to see you, too, Alb," Seamie replied. "Haifa . . . who'd have guessed it?"

Neither man said, for it was not in either's nature to be overly emotional, but they both knew what their words really meant—not so much that they had never expected to see each other in Haifa, but that they had never expected to see each other anywhere again. Ever.

The war had taken millions of lives, including those of many of their friends—men they'd known as boys, men they'd gone to school with, grown up with, sailed and hiked and climbed and drunk with. Sometimes it seemed everyone they'd ever known was gone.

"You hear much about Everton?" Seamie said now.

"Dead. The Marne."

"Erickson?"

"The Somme."

Seamie rattle off another dozen names. Albie told him that ten had been killed and the other two had been injured.

"Gorgeous George?" Seamie asked hesitantly, afraid of the answer.

"Mallory's still with us. Last I heard."

"I'm so glad," Seamie said. "Someday, when this whole damn thing is over, we're going climbing again, Alb. All of us. On Ben Nevis. Or Snowdon."

"Wouldn't that be lovely?" Albie said wistfully. "We could rent a cottage. In Scotland or Wales. Or maybe the Lake District."

"Anywhere, as long as there's a good pub close by."

"Oh, for a plate of cheese sandwiches with Branston pickle."

"You're a madman, Albie. You really are," Seamie said, laughing. "Ask any man here what he misses and he'll say women. A pint of good ale. Roast beef with gravy. Not you. You want Branston pickle." Seamie suddenly stopped laughing and turned serious. "We'll do it, Albie. We will. All of us together again. You and I, and George, and . . . well, maybe not quite all of us." He was quiet for a bit, then he said, "Do you . . . do you ever hear anything from her?"

Albie sighed. "Very little," he said. "Mother received a letter, late in 1914, from Cairo. A few more in 1915. Not much since."

"Cairo? You mean here in the Mideast?"

"I do," Albie said. "She'd followed Tom Lawrence out here, if you can believe it."

"Yes, I can."

"She arrived here in September of '14. Just after the war broke out. Lawrence got her a job under Allenby. She was working on maps. I've seen some of them. They're bloody good. Then she resigned her position. Left Cairo. Right about the same time Lawrence went into the desert. Wrote to Mother and said she was traveling east. That was the last we heard from her. I imagine she went back to Tibet, but I really have no idea."

Albie's expression was pained as he spoke.

"I shouldn't have mentioned her," Seamie said. "I'm sorry."

Albie smiled ruefully. "It's all right, old mole," he said.

No more was said about it. No more needed to be. Seamie knew Albie's relationship with his sister was a difficult one. He was glad, however, that Albie knew nothing about the relationship he and Willa had had in London, shortly after he'd married Jennie.

"Now, if I can just find those figures . . . ," Albie said, digging under a pile of papers on his desk.

"Albie, you didn't tell me . . . why the devil did London post you all the way out here, anyway? Why Haifa? Are you being sent down? Did you bugger something up? Get a code wrong?"

Albie laughed unhappily. "I only wish it was that," he said. "I'd be having myself a holiday. Buy myself a nice pair of field glasses and see the sights."

Seamie, who'd gotten out of his chair and walked over to the window, turned around, worried by the grim note in his friend's voice.

"What is it, then?" he asked him.

Albie gave Seamie a long look, then gravely said, "I shouldn't tell you this either, but I will because your life may well depend on it and because you may be able to help me. However, you must keep the information to yourself."

"Of course."

"We have a German mole in London. A very effective one. Somewhere in the Admiralty."

"What?" Seamie said. "How can that be?"

"We don't know. We've taken great pains to ferret him out—for years—but we've not been successful. I can tell you, though, that we're almost certain someone has been feeding information on our ships to German high command and that it's been happening for years. At the beginning of the war, they received intelligence on the design and capabilities of our dreadnoughts. Now they're getting information on deployment of our ships. In the European theater. And here, in the Mediterranean."

Seamie's blood ran cold.

"For a long time, Germany was not overly concerned about the eastern front," Albie said. "Now that Lawrence is making such headway in the desert—and now that it actually looks like he has a crack at Damascus—they are paying more attention. Messages appear to be going from London to a contact in Damascus. We don't know how. Or to whom. But we do know why—the Germans and the Turks want to keep hold of the city at all costs. They plan to strongly defend it— which means putting paid to Lawrence and his band. When they've done that, they want to retake Aqaba, then advance on Cairo. This entails added ground troops, of course, but they've also begun to step up their naval presence here."

"My God. The *Hawk*," Seamie said, stricken. "My men."

Albie nodded. "We don't believe it was luck that led that German gunboat to you. They knew where you were. We lost two more ships in the last three days as well. One off the coast of Tripoli, the other south of Cyprus. The Admiralty wants it stopped. Now."

"But how?" Seamie said. "You haven't been able to find the mole in London, you said. And he's been operating for years."

Albie nodded. "Captain Reginald Hall, the head of Room 40, thinks that if we can't nab him, perhaps we can nab his counterpart here. It's a long shot, admittedly, but a great deal of intelligence comes and goes through Cairo, Jaffa, and Haifa. People here hear things and see things. I'm hopeful that we can collect enough pieces to put the puzzle together. We're cultivating a lot of sources—Bedouin traders who move between Cairo and Damascus, and who courier goods and parcels. Brothel owners whose girls service Europeans. Hotel owners. Waiters. Barmen. I'm not sure whom the information is going to come from, but I'm chasing down every lead I can think of. We have to find the man and soon. Before it's too late. Before he does any more damage."

"How can I help, Albie?"

"You can keep your ear to the ground," Albie said. "It's amazing who these people are. He could be the man who cuts your hair. The one who serves your lunch. You never know how close you might be."

"Excuse me, Mr. Alden. . . ." A young woman was standing in the doorway. She was small and pretty and serious. She wore a white blouse and gray skirt. Her hair was neatly pulled back.

"Yes, Florence?"

"One more thing . . . this just arrived classified from General Allenby's office," she said, handing him an envelope.

"Thank you, Florence," Albie said. "That will be all. I shall see you tomorrow. I expect to be back here by ten o'clock."

"Very well. Good night, sir."

"Good night."

"I'll just take a quick look at this and we'll be off. Grab our jackets, will you?" Albie said to Seamie.

As Albie opened the envelope and pulled out a typed memo,

Seamie took their jackets off the coat stand in Albie's office. He was glad they were finally leaving for the officers' mess. Never mind bed rest, a tall cool gin and tonic would be just what the doctor ordered.

"You ready?" he said, turning back to Albie.

But Albie didn't answer him. One hand was over his face, covering his eyes. The other, the one holding whatever had come in the envelope from Allenby, was at his side.

"Albie?" Seamie said, alarmed. "Albie, what is it?"

Albie didn't answer him. Instead, he held the document out to him. Seamie quickly took it and started to read.

He skimmed the lines that warned the reader that this was classified information, and quickly came to the subject of the memo. A British plane doing reconnaissance in the Jabal ad Duruz hills had gone down in the desert four days ago. The pilot, Dan Harper, was killed in the crash. The plane was carrying one passenger—the photographer Alden Williams. Williams, whose body was not found at the crash site and who was presumed dead, might have been captured by Bedouin raiders, or by Turkish troops, who held the area. The wreckage was thoroughly searched, but Williams's camera was not found. Whatever information Williams was able to gain about the size and movements of Turkish troops near Damascus had been lost. There was concern that if the Turks had Williams, they might try to extract sensitive information from their prisoner. And then, at the bottom of the note, was a hand-scrawled message from General Allenby.

"No," Seamie said as he read it. "Dear God, no."

Dear Alden,

As this event concerns reconnaissance, and may come under your bailiwick, I wish to apprise you of some particulars.

Alden Williams, as you likely know, was the photographer attached to Lawrence and his camp. Williams is a pseudonym used to obscure the fact that the photographer is a woman. It is highly doubtful that the British public would approve of a woman's presence on the battlefield. Equally unpalatable to the public would be the idea of a British woman taken prisoner by the Turkish—some of whom, as you also know, have been known to treat their prisoners with the utmost brutality. Please keep me posted of any and all intelligence gathered on this particular topic.

Alden Williams's real name is Willa Alden. Same surname as your own. Is she any relation to you?

Please keep these details confidential.

Yours,
Allenby

CHAPTER FIFTY-NINE

INDIA FROWNED. SHE sat back in her chair and regarded Lindy Summers, her head nurse. "What about the new one? The blond boy who came in yesterday . . . Matthews? Any changes in his condition?" she asked her.

Lindy shook her head. "No, there isn't, Dr. Jones. Which is both good and bad. Good because I'm still convinced he has bronchitis, not the flu, but bad because he's so weak, I'm worried the bronchitis alone will be enough to finish him off." Lindy fished out a folder from the stack she'd just placed on India's desk and handed it to her. "Here's the latest on his vitals. Another lad, Abbott . . . now, he has me worried."

"Tall lad? Red hair and freckles? Facial burns?" India asked.

"That's the one. He came in feverish, complaining of headache. Now he's coughing. And his lungs sound wet."

India's expression became grim. "We have to set up a quarantine for possible flu victims. Right now," she said. "We simply cannot afford to take any chances. These men are so weak as it is that if the flu gets hold of them, they won't stand a chance. Gather the staff, tell them to go ahead and set up the ward in the attic."

"The attic?" Lindy said uncertainly.

"We had four men arrive this morning, and we're due to get another seven tomorrow. We're out of room. The attic's cramped but it's clean. It's hardly ideal, but it's all we've got," India said. She had long ago learned that when it came to medicine, ideal situations existed only in textbooks.

"Yes, Dr. Jones," Lindy said. "I'll get started right away."

At that moment, the door to India's office opened and Sid stepped inside. A visit from him during the day was very unusual. He was often so busy with the shell-shocked patients that she was lucky if she and the children saw him at suppertime.

"Sid! I'm so glad you're here. Lindy and I were just talking about the quarantine ward and . . . ," she began.

And then she stopped speaking. For as he sat down across from her, she saw that his face was ashen and his eyes were red. She had only ever seen her husband cry once. A long time ago. She could not imagine what had upset him enough to make him weep.

And then a terrifying thought gripped her. "Sid, the children . . . ," she started to say, her heart in her throat.

"They're fine. All fine," he said. "Lindy, if I could have a minute?"

"Of course. Please excuse me," Lindy Summers said. She quickly stood up, left the room, and closed the door behind her.

India got up, came around to the front of her desk, and sat down next to her husband.

"What is it? What's happened?" she asked him. "Is it Seamie? Did he take a turn for the worse?" India knew, as did the rest of the family, about the destruction of the *Hawk*, and Seamie's resulting injuries, for Jennie had received a telegram and had told them, but those injuries—the telegram said—were not life-threatening.

Sid tried to answer her and found he could not.

"You're scaring me," India said.

He swallowed hard and tried again. "Some new patients came in this morning," he said.

"Yes, I know. Four of them."

"One of them is badly shell-shocked," Sid said. "In fact, it's the worst case I've ever seen. He's gone. Totally gone. Does nothing but shake and stare straight ahead of himself." He paused, and then his voice broke as he said, "India . . . it's Charlie. My nephew. My namesake. And he doesn't know me. He doesn't even know me."

It took a minute for Sid's words to sink in. "I'm so sorry, Sid," she finally said, in a choked voice, leaning her head against his. "Is there no hope? None at all? You can do something, I know you can. I've seen what you've done with the other lads."

Sid shook his head. "Come with me," he said, standing up.

India followed him downstairs. He led her to the last room on the hall where the shell-shocked men lived. She looked through the open door and saw a young man seated on the bed, shaking horribly. He was skeletally thin, just skin over bones. His eyes were open, but they had a dead and empty look to them.

India went to him. She sat down on the bed next to him and gave him a quick examination. She talked to him as she did, trying to make some contact, trying to elicit a response, a flicker of recognition. But her efforts were in vain. There was nothing there. Nothing. It was as if all the things inside of him—his heart and his soul, his bright mind and quick sense of humor—had been ripped out, and all that was left was a shell.

"He's only seventeen, India," Sid said. "He's only seventeen years old."

India heard her husband's choked sobs then. She thought of what she had to do next—call Fiona and Joe and tell them that their precious child was here, in her hospital. That he was wounded, not dead—but he might as well be.

And then India, who had learned long ago not to cry over her patients, covered her face with her hands and wept.

CHAPTER SIXTY

"WALK!" THE MAN shouted in Turkish. "Walk or I'll kick the hell out of you!"

Willa had fallen onto her side in the dirt. Her legs didn't work. Nothing worked. She was dizzy and disoriented. Her eyes wouldn't focus.

"Walk, I said!" the man yelled.

His boot in her ribs made her scream, but it did not bring her to her feet. Nothing could do that. She was going to die here. In the dirt. In the crucifying heat. And she didn't care. She had heard the Bedouin talking to the Turks, and had understood enough of their conversation to know she'd been traveling for five days. After five days of crossing the desert, bound and slung over the back of a camel, after nights spent tied like an animal to a stake in the ground, after enduring dehydration, hunger, and excruciating pain, dying would be a mercy.

Her clothes were caked with dirt, blood, and vomit. She had soiled herself. One of her captors had tried to rape her three nights ago, but had been so repulsed by her condition that he'd turned away from her in disgust.

It didn't matter anymore. None of it mattered. It would all be over soon. She closed her eyes and waited for death. She was not frightened; she welcomed it.

But the Turkish Army had other ideas.

There was more yelling, and then Willa felt hands under her arms, hoisting her to her feet. She opened her eyes, saw a man in uniform hand a leather purse—small and heavy—to the Bedouin raiders who'd captured her. Then two men lifted her off the ground and frog-marched her inside a stone building. She had the vague notion she was in some kind of garrison town. But which one? Was it Damascus?

Her new captors continued to half drag, half carry her through the building. They went through a foyer, down a long hallway, and then down a flight of stairs. It was dark, and her vision was still coming and going, but Willa was certain that she was in a prison.

A thick wooden door was opened, and she was dumped inside a small, dark room with an earthen floor. One of the men left, then came back a minute later with a jug of water. He yelled at her again. She thought he wanted her to drink. But she didn't want the water. She'd made up her mind to die. She struggled, trying to shake the man off, but he was far too strong for her. He held her mouth open until he'd poured most of the water into her, then he held it shut so she could not vomit it back out. After a few minutes had passed, he let go of her and she slumped to the ground.

A plate of food was brought and set down on the floor. The door was closed and locked. It was completely dark in the cell. There was no window, no light at all.

Willa did not know where she was. All she knew was that Bedouins had taken her from the crash site, transported her for many miles, and finally sold her to the Turks—who likely thought she was a spy and intended to interrogate her.

She felt very afraid at the thought of an interrogation. She had heard tales of the Turks' methods and knew they would stop at nothing to get information from her. She promised herself then and there that she would tell them nothing, no matter what they did to her. They would tire eventually and would kill her, but she would give them nothing—nothing about Lawrence, nothing about Damascus.

She would need something to get her through the coming ordeal. Something she could think of to keep up her courage and her strength as they beat her bloody.

An image of a face came to her in the darkness, though she did not want it to. With a trembling hand she traced a single letter in the dirt of her cell floor—the letter S.

CHAPTER SIXTY-ONE

"SEAMIE, YOU CAN'T do this. It's madness. Total bloody madness," Albie Alden said.

Seamie, busy tightening the girth strap on his camel's saddle, did not reply.

"Allenby will send men out to hunt for her," Albie said.

"What men? In case you haven't noticed, Albie, there's a war on," Seamie replied. "Allenby's not going to use valuable troops to hunt for one person—a person who's not even supposed to be in the desert."

"But you're wounded! You can't ride with your injuries. And even if you could, you don't know what you're doing. You don't even know where you're going!"

"He does," Seamie said, pointing at a man sitting atop a second camel, his Bedouin guide, Abdul.

Albie shook his head. "The two of you . . . all alone in the desert. You'll be hopelessly lost within a day. And for what, Seamie? Willa's plane crashed. The pilot was killed. It's likely she was badly injured, and it's equally likely that she is now dead."

Seamie sighed. "That's our Albie, ever the optimist."

"What about your ship? You're supposed to take command of a new ship in just under five weeks' time. How are you going to get out to the Jabal ad Duruz hills, search the area around them, and get back to Haifa in time? If you're not at the docks the morning of the day your commission begins, you'll be classed as a deserter. You know what the British military thinks of deserters, don't you? You'll be court-martialed and shot."

"I'll make sure that I hurry then."

As Albie hectored him, Seamie looked inside his saddlebags, double checking that he'd packed both of his pistols, sufficient ammunition, basic medicines and dressings, and his field glasses; then he rechecked his food and water supplies. It was difficult to see in the darkness. The sun had not yet risen over Haifa.

He had made up his mind to find Willa right after he'd finished reading Allenby's memo. The news had devastated him. He couldn't stand the thought of Willa, possibly injured, certainly afraid, in the hands of cruel and vicious men. It nearly drove him mad.

Instead of going to dinner at the officers' mess, as he and Albie had planned, he'd spent most of the night preparing for the trip. He'd found a guide before the sun had even gone down, and they'd spent the following day gathering supplies. When night fell again, he slept for a few hours, then rose at four A.M., dressed, and made his way to the gates of the city. He'd met Abdul by the east wall just after five o'clock.

Albie, who'd been against the plan ever since he'd heard of it, had met them at the wall and was still trying to talk Seamie out of it. He'd used almost every argument he could think of—every argument, that is, except the one that mattered most to him. He hadn't want to use that one, but he saw now that if he wanted to stop his friend from doing something rash, he had no choice.

"Seamie . . . ," he said now, hesitantly.

"Yes?" Seamie said, buckling one of his saddlebags.

"What about Jennie?"

Seamie stopped what he was doing. He stared straight ahead of himself for a few seconds, then turned to Albie. Albie had never broached the topic of Seamie's affair with Willa; he'd never so much as mentioned it. For years, Seamie thought Albie hadn't known anything about it. Now he saw that he was wrong. He saw something else, too.

"It was you, wasn't it, Albie?" he said quietly. "You're the one who told Willa to go. To leave London. And to leave me. I always wondered if somebody had said something to her. Willa's note . . . her decision to go . . . it was all so abrupt."

"I didn't have a choice, Seamie. It was wrong. For you. For Willa. And for Jennie. I went to your flat one night to see you. You weren't there, but Jennie was. She was very upset. She knew, Seamie. And she was carrying your son. You and Willa are the most important people in the world to me. How could I do nothing? How could I let you destroy yourselves and everyone around you?" Albie looked at Seamie. "You're furious with me, aren't you?"

Seamie felt gutted by his friend's revelation, and by the knowledge that he himself had caused Jennie such grief. "No, Albie, I'm not furious with you," he said. "I'm furious with myself. I had no idea that Jennie knew," he said, sadly. "I thought I'd managed to keep it from her."

"I'm sorry. I've only caused more pain by bringing this all up. I made a mistake. I shouldn't have said anything."

"No, Albie. I'm the one who made a mistake. Quite a few of them. I made one when I married Jennie. And another one when I took up again with Willa. And I've tried to set things right. I've tried my best to be a good husband and a good father. And when this war is over, I will try again."

"Is going after Willa your idea of being a good husband?" Albie asked him.

"For God's sake, Albie!" Seamie said angrily. "I'm not riding out into the desert to rekindle a love affair. What do you want me to do? Sit on my backside while she rots in a Turkish prison? While her guards beat her or starve her . . . or worse?"

"Lawrence will search for her. If she is alive, he'll find her."

Seamie laughed joylessly. "And risk giving away his position? The size of his troops? Right before an offensive? I doubt it. Lawrence is a soldier through and through, Albie, and you know it. As much as he might want to rescue Willa, he cannot risk the lives of thousands for the life of one."

"You mustn't do this."

"What the hell is it with you, Albie? Don't you want me to find her?" Seamie said, but he regretted his words as soon as they were out of his mouth. The pain they caused Albie was evident on his face.

"Of course I want her found. She's my sister, Seamie. We have been at odds over the past few years, but I care about her greatly," Albie said quietly, looking at the ground. "But I don't think you can find her. I think all you can do is recover her body. Which is what I will attempt to do from here with the help of local contacts—Bedouin traders, Turkish informants, and the like. I wish you would help me in that. I wish you would stay here and . . ." He faltered.

"What?"

Albie looked at Seamie. "I'm afraid this will be it, the thing that finally kills you. I've always thought you'd do each other in, you and Willa. Always. As children on my father's boat. In Cambridge, when you climbed up buildings. You came damned close on Kilimanjaro. And then in London I thought you'd do it by breaking each other's hearts. You still might. It's a madness what you have between you. Love, I guess you call it. It almost destroyed Willa in Africa. And again in London. She's likely dead now, Seamie. I know it, and you do, too, but you can't accept it. And now you're hell-bent on destroying yourself on this impossible mission. If you're captured by the enemy, well, you know what will happen . . ." His voice trailed off.

"Albie," Seamie said. "I have no choice. Can't you see that? She is my heart and my soul. There's a chance she's still alive, even if it's a slight one, and while there is, I can't abandon her. I can't."

Albie sighed. "I knew I wouldn't dissuade you," he said heavily. He reached into his trousers pocket and pulled out a folded paper. "It's a map of the region. The most current we have. Destroy it if you're taken."

Seamie took the map. Then he pulled Albie close and hugged him tightly.

"I'll be back," he said. "She'll be back, too. In the meantime, get off your skinny, bespectacled arse and find some spies, will you? So my next boat doesn't get blown up like my last one did."

And then Seamie mounted his camel, and he and Abdul were off. As they rode away, Albie heard the song of the muezzin rising from within the walled city, calling the faithful to prayer. He was not a religious man, but he never failed to be moved by the beauty and emotion of the muezzin's voice, and as the sun rose, sending its golden rays across the desert dunes, he sent up a quick prayer of his own.

He asked God to protect Willa and Seamie, these two people whom he cared about so deeply. He asked Him to overlook the mad and reckless love that bound them, and then he asked for one more thing—he asked God to please spare him from ever knowing anything like it.

CHAPTER SIXTY-TWO

FIONA STOPPED DEAD at the front doors of the Wickersham Hall hospital—a hospital she and Joe had helped fund, one they visited often. Never did she think she would one day come here to visit her own son.

She, Joe, and Sid had come up from London early this morning on the train. A carriage had met them at the station and brought them here. She'd alighted, waited until Sid and the driver got Joe's chair down and got Joe into it, and then she'd proceeded with her husband and brother to the hospital doors. Now, however, she found she could go no farther.

Sid had come to London last night to tell her and Joe, and the rest of their family, about Charlie. They were all in the drawing room, sitting by the fire. It was late when they heard the knock on the door, and Fiona had felt her heart falter inside her. She got to her feet immediately, waiting for Mr. Foster to come into the drawing room. With a son in the army, she lived in terror of a knock on the door.

"He's *not* dead. Oh, thank God!" she said, when Sid came into the drawing room where she and Joe had been sitting by the fire. "They send a telegram to tell you when your son's died, not an uncle."

"No one's dead, Fiona," Sid had said, closing the door behind himself.

"It can't be good, though, your news, can it? You wouldn't have come all this way at this hour if it was," she said, steeling herself. "What's happened?"

Sid made her sit down first. She'd known then that whatever he had to tell her would be very bad. People always made you sit down when the news was very bad. And it was. She cried when he told her about Charlie, and then she kept crying—all night long. She wanted to leave for the hospital right away, but Sid was against it.

"He's only just arrived," he said. "Let him sleep. Maybe a good night's rest in a safe, quiet place will help calm him."

The three of them had left for Paddington Station early. They were on the first train out. Fiona left the younger children in Mrs. Pillower's care. Katie was in Oxford.

Fiona looked up at the large doors now. She had walked through them in happier days, years ago, when she'd come to visit Maud. It felt like such a long time ago, like another lifetime. She remembered another set of hospital doors that she'd walked through once. Even farther back in her past. When she was only seventeen years old. She'd walked through those doors, rushed through them, to see her injured father, right before he died.

She shook her head. "No," she said. "I can't do it."

Joe, who was by her side in his wheelchair, took her hand. "You have to, love," he said. "Charlie needs you."

Fiona nodded. "Yes, you're right," she said. She gave him a brave smile, and together they went inside.

India was waiting for them. She hugged and kissed them wordlessly, then she and Sid led them down a long hallway and into a patient's room. Fiona looked at the poor young man sitting on the bed. He was shaking and pale and as thin as a scarecrow. He was staring at the wall. She looked away again, confused.

"Where is he? Where's Charlie?" she asked.

Sid put his arm around her. "Fee . . . that is Charlie."

Fiona felt her heart shatter inside of her. She covered her face with her hands. A low animal moan of pain escaped her. She took a deep breath and then another and then she lowered her hands. "It can't be," she said. "How did this happen? How?" she asked. "Do you know?"

"We know, Fiona," Sid said hesitantly. "India and I read the medical reports yesterday."

"Tell me," she said.

"It was a hard thing to read, Fee," Sid said. "And probably it's a harder thing still to hear. I don't think—"

"Tell her. Tell us. Both of us. We have to know," Joe said.

Sid nodded. He took them out of the room and then he told them.

"According to the reports of the medical officer in the field," he said, "Charlie had been in the trenches, on the front lines, for five straight months prior to the final attack on his unit. He'd held up under terrible conditions and had always conducted himself bravely. He'd rushed enemy lines during the heat of the battle many times. And then, during an attempt on an enemy position early one morning, two shells in succession hit very close to him. One shell deafened him. The other blew his friend, a lad by the name of Eddie Easton, to bits. Charlie was covered in Eddie's blood, and in pieces of his flesh." Sid had to stop speaking for a bit. "I'm sorry," he said, clearing his throat.

"Go on," Fiona whispered, her fists clenched at her sides.

"Charlie lost his mind," Sid continued. "He couldn't stop screaming, and couldn't stop trying to shake the blood and gore off himself. He tried to crawl back into the trench, but his commander wouldn't let him. The man—Lieutenant Stevens—kept screaming at Charlie to get back out to the battlefield, but Charlie couldn't. Stevens called him a coward and threatened to have him shot for desertion if he didn't return to battle. Charlie kept crying and shaking. Another shell exploded nearby. He curled into a ball. Stevens grabbed him and dragged him back to the front lines. He hauled him into no-man's-land and tied him to a tree. He left him there for seven hours. Said it would set him straight, make a man of him. By the time the shelling stopped and Stevens finally gave the order to bring him back, Charlie was catatonic. The two soldiers who went to untie him said they could get no response from him at all. They carried him back to the trench. Stevens had at him again, yelling at him, slapping him— all to no effect. He then ordered him invalided."

When Sid finished speaking, Fiona turned to Joe, but he was facing away from her, from all of them. His head was bent. He was crying. This man, this good, brave man, who'd never cried for himself when he'd been shot, who'd never shed one tear when he'd lost his legs, and very nearly his life, was sobbing.

Reeling, Fiona walked back into Charlie's room. She took a halting step toward her son. And then another, until she was standing next to his bed. She knelt down beside him and gently stroked his arm.

"Charlie? Charlie, love? It's me, it's Mum."

Charlie made no response. He just kept staring at the wall and shaking uncontrollably. Fiona tried again. And again. And again. She squeezed his arm. Touched his cheek. She took his trembling hands in hers and kissed them. And still Charlie gave no sign that he knew her, that he knew himself, that he knew anything at all. Finally, when she could bear it no longer, Fiona leaned her head against her son's legs and wept. She thought that she had been through everything a human being could go through. Losing her family as a young girl. Losing her beloved first husband, Nicholas, and then almost losing Joe to a criminal's bullets. But she discovered now that she had not, for this pain was like nothing she'd ever known. It was new and terrible. It was a mother's pain at seeing her precious child destroyed.

And Fiona realized that for once in her life, she did not know what to do. She did not know how she would ever get off her knees and stand up again. She did not know how she would manage to take her next breath.

She did not know how to bear the unbearable.

CHAPTER SIXTY-THREE

WILLA ALDEN EXPECTED death to come.

She had hoped for it, prayed for it, and sometimes, alone in the darkness of her cell for days on end, she had begged for it. But death did not come.

Loneliness came, along with despair. Hunger came, and the bone-chilling cold of desert nights. Lice came and, with them, fever. But not death.

She learned to tell day from night by the levels of noise and activity outside her cell. Morning was when the warden walked from cell to cell, opening a small sliding hatch, peering in at his prisoners to make sure they were still alive, then closing it and moving on again.

Midday was when her jailers brought her a jug of fresh water and her one and only meal, and emptied the tin pot that served as her toilet.

Evening was when a hush fell over the prison.

Night was when the rats came out. She had learned to leave some food for them on her plate and to push her plate into a corner, so they would fight one another for the scraps and leave her alone.

She kept track of the passing days by scraping marks in the wall with a stone she'd found on the floor of her cell. She thought she'd been locked away for thirteen days.

The jailers worked in teams. They talked as they worked, but only to each other. When she was feverish, which was most of the time, she could do little but lie mute on her filthy cot. On the few occasions when she could muster the strength to sit or stand, she tried to engage her jailers. She tried to find out why they were holding her and what they planned to do with her, but they would tell her nothing. She understood a bit of Turkish, however, and from the snatches of conversation she could hear, she was able to make out the words "Lawrence," "Damascus," and "Germans."

It was still August; she was sure of that. Had Lawrence marched on Damascus so soon? she wondered. Or had the Turks held the city with the help of the Germans? And for God's sake, where was she? And what were her Turkish captors going to do with her?

Willa finally got her answer nearly two weeks after she'd been brought to the prison. Shortly after the warden made his morning rounds, her door was opened again. The warden was standing in it, along with two of his men. One of them carried a lantern. The warden wrinkled his nose at the smell, then barked at Willa to get up. She could not. The fever she'd been running off and on for most of her imprisonment had spiked up the night before. She was weak and delirious and did not have the strength to stand.

"Get her up," the warden said to his men.

One of them swore under his breath. He did not want to touch her, he said. She was filthy and full of fever. The warden shouted something at him, and he smartly did as he was told. Willa was marched out of the cell and down a long corridor. The daylight, coming in at the windows, blinded her. She had been in the dark for so long her eyes could not cope with brightness. They had adjusted somewhat, however, by the time she arrived at her destination—a small, well-lit room at the back of the prison. There was a metal chair in the middle of it. Underneath the chair was a drain. Willa's stomach knotted at the sight of it.

Please, she prayed. Make it quick. "Death rides a fast camel," Auda always said. Willa fervently hoped he was right.

The men sat her down in the chair and tied her arms behind her back. In the light of the room, she could see how filthy she was. Her clothes were in tatters. Her shoes had been taken away weeks ago. Her feet were covered in dirt. A dull red rash covered her ankles.

"What is your name?" the warden asked her. In English.

"Little Bo Peep," Willa said. She'd been asked her name several times since she'd arrived at the prison and had steadfastly refused to reveal it.

The warden slapped her across her face. Hard. Her head snapped back. She slowly raised it again, sat up straight, and stared straight ahead.

There were more questions. More smart answers, or no answers. The questions got louder. And the slaps turned to punches. Willa felt her right eye swell up, tasted blood at the corner of her mouth, and still she gave them nothing. She thought of Seamie. Of Kilimanjaro. Of their time together in London. And she gave her captors nothing.

"Do you know what I'm going to do to you, you filthy bitch?" the warden finally said to her in English. "I'm going to stick my big fat cock up your ass and make you scream. And when I'm done, my men will have a turn."

Willa, her head lolling on her chest now, laughed. "Are you? For your sake, I hope you have a cold," she said. "A bad one. I hope you can't smell a thing."

The warden cursed at her. He turned to one of his men and, forgetting to switch back to Turkish, said, "I'm not touching her. She stinks like a sewer. Her hair's crawling with lice. She probably has typhus. He's here now, isn't he? Go and get him. He can do his own dirty work. From what I hear, he's very good at it."

Typhus, Willa thought woozily. Well, that's me done for. I only wish it had carried me off sooner.

She wondered who the *he* the warden had talked about was and wondered if she would stay conscious long enough to find out. The door opened again. Someone new walked into the room. She heard harsh words. It was a man. He was speaking German. A rough hand grabbed hold of her hair and yanked her head up.

"*Um Gottes Willen!*" the man said. He was close now. His voice sounded strangely familiar.

There was the sound of laughter, mirthless and bitter. And then the man said, "I should've guessed it was you. *Namaste*, Willa Alden. *Namaste*."

CHAPTER SIXTY-FOUR

SEAMIE STARED AT the sheared and twisted metal of the Sopwith Strutter. How Willa had survived such a violent crash was beyond him. She must have been injured, he thought. Badly. The pilot certainly had been. His headless body still sat in the cockpit, festering in the desert sun.

"What do, Boss?" Abdul, his guide, said in his broken English.

What do, indeed, Seamie thought. If only I knew.

It had taken them twelve days to reach the crash site—twelve days of arduous travel in the blazing desert sun. As Seamie could speak little Arabic, and most tribesmen spoke no English, Albie thought it might be useful for Seamie to have images of Willa. They'd stopped in every village along the way, showing the pictures of Willa. They'd questioned Bedouins on the move, traders, goatherds—anyone they saw—using up precious time in the pursuit of information on Willa's whereabouts, but no one had seen her. No one had heard a thing. They'd stopped to sleep only when it was too dark to see, then risen at dawn's first light to try to gain as much ground as they could.

They'd arrived at the crash site only minutes earlier, and Seamie had been careful to search the perimeter of the site for any tracks left by Willa's abductors, but the wind had swept them away.

He turned around in a circle now, trying to take in the lay of the land, trying to piece together what might have happened to Willa and where she might be. If Turkish soldiers had taken her, she would likely be in a military prison in a garrison town or at an army camp. If tribal raiders had taken her, she could be anywhere.

Seamie told Abdul to rest himself and the animals. As Abdul dismounted, Seamie took his map—the one Albie had given him—out of his saddlebag. The map indicated known Turkish camps in the desert, watering holes frequented by the Bedouin, and desert settlements too small to have names.

Since he had not been able to discover anything during his journey east to the crash site, or from the site itself, Seamie decided that the next thing to do would be to start riding in an ever-widening circle around the site, hoping to spot tracks, a trail, anything.

He was all too aware of how little time he had before he had to be back in Haifa and on his new ship, and how much ground he had to cover before then. How he would ever find Willa in this endless godforsaken nothingness, he did not know. It was like trying to find a grain of sand in . . . well, a desert.

Abdul, already drowsing in the shade of his camel, did not see the raiding party as it approached from the south. Nor did Seamie, who was carefully studying Albie's map. He was not aware of them at all until one of their camels bellowed, and by then it was too late. All but one of the men had already jumped down from their camels and surrounded them. They wore dusty white robes, head scarves, and daggers in their belts.

Abdul woke up with a start and scrambled to his feet. "Raiders. Six of them. Very terrible news," he said.

"So I gather," Seamie said. "What do you want?" he asked the men. But he got no answer.

One of them went to Seamie's camel, opened his saddlebag, and started digging through it.

"Hey! What are you doing there! Get your hands off that!" Seamie shouted angrily.

He made a move to stop the man and instantly found a dagger at his throat. The raider pulled out a pistol, bullets, and a photograph of Willa that Albie had given Seamie. The raider handed the goods to the sixth man, a tall, fearsome-looking Bedouin who was still seated atop his camel and who seemed to be the leader. The leader examined the gun, then the photographs, and then he shouted at Seamie.

Abdul translated as best he could. "He asks why you have these photographs," Abdul said. "He asks your name."

"'Tell him I ask that he kiss my arse!" Seamie yelled. "Tell him to put my things back and take his bloody pack of thieves out of here."

Abdul, wide-eyed, shook his head no.

"Tell him!" Seamie shouted.

The Bedouin shouted at Abdul, too, until Abdul, quaking in his robes, did as he was told. The Bedouin listened to Abdul's words. He nodded, laughed, then barked an order at one of his men.

Seamie never saw the man take the pistol from beneath his robes, never saw him grasp it by its barrel and raise it high, never saw the blow coming.

CHAPTER SIXTY-FIVE

"OH, GRAN! I'M so glad you're here!" Katie Bristow said, rushing down the stairs of her parents' Mayfair house. "Come upstairs, will you?" she said, tugging on her arm.

"Goodness, Katie! Let me get my coat off first!" Rose Bristow said breathlessly. Katie had rung her an hour ago, sounding very upset. Rose had grabbed her things and come as quickly as she could. "What's going on?" she asked Katie now. "You were talking a thousand words to the minute on the blower. I could hardly understand you."

"It's Mum. She's barely eaten since she and Dad came back from hospital, and that was nearly two weeks ago! She doesn't sleep. She barely speaks. She just lies in her bed, all curled up in a ball."

Rose frowned. "Where's your father gone?" she asked.

"He went back to Wickersham Hall. To see Charlie. He's tried everything, Gran. He talked to her. Held her. Brought her cups of tea. He even yelled at her. Nothing worked. Then he called me to come home from school. But nothing I do works, either, and I've done everything I can think of. I don't know what else to do, Gran. I've never seen Mum like this. Never," Katie said, and then she burst into tears.

Rose took her granddaughter in her arms and soothed her. "Hush now, Katie. We'll sort it all out. Your mum's had a terrible shock. She just needs some time to find her feet again, that's all. Go downstairs now and get yourself a cup of tea and I'll go up to her."

Rose took hold of the banister and started up the stairs. She hadn't been to see Charlie yet. Peter, her husband, was very poorly with a chest complaint, and with that terrible influenza going around, she'd hadn't wanted to leave him in case it got worse. Joe had come to see her, though, and had told her what had happened. She'd never seen her son so broken-looking.

Life, Rose well knew, could throw some hard punches at you, but nothing hurt as much as losing a child, or seeing one of your children hurt and suffering. Becoming a parent changed you forever, as nothing else could. Not good or bad fortune. Not friendships. Not even a man or a woman.

Rose remembered how she was before she married and had children, when she was a young woman. She was slim and small, with a pretty face and figure. Several lads had wanted to court her. She had prayed and wished and hoped for all sorts of silly things then. For ribbons. For thick hair and pink cheeks. For a pretty dress. For a husband who was handsome and let her spend the pin money.

After she became a mother, she had only ever prayed for one thing: that no harm would ever come to her children.

She reached the landing now and—huffing and puffing slightly—walked down the hallway to Fiona and Joe's bedroom. She knocked on the door, received no answer, and walked in.

Her daughter-in-law was in her bed, fully clothed, with her back to the door. Rose's heart clenched at the sight of her. She knew Fiona had lost her own mother when she was young. Kate Finnegan had been Rose's close friend. They'd lived on the same street when they were newly married. For the love of Kate, and of Fiona, Rose had tried to be a mother to her daughter-in-law all these years.

"What's all this then, eh, Fiona?" she said gently. "Lolling about in bed all day, are we? That's not the Fiona I know. How about you come downstairs now? And join Katie and me in the kitchen for a nice cup of tea?"

She sat down on the bed next to Fiona and began to rub her back. "You've got both Joe and Katie at their wits' end with worry. The littler ones are running rings around poor old Mrs. Pillower. Mr. Foster's at a loss. Even the dogs look sorry for themselves. No one knows what to do without you to tell them. You've got to get up now."

Rose heard a sob, and then another. Fiona turned around, and Rose saw that her face was swollen and her eyes were red from crying.

"I try to get up, Rose," she said in a small, choked voice. "I try to get out of this bed, but when I do, all I can see are the faces of the men in the veterans' hospital. All the young men who look like old men now because of what's happened to them. And I see a new face among them—my Charlie, who doesn't even know me anymore. He's gone, Rose."

"He's not gone. He's in a good hospital in Oxford with his uncle Sid and auntie India, where he'll get good care. The best. There's no better place for him," Rose said.

Fiona shook her head. "You didn't see him. My beautiful boy is gone. There's a stranger in his place. A hollowed-out, dead-eyed stranger. How could he do it, Rose? The lieutenant . . . Stevens is his name. How could he do what he did to Charlie? Nothing happened to him. No disciplinary action was taken against him. He should be in jail for what he did. He destroyed my son. Charlie will never get better. How can he? There's nothing there anymore. He doesn't have a chance."

Rose let her weep. She let her cry the grief and rage out, and when she had stopped, when the sobs had subsided to silent tears,

Rose said, "Listen to me, Fiona, and listen well. If you really believe that Stevens has destroyed Charlie, then he has. And then you're right—the poor lad doesn't have a chance. Not as long as you stay in this bed. Not as long as you've given up on him."

Fiona wiped her eyes. For the first time since Rose had come into the room, Fiona met her eyes.

"He's still there," Rose said. "He's just gone deep inside himself. To someplace quiet and safe. Where the shells can't get at him. Where he can't see his dead friend anymore. You're his mother. If anyone can get to him and pull him back out, you can. But you've got to try. You've got to fight. I've known you since the day you were born, Fiona. You've fought your whole life. For God's sake, don't stop now."

"But I don't know how, Rose. I don't know what to do," Fiona said helplessly.

Rose laughed. She took Fiona's hand and squeezed it tightly. "Do we ever know what to do, we mothers?" she asked her. "Did I know what to do when Joe had his first bout of croup? Did you know what to do when Charlie fell out of a tree and broke his arm? No. You never know what to do. You just figure it all out somehow because you have to. If you don't, who will?" Rose said.

Fiona nodded.

"All you have to do, lass, is try," Rose said, patting her arm. "I know you can do that for Charlie. I know you can."

Fiona sat up. "Can I, Rose? Really?"

"Yes, of course you can," Rose said. "You'll find him, Fiona. I know you will. You'll find him and bring him back to us."

"Do you promise?" Fiona asked, her voice small and uncertain.

Rose thought about her damaged grandson. She thought about what had happened to him, about the horror of having to wipe his dead friend's blood off him. She thought about how cruelly he'd been abused and how people had been driven hopelessly mad over less.

And then she thought about the woman sitting next to her, and all that she'd overcome in her life, and how her losses and sorrows had not made her bitter and cruel, they'd only made her stronger, kinder, and more generous.

"I do," Rose said, smiling. "I promise."

CHAPTER SIXTY-SIX

SEAMIE OPENED HIS eyes.

"Where am I?" he muttered. "What's happened?"

He blinked a few times to clear his vision, then tried to sit up, ignoring the pain battering at his skull. Groaning, he lay back down again.

He looked around and realized he was lying on a soft rug, inside a tent. How he'd got here, he did not know. For a few seconds he could remember nothing, and then it all came back to him: He'd been at the crash site with Abdul when the raiders arrived. He'd mouthed off to their leader. One of the raiders must have coshed him.

"Bloody hell," he said. Then he called for Abdul. Loudly.

A woman, alerted by his shouts, came into the tent and looked at him. She quickly went out again, shouting herself. A few minutes later, Abdul came dashing into the tent.

"Where are the camels?" Seamie asked him. "Where are our things?"

Before Abdul could answer him, another man came into the tent. Seamie recognized him; he was the raiders' leader. Behind him came the woman. She was wrapped in robes of indigo blue, with a veil across the lower half of her face.

"This is Khalaf al Mor," Abdul said, in a hushed voice, "sheik of the Beni Sahkr. The woman is Fatima, his first wife."

"I don't care if he's George the fifth, tell him to give me back my gear," Seamie growled.

Abdul ignored him. Khalaf al Mor held up the photograph of Willa. He looked at Abdul, then nodded.

"The sheik wishes to know why you have these photographs," Abdul said.

Khalaf then held up a necklace. Seamie could not know it, but it was the very one Fatima had given Willa, the one her abductors took from her.

"The sheik also wishes you to tell him what you know about this necklace," Abdul said. In a lower voice he added, "I advise you to make no further references to your backside."

Seamie looked at the Bedouin. Why was the man so interested in Willa's photograph? He had asked about it at the crash site, too. Did he know something about her? It suddenly dawned on him that perhaps Khalaf al Mor could help him. For the first time in days, a spark of hope kindled inside of him.

"Tell the sheik my name is Seamus Finnegan and that I'm a captain with the British Navy. Tell him I know nothing about the necklace, but the photographs are of my friend, Willa Alden. She was in a plane crash. Out by the Jabal ad Duruz hills," Seamie said. "Tell him I'm looking for her. I want to find her."

Fatima shrilled at Abdul. It seemed to Seamie that she was desperate to know what he, Seamie, had just said. Abdul translated. Khalaf nodded as he spoke, but his expression—one of mistrust—never changed. Fatima chattered at her husband. Khalaf impatiently waved her away.

"The sheik wishes to know if this woman is so important to you, why is she not your wife?"

"Because I already have a wife," Seamie said. "Back in England."

Abdul related his answer to the sheik and his wife. Fatima let out a loud exclamation. She shrilled at her husband again. He flapped a hand at her then said something to Abdul.

"The sheik says that your explanation is like a cracked pot and will not hold water," Abdul said.

"Why the hell does he say that?" Seamie asked.

"Because a man may have more than one wife," he replied.

"Not in England he can't," Seamie said.

Abdul relayed that information to Khalaf. Fatima, listening, excitedly talked at her husband again, quite loudly. Khalaf barked at her, silencing her. Then he spoke to Abdul again.

"The sheik says he has heard of this custom before," Abdul said. "He admits it may have its advantages. But he wishes to know how one wife alone can give you many sons. A man must have twenty at least."

"Well, I don't have twenty, but I do have one," Seamie said. He held one hand up to show he was not reaching for a weapon, then dug into his back pocket, hoping his wallet was still there. It was. He pulled it out, opened it, and showed Khalaf the photograph of little James standing with Jennie.

Khalaf smiled. He nodded. He and Fatima spoke. Abdul quietly told Seamie what they were saying. "The sheik's wife is telling him that it is exactly as she said—Willa—the woman we are all searching for. She is telling him that you are the one that this woman spoke about. You are the reason she has no husband, no child. The sheik's wife said she told her that you had a wife already, a pretty wife back in England, and a small son, too. She is telling her husband to help you."

As Abdul spoke, a small, beautiful, dark-eyed boy came into the tent and touched the sheik's arm. The Bedouin smiled at the sight of the boy and put an arm around him. Then he grabbed Abdul's arm and spoke rapidly to him.

Abdul nodded, then he turned to Seamie and said, "Khalaf al Mor wishes to tell you that this is Daoud, his firstborn son. He wishes you to know that Willa Alden saved the life of Daoud."

Seamie nodded, alert with excitement. He was certain now that Khalaf al Mor could help him find Willa.

"The sheik also wishes you to know that his wife Fatima gave the necklace he showed you to Willa Alden and that this necklace was found in the possession of some Howeitat raiders who were trying to sell it in Umm al Qittayn, a small village at the base of the Jabal ad

Duruz hills. Some of the sheik's men were there and recognized it.
They asked the Howeitat how they had got it, but they would say
only that they'd found it—not where or how. The sheik's men were
outnumbered, or they would've simply taken the necklace. Since
they could not, they paid the Howeitat for it and brought it back
here. The sheik's wife saw it and right away knew it for her own."

"Go on, Abdul," Seamie said. "Tell me the rest."

"Khalaf al Mor says that these men call themselves Howeitat, but
belong to no tribe, no village. They are known to be robbers and
kidnappers. They have sold things—guns, information, sometimes
people—to the Turks before. Khalaf al Mor fears they have done the
same with Willa Alden."

"Ask him where they are, and how I can find them," Seamie said.

The words went back and forth between Seamie and Khalaf al
Mor quickly. Seamie learned that the raiders were thought to live a
few miles south of the Jabal ad Duruz hills and that in all likelihood
all Seamie would have to do was give them money and they would tell
him what they'd done with Willa. But, Khalaf cautioned, they were
unpredictable. They were wary and took offense easily, and under
no circumstances should Seamie try to approach them on his own.

"But I must approach them," Seamie said. "How else can I find
out if they're the ones who took Willa?"

Khalaf told him that he would help him. He would give him ten
men, with rifles and camels, and he himself would ride with him,
too, to help him hunt for Willa Alden.

Seamie said they must start out right away. Much moved by
Khalaf al Mor's kindness, he thanked the sheik for his generosity
and concern and for doing so much for him.

The sheik smiled. "I do not do it for you, my friend," he told
Seamie through Abdul. "I do it because Willa Alden is beloved of
Allah. And beloved of Khalaf al Mor."

CHAPTER SIXTY-SEVEN

WILLA OPENED HER bruised and swollen eyes.

She expected the darkness of her prison cell, but instead there was light. Bright desert sunshine poured in through a window and spilled onto the clean white sheets of the bed in which she lay.

She held her hand up in front of her face. Her skin was clean. Her nails, which had been clotted with dirt and blood, had been trimmed and scrubbed. The filthy, tattered sleeve of the khaki shirt she'd worn for weeks was gone. In its place was a sleeve of cool white cotton.

It's a hallucination, she thought, brought on by my illness. Or perhaps I'm dreaming. Perhaps the warden of the prison has finally beaten me unconscious and I'm only dreaming that I'm in a clean place, wearing clean clothes, and lying in a clean bed. She waited, her eyes still open, for the hallucination to stop, for the dream to be over. To find herself back in her cell, back in the darkness. But it didn't happen.

"Where am I?" she finally murmured.

"Ah, you're awake," a voice said, startling her. It was a woman's voice. It was brisk and businesslike and sounded German.

Willa sat up, gasping with the pain of her broken ribs. She turned her head around and saw that the woman was standing at her left, by a small sink. She was dressed all in white and her hair was tucked up neatly under a white cap.

"You've been very ill," she said, with a smile. "In fact, at one stage I was quite sure we were going to lose you. You have three broken ribs, you know. And you've just come through a terrible case of typhus. Your fever hit one hundred and six a few nights ago."

"Who are you?" Willa asked.

"I'm your nurse," the woman replied.

"But how—"

"Not so much talking. You're still very weak. Here, take this," she said, putting a small white pill in Willa's hand and holding out a glass of water.

"What is it?" Willa asked.

"Morphine. It will help with the pain. Take it, please."

Something in the tone of the woman's voice told Willa she had no choice. She dutifully washed the pill down with some water.

"Very good," the woman said. "Now lie back down. Morphine can make one a bit light-headed. Especially one in a debilitated condition. I'll be right here if you need anything."

Something inside Willa wanted to argue, to ask more questions, to put up a fight, but the drug was already flowing through her, making her feel deliciously warm and drowsy, taking the pain in her chest away, taking all her pain away. It was stronger than the opium she smoked, much stronger. And so she did not fight. She just lay on the bed, feeling as if she was floating along on a soft, hazy cloud.

How long she remained in this state, she did not know. An hour could have passed, or only a minute, before she heard the footsteps in the hallway. They were slow and measured. They stopped at her door, then entered her room.

She tried to open her eyes, to see who it was, but she was so tired now, and so weak, that she could not make even her eyelids do what she wanted.

She felt a hand stroking her hair, then her cheek. It was a man's hand. She knew because he started speaking to her in a man's voice. It was familiar, this voice. She had heard it before, but where?

And then she remembered—in the prison. In the interrogation room. For a few seconds, she was gripped by terror. She wanted to get up. To run. To get out of this room, but she couldn't. It was as if her limbs were made of lead.

"Shh," the voice said. "It's all right, Willa. Everything's all right.

I just have a few questions for you. Just one or two. And then you can sleep." The voice was low and soothing. Not angry, like before.

"Where's Lawrence, Willa?" it said. "I need to know. It's very important that I know. You'll help me with this, won't you? Just like you helped me on the mountain."

Willa tried to nod. She wanted to help. She wanted to sleep.

"No, don't nod. Don't move at all. You need to be still. To rest. Just speak, that's all. Where's Lawrence?"

Willa swallowed. Her mouth suddenly felt so dry. She was about to speak, about to tell him, when suddenly she saw Lawrence—in her mind's eye. He was crouched over a campfire in the desert. He was with Auda. He looked at her, then slowly raised a finger to his lips. And she knew she must protect them—Lawrence and Auda both. She must tell the man nothing.

"Tired . . . ," she said, trying to think clearly through the swirling fog in her head, trying to parry the man's questions.

The hand on her cheek now gripped her chin. Hard.

"Where is Lawrence?" the voice said, not so kindly now.

Willa struggled to keep her wits about her. She dug down deep, mustering her last reserves of strength, in order to think of a good answer, one that would throw the man off.

"Carchemish," she said. "He's at Carchemish, digging. He found a temple there. . . ."

Carchemish was the ancient Hittite site where Lawrence had worked as an archaeologist before the war.

The man released her. She heard him swear under his breath, then he said, "You've given her too much. Between the drugs and the fever, she's out of her mind. A bit less next time, please."

Willa heard the sound of footsteps receding, heard the door close, and then she heard nothing more.

CHAPTER SIXTY-EIGHT

"IT'S MADNESS, ISN'T it, Mr. Foster?"

"Only if it fails, madam. If it works, it's genius."

Fiona, sitting across from her butler on the 8:15 to Oxford, nodded. "Sid said some of them love to garden. Charlie used to help me with the roses. Do you remember?" she asked.

"I do," Foster replied. "I particularly remember one incident when he decided to concoct his own fertilizer. From vegetable scraps, fish heads, and some ale that had gone flat. He mixed it up in the pantry, then forgot about it, and then the scullery maid kicked it over by accident."

"I remember that, too," Fiona said, laughing. "It stunk up the entire house."

"Indeed, it did. The fumes in the kitchen were eye-watering. Cook was furious. She resigned. It took all my powers of persuasion to convince her to stay."

"I had no idea, Mr. Foster," Fiona said. "Thank you."

She looked at Foster and realized there was so much she didn't know, so many problems she'd never had to concern herself with because he was always there, fixing things, smoothing things, making sure that the headaches of running a household never troubled her. And it seemed to her now that he always had been.

He was getting on, he was nearly sixty-five and graying, and he suffered from arthritis in his knees and hands. Five years ago, she and Joe had hired another man—Kevin Richardson—to work with Mr. Foster as under-butler and relieve him of his most arduous duties, but Mr. Foster was still in charge, and that was the way Fiona wanted it. She could not imagine her house, or her life, without him in it.

Fiona and Joe had always been good to Mr. Foster. He was compensated well for his work. He had a spacious set of rooms within their house. He was respected and appreciated. But suddenly, sitting across from him in the rattling train car, a huge basket of gardening clobber on the floor between them, Fiona felt that she hadn't been good enough. That she'd never told him how much he meant to her, how much she valued him.

She cleared her throat now and leaned forward in her seat. "Mr. Foster, I . . . ," she began to say.

"There's no need, ma'am. It's quite all right. I know," Foster said.

"Do you?" Fiona said. "Do you really?"

"I do."

Fiona nodded, knowing that he was not overly fond of emotional displays. In fact, when she had finally worked up the strength and courage she needed to travel back to the veterans' hospital to visit her son, it was Mr. Foster she asked to go with her. Not Joe. With Joe, her beloved husband, the father of her damaged child, she would cry. With Mr. Foster, an ex–army man himself, she would buck up and do what needed to be done.

And what needed to be done, Fiona had decided, was gardening. Maud had kept a rose garden at her Oxford home. It contained some beautiful, blowsy, fragrant old roses, but it was not as well tended as it should be. The hospital gardener and his crew put most of their efforts into the kitchen garden, which was needed to feed both patients and staff.

Fiona had heard her brother Sid talk about the progress he'd made with some of the shell-shocked men by getting them out of their rooms and putting them to work around the hospital. Charlie had shared his father's love of gardens and orchards and had always trailed behind Joe as he rolled down his rows of pear and apple trees in his wheelchair at Greenwich, inspecting his crops. Fiona hoped that caring for Maud's roses might help Charlie recover.

Fiona felt the train slow slightly now. She looked out the window and saw the station approaching. "We're here, Mr. Foster," she said. But Foster was already up and gathering their things.

"There is one thing to keep in mind, ma'am," he said, as she reached to the luggage rack overhead for her carpetbag and umbrella.

"Yes?" Fiona said. "What is it?"

"Rome was not built in a day."

"No, it wasn't, Mr. Foster, and I will keep it firmly in mind," Fiona said.

Sid greeted them when they arrived.

"How is he?" Fiona asked her brother.

"The same, I'm afraid. No change. How are you?"

Worried, Fiona thought. Frightened. Angry. Sorrowful. Uncertain.

"Resolute," she said.

Sid smiled. "I've never known you to be anything but," he said.

"I thought we would get to work on the rose garden straight away," Fiona said. "Could we borrow a barrow?"

Sid got them all set up as Fiona changed into an old work dress. He secured a barrow, some fertilizer, and a few tools that she had been unable to bring. Then he tucked a basket into the barrow, containing sandwiches and tea. When Fiona was ready, he took her and Mr. Foster to Charlie's room.

Charlie was sitting on the bed, in the exact same place he had been the first time Fiona had come to see him. He was still shaking, still staring straight ahead of himself. For a moment, her grief came back and threatened to engulf her, but she heard Rose's voice in her head, telling her she was his mother, telling her to fight for her child. And she heard Foster's voice, right next to her, saying, "Remember Rome, ma'am."

"Hello, Charlie," she said, in a strong, clear voice. "It's me, Mum. I've brought Mr. Foster with me. I thought we'd take a walk today. Get outside for a bit and do a little gardening. It's a beautiful day, you know, and there are roses at the back of the property. August is waning, the hottest weather's over, so some of them should be re-blooming. Shall we take a look? Come on, then. There we go."

Together, Sid and Mr. Foster got Charlie to his feet. His legs shook as badly as the rest of him did, and it was slow going getting him down the hallway and out of the building. Once they were outside, the two men continued helping Charlie on the way to the rose garden. Fiona, pushing the wheelbarrow, followed them.

"Oh, Charlie! Look at them all!" she exclaimed, once they'd arrived. The garden, though neglected, was still magnificent. Roses of every size, shape, and color spilled over the willow fences, over the slate stepping-stones, and over one another.

"They all need pruning and a bit of manure turned in. I see black spot on the Maiden's Blush over there. Do you see it, Mr. Foster? And that Cecile Brunner's become very unruly. Let's start with the cleanup, and the fertilizing, and then we'll clip a few dozen blooms. We'll bring them all back to the hospital and fill vases and bottles and jam jars and anything else we can find and put them in all the rooms. Shall we do that?"

Sid said he thought it sounded like a wonderful idea and that the rooms could use some brightening, then he excused himself. He said he had to get Stephen, one of his lads, to the barn to tend to Hannibal, for Hannibal, the surly sod, was needed to harrow a field and now allowed no one but Stephen to harness him.

Fiona and Mr. Foster spread a blanket on the ground and sat Charlie down near a rosebush heavily laden with bright pink blooms. Right after they got him settled, a chattering squirrel, angered by their presence, jumped from the ground into the very same rosebush, shaking the blooms roughly and sending the dew that was still on some of them flying. Droplets of water landed on Charlie. One of the soft blooms flopped down onto his shoulder, brushing his cheek as it did.

And as it did, Fiona saw something. She saw her son's eyes flicker toward the rose. The movement was subtle and small, it happened in the space of a split second, but it happened. For an instant, there was a tiny spark of life in Charlie's dull, dead eyes.

She looked at Mr. Foster. He had seen it, too. She could tell by the excitement on his face. Fiona quickly picked up a pair of secateurs and clipped a rose from high up on the bush. Then she knelt down and put it into her boy's shaking hand. She closed his fingers gently around the stem and held his hand in her own.

"I'm stronger than Lieutenant Stevens, Charlie," she said to him. "Stronger than any bloody bomb. Stronger than all the ghosts wailing in your head. I gave you life once and the war took it away, but I will give it back to you. Do you hear me, lad?" She pressed her lips to his forehead and kissed him. "You do hear me. I know you do."

She stood up then, clapped the dew off her hands, picked up a rake, and got to work.

CHAPTER SIXTY-NINE

SEAMIE LOOKED AT the man standing before him. His name was Aziz. He wore a red head scarf and red robes. He stood, feet planted firmly on the ground, arms crossed over his chest, and demanded to know why he—Seamie—was insulting him with his questions and his presence.

Seamie, Abdul, Khalaf, and Khalaf's men had ridden into the center of the man's village only moments before. From some traders on their way to Haifa they'd learned they would find who they were looking for here. It had taken them four days to find the village.

Looking around from his vantage point atop his camel, Seamie thought that this place could hardly even be called a village. It was little more than a collection of stone hovels, twenty at the most, and some ramshackle animal pens.

Aziz had come out of one of the crumbling houses to speak with them just after they'd arrived. One of Khalaf's men who'd bought Willa's necklace at Umm al Quittan had told Khalaf that this was the man from whom they'd bought it.

"I want information on the woman," Seamie said to Aziz now, for

Aziz spoke some English. "The woman from the airplane. The one you kidnapped. What did you do with her?"

Aziz laughed. He spat. He said nothing.

Seamie reached behind himself into his saddlebag, slowly and carefully to show that he was not reaching for a gun, and pulled out a small leather sack. He shook it so that everyone could hear the coins inside it clink.

"Twenty guineas," he said, looking Aziz in the eye. "It's yours. If you tell me where she is."

Aziz laughed. He let out a cry, sudden and piercing, like that of a falcon, and suddenly two dozen men came out of the houses, each one armed with a rifle.

"Mine if I tell you," he said, nodding at the sack and smiling. "And also if I don't."

CHAPTER SEVENTY

A MINUTE? AN hour? A day? A week?

Willa Alden had no idea how long she had slept. When she woke, she saw a man sitting in the chair near her bed. He was tall and handsome, with silvery blond hair, and Willa wondered, again, if she was seeing things. She closed her eyes, waited for a few seconds, then opened them again. The man was still there.

"Max?" she said. "Max von Brandt?"

The man smiled and nodded. "We meet in the desert this time, instead of in London, or in the Himalayas." He leaned forward in his chair and touched the back of his hand to her cheek. "You feel much cooler," he said. "You look better, too. Then again, you should. You slept for four days straight."

"Max, I must tell you, this is a bit of a surprise," Willa said. She tried to sit up and gasped with pain.

"Be careful, Willa. Your ribs are still healing."

"What are you doing here? What am I doing here? What is this place?" she said, pulling herself upright with the help of her bedrail. The pain was intense. Tiny beads of sweat broke out on her upper lip.

"To answer your last question first—this place is a hospital. For Turkish and German troops. In Damascus. You are here, in Damascus, because you are a spy. I am here for the very same reason."

"You . . . you're a spy?" Willa said.

"Yes, for the German secret service. I was stationed in London for quite some time, then Paris. Now Damascus. The situation here is critical, as I'm sure you know."

"You're sure I know? Know what, Max?" Willa said, putting a note of irritation in her voice.

She had quickly assessed the situation. She was quite certain now that her Turkish jailers had kept her alive on Max's orders—though he didn't know exactly who he was keeping alive until he'd seen her in the interrogation room. The Turks, simply following commands, hadn't particularly cared if she lived or died, but Max was a different story. He'd had feelings for her once. Now he believed she was a spy, but if she could convince him otherwise, he might let her go.

Max didn't answer her question right away. He looked at her for a bit, frowning slightly, then he said, "I'm being completely truthful with you, Willa. In return, I want you to be truthful with me. . . . Where is Lawrence and when is he planning to attack Damascus?"

Willa laughed. "Max," she said, "you've got it all wrong. I'm not a spy. I'm a photographer, as you know. I needed money so I talked Pathé into footing the bill for me to come out here, and then I badgered General Allenby—I'm sure you know who he is—into letting me follow Lawrence around. I've been taking stills and shooting some film, too. It all goes back to London, gets cleared, and then goes into the newsreels shown at every movie theater in England and America. Hardly top secret spy stuff, is it?"

Willa had shifted in her bed as she spoke, waking up the pain in her ribs again. It was getting worse. She wanted some morphine to dull it.

"Hello?" she said loudly, leaning forward in her bed. "Is anybody there? *Hello?* Crumbs! Where's that nurse?"

"She'll come in a minute," Max said.

His smile was gone. There was a slight hint of menace in his voice. And Willa, sweating, was suddenly chilled by the knowledge that Max had sent the nurse out and that he would bring her back only when he felt like it.

"Listen to me, Willa. Listen very carefully," he said now. "You are in a great deal of trouble. I saved you from being very badly beaten the other day. And probably raped, too. But I cannot save you forever. I have only so much influence. A motion picture camera was found in the wreckage of your plane. The film inside it was of a Turkish camp in the Jabal ad Duruz hills."

Willa's heart sank at that. She'd hoped that the film had been ruined in the crash.

"You and the pilot were very brave," Max continued. "You flew low and got some rather comprehensive footage."

Willa did not answer him. Max stood. He put his hands on her bed rail and leaned in close to her.

"I can help you. I want to help you," he said. "But you have to help me, too. I saved you from those animals in the interrogation room, and I can do more, but only if you give me something. I must have information on Lawrence."

"I have none," Willa said stubbornly. "Yes, you are right. I was on a recon mission, but it failed. As you know. As for Lawrence, he does not share his plans with me. Only with Auda and Faisal."

Max straightened. He nodded. "Perhaps you would like a little more time to think about my request," he said.

He walked out into the hallway and signaled for two orderlies to come into the room. They did. One was pushing a wheelchair.

"Where am I going?" Willa asked Max warily.

"Sightseeing," he replied.

Wordlessly, the two men lifted Willa out of her bed. They were not particularly gentle and they jostled her. Though she tried not to, Willa cried out in pain.

Max dismissed the men, then wheeled Willa out of her room, down the corridor, and out of the hospital. The hot, dusty streets of Damascus sprawled out before her. She had never been to the city before, and she took mental notes now of which way they were heading and what buildings she passed. They traveled for five minutes or so, made two left turns, and then arrived at their destination—the prison.

Willa panicked when she saw it, and tried to climb out of the wheelchair, but a firm hand on her shoulder pressed her back down.

"Don't worry," Max said. "I'm not taking you back to your cell."

He pushed her through the arched entryway, through which camels and horses and vehicles passed, over a cobbled court, past various buildings, to a dirt yard behind the prison. It was enclosed by a high stone wall and it was empty.

"What is this?" Willa asked. "What are we doing here?"

Before Max could answer her, a group of about eight soldiers marched past them. In their midst, shackled, was a Bedouin man.

"Howeitat," Max said. "One of Auda's and a spy."

As Willa watched, the soldiers marched the Bedouin to the far wall. They tied his hands behind him, then blindfolded him.

"No," Willa said, realizing what they were about to do. "Please, Max. No."

"I think you should see this," he said.

The soldiers raised their rifles. Their commander raised his sword. When he lowered it, they fired. The Bedouin arched backward into the wall, then slumped to the ground, twitching. Red stains blossomed across his white robes.

Wordlessly, Max wheeled Willa back to her hospital room, then helped her get back into her bed. She was shaking with pain and sick with shock. Max summoned the nurse and told her to give Willa a pill. She swallowed it immediately, wanting the pain to stop, wanting the images of the slaughtered man to go away, wanting to escape this misery with a deep, narcotic sleep.

When the nurse left, Max fluffed Willa's pillow for her. Then he said, "What you just saw will become your fate. I cannot stop it. Not unless you help me. Not unless you tell me what I need to know."

Max pulled the crisp white sheet over her legs. "I care for you, Willa," he said. "I have since the first day I met you, and I do not want to see you standing in front of a firing squad."

He kissed her cheek, told her he would see her tomorrow, and took his leave. He stopped inside the doorway, turned back to her, and said, "Think about my request, but not for too much longer."

CHAPTER SEVENTY-ONE

SEAMIE RAISED HIS canteen to his lips and took a swig of water. His body swayed slightly as he drank, rising and dipping in the saddle with every plodding step his camel took. He looked ahead of himself, through the shimmering waves of heat rising off the sand, at what looked like an infinite expanse of desert. He'd been traveling across it for three weeks now.

"Do you trust him?" he asked Khalaf al Mor, who was riding next to him.

"No," Khalaf replied, "but I don't have to trust him. I know he will do as we've asked. There's too much gold in it for him not to."

Aziz rode about twenty yards ahead of them, flanked by two of his own men. They were riding north, to Damascus, but would stop at Lawrence's camp first to rest and water their animals. No one knew where Lawrence made his camp—he changed locations frequently to ensure that—but Aziz claimed that he knew where Lawrence was now, and that it was on the way to Damascus. He said there was shade there, and a well that gave plenty of fresh, sweet water.

Seamie hoped Khalaf was right about Aziz. He had been right about many things so far. That they were here, heading to Damascus—that they were here at all, actually—was due entirely to him. Khalaf was the one who'd persuaded Aziz and his village full of armed bandits not to kill them.

Only minutes after Seamie and Khalaf had ridden to the village to ask about Willa, Aziz and his men had taken the bag of gold Seamie offered him for information on Willa, and were about to take every-thing else from Seamie, Khalaf, and Khalaf's men—including their lives—until Khalaf told Aziz there would be more gold for him if he did not.

"Spare our lives, take us to the girl, and I will give you twice as much gold again upon our safe return," he said.

Instantly the guns were lowered. Warm greetings and apologies for the misunderstanding were offered, and the visitors were invited into Aziz's house for a meal. He told them how he had seen the Brit-ish plane go down, had ridden to the wreck in search of plunder, found Willa, and taken her to Damascus.

"I almost did not," Aziz explained. "She was badly injured. There was every chance she would die on the way, and then the whole trip, the time, the wear and tear on my camels—all of it would have been for nothing. But she survived. And I got two thousand dinars. So it was a profitable trip after all, thanks be to Allah."

Seamie, enraged by the man's callous cruelty, had nearly lashed out at Aziz. Khalaf's hand on his arm stopped him.

"Do not allow your anger to lead you," he said under his breath. "You can do nothing for Willa if you are dead."

"Why?" Seamie asked Aziz, barely able to keep his voice even. "Why did you sell her to the Turks?"

Aziz looked at him as if he were a simpleton. "Because they pay more than the British," he said.

The following day, Seamie and Khalaf set off again, joined by

Aziz and two of his men. They had been traveling for three days now and were still another three days from where Aziz said Lawrence's camp was. Seamie was weary. His wound was oozing and hurting him. He changed the dressings daily, but the strenuousness and constant motion of desert travel aggravated his stitches and slowed his healing. And getting to Damascus was only part of the battle.

"What will you do once you reach the city, eh?" Aziz had asked him, laughing. "Make an assault on it yourself? You are a fool, Seamus Finnegan, but I like fools. Fools and their money are soon parted."

"He will get us to Damascus," Khalaf al Mor said now, pulling Seamie out of his thoughts. "What we do once we get there, that is the question."

"It's a question I ask myself all the time," Seamie said. "I never get an answer."

"Then do not ask yourself. Ask Allah. With Allah, all things are possible," Khalaf said serenely.

Right, Seamie thought. I'll just ask God. I'll ask Him to help me find the woman I love, the one who isn't my wife. The woman with whom I've caused my wife and my best friend nothing but grief. The one I still dream about and long for, even though I know I shouldn't. I'm sure He'll understand. And oh, by the way, God, it's me and Khalaf and a few of his men against an entire Turkish garrison. Will you see what you can do, old boy?

"Have faith, my friend," Khalaf said. "Have faith."

All right, then, Seamie decided. He'd do it. He'd have faith.

It was better than having nothing.

CHAPTER SEVENTY-TWO

WILLA, DROWSING, HEARD a soft knocking sound. She opened her eyes and saw Max standing in her doorway, smiling, his hands behind his back.

"May I come in?" he asked.

"This is your hospital, Max. I am your prisoner. I should think you can do whatever you like," she replied.

"How are you feeling?" he asked her, ignoring the barb. "Are you still in pain?"

"I am," she said nodding. "You wouldn't happen to have a pill on you, would you? The ribs are still kicking up and I haven't seen the nurse for hours."

"This might help," he said, pulling a bottle of wine out from behind his back. It was a 1907 Château Lafite. In his other hand, he had two wineglasses. He filled both glasses, then handed her one. "I snuck it out of the officers' mess. I hope you like it," he said, sitting on the bed.

Willa's hands shook as she took the glass. Eyeing him warily, she sniffed it, which made him laugh.

"If I wanted to kill you, there are quicker ways. Slower ones, too. Drink up. There's nothing in your glass but wine, I swear it," he said.

Willa took a sip of the rich Bordeaux. She hadn't had anything like it in years. It tasted impossibly good. Like civilization and happiness. Like all the beautiful, peaceful nights she'd squandered. Like life before the war.

"This is wonderful," she said. "Thank you."

"It is good, isn't it? I'm glad I'm drinking it here. With you. Not with some ghastly old major general in the mess, who's reminiscing fondly—and endlessly—about the Franco-Prussian War."

Willa smiled. She swallowed another mouthful of wine, loving the feeling of it coursing through her body, warming her blood, bringing a flush to her cheeks. For a few seconds, it was as if they were back in Tibet again. They hadn't any Lafite to drink there, but they'd had tea, which they'd often drunk together in the warmth of a campfire.

Max refilled her glass. "Have you thought about my offer?" he asked.

Willa took another drink. "Of course I have," she said. "But what can I say about it, Max? What do you want me to do? Be a traitor to my own country? Could you do that?"

Max smiled ruefully. He shook his head. Willa half expected him to call for the firing squad, but he didn't.

"It's amazing how we both ended up here at the same time, isn't it?" he said. "I'd be tempted to say it was fate, if I believed in fate."

"But you don't."

"No. I believe life is what you make it," he said, refilling his own glass. "I don't want to be here, that's for certain. I don't want to be anywhere near this dreadful place, all heat and dust and soldiers." He put the bottle on the floor and looked at her. "I want to be where I was happiest, Willa. Back at Everest. With you. I feel that that's my true country—the Himalayas. It's yours, too, and you know it. It's where we both belong."

Willa didn't say anything. She looked into her wineglass.

"Let's go back there. The two of us together," he said softly.

Willa laughed joylessly. "Just catch the next train east?" she said. "You make it sound so easy."

"I never married, you know," he said, still looking at her. "You ruined me for any other woman."

"Max, I—" Willa began, not liking where the conversation was going. Wanting to stop it. Now. Before he said anything else.

"No, hear me out. At least do that much for me," he said. "I knew then, back in Tibet, that you had feelings for someone else. But

Willa, where is he? All these years later, where is Seamus Finnegan? I shall tell you: not with you. He's married to another woman and they have a little boy together."

Willa broke his gaze. She lowered her head. Tears smarted behind her eyes.

"I don't say these things to hurt you," Max said. "Just to make you see the truth. You're wasting your life longing for something that can never be." Max reached for her hand. "You don't belong with Seamus Finnegan. And you don't belong here, in this desert hell. You don't belong to this war. Neither of us does."

Max leaned in close to her. "For God's sake, Willa, just tell me what I need to know so I can get this all over with sooner rather than later and get you out of here. I've done what I had to do—scare you. I've acted the official. Now I'll protect you. I'll take care of you. Germany is going to win the war. It won't take too much longer before it's all over. And when it is, I'll marry you—if you'll let me—and take you back where you belong, to Everest."

Willa, her head still down, said, "Do you mean that, Max? Or is it just another spy maneuver?"

"I do mean it, Willa. I swear it. I give you my word."

Willa raised her head. Tears spilled from her eyes.

"You're right, Max," she said. "I'm so tired of this damned war. I'm tired of the waste and the loss. Take me there. Promise me you will. Take me back to Everest." She leaned her forehead against his, then raised her lips to his and kissed him fiercely.

He kissed her back, passionately, then with a knowing smile, he pulled away from her.

"Convince me you mean it, Willa," he said. "Tell me where Lawrence is. We know the British want Damascus. How far north has he come?"

"Nablus," Willa said.

"He's that far west?" Max said. "Why?"

"He's moving amongst the tribes. Trying to recruit from them."

"How many man has he got with him?"

"Not many. Only about a thousand or so and he's having difficulty bringing more on board. The Bedouin don't trust Faisal, and they fear the Turks."

Max nodded thoughtfully. "We can fend a thousand off easily. What about Dara?" he asked. "We have reports that say he wants to take that before he takes Damascus."

Willa shook her head. "Lawrence doesn't care about Dara. He's going to bypass it altogether."

Max looked skeptical. "I have difficulty believing that," he said. "Dara's a valuable town on the Hejaz line. The biggest town between Amman and Damascus. In fact, I very much doubt everything you're telling me."

"I'm sure you do," Willa said, "which is exactly why Lawrence is doing it. If you think about it, though, it makes perfect sense. Lawrence has to save his men for the attack on Damascus. He can't afford to lose any fighting over Dara."

"What about Allenby?" Max asked.

"General Allenby has all he can manage with Suez. His orders are to hold that at all costs. He has little faith in Lawrence's ability to gather the troops he needs to take Damascus, and even less in Faisal's."

Max narrowed his eyes. "How do you know Allenby's plans if you've been in the desert with Lawrence?" he said.

"Because I've been working with Lawrence, but for Allenby," Willa replied. "I was at the Cairo office before I went into the desert—but you probably know that already. In fact, my presence in the desert was all Allenby's idea. He wanted me to be his eyes and ears in Lawrence's camp. I've been keeping him apprised of Lawrence's every move."

"How? You've been in the desert. In the middle of nowhere."

Willa smiled. "The airplane. I did more than one recon mission, you know. I did many. And every time I went up, I radioed Allenby in Cairo. We used code of course, but I got many messages through to him."

Max nodded, and Willa saw that the suspicion that had been on his face was gone. "Thank you," he said. "For all the information. For trusting me. And for making me believe in a future again. We will leave this place, Willa," he said. "I promise you that. We'll be together again."

He kissed her once more, pulling her close, taking her in his arms. As he did, Willa gasped. "My ribs," she said.

"I'm sorry," he whispered. "I got carried away and forgot about your injuries. Forgive me. I want you so much, I didn't think. I'll call for the nurse now to give you your pill."

He gathered up the empty bottle and the glasses, kissed her goodbye, and disappeared down the hallway.

Willa watched him go, touched her fingers to her lips, and smiled.

CHAPTER SEVENTY-THREE

SID PULLED his collar up against the filthy weather, marveling at how the rain was always wetter and the sky grayer in East London. It was early September, and a Sunday. A few people, poorly dressed, heads down against the driving wind, hurried past him on the sidewalk.

Sid knew where they were going—to pubs, where they could warm their insides with gin and their outsides by a fire. Or, if they had no money, back to their small, damp, dreary rooms. Where there was no heat, no heart, no hope. He remembered those rooms so well.

Sid hurried himself, wanting to finish his business and leave this place as quickly as he could. He turned a corner, walked halfway down a narrow, winding street, and arrived at Teddy's offices. He greatly hoped that Teddy had been able to dig up some information for him in the month since they'd last met. He didn't relish the thought of making a third trip to Limehouse.

Inside the foyer, he shook the rain off himself and gave Teddy's girl his name.

"Mr. Ko is expecting you," she said, escorting him to Teddy's office. "Would you like some tea, Mr. Malone?"

"I would, darlin', thank you," Sid said.

He greeted Teddy, who was seated at his desk yelling into a telephone in Chinese, and sat down across from him. Teddy yelled for a few more minutes, then slammed the phone down.

"Sorry, Sid," he said. "Business headaches. How are you?"

"Fine, Teddy. Yourself?"

"Fine. Fine. Just found out that one of my ships is late. No one's heard from it, or seen it, and I'm thinking the fucking thing's gone down with half a ton of my opium on board."

Sid gave what he hoped was a sympathetic smile. It was just like Teddy to be worried about his opium, not the ship or its sailors. Teddy kept nattering on, talking about business deals, and Sid had the strange feeling, yet again, that Teddy was stalling for time. Why? Had he not been able to dig up anything on Maud and the morphine?

"Teddy," Sid finally said, interrupting him. "How about our own little business deal? Were you able to find anything out?"

Before Teddy could answer, the door to his office opened and closed. Sid turned around. He figured it was Teddy's girl with the tea. He was glad of it. The rain had wet him through. He felt like he could drink an entire pot of strong, hot tea.

But it wasn't Teddy's girl. It was a ghost from his past, come back to haunt him. Only the ghost was alive and well and flanked by two of the hardest-looking men Sid had ever seen.

"Well, as I live and breathe. If it ain't Sid Malone," said Billy Madden. "What a surprise. I thought you was dead, Sid. I was in the neighborhood, thought I'd pay Teddy here a call—he's always happy to see me, ain't you, Ted?—and here you are."

But Billy didn't seem surprised at all, and Sid doubted very much that his visit was a coincidence. Teddy had told Billy that Sid had been to see him, and Billy, for some reason, didn't like it. Including

Teddy, there were four of them, and one of him. Sid cursed himself. How could he have not seen this coming? He would have to tread very carefully.

"Why'd you leave us so abruptly, Sid? Without even a going away party?" Billy asked, taking the chair next to him. His thugs remained by the door.

"It was getting a bit hot for me here, Billy. Had to make a quick exit," Sid said, keeping his voice even.

"And so you did. But now you're back."

"Indeed I am."

Billy nodded. He smiled. And then he sat forward and said, "What the fuck do you want?"

"Some information from Teddy."

"Information, is it?" Billy spat. "I'll give you some information, Sid: You made a big fucking mistake coming back here. Who are you working with? Fat Patsy Giovanna? The Kenney brothers? Who?"

So that was it—Billy thought he wanted his manor back.

Sid held up his hands. "Easy, Billy," he said. "I'm not working with or for anyone. I'm just looking into a death, a suicide that happened a few years back. For a friend of mine. That's all."

"You expect me to believe that shite? Would you have believed that, Sid? Would you?"

Sid stole a quick glance at Teddy's desk as Madden ranted, desperate to see if there was anything there he could use. A paperweight. A letter opener. Just in case. Billy Madden had always been a bit barmy, but he must've really gone off his nut in the last few years. His eyes were wild. He was nearly frothing as he spoke.

"Billy, I swear to you, I'm not here after my old manor. You can have it. With my blessings," he said.

"Is that so? Then tell me what you're really doing here. Why do you care about some old tart who offed herself years ago?"

Sid could have told Billy the truth. The truth might have saved him. But he didn't. There was no way in the world he was going to tell Billy Madden that he had a wife now, and that Maud was his wife's sister, and that all he wanted to do was find out if she'd truly killed herself, so his wife could have some peace. No matter what happened to him, he was not going to tell Billy Madden a damn thing about India or their children.

"That old tart mattered, Billy. To a friend of mine. That's why I care."

Billy shook his head. "Do for him," he said.

Sid was expecting it. In a flash, he grabbed a stone lion from Teddy's desk and threw it at Teddy. It hit the side of his head hard, taking him out of the fray. Sid turned, then, and faced Billy's men. He wasn't afraid of Billy; Billy was a coward, but Billy's lads were a different matter. If he wanted to get out of here alive, he had to get through them first. Sid got a few good punches in. He split a lip and cracked a nose, but Billy's lads were younger, stronger, and bigger. Their blows bloodied Sid and weakened him. And then a well-aimed punch to the back of his head dropped him.

"Get him up and get him out of here," Billy said, looking at Sid with contempt as he lay on the floor, barely conscious, groaning, his face covered in gore.

"What are you going to do with him?" Teddy asked. He was holding a handkerchief to the gash in his left temple. The white cloth was rapidly turning crimson. The front of his suit was stained with blood.

Billy was calmer now. His eyes were clear and focused; they'd lost their mad look. He took a cigar from the box on Teddy's desk and lit it, tossing the match on the floor.

"I'm taking him to the boatyard. I'll lock him in the basement till John gets back. He's off on his North Sea run, but he'll be back in a few days. Soon as he is, I'll have him take Malone out. Way out. Past Gravesend."

"Dead or alive?" Teddy asked.

"Who cares?" Madden said. "John'll weight him and dump him over the side, and if he's not dead when he goes in the water, he soon will be."

"Good riddance," Teddy said. "Bastard cracked my skull."

"Good riddance is right," Billy growled. "He fooled everyone once, back in 1900, but he won't do it again. It's over for him. This time Sid Malone really is going to rot in the Thames."

CHAPTER SEVENTY-FOUR

THE RACKET OUTSIDE Willa's hospital window was earsplitting. Men were yelling. Camels—it seemed like there must be a thousand of them—were bawling. Noisy motorcycles were sputtering by. A woman was scolding someone at the top of her lungs. An automobile was honking its horn.

"What on earth is going on?" Willa asked Sister Anna, who had just bustled into the room, an angry expression on her face.

"The Sunday souk," Sister Anna said, firmly closing Willa's window. "It's one of the days that animals are traded in the marketplace. The other day is Wednesday. Camels, horses, donkeys, goats . . . they all pass by the hospital on the way to market, and pass by again on their way out of the city with their new owners. The noise and dust and mess are unspeakable. It's disturbing for our patients and a health hazard, too. What you're hearing right now is because a camel broke loose and upended a vegetable cart. Two people were hurt. The hospital's administrators have spoken to the city authorities numerous times, but nothing changes."

"Camels, you say? I should like to buy a camel and go riding. Right this very instant. It's been so long since I was outside," Willa said.

"Camel riding? With broken ribs?" Sister Anna said, raising an eyebrow. "I should think it will be a little while yet before you're ready for that."

"I suppose you're right," Willa said. "I'll stick to my mapmaking for now."

She had paper, pencils, and an eraser on a narrow rolling hospital table that allowed her to work in her bed, as her doctor would not allow her to work out of it. Max had asked her draw a map of the area south of Damascus, indicating what route Lawrence would take to attack the city.

"Mr. von Brandt is very pleased with your work. I overheard him talking to Dr. Meyers, asking him when he might be able to take you out of the hospital for a small jaunt," Sister Anna said. "Wouldn't that be lovely?"

Willa smiled. "I'm pleased that he's pleased," she said. Then she clumsily dropped her pencil, tried to catch it before it fell on the floor, and winced with the effort.

Sister Anna saw her. "Is the pain still bad?" she asked, frowning. Willa nodded.

"I'm sorry to hear it. A woman with three broken ribs and typhus should not have been kept in a prison cell for even one day, never mind several weeks. The disease has obviously weakened you." She reached into her skirt pocket and drew out a small glass bottle. "Here's another pill," she said. "It's been slightly less time between dosages than I would like, but I do not like to see you in pain."

Willa took the pill. She raised her hand to her mouth and took a drink of water— spilling some because her hand was shaking. Then she sat back against her pillows, her hands folded in her lap.

"Thank you," she said, giving the nurse a weary smile of relief.

"I think you should rest for a bit or you will overdo it," Sister Anna said. "You need to build your strength, not tax your body further. You can continue your work later."

"But Mr. von Brandt's maps . . ." Willa protested.

"They can wait for a bit. And if Mr. von Brandt has any objections, he may speak about them with Dr. Meyers." She wheeled the table away from Willa's bed, then walked to the window and let the blind down. "Sleep now," she said.

Willa, eyes already closed, nodded gratefully. Sister Anna quietly left the darkened room, pulling the door closed after her, and locking it—as she always did.

As soon as she heard the bolt turn, Willa opened her eyes and sat up in bed. Her movements were quicker and surer than any she'd made in front of Max or Sister Anna. She quietly got out of bed and flipped her mattress up. She took the pill Sister Anna had given her—it was still in her hand, she'd only pretended to swallow it—and pushed it into a small hole she'd made in the mattress's welting. Then she felt along the welting to make sure the other pills she'd hidden were still there. They were. No one had discovered them—yet. She lowered the mattress, got back into bed, and smoothed her sheets and blankets, then she closed her eyes to sleep.

Sister Anna was right. She needed to build her strength, for she would need it. Max had talked to Dr. Meyers about a jaunt. She doubted it would happen today, or tomorrow, but she was sure it would happen soon. Very soon. And when it did, she must be ready.

CHAPTER SEVENTY-FIVE

"IS THAT YOU, love?" India called out. She was sitting in the kitchen of the Brambles and had just heard the mudroom door open. She'd been expecting Sid for the last two hours.

"I'm afraid not. It's just me, not my handsome brother," Fiona called back.

India laughed. "Fancy a banger?" she said.

"I could murder a banger. A dozen bangers," Fiona said, walking into the kitchen. "And mash and onion gravy. Have you got any?"

"Enough to feed an army. Sit down and tuck in," India said.

She got up from the kitchen table, where she'd been reading at least twenty British newspapers—some that she'd sent for from as far afield as Glasgow and Leeds—and got a plate, cutlery, and a cup of tea for Fiona.

"Sit, India," Fiona said, rubbing her hands together. "I can see to myself." She gave her sister-in-law a quick kiss on the cheek, took the cup of tea from her hands, and took a seat at the table.

"How did Charlie do today?" India asked. "Any progress?"

"None," Fiona said, shoveling potatoes onto her plate. "We've nearly got through the entire rose garden now, but he's still exactly the same. I'd hoped for something—some small but steady improvement— ever since I saw that spark in his eyes. But there's no change. I'm starting to wonder if I only imagined his reaction to the roses."

"I'm sure you didn't. It takes time. He'll get there," India said. "With a mother like you and an uncle like Sid, he has no choice."

Fiona laughed, but India could see she was tired. She'd been working with Charlie all day long. Worried that Fiona would ex- haust herself coming and going, she and Sid had asked her to stay with them at the Brambles—an offer she gladly accepted. Mr. Fos- ter had gone back to London and Fiona had decided to return to London on the weekends, and come up again on Monday mornings. India was glad about the arrangement; she loved her sister-in-law's company.

"It's so quiet in here. Are the children in bed?" Fiona asked now, dousing her sausages and mash with gravy.

"They went up half an hour ago. They wanted to wait up for Sid— he promised them presents when he got back—but it was already eight-thirty and they could barely hold their heads up. I told them he'd give them a kiss when he got in."

"Where did he go?" Fiona asked.

"London. He went yesterday evening and spent the night. He was due back around six-thirty. I don't know what's keeping him."

"London?" Fiona said, with a slight note of concern in her voice. "Why did he go there?"

"You don't like it either, do you?" India said worriedly. "I told him not to go. But he said he had business there."

"What kind of business?"

"He said he wanted to talk to someone about medical supplies for the hospital. Drugs, specifically."

Fiona's expression softened. "Oh, it's just hospital business then, isn't it? Forgive me, India. I was being silly. It's just that given his past, I worry."

"I know," India said, gathering her newspapers into a stack. "I do, too. I'm always afraid someone from his old life will spot him in the city and try to make trouble for him. It's probably a daft notion, but I can't help it."

"Well, I'm sure he'll be back any minute. I bet he missed his train, that's all." Fiona pointed at the newspapers in front of India. "What do you have there? A little light reading?" she asked.

India suspected she was trying to change the subject. "Hardly," she said. "I'm trying to follow any and all reported outbreaks of Spanish flu in Britain. It's certainly getting a foothold here. The numbers of infected are increasing in Glasgow, Edinburgh, Newcastle, and York; holding steady in the Midlands and Wales; and starting to pick up in Weymouth, Brighton, and Dover. I've read that quite a few of the major cities are going to start spraying streets in hard-hit areas with disinfectant."

"Any sign of it in the lads here yet?" Fiona asked.

"Not yet, no. Thank God. We have a quarantine ward set up though, just in case. Harriet wrote me to say that she's seeing it starting in London. South of the river, mostly. I wish I could convince Jennie to leave the city and come here. And to bring James with her."

"Have you spoken with her about it?" Fiona asked.

"I wrote her last week, inviting her to come, but she wrote back that she can't leave her father, and he won't leave his parish. She did say, though, that they aren't seeing a tremendous amount of it in Wapping yet. She said if that changes, she'll send James to me. You must be vigilant, too, Fiona, and send the children—at least the younger ones—if the outbreak grows."

"I certainly will. I won't need telling twice," Fiona said. "You'll have us all camped out with you. Mr. Foster, too."

"That would be lovely," India said, smiling. "I think the Brambles needs a butler. We could use some poshing up around here."

The two women continued to chat as Fiona ate her meal. When she finished, she washed up her dishes, then excused herself. "I'm completely knackered," she said. "I'm going to go up to my room, write Joe a letter, and then fall into bed. Thank you for the supper, India. It was delicious," Fiona said. Then she impishly added, "What's for supper tomorrow night? Pickled whelks? Cockles?"

India laughed. She'd grown up the child of very wealthy parents. They had been served fancy dishes at every meal, she'd once told Fiona, but—being a well-bred young lady—she'd never been expected to learn to cook any of them. She'd only learned her way around a kitchen after she'd married Sid—an East Londoner who liked his native dishes. She could not cook bifteck au poivre, or Dover sole in cream sauce, but she could turn out a perfectly cooked sausage, a wonderful steak and kidney pie, and the most delicious fish and chips Fiona had ever tasted.

"I'll make you eel and mash tomorrow," she said now.

Fiona made a face. "My brother doesn't actually eat that, does he?" she said.

"I'm afraid he does."

Fiona kissed India good night. "It's late," she said. "You should get some sleep, too. He'll be home soon. Don't worry."

India smiled and nodded. "Good night," she said. "Sleep well. Send our love to Joe."

As soon as Fiona left the kitchen, India's smile faded. She reached into her skirt pocket and pulled out a small jade Buddha, about two inches long. She'd found it in the pocket of one of Sid's jackets earlier today, when she'd picked the jacket up off the back of a chair to hang it, and could not imagine where he'd got it or what he was doing with it. She stared at it for a bit longer, then put it back in her pocket. For some reason, she hated the sight of it. It frightened her. It seemed like a bad omen.

Desperate to busy herself, and so distract herself from her anxious thoughts, India rose from the table, put her newspapers away, wiped down the sink, and then went out the back door to shake out the tablecloth.

The night air was chilly, but she lingered for a few minutes, peering into the darkness, hoping to catch a glimpse of Sid coming up the drive. Trying to follow Fiona's advice. Trying not to worry.

CHAPTER SEVENTY-SIX

"OH, MAX! I don't know what to say! It's beautiful, and you shouldn't have, but I'm ever so glad that you did," Willa said happily.

"I'm so pleased you like it," Max said, smiling. "It's time you had something to wear other than a hospital gown."

Willa sat in her bed, amid pink ribbons and tissue paper. Max sat in a chair close by. Moments ago, he had appeared in her doorway carrying an armful of boxes. Inside them were a pair of calfskin shoes, silk stockings, lacy underthings, and a beautifully made lawn dress—all in ivory.

"How did you have time to get to Paris and back? I saw you only two days ago!" Willa said, teasing him.

Max grinned. "The seamstresses here are astonishing. They can copy anything. And some of the shops carry very fine goods from Europe."

"Thank you, Max. Really. You are far too good to me," Willa said. "Shall I change into it? Are we going for another outing?"

Two days ago, Max had come for her with a wheelchair and had taken her for an hour-long ride around the streets of Damascus. They'd gone to the souk, where he'd bought her a lovely necklace, and then they'd had lunch in a cafe. And then Willa's strength had faded and Max had brought her back to the hospital.

"As much as I'd love to take you for a jaunt this instant," he said now, "I can't. I have a meeting with Jamal Pasha in an hour . . ."

Willa knew the name. Jamal Pasha was the Turkish governor of Damascus.

". . . but I was wondering if you would do me the great honor of joining me for dinner at my quarters this evening. If, and only if, you feel up to it."

"I would be delighted to," Willa said.

"Wonderful. I will call for you at eight."

Willa suddenly looked down at her dress, not meeting Max's eyes.

"Is something wrong? Is eight too late?" he asked, concern in his voice.

Willa smiled ruefully. "Nothing's wrong. Nothing at all. It's just that it's so nice to have something to look forward to," she said. "It's been so long since I've had that."

Max rose from his chair and sat on the edge of her bed. He hooked a finger under her chin and lifted her face to his. "You have the rest of your life to look forward to Willa Alden," he said, kissing her mouth. "With me."

Willa kissed him back. He put his arms around her and held her close, releasing her only when he heard footsteps in the hall.

"Sister Anna will scold me," he whispered. "She'll say I'm tiring you."

"I hope you will. Tire me, that is," Willa whispered. "Later."

Max feigned shock at her words. Then, as Sister Anna came into the room, he said, "Until this evening, Miss Alden."

"Until this evening, Mr. von Brandt," Willa said.

"And how is our patient this afternoon?" Sister Anna asked. She had just started her shift.

"Very well, Sister Anna," Willa said, as Max left the room. "I've been invited to Mr. von Brandt's for supper this evening."

"So soon?" Sister Anna asked. "Are you certain you are up to it? You are still taking three doses of morphine daily."

"I will manage. One cannot always give in to pain and weakness.

That is no way to win a war, is it? And Mr. von Brandt and I have much to discuss concerning the war."

"Yes, of course," Sister Anna said. "Is there anything I can get for you? Anything that you require?"

Willa looked at her beautiful new clothes, then said, "Yes, there is. A bath."

Sister Anna smiled. "Of course. I'll run one for you," she said. "I'll fetch you in about fifteen minutes."

Willa nodded and Sister Anna left the room. As soon as she had, Willa's smile faded and her jaw took on a grim and determined set.

So soon, she thought.

She'd hoped she would have a few more days. Her side still hurt. She was still weak from the typhus. She would have to overcome both, for Max was bringing her to his house tonight. Once she was there, it would be now or never. She would do her best to look as good as she possibly could. And she would hope like hell that he had wine to drink. A lot of it.

She suddenly felt terrified. It was such a hopeless long shot, her plan. Most likely it would all go horribly wrong, and then it would be her in the yard of the prison, blindfolded and awaiting the firing squad.

She thought of Lawrence and how he had endured years of hardship and privation in the desert to further the cause of Arab independence. She thought of Khalaf and Fatima and their little son. She thought of Auda and of all the wild, indomitable Bedouin. She heard Auda's voice in her head. "Dwell not upon thy weariness, thy strength shall be according to the measure of thy desire," he told her now, just as he had so many times before in the desert. Willa snaked her hand down under her mattress and felt for the pills she'd hidden.

"Tonight, then," she whispered in the silence of her room. *"Inshallah."*

CHAPTER SEVENTY-SEVEN

WILLA WAS READY.

It was a few minutes before eight. She was washed, combed, and dressed. The gown Max had bought had been made for her. It caressed her slim body beautifully and set off her dramatic coloring—her pale skin and dark hair, her luminous green eyes. She was wearing the necklace he'd bought for her in the souk. One of the younger nurses had put her hair up in a soft, fetching twist and loaned her a tube of lipstick.

"My goodness, Miss Alden," Max said when he came for her. "You are absolutely beautiful."

Willa smiled. She was standing by the foot of her bed. Dr. Meyers had gotten her a new leg, to replace the one battered in the plane crash. It fit her well and allowed her to walk relatively easily—though no one knew that but her.

"Why, thank you, Mr. von Brandt," she said. "You look very handsome yourself."

Max bowed his head at the compliment. Willa took a few slow steps toward him, reaching for his arm.

Max frowned. "I'm going to get you a wheelchair. I saw one downstairs."

"It's not necessary, Max," Willa protested. "I can walk. I should walk."

"We'll only use it to get you to my house. Once you're there, you can walk all you like."

Willa sighed. "If you insist," she said.

As Max pushed her through the city streets, Willa commented on the number of animals in the streets and asked many questions.

Who lived in the splendid stone house? The whitewashed one? The tiled one? Where did Jamal Pasha live? What was Max's house like?

"You can see for yourself," he replied to her last question. "It's right there."

He wheeled her up to a beautiful whitewashed house, one of a row of houses about a half mile from the city square. Its arched windows were framed by intricately painted Arabic designs. The entrance—which was set back slightly from the street—was tiled in squares of blue, green, orange, and yellow. Lush red roses climbed the pillars flanking the door, and a stained-glass lantern hung over it, casting a warm glow.

"Max, it's lovely!" Willa exclaimed.

"I'm glad you like it. I'm renting it from a wealthy Turkish merchant. He and his family decamped to Aleppo."

"Are we close to the souk here?" Willa asked. "I'm afraid I haven't got my bearings yet."

"The souk is about four streets west of us. Southwest, actually. Over that way," Max said, pointing.

"Ah, that explains all the animals in the streets," Willa said.

"Yes, they're sold there on Sundays and Wednesdays. But the traders bring them in the night before, which is why there were so many of them in the streets just now. Tomorrow's Wednesday of course."

Willa knew that already. Sister Anna had told her about the animal markets. But she did not let on. The Wednesday animal market was the reason she had said yes to Max's invitation tonight. Had his offer been made for another night, one that did not precede an animal market, she would have begged off, pleading fatigue.

Max's butler, a tall Damascan in an embroidered robe and silk turban, welcomed them. He told Max that the cook had made a most divine meal and that it would be ready shortly.

"Will you show me the house before we dine?" Willa asked, getting out of the wheelchair and taking Max's arm.

Max said he would be delighted to and began to take her around, walking her from room to room.

They started in the sitting room. Willa marveled at the ornately carved chairs and settees, all upholstered in heavy silks, and the thick, patterned Persian rugs on the floor.

"Did the merchant let the house to you furnished?" she asked.

Max nodded. "He left everything in the house. Furniture, rugs, books, kitchenware. He even left some of his robes in the closet. In case I get the urge to go native, I guess."

In the billiards room, there were zebra rugs underfoot and lion and tiger heads on the walls. Antique swords and pistols were also displayed on the walls, many with jeweled hilts and handles.

"Toys for boys," Willa said, running her hand over one heavily crusted sword handle.

Max laughed. He led her into the study, where the walls were lined with books, some in English, some in Turkish and Arabic. They were all beautifully bound in leather. More books, and magazines and newspapers, were piled haphazardly on tables and chairs. A pair of Max's boots and a riding crop lay on the rug by a settee. His desk was covered by maps and memos, some of which had fallen to the floor. Willa glanced casually at the desk as she passed by it, then turned to Max and said, "Very sloppy, Mr. von Brandt. I think you need a wife."

Max walked to the desk. He shuffled the memos into a pile, then turned them over.

"Any candidates in mind?" he asked her, as he rolled the maps up.

"Let me think about it," Willa said. "Perhaps I can come up with one."

Just then, Max's butler came into the room, bowed, and informed them that dinner was served.

"Are you hungry?" Max asked Willa.

Willa reshelved a book she'd been looking at and turned to him. "Desperately," she said. She took his arm again, then added, "Hungry for good food, good wine, and good company. After years in the desert, I feel like I've suddenly stumbled into Paradise."

"Come," Max said, leading her out of the study and to the dining room. "Let's see what the cook has made for us."

The dining room was beautiful and romantic. Candles in silver holders had been set on the table. They cast a soft glow over the room. Roses in vases perfumed the air. Max seated her on the left of one of the short ends of the dining table—a long, ornate affair, made of ebony and inlaid with ivory, malachite, and lapis lazuli. He took the end seat himself, so they would be close together.

As Willa laid her napkin in her lap, he filled her glass and then his own with wine—again a rare Bordeaux.

"To you," he said, lifting his glass.

Willa shook her head. "No, Max, to us," she said.

Their meal began with mezze—a tantalizing array of appetizers. There were grape leaves stuffed with lamb and rice, chickpea patties, hummus, and a dish of grilled eggplant, sesame seed paste, olive oil, lemon, and garlic that Willa could not get enough of.

"This is so good, Max," she said, savoring a bite of stuffed grape leaf. "I've never had such wonderful food. Your cook is amazing."

Max sat back in his chair, watching her eat and smiling, enjoying her enjoyment of the meal. The mezze was followed by fattoush, a peasant salad made of toasted bits of bread, cucumbers, tomatoes, and mint. Then the butler brought out chicken kabobs and kibbeh—minced lamb balls, stuffed with rice and spices. To go with the meat dishes, there were lentils cooked with rice and garnished with fried onions, a dish of stuffed squash, and another of spiced potatoes.

"Max, did your other dinner guests cancel?" Willa asked halfway through the feast. "Your cook made enough for twenty people!"

Max laughed. He leaned forward and refilled Willa's wineglass and then his own. "It's all for you, Willa," he said. "I want to fatten you up. Make you healthy and hearty and happy again."

As they ate, Max asked her about Lawrence, about the sort of man he was. Willa told him, admiringly, about Lawrence's bravery, his intelligence, and his enormous charisma.

"Were you lovers?" Max asked suddenly.

She looked at him over the top of her wineglass, then teasingly said, "Why? Would you be jealous if we were? I should like you to be."

"Yes, I would," Max admitted.

"We were not," she said. "Lawrence has only one mistress—and it's not me."

"Who is it, then?" Max asked.

"Arabia," Willa replied.

Max nodded. "Well," he said at length, "I fear Lawrence is going to have to learn to get along without his mistress, because she won't be his for very much longer."

Willa forced herself to smile. She asked Max to pass her another chicken kabob. She wanted to eat as much as she could. She did not know when she would find food again after tonight.

"Let's not talk about Lawrence or the war," she said. "Not tonight. Let's talk about Everest instead."

They did. Max told her that as soon as he was finished here at Damascus, he would return to Germany and he would take her with him. He would be needed in Berlin until the war was over, but as soon as he could get away, they would travel east again. They talked about plans for their future for quite some time. Until the bottle of wine had been emptied, and another brought. Until the supper dishes were cleared, and a platter of fresh fruit, dates, and honey pastries had been served. Until the candles burned down and Max had dismissed the servants.

As they sat together in the candlelight, reminiscing about Rongbuk, Max suddenly reached across the table and covered Willa's hand with his own. "I want you, Willa Alden," Max said. "I've wanted you all night. All during the trip from the hospital. All through supper. I want you so much I can't bear it."

"What about dessert?" Willa coyly asked, biting into a date. "Don't you want any?"

"You are dessert," Max said. He rose from his chair then, picked her up, and carried her to his bedroom.

He put her down, kissed her, and gently unbuttoned the back of her dress. It slipped off her arms, down her slender body, to the floor, where it lay—a shimmering silk puddle at her feet. As she stood in her camisole, petticoat, and stockings, he took off his jacket and shirt. Then he stretched out on his bed, took her hand, and pulled her down to him. He kissed her mouth, her throat, the delicate bones of her neck. She buried her hands in his thick blond hair and kissed him back. He was gloriously handsome. His body was hard and smooth. His face, that of a stone god.

I could have loved you, Max, she thought, if things had been different.

She remembered his warm hands, his passionate kisses. She remembered the feel and smell of him. She saw him as he had been on Everest—strong and daring, hard and fearless. He had been her lover then. Now he was her enemy. She must not forget that, not for a second. It would cost her her life if she did—hers and many more besides.

Max untied the string at the top of her camisole. He started working at the buttons down the front of it. She stopped him.

"What's wrong?" he asked her.

"I'm . . . I'm afraid, Max," she said.

"You? Afraid? Of what?"

"I'm afraid you won't want me if you see me. Underneath these beautiful things you gave me, I'm not beautiful. I'm all bones and bruises. I look like . . . well, like I've been through a war."

Max laughed. He propped himself on one elbow and looked into her eyes. "When I first saw you, in Kathmandu, I thought you were the most beautiful woman I'd ever seen. I still do, Willa. I don't give a damn about bones and bruises," he said. "Let me see you."

"All right," she said, pulling his face to hers and kissing him hungrily. "But first, more wine."

Max started to get up, but she stopped him. "No, I can get it. You've indulged me enough this evening. Surely I can walk to the dining room and back."

She left the room walking slowly and deliberately, but as soon as she was out of his sight, she hurried. The seductive smile had fallen away. She had seconds only. Moving as quickly as she could, she hiked up her petticoat, rolled back the top of her stocking, and took out a small, folded square of paper. It contained white powder. She'd ground the pills between the soles of her new shoes earlier that day, when she was supposed to be sleeping, and brushed the powder into a piece of tissue paper from Max's gift boxes. She dumped the paper's contents into one of the wineglasses, poured wine on top of it, then stirred the mixture with her finger, praying it would speedily dissolve. She poured wine into the second glass, then picked up both glasses, careful to note which had the ground pills in it, and carried them to the bedroom.

"Here you are," she said, handing the spiked drink to him. He took a sip, put the glass down on the floor, and reached for her. He had her camisole and petticoat off in a twinkling. Then he finished undressing himself.

Willa smiled and nuzzled him as he did, but inside she was panicking. He had to drink more than a mouthful. She didn't know how strong the mixture was, or how fast it would work, but she was certain that if he became woozy, instead of unconscious, he would figure out what she'd done. And then it would all be over.

She picked up his glass and handed it back to him. "A toast, Max. To the end of this war," she said, taking a sip. Max followed her lead.

"To Everest," she added, taking another mouthful. Max did, too.

"And to us," she said. "To our future. Which begins tonight." She drained her glass then, and Max did the same.

She took his glass and put it, and hers, on the floor. "Make love to me slowly, Max. I don't want to rush this. I want it to last," she said, her voice soft and low. "I want us to take our time tonight, to forget all the bad memories and make new ones. Good ones."

She lay down on the bed and twined her arms around his neck. He kissed her mouth again, then her breasts, her belly. He kissed her hip, then parted her legs.

Willa let out a small sigh of what she hoped sounded like pleasure. She wondered, desperately, how long it would be before the pills took effect. She didn't want to do this.

"My God, but I want you," Max said suddenly, and then he was inside her.

Willa gasped loudly and not from desire. Hot tears stung behind her eyes. What did you do wrong? she silently shouted at herself. Why isn't it working?

She bit her lip as Max pounded against her. Her plan had failed. She would go back to her hospital room after tonight—if by some mercy Max didn't figure out what she'd done. And she would have to pretend, day in and day out, that she adored him; she would have to have dinners with him, and sleep with him, and all the while Faisal, Lawrence, Auda, and their soldiers would be marching to their doom.

And then suddenly, Max stopped. He laughed self-consciously and passed a hand over his sweaty face. "The wine," he said. "It must've gone to my head."

Willa laughed. "I feel tipsy, too. It's wonderful, isn't it?" She kissed him again. "Don't stop, Max. Make love to me. Now. I want you so."

Max rolled off her onto his side. He blinked his eyes a few times, then closed them and shook his head.

Terrified that he'd twigged what she'd done, Willa pretended that she thought he'd only grown tired. "You can rest," she whispered. "It's my turn now." She bent over him, to kiss him, ran a hand over his chest. He opened his eyes, caressed one of her breasts, then quickly closed his eyes again and pressed his hands to his face.

"My head . . . it's spinning," he said. Willa kissed him again. He pushed her off him and sat up, understanding dawning in his eyes. "The wine," he said, swaying slightly. "You put something in the wine." With effort, he swung his feet over the side of the bed and stood up, but his legs gave way and he fell to the floor. "Why, Willa?" he rasped, trying to pull himself up. He fell back on the floor then, toppling over with the bedcover in his hands. He groaned once. His eyes closed. He was still.

Willa was so terrified, she could barely breathe. She nudged him once with her foot, then again, then she jumped out of bed and dressed as quickly as she could. Her injured ribs were protesting, but she ignored them. She was a lot stronger than she'd been letting on.

Glancing nervously at Max, she picked his clothes up off the floor and went through them. She found nothing in his trousers, but there was a wallet in his jacket. She took the paper money from it and threw the wallet on the floor.

Next, she raced to the billiards room and grabbed an antique sword and three pistols off the wall. She ransacked the room's closets and cabinets, looking for bullets, and finally found some. Then she flew down the hall to the study and grabbed the maps she'd seen Max roll up earlier. She didn't stop to look at them, just took them all.

She was at the front door, almost out of the house, when she caught sight of her reflection in a hallway mirror, and saw a woman in a fancy dress, clutching weapons and maps. How far would she get looking like this? Not far at all. She needed different clothes. She would have to go back into the bedroom, and she had no idea how long the effects of the pills would last.

Moving slowly and quietly, she made her way back down the hallway. She peered around the door, her heart crashing in her chest, and saw Max. He was still on the floor, right where she'd left him.

Go, she commanded herself. Now. Hurry.

She put the weapons and maps on the bed then ran to the closet. "Please be here," she whispered. "Please." She rifled through the uniforms, dinner jackets, shirts, and trousers. They weren't what she wanted. "Come on, you have to be in here somewhere," she said. And then she spotted what she was after—the long robes worn by Arab men. She grabbed a blue one and a white one, and two matching head scarves. She quickly put the blue one on over her dress and wrapped a scarf around her head. The garments' dark colors would make her less visible in the city streets.

She looked at Max again; he hadn't moved. Everything inside her was urging her to run, but she knew she couldn't. Not yet. She needed something to put the sword, pistols, and maps in. Saddlebags would have been nice, and would have helped her look inconspicuous in a city where most still rode camels, but she had no time to look for them. Max could wake up at any second. As she tried to decide what to do, her eyes came to rest on the bed. She quickly grabbed a pillow, pulled off its case and stuffed her things inside it. The sword stuck out of the opening, but she would just have to make do. She'd spent too long here already; she should have been gone by now.

Willa was just lifting the case off the bed when Max's hand closed around her ankle. She screamed and tried to break free, but he jerked her leg hard and she lost her balance and fell to the floor. The pillow-case and its contents crashed down next to her.

"Morphine, was it?" Max rasped. "You should've put more in. You should've finished me off."

Willa struggled. She kicked at him with her free leg, but he caught it in his other hand and held it fast against the floor. Max woozily got to his knees and lurched toward her. His hands closed on her arm. He tried to drag her to her feet, but Willa kicked and struggled against him. She had to get free. It was over for her, and for Lawrence, if she didn't.

Max tightened his grip. Willa's hands scrabbled against his, try-ing to pry his fingers loose, but even though the drugs had made Max slow and clumsy, she was still no match for him. She kicked at him again and her foot caught him in the groin. He roared out in pain, rose up, and slapped her hard. She fell back against the floor, hitting her head. Lights exploded in front of her eyes. Her hands fell away from Max. One of them came down on the pillowcase.

The pillowcase. With every last ounce of her strength, Willa shoved her hand inside of it. Her fingers closed on a pistol barrel. It wasn't loaded, but it didn't need to be. Max was on all fours now, groaning. Willa pulled the pistol out, raised it as high as she could, and brought it down on his head.

Max shouted. Pain and rage contorted his face. His hands went to his head. That was all Willa needed. She hit him again. And again. Until he had stopped yelling, stopped groaning, until he had col-lapsed against her and was still.

Willa threw the pistol down. A small moan escaped her. Had she killed him? Oh, God, no. She didn't want to kill him. She'd only wanted to escape from him.

"Max? *Max!*" she cried. He gave her no answer. For a few sec-onds she was paralyzed by the horror of what she'd done.

Get out of here, a voice inside her suddenly said. Go. *Now.*

Sobbing, she pushed him off. His blood had spattered across her face and onto her hands. It had seeped into her robes. She got to her feet and staggered to the bathroom. She quickly washed the blood off her skin and decided not to change her robes. They were blue; the blood wouldn't show in the dark.

She stumbled back to the bedroom, picked up the pillowcase, and ran.

CHAPTER SEVENTY-EIGHT

"SOUTHWEST," WILLA WHISPERED as she ran through the night streets of Damascus. *The souk is about four streets west of us. Southwest, actually,* Max had said.

But which way was southwest? She had tried to walk back the way they'd come, but had become disoriented. It had not yet been dark when they'd arrived at Max's house. Now it was past eleven and pitch-black. There were no streetlights and no moon, and Willa, who'd been running flat out for the last fifteen minutes, realized she was lost.

She stopped, trying to make sense of her surroundings, to get her bearings, but she was unfamiliar with the city and its streets. Her heart was pounding so hard that she could barely breathe. She was panicking.

She had likely just killed a man. And not just any man, but Max von Brandt, a high-ranking German officer. If Max was dead, he would be discovered in a matter of hours when his servants arrived to begin their morning duties. But if he was still alive, if he could move, he would stagger to a neighbor's house for help. The alarm could go up at any minute, and when it did, the whole city would be searching for her. Willa knew she must get as far away from Damascus as she possibly could. As fast as she could.

She fought down her panic, looking left and right, trying to decide which way to go. A cry came from above her. She quickly looked up. A bird startled by something, perhaps a cat on the prowl, flew noisily from its nest into the sky. Willa followed, more by sound than by sight, and then she saw it—the night sky, full of stars.

She nearly laughed out loud. Of course! She'd been in shock, too upset to think straight, or she would have looked up at the stars when she'd first run out of Max's house. The stars were always there for her when she was lost. Picking out Polaris, she gauged southwest by its position, then pressed on, turned right instead of continuing straight as she'd intended to do, and ten minutes later, she was nearing the souk.

She saw the glow of lanterns up ahead, under whitewashed arches, smelled animals, heard the low, murmuring conversation of the traders who were still awake, and knew she was in the right place.

The first group she came to only had goats for sale. The next had horses. She pushed on, her head down, until she found the camel traders. The ones closest to her were Howeitat. She recognized their language and their clothing. Their camels were lying down in the dirt. She addressed the nearest man. He was standing at the edge of the group, facing away from them, eating olives and spitting the pits.

"I need a camel and bridle. Now," she told him, in his own tongue. She lowered her voice, hoping that in her robes and headscarf she would pass for a man.

The man took her to his animals, which were a few yards away, and prodded the beasts into standing. Willa picked one. The man shook his head and regretfully informed her that the camel she'd picked was his very best one and therefore very expensive.

Willa pulled the jeweled sword out of the pillowcase. She noticed for the first time that there was blood on the case. The camel trader noticed it, too.

She turned the bloodstain toward herself and said, "I will trade you this sword for the camel."

The man took the sword from her, inspected it, then handed it back to her. "It is a fake," he said. "Very nice, but a fake. I will take it as partial payment. What else have you got?"

"It is no fake. If you will not take it, perhaps another man will," Willa said, putting the sword back in the pillowcase.

"Perhaps I spoke too quickly," the man said.

"Good. But my offer's changed," Willa said. "I'll still give you the sword, but I want a saddle, a crop, and a skin of water as well."

The man bowed his head. "Very well," he said.

Willa took the sword out of the case again. She handed it to the man. He took it and grabbed her roughly by the wrist. She didn't dare scream. She couldn't afford to attract attention.

"Let me go," she hissed at him.

But he didn't. Instead he pushed up the sleeve of her robe. "Your skin's as white as goat's milk," he said, "just like the great sheik Lawrence." He pushed her scarf back on her head. "And a woman, too." His voice turned menacing. "I wonder, are you the one Lawrence seeks? The one who flew in the sky? What have you done, little bird? How did you come by this sword? Why is there blood upon the sack you carried it in?"

Terror gripped Willa. This man was a trader. He would sell her, and not to Lawrence. Lawrence was too far away. He would hand her back to the Turks. Her only chance was to somehow convince him not to.

"Let me go, Howeitat," she said. "The Turk is no friend to you. Let me go to help Lawrence and Auda abu Tayi return to you and your sons the land the Turks stole. The land of your fathers."

For a few seconds, the man's face softened, but then his eyes narrowed, and he said, "Lawrence cannot win. He has too few men."

"He can win. He *will* win. If you let me go." She shook her pillowcase. "I have information in here. Maps I took from the Turks and the Germans. They will help Lawrence find the best way to

Damascus. A great sheik from Cairo, a great warrior, will come with Lawrence. Together they will take the city."

The camel trader weighed this, and weighed her, Willa felt, and then he let her go.

"Ride due south. Lawrence's camp is past the Jabal al Duruz hills. Just north of Azraq. Well east of Minifir. Six days away, five if you're fast. Stay away from the railway. Turkish battalions are patrolling it daily. Be wary."

Willa, weak with relief, thanked him. She started walking toward the camel she'd picked, but the man stopped her. "That one is lame. Take this other. He name is Attayeh. He is young and healthy," he said, directing her to a larger animal. The trader saddled the camel, gave Willa the water and crop she'd asked for, tied her pillowcase securely to her saddle, and told her to go with Allah.

Seconds later, she was off, riding down the street to the Bab al-Jabiya gate. It wasn't far from the souk. She could see the light from the lanterns positioned at either side of the gate. Willa prayed that the gate was open. If it was closed for the night, she was finished. Willa pulled her scarf down low on her forehead.

As she got closer to the gate, she saw that it was still open. Better yet, there were no guards around it. Her heart leapt. She spurred the camel into a trot, then a canter. She'd have one chance to get through the gate and one chance only, and she wasn't stopping for anybody or anything.

When she was about twenty yards away, a guard suddenly stepped out of a small stone hut that was just to the left of the gate. He saw her and immediately yelled at her to stop. Another guard joined him. Both men had rifles. They raised them and aimed at Willa.

"Keep the gates open!" she yelled at them in Turkish, as manfully as she could. "Jamal Pasha is coming! Jamal Pasha is coming. He is behind me in his automobile! There is an emergency! He must get to Beirut by morning! Make way for Jamal Pasha!"

Surprised, the guards lowered their guns and stepped aside, trying to see past Willa, looking for the governor's car. Their surprise lasted for only a few seconds, but that was all she needed. She was past them in a flash, through the gate, and on the road out of Damascus, riding like the wind.

She heard gunshots behind her and prayed nothing hit her camel, or herself. In that order. She would keep going with a bullet wound, for as long as she could, but her camel might not. Nothing hit either of them, and within a few minutes, the hardpan road gave way to the looser sands of the desert. Willa did not let up on her camel, but kept whipping the creature, yelling at him, keeping him in a canter, afraid that the guards would send someone after her. No one followed, however. Perhaps the guards could not scare up a car or camels at this hour, or perhaps they had no wish to—not wanting anyone to know they had allowed someone through the gates whom they should not have.

Willa chanced a few glances behind her, heartened to see the city falling away. Her camel cantered up a dune and down the other side, and Damascus was gone. Willa whooped for joy and then, her robes flying behind her, disappeared into the desert night.

CHAPTER SEVENTY-NINE

SID SMELLED TEA. He heard voices. And water.

He was afraid. Water was dangerous. Water meant death. He'd heard them talking—Madden and his boys. They were going to put him in the water, dump him into the river. He would drown there. He would never see India again. Never see his children. They would never know what happened to him.

He tried to move, to get up, desperate to get away from the water, but when he did, pain—fierce, hot, and red—slammed into him. It was everywhere. Inside his head. In his gut. His knees. His back. He felt like he was made of pain. He cried out with it. He tried again, to get up, to at least open his eyes, but they wouldn't do what he wanted.

"Shh! Stop it, Sid. You're all right. Everything's all right," one of the voices said.

With great effort, Sid opened his swollen eyes. His vision was blurry. He could see a man's face leaning over him. And a woman's. He didn't know who they were.

"He sees us, John," the woman said. "I don't think he knows us, though. Talk to him, love. Tell him who we are."

"Sid? Sid, can you hear me?"

Sid nodded. He tried to get up.

"No, don't get up. Don't move. You'll start everything bleeding again. Just stay still. I'm John. This is me wife, Maggie. I used to do some work for you. Years ago. Do you remember us?"

Sid tried to think, tried to remember, but the pain wouldn't let him.

"He doesn't know us. Poor sod probably doesn't know his own name right now," Maggie whispered to her husband. "You came to our room one night, Sid. You had a lady doctor with you," she said. "She was asking us questions. About what we eat and what it costs and what John's wages were."

Suddenly Sid remembered. "Maggie Harris," he croaked, through his split lips. "Maggie and John."

"Yes! Yes, that's us," John said.

Sid's mind went back in time. To 1900. Before he'd left London. Before he'd married India. She had been at a Labour rally and had been arrested. He'd got her out of jail, but a reporter had pursued her. She hadn't wanted to speak to the man, so Sid had helped her throw him off. They'd hidden out in the tunnels under Whitechapel, had finally surfaced in the Blind Beggar, a pub, where they'd had a meal. Afterward, he'd taken her to meet the poor of Whitechapel.

One of the homes they'd visited had belonged to John and Maggie Harris, who had six small children and lived in two damp, dreary rooms. Maggie and her children—all but the youngest, who was sleeping under the table—were up late, working. They were gluing matchboxes together. He had fallen in love with India that night.

"Where am I?" Sid asked now.

"You're in the hold of me boat," John said.

"How did I get here?" Sid remembered clocking Teddy Ko and taking a few shots at Madden's men. Nothing else.

"Madden's lads brought you. They gave you one hell of a hiding."

Sid remembered that part.

"Then after you'd blacked out, they slung you into the basement at the boatyard. You've been there for days. This morning, just as I got in from one job, they told me I had another to do—picking up some swag in Margate. They carried you on board, threw you in the hold, and then Madden told me I'm to sail out into open waters before I go to Margate, weight you, and throw you in. I told them I would, but I won't. I made you a bed here. Got some laudanum into you, too."

"Why? Why did you do that?" Sid asked, knowing full well that Madden would kill John if he ever found out he'd disobeyed him.

"Because you always took care of me, Sid. So now it's on me to do you a good turn. And besides, I hate that bastard Madden. He works me to death, pays me nothing. Makes me do things I don't want to do. I mean, thieving's one thing, but murdering blokes, well, that's quite another. I want to leave but I can't. I'd have to go far away, me and me whole family, and I haven't the money. Madden's threatened he'd do for me, and for Maggie, and he'd make me kids watch, if I ever do leave."

"What are you going to tell him?" Sid asked, as he realized the full enormity of the risk John was taking on his behalf.

"I'll tell him I did the job, of course," John said. "He'll believe me. There's no reason not to. I'll take the boat out past Margate. Dump a pile of rubbish off the stern—rocks, old rope, broken tools—all wrapped up in a canvas in case someone's watching. Knowing Billy, someone will be. Then I'll continue on to the job."

"How the hell am I going to get home?" Sid asked, wincing with the effort of talking.

"You're not. Not yet. I should get to Margate after dark tomorrow.

Cargo won't be loaded until the following morning. We'll get you off the boat safely. You'll have to make your own way home from there."

Sid nodded.

John stared at Sid, frowning, as Maggie pressed a cloth to Sid's lip. All the talking had opened it up again. Sid could feel blood running down his chin. He could see the worry in John's eyes.

"You ought to have a doctor," John said. "You're in rough shape, Sid, but you've got to hang on. Do you hear me?"

Sid nodded. His vision was fading. The pain was pulling him under. He thought of India. She would be frantic with worry. He wished he could get word to her, but he'd have to tell John who she was and where she was and he didn't want to tell him—or anyone connected with Madden—that he even had a family, much less where they were.

"You hang on, Sid. . . ."

John's voice was growing fainter. It sounded farther away. Sid heard the water again, lapping at the boat's hull. It wanted to get at him. To fill his nose and mouth. To drown him. He wouldn't let it. He would fight it. There had been another time, long ago, when he'd gone into the water. It was here, on the London river. He'd been doing a job with his men. The robbery had gone wrong. He'd fallen off the dock into the river, hit a piling, and ripped his side open. He'd almost died from the wound. He'd felt, then, that he would die. And he hadn't much cared. But India had saved him. She'd fought for his life.

He pictured her now, held her beautiful face in his mind as the pain racking his damaged body pulled at him, threatening to drag him under. He'd had nothing to live for the last time, and no one to love.

This time he did.

CHAPTER EIGHTY

WILLA LEANED BACK into the furry warmth of her camel. The animal was lying down for a much-needed rest. Willa had driven Attayeh hard, but she knew she couldn't work him too hard. If something happened to him, she would never make it to Lawrence's camp.

Willa had driven herself hard, too. She had ridden all night, and all the next day, ever since she'd escaped from Damascus. It was now eight o'clock of the following night. She was hurting and exhausted, but she did not sleep. Instead, she had pulled all of Max's maps and papers out of the pillowcase and was going through them. What she'd read so far made her see that Max von Brandt had been playing her just as hard as she'd been playing him.

She'd read reports he'd made in which he stated he did not believe what she had told him about the size of Lawrence's army or its location. This disappointed her. She'd given him nothing but false information, hoping it would throw him off Lawrence's scent. In Max's opinion, Lawrence was south of the Jabal ad Duruz hills and he was going to ride due north from there to attack Damascus.

Furthermore, Willa had discovered that the Turkish Army had a second encampment ten miles west of their Jabal ad Duruz camp and directly parallel to it, so that when Lawrence rode north, Turkish troops from both camps would converge on him, making defense all but impossible—and making the slaughter of Tom Lawrence, Faisal, Auda, and the thousands of men with them all but inevitable.

And Lawrence had no idea of the trap that waited for him, not even an inkling. Because her plane had crashed, and she'd been taken prisoner, Willa had not been able to tell him about the first camp, and until this very moment, no one but the Turks had known about the second.

Willa rested her chin on her knee, thinking. Max had indicated on one of his maps exactly where he thought Lawrence might be—at Salkhad. It was well north of where the Bedouin trader in the market had said Lawrence was. According to Max's reports, he'd based the position on recon carried out by Bedouin scouts. But were those scouts reliable? Were they truly in the service of the Turks? Some of the Bedouin were extremely wily and would think nothing of taking Max's money and then taking even more money from Lawrence to feed Max misinformation. Was the trader who'd told her Lawrence's whereabouts reliable? Had Lawrence moved since that man had seen his camp? The area south of Jabal was large and desolate, and Lawrence could be anywhere in it.

Willa knew she had to get him, no matter what. She had to let him know what he was riding into. Should she trust Max's information and ride to the point he'd indicated on his map? Or would she need to ride farther south as the trader had told her to?

"How far do we go, Attayeh?" she said softly. But Attayeh had no answer for her.

She rolled up the maps and put them back in the pillowcase. Thank God she'd thought to take them; she would have no idea where she was going without them. She then gathered the memos and reports, having decided that she would finish reading them later. She was tired and needed to sleep. As she shuffled the scattered papers together, a few slipped from the pile. She picked them up, and a line at the top of one caught her eye.

It was a death warrant. Her own. Telegraphed from Berlin.

Her blood ran cold as she read it. Max, as it turned out, was not going to take her to Germany, or to Everest, but to the prison yard to have her shot. Today. The day after their dinner together. The day after he'd made love to her.

For the first time since she'd beaten him, she thought about the possibility of having killed him and she felt no remorse. He would have killed her. If not last night, when he'd beaten her as she tried to escape, then today.

The Bedouin who'd sold her the camel and given her water and some of his own food had also stashed two cigarettes and a box of matches in her saddlebag. She fished one of the cigarettes out now, lit it with shaking hands, and took a long drag.

She was still days away from Lawrence's camp—wherever it might be. She had little food and water. She had stolen vital military information from the desk of a German officer, information that might well turn the tide of the battle for the Middle East. She had likely killed that same German officer, and by now there would be a price on her head. Every desert bandit would be after her, as would every soldier in the entire Turkish Army.

She had escaped death last night, yes . . . but for how long?

CHAPTER EIGHTY-ONE

SID WINCED AS Maggie pressed a warm, damp cloth to his forehead. He was sitting shirtless, enduring Maggie's efforts to clean him up, at a tiny table in the small space belowdecks that John used for sleeping and eating when he was on the water.

It was nearly ten o'clock at night, and John had just docked at a tumbledown warehouse in Margate. He was on deck right now, pretending to check the lines, but really checking to see if anyone was about—a watchman, perhaps, or any of Madden's crew. Sid was desperate to get off the boat, desperate to get home to India and the children. He knew they'd be out of their minds with worry.

"Hold still, Sid," Maggie scolded. "You can't go out and about with blood all over you. The busies'll be on you quicker than you can blink. Surely you don't need me to tell you that. You must remember one or two things about avoiding Old Bill from your London days."

Sid smiled as best he could. "One or two, Maggs," he said.

It was Wednesday—four days since Madden and his boys had given him a beating, one day since he'd come to in John's boat, but everything still hurt. It was painful to open his eyes. To turn his head. To bend and stand and walk. It hurt to swallow, and when he'd taken a piss off the stern of the boat earlier, his water had been bloody.

"Your clothes are a lost cause," Maggie said. "John brought some of his old things for you. As soon as you're washed, you can put them on."

"You and John have been very good to me, Maggie. I owe you both."

Maggie shook her head. "You owe us nothing, Sid Malone. I couldn't even count the times you saved our bacon. With all those jobs you gave John. There were several times we would have starved without you. I don't know how I would've fed the kids without those wages."

"How are your children?"

Maggie didn't answer right away. "The younger ones are all right," she finally said. "They're still only kiddies. The older ones are a worry. Me eldest girl has trouble with her lungs. And the two boys, well . . . they're boys, aren't they? Starting to run wild. Can't blame them, I suppose, with what they see all round them. But still, once upon a time, I had hopes, you know? Hopes that it might be better for them than it was for us. Madden's already got his eye on our Johnnie. I don't want our lad near that man, but it's hard to keep him away. He gives him booze. Women, too, I've heard. Makes him feel like he's cock of the walk. He's only fifteen, Sid. He don't know any better. He won't know any better until it's too late."

Sid saw that her brow was knit with worry as she spoke. "You can't get him out of London?" he asked her. "Send him off to the country with relatives for a bit?"

"We haven't got any relatives in the country. They're all in London," she said. "As mad as it sounds, I'm thinking of talking to him about enlisting as soon as he's sixteen. If the war's still on. He's safer on the lines, with Gerry shooting at him, then he is in Madden's company."

As Maggie finished speaking, they both heard footsteps above them—two sets. And then voices. Maggie held a finger to her lips. Sid stiffened.

"You all right then, John?" they heard a man say. "All settled in for the night?"

"Aye, Bert. Right as rain," John replied.

"I'm leaving now. Harry's on in the morning. He knows to expect you. Lads should be early. Madden told me to tell them to get the goods here before dawn."

"I'll be ready for them. Ta ra, Bert."

"Ta ra, John. Sleep well."

A minute or so later, John's feet were seen climbing down the narrow wooden ladder that connected the deck to the lighter's hold.

"Coast is clear," he said, closing that hatch above him. "There was only Bert about, and he's leaving." He looked at Sid. "Well, you won't win any beauty contests, not with that face, but you look better than you did," he said.

"I wouldn't have won any beauty contests before Madden got hold of me either," Sid said.

John took a seat across from him. He reached into his jacket pocket, took out some money, and put it on the table. "That's two and six," he said. "It's all I could scrape together. Take it. Get yourself home."

Sid was deeply moved by his friend's generosity. He knew that this money was likely all John had in the world. He didn't want to take it, but he had no choice. Billy's men had gone through his pockets before they'd dumped him off with John. They'd taken all his money.

"Thank you," he said. "I'll get it back to you. I swear."

John nodded. The clothes he'd found for Sid were lying on top of the table. Sid picked up the shirt and put it on. The sleeves were too short, which made them all laugh, but it was better than what he'd had. The trousers and jacket fit. John gave Sid the layout of the town of Margate and told him the best way to go to get out of the town quickly.

When they'd finished talking, Sid readied himself to go. He stood up and tried to thank John and Maggie, but they waved his words away.

"Sid, before you go . . . can I ask you something?" John said.

Sid nodded.

"Why did you go back to Teddy Ko's to ask about that woman—the one who killed herself—Maud Selwyn Jones? Are you really looking to take your manor back, or were you feeling completely barmy that day?"

Sid raised an eyebrow. "Neither, I was just after some information. How do you know about that, anyway?" he asked. He'd told John he was at Teddy Ko's, but not why.

"Because we—me and Madden—arrived at Ko's just after your first visit. I heard everything Billy and Teddy talked about. Enough to know you was digging around for information on the Jones woman. And enough to know that you just being here made Billy furious. Did you get what you was after?" John asked.

"No, I didn't," Sid said.

John and Maggie traded anxious looks.

"What is it?" Sid asked them. "Do you know something? Can you tell me?"

"Aye, I know plenty," John said. "Enough to maybe put Billy Madden in front of a firing squad. Which I'd quite like. And meself as well. Which I wouldn't."

Sid sat back down. "Tell me, John," he said. "I'll keep you out of the shite no matter what. I promise."

John took a deep breath. "Years back, right before the Jones woman's death, a man by the name of Peter Stiles bought morphine and a syringe off Teddy Ko. I was at Ko's that day, picking up his weekly payment to Billy. I saw Stiles come in. I saw him pay Teddy for something in a small brown bag. After he'd gone, I asked Teddy what it was and he told me."

"I don't see the connection," Sid said. "The name Stiles doesn't ring a bell. It's never come up in the police reports on Maud's death," Sid said. "Lots of people buy drugs from Teddy."

"Hear me out," John said. "I knew Stiles. He'd come to the Bark, to see Madden, earlier in the year. This is 1914 I'm talking about. He had made certain arrangements with Madden. . . ." John's voice trailed off. He looked pained. Sid could see that talking about Peter Stiles was difficult for him.

"Go on, John," he said.

"These arrangements concerned taking a mate of Stiles's—a man named Hutchins—out on me boat. Every fortnight. To the North Sea. To certain coordinates, to meet another boat. Stiles was moving swag to the continent. Jewelry. At least that's what he said. Meself? I don't think it was jewels that he was moving. We were always met there by a boat. Hutchins would give a box to the captain. He sounded as English I do, Hutchins that is. The captain of the other boat, though? And the crew. They were speaking German."

"Christ, John," Sid said. "How long did this go on? When did it stop?"

"That's the thing—it didn't," John said. "Hutchins is dead. Another bloke did for him back in '14, but I'm still meeting the boat. With a new man—Flynn. I don't want to do this, Sid. I never wanted to do it. I'm running secrets to the Germans. I know I am. Our boys are dying over there and I'm helping Gerry kill them. I want to stop but I can't. I'm in too deep. Madden'll do for me. And then what happens to me kids?" His voice broke. He looked away from Sid, but before he did, Sid saw the anguish in his eyes—and recognized it. It had been his own once.

"Madden's a bastard, well and truly," Sid said. "We'll get round him, though, John. Don't worry. We'll figure something out. I'll fix this somehow. But first finish your story. Tell me all of it. I still don't understand how this ties in with the death of Maud Selwyn Jones."

John wiped his eyes. "Her death was a big news story, wasn't it? It was in all the papers. HEIRESS TAKES HER OWN LIFE, the headlines said. There were pictures of her. I saw them. And when I saw them, I recognized her. I'd seen her before. And Stiles, too. I saw them together. Only he wasn't Stiles then."

"Hold on, John. Slow down. I'm not following you," Sid said.

"We was casing a house, me and a few more of Madden's crew. In the West End. Belonged to some toff who had lots of silver, paintings, the usual. We was going to knock it off one weekend when he was away. We went in one afternoon—me and another bloke—posing as inspectors from the gas company. Wanted to get a gander round the place—see what was where upstairs, and get the lay of the basement doors and windows. While we was in the foyer, messing about with a gas lamp, I saw them come in—the Selwyn Jones woman and Peter Stiles. Only she called him Max, and she introduced him to the lady of the house as Max von Brandt. After her death, I checked out this Max von Brandt. Found out he was from Germany. He only posed as Stiles, an Englishman, to get the use of Madden's boat. I don't see him anymore—Stiles, that is. And I never told Billy about him being von Brandt. But I still see his man Flynn. Every fortnight. And whatever he's giving the Germans . . . well, it ain't diamond earrings."

Sid sat back in his chair, gobsmacked. So many questions were whirling around in his head, he barely knew which one to ask first.

"John," he said at length. "I believe what you're telling me—that Stiles or von Brandt is passing documents to Germany, but it doesn't follow on that he killed Maud. Max von Brandt's alibi was solid. He was completely cleared of any connection in Maud's death. The police reports said he didn't do it. They said she killed herself with an overdose of morphine."

"I know what the reports said. I read the papers," John said. "But since when do the busies have the last word on anything? What are they now, geniuses? They say he didn't. So what? I say he did."

"How?"

John shook his head. "That's the rub, isn't it? I don't know. Maybe he was quick and injected her right then and there when he took her home. Maybe he paid off the cabbie to say he'd only been in her house a minute or two, when he'd actually been in there longer. Maybe he had a key on him and snuck back later that night. Maybe he didn't need a key. Maybe he went back all nice-like, pretending he wanted to make up, and she let him in. If anyone could've pulled it off, he could've. He's one clever sod."

"But why? Why would he want to kill her? He finished with her, not the other way round."

John thought for a bit, then he said, "Maybe it had nothing to do with their love affair. Maybe she knew something. Maybe she'd seen something she shouldn't have."

"Maybe you're right," Sid said slowly. "Here's another question: Where is von Brandt or Stiles or whatever he calls himself now?"

"I don't know. I haven't seen him since the war started."

"But you're still taking Flynn and the documents out to the North Sea?"

John nodded.

"So Billy's still getting paid," Sid said. "Or else you wouldn't be. He doesn't do anything from the goodness of his heart, not our Billy. Somebody's still sending the money." Sid thought for a minute, then he said, "How does Flynn get the documents?"

"I don't know. He doesn't say much. He just appears at the boatyard every fortnight. Like clockwork. I just took him out this past weekend. Due to go again not this coming Friday, but the next one."

Sid took a deep breath, then blew it out. "Well, John, I have to say . . . this is one fine fucking mess. We could go to the police, tell them all you know about von Brandt and Flynn and Madden. Maybe get you some sort of informant's deal. But then what? Madden just denies everything. There's no proof of any of this, right? It's just your word against his. Old Bill does nothing, much as they'd like to, because they can't. Madden knows you snitched and comes after you. Not what I'd call a good result."

"Nor I," said Maggie.

"We go to the government," Sid said. "Tell them about von Brandt and Flynn. Tell them they can't implicate you. They nab Flynn at the boatyard with the documents on him. He's in the shit. You say you've never seen him before. You have no idea what he's doing in the boatyard. You're in the clear. That way, we put an end to the passing of any secrets to Gerry, but you still belong to Billy. Also not good."

Sid put his elbows on the table and his head in his hands, trying to come up with a solution. After a few minutes, he raised his head and said, "John, Maggie . . . how would you fancy a trip to Scotland, followed by an even longer one to America?"

"What?" John said.

"Listen, what I'm going to tell you now you can't tell a soul."

John and Maggie nodded.

"I have a place. In America. It's a huge ranch in California. Right on the coast. I have a family, too. They came to England right before the war started and then got stuck over here. I got myself over here because I didn't want them here without me for all these years. When this bloody war ends—if this bloody war ever ends—we're all going back. I left the ranch in the hands of my foreman. He's a capable man and I think he's taking good care of it, at least I hope he is, but I'm always looking for good help. What if you were to go to Scotland, to someplace nice and quiet in the country, and stay there for a bit, and then make the trip to California when all this nonsense is over?"

It was John's turn to look gobsmacked. "But how, Sid? We have no money," he said

"I do. I'll pay for it. All of it."

"We couldn't do that," Maggie said, shaking her head. "Couldn't ask that of you."

"Yes, you could. Because of you, my wife's not a widow tonight. My children still have a father. I'm in debt to you the rest of my life for that. Let me start paying you back."

John and Maggie looked at each other. Sid could see that he almost had them.

"Think of it . . . you'd be out of London, away from Madden. Safe. Your kids would grow up in the most beautiful place you can imagine. With green grass and blue skies and the whole Pacific Ocean right there. I'd get your sons ranching instead of breaking heads and thieving. Your daughter will have clean air. Sunshine. Come on, Maggs . . . John . . . what do you say?"

Maggie nodded at John, and then John said, "Can you really do all that? Get us, all of us, all the way to California?"

"I can."

"All right, then. Yes. We'll go. But how? When? And what do we do about Flynn? And Madden?"

"I don't know. Not just yet. But I'll figure it out. We've got to stop Flynn before your next North Sea run, get you away from Madden, and make sure no one twigs any of it until it's too late."

"That's one tall order, Sid," John said.

"Aye, it is, but if anyone can figure out how to get you lot out of London, it's me. I'm a master at disappearing. I've died in the Thames three times already. What's going to take a bit more maneuvering is nabbing Flynn. But we'll worry about that a little later," he said, standing up and scooping the money John had given him off the table. "Right now, my biggest problem isn't Germans or spies or Billy Madden. It's how the hell I'm going to get all the way from Margate to Oxford on two pounds and six shillings."

CHAPTER EIGHTY-TWO

WILLA, SITTING ATOP her camel, leaned over to one side and vomited into the sand. She did not stop the animal while she was sick, but kept him going. The punishing sun beat down upon her, making the desert air shimmer, making her feel a thousand times worse than she already did.

She didn't want to even acknowledge what she was feeling—the nausea, the cramps in her gut and in her legs. They were all signs of cholera. If she acknowledged them, she would dwell on them and worry about them. And she could not afford to do that.

Willa had stopped at an abandoned well yesterday. It was old and disused, and had been left for a reason. The water—what there was—had a dark look to it and a musty smell. She knew better than to drink it, but she'd had no choice. She had already emptied the one skin of water the camel trader had given her. Attayeh had become stubborn and unbiddable, a sure sign that he needed water, too. They'd both drunk their fill, rested for a few hours, then moved on. Twenty-four hours later, Attayeh seemed no worse for the well water, but she was.

She had consulted Max's map a few hours ago. According to it, she would soon come to a small village. She still had Max's money on her, and the remaining two pistols she'd stolen. She hoped to be able to barter something for water and medicine there—if the people there were friendly, if the village wasn't a dwelling place for raiders, or an outpost for Turkish soldiers. If she could rest there for half a day or so, patch herself up a bit, and make sure Attayeh got plenty of water, then she could make Lawrence's camp in a day if it was where Max thought it was, or two days if it was where the camel trader said it was. But those were a lot of ifs, and she knew it.

She leaned over Attayeh's side again, retching violently, her eyes tearing with the force of the spasms. When it was over, she spat into the sand, then wiped her mouth on her sleeve.

Turkish soldiers, Bedouin raiders, the killing sun, cholera, the threat of dehydration if she didn't stop throwing up . . .

Willa wondered, ruefully, which one would get her first.

CHAPTER EIGHTY-THREE

"SEAMIE, YOU CAN'T do it. It's madness. You'll never make it. Damascus is at least five days from here. That's five days to get there, and what? Another eight or nine days to get from Damascus back to Haifa? And that's not including the time it takes to track down news of Willa in the city, while somehow managing to not be recognized. You told me you need to be back in Haifa in eight days. What you're proposing simply cannot be done," Lawrence said.

"Are you certain it's five days to Damascus?" Seamie said. "Has it ever been done faster?"

"Perhaps," Lawrence said, "but you still have to turn around and head south again once you've reached Damascus. Unless, that is, you fancy a court-martial. Even if you got there, and found Willa, what do you plan to do? Do you think the Turkish Army will just allow you to waltz off with her?"

Seamie had no answer for him.

"We start our march on the city in a matter of weeks. If she's in Damascus, I will find her. Let me do it. Let me find her. You must go back to Haifa. It's the only possible course," Lawrence said.

Seamie nodded, defeated. There was nothing else he could do.

He had ridden into Lawrence's camp a day ago, with Khalaf, Aziz, and their men—Lawrence's *new* camp. Spooked by rumors of Turkish patrols, Lawrence had broken his last camp earlier than he'd intended and moved farther east, to a new position. When Seamie and his comrades had found the new camp—thanks to word from a passing cloth merchant—they'd nearly been shot for their troubles. A sentry had spied them and ridden out with fifty men, all of whom had rifles. They were surrounded and led back to camp. Lawrence recognized both Seamie and Khalaf immediately and embraced them warmly. Their animals were seen to, and they were all invited into Lawrence's tent to eat and drink. There, they met Auda, and then explained why they had come. Lawrence had been elated to hear that Willa had survived the plane crash, but furious at Aziz for selling her to the Turks.

"You should have brought her to me!" he thundered at him.

Aziz had merely shrugged. "You should have paid me better for the last hostage," he said.

Seamie had to admit now that his attempt to find Willa had failed. He would return to Haifa tomorrow with no idea where she was, or if she was even still alive. He knew that what Lawrence had said made sense, but it was so hard to turn back to Haifa. He couldn't believe he had ridden all this way, and against all odds found Lawrence's camp, only to have to give up now. And yet if he did not, if he pushed on and got back to Haifa late, he would be accused of desertion.

"I will go to Damascus with Lawrence," Khalaf told him now. "I will find Willa Alden. If she is not there, I will search elsewhere. I will not give up until I have her, and when I do, I will send word to you."

Seamie nodded. He had to accept Lawrence's offer, and Khalaf's. He could do nothing else. As he thanked the two men, they all heard shouts from outside the tent. A minute later, a young man, a Howei-tat, was inside the tent, excitedly telling Lawrence, and everyone else, that an airplane was approaching from the west.

"One?" Lawrence asked tersely.

"Just one," the young man said.

"Ours or theirs?"

"Ours, *Sidi*."

Lawrence rose. Outside the tent, he motioned for the young man's field glasses and raised them to his eyes. Seamie was following the plane with his own field glasses. It was circling low now. As they all watched, the pilot brought it down on the flattest, hardest part of the camp's terrain, near the camel pen. Bellowing, spitting camels welcomed both the pilot and his single passenger as they climbed out of their seats.

"Is that . . . ," Lawrence began, his glasses still trained on the two men.

"Albie Alden," Seamie said quietly, his heart filling with dread. Seamie knew that Albie believed that Willa was dead. Is that why he was here? To tell them to call off the search? To let them know he'd found her body?

It's probably nothing to do with Willa. It's something to do with the march on Damascus, Seamie told himself, willing it to be so.

Albie and the pilot, who'd immediately been surrounded by gun-toting men, were quickly marched to Lawrence's tent. Lawrence greeted the two men as they approached him, but Albie, dusty from the plane ride and breathless from the march, cut him off.

"She made it out of Damascus alive," he said. "And she's trying to get to your camp, Tom. You've got to find her. Immediately. She's got maps on her showing the size and location of Turkish troops stationed between here and Damascus. They've set a trap for you. You've got to go after her. Now. The Turks are hot on her trail. They've put a price on her head. Anyone who finds her is under orders to recover the maps and bring her back to Damascus."

"How do you know this?" Lawrence asked.

"A camel trader in Damascus swears he sold her a camel and sup-plies the night she escaped from the city. She was on the run, dressed as a man. She told him she was in the service of the great sheik Law-rence, and he told her where your camp was. After she'd got out of the city, he told the story to his brother, a spice merchant who works the backcountry between Damascus and Haifa. The merchant, who visits a whorehouse in Haifa, told the madam who runs it, and the madam told me. For a fee, of course. But I trust her information. My colleagues tell me she's never been wrong."

"How long ago did she leave Damascus?" Seamie asked

"I'm not sure. Four days, maybe," Albie said.

"Then she should be close by now," Tom said. "She's an excellent navigator. She wouldn't have got herself lost."

"That's the problem," Albie said. "The trader who sold her the camel told her where to find your camp, Tom, but since then, you've moved camp."

"Bloody hell. She's trying to ride to the old camp," Seamie said. "And there's nothing there." He turned to the pilot. "Can you fly out to the old campsite?" he asked.

"It's about a seventy miles west of here," Lawrence added. "Have you got enough petrol?"

"Petrol's not the problem," the pilot said. "I know that area. It's all dunes. I can't land. If I got down, I'd never get back up again."

"Fly a recon, then," Seamie said. "I'll go with you. If we can spot her, we can turn around, get back here, and get a party of armed riders out to her straightaway."

"Let's go," the pilot said, starting back toward his plane. Seamie was hot on his heels, but Albie called to him, stopping him.

"What is it?" Seamie said.

"There's more to the story. According to the camel trader, Willa killed a high-ranking German officer—one Max von Brandt."

"*What?* The same Max we knew in London? The bloke who came to my wedding?"

"Yes. I think he's the spymaster, Seamie. The one I've been hunting. I think he worked for the German government while he was in London, that he established a link with an informant in the Admiralty while he was there, and that that link is still active. Still feeding information to the Germans on the whereabouts of our ships."

Seamie couldn't believe what he was hearing. "Do you have proof of this?"

"Not yet. Just a strong hunch. Von Brandt was in London as the information was beginning to flow to Berlin. Now he's here. Or rather, he was. It's too much of a coincidence. He was very valuable to the Germans, and they can't be happy about what happened to him." Albie paused for a few seconds. He swallowed hard, then said, "The camel trader said that when the Turks get her back to Damascus, they're going to shoot her. Find her, Seamie. Please. Before they do."

CHAPTER EIGHTY-FOUR

"HERE THEY COME," Willa said, stiffening in her saddle.

"Remember please that you are mute," Hussein said.

"I'll remember. And you remember that if you pull this off . . . if they let us through . . . that the pistol is yours," Willa said.

The boy Hussein grinned. His eyes sparkled. He was only fifteen or so. This was an adventure to him, a game. If he played it well, he would win a prize. For Willa, it was life or death.

Hussein spurred his camel on. Willa followed close behind on Attayeh, who had been fed and watered and was tractable once more. Which was a good thing, for Willa had to keep him closely reined in to make sure he didn't step on or kick one of the two hundred goats walking ahead of them. Attayeh, it turned out, didn't care much for goats.

Willa had arrived in Hussein's village early that morning. It was situated near a small oasis and had provided plenty of water for herself and her camel. Luckily it had not been home to raiders, or a Turkish outpost, and she was able to trade Max's money for food and water for Attayeh and a bottle of some horrible bitter liquid that was supposed to help with stomach ailments. She still could keep nothing inside her. The illness, whatever it was, was taking a toll on her.

The village was inhabited by goatherds mainly, many of whom pastured their animals at a nearby spring. Willa planned to stay there for a day, resting and recovering her strength. She and Attayeh had napped a bit under the shade of some date trees in the center of the village. Afterward, she'd asked a village elder if he knew where the sheik Lawrence camped. The man had shaken his head no, smiling regretfully.

"The other visitors wish to know the same thing," he told her.

The hairs on Willa's neck prickled. "What other visitors?" she asked, warily.

"The soldiers who come through. Most every day now. The Turks."

Willa had jumped to her feet. "Which way do they ride?" she asked the man.

"All ways," the man told her, making a back-and-forth motion with his hand. "They are looking for Lawrence. They stop here for water."

Willa panicked. An entire Turkish patrol could be here any minute. And from any direction. She quickly gathered her things, refilled her skin with water, and saddled Attayeh. She was looking all about as she did, nervously scanning the horizon for rising dust. As she rode out of the village, she saw two boys saddling up their camels—one about her height, one smaller. A herd of goats was milling about them.

Looking at them, she got an idea. She rode up to them and quickly told them that she needed to get past the Turkish patrol.

"Trade clothes with me," she said to the taller boy, "and stay here in your house while I pretend to be you and ride out with your brother. If I get past the patrol, there will a reward for you both. If I do not, I will say I kidnapped your younger brother while you were still in your house and forced him to ride out with me."

"The soldiers will know you are not one of us the minute you speak," the boy said.

"Then your brother must tell them I cannot speak. He will tell them I am deaf, too. And not right in my mind."

"You must not show your eyes. They are green, not brown like ours."

"I will look at the ground."

The older boy snorted. "You are a fool. It will never work. You must go with me instead," he said matter-of-factly. "You must wear a veil. I will say you are my sister and a mute and that I am bringing you to marry a man in the village south of the spring and that fifty of the goats are your dowry."

Willa blinked at him. "That's a brilliant plan," she said. "Simply brilliant!"

"Yes, it is. But I have not yet said I will do it. What is the reward?" he asked.

"One of these," Willa said, showing him one of the jeweled pistols she had stolen. His eyes widened. Willa knew the pistol was worth more money than he would make in a lifetime.

The boys talked among themselves, then the older one, Hussein, sent his younger brother home for women's robes. When the boy came back, Willa was pleased to see that the robes included a full head covering, with only a small cloth mesh for her eyes. Hussein was a genius. If she ever found Lawrence, she would tell him about the young man. He would be an asset to anyone's army. Willa quickly put the robes on. She hated the head covering, hated how it impeded her vision and her mobility, but she was glad of it also. Under it, she was a village woman, and as such, invisible to all but her family.

She and Hussein set off. They had ridden for half an hour before they saw a patrol on the horizon.

"Stay behind me," Hussein said now. "Bow your head. Like a village girl would."

Willa did as she was told. The Turkish soldiers stopped them and spoke rudely to Hussein.

"You there!" their captain shouted. "Where do you come from and where are you going?"

He told them, adding that he was taking his sister to her new husband's village.

"What is your name, girl?" the captain shouted at Willa.

"She cannot answer you, she is mute," Hussein said. "That is why I have so many goats. Because she is mute, my father must give fifty goats instead of twenty-five to marry her off."

"Is that so? And you are paying the husband extra? For a wife who cannot speak? That is a rare and wonderful thing. I wish my wife could not speak," the captain said, laughing. "My boy, the man should pay *you* extra!"

The captain circled around Hussein and Willa, fording his way through the bleating goats, never taking his eyes off Willa. She could see him through the mesh of her head covering. Her heart was pounding. Why did he not let them pass? Hussein's story was perfectly credible.

A split second later, Willa found out. The captain raised his riding crop and brought it down hard on her leg. Willa, expecting such a rotten trick, was ready for him. She doubled over in her saddle, noiselessly cowering, and grabbed her leg, rocking back and forth as if it hurt her terribly, when actually it didn't hurt a bit, as the captain had lashed her false leg.

Satisfied, the captain said, "Forgive me, my boy. I had to make sure of your story. There is another woman at large in the desert, and she is not mute. She is an Englishwoman, one of Lawrence's, and very dangerous. If you should see such a woman, please report her to me, or to any member of the Turkish Army, immediately."

"I will, sir," Hussein said. He told Willa to stop sniveling and follow him, then whipped his camel into a trot. Willa did the same with Attayeh. Half an hour later, when they were well out of sight of the patrol, she shouted at Hussein to stop. She tore her robes off and tossed them to him. Then she dug in her saddlebag for the pistol she'd promised him and tossed that to him, too.

"Thank you, Hussein. I owe you my life, and many others' besides," she said, wrapping a scarf around her head.

Hussein smiled, told her to go with God, then spurred his camel west. Willa turned Attayeh south. She would reach Salkhad soon, where Max thought Lawrence was. It was about a day's ride. If he was not there, she would press on, riding farther south. She was weary and ill and in pain; the horizon swam sickeningly before her eyes, but she did not stop, she did not even falter.

"One more day, Attayeh, old boy," she said aloud, trying to ignore the pain in her gut. "All we have to do is keep going for one more day."

CHAPTER EIGHTY-FIVE

"WHERE IS IT?" Willa mumbled, through cracked, blistered lips. "Where the hell is it?"

She turned in her saddle, looking all around, but could see no camp.

"Where is it?" she shouted hoarsely. Her voice, floating over the dunes that surrounded her, echoed back at her mockingly.

She had looked for Lawrence's camp at Salkhad, questioned some local boys, but had heard nothing of Lawrence, and had found nothing of him. Then she'd continued south, to where the camel trader had said he was—north of Azraq and east of Minifer. And again, she'd found nothing. Perhaps both Max and the trader were wrong. Or perhaps she'd simply missed the encampment, or missed signs like tracks or camel scat, that could have led her to it. It was hard to hold her head up now, to even see straight. It was hard to think. It hurt to even try. She had so little strength left.

Attayeh stumbled suddenly, and Willa lurched dangerously in her saddle. "Keep your seat, old girl," she told herself, her voice little more than a croak now. Her throat was as dry as dust. She'd drunk the last of her water yesterday. She couldn't remember exactly when. She had not stopped for the last forty-eight hours, but had driven Attayeh mercilessly. She had no choice. She was dying, she knew she was, and she had to get to Lawrence before the sickness in her gut finished her off.

It was certainly cholera. People sometimes recovered from it. If they had the proper medicines, and rest. She had neither. She desperately wanted to climb down. To stop. To rest. But she knew that if she did that, she would not get up again. She would die where she lay, for she would not have the strength to pull herself back up into the saddle.

Attayeh, exhausted and confused, stumbled again and wept. Willa knew that camels cried tears when they became dehydrated, and Attayeh had been ridden too hard and too long without rest, food, or water. Willa wanted to speak to the animal, to comfort him and encourage him, but she no longer had the strength to do so. She hoped she might be near a village, or a Bedouin camp, and that Attayeh, sensing the nearness of other camels, and water, might be able to get there on his own. She hoped so. She had to, for hope, fragile and fading, was all she had left.

Willa rode on for another half hour, her head lolling as Attayeh plodded along. The camel bellowed suddenly. He stopped short, then started walking again, at a brisker pace. Willa picked her head up; she squinted into the distance, hoping that by some miracle the camel had spotted an oasis, a small settlement, something. Instead, she saw dust on the horizon. She wondered for a moment if she was seeing things. She knew that people who were suffering from dehydration started to hallucinate. She squinted again. There *was* dust on the horizon, she was sure of it. She shaded her eyes and saw riders—three of them. One was in the lead, streaking ahead of the others, though they were all coming on fast.

Please, she prayed, don't let them be Turkish soldiers. Or raiders. Please. I've brought the maps this far, let these be good men. Willa knew she would never see Lawrence again, but she hoped these riders, whoever they were, would take the maps the rest of the way.

After what seemed like an eternity, the lead rider drew up to her. Willa saw that he was wearing plain white robes, dirtied by dust and sweat. He unwound his head scarf, and Willa knew then that her death was very close.

He was a real man, she was quite sure of that, because he was shouting at her, but his face . . . his face was a hallucination, a vision. For one last time, her fevered mind was showing her the one she most wanted to see—Seamie Finnegan.

"Willa, my God," he said. "It's all right. You'll be all right now,

Willa. We're here. We'll get you back to camp." There was fear in his voice as he spoke, and in his eyes.

His voice . . . it even sounds like Seamie's, she thought. And he knows my name. He must be one of Lawrence's. Oh, thank God!

Willa tried to speak to him, she tried to answer him, but she couldn't. Her throat worked, but no sound came out. Her voice was gone. She motioned for water. The man gave her some. She drank, then gasped as her gut was gripped hard by a fresh wave of cramps.

When the pain subsided, when she could breathe again, Willa rasped out her final words. She was swaying in her saddle now. There was nothing left inside her, no strength, no will. She was played out, but it was all right. She could let go now. This man would help her.

"Please . . . I have maps . . . documents . . . give them to Lawrence . . . tell him Jabal ad Duruz is a trap . . . tell my mother I'm sorry . . . tell Seamus Finnegan I love him . . ."

CHAPTER EIGHTY-SIX

"HE'S DEAD, I know he is," India said, dully. "That's the only explanation. He wouldn't not come home for days for the sheer hell of it. Something's happened to him. Something terrible."

It was a Sunday morning. Fiona was sitting with India and Jennie in the Brambles kitchen. She'd just cooked everyone breakfast and had sent the children outside to play. Charlotte and Rose had Wish, Elizabeth, and little James with them, as well as Fiona's younger children. Fiona and Jennie had brought their children with them expressly to keep India's children occupied, and to keep their minds off their missing father. India kept telling them that their dad had business in London, and that's why he wasn't home, but it had been a week since he'd left for London, and she couldn't go on saying that forever.

Fiona reached across the table and took India's hand. She'd been doing her best over the last few days to keep India's spirits up, and her own, but it was getting harder by the minute. India was right, of course, Sid would never simply take off on a jaunt, or a drinking binge, or some sort of mad spree. He would never have worried India that way. Fiona was frightened, though she refused to let on, that something terrible had indeed happened to him. And someone from his past was involved. She felt it in her bones.

"Joe will be here any minute now," she said. "He'll tell us what he's found out. He hired one of the best private investigators in London. The man's bound to have turned up something."

India picked her head up and looked at Fiona. "Yes, but what?" she said, her eyes filling with tears. "I'm sure he'll have found out something, but I'm not sure I'll want to hear what it is."

A few minutes later, there was a knock at the front door. Fiona ran to answer it. It was Joe, assisted in his wheelchair by Mr. Foster.

"Hello, love," Fiona said, kissing her husband. She greeted Mr. Foster. "What news?" she asked them.

Joe shook his head. "It's not good, Fee."

Fiona's heart sank. Not Sid, she thought. Please. "Come inside. Into the kitchen," she said in a hollow voice. "That's were India and Jennie are. It'll save you telling it twice."

Joe greeted both women. As Jennie poured tea for Joe and Mr. Foster, Joe asked India how she was holding up.

"Not very well, I'm afraid," she said.

The fear in her eyes was so great that it hurt Fiona to look at her. Sid was Fiona's brother, and she loved him, but he was India's whole life. They'd been through so much already. It wasn't fair that he should be taken from her now.

"What's happened to him, Joe? What did the investigator find out?" Fiona asked.

"We don't know what's happened," Joe said. "The investigator—

Kevin McDowell's his name—managed to find out that Sid was last seen going into Teddy Ko's offices in Limehouse last Sunday. Ko's an importer. Does his trade with China."

India remembered the little Buddha she'd found in Sid's pocket. "Teddy Ko . . . ," she said slowly. "I know that name. He's also an opium peddler. I once tried to get his place shut down."

"He still is an opium peddler. The biggest in London," Joe said.

"Why was Sid there?" India asked. "What on earth could he have wanted with Teddy Ko?"

"I don't know. All I know is that he was seen going into Ko's, but was not seen coming out," Joe said. He hesitated before continuing. It was the briefest of pauses, but Fiona felt it and so did India.

"What, Joe?" India said, in an anguished voice. "What are you not telling me?"

Joe took a deep breath, then said, "Billy Madden and two of his heavies were also seen going into Ko's. About five minutes after Sid went in."

India shook her head. She knew that name, too. They all did. "Why, Joe? Why did he go there?" she said, her voice breaking. She started to weep.

Jennie went to her side. She put her arms around her.

Fiona looked at Joe. "Billy Madden?" she said, tears starting in her own eyes. "What was Sid doing mixing with the likes of Billy Madden? Years ago, yes. But why now? He must've been mad, Joe. I don't understand it. I don't—"

Her voice was cut off by the sound of a door slamming. "Peter, is that you?" she sharply called to her son. "Go back outside, will you? And don't slam the door! I've told you a thousand times not to!"

"Sorry," a voice said.

It wasn't Peter.

"Bloody hell!" Joe said as Sid walked into the kitchen. "Look at your face! What happened to you?"

India's head snapped up. She leapt out of her chair, ran to Sid, and threw her arms around his neck. "I thought you were dead!" she sobbed. "I thought I'd never see you again!" She let go of his neck, grabbed fistfuls of his jacket, and shook him. "Why did you go to see Teddy Ko? And Billy Madden? Why did you do it?" she shrilled at him. "They could've killed you. It looks like they almost did!"

"India, how do you know all this?" Sid asked, looking stunned.

"We hired an investigator," Joe said.

"Mummy!" Charlotte said loudly. She was suddenly in the kitchen with Wish and the other children. "Was that Daddy who just came in?" Her excited smile fell when her father turned to her. "Daddy? What happened to you?" she asked, ashen-faced. Little Wish burst into tears. Sid's face was still a swollen mess of cuts and bruises.

"Excuse me, ma'am," Mr. Foster quietly said to Fiona. "But could you tell me where the brandy is kept?"

"In the cabinet above the sink, Mr. Foster," Fiona said, taking a semi-hysterical India by the arm and leading her to a chair.

While Sid comforted his children—telling him he'd been in a bit of an accident, that's all, and that's why he looked so terrible and hadn't come home to them right away, but now he was here, home again, and Mummy would take care of his hurts—Jennie herded James and the other children back outside into the garden. Foster poured brandy for the adults, then made some hot chocolate. He poured it into mugs, put some biscuits on a plate, and asked Charlotte, who was still in the kitchen, if she could help him carry the treats out into the garden.

"Thank you very much, Mr. Foster," Charlotte said politely. "But I do not require cocoa and biscuits. I require a proper explanation."

"It's all right, Mr. Foster," Sid said. "She's old enough to know what's going on now. She can stay." To his daughter, he said, "You were going to have to find out the truth about me and my past sometime. Might as well be now."

By the time Mr. Foster had gone outside, India had emptied her brandy glass and stopped sobbing. Fiona, Joe, and Jennie had drunk theirs, too. Sid sat down at the table and emptied his in one swallow.

"You can usually be counted on to turn up," Joe said. "Even when all the odds are against you. This time, though, you had even me worried. What the devil happened to you?"

Sid picked up the bottle and refilled everyone's glass.

"I'll tell you everything," he said. "Every last thing. But get that down yourselves first. Otherwise, you're never going to believe me."

CHAPTER EIGHTY-SEVEN

"DO YOU REMEMBER it, Willa? Mombasa? Do you remember the turquoise sea? And the pink fort? And the white houses? Do you remember the hotel where we spent our first night? They didn't have two rooms for us. We had to share a bed. I don't think I slept at all. I stayed up all night, just listening to you breathe. You didn't. Stay up, I mean. You fell asleep and snored."

Seamie was talking fast.

I sound like a madman, he thought. No, a salesman, rather.

For that's what he was doing—trying to sell Willa on the idea of staying. Here. In this world. He was trying to sell her on the idea of life. Her life. He talked to her of their childhood. Of sails with her, Albie, and her parents. Of climbs on Snowdon and Ben Nevis. Of rambles in the Lake District. He talked to her of Kilimanjaro and their time together in Africa. He reminded her of the animals moving across the veldt, the sunrises, the impossibly vast sky. He told her how much he loved her photographs of Everest. And how he dreamed, still, of going there with her one day. He tried to bring back her best memories, tried to create images for her fevered mind of the things she loved most in this world. He tried to make her hold on, to stay with him.

She was sick. God, she was so horribly sick. He'd given her aconite and opium. He'd tried quinine. Nothing worked. Nothing broke her fever, nothing stopped the spasms that racked her body. No food stayed in her. No water, either. It was as if her body, battered and broken from the years of punishment she'd meted out to it, was trying to expel the fierce and terrible spark that animated her—her will, her drive, her very soul.

He told her of the search for the South Pole, and how the howling of the Antarctic wind and the ceaseless groaning of the sea ice could drive a man mad. He told her about existing in a world devoid of all color, a world of white, and of the infinite ocean of stars at night.

He ran out of adventures to talk about, and so he told her about the rest of his life. About James, the son he loved beyond all reason. He told her about the small cottage in Binsey, where the boy was born. He told her about the mistakes he'd made, the things he regretted, and the things he refused to regret. He told her about Haifa and the ship that waited for him there, and that he had to go, but didn't want to leave her.

And then he stopped talking suddenly and rested his head in his hands. For two whole days he'd nursed her, watching over her, bathing her blazing skin, holding her as she shivered and retched and arched against the pain inside her. He had barely slept since he'd first arrived at Lawrence's camp, and was so exhausted now, he was nearly delirious himself. He had searched for her by plane but hadn't been able to spot her from the air, so he had ridden out from Lawrence's camp and during his second day of riding, had found her.

"Please don't die, Willa. Don't go," he said. "Don't leave me here in this world without you. Just knowing you're somewhere on this planet, doing something brave and amazing, makes me happy. I love you, Willa. I've never stopped loving you. I never will."

He raised his head and looked at her, at the ruined wraith of a woman lying on the ground in a tent in the middle of this godforsaken desert, in the middle of this godforsaken war. Yes, he loved her, and she loved him, and their love had brought them only grief. Was it love at all? he wondered now. Or was it merely madness?

"I love you, too, Seamie," Willa said, her eyes suddenly open.

"Willa!" Seamie said, reaching for her hand and squeezing it. "You're awake!

She swallowed, grimacing, then motioned for water. Seamie got her some, and sat her up to drink it. When she finished, he gently eased her back down on her pillow. Sweat had broken out across her brow, and her breathing was shallow and labored. He could see the effort it had cost her merely to drink.

"Lawrence?" she said, her voice raspy.

"On his way to Damascus with Auda and an army. They're heading well west of Jabad al Duruz, and the traps set for them there. Because of you."

Willa smiled. She gazed at him for a while, gathering her strength, then said, "You have to go now."

"How, Willa? I can't leave you here . . . you'll die . . . I can't . . ."

"I'm finished, Seamie," she said. "I'm so tired . . . so ill . . . I'm played out."

"No, Willa, don't say that," Seamie said, his voice breaking.

"I . . . I heard you . . . talking," she said. "About us. James. Your ship. Go, or you'll be court-martialed and shot." She swallowed again. Her eyes were filled with pain. "Is that what you want for your son?" she finished softly.

"No, but—"

She cut him off. "We have to let go, Seamie. Once and for all. We've hurt each other long enough. Hurt too many others." There were tears in her eyes now. "Go to Haifa," she said. "Stay alive. Please. Survive this damn war and go home again. Jennie . . . and James . . . they need you—"

Willa abruptly stopped talking. She leaned over and vomited into the brass urn at the side of her bed. Seamie held her head, then wiped her face. As he settled her down on her pillow once more, he felt her body go limp in his hands.

"No!" he shouted, terrified that he'd lost her. "Willa, no!"

He quickly checked her breathing and her pulse. She was still alive, but unconscious again. Her skin was horribly hot to the touch. Grabbing a rag, he dipped it into a bowl of water, and sponged her face and body.

"Don't go, Willa," he whispered. "Please don't go."

As he sat in the tent, in the stench and heat of Willa's sickness, trying desperately to cool her, he suddenly heard bells in the desert and the sound of camels bawling. He wondered who was coming. The camp was nearly deserted. Lawrence, Auda, and Khalaf, together with four thousand troops, had left this morning. They were going to ride east, not north, turn west again to meet Faisal at Sheik Saad and then march to Damascus, avoiding certain slaughter at Jabal ad Duruz. Because of Willa. If it hadn't been for her, for her courage, her luck, her refusal to quit, they would have ridden into a trap, one they could not possibly have fought their way out of.

Only a few men remained behind to guard Seamie and Willa. Seamie stood up now, stepped outside of the tent, and shaded his eyes against the sun. What now? he wondered, too spent to be afraid. What the hell is happening now?

He quickly saw that it was not the Turks. That's something, he thought. It was a group of Bedouin, some fifty strong. Men were in the lead, followed by a litter. More men brought up the rear. When they got close to him, the lead man, tall and angry-looking, dismounted from his camel, walked up to Seamie, and bowed.

"I bring Fatima, first wife of Khalaf al Mor, and her women. She has heard that the woman Willa Alden is here and in need of help. You will take her to see Willa Alden. You will do this now."

Fatima and her women, all heavily veiled, came forth. When she saw Seamie, Fatima removed the veil from her eyes.

"You found her, Seamus Finnegan," she said.

Seamie bowed. "I did. With your help."

"Not with my help. With Allah's help," she said. "Take me to her."

"She is very sick, Fatima," he said brokenly. "I've tried everything. For two days, I've tried everything I can think of."

"I have remedies. Desert herbs. They may help," Fatima said. "And I have her necklace. The one I gave her to keep evil spirits away. She will need it now."

Seamie led Fatima to Willa's tent. He went inside with her. Fatima tried to hide her shock at the sight of Willa's emaciated body, but failed.

"She's very bad, isn't she?" Seamie said.

"You will go to another tent now and sleep or I will be nursing two sick people, not one," she said sternly, fastening the necklace around Willa's neck.

"I can't. I have to leave. I have to get to Haifa."

"You will sleep first. If only for a few hours, or you will never make it to Haifa," Fatima said.

Seamie was too tired to argue. "Thank you for coming," he said. "Please save her."

"I will do all that I can for her, but it is in Allah's hands, Seamus Finnegan, not mine."

Seamie nodded. "Talk to Him, Fatima. He listens to you. Tell Him if He wants a life, He can have mine. A life for a life. Mine, not hers. Tell Him, Fatima. Tell Him to please let Willa Alden live."

CHAPTER EIGHTY-EIGHT

". . . AND JENNIE'S GATHERING the statistics on the number of single London women under thirty who own property, which we'll need for the letter-writing campaign to the Commons," Katie Finnegan was saying.

But Jennie didn't hear her. She was sitting in Fiona and Joe's drawing room, attending her Tuesday-night suffrage meeting, but she was a million miles away. Katie was talking about the group's latest campaign—a push to lower the voting age for women—but Jennie was back at the Brambles, two nights ago, listening to Sid's dreadful story. She was feeling her blood run cold as he told them why he had gone to Teddy Ko's, what had happened to him, and what he had learned— about Maud, and about Max von Brandt. She was remembering how she had sat there, barely moving, barely breathing, as Sid told them that Max was in all likelihood a German spy, and a murderer, too—Maud's murderer. She remembered India's terrible shock at the news—and her grief. And she remembered Joe's fury.

"We have to tell the PM about this. Immediately," he'd said. "Von Brandt left London, but it sounds like his man Flynn's still moving information. He has to be caught. And stopped. Now. Before any more British lives are lost."

"Hold on, Joe," Sid had said. "John Harris—the man who saved my life—is all mixed up in this. He never wanted to be, but he had no choice. Madden threatened him. I promised I would help him, that I would get him and his family out of London. We can't make a move on Flynn until we figure out a way to do it that won't land John in prison."

"But we can't allow Flynn to remain at large," Joe said. "He could do a runner at any second."

"We have a few days," Sid said. "Today's Sunday. John told me that the next rendezvous would be this Friday. That's when we have to move. We have to catch Flynn with the goods on him or we've got nothing—just an innocent man, wrongfully accused."

Nobody had noticed Jennie as they talked. Nobody noticed how pale she'd suddenly gone, or that her whole body had begun to tremble. And ever since then, she'd been veering wildly between belief and denial, between terror and despair, and it was tearing her in two.

One minute she would tell herself that Sid had made a mistake—Max was on the side of peace, just as he'd told her. The next minute, she would believe that he was all the things Sid said he was. After all, what reason did John Harris have to lie? No honorable man engaged in a good endeavor would have anything to do with the likes of Billy Madden. No honorable man would buy morphine from a drug lord, and no honorable man's paramour would turn up dead from an overdose only days after he'd bought it. Max von Brandt was a German spy. He'd been hurting the Allies, not aiding them. He'd been sending thousands upon thousands of British fighting men to their deaths. And she, Jennie herself, had helped him. She had blood on her hands as surely as he did.

The truth of this was so unbearable that Jennie could not accept it. So she didn't. She told herself, again, that Sid was wrong. And John Harris, too. And that it would all come out when they found the man they were searching for—Flynn. He would tell them who Max really was and what he was doing. He would set them all straight.

"Do you think you could have those figures ready by early next month, Auntie Jennie? Auntie Jennie?"

It was Katie.

"Oh! I'm so sorry, Katie. I don't know where my head is tonight," Jennie said.

"You look a little peaky. Are you all right?"

Jennie, smiling, waved her concern away. "I'm fine. Just a little tired."

Katie asked her question again, and Jennie said she would indeed have the figures ready for her next month. Katie thanked her, smiling sympathetically. Jennie knew that Katie would attribute her fatigue to the scare the whole family had been through with Sid, but in reality it was the dreadful doubts she'd been entertaining about Max that made her feel ill. She had a headache all the time now, and often felt attacks of nausea, or shivered with a sudden chill.

With difficulty, she forced herself to listen and participate in the rest of the meeting, but she was glad when it was over and she could return to Wapping—to James and her father. As usual, she walked to the bus stop with Gladys Bigelow. They rode the same bus east, though Jennie got off it earlier than Gladys did. When the bus had stopped for them, and they'd climbed aboard and seated themselves, Gladys wordlessly handed Jennie an envelope, as she had been doing for more than three years now.

Jennie was just about to put the envelope in her carpetbag, when instead she took hold of Gladys's hand.

"What is it?" Gladys asked her, in that flat, dead voice of hers. "What's wrong?"

"Gladys, I have to ask you something," Jennie said.

Gladys's eyes grew wide. She shook her head. "No, you don't," she said.

"I do. I have to know about Max."

Gladys yanked her hand free of Jennie's grip.

"I have to know, Gladys," Jennie said. "I have to know that he's who he says he is. He told me he was a double agent. That he's helping sabotage Germany's war efforts. I have to know what's in this envelope."

Gladys shook her head. She started laughing, but her laughter quickly turned to tears. She turned away from Jennie and would not speak. Watching her, Jennie realized with a sickening certainty that Sid was right—Max was a German spy.

"Gladys," she said. "We have to tell someone. We have to stop him."

Gladys turned around. She grabbed Jennie's arm and squeezed it hard. "You shut your mouth," she hissed. "You don't tell anybody anything! Do you hear me? You don't know him. You don't know what he's capable of. But trust me, you don't what to find out."

"Gladys, you're hurting me! Let go!" Jennie said.

But Gladys didn't. She tightened her grip. "You keep delivering that envelope. Just like you're supposed to. The war will end one day, and then we can put it all behind us and never talk about it, never even think about it, again."

And then she stood up, took a seat away from Jennie, and stared out of the window into the darkness. She was still sitting like that when Jennie reached her stop.

As Jennie walked home from the bus stop, she felt anguished. She didn't want to believe the worst of Max, but it was getting harder and harder not to. If he was indeed working for Germany, she had to tell someone. It was the right thing to do. The only thing to do.

But then something that Gladys had said came back to her: *You don't know what he's capable of. But trust me, you don't want to find out.*

Jennie thought back to the time that Max had come to visit her in the rectory. She remembered how he'd told her of his mission and had asked her to help him. He'd been courtly and kind, as he always was, but when she wavered, when she tried to say no to him, his eyes had hardened and he'd threatened to tell Seamie about Binsey.

The memory was like a knife to her heart now. She'd just sent Josie Meadows a letter, with a picture of James. In it, she'd told her old friend what a beautiful child James was, that he was growing strong and healthy, and that he was loved. So dearly.

She'd addressed it to Josephine Lavallier—Josie's new stage name. She felt frightened now to think that Max knew about Josie, about their letters, about James. She could not bear for Seamie to know the truth about what she'd done, could not bear for James to one day know that she and Seamie were not his real parents.

Jennie arrived at her father's house. A light was on in the hallway, but the rest of the house was dark. Her father and her son were already asleep. She did not take off her coat and jacket, but hurried directly into the kitchen.

There, she put the kettle on, but not for tea. She was going to steam the envelope open.

It was time to find out once and for all just who Max von Brandt really was.

CHAPTER EIGHTY-NINE

JENNIE SAT AT the kitchen table, in the light of a small, single lamp, and stared at the large manila envelope in front of her. The house was quiet except for the ticking of the clock atop the mantel. She was supposed to take the envelope to the church basement and put it in its usual hiding place. Instead, she had steamed it open. She had not yet pulled its contents out and read them, though. She was too afraid.

There would be no going back once she read whatever was inside the envelope. She would find out who Max von Brandt really was. And she would find out what she really was. She would learn if she'd helped him save innocent German lives, or helped him destroy British ones.

"You should have done this years ago," she whispered to herself. But it had been easier not to. Easier not to know the truth, to believe she was doing good. Easier to accept Max's help with Willa, than to earn his enmity and have him reveal the truth of James's parentage.

As Jennie reached for the envelope, a sudden wave of nausea gripped her. She ran to the sink and was sick. When the heaving had stopped, she rinsed her mouth out, wiped her face, and sat down again. She had felt horribly unwell ever since Sid arrived at the Brambles with his news. Her headaches and sour stomach had got worse over the last few days, and she felt feverish now, too. She was certain it was all a reaction to the shock of Sid's allegations against Max.

"It has to stop," she said. "Now."

She pulled out the envelope's contents, praying hard that all would be as Max had said. What she saw told her instantly that it would not.

The envelope contained carbons of letters from Sir George Burgess to Winston Churchill, First Sea Lord, and to various other high-ranking naval officers, cabinet ministers, and the prime minister himself. In them was information on the movement of British ships, the size of their crews, the number and sizes of their guns, the objects of their missions.

Jennie saw the names of ships: *Bellerophon*, *Monarch*, *Conqueror*, *Colossus*, and *Exeter*. Some were in the Atlantic Ocean. Some in the Mediterranean. There was information on Britain's oil fields in the Mideast, their production capabilities, and their security.

There were no identity papers of any nature. There were no names of safe houses in Germany and France. No contact information for the people in Britain who were supposed to be providing homes and employment for the dissenters smuggled out of Germany.

It was all a lie.

Jennie stuffed the carbons back into the envelope then put the envelope back into her carpetbag. She couldn't bear to look at it. She covered her face with her hands and moaned with the horror that confronted her. What had she done? How much information had she helped feed to Berlin? How many men had she helped Max kill?

She was filled with guilt, sick with remorse. She knew she should immediately take the envelope to her brother-in-law, Joe. He would know what to do with it. But she was also frightened. If she took the envelope to Joe, the authorities to whom he showed it would want to know how he'd got it. He would have no choice but to tell them. Would they arrest her? What about her father? It was his church that she'd used to move the documents. Would they arrest him, too? If they did, what would become of James?

Her stomach squeezed again. She tried to quell the nausea roiling inside her. As she did, a fresh, and terrible, realization hit her—those ships, the ones mentioned in Burgess's letters—some of them were in the Atlantic, others in the Mediterranean.

The Mediterranean.

"That's where Seamie is," she said aloud.

Jennie didn't know the name of his new ship. Seamie was not allowed to mention it in his letters to her, but she knew he would soon be on it, as soon as the injuries he'd received when the *Hawk* was sunk had healed. Maybe he was already on it, patrolling off the coast of Arabia again. And, thanks to Max's efforts over the last few years—and her own—maybe German submarines were waiting for him.

"Oh, God," she cried. "Oh, Seamie, no."

She saw, with a sudden, wrenching clarity, what she had done: She had helped Max von Brandt because she hadn't wanted him to tell Seamie the truth about her, and about James, but by trying so desperately to hold on to the man she loved, she had likely doomed him.

She bent down to pick up her carpetbag; she knew what she had to do. She would take the envelope to Joe. Now. Immediately. Word had to be got to Burgess and the Admiralty that the Germans knew everything, and that British ships were in greater danger than anyone could imagine.

As Jennie put her coat back on, the nausea overwhelmed her and she was sick again, violently so. When she finished, she stood over the sink for a few minutes, shaking and gasping. As soon as she caught her breath, she opened her eyes and that's when she saw it—blood in the sink.

Jennie touched her fingers to her lips, but they came away clean. She realized that the blood was coming from her nose. She reached into her pocket to get a handkerchief to stanch it, but the blood was coming faster now. As she pressed the cloth to her face, the room swam suddenly, then came back into focus.

"Mummy?" a little voice said.

Jennie turned around.

"I heard a noise," James said. "Mummy, your nose is bleeding."

"James," Jennie said. Her son looked blurry and far away.

"What is it, Mummy? What's wrong?"

"James," Jennie said, right before her legs gave way. "Run and get Granddad. . . ."

CHAPTER NINETY

"WHERE AM I?" Jennie Finnegan said, looking around herself. She was lying in a bed that was not her own, in some sort of nightgown that was not her own, in a room she didn't recognize, next to people she had never seen before.

Frightened, she sat up. She swung her feet over the side of the bed and tried to get up but was gripped by a fit of coughing so severe, it left her weak and breathless.

"Mrs. Finnegan!" a voice said. "Please lie still! You mustn't bring the coughing on."

Jennie looked up and saw a young woman—a nurse—hovering over her. She wore a white cotton mask over her face.

"Where am I? What's happened?" Jennie asked, panic-stricken.

"You're in hospital, Mrs. Finnegan. On the quarantine ward. You're very ill, ma'am. It's the flu. The Spanish flu," the nurse said, easing Jennie back into bed.

"The flu? My God," Jennie said, slumping back against her pillow.

She remembered now. She remembered standing in her father's kitchen, devastated by what she had learned about Max von Brandt. She remembered being sick, and dizzy, and the blood . . . she remembered the blood.

"What day is it? How did I get here?" she asked. And then a terrifying new thought occurred to her. "Where's my son? Where's James?"

"Please calm down, ma'am. Everything is all right," the nurse said. "It's Wednesday. Your father brought you here last night. He wanted to stay with you, but of course we couldn't allow it. He told me that if you woke, I was to tell you he had a neighbor woman, a Mrs. Barnes, come to stay with James last night. And that he would be taking the boy to your sister-in-law's—a Mrs. Bristow's—later today."

Jennie felt so relieved. James was in good hands; he would be well cared for.

"I'm Sister Connors, by the way," the nurse said. "I'm one of the nurses who'll be looking after you."

Jennie nodded. "Are my things here?" she asked her. "My carpetbag?"

"No. Your father didn't bring anything with him. Is there something you need? Something I can get for you?"

"Listen to me, please," Jennie said urgently. She had remembered something else—her determination to stop Max, to stop the flow of military secrets to Berlin. "You must get my brother-in-law here. Joseph Bristow. He's an MP. Something terrible is going on and he must know about it immediately."

"I'm afraid he won't be allowed on the quarantine ward, either," Sister Connors said gently.

"I must get word to him. Can I write him?"

"I'm afraid not. We can't pass along anything handled by the infected."

"What am I going to do, then?" Jennie said, agitatedly.

"I can't just go summoning MPs, Mrs. Finnegan. If you could just tell me what it's about," Sister Connors said kindly.

Jennie didn't want to, but it seemed she had no choice. "There is a spy ring at work in London. They're passing secrets to Berlin through a network of tunnels under the river. I know about it because I helped them," she said. "Now, can you please get Mr. Bristow? He has a telephone at his home and also at the House of Commons. Do you have a telephone on the ward? Perhaps I could get word to him that way."

"One moment, please, Mrs. Finnegan," Sister Connors said.

Jennie watched as she walked to the center of the room, where the ward sister was standing with a clipboard, writing something down. Sister Connors tried to keep her voice down, but Jennie heard every word that she said.

"The new patient—Mrs. Finnegan—she's talking about spies, Sister Matthews, and says she's helping them. I believe she's delirious."

The ward sister nodded. She came over to Jennie's bed. Her eyes were troubled. "Hello, dear. I'm Sister Matthews. Sister Connors tells me that you're rather upset. You must calm yourself," she said through her mask. "You are very ill and you need to rest."

"I know you think I'm off my head," Jennie said. "I promise you I'm not. My husband, and many others in the Mediterranean, are in great danger. I must speak with my brother-in-law."

Sister Matthews nodded. "Get Dr. Howell, please," she said to Sister Connors.

Thank God, Jennie thought. The doctor would listen to her. He would ring up Joe and tell him she needed to see him.

A few minutes later, a brisk, bearded man appeared. He looked weary and careworn. A stethoscope hung from his neck. The front of his white coat was flecked with spots of dried blood. He was holding a cup.

He introduced himself, and then before Jennie could speak, he said, "Now, now, Mrs. Finnegan. What's all this I'm hearing about spies? You mustn't worry yourself about such things. Your husband is quite safe, I'm sure. We have spies of our own, you know, working very hard to catch the baddies. That's their job. Yours is to get better. Now, drink this, please."

Jennie eyed the cup suspiciously. "What is it?" she asked.

"Medicine," the doctor replied.

Jennie shook her head. "It's a sedative, isn't it? You think I'm raving, but I'm not. You have to believe me, Dr. Howell. You have to—"

"Mrs. Finnegan," Dr. Howell said, interrupting her, "if you will not drink the medicine willingly, I shall have to resort to other means."

"No! I can't. I must speak with Joseph Bristow! Please!" Jennie said, her voice rising. Her agitation set off another round of coughing. It was so harsh and racking that blood dripped from her nose again.

Dr. Howell wiped the blood with a cloth and showed it to her. "You have a young son, do you not? And a husband," he said. "What would they say to you if they knew you were not doing all in your power to recover and return to them? What would they say to me for allowing it?"

Jennie realized that Dr. Howell did not believe her and that he would not be sending for Joe. She realized, too, what he was trying to say—that she was gravely ill and that there was a very real possibility that she might not return to her husband and son . . . ever.

With tears in her eyes, Jennie took the cup from Dr. Howell's hand and downed the bitter liquid inside it. It took only seconds to work. Almost before she knew it, her eyes were closing, and she felt herself being pulled under, into a deep and heavy sleep.

The last thing she felt was Sister Connors's gentle hands smoothing her hair back from her face. The last thing she heard was the nurse's voice saying, "Poor woman. I'm sure the barmy things she's saying are all coming from her worries about her husband, from him being in the war and all."

And Sister Matthews replying, "She should worry about herself. She has a fight ahead of her as bad as any of our boys on the front are facing. And about as much chance of winning it."

CHAPTER NINETY-ONE

"HELLO, MUM! YOU all right?" Gladys Bigelow said loudly, poking her head into their small sitting room. Her mum was a bit hard of hearing. Gladys had just put her umbrella in the hallway stand and her bag of marketing on the floor and was now unbuttoning her dripping raincoat.

Mrs. Bigelow, in her usual seat by the window, smiled tiredly and said, "Right as rain, love. How was your day?"

"Beastly. I'm glad it's over."

"And I'm glad you're home. It's a filthy night. Awfully wet for September."

"You don't have to tell me. I'm half-drowned. I bought us some nice gammon steaks for our tea. And a tin of pineapple rings to put on them. And peas. I think I'll make some mash, too. I know you're partial to gammon steaks with mash."

"Oh, Gladys. You shouldn't have to do it."

"Do what, Mum?" Gladys said, shrugging out of her raincoat.

"Work so hard all day, then come home and cook for me. It's too much for one person," Mrs. Bigelow said, fretting at the kerchief in her hands.

Gladys frowned at that. She put her raincoat on a peg near the door, sat down next to her mother, and took hold of her shaking hands. "What's the matter, Mum? Are you feeling low again today? What's happened?"

Mrs. Bigelow turned her head away.

"Come on now. Out with it. Tell me."

"Well, Mrs. Karcher came over today. She brought me some biscuits she'd made. . . ."

"That sounds very nice," Gladys said.

"Oh, it was. She's a lovely woman is Mrs. Karcher. She told me that her middle girl—Emily, her name is—is engaged to be married. Her fiancé's fighting in France, but he wrote her a letter and asked her would she marry him and said he's sorry he couldn't put a ring in the envelope, but he'll buy her one as soon as he gets home."

"Why would that make you sad, Mum?" Gladys asked. "That's a lovely story."

"It *is* a lovely story, Gladys, that's why it makes me sad. You should be telling stories like that. You should have lads asking you to marry them. But you don't. Because you can't. Because you're saddled with me."

"Oh, Mum, you silly thing. Is that what has you all teary?"

"I'm not silly, Gladys. It's not natural, a young girl like you stuck looking after her mother. You should have a lad of your own. And a place of your own. And children one day."

"I will, Mum. One day I will," Gladys said.

"Whatever happened to that one you were seeing . . . that Peter lad? A sailor, he was."

"I've told you, Mum. He was killed in the war. Early on."

"That's right, you did. What a shame, that. He sounded like such a nice lad, too. And none since? In all this time?"

"Well, they're a bit thin on the ground just now, aren't they?" Gladys said. "I mean, with a war on and all."

"I suppose they are," Mrs. Bigelow said.

"Just wait until the war's over and they all come back home. They'll be so tired of living in the trenches, with only other blokes for company, that they'll all be mad to find a girl. Then all of us unmarried girls, we'll just be able to pick and choose, won't we?" Gladys said, smiling, trying to jolly her mother into a better mood.

"I hope so," Mrs. Bigelow said.

"And I know so. No more of this silly talk from you. You're no trouble at all. I love to come home and tell you all about my day. What would I do if I didn't have you to talk to? Have to get a budgie, wouldn't I? And I can't stand the bloody things."

"Gladys!" Mrs. Bigelow said. "You shouldn't use such language. It's not ladylike."

But Gladys could see she was trying not to laugh. She kissed her mother's cheek and said she would have to start their tea, or they wouldn't be eating until midnight.

"Did the postman come today, Mum?" she asked on her way out of the sitting room.

"Yes, he brought a letter or two. Mrs. Karcher put them on the kitchen table."

Gladys picked up her marketing and walked down the short hallway into the kitchen. She put her groceries away in the icebox, then grabbed her pinafore from its hook on the back door and tied it around herself. She was worried about her mother. Her spirits were often poor, but lately the bouts of tears and anxiety had grown more frequent. She had talked to Dr. Morse about it just yesterday, and he said low spirits were common in the housebound. She'd asked, too, if there was any hope that the palsy that afflicted her mother so badly—Parkinson's disease, the doctor called it—would ever improve.

"I'm afraid it will not, Miss Bigelow," he'd said. "Parkinson's is a progressive disease. It will continue to cause degeneration in the central nervous system. Your mother's motor functions, and her speech, will only grow worse. You must be prepared for that."

Gladys did not know what she would do when her mother got worse. It was hard enough to care for her now. She wished she could be at home with her all day, but that was impossible. She had to work. They needed the money that she earned. The neighbors were wonderful, of course, and looked in on her during the day, but what would happen when she could no longer walk at all? Or talk? Or eat?

Gladys sighed. She wouldn't think of that now. Not tonight. She would get the tea, that's what she would do. Then she would wash the dishes and get her mother to bed. And then scrub the floor or wash a few things. Anything to keep herself busy. Gladys needed to be busy. Being busy kept her from thinking too much.

She set a pot of water to boil on the stove and smiled as she turned the knob on her new cooker. She'd just bought it last week. The old one had finally given out, and the man at Ginn's Appliances said it would be better to buy a new one than to keep repairing the old one. So she had. She'd splurged on a deluxe model. It was the best one in the shop Mr. Ginn had said—all cream enamel with bits of green here and there, four burners, a grill, and a roomy oven. It was a gas oven and ever so much nicer than the old one, which had been coalfired. There was just one thing to be careful about, Mr. Ginn had said, and that was to make sure the knobs were turned off completely when she was finished using it.

"Otherwise, you'll gas yourself to death, Gladys," he said, "and we certainly don't want that. You're one of me best customers!"

She was, too. Just last year, she'd bought the icebox from him.

When Gladys had the potatoes boiling and the peas opened and on the stove, she set the table. Then she turned her attention to the day's post. There was a bill from the gas company and something from the savings and loan about buying war bonds. There was another envelope, too—a small buff-colored one with her name and address on it and nothing else, no return address. The postmark was from Camden Town. It had been mailed yesterday. Puzzled, Gladys opened it. She gave a small cry when she saw what was inside.

"Gladys? Was that you?" her mother called from the sitting room. "Are you all right?"

Gladys swallowed hard. "I'm fine, Mum!" she called back. "Just burned myself on the pot handle, that's all."

"Be careful, love."

"I will."

Gladys stared at the ugly photograph in her hand. It was of her. Max von Brandt had taken it nearly four years ago. In a boarding-house in Wapping. Feeling sick to her stomach, she turned it over. There was nothing written on the back of it. There was nothing else in the envelope. There was no message at all, but there didn't have to be. It was a warning. Something had gone wrong. And the person who'd sent the photograph was telling her she'd better put it right.

But what could have gone wrong? Whatever it was, Gladys was certain it involved Jennie Finnegan. She immediately thought back to last night, and the conversation she'd had with her on the bus on their way home from the suffrage meeting; she'd been able to think of nothing else the entire day.

Jennie had wanted to know about Max. She'd wanted to know what was in the envelope Gladys had given her. She'd even talked about going to the authorities. Had she actually done so? Could she have been that foolish? Gladys had warned her. She'd told Jennie to not open the envelope, to deliver it just as she'd always done, or she'd find out exactly what Max von Brandt was capable of. Surely Jennie had listened to her.

But if Jennie *had* listened, then why had this picture been sent?

Maybe, a small voice inside her said, someone else had been listen-ing, too. There had been other people on the bus—a handful of men. Was it possible one of them was working for Max, had been told to watch his couriers, and had overheard them? Yes, Gladys realized with a cold dread, it was. Anything was possible where Max von Brandt was concerned.

The photograph was a warning, all right—a warning to her to keep Jennie Finnegan in line.

"My God, what am I going to do?" Gladys whispered, numb with fear.

If Jennie decided to open the envelope, and discovered what was really in it, she would certainly go to the authorities. And when she did, government men would come for her—Gladys. She would be arrested, tried, and found guilty of treason. If she wasn't executed, she would spend her life in jail.

To prevent this, she would have to frighten Jennie. She'd have to intimidate her into continuing to deliver Max's envelopes. But how? She believed that Jennie honestly hadn't known she was helping German spies smuggle British military secrets to Berlin. Jennie was an innocent; Max had told her he was on Britain's side and she believed him. But for some reason, she now no longer believed him. And what was she, Gladys, supposed to do about that? Force an innocent woman to betray her own country? Even if she had an idea how to go about such a thing, she had no stomach for it. She would not do to someone else the dreadful thing Max von Brandt had done to her.

Just as she had the first time Max had shown her the pictures, Gladys once again thought of killing herself. But now, as then, she could not bring herself to do it, because she did not want her mother to be taken to a home where no one would look after her properly.

"What am I going to do?" she whispered again, in despair.

Moving woodenly, she tore the picture into bits and put the pieces into the rubbish bin. She opened the tin of pineapple rings, took the gammon steaks out of the icebox, put them in a bowl, and poured the juice from the tin over them. While they sat in their marinade, she mashed the potatoes, drained the peas, then added butter and salt to both. Next, she put the kettle on for a pot of tea, struck a match, and lit the grill. As the gas hissed, then whooshed into bright orange flames, she found her answer.

When she finished grilling the steaks, she put them on two plates and decorated them with the pineapple rings. Then she put the mash and peas on the table, followed by tea made in the best teapot. The meal looked very inviting. She thought her mother would like it very much.

"Tea's ready, Mum!" she shouted as she went down the hall to get her mother. "It looks good, if I do say so myself. I hope you've an appetite tonight."

Gladys helped her mother down the hallway to the kitchen and eased her into her chair.

"Sit down now, Gladys," Mrs. Bigelow said. "You must get off your feet for a bit."

"I will do, Mum. It's drafty in here. I'm just going to close the window so we don't get a chill."

She did so, and then kicked a floor rug up against the bottom of the back door. Just before she sat down, she turned the gas on for all four burners, the grill, and the oven, pretending, as she did, that she was turning them off. She knew that her mother, with her bad ears, would never hear the hissing.

"This is lovely, Gladys!" Mrs. Bigelow said, as she struggled to cut her steak with her trembling hands. "It's just the thing to take the gloom off a miserable, rainy night."

"Thank you, Mum. I'm glad you like it," Gladys said.

Mrs. Bigelow must've heard the sad, strange note in Gladys's voice, for she suddenly looked up. "You all right, Gladys?" she said.

Gladys nodded. She smiled.

She had wiped away her tears before her mother could see them.

CHAPTER NINETY-TWO

"SHALL WE TRY again, gentlemen?" Joe said, wheeling himself into Sir George Burgess's office. Sid Malone came in behind him. "Can hostilities cease for the duration of this meeting?"

Sid nodded. Burgess, standing behind his desk, did the same. "Please sit down," he said, gesturing to the two chairs on the opposite side of his desk.

Sid pulled one of the chairs out of the way of Joe's wheelchair, then sat down in the other. Burgess poured tea for both of them from a big silver teapot. He splashed some on Joe's saucer as he did.

"Forgive me. I usually have a girl to do this— you know her, Joe—Gladys Bigelow—but she hasn't come to work today. Most unlike her. I hope it's not the Spanish flu. Just sent my man, Haines, around to her flat to see what's going on. I hear your sister-in-law's laid up with it."

"She is, indeed," Joe said. "She's in hospital."

"I'm very sorry to hear it."

"Thank you, Sir George," Joe said. He paused, then said, "All right, then. Let's get down to business. We've a spymaster, von Brandt, whom, it seems, we can't touch, and we've a courier, Flynn, whom we can catch. We know where to find him, and when. What we don't have is our inside man. The person inside the Admiralty who's getting the information to the courier. Are we agreed on that much?"

Both Sid and Burgess said that they were.

"Good," Joe said, relieved. "That's a start."

He had brought Sid to Burgess's office at the Admiralty two days ago so that Sid could tell Burgess everything he'd told Joe about Max von Brandt and the man called Flynn. Without naming him, Sid had also told Burgess about his friend John, who'd been ferrying Flynn to the North Sea, and who'd saved Sid's life.

Burgess, alarmed, had wanted to immediately take John in for questioning and to nab Flynn, too. Sid had told him they could not immediately nab Flynn, for he only came to John's boatyard every fortnight. He'd also informed him that he would not allow John to be taken in or questioned, because to do so might endanger his life. He explained Billy Madden's role in the proceedings and told Burgess that Madden had threatened John and his family.

Burgess, however, made it clear he didn't care about Billy Madden or his threats; he wanted John, and he wanted him now. Sid refused to give John up, and the meeting had devolved into a shouting match.

"God only knows how much havoc this network has wreaked, how many deaths it's caused!" Burgess had yelled, banging his fist on the table. "I must have the name of your contact, Sid. I demand that you give it me."

"You what?" Sid said, leaning forward in his chair. "You *demand* it?"

"I do indeed."

Sid laughed. "I'm giving you nothing. No names, dates, or places," he said.

"I could have you arrested. It's certainly within my power."

"Go ahead. I'll deny everything I've told you. You'll look even more of a git than you already do."

"Now, see here!"

"No, *you* see here. You've no understanding—none at all—for the hardship that drove my friend to do what he's done," Sid said. "I'll not have him sacrificed."

"What about all the other men who are being sacrificed? Right this very minute. Because of a spy ring that is operating in London. What about them?" Burgess had asked.

Sid, glowering, said, "Well, we'd better sit down and hash out a plan then, hadn't we?"

And they'd tried, but they'd failed. Neither man would give an inch. Sid would do nothing to endanger John and his family. Burgess would give no guarantees that he would spare them. Sid had finally stormed out, disgusted. He and Joe had left Burgess's office no closer to capturing von Brandt's spy than they had been when they walked in.

"We got nothing done, Joe," Sid had furiously said afterward. "Bloody nothing!"

"Welcome to the wonderful world of politics, old son," Joe replied.

Now, two days later, they'd decided to meet again in Burgess's office, to see if they could work together to fashion a plan. Joe knew, as did they all, that they could not afford to leave the premises today without one. Too much was at stake.

"So, chaps," Burgess began now, "the question remains: How do we take Flynn without implicating Mr. Malone's friend?"

Sid, apparently, was ready for the question. "We don't," he said. "At least not right now."

Burgess raised an eyebrow.

"Hear me out," Sid said. "You don't want Flynn by himself. Flynn's low-hanging fruit. Take him and you break the pipeline from London to Berlin, sure . . . but for how long? Von Brandt, wherever he is, just puts another courier into play. There are probably a dozen of them in London right now, just waiting for the nod. If you want to stop the flow of secrets to Germany, you have to find out who the inside man is—the man in the Admiralty—and get him at the same time that you get Flynn."

"Go on," Burgess said, intrigued.

But before Sid could, there was a knock on the door.

"Come in!" Burgess barked.

A young man hurried into the room and closed the door behind him.

"My assistant, William Haines," Burgess said. "What is it, Haines?"

"Sir George," the young man said breathlessly, "there's been a rather important development in the matter we were discussing earlier, and I—"

"What matter would that be? We discussed several."

"Well, sir, it's one of rather sensitive dimensions. . . ." Haines paused, glancing at Joe and Sid.

"Speak freely, old chap," Burgess said.

"Thank you, sir, I shall. We have just received a communication from Haifa indicating that a person of particular interest—a Mr. Max von Brandt—is thought to have been killed in Damascus. By a person close to Lawrence. A chap by the name of Alden Williams."

"Well, that's good news. One less spymaster to worry about, but unfortunately, his protégés are still at large in London. Thank you, Haines," Burgess said, waving the man away.

"There is one other thing, Sir George . . . ," Haines said.

"Yes? What is it?"

"The matter of Miss Bigelow's whereabouts. I'm sorry to tell you that Gladys has been found dead in her home."

"What?" Burgess said, shocked. "Gladys is *dead*?"

"Yes, sir. We were all rather upset about it, I might add. It was gas inhalation. Given where she works—worked—the police notified us immediately. The press was already sniffing about. At our request, the police have put it about that she accidentally left the gas turned on. She'd just bought a new oven, you see. But they—and we—actually suspect she committed suicide."

"Good God, man. Why do you think that?" Burgess asked.

"Because sir, all four stove burners were turned on. One doesn't leave all four on accidentally. And the grill. And the oven. The kitchen window was shut tight, and there was a rug pushed up against the bottom of the door."

"I see," Burgess said.

"Miss Bigelow's mother was with her in the kitchen. She, too, died from gas inhalation. Miss Bigelow left no note, but the two officers who found her also found this in the rubbish bin. They pieced it back together and gave it to us," Haines said, handing Burgess a glued-together black-and-white photograph.

"Bloody hell," he said. "Thank you, Haines, that will be all for now," he added, pushing the photograph across the desk to Joe and Sid.

"Somebody was blackmailing her," Joe said, as Haines closed the door behind him. "She looks drugged in this photograph. Or drunk. Somebody slipped her something, took this picture, then used it to make her do what he wanted—which was to smuggle secrets out of your office. Bet you a hundred quid it's von Brandt. Or rather, it *was* von Brandt."

"Looks like we've got our inside man," Sid said. "Sooner than we thought we would. Only she's a woman. And she's dead."

Burgess was silent for a bit, then he shook his head and said, "No, it's not possible. There is simply no way that Gladys Bigelow took those documents to Flynn."

"How can you be sure?" Joe asked.

"Because we had her watched and followed. On numerous occasions."

"You suspected her?" Sid asked.

"Not at all. In fact, if there was one person I trusted above all, it was Gladys," Burgess said sadly, "but when war was declared, we watched everyone. As a matter of course. To be absolutely certain of them. I am quite sure that I myself am regularly followed. At least I hope I am."

Burgess paused to pour more tea, then continued. "I read the surveillance reports on Gladys myself. Her movements were as regular as the rain. She had her knitting club and her suffrage meetings. She did her marketing at Hansen's. Bought her clothes at Guilford's. On Sundays she took her mother to the park. There were no men in her life, not one. I can tell you with utmost confidence that Gladys Bigelow was not meeting German spies in smoky pubs or on the riverfront in the dead of night or anywhere else. So how the devil did the documents get from her hands to Flynn's?"

"You think there was yet another person involved?" Sid asked. "Someone who took the documents from Gladys and got them to Flynn?"

"There had to be," Burgess said.

"So we're only slightly better off than we were ten minutes ago. We've got the inside man accounted for, but now there's another courier to find. And we've no idea who he is," Joe said.

"I'm afraid so," Burgess said. "I'm also afraid that we cannot wait to find out who he is. When we first spoke, Sid, you told me your friend is scheduled to depart on his North Sea run on Friday— tomorrow. Flynn undoubtedly reads the papers, just like the rest of us. He'll find out that Gladys Bigelow is dead. Without her, he can't get his information and has no reason to stay in London. He'll go underground or leave England altogether. We'll lose him, and more importantly, we'll lose any information we could've squeezed out of him." Burgess looked at Sid. "We have to make a move. There is simply no other choice. I am asking for your help. Not demanding, asking."

Sid nodded. "Give me a few hours. I'll come up with something," he said. "Give me until tomorrow morning."

Burgess nodded. "Until tomorrow morning," he said.

There was another knock on the door. "I'm sorry to interrupt again, Sir George," Haines said, "but we've just had an urgent message for Mr. Bristow, from his wife."

"What is it?" Joe asked, alarmed.

Haines read from the piece of paper in his hand. "Mrs. Bristow asks that you meet her at the Whitechapel Hospital immediately. She says that your sister-in-law is in a very critical state and not expected to live much longer." Haines looked up at Joe. "I'm so terribly sorry, sir," he said.

CHAPTER NINETY-THREE

"HOW IS SHE?" Joe asked Fiona, as Sid wheeled him into the lobby of the Whitechapel Hospital.

Fiona, her eyes red with tears, shook her head.

"It won't be much longer," India said. She'd also been crying. She'd loosened the mask she'd been wearing on the quarantine ward; it was hanging around her neck. "She's been in and out of consciousness for the last few hours. She's been asking for you, Joe."

"Me?" Joe said, puzzled. "Why?"

India took a deep breath, then said, "She says she needs to tell you something—something that concerns Max von Brandt . . . and the Admiralty."

"*What?*" Joe said, stunned. "What does Jennie know about von Brandt and the Admiralty?"

"We're not sure. At first the nurses and the ward doctor—Dr. Howell—thought she was delirious," India said. "But she's persisted in her claims, and earlier this afternoon, when I came to visit her, she made me fetch her carpetbag from home. She wouldn't settle until I'd done it. There was an envelope in there. It contains carbons. She says they're from letters sent by Sir George Burgess at the Admiralty."

"My God. How did Jennie get those?" Joe asked.

"I don't know. She didn't tell me. The whole thing sounds mad, but after the other night—after all the things that Sid told us about Max von Brandt—I couldn't dismiss it. I had to bring you here."

"I'm glad you did, India. Can I go in to her?"

"Normally the hospital won't allow anyone but medical staff in a quarantine ward, but I've explained to Dr. Howell that Jennie has critical information that needs to be shared with a member of government and he's agreed to let you on the ward for ten minutes. The Reverend Wilcott's with her, too. He's her minister as well as her father, and clergymen have special privileges. You'll have to wear this," she said, handing a mask to Joe. "And I must tell you that you are taking a great risk. The Spanish flu, if contracted by an adult, is often fatal."

"Let's go," Joe said, without hesitating.

"Sid, Fiona . . . we'll be back shortly," India said.

"Please give her our love. Tell her James is fine. That his cousins are taking good care of him . . . ," Fiona said, her voice breaking with grief.

Sid went to her and put his arm around her. "Go," he said quietly to India and Joe. "Hurry."

After a brief elevator ride, India and Joe were at the doors to the quarantine ward, on the hospital's second floor. India tied Joe's mask around his nose and mouth, and then he followed her through the ward's large double-door entry.

He stopped short a few feet into the ward, momentarily stunned by the sheer number of people there, and by their suffering. He saw one woman coughing up blood, another struggling grievously for air. A man, skeletally thin, was moaning deliriously.

"Where is she?" he asked.

"She's down this way," India said. "Are you all right?"

"I will be," he said.

He and India continued down the walkway. "Dad?" he heard a small, weak voice say, as they neared a bed in the center of the ward. "Dad, is that Joe? I thought I heard him. Will you get him for me?"

India stopped. Joe did, too. He looked at Jennie, but barely recognized her. She was horribly thin and her skin had a frightening blue tinge. Her breathing was labored. Her eyes were open. They were wild and glassy. He looked at the Reverend Wilcott, and the grief he saw in the older man's eyes was devastating.

"Dad!" she said again, louder this time.

"I'm right here, Jennie," the Reverend Wilcott said, rushing to take her hand.

"I need my bag," she said. Her voice was thin and agitated.

"It's right here, Jennie. Please calm down. You mustn't worry yourself over—"

"Please, Dad!"

"All right . . . yes, yes . . . it's here, right here," the Reverend Wilcott said, pulling a carpetbag out from under the bed. "What do you need from it?" he asked.

"There's an envelope inside it," she said. "Get Joe, Dad. Promise me you will. Get him and give him the envelope and tell him to read what's inside of it. Tell him—"

"Jennie, darling, Joe's here. He came. He's right here," the reverend said.

Jennie tried to sit up, but could not. Her father caught her in his arms and helped her.

"Jennie, what is it?" Joe said gently, wheeling himself over to her and taking her hand.

Jennie coughed hard; blood dripped from her nose. As her father wiped it away, Joe could see the effort it cost her to talk, to merely breathe, and he knew that she was fighting—not for her life, which was lost, but for a few extra minutes.

"I have to . . . I have to tell you something. In 1914, Max von Brandt came to me. . . ."

So it's true, Joe thought. No. God, no. Not you, Jennie.

". . . He told me he was a double agent and that he needed help smuggling forged papers to Germany, in order to get German dissidents out of the country. He told me I would receive an envelope—"

"From Gladys Bigelow," Joe said.

Jennie nodded. "How do you know?" she asked him.

"Gladys killed herself. We think she was being blackmailed," Joe said. "Jennie, we think Max is dead, too," he added, hoping it would give her some comfort.

Jennie closed her eyes. Tears slipped down her cheeks. A few seconds passed before she could continue. When she started speaking again, she sounded even weaker.

"He told me to put the envelope in the basement of the church, inside the statue of St. Nicholas, and that a man would come for it. He told me I'd be helping him save innocent people. And so I did it. But he lied. I opened the envelope last week. I should have done it years ago." She pushed her bag toward Joe. "It's in there. Take it. He's a spy and I've been helping him. All these years. They know, Joe. About Seamie. About all the ships. The Germans know. Please help him . . . help Seamie. . . ." She stopped talking, closed her eyes, and collapsed back against her father.

Joe opened the envelope. His blood froze in his veins as he saw the carbons from Burgess's office. He held one after another up to the light and read information on ships—their names, captains' names, the size of their crews, their whereabouts.

"Jennie . . . ," he started to say.

"Don't," the Reverend Wilcott said, crying. "She hasn't the strength. Can't you see that?"

But Jennie opened her eyes again. She looked at Joe.

"When were you supposed to put the envelope in the basement? What day exactly?"

"Wednesdays," Jennie said. "The day I always clean the sacristy."

"Does the courier—Max's man—pick them up on Wednesdays?"

"I don't know. I never checked. Every time I went down with a new one, the old one was gone," Jennie said.

"Thank you, love," Joe said. He squeezed her hand tightly. "We'll fix it, Jennie. I promise you. We'll set it to rights."

Jennie gave Joe a tearful smile. "Take care of James," she said. "Promise me you will. Tell him that I loved him . . . that he was always my beautiful boy, no matter what happens. Will you tell him that? Will you?" she said, suddenly agitated again. "Please tell him that. . . ."

"Shh, Jennie. Of course I will. James is fine. He's with his cousins and they're taking good care of him. He sends his love to you. Fiona and Sid, too."

Jennie closed her eyes. "Tell Seamie I love him, too . . . and tell him I'm sorry," she murmured.

"Oh, my darling girl, you've nothing to be sorry for. Nothing at all. Do you hear me, Jennie? Do you?" the Reverend Wilcott said.

But it was too late. Jennie was gone. The reverend leaned his head against hers and wept. India went to him. She put a soft hand on his back. Joe, still holding the envelope, quietly left them. A nurse stopped him outside the ward, took his mask off, and had him wash his hands. Then he went to find Fiona and Sid again.

"She's gone," Joe said, when he saw them.

Fiona shook her head. "James is home with Mr. Foster and the children. How will I tell him his mother is gone? How will I tell Seamie?" she asked. She wiped her eyes.

"Fiona, love," he said. "I'm sorry, but I have to go now. I'll be back and I'll do my grieving later, but if I don't get to Sir George right away, we might all be grieving another family member soon— Seamie."

"What Jennie told you . . . the things you asked her . . . they all have to do with what Sid told us the other night, don't they? With John Harris and Madden and Max von Brandt?"

"Yes, they do," Joe said. "Seamie's in great danger. Many men are."

"Go," Fiona said tearfully. "And for God's sake, stop that man Flynn."

Fiona went to wait for India, and Joe took Sid aside. He quickly explained to him exactly what he'd learned from Jennie.

"I'm going to the Admiralty," he told him. "I've got to tell Burgess what I just found out. Are you coming?"

"You go," Sid said. "Tell Burgess what you know, but give me the envelope."

"Why?"

"It's our only chance of catching Flynn. You said Jennie doesn't know what day he picks up the envelope. Maybe it's Wednesday. But maybe we'll catch a bit of luck and it's today—Thursday. If it is, we've got to make sure it's there—just like it always is—or he'll spook. If we're really lucky, he hasn't read about Gladys. And he can't know about Jennie—why would he? Hopefully, he'll come today, take the envelope, go on his merry way, and show up at the boatyard tomorrow night, right on time. Only difference is, I'll be there waiting for him. And you'll be waiting for me. Upriver. With a carriage."

Joe smiled.

"I'll meet you at your house," Sid said. "Tomorrow night. At five o'clock. Tell Burgess he's to be there, too. Waiting upriver with you."

"I'll have the carriage ready. Anything else I can do?" Joe asked, handing Sid the envelope.

"Yes, one other thing," Sid said.

"What?"

"Hope like hell we're not too late."

CHAPTER NINETY-FOUR

"HE'S NOT COMING," Sid said.

"He is. He's never here on the dot. Sometimes it's ten. Eleven. Midnight. It's always different," John Harris said.

"Something spooked him."

"The rain slowed him. It's pissing it down, in case you haven't noticed."

"He's twigged. I know he has. He's a wily one, our boy. He's managed to not get himself captured all these years. He's cagey and cautious and he can likely smell trouble from ten miles away. He'll not come tonight. I know it."

John threw the hand he was playing down on the table. "You're a right old woman, you know that, Sid?"

It was Friday night, nearly eleven o'clock. Sid and John were sitting playing spoil-five in the hold of John's lighter, which was moored at Billy Madden's boatyard. Sid's mind wasn't on his cards, though. He was too tense. John was as well, though he was doing a better job of not showing it.

They were waiting for Flynn. Sid had taken the envelope Jennie had given Joe and hidden it in the basement of St. Nick's, inside the broken statue of the saint. He'd done it immediately after he'd left the hospital, but had he been early enough?

He had no idea when Flynn came through the tunnels to pick up the envelope. What if he'd come earlier in the week? What if he'd heard about Gladys Bigelow? Burgess's office had told the newspapers to hold their stories for a day, but they couldn't keep Gladys Bigelow's neighbors and friends from talking. Or her landlord. The man who'd sold her a pound of apples the day before. Or the newsagent at the corner.

So much depended on timing tonight. On sheer bloody luck. Burgess needed Flynn. He needed to find out from him just how much Berlin knew. Sid needed him, too. He needed to find out how much trouble his brother Seamie was in. And John needed him. He needed Flynn to show up and get on the fucking boat. Now. He needed to look as if he was headed to the North Sea, as usual, so he could get a good three days' head start before Madden figured out he was gone for good.

"Go above and see if he's—" Sid started to say. And then they both heard it—the sound of footsteps on the dock. Sid rose from the table wordlessly and positioned himself so that he was close to the ladder, but so that Flynn would not see him as he came down it. John had told him that Flynn always climbed down facing the rungs.

Sid saw a pair of booted feet, then strong, slim legs, a satchel hanging down from a shoulder strap, and then the rest of what was a good-sized man. Looking at him, Sid was glad he'd taken Joe up on the offer of a pistol earlier in the evening.

As Flynn climbed down the last rung of the ladder, Sid stepped forward noiselessly and pressed the barrel of the gun to the back of his head. He cocked the trigger. The sound it made was unmistakable. Flynn froze.

"That's far enough, old son," Sid said. "Hands up now, where I can see them."

Flynn did as he was told. And then, just as Sid was going to snap a handcuff around one of his wrists, Flynn suddenly ducked, whirled around, and drove his fist into Sid's gut, knocking the wind out of him.

Sid staggered away from the ladder, his hands clutching his gut, trying to breathe, and Flynn scrambled up it.

No! Sid shouted silently, stumbling toward the ladder. But John was ahead of him. He shot up the ladder in a blur of speed, wrapped one arm around Flynn's neck, grabbed a fistful of his hair, and drove the man's head into a ladder rung.

Flynn screamed in pain. His hands came off the ladder. He lost his balance and fell, with John still hanging on to him. Both men crashed to the floor. John gave Flynn no time to recover. He was nowhere near as big as Flynn, but he was quick. He straddled the man and started throwing vicious jabs to his face. Flynn swung wildly at him, trying to knock him off. John ducked some blows and took others, but they didn't stop him. They didn't even slow him. He was fighting for his life—his and his family's.

Sid, in the meantime, had caught his breath. He found the handcuffs he'd dropped and snatched them off the floor. Flynn, already bleeding and bruised, was no match for two men. In a matter of minutes, Sid and John were able to cuff his hands behind his back, gag him, and bind his ankles.

"Well done," Sid said to John when they'd finished with him. Sid was breathing heavily. John was bleeding. But they'd both be fine.

"For a minute there, I thought we'd lost him," John said.

"Me, too. I—"

"John!" a voice bellowed from above. "John Harris!"

Sid and John froze. They knew that voice. It was Billy Madden.

"John! You down there?"

"Go up!" Sid hissed at him. "Act like you're waiting for Flynn."

"Right here, Billy!" John shouted.

Flynn's eyes followed him. Sid picked up a long, thin, horribly sharp knife that John used for cutting lines. He quietly bent over Flynn.

"One sound from you and I go up and shoot Madden. Then I come back down here. I won't shoot you, though. I'll cut your throat," he said. "Ear to ear and very slowly."

Flynn's eyes widened. He nodded.

"Where's Flynn?" Billy barked when John was abovedecks.

"He hasn't shown yet," John said.

Billy swore. "Bastard owes me money. Or rather his master does. I was getting an envelope every month, nice and regular. This month I've got nothing. You tell him—"

"Billy! Come on, darlin'!" a voice called. A woman's voice. It sounded farther away. "You said we wuz going to the Casbah, not a manky old boatyard!"

"Shut your mouth, you silly bitch!" Billy shouted. "Or I'll throw you off the dock!"

"Billeeee!" the woman whined.

"She doesn't watch herself, I'll have another body for you to dump off Margate," Billy said darkly. "Anyways, when Flynn shows up, you tell him I want to see him. The minute he sets foot back on land. I'm running a business here, not a charity."

"Aye, Billy, I'll tell him."

"When are you back?"

"Three or four days, as usual. Should be fair on the way out. Might get some weather on the way back. If we do, it'll slow us."

"Come see me when you're done. I've got another job for you. Paintings this time. Got 'em out of a big manor house in Essex. They need to go south."

"Will do."

Sid heard footsteps on the dock. He waited for John to come back belowdecks, but it was a good, and nerve-racking, ten minutes, before he did.

"Christ, lad, where were you? I'm nearly shitting meself here!"

"Making sure Billy was gone."

"Is he?" Sid asked.

"Aye. I watched him. Waited till he and his tart got back in his carriage."

"Let's go," Sid said.

John didn't need telling twice. He'd already untied the lines. Minutes later, he had the boat's engine going and they were off. They needed to make Millwall by one o'clock, and it looked like they would. About half an hour later, John and Sid were bringing the boat alongside a small dock behind the Wellington, a riverside pub. To both men's great relief, Maggie Harris and her children were on the dock waiting for them.

"Come on! Hurry!" John hissed at them, not even bothering to tie up. One by one, he got his family on board, looking fearfully about the whole time.

Earlier that day, Sid had gone to John and Maggie's rooms. He'd given Maggie five hundred pounds, an enormous sum of money that she'd been terrified to take, and a piece of paper with two addresses on it—one in Inverness, one in Point Reyes.

"You'll go to Inverness first," he had told her. "To Smythson's Estate Agents. A man there—Alastair Brown—will look after you. There's a little house waiting for you there. Rent's all taken care of. When the war ends and you can travel across the Atlantic again, you can sell your boat, get yourselves to New York, and then to California. I'll be waiting there for you. Hope you like cattle. I've got four hundred head."

Maggie had burst into tears then, and Sid had had to wait until she'd calmed down to explain the rest of the plan to her. He had to make sure she was listening, that she understood what he was telling her. There was no room for error.

When she'd dried her eyes, he told her that just before teatime, she and the children must leave their rooms with nothing but the clothes on their backs, and that they must get to Millwall, to the Wellington, check into the room he'd booked under a fake name, and stay there.

"You lot," he'd said to three of the older children, "you leave home one by one. As if you're going out to see a friend, or do an errand. Maggie, you take the others, and your basket, as if you're going to the market. No suitcases, you understand? You mustn't look as if you're leaving. Madden's got eyes and ears all over East London."

Maggie said she understood. The children all nodded.

"Good. Get yourselves to the Wellington and stay in the room. Just before one o'clock in the morning, get downstairs to the dock in back of the pub and wait there. Do it as quietly as you can. John and I will come for you then. Don't say a word about any of this to anyone."

As soon as the last of John's brood was belowdecks, with a caution to leave the man lying on the floor there alone, Sid pushed off, John gunned the engine, and they were under way again. It took only a quarter of an hour to get to their second destination, a Millwall wharf. BRISTOW was painted on the old brick building, in tall white letters. Two men were waiting for them on the dock there—one was in a wheelchair, the other was pacing and smoking a cigar.

Burgess stopped pacing when he saw the boat, and went to the edge of the dock to catch the line Sid threw him. When the boat was tied, Sid went belowdecks, cut the ropes that bound Flynn's legs, and told him to climb the ladder. Sid helped him from below, since his hands were still cuffed, and John from above. Together they got him off the boat and onto the dock.

"George, Joe," Sid said, "I'd like you to meet Jack Flynn."

Sir George shook his head in amazement. "I'll be damned," he said. "You did it."

"Keep hold of him," Sid cautioned, making Flynn sit down on the dock. "He's slippery as an eel."

Sid turned back to John. "Go now," he said quietly. "Get out of London. Get out of the life."

John nodded. "Sid, I . . . I don't know how to thank you."

"Because of you, I get to watch me kids grow up. That's all the thanks I need," Sid said. "Go. The more distance you can put between yourself and Billy Madden, the better."

"I'll see you again, Sid," John said. "One day."

Sid smiled. "You will, John."

Sid untied the line and threw it to John. He waved as the boat pulled away from the dock. He hoped he would see John again. He truly did. He wanted things to go well for John and his family, but there were no guarantees. It took a long time to outrun your old life. He knew that well enough.

Sid gave one last wave, then he turned around. "That's one problem solved. Now, let's get Mr. Flynn up and out of here," he said.

He and Sir George hoisted Flynn to his feet. They half marched, half carried him down the dock, to the warehouse. Joe came behind them in his chair.

"Were you able to get the telegram sent off?" Sid asked Burgess.

Ever since he'd seen the contents of the envelope Jennie had given Joe, with all of its information on British ships in the Mediterranean, Sid had been worried sick about Seamie. As they left the hospital where Jennie had been quarantined, Joe had promised him he'd get Sir George to telegraph warnings to naval command in the Mideast and to the ships themselves.

"We were," Burgess said now, "but it's a long and arduous chain of telegraphing to get a message from London to the Mideast. We cabled our offices in Haifa and we cabled the *Exeter* herself, but we're still awaiting confirmations. We hope to have them in another day or two."

"Thank God," Sid said. "That's a relief. A huge, bloody relief."

Sid, Burgess, Joe, and their prisoner were just about to enter the warehouse when they were hailed from the dock by a boat that had just pulled up to it.

"Jack Flynn!" shouted a male voice. "This is Chief Superintendent Stevens, of Scotland Yard. You are under arrest. Give yourself up immediately!"

"What the——" Joe started to say.

"Bloody hell!" Sid bellowed, as a beam from a bull's-eye lantern was shined in his face, blinding him.

"Stop! All of you!" It was the voice again. "Grab them!"

Sid heard footsteps—many of them—on the dock. Within seconds, he, Joe, and Sir George were surrounded by police officers.

"Who are you? What are doing? What is the meaning of this?" Burgess spluttered.

"I'm Chief Superintendent Stevens," a tall man in uniform said. "I'm here to arrest Jack Flynn on suspicion of receiving stolen property. I'll be taking you in for questioning as well."

"You'll be doing nothing of the sort!" he said, blocking Stevens's access to Flynn.

Stevens gently, but firmly, pushed Burgess aside. "Your name, sir?" he said to Burgess, as he took Flynn's arm and pulled the man toward him.

"Do you not *know* who I am, you damned ninny? I am Sir George Burgess, Second Sea Lord! Put your hands on me again, and I'll personally see to it that you're demoted to constable. Walking the beat in a one-horse village in Cheshire! Unhand that man! He's a German spy."

Stevens gave a quick nod to one of his men. In a twinkling, the officer had slapped handcuffs on Burgess, Joe, and Sid.

"You're making a mistake, Chief Superintendent," Joe said.

Stevens turned to him. "Am I now? And who might you be?"

"Joe Bristow, MP for Hackney. Sir George is right about Flynn—he's a German operative. I can prove it. He has an envelope on him. It contains carbons of letters written by Sir George and stolen from his office. The letters detail secret information on the whereabouts of British ships—information that Flynn's been passing to Berlin via ships in the North Sea. Open it. You'll see."

Stevens weighed Joe's words. Looking skeptical, he walked over to Flynn and opened the man's jacket. He found a large yellow envelope, folded over, inside the breast pocket and pulled it out.

Sid, who'd been holding his breath, quietly let it out, relieved. That was the same envelope Joe had received from Jennie. He recognized it. Now Stevens would see that they were right. He'd release them and allow them to take Flynn with them, to be held and questioned by Burgess and the Secret Service.

Stevens opened the envelope. He looked inside and smiled, then he tilted it and poured its contents—an assortment of diamonds, rubies, and emeralds—into his hand. Some of his officers moved in for a closer look.

"You're looking at about fifty thousand pounds' worth of stones, lads," he said. "Stolen from a jewelers' in Brighton and bound for Amsterdam." He threw a dark look in Joe's direction. "I don't know who those three are, or what they're doing here on a wharf in the middle of the night with Jack Flynn, but I mean to take them in and find out. What I do know is that Flynn is a notorious fence. We've been following him for some time, but we've never been able to catch him with the goods on him. Not until tonight, eh, Jack?" Stevens said, winking at Flynn. He carefully poured the jewels back into the envelope. "I only wish we'd been able to catch the boatman, too. The one who's been helping Flynn get his swag to Holland. He was moving too fast, though. It was either follow him or nab Flynn. Take them aboard, lads. All of them."

The three men were seated together on the deck of the boat. Joe's chair was secured so that it could not roll about the deck as the boat turned and maneuvered back upriver. Flynn was taken belowdecks. Sid looked at him as he was walked past them, and he could've sworn that he saw the ghost of a smile on his face.

"This is preposterous. A complete and utter farce!" Burgess spat, when they were under way. "It was the same envelope that came from Jennie Finnegan. The very same. I'm positive of it," he added. "There was even a carbon smudge on the flap. I distinctly remember it. What the devil happened?"

"Someone got to Flynn," Sid said. "Told him he was about to get nicked. Someone who didn't want him sent down as a spy. They got to the envelope, too. They took out the carbons and put in the jewels. Told him to go through with the run as usual. That's all worrying . . . but what's really worrying is that the someone is powerful enough to get the Yard to play along with it all."

They all fell silent as Sid's words sank in, then Burgess said, "But why? Why not just tell him to bolt? To get out of London? Go underground? Why go through the whole elaborate charade of arresting him as a fence? And taking us in, too? I'm sure they'll hold us for all of ten minutes, then release us with full apologies."

"Because that same someone wanted to prove us wrong. To discredit us. To put paid to our theories about von Brandt, Flynn, and Gladys Bigelow. Make it all look like utter nonsense," Sid said.

"But who would want to do that? Who else knew?" Burgess said. "Whom did you tell?"

"No one," Joe said.

"Likewise," Sid replied. "No one knew except the three of us. Unless *you* told someone, Sir George."

"I told Churchill. He told Asquith," Burgess said. "It can only mean one thing . . ."

"That Churchill's working for the kaiser," Sid said drily. "And Asquith, too."

Joe laughed, but his eyes turned hard and his voice grim as he said, "It means that Max von Brandt is still alive. He has to be. Because someone, someone quite high up, is working very bloody hard to protect him."

CHAPTER NINETY-FIVE

WILLA HEARD A woman singing, soft and low. She had heard the song before, but she couldn't remember where. Gentle hands sponged her brow, her cheeks, her neck. Her body felt cool. The terrible burning had stopped. She felt peaceful and light, as light as a desert breeze. She felt as if she were floating in a clear oasis lake, and that Seamie was nearby. She wanted to stay this way forever. In this beautiful place. With Seamie. And yet she could not, for something was not right. There was something she was supposed to remember, something she was supposed to do.

She sat up with a gasp and opened her eyes. "Lawrence," she said hoarsely. "The maps . . . I have to get to Lawrence. . . ." Her head started spinning from the sudden motion. She groaned.

"Shh, Willa Alden. Lie down," a woman's voice said. "Lie down now."

Willa looked behind herself, in the direction the voice had come from. A Bedouin woman stood there, wringing out a cloth over a basin. She turned around and smiled. Willa knew her face.

"Fatima?" she said. "Is that you?"

"It is."

"Fatima, I have to get to Lawrence. I have to tell him about the maps. I have to go."

Fatima hurried to the bedside and eased Willa back against her pillow. "Everything is fine. Just fine. Now, lie down."

"But there's a trap. The Turks are waiting for Lawrence!"

"Lawrence is safe. Faisal, Auda, Khalaf al Mor—all of them are safe. Do you not remember?"

"No. I . . . I can't remember anything. Everything's so hazy. Where are they?"

"In Damascus, of course."

Willa blinked. "You mean . . . ," she started to say.

Fatima smiled. "They have taken the city, Willa. Damascus is in the hands of the British, and Arabia, at long last, is once again in the hands of the Arabs. Allah be praised!"

Willa closed her eyes. She whooped for joy, then laughed out loud, then started to cough.

"Quiet yourself, please," Fatima scolded. "You have been very ill. It was cholera. We despaired of your life. More than once. You are not out of danger yet and must spend many days recovering."

"Tell me what happened, Fatima. My mind is so foggy. I remember being at a village with some goatherds, and nothing after that," Willa said.

"You rode almost all the way into Lawrence's camp," Fatima said, "but it was his old camp. Lawrence's riders found you, though you were half-dead when they did, so I am not surprised you remember nothing. You talked of maps. Lawrence searched your saddlebags after you were brought into camp. He found all that you had brought him. He saw how the Turks had positioned themselves, how they had set a trap for him."

"What did he do?"

"He avoided it, of course! He and his troops rode east of the Turks. Beni Sakhr, Howeitat, Rwala—all rode as one. They skirted the danger. The English sheik Allenby met them at Damascus, and together they took the city."

"They did it, Fatima," Willa whispered.

"Indeed they did," Fatima said. "Because of you, Willa Alden. Had you not arrived with the maps when you did, they would have ridden directly towards the Turkish soldiers and would have been attacked."

"How do you know all this?" Willa asked.

"We have had a messenger from Damascus. A man whom Khalaf sent. Here, drink this. You must have water now."

Fatima helped her sit up a little and held the glass while Willa drank from it.

"Thank you," Willa said when she had finished.

"It is nothing," Fatima said. "Only a little water."

"I mean thank you for saving me, Fatima. More people die from cholera than survive it. I owe you my life now."

"Oh, no. Not me," Fatima said. "I did very little. The credit belongs to another."

"Really?" Willa said. "Who?"

"Captain Seamus Finnegan."

Willa thought she might be hallucinating again. "What did you say?" she whispered.

"Seamus Finnegan. He was in Haifa when he heard what had happened to you. Apparently, your brother, too, is in Haifa, and word got to him that an airplane you were riding in crashed in the desert." Fatima explained how Seamie had hunted for her and how he'd finally found her. "He brought you back here," she said, "and somehow, only Allah knows how, he kept you from dying. I only arrived when the worst was already over."

Seamie, here with her. In the desert. Willa couldn't believe it. It was so unreal that it made her head spin all over again. Her heart filled with love and gratitude and sadness for this man whom she loved so much, whom fate brought back to her again and again, and yet never allowed her to have.

"I *thought* he was here, Fatima," she said. "The whole time I was

sick, I thought he was here. I remember him talking . . . talking to
God, I think. No, talking to you. Asking you to bargain with God.
Asking Him to take Seamie's life and spare mine. But when I woke
up, I was sure I'd only dreamt it."

"You did not. He was truly here."

"Where is he now? Could you ask him to come, Fatima?" Willa
asked. "I want to see him."

Fatima looked at her sadly. "I cannot. He left camp. He's gone."

"But why? Why would he do such a thing? Why would he leave
without even saying good-bye?" Willa asked, stricken.

"He had to get to Haifa. To take command of a ship," Fatima said.

"Yes, I remember now. He told me he had to go," Willa said
tiredly. "Things are coming back to me, but in bits and pieces."

"He left a letter for you," Fatima said. She went to the small table
where the basin of water stood and picked up a piece of paper, folded
in two, that was next to the basin. Willa opened the letter with trembling hands and read it.

My darling Willa,

*I am sorry to leave you before you are awake, but I know that you
are out of the woods now and will only get better under Fatima's care.*

*I hope you will understand that I had no choice but to leave. I
am due to take command of the ship* Exeter, *and must get back to
Haifa quickly.*

*Perhaps someday I will see you again and you can tell me exactly
how you came to be riding alone through the desert, so sick and so
weary, with maps from the German high command in your possession.
I'm sure it will be a hell of a story. Most everything that you do is.*

*Take care of yourself, Willa. Please. You have no idea how close
you came this time. Closer, I think, than you came when you fell at
Kili. Stop punishing yourself. For my sake, if not your own. We've
made our mistakes. We're paying for them. But I don't know how
I'd go on if something happened to you. I don't know what I'd do if
you weren't there in my head, and my heart, every time I look up at
the night sky or smell the sea or climb to the top of something—a*

mountain, an ice wall, or a bloody great sand dune—just to see what's beyond it.

I love you, Willa. Whether it's bad or good, I love you. I always have and I always will. Don't you ever take that away from me.

Yours, Seamie

Willa folded the letter closed. She wished she could cry. Crying would help. But she couldn't. The pain she felt was too deep for tears.

Fatima took the letter and put it back on the table. "The letter has caused you grief. I can see it. I would not have given it to you if I had known it would. You must ask Allah for help. He listens. He hears. He answers our prayers. He has answered mine. He will answer yours. And Seamus Finnegan's, too."

Willa smiled tiredly. She was quite sure God listened to Fatima, but He did not listen to her. And she doubted He listened to Seamie, either.

She thought again of how Seamie had asked Fatima to ask God to spare Willa's life. He'd said he'd give his own, if only God would spare hers.

A sudden chill gripped her at the memory. Why had he said that? she wondered. He shouldn't have.

She fervently hoped that Fatima was wrong and that she was right. She hoped that God did not listen to Seamus Finnegan.

CHAPTER NINETY-SIX

"REPORT, MR. WALKER?" Seamie asked his lieutenant.

"All clear, sir. We've sighted nothing all morning. Not even a fishing boat."

"Strange," Seamie said. "Captain Giddings was certain he'd seen something. Right about where we are now. He was certain it was a German gunboat. Said he pursued her, but she eluded him."

"She must've realized she'd been spotted. Probably cleared off," Walker said.

Seamie, squinting out over the brilliant blue sea, nodded. "Could well be. Keep me informed, Mr. Walker."

"Of course, sir."

"Set a course for north-northeast, Mr. Ellis," Seamie said. "Tell the gunners to take their positions. I'd like to take a look around the northern coast of the island."

"Aye, aye, sir," the quartermaster said.

Seamie and the crew of the *Exeter* were patrolling off the coast of Cyprus. Shortly before they'd left port—about twenty-four hours ago—Peter Giddings, the captain of a ship that had just returned to Haifa to refuel—had come aboard to tell Seamie that he'd seen a German gunboat at the top of Famagusta Bay. He'd followed it, but the gunboat had disappeared around the island's northeastern tip. His fuel was low, Giddings said, or he would've given chase. He cautioned Seamie to keep his eyes open for the boat.

"I'm worried that Gerry may be using it as a decoy," Giddings said. "He may be hoping to draw us around the point, where other gunboats are lying in wait."

Seamie thanked him for the information, and shortly afterward the *Exeter* had left port. It almost didn't leave at all. At least, not with Seamie at the helm.

He'd only made it back to port by the skin of his teeth. He was due to assume command of the *Exeter* at 0800 hours today. He got back into town just before six A.M., on a camel. He rode the animal to Albie's house and banged furiously on his door. When Albie opened it, rumpled and bleary-eyed, Seamie handed him the camel's reins and rushed past him, saying he needed to bathe and shave. Luckily, he'd thought to leave his uniform with Albie. He was washed and dressed by seven. He ran back downstairs, told Albie that his sister was alive, if not exactly well. He explained what had happened, and where he could find her, and told him to take his camel to go fetch her. Then he slurped down a cup of tea, crammed a slice of toast into his mouth, and ran out the door. He made it onto the ship at exactly twelve minutes to eight.

It had been an uneventful few hours since he'd left port, but now, as the *Exeter* headed north-northeast, Seamie felt uneasy. He wondered if the gunboat had truly cleared off, or if Giddings was right and it was trying to lure them into a trap. They would have to proceed cautiously.

As he was about to leave the bridge to inspect his guns, the radio suddenly crackled and popped. He turned around. They were too far away from port to be receiving any messages from naval command in Haifa. This had to be a ship-to-ship communication, which told Seamie there was some urgency to it. Ensign Liddell, the radio operator, dove for his headphones. He started twiddling knobs and pressing buttons, and then suddenly he was scribbling furiously. He stopped writing once or twice to ask for clarification, and two minutes later, he signed off. He pulled his headphones off and stood up. Seamie saw that his usually ruddy cheeks had gone white.

"Captain, sir," he said, "we've just received a message from the captain of the *Harrier*, which is currently southeast of us, approximately halfway between us and Haifa. Since naval command cannot reach us, they've asked the *Harrier* to relay the following message from London, from Sir George Burgess himself."

"Read it," Seamie said tersely.

"We are ordered to abandon our position immediately and return to port."

"*What?*" Seamie said. "We just bloody got here!"

"The SSB has confirmed intelligence reports that a German fleet has moved into the southeast Mediterranean and is massing off the eastern coast of Cyprus, a fleet of—"

"Fleet? What fleet? There isn't one bloody boat here!" Seamie said. "Not one! This is madness! We can't turn around now!"

"Begging your pardon, Captain Finnegan," Ensign Liddell said. "Allow me to clarify. Not a fleet of war ships . . . a fleet of U-boats."

The bridge went completely silent.

"Mr. Ellis," Seamie said, "Bring her about. Now. Set a course for—"

He never got to finish his sentence. The first torpedo clipped the *Exeter*'s starboard bow. The second one broadsided her. She burst into flames, and ten minutes later she sank to the bottom of the placid blue sea.

PART THREE

DECEMBER
1918

LONDON

CHAPTER NINETY-SEVEN

"OI! MISSUS! IF I was yer husband, I'd poison yer tea!" a drunken heckler shouted.

"And if I was your wife, I'd drink it!" Katie Bristow shouted back, laughing cheekily.

The heckler scowled; the crowd in the packed market hall erupted into laughter. She'd just proved to every man and woman present that she was one of them—tough, scrappy, able to take a jab.

Joe, whose mouth had been set in a hard, angry line, whose hands had been clenched into fists, laughed, too. He'd wanted to wallop the bollocks who'd just shouted at her, but he knew that Katie would be angry with him if he so much as traded words with the man. She'd warned him about interfering at her speeches, no matter how unruly it got.

"Listen, Dad, you can't come if you're going to get shirty every time some silly bugger opens his gob," she'd said to him. "How will it look? Like I need my father to fight my battles for me, that's how. That won't go over well—not for Sam's campaign, and not for my own one day. So if you do come, you've got to keep quiet."

Joe had promised her he would. He didn't want to be banished. He didn't want to miss a single word his daughter said. She was a dazzling speaker—quick on her feet and inspiring. But it was so hard for him to keep quiet. He had many campaigns under his belt—for himself and for other Labour candidates he'd come out to support—and he well knew the ugliness of which crowds were capable. But nothing he'd ever encountered in his entire career as a politician matched the vulgarities thrown at Katie.

A general election had been called for December 10, and Katie, a

popular figure in East London with her pro-Labour newspaper and
pro-union activities, was spending her Christmas holiday stumping
for Samuel Wilson, Labour candidate for the Tower Hamlets seat,
which included Limehouse, where they were now. As soon as she'd
started campaigning for Wilson, the newspapers had jumped on
her—calling her unladylike and unnatural. Some of the people she'd
hoped to pull to Wilson's side called her far worse. Grown men cat-
called and heckled and said things better suited to a barnyard than a
public hall, things that would have made most women—and even
some men—blush and falter and run from the podium.

Not his Katie. She simply clasped her hands in front of her, waited
for her antagonist to finish, then gave it back to him twice as hard.

"Oh, Katie," Fiona had fretted, after she'd attended her daughter's first speech. "Those men were truly horrible. Doesn't it upset
you?"

"I don't let it, Mum," Katie said. "I can't. One day I'll be campaigning for myself, and that will be even tougher. I've got a chance
to learn how to deal with crowds now, during Sam's campaign. It's a
good way to gain experience. I've got to be able to take what people
throw at me and throw it right back at them."

Now, as Joe continued to listen to Katie, one bright spark pointed
out that she was a woman and that a woman's place was in the house.

"Oh, I couldn't agree more," Katie said, smiling her impish smile.
"That's partly why I'm here, you see. Because I very much want to
be in the house one day—the House of Commons."

There was a great deal of laughter, and she joined in, but then she
turned serious.

"Yes, I'm a woman," she said, suddenly steely-voiced. "And very
proud of it. The war is over now. Armistice Day has come and gone.
But let us never forget that it was women who held their homes together while their men were away. It was women who worked in the
munitions factories and then came home and scraped meals together
out of rations, night after night. It was women who kept families of
this country going single-handedly for four long years. So yes, I am
proud, but proud as I am, I do not stand here before you today and

ask you to vote for my candidate because I'm a woman, I ask you to vote for Sam Wilson because I'm a member of the Labour Party and he is, too."

Cheers went up—the first of the evening.

"You women out there—your country called upon you in her time of need, and you answered that call," Katie said, hotly. "You worked and sacrificed and went without, never knowing if you would see your sons, brothers, and husbands again. Some of you got telegrams telling you that you never will. Who will be there for you now? During *your* time of need?"

A group of women seated near the front of the hall burst into applause.

"You men—you did not ask for this wretched war, but you got it," Katie continued. "You endured a living hell on the banks of the Somme and the Marne. In the Atlantic Ocean. The Mediterranean Sea. Hundreds of thousands . . . no, *millions* of your comrades died, leaving behind grieving mothers and fathers, wives, children. Many of you have returned to us injured, unable to work, sometimes too damaged to ever rejoin society at all. You fought for us—now who will fight for you?"

A new cry went up—no catcalls, no insults, just one word, loud and strong: "Labour! Labour! Labour!" Katie did not hush the voices, but let them chant their battle cry until the rafters of the market hall shook with the noise.

When the crowd had quieted again, she said, "Ladies and gentlemen, we are not the same people we were four years ago. We live in a changed world now, one of war's making, and we cannot accept tired, old-world policies. Give Sam Wilson a chance, give Labour a chance, to represent you in this new world. You fought, you gave, you endured . . . now it's Labour's turn. Let Sam fight. Let him fight for better jobs for the men who've come back, for better pensions for the families of those who didn't. Let him fight for more hospitals for the injured, for more schools for the children of our courageous soldiers and sailors. Ladies and gentlemen of Limehouse, let Sam Wilson fight for *you*."

A roar went up. Hats went up in the air. Voices, some five hundred strong, chanted, "Wilson! Wilson! Wilson!"

As Joe looked at his daughter—her cheeks flushed, her blue eyes shining, her head held high—he thought he would burst with pride. He didn't know many twenty-year-old girls who were pulling down excellent grades in their final year of university, publishing their own newspapers, and campaigning on behalf of a would-be MP during their school holidays.

"Looks like the acorn doesn't fall far from the tree," a man beside him said.

Joe turned toward him. He knew his voice very well. "Why, if it isn't Jimmy Devlin," he said.

James Devlin was the editor and publisher of the *Clarion*, an East London newspaper. Katie printed her paper, the *Battle Cry*, on the *Clarion*'s presses.

"She's a brave one, Joe. I have to give her that. I've seen men— seasoned politicians—turn tail and run when confronted by crowds like this."

"She's the bravest woman I've ever known. Besides her mother, of course," Joe said.

"She's read this crowd right," Devlin said admiringly. "Telling them how the war's changed things. It certainly has. And not for the better. But not every candidate's coming out and saying that. Armistice Day was a month ago, but a lot of them are still beating the drum, talking about honor and glory and all of that. Not a lot of glory in death. Is there?"

Joe shook his head. Devlin was right. The war was over, and the world, weary and heartbroken, was grateful for it, but it had changed things forever. Nothing was the same. No family was untouched. His had certainly suffered its share of losses. Poor, damaged Charlie was still battling shell shock. His progress was painfully slow. Jennie was dead. And Maud. Seamie, too. His ship had gone down in the Mediterranean and his body had never been found. They'd had nothing to bring home, nothing to bury. His little son, James, nearly four years old, was now an orphan. Joe and Fiona had taken him in immediately, loving him every bit as much as if he'd been one of their own. He had no one else. Jennie's father, the Reverend Wilcott, had succumbed to the Spanish flu shortly after his daughter. The man behind Maud's death, and Jennie's tortured conscience, and likely Seamie's death, too—Max von Brandt—was thought to be dead. But Joe didn't believe it—no one had been able to confirm or disprove the reports from Damascus—and he doubted that anyone ever would.

India and Sid had returned to California. The Harrises, who'd ridden out the war in Inverness, had followed them. The hospital India and Sid had started at Wickersham Hall continued to take in war veterans and rehabilitate them. India had handpicked her successor, Dr. Allison Reade, a young woman whom Harriet Hatcher had recommended. India and Sid, together with Joe and Fiona, continued to fund the hospital.

"You finding time to campaign for your own seat?" Devlin asked.

"Just barely," Joe said. He'd been appointed leader of his party and, as such, was busy traveling the country, supporting candidates for seats in constituencies far away from London.

"Well, see that you don't lose it," Devlin cautioned. "This time out, Labour really does stand to make gains. I've seen the proof of it. At rallies all across London."

"I think the best we can hope for is that Labour gains and the Liberals win," Joe said. "It will still be some years before we see one of our own in Number 10. Very likely it won't happen in my time, but I'm hoping it will happen in Katie's. Perhaps I'll still be alive to see it."

"You're going to stay in the fray for some years, then?" Devlin asked. "No nice, peaceful retirement for you?"

"Chance would be a fine thing, Jimmy," Joe said.

"Why not? The war's over. Haven't you heard?" Jimmy joked.

"I have, but I wonder sometimes if the war—the one we're fighting, the same one we've always fought—will ever be over. It's hard, Dev. It tires a body after a while."

"Yes, it does," Devlin said. "Especially old bodies. Like ours."

Joe laughed. He was now fifty-three years old, and though there

were days—many of them—when he felt his age and longed to lin-
ger in his bed with a pot of tea and the morning papers, there were
many more days when he felt every bit as passionately committed to
the cause of social reform as he ever had. In fact, even more than he
ever had. In addition to becoming head of his party, he'd also taken
on the leadership of several government committees, on veterans'
affairs, education, and unemployment. Fiona had had mixed emotions about his taking on all this extra work at his age. She'd asked
him if he could maybe just take up stamp collecting and had wondered, as Devlin had, if he would ever live a peaceful life. But Joe
knew that he wouldn't, because there was no peace to be had.

The pain of what had happened to Charlie made sure that there
never would be. Not for him. Peace and contentment went out the
bloody window every time he saw his damaged son, and the other
poor ruined young men who still lived at Wickersham Hall and probably always would, because there was no other place for them. Peace
and contentment went out the window every time he rode through
the slums of East London, and the slums in Liverpool, Leeds, Glasgow,
and Manchester, and saw that the war that had changed everything
had changed nothing—not in those places.

"How about you, Dev?" Joe asked. "You're hardly a spring chicken.
Are you going to give it up anytime soon? Leave your typewriter and
take up fishing?"

Devlin snorted. "And leave London's news in the hands of Fleet
Street? Certainly not. Somebody's got to put the truth out there."

Joe smiled. James Devlin had, in his own way, been fighting the
good fight, too. He liked his blood and thunder—the murders and
robberies, all the blood and gore that sold newspapers—but he'd run
countless stories about dangerous working conditions at the docks
and the sweatshops, and threats to the public health from unsanitary
and crowded living conditions in the slums. In his own way, Devlin
had done as much as Joe had to bring the public's attention to the appalling privations suffered by the poor of East London, and Joe
knew that a strong sense of social justice was what got James Devlin
up in the morning.

"Tell you what," Joe said, offering Devlin his hand, "when we've won our war—that one that's still raging—then we'll worry about the peace. Not before. Do we have a deal?"

Devlin smiled. "We do indeed," he said, taking Joe's hand and shaking it.

Another huge roar went up from the front of the market hall. Both Joe and Devlin turned in time to see several members of the crowd surge up to the podium and lift Sam Wilson, who'd just finished his own speech, onto their shoulders. When they'd got him, they reached for Katie and lifted her up, too. Then they marched through the hall and out the door into the streets, where even more people were cheering.

"Should be quite a contest," Devlin said, watching Sam and Katie disappear down the street. He shifted his weight from one foot to the other, groaning a bit. "Arthritis," he said, shaking his head. "Plays up a lot more now than it ever did before. Glad it's the young ones fighting it, I must say." He pushed his hat back on his head. "Wouldn't miss it, though."

Joe smiled. "Nor I, Dev," he said. "Not for all the world."

CHAPTER NINETY-EIGHT

"HOLD STILL, OSCAR," Willa said. "Just a few more and I'll let you get up. I promise. The light's so amazing right now and it won't last much longer. The days are far too short in December. Look out the window, will you?"

Oscar Carlyle, a musician, crossed his hands over his trumpet, turned, and gazed out of the window.

"That's it . . . perfect!" Willa said.

His eyes widened, just as Willa knew they would. A smile played upon his lips. The light from the sunset, streaming in through the giant windows of Willa's west-facing atelier, did that to people. It captivated them. Enchanted them. It softened them, made them drop their guard, opened them up for a few seconds, just long enough for her to capture the breathless surprise, the sense of wonder, on their faces. Just long enough for her to snatch a tiny bit of their souls and affix it to film forever.

"The sun going down over Paris. What an incredible sight," Oscar said, in his hard Brooklyn voice. "How do you get any work done here? I'd be staring out of the windows all day."

"No talking!" Willa scolded. "You'll ruin the picture."

She took shot after shot, working as rapidly as she could in the last few minutes of light left to her. She wanted something magical out of this sitting, something extraordinary.

The sitting had been commissioned by *Life* magazine; they were doing a piece on Oscar, a young, avant-garde composer, and they wanted an equally avant-garde photographer to shoot him.

The war had ended a month ago, and the world was beginning to pick itself up and dust itself off. Already people were starting to clamor for news of something other than death, disease, and destruction. Some of Willa's recent assignments had included portraits of the Irish writer James Joyce and of the fiery Spanish painter Pablo Picasso.

When *Life*'s editors heard that Oscar was traveling from his home in Rome to Paris to perform there, they immediately wrote Willa to schedule the sitting. She'd only been in Paris about two months— since early November—and already she'd made a name for herself.

After another thirty-odd frames, the sun dipped beneath the city's rooftops; its last golden rays disappeared, and Willa put her camera down.

"That's it," she said. "We're done."

"Thank God," Oscar said, standing up to stretch.

"I think I got some good shots. You have an amazing face. Sensitive and intense. It's a photographer's dream."

Oscar smiled. "Well, let's hope my pretty face can sell out a few music halls," he said. "God knows my agent isn't."

"Have a seat on the divan," Willa said. "Make yourself comfortable. I won't be a moment."

"The very last thing I want to do is sit down again," Oscar said, walking over to a wall where various black-and-whites were tacked up. "I'd much rather look at your work. I've been wanting to nose around ever since I arrived."

Willa lived and worked in what used to be a milliner's atelier in Montparnasse, on Paris's Left Bank. She'd just moved in a fortnight ago from the flat she'd had near the river. The atelier was at the top of a dingy, rundown building, but the space was much larger than her old flat, filled with light, and quite cheap.

"Suit yourself," she said.

She carried her camera to her darkroom—a small alcove she'd made by hanging blankets around the atelier's lone, cold-water sink—and carefully set it down on the counter. She would develop the film later, when she was alone. Next to the sink was a syringe, a length of rubber tubing she used as a tourniquet, and a vial of morphine. She would attend to those later, too. When Oscar was gone. When the film was developed. When she'd got back from haunting the late-night cafes with her friend Josie. When there was nothing else to do and nowhere to go and she was all alone with her ghosts and her grief.

A doctor had given her the morphine when she'd first arrived in Paris. She told him she needed it to control the pain in her damaged leg. It was true, sort of. The leg didn't pain her so much anymore, but other things did. It was peacetime now, but there was no peace, not for her, and there never would be.

Willa took a half-empty wine bottle down off a shelf, tugged the cork out of it, and filled two glasses. "Cheers," she said, as she re-emerged from the darkroom. "Thank you for being such a wonderful subject."

Oscar seemed not to hear her. He was walking around her flat, peering at the photographs on the wall. She walked up to him and handed him one of the glasses. "I came to your concert, by the way. The one you gave two nights ago at the Opera. I loved it," she said. "What are you working on now?"

"A new symphony. A new musical language for a new world," he said absently.

"Is that all?" Willa joked, sipping from her glass.

Oscar laughed. "I sound like a jerk, don't I?" he said, turning to her. "Sorry, I was distracted. How could I not be? This is incredible," he said, pointing at a silvery black-and-white nude.

Willa glanced at the shot. It was a self-portrait. She'd taken it about two weeks ago and had exhibited it, along with a few other photographs, at a local gallery. It had caused quite a stir. Titled *Odalisque,* it showed her sitting on her bed, without her artificial leg, completely bare, her body taut and scarred. She had not modestly turned her gaze away from the camera, but instead had stared into it nakedly and challengingly. It had been called "shockingly brazen" and "subversive" by the mainstream press, but other, more forward-thinking critics had called it "brilliantly symbolic," "wrenching," and "a modern, war-torn Odalisque for our modern, war-torn world."

"Weren't you afraid? To be so naked? So vulnerable?" Oscar asked her.

"No, I wasn't," Willa said. "What's left to be afraid of? I'm scarred. Damaged. I'm missing pieces of myself. After the last four years, aren't we all?"

Oscar smiled sadly. "Yes," he said. "Yes, we are."

He kept walking from one shot to the next. Some were framed. Some were simply pinned to the wall. More were fastened with clothespegs to a length of rope stretched from one end of the room to the other.

"I've never seen anything like these," he said quietly.

"No," Willa said. "Most people haven't. Which is the whole point, I suppose."

The shots Willa had taken were not pretty images of children and parks and bourgeois Parisians out for a Sunday stroll. They were photographs of prostitutes and pimps. Shots of armless and legless soldiers, begging on the streets. A drunk man lying in the gutter. A skinny, dirty girl singing for pennies outside of a restaurant. They were ugly, many of them, harsh, raw, and utterly compelling.

They showed the souls of a war-weary people, and they showed her own soul, for Willa poured everything inside her—her emotion, her passion, and her sorrow—into them. Her art was the only solace she had, the only thing that allowed her to express the inexpressible— the sadness and anger she felt at having survived the great war and its horrors, only to wish she hadn't.

"There are so many," Oscar said quietly. "You must never sleep."

"No, not if I can help it," Willa said. "I'm sitting down, even if you're not. I'm knackered," she added, flopping down on a cracked and torn leather divan.

Oscar sat down in a battered old armchair across from her, and Willa refilled their glasses.

"What happened to you? During the war, I mean," he asked, giving her a searching look.

"I rode with Lawrence, in the desert. I photographed him and his men."

"It sounds exciting."

"It was."

"What else happened? Something must have. These pictures . . ." His voice trailed off as his eyes lit on even more prints, stacked haphazardly on the table between them. "You must have experienced a very great sorrow to be able to so easily recognize it in others."

Willa smiled sadly. She looked into her wineglass. "I lost the person I loved most in the whole world," she said. "He was a naval captain. His boat was sunk in the Mediterranean."

"I'm so sorry," Oscar said, visibly moved.

Willa nodded. "So am I," she said.

She remembered that day now, the day she'd learned Seamie was dead. She'd been in Lawrence's camp, recovering from cholera. She'd been lying in her bed, eating some soup, when Fatima suddenly came into her tent, talking excitedly.

"Willa, you have a guest," she said. "He's tall and handsome and says that he knows you."

Willa put her soup bowl down. Was it Seamie? she wondered. Could he have come back? Her heart began to race.

The flap to her tent opened again and her brother came inside. His face was tanned. He was wearing a uniform. He took off his hat and held it in his hands.

"Hello, Willa," he said. "I've come to see you. And to bring you back to Haifa. To stay with me there. In a house. A rather nice one. If you'd like to come."

"Albie?" Willa said. "My goodness, this is a surprise! I thought . . . I thought that—"

"You thought that I was Seamie," he said, then quickly looked down at his hat.

"Yes, I did," she said awkwardly. "But I'm very glad to see you, Albie. I really am. Sit down."

Albie sat on the cushion next to her bed. He leaned over and kissed her cheek. "It's good to see you, Wills. It's been yonks, hasn't it. I've heard all about your exploits," he said. "How are you?"

"Much better. Getting stronger every day, in fact. My food and drink stay in me now. It doesn't sound like much, but believe me, it's a huge achievement."

Albie laughed, but his eyes were sad. Willa knew her brother well. They hadn't been on the best terms, hadn't even seen each other for years now, but it didn't matter—she knew him. And she knew when something was wrong.

"Albie, what is it?" she said.

"Oh, Willa," he said. "I'm afraid I've got some very bad news."

Willa grabbed his hand. "Is it Mother? It is, isn't it? Albie, what's happened to her?"

"It's not Mother. I received a letter from her just last week. She's fine." Albie stopped speaking. Willa saw that his throat was working. "It's Seamie," he finally said.

Willa shook her head. "No. No, Albie. Please."

"I'm sorry," he said.

"When? How?" Willa asked.

"A few days ago. Off the coast of Cyprus. His ship was broadsided by a German U-boat. It burned and then sank. No survivors were found."

Willa let out a long, trailing moan. She felt as if her heart was being ripped from her. He was gone. Seamie was gone. Forever. The pain of it was beyond bearing.

As she wept, she remembered what Seamie had said while he nursed her. She remembered how he'd asked Fatima to pray for Willa. She'd heard his voice in her fevered dreams then, and she heard it still—in her nightmares.

Talk to Him, Fatima. He listens to you. Tell Him if He wants a life, He can have mine. A life for a life. Mine, not hers. Tell Him, Fatima. Tell Him to let Willa live.

God had listened. And God had taken him.

"And you came here after the desert? Right to Paris?" Oscar said now, breaking in upon her sad memories.

"No," Willa said, shaking her head. "I stayed with my brother for a few days. He was stationed in Haifa. Then I went home to England. I stayed with my mother in London, but London was gray and sad and full of ghosts. Everywhere I looked, someone was missing. That, too, only lasted a few days and then I came to Paris, where the ghosts all belong to other people, not me."

She didn't tell Oscar how unhappy her mother was that she'd gone to Paris, or that she'd sent Albie to fetch her after he'd arrived home from Haifa. He'd come to her flat, taken one look at her, and said, "Still trying to kill yourself, eh? Only this time it's with a needle." He'd returned to London without her.

Oscar picked up a print of an actress painting her face. Willa had shot it as the woman was looking into her dressing room mirror. Her hair was twisted up in pin curls. Her enormous breasts were nearly popping out of her black corset. Her expression, as she rubbed white greasepaint onto her skin, was searching and intense, as if she'd hoped the mirror might tell her who she was.

"Josephine Lavallier, *l'Ange de l'Amour,*" Oscar said.

"You know her?" Willa asked.

"I think all of Paris does. Thanks to that photograph of her at Bobino's, standing onstage in a pair of feathery wings and very little else. I saw it a few nights ago, hanging on the wall at La Rotonde. Did you take that one, too?"

Willa nodded. "That shot was published in one of the daily papers here. The editor was outraged such an act is permitted on a Paris stage. Ever since he ran it, Josie's show has been sold out," she said, laughing. "The show's very cheeky. Have you seen it?"

Oscar said he had not, and Willa said he must. "We'll go this very evening," Willa said. "I'll take you. Are you free?"

Oscar said he was, and Willa said it was a date, then. They'd get a bite at La Rotonde first.

"I thought you said the show's been sold out. Will we be able to get tickets?"

"Josie will get us in," Willa said. "We've struck up quite a friendship, Josie and I. We get along quite well. In fact, we've made a pact—neither one of us is allowed to talk about the past. There *is* no past when we're together, only the present. We don't talk about the war, or what we've lost. We talk about paintings and the theater and what we had for dinner, and whom we saw, and what we wore. And that's all. She's originally an English girl. Did you know that?"

"No, I thought she was as French as onion soup."

Willa laughed. "She lets me come backstage and photograph her and her fellow actresses. I get shots of everyone and everything. The stage manager. The back-door johnnies. The girls in their costumes. The romances and the rows. In return, I give her prints of anything I take of her."

Willa looked at the shot Oscar was holding and smiled. She was quite proud of it. "Josie's a fascinating entertainer," she said. "Even though she's English, she embodies Paris, a place that's been battered but not broken. A place that's still beautiful, still defiant."

Willa gazed at the photograph for a bit, then said they should get going. Coats and hats were gathered. As they walked toward the door, another photograph, one hanging over another divan—that Willa used as a bed—caught Oscar's eye. It showed a young man standing on top of a mountain peak, with what looked like the whole world spread out behind him.

"Where was that taken?" he asked.

"On Kilimanjaro. On top of the Mawenzi peak," Willa said.

"That's him, isn't it? The naval captain?"

"Yes, it is. It was taken just after we'd summitted. And just before I fell. And shattered my leg."

Willa told him the story.

"My God," he said, when she finished. "Can you still climb?"

"Only foothills," she said, touching the photograph gently. "I loved climbing more than I loved anything or anyone, except for Seamie. We had such plans, he and I. We were going to climb every mountain in the world. We used to talk about what made a good climber. We decided it was longing—the overwhelming desire to be the first, to lay eyes on a view no human being had ever seen before." She smiled ruefully, then added, "That was many years ago. Before I lost my leg. And Seamie lost his life. But I still think about it—Kilimanjaro, Everest, all of them. And in my dreams, I climb them. With him."

The aching note of sadness in her voice was not lost on Oscar. "It's an awful thing, isn't it?" he said quietly, as Willa opened the door for him.

"What is?" she asked, fishing her key out of her pocket.

"That which drives us," Oscar said, starting down the stairs. "The quest. We are prisoners, both of us. One of music. One of mountains. And neither will ever be free."

"Perhaps freedom is overrated," Willa said, locking the door. "What would either of us be without our quests? Me without my mountains. You without your music."

Oscar stopped midway down the flight of stairs. He looked up at her.

"Happy," he said. Then he turned and kept on walking.

Willa, laughing ruefully, followed.

CHAPTER NINETY-NINE

HE WAS GOING to die. He knew that now. He hadn't eaten for three days. Hadn't drunk for two. There was no more food, no more water, and no hope of getting either of those things.

The guards were gone. Two weeks after Armistice Day, they'd heard the war was over, and they'd left. News traveled slowly in the desert. They'd taken the camels, the goats, all the weapons, and plenty of food and water, and they'd buggered off, leaving their charges—seventy-two British prisoners of war, survivors of U-boat attacks in the Mediterranean—to fend for themselves. In the middle of the desert.

They'd unlocked the doors to the cells. That was something. It had enabled the men to get out—those who could walk, at least—and reconnoiter the prisoner-of-war camp to take stock of supplies.

It had been a very quick exploration. The prison, such as it was, was merely a series of stone huts—the remains of a small village, the men guessed—that had been fashioned into cells by bolting strips of sheet metal over the windows and adding padlocks to the doors. There were no toilets, no sinks, no cots. Just some rags on the ground upon which to sleep. For meals they had got whatever half-rotted mess their jailers saw fit to feed them. Temperatures usually reached 110 degrees during the day and often sank into the fifties at night.

Out of the seven who'd survived the U-boat attack with him, three had died of their injuries during the first week. Walker had starved to death three days ago. Liddell, last night. Benjamin was hanging on, but only barely. He'd likely be gone by nightfall.

And Ellis, well . . . he didn't know if Ellis was alive or dead.

Ellis had walked out with two other men nine days ago, vowing to
make it to Damascus, but there were more than one hundred and
fifty miles of heat and sand between this godforsaken place and that
city, and he and his comrades had been sick, weak, and malnour-
ished. Most likely, they'd dropped down dead one by one in the
desert.

Which would mean that no one on their side knew now that he,
Benjamin, and the other prisoners were even here.

The Germans had pulled him from the sea three months ago. He'd
been clinging to a piece of wood. His clothes had been in shreds.
Blood had been seeping from his nose and mouth. He'd had a deep
gash across the back of his head. His right side was burned down the
length of it—arm, torso, and leg.

"You were nearly dead by the time they pulled you out," Ellis, his
quartermaster, had told him. "You were raving. Out of your mind.
You didn't even know your own name."

Bir Güzel, the Turkish guards had called him—"beautiful one."
It was their little joke, for with his bruised and swollen face, he'd
been anything but beautiful.

When he was better, when he could open his eyes and talk, Ellis
told him that he'd been unconscious for days. They'd tended to
him—Ellis and the others—they'd kept him alive.

He couldn't remember a thing when he'd first come to. Little by
little, though, the memories returned. The ship-to-ship message. The
German U-boat. The torpedoes. The horrible way the rest of his crew
had died. The noise and the fire and the screaming. And then the awful
silence as the ship went under.

The guards told them little. They'd had no idea the Allies had won
until the day the guards let them out of their cells and informed them
that the war was over and they were free to go. They pointed south
and told them Damascus was that way, and that it was in the hands
of the British now, and that it would take them five days to reach it.
On a camel. If they could find one. And then they'd ridden off. One
had looked back and tossed Ellis a compass.

They'd talked among themselves that night, all the men, after they'd seen how little food and water they had, and decided to send a party south to the city. The three strongest would go. Hopefully they'd be able to get to Damascus and bring help back before it was too late for the ones left behind.

His burned legs had not healed and he could not walk. He could barely sit up. There was no question of him walking to Damascus. He had lain in his cell for most of the past eleven days, drinking and eating what little the others brought him. Until, finally, there was no more to bring.

They were good men, his fellow prisoners, and he hoped they survived. It was too late for him, but he hoped desperately that help would come for them.

He closed his eyes and fell into a deep sleep, hoping he would not wake again to the horrifying thirst and the gnawing pain in his guts. He dreamed of his young son. And of the boy's mother. He dreamed of a dark-haired woman with green eyes. She was standing at the foot of a mountain, smiling at him. She was so beautiful. She was a rose, his wild rose. He would let go now—let go of the pain and the sorrow and the suffering, let go of everything. But he would find her again one day. He knew he would. Not in this life, but in the next.

He was ready to die, death held no terror for him, but the sound of men's voices, loud and urgent, pulled him back from it.

"Holy Christ! There's a dead body in here! And another one there!"

He heard someone kicking at his door—closed most of the way against the fierce heat.

"This one's gone, too, Sergeant," a second voice said, a voice that was very close by. "Wait a minute! He's not . . . he's breathing! He's still alive!"

He opened his eyes and saw a soldier standing over him, a British soldier. He saw him kneel down, then he felt water on his lips and in his mouth, and he drank it greedily, clutching at the canteen with shaking hands.

"There you are, that's enough. Slow down or you'll be sick. There's plenty more where that came from. What's your name, sir?"

"Finnegan," he said, blinking into the bright desert light flooding into his cell. "Captain Seamus Finnegan."

CHAPTER ONE HUNDRED

"HERE, JAMES, LOVE, give one of these to Charlie and one to Stephen," Fiona said, handing her nephew two ornaments she'd taken from a huge box. It was Christmas Eve, and she, Joe, their children, and little James, were spending it with the men at the Wickersham Hall Veterans' Hospital.

James carefully took the ornaments from her, then walked over to a young man who was standing by the tree. "Here, Stephen," he said, handing him a snowman. "Put it high up. No, not there. Higher. Where we haven't got anything yet."

James then walked over to Charlie, who was sitting on a settee, staring ahead of himself. He placed the second ornament in Charlie's hand, but Charlie made no move to get up and hang it on the tree. James, too little to know what shell shock was, or to feel the tragedy of it in a seventeen-year-old boy, simply got impatient with him. "Come *on,* Charlie!" he said. "You've got to do your share, you know. That's what Granddad always said. He said we've all got to do our share and no shirking." When Charlie still didn't move, James took hold of his free hand and tugged on it until he did. "Go put yours by Stephen's," he said.

"A right little general, isn't he?" Joe said fondly.

Fiona, watching the two cousins, one tall and one so small, nodded and smiled. It was the simplest of actions—putting a Christmas ornament on a tree—and yet seeing Charlie do it made Fiona so happy. He was making progress—slowly, but steadily.

In the months since he'd come back from the front, his shaking had lessened, he'd learned to feed himself again, and he could now help with simple chores. He still had difficulty sleeping, though, and almost never spoke.

They had tried taking him home, Fiona and Joe, back in October, hoping that the sight of his old house might help to bring him out of himself. It had been hard going, though. The younger children had been devastated by the sight of him and day-to-day life with him was arduous. He had difficulty eating and sleeping. He had nightmares. It was hard for him to go up and down stairs. Reluctantly, she and Joe had decided to bring him back to Wickersham Hall, for he did better there. It was quieter and things were done on a schedule. Routine seemed to comfort him.

Fiona and Joe sent to Europe for specialists and brought them to the hospital, one after the other. None of them had helped Charlie at all. During one terrible visit, the doctor, a man from Prague, had decreed that Charlie was hopelessly insane, and said that he could only benefit from something called convulsive therapy—a new treatment he'd invented. A high does of a stimulant drug—the name of which Fiona couldn't even pronounce—would be administered to Charlie. It would induce a grand mal seizure.

"That's a generalized seizure," the doctor said, "one which affects the entire brain. It is my hope that by inducing the seizure, I will re-order the damaged pathways in his brain. Have no fear, Mrs. Bristow. He will be properly restrained. Leather straps and shackles work quite well, with little bruising or chafing to the patient." He'd smiled cheerily, then added, "And even less to the doctor!"

Furious, Fiona had told him to get himself back to Prague and out of her sight. She'd grabbed her unhappy child's hand and dragged him out of the room and off to the hospital's orchard. She sat him down in the grass so he could not hurt himself, then went to pick some pears for the cook. She'd only taken her secateurs with her, not a basket, so she gave the fruit—she'd cut off a lot—to Charlie to hold, forgetting in her anger and sadness that he shook so, he could hold nothing. When she turned around again, he had stopped shaking. Not entirely, but mostly. He was holding one of the pears and looking at it. He lifted it to his nose and inhaled its scent. And then he looked at her, really looked at her, for the first time since he'd come home, and smiled. "Thanks, Mum," he said, quite clearly.

Fiona had nearly shouted with joy. She'd hugged him and kissed him. He'd dropped his head again, looked away, as he always did when people came too close. But he'd made gains since then, talking every now and again, making eye contact. It was a slow awakening, a slow returning to them. But Fiona was convinced that she would have her son back one day.

The very next day, back in London, she turned over the running of her tea businesses to her second in command, Stuart Bryce. She made him chairman, and gave him absolute authority, letting go, in a matter of mere hours, the business she'd taken a lifetime to build.

"Are you sure, Fee?" Joe had asked her, when she told him of her decision.

"I am," she said, without a doubt, without a tear, without a second's hesitation. Her tea empire was important to her; she loved it, but she loved nothing else in the world as much as she loved her children. Her son Charlie needed her desperately, and now so did her little nephew James.

She spent as much time as she could at Wickersham Hall, always taking James with her, and sometimes the twins, too, and staying at the Brambles. Together, she, Charlie, and the children did the work that Wickersham Hall's gardener couldn't manage. They dug and planted and clipped and pruned, preparing the plants and trees for the winter. They planted two hundred crocus bulbs. Three hundred tulips. Five hundred daffodils.

Autumn had come, and with it, a gathering sense that the war would be over soon. The Americans had come into it, fighting on the side of the Allies. Their numbers tipped the balance. The kaiser couldn't hope to hold out much longer. Day by day, Fiona's hopes grew—hopes for a quick end to the fighting, and for the safe and speedy return of her brother, Seamie.

And then came the awful day Joe had arrived at the Brambles

unexpectedly and Fiona knew immediately what had happened. She didn't need to read the telegram he was holding; she could see it in his eyes.

"I'm sorry, Fiona," he said. "I'm so sorry."

Charlie had been the first one to go to her. The first one to put his arms around her. "There, there, Mum," he'd said to her as she sank down in a chair, keening with grief. For herself. And for James, who in the space of mere weeks had lost both of his parents. "There, there," Charlie had crooned to her, just as she had to him when he couldn't eat and couldn't sleep. When the memories were too much for him.

Sid had grieved, too. Deeply. The loss of his brother had hastened his decision to return to America. To a place that contained no memories of Seamie. India had hired another doctor—one who could take over her responsibilities: Dr. Reade. She'd left the hospital in her care, and then she, Sid, and the children had left for Southampton and America. They'd made it safely to New York, and then across the country to California and Point Reyes, the place they loved so much. Fiona missed them terribly, but she understood their wanting to leave.

Seamie's personal effects had arrived from Haifa a few weeks later. She had nothing of him to bury—there were no remains—so she simply put a headstone next to Jennie's, in the Finnegan family plot in a churchyard in Whitechapel, and then she and Charlie planted a yellow rose between the two graves. Yellow for remembrance. She would never forget the brother whom she loved so much. She knew he was with their parents now, and with their baby sister, Eileen, and with his wife, Jennie.

Whenever she went to visit her family's graves, Fiona asked her parents to hug Seamie for her, the poor, restless soul. Happiness wasn't his gift. Once, years ago, it had seemed that he'd found at least some happiness, when he'd found Jennie and they married. But even then, there was still something sad and restless about him. Fiona knew that he'd seen Willa Alden again, at her father's funeral, and she suspected that Seamie had married Jennie even though he'd never got over losing Willa. She understood the pain that came from that. She had very nearly done the same thing herself. A long time ago in New York, when she thought that Joe was lost to her forever, she'd nearly married another man whom she thought she loved— William McClane. Had she done so, she would have lost the chance for true love forever. She could hardly bear to imagine that, to imagine her life without Joe in it, and her heart hurt anew for her brother as she thought how he had missed out on a life with Willa, his own true love.

Fiona glanced at the Christmas tree now. James had at least eight men gathered around it, and Joe, too, and was still handing out ornaments. It seemed to do them good, the patients—having a tree in their midst, records on the gramophone, and cups of mulled cider and hot chocolate to drink. It was the first real Christmas most of them had had in the last four years.

Fiona was glad of the cheer the holiday brought, for the veterans' sakes—and for her family's. Earlier in the month, Joe had won a grueling campaign to retain his Hackney seat. The prime minister had been ousted, but Joe had been returned. In fact, he'd been appointed Labour secretary by David Lloyd George, the new prime minister. Sam Wilson—whom Katie had campaigned so hard for— had won his seat, and Labour as a whole had made many gains. It had been a hard contest, and Joe and Katie were exhausted. It would do them good to rest for a few days.

"Come, James, you take this one and put it on," Fiona said now, lifting another ornament out of the box and handing it to him. "You've got all the lads hanging ornaments, haven't you? It's time you put some on yourself."

"It's an angel, Auntie Fee," James said, admiring the pretty porcelain ornament as he took it from her.

"Yes, it is," Fiona said.

"My mummy's an angel," the little boy said. "My daddy, too. They're in heaven now."

Fiona had to steady her voice before she could reply. "Yes, my darling," she said, "they are."

Fiona watched as James put his angel on the tree. She was thinking that Seamie had been the same age as James when he lost both of his parents. She had raised him. Now she would raise his son.

When James had hung the ornament, he turned to her and said, "I'm hungry, Auntie Fee. Stephen ate all the mince pies." He left the common room, where they'd been working, and took off down the hallway, toward the kitchen.

"James? Come back, will you? Where are you off to now, you little monkey?" Fiona called after him. "To pester Mrs. Culver for another mince pie, no doubt," she said, sighing as she climbed down from the stepladder she was standing on. "Charlie, love, you can put some more ornaments on the tree, if you like. I've got to go after James." Charlie nodded.

Always exploring and roaming, our James, Fiona thought as she hurried down the hall after him. Just like Seamie when he was little. She doubted very much that her brother was in heaven, despite what James had said. Heaven couldn't hold him. He was at the South Pole, or the North Pole, or on top of Everest. She hoped that wherever Seamie was, he was finally at peace.

"There you are!" Fiona said, when she caught up with her nephew. He was sitting at the cook's worktable, next to his cousin Katie, who was laying out next week's edition of the *Battle Cry* and drinking a cup of tea. He was watching the cook roll out pastry for the meat pies she was baking. "I hope you're not bothering Mrs. Culver," Fiona said to him.

"Oh, he's no bother at all," Mrs. Culver said. "He's right good company, aren't you, laddie?"

James nodded. His mouth was full of mince pie. Mrs. Culver had readied two more platters of them for the common room.

"Leave him here, Mrs. Bristow. I don't mind a bit. He can help me roll out the dough."

"Are you sure, Mrs. Culver?"

"Quite."

"All right, then," Fiona said. "I'd very much like to finish with that tree." She touseled James's hair, picked up a platter of mince pies, and turned to leave the kitchen. As she was walking past the windows toward the hallway, she glanced outside and saw an older man, a hard-looking man, walking with one of the patients.

"Who is that? I don't think I've ever seen him here before."

Katie looked up from her paper. She followed Fiona's gaze. "That's Billy Madden," she said. "*The* Billy Madden."

Fiona stared, stunned. "How do you know that, Katie?"

"I spend a lot of time in Limehouse. So does he," Katie said wryly.

"Billy Madden . . . *here?*" Fiona said. "Why?"

She remembered, very well, how Billy Madden had tried to kill her brother Sid.

"He's here to visit his son. His youngest. The lad just arrived last week," Mrs. Culver said.

"Peter Madden," Fiona said. She'd seen his name on the roster of incoming patients last week, but she'd never imagined he was Billy's son.

"Aye, that's him. Billy's two older boys were killed on the Somme, I heard. The one here with us was shot in the head. He has brain damage. Dr. Barnes says there's no hope for him. He'll never be right," Mrs. Culver said.

"I know Peter," James said. "He's new. He's very quiet."

Watching the man, stoop-shouldered and broken-looking, walking past with his silent, shuffling son, Fiona almost felt sorry for him. Almost.

"I've heard such dreadful things about him," Mrs. Culver said, looking out of the window, "but they're hard to credit. I mean, look at him . . . he hardly looks like a fearsome villain, does he? He looks like he's been gutted."

"Who's gutted? Who's a villain?" James asked, looking out of the window, too.

Fiona, her eyes still on Madden, felt a shiver go up her spine.

"Auntie Fee? Who's a villain?" James asked again. "That man out there? Is he Peter's daddy? He doesn't look like a villain. He just looks sad."

"No one's a villain, James," Fiona said. "Eat your mince pie, love," she said, still gazing at Madden.

Madden, who had his son's arm, pointed at something, smiling. Fiona followed the direction of his finger. It was a huge hawk, circling a field.

Mrs. Culver thought Madden a broken man, a changed man, but Fiona wasn't so sure. Men like Madden never really changed. She knew that well enough. The violence never left them. It stayed inside, coiled like a viper.

Fiona suddenly heard a door open and bang shut again, and the next she thing saw was James running across the lawn. Running to Billy Madden. He had something in his hands.

"James!" she shouted, banging the platter of mince pies down and running after him. "James, come back!" she shouted again, once she was outside.

But James was already at Billy Madden's side. He tugged on Madden's jacket. Madden turned around and James handed him something. As Fiona drew closer, she saw it was a mince pie. He gave one to Peter, too.

"Merry Christmas," he said.

Madden, still holding his pie, knelt down to the boy. His face had gone white. As if he'd just seen a ghost. As Fiona watched, he reached out and took hold of James's hand.

"William?" he said. "Son, is it you?"

His voice sounded tortured. His eyes, huge in his pale face, were boring into James. He was scaring him.

"Let go of me," Fiona heard James say, as he tried to break free of his grasp.

Fiona, panting, finally reached them. "Let go of him," she said, her voice low and hard. "Now."

As if suddenly remembering himself, Madden released the boy.

He looked up at Fiona. "I'm . . . I'm sorry, ma'am," he said, sounding confused. "I didn't mean to frighten the lad. Or you. It's just . . . it's just that he gave me a bit of a shock. You see, he looks exactly like my oldest son William did when he was a boy. Spitting image. It's . . . it's downright uncanny." He swallowed hard, then said, "William was killed in France, ma'am. Last year."

"I'm very sorry," Fiona said. "I see you're walking with Peter. We won't disturb you. Come along, James."

James took Fiona's hand and together they walked back to the kitchen. Fiona could feel Madden's eyes on them as they did.

"What was that about, Mum?" Katie asked, as Fiona stepped back inside, shepherding James before her.

"Run along into the common room and check on your cousin for me, will you, love?" Fiona said to James.

"I'm not sure what that was about," Fiona said to Katie when he'd gone. "But I don't want James near that man again. You'll keep him inside, Mrs. Culver? If he comes in here again?" she asked, for suddenly, and quite inexplicably, she was afraid for the boy.

"I will, Mrs. Bristow. But you've nothing to fear from Billy Madden. He's been here three times already, and he's always the perfect gentleman."

Fiona nodded. She picked up the platter of mince pies again. You're being silly, she told herself. And yet, for some reason she could not explain, before she left for the common room she locked the kitchen door.

"ARE YOU TRYING to be funny, Mr. Simmonds?" Admiral Harris bellowed, from within the confines of his office. The door was open, and Seamie, who was sitting on a bench outside the admiral's office, could hear everything. "Because I'm trying to relocate four warships, three gunboats, eight submarines, and two hundred sailors from the Mediterranean to the Atlantic at the moment and I haven't the time for pranks."

"I assure you sir, I am most definitely not being funny," Mr. Simmonds, the admiral's secretary, said.

Seamie, dressed in an army uniform loaned to him by the men of the unit who'd saved him and his fellow prisoners of war, had approached Mr. Simmonds only moments ago in his office at the Royal Navy's headquarters in Haifa and told him his story.

He listened now as the admiral said, "What I would like to know, Mr. Simmonds, is *how*. How, exactly, did this happen?"

"I don't know, sir. I gather the army had something to do with it. A unit stationed just west of Hama. Though I rather thought it might be best to allow Captain Finnegan to explain the details to you himself."

"Where is he now?"

"Right outside, sir."

"For God's sake, man, bring him in!"

Mr. Simmonds popped his head out of the doorway and motioned for Seamie to join them. Seamie walked into Admiral Harris's office, slowly and stiffly, and snapped him a sharp salute. The admiral stared, then blinked, then returned the salute.

"I'll be damned," he said softly. And then, much louder, "Sit down, lad! Where the devil have you been?"

"It's rather a long story, sir. Before I tell it, I should like you to know that Quartermaster Ellis and Midshipman Benjamin are also alive, if not exactly well, and will be traveling from Hama to Damascus as soon as they are able. Might I ask you, sir, if you have word of any other survivors from the *Exeter*?"

"I'm afraid not. You, and now Ellis and Benjamin, are the only ones I know of."

Seamie nodded sadly. He had hoped, foolishly, that more men had somehow survived. That they'd been missed by the Germans and taken by a British rescue boat, or that they'd washed up on the shores of Cyprus. Something. Anything.

"The *Brighton* received your distress call," the admiral said. "She arrived at Famagusta about an hour after the *Exeter* went down. She searched as best she could. A storm had blown in and the seas had become rough. They could find no survivors and did not know that a German ship had picked any up." The admiral paused, then said, "I imagine you are blaming yourself for what happened. You must not. You had no way of knowing about the U-boat."

"And yet I do blame myself," Seamie said.

The admiral sat back in his chair. "Of course you do, lad. Never had a captain under my command who didn't. The pain of it lessens, though. In time."

Seamie nodded. He didn't believe that. He doubted the admiral believed it himself.

"Deserted the navy for the army have you?" the admiral said, nodding at Seamie's uniform and trying to lighten the mood.

Seamie smiled. As Mr. Simmonds bustled in with a teapot and some biscuits, he told Admiral Harris what had happened aboard the *Exeter*, the injuries he'd sustained, and how he and the other survivors had been picked up by a German ship and handed off to the Turks, who'd thrown them into a terrible prison camp in the desert. He told the admiral how Ellis and the two other men had started out for Damascus, but had mistakenly veered east and ended up at Hama instead. It was an incredible piece of luck that they had, for they'd barely survived the trek to Hama and never would have made Damascus. They'd stumbled to the army barracks there and told the CO about the prison camp. He'd promptly dispatched twenty men on camels, each laden with food, water, and medicine, to the camp. They'd been too late to save some men, but they'd saved many of them.

"Incredible," the admiral said. "Absolutely astonishing. And the burns . . . they're healing?"

"They've begun to. I received good care at Hama, but I still can't move as well as I'd like," Seamie said.

"We'll have a doctor here take a look at them. At the rest of you, too. We'll wire your family to let them know the wonderful news." He paused for a few seconds, then said, "Captain Finnegan . . . Seamus . . . before I do that, I'm afraid I've got some rather bad news for you."

Seamie steeled himself. He'd heard about the terrible influenza epidemic and the havoc it had wreaked back home.

"Not my son," he said. "Please."

The admiral shook his head. "No, it's not your son. I'm afraid it's your wife. Mrs. Finnegan was stricken by the Spanish flu. She passed away last autumn."

Seamie grabbed the front of the admiral's desk to steady himself. He was reeling. He couldn't believe that Jennie had been taken ill, that she was gone. For a few seconds, he panicked, wondering where James was. Then he reminded himself that his family was in London. James would be with Fiona and Joe. He was certain of it. The knowledge helped to calm the panic, but did nothing for the grief he felt. Or the guilt. He'd wanted to be a better husband to her. He'd promised himself that when he got back home, if he got back home, he *would* be better. He'd be the man she truly deserved. But it was too late now. He would never have the chance.

"I'm so sorry, Captain Finnegan. I'm sure you would appreciate a bit of privacy just now. Another officer just left for England two days ago. His rooms have been cleaned and readied for their next occupant. I will have Mr. Simmonds escort you to them. And I will do everything in my power to get you back to London as quickly as possible."

"Thank you, sir," Seamie said softly. "I almost don't want to go. A part of me wishes I could stay here. If it wasn't for my son, I would."

"I think you'd have a good deal of company," the admiral said. "Most every man in this building would like to stay here. Myself included. It's easier, in many ways, than returning home to the graves and the grief. And yet we must do what we must do. Your son has lost his mother. He needs his father now as never before."

The admiral stood. Seamie did, too. "It's time we got you to your rooms now. You've had a terrible shock. You should rest. I'll have proper clothing sent over to you, some food, and a good bottle of wine."

"I appreciate it, sir. Very much," Seamie said.

The admiral put a kind hand on Seamie's shoulder. "It's hard to lose those whom we love, lad. Especially a beloved wife. It's the hardest bloody thing in the world."

Seamie nodded. The admiral's words, so well intentioned, caused him more pain than the man would ever know.

If only I *had* loved her, he thought. If only I had.

CHAPTER ONE HUNDRED TWO

"COME ON, WILLS, let's go," Josie Meadows said, pulling her fox stole around her shoulders. "I'm freezing my arse off. It's bloody cold in here!"

"We can't leave. We just got here," Willa said, opening the back of her camera and pulling out a spent roll of film. "I'm getting good shots."

"And I'm getting nervous," Josie said, looking around herself unhappily.

"They won't hurt you. If anything, they're afraid you're going to hurt them. Have another glass of wine, Jo. Relax," Willa said, holding her camera closer to the candle on top of the tiny table in the corner of the tattered, garish tent in which they were sitting.

It was a gypsy tent. It had been set up in a wild and remote corner of Paris's Bois de Boulogne. Willa had discovered it, and the people to whom it belonged, two weeks ago, as she was walking through the park, photographing prostitutes, vagrants, and other night people.

Willa had fallen for the gypsies instantly. Their hard beauty captivated her. Everything about them begged a photograph—the dark, haunted eyes of an old woman; the glint of an earring against black hair; the flash of a smile, sudden and unexpected and gone so quickly; the way a young man held a battered trumpet in his arms so tenderly, as if he were holding an infant; the wonder in the children's faces when a stranger appeared, the fear in the faces of their elders.

Willa had tried to photograph them right away, but they were shy, superstitious, and wary—always wary—and they would not let her. They were afraid of the police. Afraid of soldiers. Afraid of ordinary people who did not like them and wanted them to move on, and sometimes came armed with clubs in the middle of the night to make sure they did.

Determined to win them over, Willa had visited them every day, bringing small gifts—loaves of bread, a basket of apples, coffee, warm jumpers for the children. She tried to make them see that she meant them no harm, that she would not tell the police about them, not rile up a band of citizens against them. And little by little, they had warmed to her. A few of the men talked with her. One of the women made her a strong cup of coffee. A few of the children asked to see her camera.

And then finally, they had invited her to their tent. It was separate from their caravans—farther into the woods. It was where they sang and danced. One could go there, if one was known to them. One could buy a bottle of wine, a bit of cheese and bread, and listen as they poured out their stories in music and song.

She had told Josie about them, told her that she was going to their tent tonight in the hopes of photographing them. Josie thought it sounded like a grand adventure and had begged to come along.

Now, though, she was jittery. "They scare me," she said.

"I've already told you they won't hurt you," Willa replied impatiently, putting a new roll of film into her camera. It was hard going tonight. The gypsies had allowed her to photograph them, but they were still difficult, still shy about the camera. The light in the tent— from lanterns and candles—was horribly low. Now she had Josie's nerves to contend with, too. "What do you think they're going to do? Kidnap you? Sell you to their king?" she asked her.

"They've got magic. That one over there? With all the knives? He's got the eye."

"What on earth are you talking about?"

"He can see things. He can see right inside a person. I know it. I can always tell when someone has the eye. My mam had the eye. It's nothing to trifle with. Let's go."

"I didn't think l'Ange de l'Amour, the woman who shows le tout Paris almost everything God gave her every night but Monday, would be afraid of anything, never mind a few gypsies," Willa teased.

"Yes, well, l'Ange de l'Amour translates to 'the Angel of Love.' Not 'the Angel of Bloody Stupid Stunts That Will Surely Get Every-one Killed.'"

Willa took a small bottle from the pocket of her trousers. She shook out two white pills and washed them down with a slug of wine.

Josie saw her take the pills. "What are those?" she asked.

"Painkillers."

"Do they work?"

"No."

"Your leg still hurts?" Josie said, concerned.

"My leg's fine," Willa said.

Josie gave her a long look. "The dose you gave yourself in your darkroom, right before we left, that wasn't enough? Oh, don't look so surprised. I know what you do in there. Making pictures is only half of it."

"All the morphine in the world's not enough, Jo," Willa said.

"Bloody right about that," Josie said with a sigh. "Nor all the wine, men, money, jewels, and dresses. Go on, then, Wills. Go take your snaps. What's the death of a chorus girl in the service of great art?"

Willa laughed. She kissed Josie's cheek. Josie was the only one who understood. Even Oscar Carlyle, who'd recently become her lover, didn't.

Morphine didn't stop the pain, it only dulled it. For Willa, there was only one thing that stopped it—taking pictures. When she was behind a camera lens, concentrating on a shot, she forgot everything. Forgot she even existed.

As she advanced the film in her camera, the two musicians—a violinist and a singer—whom she'd been shooting left the small stage they'd been standing on. A girl, young, voluptuous, and scantily clad, took their place. She stood against the stage's wooden backdrop, placed her hands on her hips and her legs wide apart in a V.

As Willa and Josie watched, the man—the one who Josie said had the eye—stepped forward. He had half a dozen daggers in his hand. A boy dropped a basket at his feet that contained even more. Another man, short and sprightly, jumped up on stage and announced that the Amazing Antoine, knife-thrower extraordinaire, would now take the stage. He jokingly advised any in the audience with an aversion to blood to leave now. Then he quickly jumped down.

Willa quickly reached into her pocket. She pulled out a few francs, walked up to Antoine, and offered them to him, hoping the money might persuade him to allow her to photograph him. Antoine looked at the money and then at her. He shook his head, and Willa's heart sank, but then he pointed to her, and the stage.

Willa didn't understand at first, but then, looking into his dark eyes, the eyes that Josie was sure could see inside someone, she did. "All right, then. Yes," she said.

"What?" Josie said loudly. "What's going on? What did he say? Willa . . . you're not . . . you can't be serious. Have you lost your bloody mind?"

Willa held a finger to her lips.

"Don't, Willa! Please!" Josie said. "He's been drinking! I saw him!"

But Willa was already on the stage.

"I'm not watching this," Josie said. "I can't." She covered her face with her hands, then peeked through her fingers.

The man barked at the girl onstage and she quickly left it. Willa took her place. She positioned herself against the back drop, legs in a V, just as the girl had done, but instead of putting her hands on her hips, she raised her camera—a little Kodak Vest Pocket. She'd brought it with her tonight because it was small and unobtrusive, and had a quick shutter speed.

Willa steadied herself now, then gave the man a quick nod. Low, urgent murmurs rippled through the crowd. Willa ignored them. Every fiber of her being was focused on Antoine, waiting for the look or the movement that would signal the first throw. A drumroll was heard. Antoine paced. He spat on the ground. Then he took a deep breath and threw the first knife. It landed with a sharp *thuk* only inches from Willa's right ankle. There was applause, and a few gasps. Willa didn't even hear them. She'd got off a shot, but had she caught the throw? She wound her film forward and readied herself for the next one.

The man started throwing in earnest now. To Willa's left. To her right. Josie was shouting, but Willa couldn't make out her words. People were clapping, yelling, gasping. And the man kept throwing. Faster now. One knife pinned her trousers to the board. Josie screamed. Willa never moved. She never so much as flinched. She just kept clicking and winding as fast as she could, trying to capture the man's face as he took aim, the knife as it came speeding toward her, and the crowd in the background, their faces lit by candlelight and hidden by shadow. She never stopped, never lowered the camera, never lost her nerve. The knives kept coming, traveling up her legs. To her torso. Her shoulders. Her neck. And finally, her head.

"Stop it! Stop it, you'll kill her!" Josie shouted.

The gypsy threw the last of his knives rapid-fire. They made a halo around Willa's head. He paused, then threw his very last one. It landed an inch away from her left ear. He bowed then, to wild applause and ringing bravos, then swept his arm toward Willa. She, too, took a bow, to even louder cheers.

Her cheeks were flushed, her heart was pounding. She was certain she'd got something on film. Maybe even something amazing. Everyone was excited and happy. Everyone, that is, except Josie, who was flushed and furious.

Josie stood up, now that it was over, walked to the knife-thrower, and gave him what for.

Her harangue lasted a good two minutes and made both the knife-thrower and the audience laugh. Willa tried to get down and go to her friend but found she was pinned in more than one place. The knife-thrower's girl assistant came to her aid, pulling two knives out of the cloth of her trousers.

Willa jumped down off the stage. She trotted over to Josie just in time to see her poke a dainty, gloved finger into the knife-thrower's chest and angrily say, "That was a very stupid thing to do! You could've killed her!"

And just in time to see the gypsy smile and say, "No. Never. How can I kill what is already dead?"

CHAPTER ONE HUNDRED THREE

"CAPTAIN FINNEGAN! CAPTAIN Finnegan, over here, please!" the photographer shouted.

Seamie, walking to the door of his sister and brother-in-law's house, turned around. A dozen flashes went off, nearly blinding him.

"Captain Finnegan! How does it feel to be home?"

"Wonderful, thank you," Seamie said, dazed. "I'm very happy to be back in London."

Seamie had not expected this. He had expected an uneventful ride to Mayfair and a quiet arrival, but reporters and photographers had swarmed him the second he'd stepped out of the carriage. He'd quickly forded his way through them and made his way up the steps. He was about to knock on the door when it suddenly opened.

Joe was there, in his wheelchair. "Come inside, lad. Hurry. Before the piranhas eat you alive."

Seamie did as he was told, grateful to be out of the scrum of shouting, jostling men. Questions, shouted loudly, followed him.

"Captain Finnegan! Tell us about the attack on your ship!"

"Captain Finnegan! When did you find out your wife died?"

"Captain Finnegan! Is it true you married an Arabian girl?"

"That's all for today, lads," Joe shouted. "Captain Finnegan's very weary from his long voyage."

"Mr. Bristow! When did you learn that your brother-in-law was alive?"

"Has Captain Finnegan seen his son yet?"

"What was Mrs. Bristow's reaction?"

"Diabolical, that lot," Joe said as he wheeled himself back inside the house and slammed the door behind him.

In the foyer, Fiona, weeping, had already thrown her arms around her brother.

"We thought you were dead, Seamie. I can't believe you've come back to us," she said through her tears.

"It's all right, Fee. It's all right . . . ," Seamie said, holding her tightly. Admiral Harris had telegraphed Fiona and Joe back in January. It was nearly the end of March now. The doctors in Damascus hadn't wanted him to travel until his burns had healed further. That had taken a month. And then the boat had taken another six weeks to get to England. The separation had been hard on them all.

When Fiona could bear to let go of him, Peter hugged him. Then Katie, and the twins. Everyone was there to greet him but Rose and James.

"How is James?" Seamie asked, when they finally released him.

"He's a little nervous," Fiona said.

"I would think so," Seamie said.

James was bound to be nervous, if not downright frightened. He had recently lost his mother. And his father—or so he'd been told. But now his father—a man he didn't even know very well—was coming back into his life. Seamie had only seen James a handful of times, when he was just a baby. He doubted very much that James, who was four now, remembered any of them. He knew he would be a stranger to the boy.

"Does he want to see me?" Seamie asked.

"Yes, he does. He's upstairs with Rose right now. I thought it might be better to bring him down after we'd all calmed ourselves a bit. Me especially. We've told him all about you. He's quite impressed. He wants to hear all about the *Exeter*. And how you survived the attack. Shall I get him?"

"Yes," Seamie said.

Fiona sent a maid upstairs to fetch Rose, then suggested everyone follow her into the parlor. When they'd all sat down, Rose came in, holding hands with a little boy.

Seamie's heart melted at the sight of his son. Seamie had teased Jennie that he was the milkman's son, for he had nothing of the

Finnegans in him. He was fair-haired, with hazel eyes, like his mother. And, like her, he was beautiful.

James left Rose and went to stand by Fiona.

"Is he really my daddy, Auntie Fee?" Seamie heard him whisper.

"He really is, James," Fiona said. "Would you like to say hello?"

James nodded. He approached Seamie shyly and manfully offered him his hand. Seamie could see James was being very brave, and his son's courage touched him. He took the small hand in his and shook it.

"Hello, James," he said.

"Hello, sir," James said. He looked Seamie over uncertainly, then added, "My uncle Joe is a member of Parliament."

"Is he now? Then I shall have to be very careful how I tread around here," Seamie said.

"Are you a bloody Tory?" James asked cautiously. "The bloody Tories make him very angry."

Fiona gave Joe a look. "I told you not to bellow so! I told you the children could hear you!" she whispered scoldingly. Joe looked at the ceiling.

"I see," Seamie said, biting back his laughter. "Well, I'm a Labour man myself, so I don't think I'll have any trouble there."

"Have you come to take me away?" James asked suddenly, plaintively.

Seamie could see the worry in his eyes. The poor little blighter, he thought. He's been through so much.

"No, James," he said gently. "In fact, I was wondering if you would let me stay here for a bit. With you and your aunt Fiona and your uncle Joe. I'd like very much to stay. But only if you want me to."

James's little face brightened. He turned to Fiona. "Can he, Auntie Fee? Can he stay with us?"

"He certainly can," Fiona said. "We'll make up a bed for him."

James smiled. "I got a train set for Christmas," he said to Seamie. "Would you like to see it?"

"I would like that very much," Seamie said.

"Come on, then," James said, offering Seamie his hand.

Seamie took it. He followed James. For the first time in months, ever since the *Exeter* had gone down, he felt glad.

Glad he'd survived.

Glad to be home.

Glad for the one thing he'd managed to do right in his life. Glad for little James.

CHAPTER ONE HUNDRED FOUR

WILLA STRETCHED LANGUIDLY in her bed, then sat up. It was three A.M. She would get up soon. Make some prints. She was wide awake and full of energy. Making love had always had that effect on her.

She looked over at Oscar Carlyle, her handsome American lover. He was lying sprawled out on his back in a tangle of sheets, eyes closed.

Lover, she thought now, as she turned away from him and gazed at the night sky out of her huge windows. What a strange word for what he is to me.

Willa didn't love Oscar, or any of the men she'd been with since she came to Paris. She wished she did. She wished she could.

"I love you, Willa."

She'd only ever loved one man, and she knew, deep inside, that she would give her body now and again, but she would never, ever give her heart. She could not. It was gone. She had given it to Seamie, and Seamie was dead.

"I love you, Willa."

Grief filled her—thick, black, and choking. She couldn't bear that he was gone. She didn't know how to go on in a world that didn't have him in it. In her head and in her heart, she still talked to him. Still marveled at sunsets with him. Told him about her work. Shared her wishes to return to Everest one day. And in her head and her heart, she heard him answer her. How could he be gone?

Willa felt a hand on her back. She jumped, startled. "Where are you, Willa? Where'd you go?" Oscar said.

Willa turned to him and smiled. "Nowhere. I'm right here."

"I said I love you. Fifteen times."

Willa leaned over. She kissed his mouth. And said nothing in return.

"I'm starving," Oscar said. "You have any food in this joint?"

"Some chocolate, I think. And oranges," Willa said.

Oscar got out of bed. He was young—only twenty-seven. He had a glorious body, all bronzed, rippling muscle. They'd gone out on the town, more than three months ago, after she'd photographed him for *Life*, and had had a good time. That same night, they'd ended up in bed. He was kind and smart and funny. He was something warm to reach for in the middle of the night. He would have to return to his home in Rome in a fortnight. She would miss him when he left.

He grabbed a silk kimono of hers now and shrugged into it.

"You look very fetching, Madame Butterfly," she said.

He picked up a magazine and held it in front of his face, like a fan, then walked daintily across the room like a geisha, to fetch the bowl of oranges, which made her laugh.

He put the oranges on the bed. He found half a bar of chocolate, wrapped in silver foil, and another bottle of wine—they'd already emptied one—and brought them to her, too.

"It's cold in here!" he said, belting the kimono around himself. He padded over to the small iron stove, on the far side of the room near the windows, opened its door, and tossed in a few lumps of coal. As he was making his way back to the bed, he stopped suddenly, to look at a row of prints spread out on a long worktable.

He was silent for a few minutes as he looked at them. Picking some up. Shaking his head. Saying, "Damn, Willa."

Willa knew what he was looking at it—it was a series she'd taken two days ago, at a brothel. The photographs portrayed the prostitutes during the day, when they were off-duty. It showed them washing their sheets, their underthings. It showed them cooking, eating, and laughing. Taking care of their children. It showed them as human beings.

"These are astonishing," Oscar said quietly. "Totally amazing. The critics are going to go nuts."

"Good nuts or bad nuts?" Willa asked, smiling at his Brooklyn voice.

"Both," he said, getting back in bed. "You're fearless, Willa. But it's not because you're brave. It's because you don't give a damn what happens to you. You don't care if the tarts beat you up, or the gypsies, or the cops, or the critics." He looked at the oranges and frowned, then took a big bite of the chocolate. "You got anything else to eat here?"

"I don't think so."

"No wonder you're so thin," he said, breaking off a piece of chocolate and popping it into her mouth. "Come to my place tonight. I'll make you steak frites."

"That sounds delicious. I think I will," she said.

As Oscar poured them both more wine, Willa reached over to her night table, for the bottle of pills that was there. She tried to take two, discreetly, to help her cope with the sorrow she was still feeling over her memories of Seamie. Oscar saw her, though, and said, "More pills? Again?"

"I need them. For the pain," she said.

"What pain? Where?" he asked her.

"My leg," she said.

Oscar shook his head. "No," he said. "The pain's not there." He slid his hand under her breast, pressing his palm against her heart. "It's here," he said.

Willa looked away. She didn't want to talk about it.

Gently, tenderly, Oscar took her chin in his hand and turned her face to his. "Look at me, Willa. Why are you so sad, huh? Always so sad? Thin and sad." He took her arm, stretched it out, kissed the inner bend of her elbow. "Why do your arms look like pincushions? Why do you gobble all those pills?"

"Oscar, don't . . . ," Willa said.

"Because you lost someone? In the war? Yeah, I know. I've seen the picture you took of him. The one on your wall. But hey, here's some news: Everybody lost someone." He went quiet for a bit, then he said, "But you found me and I found you, and that should count for something. It could, too, if you would let it."

Oscar popped the last piece of chocolate into his mouth, then he took the silver foil that had covered it and twisted it into the shape of a ring, complete with a knobby diamond. He took Willa's hand in his, slipped the ring onto her finger, and said, "Marry me, Willa."

"Stop it, you fool."

"I'm dead serious. Never been more serious. Marry me."

Willa shook her head.

"Come on, Willa. Be my wife. I'll get you out of this dump. Take you back to Rome with me. Get you a nice house somewhere pretty. One with radiators. You can have a garden. And a kitchen. I'll buy you an apron. And a set of china . . ."

Willa burst out laughing.

". . . and a vacuum cleaner, too." Oscar's voice dropped. "I'm serious. We can have kids. And toast in the morning. And dinners at night. Real ones. Just like normal people."

"That sounds nice, Oscar. It really does," Willa says softly. The thought that he cared enough to want these things for her, these good and real things, touched her deeply.

"It *is* nice. It will be. Do it. Leave your ghost in the graveyard where he belongs and do it, Willa."

Willa knew he was a good man. A talented musician. And as handsome as a god. Most women would have killed to have a man like that propose to them.

"Come on, Willa. Marry me," he said, pulling her close. "I love you like mad. Whaddya say? I'm throwing you a lifeline here. Don't be a jerk. Take it."

Maybe he was right and she was wrong. Maybe there was a

chance for her. For them. Nothing she'd done had ever been able to make her forget Seamie, but then again, she'd never done anything this mad or this foolish. Maybe she could be happy married. In a house. With a vacuum cleaner. Maybe she could. At the very least, she owed him for that. For caring enough to try.

"All right, then, Oscar," she said. "Why not? Yes. I'll marry you."

CHAPTER ONE HUNDRED FIVE

"EXCUSE ME, PRIME MINISTER," said Amanda Downes, David Lloyd George's secretary, "but you and the cabinet are due downstairs now for photographs with the German trade commission."

Lloyd George, who'd replaced Asquith in the general election, and who was in the midst of haranguing his chancellor of the exchequer, Andrew Bonar Law, over the government's proposed budget, paused. "Thank you, Amanda," he said. He turned to his minister of trade, Archibald Graham. "Remind me, Archie, why we are going along to this dog and pony show. This was your idea, wasn't it? What's it all about?"

"Reestablishing trade with Germany. Lifting embargoes. Making loans. Abolishing tariffs," Graham said.

"Business as usual," Joe Bristow said, with a note of bitterness in his voice.

"Precisely. They want our tea. We want their motorcycles," Graham said.

"But none of it can happen until we put that slight incident behind us," Joe said.

Graham raised an eyebrow. "Slight incident?" he said.

"The war."

"I wouldn't have put it exactly like that," Graham said, "but yes, that is correct."

Lloyd George sighed. He stood up and picked his cravat up off his desk, where he'd tossed it earlier. "I suppose there will be press?" he asked, tying the cravat around his neck.

"Quite a bit from what I understand," Graham said. He, and the ten other men seated around the large mahogany table in Lloyd George's office, also rose. All but Joe, who pushed his wheelchair away from the table.

"The kaiser starts a war, kills millions, then he wants to sell us motorcycles," he said, disgustedly. "I want no part of this."

"What we want to do and what we must do are two separate things," Graham said patronizingly. "In politics we must sometimes make deals and compromises. You've been in the House a long time. You know that well enough. This particular compromise is for the greater good."

Joe cocked an eyebrow. "Is it?" he said.

"It will create trade. And trade creates jobs. Which the men who have fought for this country, and have returned home to it, desperately need. We treat with the enemy to secure our advantage."

Lloyd George sighed deeply. "You're right, of course, Archie."

"I usually am, sir," Graham said. "Now, gentlemen, if we can please present a united front to the press on this issue. Smiles and warm words would be helpful."

Joe, who had wheeled himself to the doorway, now turned his chair around, blocking everyone else's way out. "A united front?" he said, shaking his head regretfully. "I don't know, Archie. I have to tell you that this is going to be a very hard sell in East London," he said.

"Ah. Now we come to the heart of the matter. I'm surprised it took you so long," Graham said archly.

"I'm going to need something I can take to my constituents."

"Have you any ideas on what that something might be?"

"As a matter of fact, I do."

"I somehow thought you would."

"I'll want three new factories. One in my constituency, Hackney.

One in Whitechapel and one in Limehouse. If Gerry wants to sell us motorcycles, he can bloody well build them in East London." He paused, then said, "In politics, Archie, we must sometimes make deals and compromises. You've been in the House a long time. You know that well enough."

Graham crossed his arms over his chest. "Two factories," he said at length. "Put them wherever the hell you like."

"Done," Joe said, flashing the man a wide smile.

"If you gentlemen are finished?" the prime minister said.

"We are," Joe replied, wheeling himself out of the way so that Lloyd George could pass him.

The prime minister led the way from his office, down a series of corridors, to the foyer of Number 10 Downing Street, his ministers following in his wake. There, Lloyd George stiffly shook hands with the head of the German trade commission—Wilhelm von Berg—as his ministers mingled with the delegates. The conversation was cool. Both sides were coming together because they had to, not because they wished to.

Joe made small talk with a coal baron from the Ruhr Valley, an economist from Berlin, and a manufacturer of farm equipment. The atmosphere was stiff and uncomfortable, and Joe found himself actually wishing to be outside, in the bear garden of journalists and photographers that awaited.

"Congratulations on your reelection, Mr. Bristow," a voice behind him said, in impeccable, polished English. Joe turned. A tall, blond man stood nearby. As Joe looked at him, he realized he knew him. His hair was shorter than the last time Joe had seen him, and there was a vicious scar running down the left side of his face, but even so, he had not changed greatly over the last four years.

"Max von Brandt," the man said. "We met before the war. At Holloway prison. You invited me to your home. For your brother-in-law's wedding."

"Yes," Joe said coldly. "Yes, I did."

"I'm pleased to see you again," Max added, "this time in my role as delegate to the trade commission."

A terrible anger rose inside Joe at the sight of von Brandt. With great effort, he forced himself to contain it. He was conducting the people of Britain's business here, not his own. He had words for von Brandt, but they would have to wait. He forced himself to listen, politely and attentively, while Max, and two more men who'd joined him, greeted him and congratulated him.

"Gentlemen, this way if you will . . . ," Joe heard Archie Graham say.

They were all shepherded outside, in front of the prime minister's residence. Hordes of reporters, jostling behind a cordon, started peppering them with questions.

"Rather reminds one of standing in front of a firing squad," Graham, who was standing next to Joe, said.

"I think the firing squad would go easy on us compared to this lot," Joe replied.

It was announced that the prime minister, his cabinet, and their German guests would stand for pictures first and then take questions. Joe looked out over the sea of press and saw his daughter in the scrum. She had her notebook out and was scribbling in it furiously. She had a photographer with her. Joe frowned at her. She was no longer on her term holidays. She should have been up at university and must have skipped classes to come to London. Fiona would certainly be unhappy if she knew, and there would be a row. Joe was proud of Katie for her devotion to journalism, but that paper of hers could sometimes cause a good deal of trouble, too.

After three or four minutes of picture-taking, the questions started. Reporters were shouting, interrupting, demanding answers. An irate Fleet Street wanted to know why the government was holding trade talks with Britain's erstwhile enemy.

Graham spoke first, telling them how renewed trade ties would help strengthen Britain's economy. The prime minister followed, urging for magnanimity in victory, and then it was the Germans' turn. Max von Brandt, their spokesman, stepped forward. He carefully and cogently outlined his commission's plans, detailing benefits for both Britain and Germany. He talked for about ten minutes, then finished by saying, "We will, of course, explain our plans more fully during our meetings with our British counterparts here in London over the next few weeks, but we appreciate being able to outline our ideas for you here. Fleet Street has been ill-disposed toward us, and understandably so, but I wish to assure you that it is my sincere hope, and the hope of the German people—now that the hostilities between us have ended—that we can work together for peace and prosperity, and for the benefit of both our nations. Good day, gentlemen."

Throughout Max's speech, Joe sat in his chair smiling woodenly and all the while raging inside. Von Brandt's presence was a cruel taunt to him. It was unbelievable that this man who had caused so much damage to his family, and to countless others, could stand here, smiling and talking about better days to come, as if nothing had ever happened. Joe's rage boiled up inside him and he could not contain it.

After a few more minutes of questions, the prime minister gave the members of the press a wave good-bye and headed back inside Number 10.

"Mr. von Brandt," Joe said, as German and British statesmen followed him. "Might I have a moment?"

Max stopped. He turned around, a questioning expression on his face.

"In here, please," Joe said, gesturing toward a receiving room off the foyer.

Max followed Joe. Once they were both inside the room, Joe closed the door. "Berlin should have sent someone else. Anyone but you," he said.

"I'm sorry to hear you feel that way, Mr. Bristow. I hope my work has not been lacking in some way?"

"I know who you are. And what you are. Maud Selwyn Jones died at your hands, didn't she? Why? Because she saw something she shouldn't have? Gladys Bigelow killed herself because you were blackmailing her. Jennie Finnegan went to her grave tortured over the fact that she'd helped you, a German spy. Her husband was very nearly killed by the information your network passed to Berlin. But I guess all's fair in love and war, isn't it?" Joe said.

Max shook his head. He gave Joe a puzzled smile. "I'm afraid I have no idea what you're talking about, Mr. Bristow," he said. "But before you destroy a man's reputation by accusing him of espionage and murder, you'd better have proof. A good deal of it. British libel laws, from what I understand, are highly punitive."

Max was right, of course. Joe had nothing concrete with which to hang him. He believed Jennie Finnegan's and John Harris's stories, but others would not. And he remembered, too, what had happened with Jack Flynn when they'd tried to bring him in for spying.

"You heartless bastard," Joe said. "I'd nail your head to the floor if I could only get out of this chair."

"How lucky for me, then, that you cannot," Max said. The smile was gone. His blue eyes were cold and hard. "A bit of advice, if I may: Things are not always what they seem, Mr. Bristow, especially when it comes to politics. The war is over. The entire world has accepted that. I urge you to do the same. Good day."

Max smiled icily, then left the room, slamming the door behind him. Joe stared after him, knowing he couldn't touch Max. Knowing he had only theories and hearsay, no proof. Knowing a treacherous and deadly man once again walked the streets of London and that he had no way to stop him. If only he did. If only there was some way, some one, some thing, *anything*, that could show the world what Max von Brandt was.

"Damn you," Joe said aloud. He picked up a glass paperweight and hurled it at the door. It shattered into a million useless pieces.

CHAPTER ONE HUNDRED SIX

WILLA LAY SPRAWLED out on her bed, tangled in her sheets, dreaming. She had fallen into a deep, narcotic sleep. A length of rubber tubing lay on the floor next to the bed, along with a syringe. A thin trickle of blood dripped from the inside of her right elbow.

She dreamed that she was standing on a platform at a train station, all alone. It was late and dark. A cold wind howled. It was a dangerous place. She knew she had to get out of there, but she didn't know how. There were no exit signs, no doors or stairs, no way out.

She couldn't quite remember how she'd got here. The pain had been very bad tonight—she remembered that. She'd been walking by the Seine earlier in the evening. She'd gone to buy wine, bread, and cheese. She'd seen a man walking toward her. He was handsome and tall and had red hair, and for the merest of seconds, her heart had leapt and she though it was him: Seamie. But of course it wasn't. Seamie was dead.

She'd felt so heartbroken afterward, so crushingly alone. The pain of knowing that she'd never see his face again had been agonizing. She'd rushed back to her flat, thrown her food down on the table, tied the tourniquet around her arm, and shot herself full of morphine. Nothing could save her. Not her work. Not Oscar. He was a good man, but she didn't love him. Couldn't love him. Something in her had died when Seamie died—her heart. She wanted the rest of her to die now, too.

The train pulled in, billowing steam. She was so glad. The wind had grown colder, the darkness more menacing. She desperately wanted to get on board. Faces, gray and expressionless, looked at her from the windows, but she wasn't scared of them. Seamie will be on this train, she thought. I know he will. More than anything, she wanted to see his face again, to hear his voice, to touch him. She climbed the steps from the platform to the train, turned into the car itself, and started to walk down the aisle, looking around expectantly for Seamie, but she could not find him. She walked into the next car, and the next. "Where is he?" she said aloud. "Where?" She was running now. Calling his name. But he was not there.

"Willa!"

She stopped and turned around. Was that him? It must be. But where was he?

"Seamie!" she called out. "Seamie, where are you?"

"Willa. Come on, Willa, sit up. . . ."

She felt pain, sudden and sharp. Someone was slapping her face. Hurting her. Again and again.

"Stop it!" she cried. "Let me go!"

"You're conscious. Oh, thank God. Willa, open your eyes."

She tried. But it was so hard.

Hands pulled her into a sitting position. A glass was pressed to her lips. The voice urged her to drink. Willa did so, then forced her eyes open. Josie was leaning over her. She looked terrified. And well dressed.

"You look so nice. Going out?" Willa mumbled.

"That was the idea," Josie said tightly. "We were going to meet you for dinner. Oscar and me. Remember? How much did you take?"

"Not enough, apparently," Willa said.

"Come on. Get up," Josie barked. "You're going to drink some coffee and walk this off."

As Josie tried to get her out of bed, another voice was heard—a man's. It was coming from the doorway. "Damn it, Willa," he said. It was Oscar. He looked heartsick.

"I'm sorry," Willa whispered.

"How could you do it?" he asked her.

"Oh, Oscar," she said brokenly. "How could I not?"

CHAPTER ONE HUNDRED SEVEN

BILLY MADDEN PICKED up his glass of whiskey—his fifth in the last hour—and downed it. On the table in front of him—next to the bottle—was a photograph of his three sons. It had been taken right before they'd shipped off to France. All three were in uniform.

"I still can't believe it, Bennie," he said. "William and Tommy dead. And Peter in hospital and a right fucking mess. He can't talk. He can barely walk. All he can do is shake—so fucking hard that he can't hold a spoon, or a pen, or his own fucking cock. The nurses have to do everything for him."

Bennie Deen, one of Billy's heavies, was sitting across from him at a table in the Bark. He was reading a newspaper. It was four o'clock. The pub was quiet. Only a few other men were in it. Bennie lowered his paper now and said, "You've got him in a good place, guv. The best place. He'll get better there. Didn't that doctor—Barnes, was it?—say that they're making strides with some of the worst of the lot?"

"Better? What's better? Maybe one day he'll be able to walk by himself. Or eat by himself. But he's never getting out of there. He'll die in that place. He'll never have a life, a woman, kids, nothing. He might as well be dead, too."

Billy poured himself another whiskey. "It's hardest on me wife," he said. "She don't do nothing anymore. She won't talk. Won't eat. She just sits in the kitchen, looking out the window. Like she was waiting for them all to come home."

"Can't she have no more?"

"No more what?"

"Kids."

"No, you stupid git, she can't. She's old. Forty, forty-one . . . I don't know. And even if she could, kids aren't hats, you know. You lose one, you can't just fucking replace him. For Christ's sake, go back to reading the funny pages, will you?"

At that moment, the door to the Barkentine opened and a young, well-dressed woman came inside. She was carrying a stack of newspapers.

"Is Mr. Madden about?" she asked the bartender. The man was just saying no, when she spotted Billy seated in his usual spot by the windows. "Ah! There he is. Thank you so much!" she said to the barman.

"Mr. Madden, might I join you for a moment?" she asked, as she approached his table. "My name is Katie Bristow. I'm the editor and publisher of the *Battle Cry,* and I work for Sam Wilson, your local member of Parliament."

"I don't care who you are, lass, you're not welcome here," Billy said. "This ain't a pub for ladies."

"Mr. Madden, Sam Wilson has a matter of great importance that he wishes to discuss with you," Katie said.

"Then why doesn't he come here himself?" Madden growled.

Katie frowned. She looked down at the floor, then back up at Billy. "Just between us, Mr. Madden . . . I think he's afraid," she said. "It's not everyone who'll come down to this part of Limehouse."

"Oh, aye? And why aren't you afraid, you cheeky little snip?"

"Because I've seen you with your son Peter. At Wickersham Hall. At Christmastime. You ate mince pies and didn't seem terribly fearsome."

Billy sat back in his chair, dumbfounded that this girl knew about Peter and, moreover, that she had the stones to talk to him so plainly.

"My brother Charlie is a resident of Wickersham Hall, you see," Katie explained. "He came back from France with severe shell shock. Members of my family founded the hospital. My parents contribute to its upkeep. I go there as much as I can. It's difficult though, what with my classes, and the paper, and my work for Mr. Wilson. I was there in December, though, and I saw you both—you and Peter."

"What do want?" Madden said gruffly. He didn't like talking about his son with strangers.

"The government is in talks with the Germans about siting two motorcycle factories in London. One possible site is in Limehouse, but there is competition. Other MPs are against us. They want the factories situated in their own constituencies. Sam Wilson is going to hold a rally next Saturday in support of the factory. He wants you to come."

Bennie burst into laughter. "Maybe you can carry the banner, Boss. Hand out badges."

Madden laughed, too. "You must be joking. You want *me* to come to a rally . . . for the Gerries? The same people who started the war that killed two of my sons and damaged the third one?"

"It is not a rally for the Gerries," Katie said. "It is a rally calling on government to site a German factory here in Limehouse instead of somewhere else. Because the people of Limehouse desperately need work, Mr. Madden. It is one of the poorest areas of London, of the entire United Kingdom. Life expectancy rates here are among the lowest in the country, and everything else—infant mortality, unemployment, crime, malnutrition—are extremely high. You are a powerful figure in Limehouse, Mr. Madden . . ."

"Too right!" Bennie chimed in.

". . . and if people see you come out for it, they will come out for it, and we need numbers if we are to convince government to put the factory here."

Madden was getting tired of this girl and her tedious speeches. "You've got the wrong man," he said. "Rallies ain't in my line of work."

But Katie was not to be deterred. "I know what your line of work is. Must it always be? I saw you with your son, Mr. Madden," she said quietly. "You were kind and concerned. You were—"

Billy Madden had had enough. Talk of his son made him feel helpless, and feeling helpless made him furious.

"My son is none of your bloody business. Get out. Now," he said, his voice rising.

Katie blinked, but did not falter. "Can I leave a copy of my newspaper with you? It has a story on the factory. Maybe you could take a look at it sometime."

Billy was barely keeping his temper under control now. "If I say yes, will you fuck off out of here?" he asked.

"Right away," Katie replied.

"Yes, then. Leave your bloody paper. If nothing else, the pictures will keep Bennie here amused."

"Good-bye, Mr. Madden, and thank you," Katie said, as she placed a copy of the *Battle Cry* on top of his table.

Madden, staring out at the river, made no reply.

"The fucking cheek," he said when she was gone. "Wilson can take his bloody factory and stuff it up his arse. I'll never have anything to do with it or with the bloody Gerries." He pointed at Katie's paper. "Take that rag and burn it," he said to Bennie. Then he poured himself another drink and continued to stare at the river, remembering Peter as he once was.

Bennie reached for the *Battle Cry*. As he lumbered over to the fireplace with it, he read the cover article. There were photographs to go along with the story, photos of the prime minister and his cabinet and the German trade commission. He stopped short, staring at one of the pictures.

"Oi, guv," he said, walking over to Madden. "Take a look at this. . . . Isn't this the bloke who used to come here? The one who hired a boat from you to take his man out to the North Sea? Name's different, but I could swear it's him."

"What are you on about now?" Madden said.

Bennie put the paper on the table in front of him. "There," he said, pointing at a picture. 'Maximilian von Brandt, Spokesman for the German Trade Delegation,' it says. See him? Second from the left."

Billy squinted at the photograph. The whiskey had made his mind foggy. "You're right. It is him. Without a doubt," he said at length. "Peter Stiles he called himself. Says here his name is von Brandt, though. Well, whatever it is, the son of a bitch cost me a good boatman.

John Harris disappeared right after the busies took his man Flynn. If I ever see Harris again, I'll gut him for walking out on me."

Billy kept reading and as he did, the whiskey fog lifted. "Bennie, listen to this. It says here that von Brandt was an officer in the German Army during the war and was pals with the kaiser, and that he's now a high-ranking government man and that the new guv'nor, Friedrich Ebert, handpicked him to come over to London and make nice."

"Yeah? So?"

"So? *So?*" Billy said angrily. "So he lied to us! He came here to the Bark sounding as English as me grandmother. Made out like he was one of us. But that wasn't true. He was *German*, Bennie. An officer in Gerry's army. Pals with the kaiser . . . it says so right here!"

"So?"

"So, I'll bet you my right ball that it wasn't jewelry his man was taking to the North Sea!"

"You . . . you don't think he was a spy, guv?" Bennie said slowly.

"No, you daft bastard, I *know* he was a spy!" Billy said. He shook his head in disbelief. "All that time, Bennie . . . all that time I thought he was a villain moving some swag. But he wasn't. And me, Bennie? What was I doing? I was helping Max von bloody Brandt feed secrets to the Gerries. I was helping a dirty spy. Fuck me! No . . . fuck *him*!"

Billy stood up, grabbed the whiskey bottle, and threw it across the room. It nearly hit the barman and it shattered the mirror behind him.

"Easy, guv," Bennie said.

But it was too late. The table Billy had been sitting at went over. Then every table in the room did. Pictures were smashed. Windows, too. Chairs were thrown against the wall. Billy was screaming and cursing, out of his mind. He only stopped his mad rampage when there was nothing left to break.

"I bet it was him who did for my boys," he said then, wild-eyed and panting. "I bet it was him who gave the Gerries all the information they needed. It's his fault, Bennie. It's Max von Brandt's fault William and Tommy are dead and Peter's off his nut."

"You've got to calm down, guv. This is no good."

"Oh, I'll calm down all right, Bennie. Just long enough to find von Brandt."

"Billy, be reasonable," Bennie said. "Von Brandt's a government man. He spends his days with the likes of the prime minister. We couldn't even get close to him."

"Oh, but I am being reasonable," Billy said, his eyes blazing with rage. "In fact, I've reasoned it all out very nicely. I'm going to make his father grieve the way I'm grieving. I'm going to make the man know what it feels like to lose a son."

"You don't mean that. We can't just—"

"We can, Bennie," Billy said. "And we will. There's got to be a way. Whatever it is, I'll find it, and when I do, Max von Brandt is a dead man."

CHAPTER ONE HUNDRED EIGHT

MAX VON BRANDT poured himself a cup of strong coffee and sat down at the desk in his hotel suite. It was only half past three, but he was already exhausted. The day, full of meetings at Westminster and interviews with the London dailies, had been a grueling one.

He was due at the chancellor's house for supper tonight—an event which would likely go quite late, and before that, he had a dozen telephone calls to make and a thick stack of reports to read through. He was just reaching for the telephone when he heard a knock on his hotel room door.

"Telegram for Mr. von Brandt," a man's voice called.

"One moment, please," Max called back.

He rose, quickly crossed the room, and opened the door. Before he could even shout, the two men were on him. The first man, a broad-shouldered giant, drove his fist into Max's face, knocking him to the floor.

The second man quickly closed the door and locked it. "Get him in the chair, Bennie," the first man said. "Over there. Tie him."

Max, dazed from the blow and bleeding from the gash it had left on his jaw, felt himself being lifted up and dragged backward. He tried to reach into his pocket, to get hold of the knife that was there, but before he could, he was dumped into a chair and a length of rope was wound around him, pinning his arms tightly against his body.

"Well done, lad," the second man said. "He won't be going any-where soon. Will you, Mr. Stiles?"

Max, who'd been straining against his bonds, looked up just in time to see Billy's fist come flying toward him. The blow opened up another gash—this one across his cheekbone. His head snapped back. Blood sprayed across the wall behind him in an arc.

When the pain had subsided a bit, when he could see properly, and speak, he said, "Hello, Billy. What a pleasure it is to see you again."

"Shut your mouth, you bastard. You cunt. You filthy spy."

"Billy, I don't—"

"Shut your mouth!" Billy screamed.

He pulled a pistol out of his coat pocket and pointed it at Max.

"You killed them," he said. "You killed my boys William and Tommy. You put Peter in hospital for the rest of his life."

Max realized he was in very great danger. Billy Madden had never been entirely right; now he seemed to have gone completely insane. His eyes were dark and mad and full of rage. Flecks of spit flew from his lips as he spoke. He was sweating and shaking.

"Billy, let me talk, listen to me. . . . I did not hurt your sons. I swear it."

"Listen to him, will you, Bennie? Listen to his lies. You *did* kill them," Madden shouted. "I saw you, von Brandt. I saw your picture in the paper. The German guv'nor himself sent you here to make nice with the prime minister. How stupid do you think I am? You're not Peter Stiles. You're not English. And that wasn't swag you were

sending to the North Sea. You and that murdering bastard of a kaiser were thick as thieves. You stole information here, you and your
men, and you gave it to Germany. You told the kaiser where my
boys would be and he dropped his shells on them. You killed them
sure as I'm standing here, and now I'm going to kill you."

Madden raised the gun again, and Max knew he had seconds,
only seconds, to save his own life.

"It would be a terrible mistake to kill me, Billy," he said.

"I don't think so," Madden replied. He walked over to Max and
pressed the pistol's barrel against his head.

"You have another son."

"The fuck I do," Madden said, cocking the trigger.

"Josie Meadows," Max said. "She was pregnant when she gave you
the slip, wasn't she? Pregnant with your child. Put the gun down,
Billy, and I'll tell you where she is."

CHAPTER ONE HUNDRED NINE

"DADDY?" JAMES SAID.

Seamie smiled. He loved the sound of that word on his son's lips.
If he lived to be a hundred, he would never tire of hearing it.

"Yes, James?"

"Tell me about Lawrence again. And Auda and Faisal. Tell me
about the desert."

Seamie, sitting on an old, squashy settee by the fireplace in the
Binsey cottage, said, "Isn't it past your bedtime, lad?"

"Just one more story. Please, Daddy?"

Seamie smiled. He would happily have told him twenty stories.

"Did you wash your face?"

"Yes."

"Clean your teeth?"

"Yes."

"Come on then, come sit by me," Seamie said, patting the cushion next to him.

James, in his pajamas and clutching Wellie, his teddy bear, bounded onto the settee.

They'd come up to Jennie's old cottage, which belonged to Seamie now, to spend a week together, just the two of them. They'd got to know each other at Fiona and Joe's house over the last few weeks. James had been reticent at first, but had gradually warmed to Seamie and had even started to call him Daddy on his own. When Seamie asked him if he might like to visit the cottage in Binsey and do a little winter rambling around the Cotswolds, James had immediately said, "Would I! Let's go!"

Seamie had taken James into an outfitters on Jermyn Street and made a big production of getting him kitted out with a pair of hiking boots, gaiters, a small walking stick, a waterproof, mittens, and a good warm hat. They'd arrived at the cottage three days ago and had been having a wonderful time cooking for themselves, walking, having pub lunches, talking, and sitting by the fire. Seamie hoped to eventually be able to go on proper treks and climbs with James, but his injuries were still not fully healed.

"If you could have seen Lawrence in the desert just one time," Seamie began now, "you would want that one time to be right as he set off to take Damascus."

"Why, Daddy?"

"Listen and I'll tell you," Seamie said. "Lawrence was about to wage the biggest campaign of his life, a campaign that would affect the fate of nations, and of all the people living in them. He was going to try to take a desert city heavily fortified by Turkish forces. If he succeeded, he would deal a lethal blow to England's enemies, and he would accomplish nothing less than the liberation of all of Arabia. . . ."

Seamie went on to describe for a wide-eyed, spellbound James the scene in Lawrence's camp right before the march to Damascus. He told him about the yelling and bawling camels, the thousands of fearsome Bedouin fighters. He told him about Lawrence, riding at the head of the Arab irregulars with Faisal and Auda. He painted a picture for the boy of the sight the three men made in their robes, rifles slung over their backs—the regal Faisal; the warrior Auda, with his sharp features and piercing hawk's eyes; and Lawrence in his white robes, at once so English, with his blue eyes and easy smile, and yet a son of Arabia, too, belonging, at that moment, entirely to the desert and its people.

Seamie told James how it had taken hours and hours for all the soldiers to leave. How the dust clouds had risen in their wake, how they looked as if a sea of men was marching to Damascus.

And then James said, "But, Daddy, what were you doing there?"

"Where? At the camp?"

"In the desert. You're a sea captain, aren't you? There are no oceans in the desert."

"Right you are, James. Well observed."

James smiled proudly.

"I had been hunting for a friend in the desert. This friend had fought very hard on behalf of Major Lawrence, had been captured by the Turkish Army, but had escaped."

"Did you find him?"

"Her, actually. Yes, I did. And I took her back to Lawrence's camp."

"Her?" James said, wrinkling his nose. "You had a girl for a friend?"

Seamie laughed. "I did."

His voice was wistful now, his expression sad. He wondered what had become of Willa. He had not seen or heard from her since he'd left her with Fatima at Lawrence's camp. His ship had been attacked only days after he'd said good-bye to her. Albie, who was back in Cambridge, and whom he'd written to, said she was in Paris. He had no current address for her, though. He'd tried to fetch her home once, but it hadn't gone well, and they hadn't corresponded since.

He gave Seamie the last address he had for her, but she must've moved because his letter to her had been returned to him unopened. He wondered if she'd heard he was dead, wherever she was, and if she'd now heard the opposite. He would go to Paris soon. As soon as he and James were a little more settled. Not just yet, though. He'd just come back into the boy's life and felt he must not leave him again so soon.

"She must've been a very good friend for you to hunt for her all over the desert."

"She was a good friend. Even though she was a girl," Seamie said conspiratorially.

"Mummy was a girl," James said. "Did you love your friend like Mummy?"

Seamie faltered for a second, as all the old pain flooded back. He thought about the mistakes he'd made and the betrayals. He thought about the sorrow, the regret, the guilt, and the loss. How in the world could he ever explain that to anyone, never mind a small boy?

"You know what, lad?" he finally said. "That's a story for another day. Off you go now. It's late. Time for bed."

"All right," James said. He kissed Seamie's cheek. "I love you, Daddy."

Seamie was stunned. It was the first time James had said that. He leaned his head against his son's and quietly said, "I love you, too, James."

They sat close beside each other, father and son, staring at the fire. Seamie forgot all about bedtime. He forgot the painful thoughts he'd just been thinking, the painful emotions he'd just felt.

For the first time in a long time, he didn't think of the past. And of all the things he'd lost. He thought only of the present, and what he had. And how it was so much more than he deserved. And he prayed then that he would never, ever lose it.

CHAPTER ONE HUNDRED TEN

"IT'S A LIE," Billy Madden said. "You're making the whole thing up to save your hide."

"It's no lie. Untie me and I'll tell you more," Max said, hoping to convince Billy of the truth. Hoping to save his life.

"Maybe I'll just beat the shite out of you instead. That's another way of getting you to tell me more."

"I hope you're feeling strong. Or, rather, that your gorilla here is. I can take a beating, Billy. In my line of work, it's an essential skill. Go too far with the fists, though, and you might kill me. That would be unfortunate. Because I'm one of only two people who knows that you have a son. Josie also knows where the boy is. But you have no idea where she is, do you? Kill me, and you'll never find out."

Madden stared at Max thoughtfully, then said, "Untie him, Bennie."

As soon as the ropes had been removed, Max stood. "He leaves, first," he said, pointing at Bennie, "and then you unload the pistol and give me the bullets."

Madden did as Max asked.

When Bennie was on his way to the hotel's lobby, and the bullets were safely in Max's pocket, Max looked at Madden and said, "Listen carefully, I'm only going to say this once. And then you're going to leave."

Madden nodded.

"She's in Paris. I've kept tabs on her. She's an actress. She goes by the name of Josephine Lavallier. She performs at Bobino's in Montparnasse. She hid from you back in 1914, had the child—a boy—and gave him away. Then she left England for the continent."

"Gave him away? To who? Is he here in London? Is he at an or-phanage?"

"She gave him to a woman. The woman died. The boy is still well. He lives with the woman's husband—a man whom he knows as his father."

"What woman? Stop playing silly buggers and tell me the husband's name!"

"Sorry, Billy, but I'm afraid that's not possible. That bit of infor-mation buys me a bit of time. It's my insurance policy against another afternoon like this one. As long as I know where your son is, you can't kill me."

"I'll still kill you, von Brandt. I'll just wait until I find that bitch of a Josie and get the name of the ones she gave my boy to. Then I'll nip right back and do for you. Nab you some night when you least expect it."

"I don't think so. By the time you get to Paris and find Josie and then get back to London again, I'll be back in Berlin. I'd advise you not to come after me there. I have many friends in that city."

Without another word, Billy Madden left, slamming the door behind him. Max locked it after him. He walked back to the sitting area, picked the rope up off the floor, and put it in his briefcase. He would dispose of it later. He got a facecloth from the bathroom, wet-ted it, and rubbed his blood off the wall.

Next he went into the bathroom and attended to his face. He would tell Lloyd George, Bonar Law, and the others at the dinner to-night that he'd got into a scuffle on the street with a man who'd lost his son in France and wanted to take it out on a German, any Ger-man. It wasn't so far from the truth.

After he'd cleaned himself up, Max poured himself a whiskey to steady his nerves. He'd very nearly had a bullet put through his head. As he downed the contents of the glass, he thought it would be a good idea to kill Billy Madden. Right away. Tonight. But he knew that was impossible. Madden always had at least one of his men around him, if not more. Max was too visible now to move around London freely, and even if he could put together some sort of disguise, how would he get the time to go after Madden? His evenings were full of parties and dinners. He was supposed to be acting the part of the civilized diplomat now, not making shadowy visits to East London, as he used to do.

He would have to let it go. There was no other choice. He felt a momentary ripple of unease over having told Madden about Josie, and about possibly endangering both Josie and her son. In his current state, Madden was probably insane enough to actually go to Paris.

What would Madden do if he found Josie there? Max wondered. He'd probably question her about the child. Probably rough her up a bit. She might tell him where the boy was and she might not, but even if she did, was Billy Madden crazy enough to try to take a child from the likes of Seamus Finnegan? The man was a war hero. He'd survived the best efforts of the German Navy. He'd kill anyone who tried to take his son, and even if Billy did get hold of the boy, once the story made the newspapers, the entire country would be looking for him.

No, Max decided, Billy Madden was currently unhinged because of grief over his sons. Once he calmed down a bit, he would see the lunacy of the whole thing and let it go. Of course he would.

Max finished his drink and tried to put the whole incident out of his mind. He had things other than some East End madman to worry about. He'd managed to accomplish none of the things he ought to have done. No telephone calls had been made, no reports had been read. And he now would need to bathe and dress if he had any hope of getting to his dinner on time.

And after his dinner, he had one more meeting to attend. A very private meeting. Back here, in his rooms. Quite late.

Max von Brandt had been put in charge of the trade and finance delegation for a reason, and it wasn't because he was all gemütlich with the German president, no matter what the papers might say. It was because he had other business in London, for which the delegation was merely a convenient cover. He had something far more important to achieve than selling motorcycles.

He had a chain to mend.

"*BONJOUR*, WILLA!" THE baker's wife called out, as Willa entered her shop.

"*Bonjour*, Adelaide. *Ça va?*" Willa called back.

"*Oui, ça va! Et toi?*"

"*Je suis bien, merci, mais j'ai faim. Un croissant, s'il vous plaît, à aussi une baguette.*"

As the baker's wife assembled Willa's order, she told Willa that she was too thin and would never get a man because what man wanted to embrace a woman who looked like a garden rake? She said she was going to give Willa two croissants, not one, and that she must promise to eat them both.

Willa forced a smile and said she would. She paid for her purchases and slowly walked back to her flat. There was no reason to hurry. No one was waiting for her there. When she got to her rooms, she put her croissants and the milk she'd bought on her table, then heated a pot of water for coffee. She hung up her coat and then, still cold, shrugged into the woolly cardigan that Oscar had left hanging on a hook by the door. It was soft and warm, and of a good quality. I should really give it back to him, she thought. I will. If I ever see him again.

Oscar had decided that a nice house with a set of china and a vacuum cleaner in it was not the answer to Willa's problems—and neither was he. They had parted company a few days after her overdose and he'd returned to Rome. Willa didn't blame him. She wasn't angry with him. She didn't want to live with herself. Why should he?

The water boiled. Willa ground some coffee beans, put them in her press, and poured the water over them. She poured some creamy milk into a bowl, added some coffee, then carried the bowl to the table. Morning sunshine was streaming in the windows. She turned her chair so its heat warmed her back. Then put her head in her hands and wept.

It was like this every day now. Sadness had overwhelmed her; it had nearly immobilized her. She could barely eat or sleep and didn't work at all anymore. She wished that Josie and Oscar hadn't found her. She wished she had died the night she'd overdosed. She would have been with Seamie, then, instead of always being without him.

She pushed her breakfast aside and grabbed the bottle of pills on her table. She'd run out of injectable morphine. The pills weren't as strong, but they were all she had left.

As she swallowed three, she heard a knock on her door. "Who is it?" she called out.

"It's your aunt Edwina! Let me in!"

"Aunt Eddie?" Willa said, in disbelief. She hurried to the door and opened it. Her aunt stood there in a traveling coat and hat, a valise in her hand.

"Oh, dear," she said in a dismayed voice, her eyes traveling over Willa. "That man was right. You do look a wreck. May I come in?"

"Of course, Aunt Eddie," Willa said, taking her aunt's valise. "What man? What did he say? Why are you here?"

"What a lovely greeting," Eddie sniffed. "And after I've come all this way."

"I'm sorry, Eddie," Willa said, hugging her aunt. "I'm glad you've come, of course I am. I'm just confused, that's all. About this man you mentioned."

"Some man wrote to Albie," Eddie explained, as she took her coat off and laid it over a chair. "Said he got Albie's address from a stack of old letters he found in your flat. He said you were in an awfully bad way and that he—Albie—should come and collect you. Since Albie already tried that once—with no luck—I decided to come. I'm here to bring you home, Willa."

"Wait a minute, Aunt Eddie . . . what's the man's name?" Willa asked, still puzzled.

"Oscar Something-or-Other. I can't remember. He said he knew you and cared for you but couldn't seem to do anything for you. He didn't think you should be alone. Is that coffee I smell?"

"Yes, it is," Willa said. "Let me get you some." So Oscar was behind this. He'd written to her family out of concern for her. That he would do that, after what she'd done, touched her so deeply she felt like crying again.

"Willa, I came because of Oscar's letter, because I was worried about you, but there's also another reason for my visit," Eddie said.

Willa, who'd been stirring milk into her aunt's coffee, turned around, alarmed.

"Don't look so worried. Your mother and brother are both fine. I have some news for you. It's good news, but rather shocking. I think you should sit down. Come," she said, patting the empty space next to her on the settee.

Willa sat. She handed her aunt a hot cup of coffee. "I must say that this is all very strange, Aunt Eddie. What news? What is it? Couldn't you have just written instead of making the trip all the way from Cambridge to Paris?" she asked her.

Eddie didn't reply. She leaned over to her valise, drew a newspaper out of it, and handed it to Willa. Willa saw that it was a copy of the London *Times* and that it was several weeks out of date.

"Read it," Eddie said.

The headlines talked of the transfer of Alsace from Germany to France, of reconstruction projects in the Marne area, and of the Belgian king's visit to Paris. Willa quickly scanned the articles, sipping her coffee as she did. "What is it I'm supposed to be looking for?" she asked.

Then she saw the photograph at the bottom right of the page, and the coffee bowl slipped out of her hand, bounced off the table, and smashed on the floor. Willa didn't hear it smash. She didn't see the mess on the floor. All she saw was Seamie's face.

"My God, Eddie . . . it can't be," she whispered. But it was.

BRITISH SEA CAPTAIN RETURNS FROM THE DEAD, the headline said. "Seamus Finnegan, captain of the *Exeter*," the caption read.

Willa touched the image with trembling fingers. She started to read the article and learned what had really happened to Seamie after his ship had been attacked. She started to laugh, then burst into tears, and then laughed again. She kept reading and learned that he'd arrived in London a month ago and planned to stay with his sister and her husband. At their home, he would be reunited with his young son, James, who'd been staying with his relatives. Willa was stricken to find out that the reason the boy was not with his mother was because he had lost her to influenza. Captain Finnegan had told the press that he would eventually be relocating with his son to a family cottage in the Cotswolds.

"I can't believe it. I simply cannot believe it," Willa said. "He's alive, Eddie."

"I know. Wonderful, isn't it? I wanted you to hear it from me. I hoped I would reach Paris before any of the London papers did. Oscar said you were in such a fragile state, I wasn't sure how you'd react."

Willa stood up, elated. She was crying again, but this time her tears were tears of joy. Seamie was alive. He was in this world still, not the next.

"Do you know where Seamie is in the Cotswolds?" Eddie asked.

"The paper said he was moving to a family cottage. I think it's in Binsey. He mentioned a cottage in Binsey once. It belonged to his wife. Perhaps you can go see him there. After we return home," Eddie said.

The smile on Willa's face faded. She shook her head. "No, Aunt Eddie, I can't," she said.

"Why not?"

Willa was silent for a moment, then she said, "Because back in the desert, after Seamie found me and brought me back to Lawrence's camp, I told him we had to let go of one another. To stop hurting ourselves and the people around us. It's not good, what we had. Or what we did. Before the war." She looked down at her hands. "Perhaps you don't know about that. Or perhaps you do."

Eddie nodded. "I didn't. I do now."

"Yes, well," Willa continued, "it's a hard, destructive thing to love someone you shouldn't, and it's caused nothing but grief."

"His wife's passed away, Willa," Eddie said gently. "He's a widower now."

"So what should I do, Aunt Eddie?" Willa said bitterly. "Run to him like some she-vulture? I won't. Too many mistakes were made, too many sins committed. Jennie deserved better. Albie did. Seamie himself did. No, I'm staying here. We ended it for a reason, and that reason remains—we're no good for each other. We weren't in Africa. We weren't in London back in 1914. And we wouldn't be now, either. I know that." Eddie let out a long, heavy sigh. Willa took her aunt's hands in hers and said, "I appreciate you coming here. I know you did it out of concern for me and I love you for it, Aunt Eddie, but I can't go back. I can't. It's far too painful."

Eddie nodded. "I understand, Willa. God knows what I'll tell your mother, but I do understand."

Willa kissed her. "Thank you. You won't go back right away, will you? Stay with me for a bit."

"Yes, I think I shall stay," Eddie said. "I quite fancy a bit of a holiday and some good French food." She frowned, then said, "Your hands are trembling, Willa, I can feel them. You were already in a state when I arrived and I fear I've made things worse."

Willa shook her head. "You've done no such thing. I'm happy, so deeply happy, to know he's alive," she said. "He is my heart, and my soul, and to know that he didn't die, that he . . ." Her voice trailed off as tears threatened to overtake her again. She struggled to gain control over her emotions, and when she had, she said, "I believe I'm in need of some air, a walk, something."

"That sounds like a good idea. A walk will clear your head. I'll help myself to more coffee while you're gone, and when you get back, perhaps you can show me around Montparnasse," Eddie said.

Willa kissed her aunt again then she grabbed her coat and got down the stairs from her flat to the street as fast as she could, forgetting her scarf, forgetting her hat, forgetting everything but the amazing, impossible news that Seamus Finnegan was alive.

CHAPTER ONE HUNDRED TWELVE

"JOSIE!" WILLA SHOUTED, knocking on the door to her friend's flat. "Jo, it's me, Willa! Open up, will you?"

She'd been knocking for a whole minute already, but Josie had not answered. Willa knew she was there. There was no way she would have left the flat this early. Not Josie. She usually slept until noon.

Willa wanted to see her. Josie was her closest friend and she wanted to tell her about Seamie. She wanted to have a good long talk. And a good long cry, too.

"Come on, Josie, you lazy wench! Wake up and open the door!" Willa shouted, banging on the door again.

But still there was no answer. "That's odd," Willa said. She tried the doorknob; it turned in her hand. That was odd, too. She pushed the door open. "Jo?" she called again, uncertainly.

It was dark inside the foyer. Willa's eyes took a few minutes to adjust. As soon as they did, and as soon as Willa walked into the flat proper, she saw that something was terribly wrong. The place looked as if it had been upended. Pictures were off the wall. Vases and statues lay on the floor in pieces. The draperies had been shredded. Cushions had been torn apart. The fine silk upholstery on Josie's furniture had been cut open. Stuffing spilled out of chairs and settees.

"Josie?" she called out, suddenly afraid. She heard a sound, like a moan, coming from the bedroom and hurried toward it.

The sight that greeted her as she entered the room made her scream.

Josie lay on her bed. Her face had been battered so badly that she was nearly unrecognizable. Blood had dripped down the front of her dress and all over her bedding.

"Josie . . . my God . . . ," Willa cried, running to her friend.

Josie reached for her. "I didn't tell, Willa," she sobbed. "I didn't tell him."

"Tell who? Who did this to you?" Willa said, taking her bloodied hand. She knelt down on the floor. "No, don't speak. Don't move. Don't do anything. I'm going to run for help."

"No!" Josie moaned.

"You need a doctor!" Willa said.

"There's no time. Listen, Willa, please. . . . I have a son," Josie said, with effort.

"*What?*"

"A little boy. Back in England. James. I used to go round with a villain . . . Billy Madden. He put me up the spout, then wanted me to get rid of it. I couldn't. I had the baby. Gave it to my friend Jennie. She used to be my teacher. She'd lost her baby. Her husband didn't love her and she thought he would, if she could give him a child, but she couldn't. She'd had an accident. I left London and hid in her cottage. In the Cotwolds. . . ." Josie stopped speaking for a minute. She closed her eyes, breathing heavily.

Willa felt her whole body go cold. Seamie's late wife's name was Jennie. She'd had a cottage in the Cotswolds. Their son's name was James. James was four years old. No, she thought, it can't be. It's a coincidence, that's all.

Josie opened her blackened, swollen eyes again. Willa could see the pain in them.

"Josie, don't talk," she said. "Save your strength. Let me go for a doctor. *Please.*"

"There's no time," Josie said. She gave a small groan, stiffening against something that hurt her terribly. "I told the doctor who delivered my baby that I was Jennie, so the right names would be on the birth certificate," she said. "I gave James to Jennie the day after he was born and then I left for Paris. Jennie lied to her husband . . . she pretended to be pregnant, then told him she'd had the baby herself. I asked her would she write me now and again . . . send me a picture . . . oh, God . . ." Josie's words became a whimper of pain.

"Josie, please . . . you must let me go for help."

Josie shook her head. "Somebody told Billy about the child, and now Billy wants him. He's gone mad, Willa. I thought he would kill me. He said he lost his sons in the war and now he's going to take James. He tried to get Jennie's name from me, and her husband's, but I wouldn't give them to him . . . I wouldn't . . . so he did this to me. He's going back to England. He's going to find James somehow and take him," Josie sobbed. Tears leaked out of her eyes. "Don't let him, Willa. Don't let him take James. . . ."

"Shh, Josie, shh . . ."

"I hid the letters," she said, hysterical now. "The ones Jennie sent me. Billy pulled the place apart, but he didn't find them. They're in my jewelry box. Take them. They have Jennie's address on them. Tell her what happened. There's money in there, too. Take it, Willa. Go to her. Warn her. Hurry."

"Where, Josie? Where's the jewelry box?" Willa said. She would find it. That would calm Josie down.

"In the sitting room."

Willa ran into the other room and searched through the wreckage for Josie's jewelry box. She found it near the window, but it was empty. The jewels it had contained had been dumped onto the floor. There were no letters inside it, no money, nothing.

"Damn it!" Willa hissed. "Where are they?" She knelt down again and start ripping the box apart. She ripped out the lining, tore out the drawers and shelves, but still she found nothing. She raised the box over her head and slammed it against the floor. Once, twice. On the third time the bottom splintered. Willa pulled the pieces apart, and there they were—a stack of letters, neatly tied with a ribbon, and a small leather pouch containing franc notes and pound notes, rolled up together.

Willa pulled a letter out of the stack and turned it over, dreading what she might find. "Oh, no. Oh, God," she said. The return address was in London. Willa recognized it. It used to be Seamie's. She recognized the name above it, too: Finnegan. J. Finnegan. Jennie had died, and Josie hadn't known it. And Jennie had been married to Seamie. And her son . . . James . . . he was the boy Billy Madden was after. And Seamie had no idea about any of this.

"Did you find them?" Josie asked weakly when Willa returned to her bedroom.

"I did," Willa said, putting the letters and the money on Josie's night table.

"You've got to tell her. Promise me!" Josie said fiercely.

Willa couldn't bear to tell Josie that her friend was dead. "I promise you, Jo. I swear. I'll do something . . . ring her . . . or . . . or send a telegram. Soon. Very soon. But right now, I'm going to see to you."

There was a lot of blood on Josie's clothing, and in the bed. Too much blood.

"What am I going to do? What the hell am I going to do?" Willa whispered to herself. An image flashed in her mind—of her pill bottle. She'd taken three morphine pills. No wonder she couldn't think straight. "Come on, Willa, shake it off," she told herself. "You've got to think!"

Two seconds later, she was out on the landing, battering on the neighbor's door. A man answered it. She quickly told him that her friend had been attacked and that she was badly injured and needed a doctor. The man said a doctor lived on the top floor of the building and then ran upstairs to fetch him. A few minutes later, the doctor was at Josie's side. Her attacker had split a vein in her chin, he told Willa, that's where most of the blood was coming from. He said he would cauterize it and then stitch up the worst of the wounds on Josie's face.

"She's going to be all right," he told Willa. "She might've bled to death if I hadn't got here when I did, though."

As the doctor set to work on Josie, Willa raced back into Josie's sitting room. The telephone was on the floor. Willa prayed that it still worked. She set the base upright and put the receiver in its cradle. After waiting for a few seconds, she picked the receiver up again and dialed for the operator. Almost instantly, she heard a woman's voice. She asked to be put through to the address on the envelope. No luck. Service to that address had been terminated, the operator informed her. She asked to be connected to the home of Miss Edwina Alden, at Highgate House, Carlton Way, Cambridge.

After a few minutes, a male voice, crackly and faraway-sounding, said, "Highgate House. Hello?"

"Albie?" Willa shouted. "Oh, thank God!"

There was a pause, then "Willa? Is that you?"

"Yes, it's me. Albie, I need your help. You've got to get hold of Seamie. His son, James, is in terrible danger. He's not really his son. The boy was given to Jennie by another woman—Josie Meadows. His real father is Billy Madden, a villain. From London. He's coming after the boy, Albie. He's just been here in Paris and he's beaten Josie very badly—"

"Willa," Albie said, cutting her off.

"Albie, don't talk. Just listen to me."

"No, I'm not listening. Not anymore. You're obviously off your head, Willa. And we both know why."

"Albie, I'm *not* off my head. This is real. You've got to call Seamie and tell him. Now!"

"Aunt Eddie's supposed to be there with you. Is she? Put her on the phone."

"I can't. She's at my flat. I'm at my friend's flat. Albie, you've got to listen to me." Willa's voice was shaking badly. She tried to keep it steady, but she couldn't.

"This is pathetic," Albie said. "I can't bear to listen to you. Don't ring me again, Willa. Not in this state. Not until you've quit the drugs."

"Albie, no! Wait! Don't hang up!"

"Just answer me this: Did you take anything today?"

She did not want to answer him. "Yes, but Albie, I—" she finally said.

"I thought so." There was a loud click and then a dull, dead tone.

"He thinks I'm a raving lunatic. Because of the morphine," Willa said out loud.

Of course he did. When he'd come to Paris to fetch her home, he'd been able to tell just by looking at her that she was addicted. And now she'd called him out of the blue with this outlandish story.

She started to panic. If she couldn't get hold of Seamie, and if Albie wouldn't help her, who would?

"Think, Willa, think," she told herself. She got an operator again and asked to be connected to Westminster, hoping to talk with Joe Bristow. This time it was the operator who hung up on her.

Willa was frantic, then she remembered the cottage—at Binsey. In the newspaper article, Seamie had said he was going to relocate to a family cottage in the Cotswolds. It had to be the Binsey place. It just had to be. A few seconds later, she was on the line again, asking the operator to see if she could connect her with a Seamus Finnegan in Binsey, but again she had no luck. The woman said she had no such listing.

"Is there *anything* in Binsey with a telephone in it?" Willa asked. "A church, a shop, a pub, anything?"

The operator said there was an inn and then put her through.

"The King's Head. May I help you?" a woman's voice said.

"Hello. Yes," Willa said. "I was wondering if you know of a Captain Seamus Finnegan?"

There was a slight pause, then "Is this another reporter? I've told you lot time and again—leave that poor man alone!" the woman said angrily.

"I'm not a reporter. I'm a friend of Captain Finnegan's," Willa said.

"Pull the other one. It's got bells on," the woman said. And then she, too, hung up.

Willa stood in the silence of Josie's flat, the phone in her hand. She didn't know who else to ring for help. She didn't know how to get hold of Seamie, to warn him. All she knew was that Billy Madden was on his way back to England. On his way to find James Finnegan.

And he would stop at nothing to get him. The battered woman in the other room was proof of that.

And suddenly, Willa knew exactly what to do.

She ran into Josie's bedroom and knelt down by the bed. "I'm sorry, Jo. I'm so sorry for what happened to you. And I'm sorry to leave you like this, but I have to go now. Back to England. I'm going to find Seamie—James's father—and tell him what's happened. I'm going to make sure Billy Madden is stopped. I promise you."

"Take the money, Willa. Get on a ferry. Hurry."

"I will, Josie. And I won't leave you alone. My aunt Eddie just arrived. She was supposed to fetch me home with her. I'm going to send her over. She'll take care of you."

Willa leaned over her poor friend and kissed her forehead. Then she stood up, grabbed the bundle of letters and the wad of bills from the night table where she'd put them, and shoved them into her trouser pocket.

"Good-bye, Jo," she said, then she left Josie's flat, let herself out of the building, and broke into a shambling run.

CHAPTER ONE HUNDRED THIRTEEN

"I CAN'T BELIEVE this," Willa said. "I can't bloody believe this!"

She had traveled all the way from Paris to Calais, and then Calais to Dover in just under twenty-four hours. She'd taken a hackney from the ferry terminal to the train station, yelling at the man to driver faster the whole way, only to discover that she'd missed the Dover to London train by six minutes. Six bloody minutes! And the next one was not for another five hours.

She didn't have five hours to waste twiddling her thumbs here.

Seamie and James didn't have five hours. God only knew where Billy Madden was. Fear chattered at her, telling her he could be back in London by now, looking for them. She clamped down on it, reminding herself—as she'd done ever since she'd left Josie's flat—that Josie had *not* given Madden Jennie's name. Or Seamie's. Without those names, he couldn't track James down. Without those names, there was still time. But then she remembered that someone had told Madden that Josie had a son—did that someone also know where the boy was now?

There had to be another way to get to London, and to Paddington Station, where she could get a train to the Cotswolds. Perhaps there was a bus going there, perhaps she could hire another hackney to at least take her partway. As she walked out of the train station, looking around, trying to figure out what that other way might be, she spotted a delivery boy on a motorbike with a wooden crate strapped to the back. He'd just dropped off a bundle of papers at a newsagents and was about to motor off again.

"Wait!" she shouted. "Don't go!"

The boy turned. She started running toward him, waving. He gave her a quizzical look and pointed at himself.

"Yes, you!" she shouted. "How much for the motorbike?" she asked breathlessly, when she reached him.

"Depends where you want me to go. For local deliveries, I charge by the mile. For trips to Canterbury, or any of the outlying towns, I charge a flat rate."

"I don't want to hire the bike. I want to buy it. How much?"

"It's not for sale, miss. It's me livelihood, that bike."

"I'll give you twenty pounds," Willa said, digging in her satchel for her wallet.

The boy's eyes narrowed. "You're not a fugitive, are you?"

"No. I have a very great emergency, though." Willa found her wallet, opened it, and pulled out a twenty-pound note. "Will you sell me the bike or not?"

The boy nodded. "Have you driven one of these before?" he asked her.

Willa told him that she had. She'd done so in Cairo countless times.

"Tank's half-full," the boy said, taking off his goggles and handing them to her. "You should buy petrol at Broughton's—it's on the west edge of town. You'll pass it on the way out. There's a petrol station another twenty-five miles down the road, but it's closed as often as it's open."

"Thank you," Willa said.

She put her satchel in the crate, started the engine, and put the bike into gear. She found the petrol station a few minutes later and asked the proprietor to fill the tank. As she waited, she walked around in the brisk air and stamped her feet, trying to wake herself up. Trying to shake off the nausea and headache that were plaguing her. She'd had no morphine for more than twenty-four hours and was feeling the symptoms of withdrawal. She'd tried to sleep on the ferry, hoping that would help to take the edge off, but it hadn't. If anything, it made things worse. Every time she closed her eyes, she saw Josie's battered face.

Willa had run straight home from Josie's flat. She'd told her aunt Eddie what had happened. Not much could shock her aunt, but that did. When Willa asked her if she would take care of Josie, Eddie jumped off the settee, put her coat on, and asked for the address. She was just heading out the door when Willa grabbed her arm.

"Aunt Eddie, after you see to Josie, will you please ring up Albie and tell him what's happened?" she asked her. "There's a telephone in Josie's flat. I rang him. I tried to tell him, but he wouldn't listen to me. He's thinks I'm mad. He'll listen to you."

"I'll ring him as soon as I get your friend seen to. Hurry, Willa. Go," she said.

Willa had quickly put a warm jumper on, a sturdy pair of boots, and a thick coat. Then she'd put Josie's money and letters into her satchel. She'd closed the door to her flat, run down the stairs, and headed for the train station, where she'd managed to get a ticket on a 4:30 P.M. train to Calais. When she arrived, she found that the next boat to Dover was full, so she'd booked a passage on the night ferry. It was early morning now, about eight o'clock.

When she'd first got back to her own flat, she'd thought about going to the police and telling them what had happened to Josie, and that the same man who'd beaten her was now trying to kidnap a child. But then she thought, What if they don't believe me? Worse yet, what if they do? They'll insist I come into the station with them. They'll ask me a thousand questions. Their first job will be to investigate what happened to Josie, not to protect a child in England. I'll be sitting in the station house, reconstructing the crime scene for them, and Madden'll be halfway across the channel.

Going to the Paris police would have done no one any good—not James and not Josie. What she needed to do was to warn Seamie that Billy Madden wanted his son. Since she had failed to get Albie to do that, or Joe Bristow, or the publican at Binsey, she would have to do it herself.

"You're all set, miss," the petrol man said. "You'll have to fill her up again just as you're nearing London."

He gave her the name of a town with a good petrol station and a good pub, in case she fancied a break from the road and a nice hot meal. Willa thanked him. She pulled her goggles down over her eyes, kick-started the bike's engine, and flew out of Dover.

As the town fell away behind her, she decided she would try Albie again when she stopped—if the pub the petrol man mentioned had a telephone. Maybe Eddie would've gotten through to him by then. And maybe this time she—Willa—could convince him to drive down to Oxford, find Seamie and James, and get them out of harm's way.

Just in case she was wrong. Just in case Billy Madden was a lot closer to Binsey than she thought.

CHAPTER ONE HUNDRED FOURTEEN

ALBIE ALDEN HEARD the telephone ringing all the way from the garage. He lifted his marketing out of the car and made a run for it. The weather was filthy; he got soaked through running the few yards between the garage and the back door.

"Yes? Yes? Speak up, please, I'm hard of hearing!" he heard as he entered the kitchen. It was Mrs. Lapham, a cleaning woman his aunt Eddie insisted they have in twice a week. "Will? Will who?" she yelled.

Albie winced. It was Willa. It had to be. He set his basket down on the table and walked over to where the telephone stood on a small round table.

"I'll take it now, Mrs. Lapham. Thank you!" he bellowed.

Mrs. Lapham jumped. "Oh, Albie, dear! Gave me a right good startle, you did! There's someone on the blower," she said.

"Yes, I gathered," Albie shouted.

Mrs. Lapham handed him the telephone and went back to her cleaning. Albie held the receiver to his chest, waiting until she was out of earshot, then remembered that the poor woman was always out of earshot.

"I thought I told you not to call until you'd stopped using morphine," he said into the mouthpiece.

"I *have* stopped. I've had nothing for well over twenty-four hours, and it's killing me. I feel like my head's going to explode," Willa replied.

Albie heard wind blowing and what sounded like rain sheeting down. The line crackled, went out for a few second, then came back again. "Where are you?" he said.

"At a petrol station just west of London."

"*What?* What the devil are you doing there?"

"Did Aunt Eddie call you?"

Albie looked around for a note. "No. I don't think so. But I've been out a good deal of the day," he said. "Why?"

Albie heard Willa groan. "I'm trying to get to Binsey. To Seamie."

"Willa, you must tell me where you are. Right now. I'll send someone to get you," Albie said sternly.

"Someone with a big net? Holding a jacket with buckles down the back?" Willa shot back, her voice breaking. "Albie, I've just seen my best friend beaten to within an inch of her life. I'm trying to save another friend from something far worse. I've been traveling for hours and hours—far too many of them in the soaking rain on a sputtering bastard of a motorbike. I'm not under the influence of anything now, and I'm not mad, either. Madness can only take you so far. It can't take you from Paris to Oxford in twenty-four hours. You have to be sane to pull that off. Which is what I am. I swear it. Terrified, yes. In shock, yes. But sane." She paused for breath, then said, "This is life or death, Albie. Seamie's and his son's. Ring the inn at Binsey. The King's Head. Ask them if they can get Seamie to the telephone. Maybe they can send a lad to his cottage for him, and he can walk to the pub and ring you back. If he does, tell him what I told you yesterday. Please, Albie. Do this for me and I'll never ask you for anything again. I'm on my way there, but I've still a ways to go. Please, please, please do this."

"Yes, all right. I'll ring the pub," Albie said, very worried now. "Just calm down, Willa."

There was more crackling and then the line went dead. Albie put the receiver back into its cradle and set the tall, candlestick telephone down on the hallway table. He took a deep breath, then blew it out again, trying to decide what to do.

Even without the influence of morphine, Willa had always been rash and unpredictable, heading up mountain peaks as a young girl that daunted many men. And later, heading off to Africa on a whim, then to Tibet, Arabia, Paris. She'd been heedless, thoughtless, even, at times, ruthless. Ruthless in her pursuit of what she wanted, ruthless to others if that's what it took to get it. Ruthless, most of all, in the way she drove herself. In one thing, however, she had always been constant, always steady, no matter how dearly it cost her: her feelings for Seamus Finnegan. It was those feelings, Albie thought now, and not the morphine, that had finally done her in. Being told he was dead, and then finding out he wasn't—it must have been a shock for her. Too great of a shock.

A few seconds later, he picked up the phone again. "Binsey, near Oxford, please," he told the operator. "The King's Head."

It took a few minutes to get the call through. "Trouble with the lines," the operator told him. Finally, he heard a man's voice say, "Good afternoon. The King's Head. Mr. Peters speaking."

"Hello, my name is Albert Alden. I'm a friend of Captain Finnegan's. I need to speak with him."

"Ah! You're in luck! They're here just now—Captain Finnegan and his son. Having their dinner. I'll fetch him for you."

Seamie got on the line. He was surprised, but pleased, to hear Albie's voice. Albie told him it was nice to hear his voice, too, and that he was sorry to disturb his supper, but he had something rather troubling to discuss with him.

As he finished talking to Seamie, he said he hoped he would come up to Cambridge one day soon, with James, for a visit. Seamie said Albie could count on it.

Albie said good-bye and hung up. Seamie and his son were just fine. No one had been beaten or murdered or kidnapped. Quite to the contrary. They'd just enjoyed a nice meal at a Cotswold pub and would soon be enjoying a leisurely walk back to their cottage.

"I should have known," Albie said to himself. "This is all utter nonsense. Just more of Willa's lunacy. Why do I even listen to her? If anyone's mad, it's me for taking her telephone calls."

He looked out of the window. The rain was still lashing down. It was cold, and getting dark as well. It was hardly a good time for a drive, and yet what choice did he have? His insane sister was about to descend on his best friend. Seamie couldn't be expected to deal with her. No one could. He would collect her and bring her back here, and then he would see about a doctor for her. It was time somebody did.

"Albie dear, are you off the blower yet?" Mrs. Lapham shouted from the sink.

"Yes, I am!" Albie shouted back, walking over to her.

"Oh, good! Before I forget, your aunt Edwina rang up . . ."

Albie groaned. Eddie was supposed to have brought Willa home with her, not allowed her to make a dash for it. He could only imagine what she wanted to tell him and he didn't want to hear it. Not now. He had one loonie to deal with this evening; he didn't need two.

". . . and she wants you to ring her back. Here's the number," Mrs. Lapham said, pulling a piece of paper from her pinafore pocket and handing it to him.

"Thank you," Albie said.

Mrs. Lapham smiled and went back to her work.

Albie stuffed the paper into his trousers pocket, then loudly said, "Mrs. Lapham, I'm going out for a bit. In the automobile. I won't be back before you finish. Please lock the door when you leave."

"Of course," Mrs. Lapham said, not looking up from her polishing. "Where are you going, Albie dear?"

"On a wild-goose chase."

"Mongoose Place?" Mrs. Lapham said. "What a strange name. Never heard of it. Sounds lovely, though! Have a good time, Albie. And don't forget your wellies."

CHAPTER ONE HUNDRED FIFTEEN

WILLA GUIDED HER motorbike down the long, trailing drive that led to Seamie's cottage. At least, she hoped it did. If the directions Mr. Peters at the pub had given her were any good, it would.

It was dark now, and the drive was rutted and muddy from the rain. It took all the strength Willa had left to keep the bike from skidding and going over. She was soaked, cold, and exhausted. Most of all she was frightened—frightened that she was too late, that Billy Madden had somehow got here before her.

"He can't have," she told herself yet again. "He doesn't know Jennie's name. He doesn't have the address of her cottage."

After a few minutes, a small stone house came into view. Willa rode up to it and cut the engine. As she was getting off the bike, the door to the cottage opened. Seamie came out. He held a lantern in one hand. He held his other hand over his eyes, as a block against the rain. He squinted into the darkness, unable to see her yet.

Willa's heart clenched at the sight of him—with love, so much love. Still. Always. She took her goggles off, wiped as much mud off her face as she could.

"Hello, Willa," he shouted into the rain. "Come inside."

Willa, who'd been walking toward the cottage, stopped short.

"Seamie . . . how . . . how did you know it was me?"

"Albie rang me."

Relief flooded through her. "Oh, thank God!" she said, walking up to him. "Then you know—"

"I do. He told me everything," Seamie said.

He pulled her to him and held her tightly, pressing his lips to her cheek. She melted into his embrace, craving the feel of him, his warmth and his scent, this man whom she'd loved her whole life, who'd come back from the dead.

"I thought you were gone," she said, fighting back tears. "I thought I'd never see you again." She pulled his face to hers and kissed him deeply. She wanted to stay like this, folded in his arms. She wanted it so much, but she knew she couldn't, not when Billy Madden could be close.

"Seamie, we have to—" she started to say.

"I know. We will. Come inside now," he said, "before you catch your death."

Was it her imagination or did his voice sound sad? Alarmed is what he should be right now, she thought. Not sad.

"I don't need to come inside. Is James with you?" Willa asked. "Is he all right?"

"What? Yes. Yes, he's fine. He just went to bed."

"He went to *bed*? Seamie, you have to get him up. You have to leave. Right now," Willa said. "Albie told you some of what's happened, but there's more to tell you. I'll explain everything later, when we're on our way, but right now, you have to pack a few things and go to Cambridge. To my aunt Eddie's house. You'll be safe there and—"

"Willa, come inside. You can get out of those wet clothes. I'll get you a glass of brandy."

Willa shook her head. Something wasn't right. This wasn't how Seamie should be acting. She wondered, for a second, if there was something wrong with him. Did he not understand the danger he and James were in?

"There's no time for brandy, Seamie," she said tersely. "Have you got a car?"

"Yes, but—"

"Where is it? I'll start it up."

Seamie stared at her. His eyes traveled from her gaunt, mud-splattered face, to her thin body, to her hands, blue with cold. His eyes, already filled with sorrow, suddenly filled with tears.

"Oh, Willa, what's happened to you?" he asked her. "Come inside. Please. You need to rest."

"Seamie, for God's sake! You and James are in danger. Very great danger."

"Willa . . . I know," Seamie said.

"You do?"

"I know about the morphine and your addiction," Seamie said. "Albie rang up the pub earlier tonight while James and I were having our supper. He told me about you, and Paris. About Oscar Carlyle and how you almost killed yourself one night. He told me everything."

Willa realized why Seamie looked so sad. Why James was asleep. Why no bags were packed. She realized what her brother had done. He'd told Seamie nothing about Madden, even though she'd begged him to. Instead he'd told Seamie that she was a morphine addict, out of her mind and raving about imaginary villains.

"Albie told you everything, did he?" she said now, angrily. "What did he tell you? That I'm a drug fiend? Well, sod him. And sod you, too! I survived Mawenzi, and Everest, and Damascus. I survived losing you. Over and over again. But now, apparently, I'm such a fragile thing that a bit of morphine's addled my brain and I'm making up stories about villains and switched children and I'm traveling from Paris to Binsey in the rain, in record time, for the sheer bloody hell of it."

"What? Willa, what are you saying? What villains? What children? Albie didn't mention anything like that."

Willa opened the crate on the back of her motorbike and grabbed her satchel. She walked past Seamie into the cottage. It was small inside. There was no foyer. They were standing in an open room that served as both sitting room and kitchen.

"I wanted this to be kinder, Seamie, I really did," she said. "I wanted you to hear it from Albie or from me. But since I'm totally bloody crackers, you'll have to find it out for yourself now."

She dug the letters out of the satchel and handed them to him. "Read fast," she said. "As soon as you finish, we're leaving."

Then she pulled a chair out from the kitchen table. "Take a seat," she added. "You're going to need it."

CHAPTER ONE HUNDRED SIXTEEN

SEAMIE WAS DIMLY aware that Willa had found the brandy he'd mentioned. She opened it, poured two glasses, and placed them on the table. Then she sat down and waited for him to finish reading.

About twenty minutes later, he looked up at her uncertainly. "Willa, I don't understand," he said. "Who is Josie Meadows? How did Jennie know her? How do you?"

"I met Josie in Paris a few months ago. We became friends. She was raised in East London. She told me that she went to Jennie's school. That's how they knew each other. When Josie got older, she performed in the East End music halls. That's how she met Billy Madden."

"But what do these letters mean?" Seamie asked, though deep inside himself he knew.

Willa took a slug of her brandy. "They mean that James is not your son," she said.

"But how . . . Jennie had a baby . . . at Binsey . . . she—" he said, feeling as if someone had taken his legs out from under him.

"Jennie lost the baby. Early on in the pregnancy. She couldn't have children, Josie told me. There was some reason. An—"

"An accident," Seamie said dully. "She was hit by a carriage when she was a child. She was badly injured."

It was all making sickening sense to him now. All of it—Jennie's unwillingness to sleep with him while she was pregnant, to even let him touch her. Her constant trips to Binsey. The telegram from her saying that she'd had the baby there and not to be alarmed, she was fine. They were both fine. God, how could he have been so blind? So stupid?

"Josie said that Jennie only pretended she was still pregnant. Josie, who really was pregnant, had the child—had James—in Binsey. She told the doctor she was Jennie, so the right names would be on the birth certificate. Then she gave James to Jennie. He wasn't Jennie's and your son." She shook her head. "No, I don't mean to say that. He *is* your son. But not your flesh and blood. He was Josie Meadows's—Josie's and Billy Madden's."

Seamie recognized that name. He knew Billy Madden was a villain and that he'd tried to kill Sid. "Did Madden know about James?" he asked Willa.

"He didn't know James had been born. Josie said he wanted her to get rid of the baby, and she didn't want to, so she fled London. She went to Binsey and stayed here in the cottage until she'd had the baby. Then she left for Paris."

"But he knows now," Seamie said.

"Yes, he does. Somehow he's found out that he fathered James. And he wants him back. Josie said that he's gone mad. That he told her he lost his sons in the war and now he wants his other son—James."

Willa paused here. In a weary, broken voice she said, "He beat her almost to death, Seamie. I saw what he'd done. He beat her to get information on James, but she wouldn't give it to him."

"So he doesn't know who Josie gave James to. He doesn't know about Binsey, doesn't know that I have him now."

"I don't know what Madden knows. Someone told him about James. I don't know who. Josie didn't know either. I'm worried that the same someone who told Madden about James knows about Jennie and Binsey and you as well. I'm worried that Madden went back to this person and got more information out of her. Or him. I'm worried—no, actually I'm scared to death—that he'll find out where you both are. That's why I want you both to leave the cottage. Right now."

"Willa, James is asleep. It's late. I can't just pile him into the car and show up on Eddie and Albie's doorstep. Surely, Madden couldn't find out any more information so fast. And even if he did, he wouldn't come out here and just snatch James—"

Willa stood up so quickly, so violently, that the chair she'd been sitting in went over. "For God's sake, Seamie, that's *exactly* what he would do! You didn't see Josie. I did! I saw what he'd done to her. She'll never be the same. She'll never be on stage again," she shouted. "*That's* why I traveled all the way here from Paris. Not because I'm mad. Not because I'm drug-addled. Because I've seen what Billy Madden is capable of. You have to leave. I don't care if it's late. You have to go to Cambridge and you have to go now. Until Madden is found and stopped, you have to hide James."

"All right, Willa, I—" Seamie started to say. He was interrupted by a little voice.

"Daddy? Daddy, are you all right? I heard voices."

A sleepy-eyed, pajama-clad James stumbled into the kitchen.

"Hello, lad," Seamie said. "I'm sorry we woke you. I'm fine. Everything's fine. I was just having a chat with my friend. James, I would like you meet Miss Alden. Willa, this is my son, James."

"Pleased to meet you, Miss Alden," James said. "Are you my father's friend from the desert? The one who rode with Major Lawrence?"

"I am, James. And I'm very pleased to meet you, too. Please pardon my appearance. I've been riding on a motorbike in the rain. Got myself rather soaked," Willa said, smiling.

Seamie looked at Willa as she spoke. She looked so haggard, so tired. She was soaking wet and trembling, from fear, or exhaustion, or the cold—he didn't know. She was scared and sorrowing for her friend and in shock, and yet she had raced here. She had got herself to Calais and Dover and had somehow got hold of a motorbike and ridden for hours through the rain and the mud to get here. For him and for James. Now she looked like she was going to collapse any second, and yet she was smiling, speaking in a gentle voice, trying her best not to upset a small child.

"James," he suddenly said, "we're going to take a ride together. You and I and Miss Alden. Can you be a good lad, go back into your room, and put some warm clothes on?"

"Isn't it a bit late to go motoring?" James asked.

"It is, but I'll make you a nice bed on the backseat and we'll pack some biscuits and make an adventure out of it. Would you like that?"

James nodded. He padded back to his bedroom.

"Make sure you put a jumper on!" Seamie shouted after him.

"He's the spitting image of her, of Josie," Willa said softly, as soon as the boy was out of earshot.

"He's my son, Willa. I don't give a damn who fathered him, who carried him, who gave him up to whom. He's *my* son."

"I know he is, Seamie. I know. That's why I came," Willa said, turning to him. "We need to go. Do you want to pack some things?"

"Yes," Seamie said. "I will." He turned and walked stiffly down the hall.

"What happened?" Willa asked, following him.

"Burns. All down my right side. I got them when my ship was torpedoed."

"We make quite a pair, don't we? Stitch us together and there might be enough working parts to make one good human being," she said wryly.

As Seamie packed his things, Willa went into James's room, found a suitcase, and put clothes into it for him. When she was finished, she carried the suitcase to the front door.

James and Seamie were already there. James was holding his stuffed bear. "Can Wellie come?" he asked.

"Of course, he can," Seamie said. "I wouldn't dream of leaving Wellie behind."

"Don't forget the biscuits."

"I won't. We'll take the whole tin."

"And tea? Can we have tea in a flask, Daddy? With lots of milk?"

"We haven't time to make it, James, but we'll take some—"

Seamie's words were cut off by a small, scraping sound. They all heard it at the same time and they all turned toward its source—the front door. As Seamie watched, he saw the doorknob turn—first to the right, then to the left. Then whoever was standing on the other side, rattled it. He knew the door would not open; he had locked it after he and Willa came inside. He knew, too, that the door was old, and the hinges rusty, and that he probably had only seconds.

Seamie grabbed James's hand and pulled him down the short hallway into his bedroom. He quickly opened his window. "Listen to me, James, and do exactly as I say. Lock your door, crawl out the window, and run to the village. To the King's Head. Tell Mr. Peters that your father needs help. That he's to send the constable."

"But Daddy . . ."

"Pretend I'm Major Lawrence. And you're Auda and that you're going to get help from Khalaf al Mor. The Turks are all around the fort. Don't let them see you."

James's little face brightened. He saluted.

Seamie saluted back. "Hurry, James. Lock the door behind me!" he said. "Go now!"

He closed the door, then listened as James shot the bolt. There was an old saber over the fireplace, if he could just get it down in time. He ran back to the sitting room and saw Willa desperately trying to lug the settee to the door, to block it. He lunged at the mantel and pulled the saber down off the wall. He was just raising it, his fingers tightening on the handle, when the door was kicked in.

CHAPTER ONE HUNDRED SEVENTEEN

"DROP IT. NOW. Or I'll shoot her," Billy Madden said.

He was quicker than any of them. He'd got into the house and across the room in seconds. Willa had had no time to run. He'd grabbed her hair with one hand and pressed the barrel of his pistol into her head with the other.

Seamie lowered the saber, but he did not put it down.

"Fucking drop it!" Madden yelled, yanking Willa's head back cruelly. She cried out in pain. Seamie did as he was told. "Make one move, and she's dead," Madden said to Seamie. He turned to the man with him. "Bennie, get the boy," he said.

"No!" Seamie shouted.

Willa couldn't see what was happening, but she could hear scuffling. She heard the horrible crack of bone against bone, heard someone fall heavily to the floor, then heard Seamie groaning. Next, she heard Bennie's footsteps going down the hallway. He tried the door, then kicked it open.

"Stop this," she said, in a strangled voice. "Please . . ."

"Shut yer gob," Madden growled, tightening his grip. He'd pulled Willa's head so far back, it had become hard for her to breathe.

Bennie came back into the room. "The boy's not there, guv," he said.

"What?" Madden said.

"He's not there. He's gone. The window's open. He must've climbed out."

"Where is he?" Madden shouted at Willa. He let go of her hair and slammed her against the wall, pinning her there by her neck, squeezing so hard, Willa thought he would crush her windpipe. "Bennie, go after him!" he yelled, when Willa would not answer.

Bennie lumbered out of the door, and Willa saw that he was also carrying a pistol. Madden turned back to her. "I'll do for you, I swear I will. And then I'll do for him," he said, pointing his gun at Seamie. "Where's the boy?" He was squeezing her throat so hard now that she was gasping for air. She scrabbled at his hand. Kicked at him. "Where's the boy?" he said again, when she finally stopped struggling. He waited for what seemed like an eternity, slowly choking the life out of her. The minutes dragged by, but Willa would not answer him. "I'm going to ask you one more time," he said. And then he raised his pistol again, pressed the barrel into her cheek, and cocked the trigger.

"Easy, Billy, there's no need for that," a voice said—a voice from Willa's nightmares. "We talked about this. There's to be no blood. Not in the cottage and not outside of it, either. We can't have the police suspecting foul play. It will ruin everything."

No, it isn't him, Willa thought. It can't be. It's the DTs. Or a lack of oxygen. Or maybe Albie's right. Maybe I am mad. Maybe my mind's finally come apart.

Madden relaxed his grip somewhat and Willa was able to breathe again. She looked to her left, toward the doorway, and saw him—a tall, blond man. He had a scar on the side of his face. She herself had put it there.

"*Namaste,* Willa Alden," Max von Brandt said, bowing slightly. "Once again."

CHAPTER ONE HUNDRED EIGHTEEN

"I KILLED YOU," Willa said, stunned, unable to believe what her eyes were telling her. "In Damascus."

"Almost," Max said. "But not quite. I'd tell you to be more thorough next time, but I'm afraid there won't be a next time."

Madden, still holding Willa by her throat, swung his pistol toward Max. "What are you doing out of the car? Don't you move! Don't move a fucking muscle, von Brandt, or I'll shoot you where you stand!"

"Easy, Billy," Max said again, as if he was trying to calm a wild animal. "You and Bennie are the ones with the guns, not me, right?" He slowly raised his hands, palms out, to show Madden he was carrying nothing.

"Where's Bennie?"

"Bennie's outside. He told me to come in after you. He's got the boy. He's got him tied up and in the car. He's ready to go."

"No," Seamie said groggily, trying to get off the floor. "You leave him alone. . . ." Blood dripped from a gash in his lip. Willa could see the terror in his eyes. She struggled against Madden. He banged her back into the wall.

"Max, you bastard!" she screamed at him. "How can you do this? James is a child! An innocent child. And you're delivering him to a criminal. A murderer!"

Madden hit her across the face with the butt of his pistol. To Max he said, "You know her?"

"Very well," Max replied. He was carrying two lengths of rope.

"I say we do them both right here. Right now. And be done," Madden said.

"No," Max said.

As Seamie, still dazed, tried again to get up, Max put a foot in the center of his back, grabbed his hands and tied them. He then tied Willa's.

"I've told you before, Billy," he said when he'd finished, "it has to be clean and neat or else you'll have every police officer in the country looking for the boy. Remember, Billy? Remember what I told you?"

Billy nodded. Willa chanced a glance at him. His eyes were dark and empty. This is what madness looks like, she thought. He would have killed them both, without a second's thought or remorse, if Max had not stopped him. But why had he stopped him? she wondered. She soon found out.

"A coat on the riverbank—Captain Finnegan's," Max said to Billy. "A walking stick. Field glasses. Broken ice. It will look like Captain Finnegan and his son went for a winter ramble. James walked out too far on the ice. He fell through. His father tried to save him, but he could not; his injuries had left him too weak. They both drowned—"

"No!" Willa shouted, cutting Max off. "It won't work. My brother . . . my aunt . . . they know—"

A vicious backhand from Max silenced her. Billy's eyes flickered uncertainly between Willa and Max, but Max, unconcerned by what Willa had said, continued to talk, his voice calm and measured.

"Pay no attention to her, Billy. She's the cleverest little liar I've ever met, and I've met quite a few. It *will* work. It will look so tragic, Billy, especially given all that Captain Finnegan has been through. His body will be found downriver. In the spring. Poor little James's never will. It'll be said that he was swept away by the currents, but really, he'll be living life with his new father. His real father. And I'll be happily back in Berlin, because I held up my end of the bargain—I helped you get him." Max paused. His eyes sought Billy's. "That's the plan, right, Billy? And we must stick to it. That's how we make sure you not only get James, but you get to keep him."

Max moved around the cottage as he spoke. He shoved the settee back in place, righted a small end table that had gone over, and cleaned up some splintered wood that had fallen on the floor near the front door.

"Right. That's right. All clean and neat-like. No messes and no clues," Billy said.

"Good," Max said. "Let's get Finnegan outside. A bash to the head and then into the water."

"You can't do this. Please, Max," Willa begged.

"What about her?" Billy said, ramming the pistol's barrel into Willa's head again.

Max smiled. "Don't worry about her. She's my problem and I'll take care of her. In fact, this is one problem I'll take great pleasure in resolving. Come on now, Billy, let's go."

He grabbed Seamie's jacket and walking stick. After getting Seamie up off the floor, he half marched, half dragged him outside. Madden followed with Willa, closing the cottage's door behind them.

"Let's be quick," Max said. "I want to get back on the road. We've been here too long as is," he said.

Outside, Willa saw Madden's car. He'd parked it up the driveway a fair bit. Probably to keep herself and Seamie from hearing it as the three of them drove in. Looking at it now, Willa knew that any ride she took in that car would be the very last ride of her life. She tried desperately to think of a way to save James, to save all of them—but there was none. Max and Madden were walking them toward the river. She and Seamie were bound. They were outnumbered. Madden had a gun and Bennie did, too. There was nothing she could do.

"I'll take this one to the car," Madden said. "You do for Finnegan."

"No, Billy," Max said. "Bring her to the water. I want her to see it. She nearly killed me. I spent a month in a hospital bed because of her. I want her to see him go in."

Madden, squinting in the darkness at the car and frowning, hesitated. "Where's that fucking Ben—" he started to say.

"You owe me that much, Billy," Max said tersely. "I got you the boy. Without me, you'd never even have known about him."

"All right, then," Billy said. "But be quick about it. Like you said, we've been here too long already."

It was over. Willa knew that now.

She had tried her best to save James, but she had failed. And now she would pay for her failure, she and Seamie both. With their lives.

CHAPTER ONE HUNDRED NINETEEN

"WALK, DAMN YOU!" Madden shouted, shoving Willa ahead of him toward the river. "Where's that bloody Bennie?"

"I told you, he's in the car with the boy," Max said. His grip on Seamie tightened. "Don't do anything foolish," he told him.

Seamie made no reply. He was looking ahead of himself, past Willa and Madden. He was looking at the river, trying to see a way out of this. The blow he'd taken had dazed him, but his head had cleared now. He could take von Brandt, if only he could get his hands untied. But even if he got Max, Madden had a gun on Willa. And Bennie, who also had a gun, was inside the car with James.

They got closer to the water. They were only about ten yards away now. Seamie strained against his bonds.

"Please," he said. "Don't do this. Not to her. Not to my son."

Max said nothing. His eyes were fixed on Willa, who had started to struggle with Madden. Max's grip on Seamie was steel-like.

"Stay still," he said quietly. "Don't move or I'll shoot her."

Willa kicked at Madden. She connected with his leg, causing him to stumble. He righted himself and hit her savagely. She staggered backward from the blow and fell to the ground.

"You bitch!" Billy shouted. "I'll fucking kill you!" He raised his gun and pointed it at Willa.

"No!" Seamie shouted.

They all heard the shot.

Billy's head snapped up. Seamie spun around. They both looked at Max at the same time, both saw the shiny glint in his hand, both realized that he was holding a smoking, silver pistol.

WILLA FELT BLOOD, hot and wet, on her face and neck. Its thick, coppery smell was heavy in the damp night air.

Max had shot her. Not Madden, Max. She'd seen him raise the pistol and fire. There was no pain, though. She had been close to death before and the pain had been terrible. Now she felt nothing at all. Is this what it's actually like to die? she wondered. She looked down at her chest for a bullet hole. There was blood spattered across her jacket, but she could see nothing else. Had he hit her in the neck? The head?

"It's all right, Willa," Max said. "You're all right."

Willa, still on the ground, realized that Madden was no longer standing over her, screaming at her. Where was he? She sat up and saw that he was lying on the ground next to her. His eyes were lifeless. There was a dark, wet hole in his forehead.

She turned and looked up at Max. He untied her hands, then he took Madden's gun from the dead man's hands and shoved it into the waistband of his trousers.

"Where's James?" Seamie was shouting. "Where's my son?"

"I don't know, Mr. Finnegan," Max said.

"You said he was in the car!"

"I lied. Turn around. Let me untie your hands."

As soon as Seamie's hands were free, he raced off to Madden's car, shouting for James. Willa struggled to her feet and raced off after him.

She found him opening all the car doors. "He's not here," he yelled. "Oh, God . . . where is he?"

"Look in the boot," Willa said.

Seamie wrenched the boot's lid up and Willa screamed. Bennie, a livid gash across his throat, was lying inside it.

"James!" Seamie shouted, spinning in circles. "James, where are you?"

Willa was about to slam the boot lid down again when Max, suddenly close by, asked her not to. She turned and saw that he had his arms around Madden's chest. He had dragged him all the way from the river to the car.

"I . . . I don't understand," Willa said. Nothing made sense to her. Nothing at all. She felt as if she was in some horrible nightmare, one from which she could not wake.

As she stood there, trying to figure out what was happening, Max tumbled Madden's body into the boot, then slammed it shut.

"James!" Seamie called out again. His agonized cry echoed through the woods.

"We must help Captain Finnegan find his son," Max said to her.

"His son's fine," said a new voice. Slowly, a man emerged from the darkness. He was holding a shotgun and it was trained on Max. "I know where he is and he's safe."

It was a very disheveled Albie.

CHAPTER ONE HUNDRED TWENTY-ONE

"JAMES IS NEARBY, Seamie. He's in good hands," Albie said, still holding the shotgun on Max.

"Albie, what are you doing here? How did you get here?" Willa asked.

"By car. After you called, I thought I should come to Binsey, meet you here and take you back to Cambridge," Albie said. "I took Eddie's automobile, but it ran out of gas a few miles outside of the village. I left it at the side of the road and walked the rest of the way. When I got to the drive, I ran into James—literally. He was very frightened, but he managed to tell me what was happening. I took him to a neighbor's house, the Wallaces'. Mr. Wallace and James went to the village to get the police. They'll be here shortly."

"Did you borrow that gun from the neighbor, too?" Max asked, looking at the shotgun.

"Mr. von Brandt," Albie said, "I've been after you for a very long time, but never in a million years did I expect to find you in Binsey. I'd like to know what you're doing here."

"It's a long story, Mr. Alden," Max said.

"That's all right. You're not going anywhere."

Max told them all about Billy Madden's first visit to him at his hotel, and how he'd had to tell Billy about James in order to save his own life.

"I never expected Madden to actually track Josie Meadows down," he said. "I thought he was in a bad way due to his grief over his sons and that it would wear off in a day or two. I was wrong. He paid me a second visit this evening, as I was getting out of a carriage in front of my hotel. He was waiting by the door for me with a gun. He forced me into his car and told me he'd been to Paris and had found Josie and that she wouldn't tell him the boy's name or where he was. Then he threatened to kill me if I didn't take him to the boy. So I did, figuring the ride would give me time to think, time to figure out a way to kill him, for I saw then that he would never stop. Not until he had James, and I did not want that to happen. I did not want an innocent child's abduction on my conscience. I knew I could take Bennie if I could just get them apart. Sending James out of the window was a great help. Bennie went after him. I saw him go. And then I went after Bennie. I was able to get his gun off him, kill him quietly with a clasp knife Billy foolishly left in my trouser pocket, and get him into the car boot."

"But Max, how did you know Billy Madden in the first place? And Josie Meadows? And Binsey?" Willa asked.

"Mr. von Brandt knows a lot of things, Willa," Albie said. "Too many things. He was a spymaster in London before the war even started. That's how he knows Madden. He used one of Madden's boats to get naval secrets to the North Sea. He's going to tell us what he knows. Every last thing. Raise your hands, Mr. von Brandt. You're under arrest."

"No, actually, I'm not."

"I have a gun. I'm not afraid to use it," Albie said menacingly.

"You won't shoot me, Mr. Alden," Max said, a note of weariness in his voice. "You can't. That shotgun's ancient. The trigger's rusted. And you're holding it incorrectly. It's probably not even loaded, is it? And even if it is, I have two pistols and I'm a much better shot. I'll get you first."

Albie still refused to lower the shotgun.

"Mr. Alden, two prime ministers will be most unhappy with you if you shoot me. Mr. Asquith, who protected me for the duration of the war. And Mr. Lloyd George who continues to protect me. You are right, Mr. Alden . . . I am a spy. But I'm not working for Germany. I never was."

"My God. That . . . that means," Albie said, as the full weight of Max's words hit him.

"That you're a double agent," Seamie said. "Fucking hell."

Max smiled ruefully. "Yes, Captain Finnegan, that's it exactly—a total fucking hell."

CHAPTER ONE HUNDRED TWENTY-TWO

"WHEN, MAX?" WILLA asked. "When did you turn? When did you become a double agent?"

"I never turned. I was a double agent all along," Max replied. "I'm a high-ranking member of the British Secret Service and have been for quite some time. I long ago saw the writing on the wall. I saw that the kaiser was a madman who would find any pretext for going to war. Had it not been Sarajevo, it would have been something else. I wanted to do what I could to stop him, to stop the war."

Willa shook her head in disbelief. "But how? How did you pull it off?" she said. "It seemed very clear to me in Damascus which side you were on. And it wasn't the Allies'. I would never have even suspected you for a double agent."

"It was difficult," Max said, "but I had a part to play, and I played it. I first had to convince Berlin that I was a loyal to the kaiser. That was easy enough. I'd had a sterling record of military service, after which I became a member of the German Secret Service. They found out I had family in London and wished to exploit that. So they had me stage a fight with my uncle—an industrialist and the head of our family's firm, and a big supporter of the kaiser's. We had a public falling out—or what looked like one—in a restaurant over my dissatisfaction with the kaiser's policies. A few days later, banished by my uncle, I arrived in London. Because of my family connections there, and because I had been publicly critical of the kaiser, I was welcomed everywhere."

"You were above suspicion, which made it easy to run a spy ring and which is exactly what Berlin wanted," Albie said.

"Yes, of course. I assembled the ring as soon as I got to London. I had to feed Berlin information. Good information. Constantly. If I hadn't done so, they would've suspected me—hence the documents in the packets that Gladys and Jennie couriered. But I gave London far more than I ever gave Berlin. No one knew about me except Asquith. Not you. Not Burgess. Not even Churchill. They couldn't know; it would have been too dangerous for me. Asquith played along quite well, I must say. He even invited me to his country home at the same time as he invited other spies—German agents who he knew were in constant contact with Berlin—people who would report back that I was doing my job. In fact, Asquith himself told me, just two nights ago, that I'm the reason the Allies won the war. Though I have to share credit with the Spanish flu, I suppose. It carried off more German and Austrian soldiers than it did Allied ones."

"People died because of your activities in London," Seamie said angrily.

Max's eyes turned hard. "Yes, they did," he said. "Once I was here, it was very important to look like a German spy to other German spies. That involved cruel, even brutal actions. I regret Maud Selwyn Jones's death. And Gladys Bigelow's. I regret any suffering I caused Jennie Finnegan. But that is the cost of what I do, and it is a very high one."

"Jennie Finnegan was my wife. *My wife*," Seamie said. "You had no business . . . you had no right . . ."

"Yes, she was your wife. And all those German sailors you sent to the bottom of the Mediterranean, Captain Finnegan, who were they? I shall tell you. Each of them was some mother's son. And probably some woman's husband, some child's father. Jennie suffered, yes. Maud and Gladys are dead—all at my hands. But how many more were saved because of what I did? How many were spared because I, and others like me, helped to shorten the war? Hundreds of thousands? Millions? Do we sacrifice the many for the one? Or the one for the many? It's a question that I'll never answer, Captain Finnegan, and one that will always haunt me."

In the distance, lights were suddenly seen shining through the trees.

"The constable, no doubt. With Mr. Wallace and James. It looks as if they're still a fair ways off, but even so, I must be going," Max said. "When they arrive, please tell them that Madden and his man were trying to break into the cottage to rob it. You, Captain Finnegan, shot at them with a pistol you keep in the cottage." He pulled Madden's gun from his waistband and handed it to Seamie. "Now is your chance, Captain Finnegan," he said quietly. "Take it, if you must."

Seamie shook his head. "The war's over," he said.

"Good-bye, Captain Finnegan," Max said. He offered Seamie his hand, but Seamie would not take it.

"Good-bye, Mr. von Brandt," he said. "Thank you for saving my son." He turned away and started walking toward the cottage. Albie followed him.

Willa stood where she was, too stunned and tired to move.

Max turned to her. "I am very sorry that I hit you. Back in the cottage," he said. "Forgive me, I had no choice. I had to quiet you. If you had kept talking about your brother and aunt, and what they knew, you would have spooked Billy, and he might've killed both you and Captain Finnegan right there."

"Oh, no worries, Max," Willa said bitterly. "I've no hard feelings toward you. Not for that, or anything else. None at all."

Max looked at the ground. "What will you do after tonight?" he asked.

"I don't know. Get out of these clothes. Sleep. Then go back to Paris, I suppose," she said wearily.

"Why? So you can finish the job?" he asked, looking up at her again.

"What job?"

"The job of killing yourself. You were always trying to. On Everest. In the desert. And now, apparently, with a needle. Oh, you needn't look so surprised. I know an addict when I see one. You must stop, Willa."

"Strange sentiments coming from you, Max. I should think you would want me dead. You were going to kill me yourself in Damascus. I saw the order. From Berlin. It was in with the maps I stole from your desk."

Max shook his head. "I follow most of my orders, but not all of them. I never would have killed you. Not you. I would have stalled Berlin. Told them you still had valuable information. I might have locked you up for a bit, but I never would have had you shot. I couldn't have. It would have been like killing myself." He paused, then ruefully added, "The best part of myself, that is."

It was Willa's turn to look away.

"Stop it, Willa. Once and for all. You're here. Seamie is here. You have always wanted to be together. You should stay with him now."

Willa laughed. "After everything that's happened? What I did to his wife?"

"What you did, eh?" Max said. "What did Seamie do, meeting you all those times at the Coburg? What did Jennie do, lying to him about their son? What have I done, Willa? To you in Damascus . . . to Jennie . . . to dozens more." He fell silent for a bit, then said, "Think about the boy. James would likely not be with his father right now if it wasn't for you. Seamie would not be alive. I doubt very much that things would have turned out the way they have without you. Think on that, and perhaps, in the days to come, it might help to balance the scales a little."

Willa looked at him. Her eyes filled with tears.

"Don't be stupid, Willa. Take what love you can find in this wretched world. There's little enough. Grab it with both hands. For yourself. For Seamie. For the boy."

Max gathered her in his arms then and held her tightly. He kissed her lips, then released her. It was time to go.

"Good-bye, Willa," he said.

"Good-bye, Max," she said.

She turned away and started walking toward the cottage. He opened the driver's side door of the car. As he was about to get in, he glanced up at the sky, hoping to get his bearings, to get an idea of which way he should head in order to get back to the main road. He saw something there that made him smile.

"Willa!" he called out, remembering her and how she looked at Rongbuk. So long ago. Sitting on a rock, staring up at the sky.

Willa turned. "What?" she said brokenly.

"Look," he said, pointing up.

She followed his gaze, and Max saw the tears on her cheeks, silvery bright. High above them the Great Hunter drew his bow. In the vast and infinite night, Orion sparkled.

EPILOGUE
Kenya, September 1919

WILLA WATCHED THEM, Seamie and James, as they ran through the grass, trying to get aloft a kite that they'd made out of newspaper.

She was sitting on the porch of a bungalow. The house was about twenty years old and had lovely, mature gardens. There were roses planted around the porch, and they were in full bloom now.

"Wild roses," said Arthur Wayland, the man who'd sold it to them. "Clipped from a hedgerow and brought all the way from England. They were my wife's favorites and she couldn't bear to leave them behind. They've done marvelously well here."

They'd just bought the bungalow, and two hundred acres of land that went with it, last week. Mr. Wayland was returning home to England after forty years in Africa. His wife had died. His two sons were in London. It was time to go back.

Willa had fallen in love with the house immediately. It faced west, giving them the most spectacular view of Kilimanjaro. They had been happy to move in and finally put their bags down. They'd spent months in ships, trains, hotels, and tents.

As she watched Seamie and James, Willa noticed that Seamie was moving slowly. The scars from his burns still troubled him sometimes. They ached. Willa's leg still hurt, too. In fact, it was why she was sitting down now instead of joining in the kite-flying. She was still getting used to the new prosthesis she'd bought right before they'd left England. The lightness and range of motion was better than anything she'd had before, but she'd had to adjust her gait, and she'd had to put up with soreness and chafing. Prosthesis manufacturers had made vast improvements to the artificial legs and arms they made. They'd had to. Thousands of men had come home from the front missing limbs. They needed to be able to work. To walk. To hold their children.

We're all scarred, all three of us. We're all damaged, Willa thought as she massaged her knee. Some of the wounds were on the outside. Some of them went a lot deeper. There were days when James still wept for his mother. And there were nights when he still woke up screaming that bad men were coming to get him.

Seamie, too, had his dark days. The aftermath of Billy Madden's visit to Binsey had been very hard on him. He'd had to come to terms with Jennie's lies, and why she'd told them. He was angry at times, he said, but mostly he felt deeply sad—sad that he'd failed Jennie. Sad that she'd been so desperate to hold on to his love that she'd deceived him, passing another woman's child off as her own. Sad that Josie Meadows had suffered for that deception at the hands of Billy Madden.

Willa had her doubts and fears, too—some of them were so strong, they sometimes made her want to reach for a syringe again, but she didn't. She had doubted that they could ever make a go of it—she and Seamie. She was afraid that too much had happened, that they would always be haunted by the mistakes of the past, that their love would always be a destructive one.

After Max had driven away, she had gone inside the cottage and collapsed in a chair. The constable arrived a few minutes later with Mr. Wallace and James. Seamie had explained to them what had happened, using the story Max cooked up. After he'd thanked both men and said good-bye to them, he put James to bed. Albie stoked the fire, made a platter of cheeses, pickles, ham, and bread, and got out the bottle of brandy.

They'd drunk the brandy, eaten the meal, talked for hours, and then they'd all fallen asleep—Albie in an armchair, Willa in another one, and Seamie on the settee. They had not been together like that for years, since they were teenagers. In the morning they'd decided they would tell Joe and Fiona what had happened, and Sid and India, but no one else. Telling anyone else, including the police, would only hurt James. Seamie would tell his son the truth. One day. When he was much older.

The next morning, Albie offered to take Willa back to Cambridge with him.

Seamie answered for her. "No," he said. "Stay, Willa. Please."

"Are you sure?" she'd asked him. He'd been through so much—he and James both—she thought they would want time to themselves. She loved him and she wanted to be with him, but she had no idea if he felt the same way—not with all that had happened.

"Please," he'd said again. And so she'd stayed.

They had talked—not of their feelings for each other, not of Jennie or Max or things long past, but of their more recent lives. Seamie told her about the prisoner-of-war camp, and how a part of him had very much wanted not to come back to England after the war. He told her he didn't know what his next step would be. What he would do with himself. Or how he would raise James. Willa told him of her life in Paris, and her photographs, and said she would have to go back eventually, for she found it impossible to be in London.

They were weary and shaken by what had happened, and what had almost happened. They lived quietly—just going for walks with James, or to the village market. Going for rides into the countryside or for lunch at the King's Head. Cooking breakfast. Reading. Playing games with James.

Seamie did not touch her or kiss her, and she understood. He was grieving. He was angry. He was tortured by guilt. She did not touch him, either, for fear of being turned away.

A week passed, and a month, and Willa realized she did not know what to do. She didn't know whether to stay or go. She wanted to know Seamie's feelings, but was afraid to ask. For once in her life, she was afraid. It was better not to know, to live in hope, than to know for sure that he no longer felt for her what she felt for him. That he no longer loved her.

And then, one night, he suddenly answered her questions.

"I don't want this," he said abruptly, while they were sitting by the fire.

Willa's heart sank. She thought he meant her. Them. She had hoped they might have a chance, but then again, how could they? There was so much hurt between them. So much sorrow. She was not surprised, but she was devastated.

She was also wrong.

"I don't want to be here in Binsey anymore," he said. "I can't bear it. I've tried to like it. For James's sake. Because he likes the country. And for yours, because you don't like London. But I don't. In fact, I hate it here. I hate this cottage. There are too many ghosts in it. I don't want to be in England anymore. I want to go back to where it all went wrong and put it right. I want to make a new start. With you and James. In Africa."

Willa was speechless.

"You think it's a bad idea," Seamie said, his disappointment evident on his face.

"No, I don't. In fact, I think it's a wonderful idea. How soon can we go?"

"As soon as you marry me."

"Seamie, I—"

"Say yes, Willa. Say yes right now or go back to Paris," he said, with an ache in his voice. "If you're going to walk away again, do it now. Before James loves you as much as I do. I can take the blow. He can't. He's been through too much."

"Yes," Willa said.

Seamie looked at her long and hard. Then he grabbed her hand, pulled her out of her chair, and led her to his bedroom. They made love there, in the darkness, fell asleep, and woke up together in the soft light of morning.

Seamie drove to Oxford the next morning. He put Willa on a train there so that she could return to Paris, for just a few days, to pack her belongings and have them sent to her mother's house. Then he went to a jeweler's and bought two gold rings. They were married in London at Willa's childhood home three weeks later. Albie gave her away. Mrs. Alden arranged a lovely breakfast for them. Fiona and Joe came. Charlie, who was talking again now, and Katie, who'd just graduated from Oxford and was preparing to stand as the Labour candidate for Southwark, and all the rest of their children were there, too.

The day after their wedding, Seamie and Willa walked up the gangplank of a steamer bound for East Africa, with James between them. They hired porters in Mombasa, as they had years ago, and took a long, leisurely trip from there, introducing James to Africa. They'd decided to settle here, in Kenya, near Kilimanjaro.

Willa finished rubbing her knee now. The pain had diminished. She knew that it would go away completely as time went by, as her body adjusted fully to the new leg. She stood now, shading her eyes, smiling at her husband, and at James. He was not her son, not yet. Perhaps one day. If he wanted to be. For now, he called her Willa and she called him James, and both of them were happy with that.

Willa put her full weight on her leg, stepped down off the porch, and walked toward Seamie and James. Her stride was easier and smoother than it had been since she'd lost her real leg. It was good, the new leg—so good that she thought that one day she might even be able to climb again. Not the Mawenzi peak, not this time—the Uhuru peak. She might be able to manage that one. It was a bit of a doddle, that climb. But that was all right.

Once, long ago, she had wanted to be bold. To be daring and brave. To be the first.

Now she just wanted to be.

She wanted to be still at night, to look up and admire the stars without asking them which way to go. She wanted to walk slowly over the veldt and through the jungle, not hurrying to make camp, but stopping to rest, to gaze at a herd of antelope, to call back to the beautiful birds who called to her. She wanted to watch, delighted, as little James marveled at an African sunset, watched a cheetah run, or made friends with a Masai boy just his age.

She wanted to sit by the fire at night with Seamie. Talking sometimes, and sometimes just listening silently and with wonder to the wild African night.

They had torn themselves apart, she and Seamie. Years ago. Here in Africa. And then in 1914, the world had torn itself apart. Now they, and the world, would put themselves back together. Slowly, with pain, regret, and with hope, they would find the way forward.

She didn't know how, exactly. She had no map. No answers. No guarantees.

All she had was this day.

This impossible mountain rising before her.

This sun and this sky.

This man and this child.

This terrible, wonderful love.

ACKNOWLEDGMENTS

I am indebted to the following works: *Everest: The Moutaineering History* by Walt Unsworth, *Lawrence of Arabia* by B. H. Liddell Hart, *Setting the Desert on Fire* by James Barr, and *Seven Pillars of Wisdom: A Triumph* by T. E. Lawrence—and to the following websites: www .firstworldwar.com; Wikipedia; www.parliament.net; www.bbc.co .uk/history; virus.stanford.edu/uda; www.cliffordawright.com; www.jordanjubilee.com; and the digital library at Cornell University, where I viewed online volumes of *Littel's Living Age*, a general interest magazine published from 1844 to 1900.

I would like to thank the late Sheri Nystrom for graciously sharing her knowledge and experience of limb amputation and its after-effects with me. And I would like to thank Clay Nystrom, her husband, for sharing Sheri.

Thank you, as always, to my wonderful family for seeing me through.

Thank you, too, to my agents, Simon Lipksar and Maja Nikolic, and to my editors, Leslie Wells and Thomas Tebbe.

And last, but very far from least, thank you to the wonderful readers, booksellers, bloggers, and reviewers who've embraced the Rose books so warmly. I appreciate your enthusiasm, emails, and kind words more than I could ever say.

BIBLIOGRAPHY

The Rose stories never would have been written had I not, many years ago, stumbled across a four-volume survey of working-class Victorian London by Henry Mayhew titled *London Labour and the London Poor*. Mayhew interviewed everyone—costermongers, thieves, prostitutes, mudlarks, even people who made a living by picking up cigarette butts. He gave detailed descriptions of their work and how they carried it out, and best of all, he let them tell their own stories, in their own words. These books are pure magic. If you ever get the chance to read them, grab it.

Many other books helped me re-create the London and New York of my novels, various other locales, and the people in them. A bibliography for the entire Rose series follows.

Abbot, Willis John. *The Nations at War: A Current History*. New York and London: Syndicate Publishing Company, 1915.

Balson, Consuelo Vanderbilt. *The Glitter and the Gold*. New York: Harper & Brothers, 1952.

Barltrop, Robert, and Jim Wolveridge. *The Muvver Tongue*. London: Journeyman Press, 1980.

Barr, James. *Setting the Desert on Fire: T. E. Lawrence and Britain's Secret War in Arabia, 1916–1918*. New York & London: W. W. Norton & Company, 2008.

Beckett, Stephen. *In Living Memory: Photographs of Tower Hamlets*. London: Tower Hamlets Local History Library & Archives, 1989.

Berridge, Virginia, and Griffith Edwards. *Opium and the People: Opiate Use in Nineteenth-Century England*. New Haven and London: Yale University Press, 1987.

Black, Mary. *Old New York in Early Photographs 1853–1901*. Second revised edition. New York: Dover Publications, Inc., 1976.

Blair, Richard, and Kathleen Goodwin. *Point Reyes Visions*. Inverness, Calif.: Color & Light Editions, 2002.

Bonner, Thomas Neville. *To the Ends of the Earth: Women's Search for Education in Medicine*. Cambridge, Mass.: Harvard University Press, 1995.

Booth, Martin. *Opium: A History*. London: Pocket Books, 1997.

Boyles, Denis. *African Lives*. New York: Ballantine Books, 1988.

Breashears, David, and Audrey Salkeld, with a foreword by John Mallory. *Last Climb: The Legendary Everest Expeditions of George Mallory*. Washington, D.C.: National Geographic Society, 1999.

Burnett, John. *Plenty & Want: A Social History of Food in England from 1815 to the Present Day*. Third edition. London: Routledge, 1989.

Burrows, Edwin G., and Mike Wallace. *Gotham: A History of New York City to 1898*. New York and Oxford: Oxford University Press, 1999.

Byron, Joseph. Text by Clay Lancaster. *Photographs of New York Interiors from the Turn of the Century*. New York: Dover Publications, Inc., 1976.

Cannadine, David. *The Decline and Fall of the British Aristocracy*. New York: Vintage Books, 1999.

Chauncey, George. *Gay New York: Gender, Urban Culture, and the Making of the Gay Male World 1890–1940*. New York: Basic Books, 1994.

Chesney, Kellow. *The Victorian Underworld*. London: Penguin Books, 1989.

Churchill, Winston Spencer. *My African Journey*. London: Hamlyn Publishing Group, 1972.

Coleman, Elizabeth Ann. *The Opulent Era: Fashions of Worth, Doucet and Pingat*. Brooklyn, N.Y.: Brooklyn Museum, 1989.

Cooper, Diana. *The Rainbow Comes and Goes*. London: Rupert Hart-Davis, 1958.

Cox, Steven M., and Kris Fulsaas. *Moutaineering: The Freedom of the Hills*. Seattle, Wash.: The Moutaineers Books, 2003.

Darby, Madge. *Waeppa's People: A History of Wapping*. Colchester: Connor & Butler on behalf of The History of Wapping Trust, 1988.

Davies, Jennifer. *The Victorian Kitchen*. London: BBC Books, 1991.

Dickens, Charles. *The Uncommercial Traveller*. New York and Boston: Books, Inc., 1860.

Digby, Anne. *The Evolution of British General Practice 1850–1948*. Oxford: Oxford University Press, 1999.

Dudgeon, Piers. *Dickens' London*. London: Headline Book Publishing PLC, 1989.

Ellmers, Chris, and Alex Werner. *London's Lost Riverscape: A Photographic Panorama*. London: Viking, 1988.

Fido, Martin. *The Crimes, Detection & Death of Jack the Ripper*. London: Weidenfeld and Nicolson, 1987.

———. *Murder Guide to London*. Chicago: Academy Chicago Publishers, 1986.

Fishman, William J. *East End 1888*. Philadelphia: Temple University Press, 1988.

Flanders, Judith. *Inside the Victorian Home: A Portrait of Domestic Life in Victorian England*. New York and London: W. W. Norton & Company, 2004.

Foote, Edward B., M.D. *Plain Home Talk Embracing Medical Common Sense*. Chicago: Thompson and Thomas, 1870.

Foreman, Freddie, with John Lisner. *Respect*. London: Arrow Books, 1997.

Fraser, Frankie, as told to James Morton. *Mad Frank: Memoirs of a Life in Crime*. New York: Warner Books, 2000.

Fraser, Frankie, with James Morton. *Mad Frank's London*. London: Virgin Books Ltd., 2002.

Fried, Albert, and Richard M. Elman, editors. *Charles Booth's London: A Portrait of the Poor at the Turn of the Century, Drawn from his "Life and Labour of the People in London."* New York: Pantheon Books, 1968.

Gann, L. H., and Peter Duignan. *The Rulers of British Africa 1870–1914*. Stanford, Calif.: Stanford University Press, 1978.

Geniesse, Jane Fletcher. *Passionate Nomad: The Life of Freya Stark*. New York: The Modern Library, 1999.

Gernsheim, Alison. *Victorian and Edwardian Fashion: A Photographic Survey*. New York: Dover Publications, 1981.

Gilmour, David. *Curzon: Imperial Statesman*. New York: Farrar, Straus and Giroux, 2003.

Grimble, Frances, editor. *The Edwardian Modiste*. San Francisco: Lavolta Press, 1997.

Hart, B. H. Liddell. *Lawrence of Arabia*. A Da Capo Press reprint of *Colonel Lawrence: The Man Behind the Legend*. New York: 1935.

Heussler, Robert. *Yesterday's Rulers: The Making of the British Colonial Service*. Syracuse, N.Y.: Syracuse University Press, 1963.

Hood, Clifton. *722 Miles: The Building of the Subways and How They Transformed New York*. Baltimore and London: Johns Hopkins University Press, 1993.

Hughes, Kristine. *The Writer's Guide to Everyday Life in Regency and Victorian England*. Cincinnati, Ohio: Writer's Digest Books, 1998.

Hughes, M. V. *A London Girl of the 1880s*. Oxford and New York: Oxford University Press, 1988.

Huxley, Elspeth. *The Flame Trees of Thika: Memories of an African Childhood*. New York: Weidenfeld & Nicolson, 1987.

Huxley, Elspeth, and Arnold Curtis, editors. *Pioneers' Scrapbook*. London: Evans Brothers Limited, 1980.

Jackson, Kenneth T., editor. *The Encyclopedia of New York*. New Haven and London: Yale University Press, 1995.

Jalland, Pat, editor. *Octavia Wilberforce: The Autobiography of a Pioneer Woman Doctor*. London: Cassell, 1989.

Jasper, A. S. *A Hoxton Childhood*. London: Readers Union, 1971.

Johnson, Boris. *Friends, Voters, Countrymen: Jottings on the Stump*. London: HarperCollins Publishers, 2001.

Johnstone, R. W., C.B.E. *William Smellie: The Master of British Midwifery*. Edinburgh and London: E. & S. Livingstone Ltd., 1952.

Kisseloff, Jeff. *You Must Remember This: An Oral History of Manhattan from the 1890s to World War II*. San Diego: Harcourt, Brace, Jovanovich, 1989.

Knight, Stephen. *Jack the Ripper: The Final Solution*. London: Granada, 1983.

Lambert, Angela. *Unquiet Souls: The Indian Summer of the British Aristocracy*. London: Macmillan, 1984.

Lawrence, Lady (Rosamond Napier). *Indian Embers*. Palo Alto: Trackless Sands Press, 1991.

Lawrence, T. E. *Seven Pillars of Wisdom: A Triumph*. New York: Anchor Books, 1991.

Llewelyn Davies, Margaret, editor. *Maternity: Letters from Working Women*. London: Virago, 1989.

———. *Life as We Have Known by Co-operative Working Women*. New York: W. W. Norton & Company, Inc., 1975.

London, Jack. *The People of the Abyss*. Chicago: Lawrence Hill Books, 1995.

MacColl, Gail, and Carol McD. Wallace. *To Marry an English Lord or, How Anglomania Really Got Started*. New York: Workman Publishing, 1989.

Manton, Jo. *Elizabeth Garrett Anderson*. New York: E. P. Dutton & Co., Inc., 1965.

Maxon, Robert M. *East Africa: An Introductory History*. Second revised edition. Morgantown: West Virginia University Press, 1994.

Mayhew, Henry. *London Labour and the London Poor*, Vol. 1–Vol. 4. London: George Woodfall and Son, 1851.

McCormick, J. H., M.D., editor. *Century Book of Health*. Springfield, Mass.: The King-Richardson Company, 1907.

McGrath, Melanie. *Silvertown: An East End Family Memoir*. London: Fourth Estate, 2003.

McGregor, Deborah Kuhn. *From Midwives to Medicine: The Birth of American Gynecology*. New Brunswick, N.J.: Rutgers University Press, 1998.

Morton, James. *East End Gangland*. New York: Warner Books, 2000.

Naib, S. K., al-, editor, with R.J.M. Carr. *Dockland: An Illustrated Historical Survey of Life and Work in East London*. London: North East London Polytechnic, 1988.

National Cloak & Suit Co. *Women's Fashions of the Early 1900s: An Unabridged Republication of New York Fashions, 1909*. New York: Dover Publications, Inc.

Nevill, Lady Dorothy. *The Reminiscences of Lady Dorothy Nevill*. Sixth edition. London: Edward Arnold, 1902.

————. *Under Five Reigns*. New York: The John Lane Company, 1910.

Newsome, David. *The Victorian World Picture*. London: John Murray, 1997.

Nicolson, Juliet. *The Perfect Summer: England 1911, Just Before the Storm*. New York: Grove Press, 2006.

Nicolson, Louise. *Fodor's London Companion: The Guide for the Experienced Traveler*. New York and London: Fodor's Travel Publications, 1987.

Novak, Emil, A.B., M.D., D.Sc., F.A.C.S., F.R.C.O.G. *Gynecologic and Obstetric Pathology with Clinical and Endocrine Relations*. Third edition. Philadelphia and London: W. B. Saunders Company, 1952.

O'Neill, Gilda. *My East End: Memories of a Life in Cockney London*. London: Penguin, 2000.

Pratt, James Norwood. *The Tea Lover's Treasury*. San Ramon, Calif.: 101 Productions, 1982.

Peterson, Jeanne M. *The Medical Profession in Mid-Victorian London*. Berkeley: University of California Press, 1978.

Pullen, Bob. *London Street People: Past and Present*. Oxford: Lennard Publishing, 1989.

Reeves, Maud Pember. *Round About a Pound a Week*. London: Virago, 1988.

Rey, H. A. *The Stars: A New Way to See Them*. Boston: Houghton Mifflin Company, 1980.

Roberts, Bob. *Last of the Sailormen*. London: Seafarer Books, 1986.

Roberts, Robert. *A Ragged Schooling: Growing up in the Classic Slum*. Manchester, UK: Manchester University Press, 1987.

————. *The Classic Slum: Salford Life in the First Quarter of the Century*. London: Penguin Books, 1971.

Ruffer, Jonathan Garnier. *The Big Shots: Edwardian Shooting Parties*. Debrett-Viking Press, 1978.

Rumbelow, Donald. *Jack the Ripper: The Complete Casebook*. Chicago: Contemporary Books, 1988.

Scannell, Dorothy. *Mother Knew Best: Memoir of a London Girlhood*. New York: Pantheon Books, 1974.

Shonfield, Zuzanna. *The Precariously Privileged: A Professional Family in Victorian London.* Oxford and New York: Oxford University Press, 1987.

Speert, Harold, M.D. *Obstetrics and Gynecology: A History and Iconography.* Revised third edition of *Iconographia Gyniatrica.* New York: Parthenon Publishing, 2004.

———. *Obstetrics and Gynecology in America: A History.* Chicago: The American College of Obstetricians and Gynecologists, 1980.

Traxel, David. *1989: The Birth of the American Century.* New York: Alfred A. Knopf, 1998.

Trzebinski, Errol. *The Kenya Pioneers.* New York and London: W. W. Norton & Company, 1986.

Tuchman, Barbara W. *The Guns of August.* New York: Ballantine Books, 1962.

———. *The Proud Tower: A Portrait of the World Before the War 1890-1914.* New York: Bantam Books, 1989.

Unsworth, Walt. *Everest: The Mountaineering History.* Third Edition. Macclesfield: Bâton Wicks, 2000.

———. *Hold the Heights: The Foundations of Moutaineering.* Seattle: The Moutaineers, 1994.

Wallach, Janet. *Desert Queen: The Extraordinary Life of Gertrude Bell: Adventurer, Adviser to Kings, Ally of Lawrence of Arabia.* New York: Anchor Books, 1999.

Weightman, Gavin. *London Past.* Collins & Brown Limited, 1991.

White, Jerry. *Rothschild Buildings: Life in an East End Tenement Block 1887-1920.* London: Routledge & Kegan Paul, 1980.

Wohl, Anthony S. *Endangered Lives: Public Health in Victorian Britain.* Cambridge, Mass.: Harvard University Press, 1983.

Wolveridge, Jim. *'Ain't it Grand?' or 'This was Stepney.'* London: The Journeyman Press, 1976.

Woodward, Kathleen. *Jipping Street.* London: Virago Press, 1983.

Youngson, A. J. *The Scientific Revolution in Victorian Medicine.* New York: Holmes & Meier Publishers, Inc., 1979.